SONG OF DRAGONS

SONG OF DRAGONS

OMNIBUS: BOOKS 1 - 3

DANIEL ARENSON

ISBN: 978-0-9878864-3-9

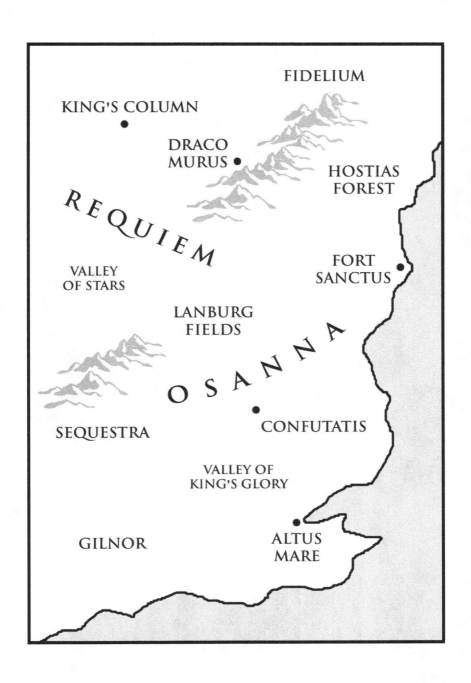

BOOK ONE:
BLOOD OF REQUIEM

PROLOGUE

War.

War rolled over the world with fire and wings.

The Vir Requis marched. Men. Women. Children. Their clothes were tattered, their faces ashy, their bellies tight. As their cities burned behind them, they marched with cold eyes. All had come to fight this day: the young and the old, the strong and the wounded, the brave and the frightened. They were five thousand. They had no more places to hide.

The dying sun blazed red against them. The wind keened. Five thousand. The last of their race.

We will stand, we will fly, we will perish with fire and tooth, Benedictus thought, jaw clenched. *Men will say: Requiem did not fade with a whimper, but fell with a thunder that shook the mountains.*

And so he marched, and behind him his people followed, banners red and gold, thudding in the wind. *Last stand of Requiem.*

It was strange, he thought, that five thousand should move together so silently. Benedictus heard only thumping boots. No whispers. No sobs. No whimpers even from the children who marched, their eyes too large in their gaunt faces. The Vir Requis were silent today, silent for the million of their kin already dead, for this day when their race would perish, enter the realm of memory, then legend, then myth. Nothing but thudding boots, a keening wind, and a grumbling sky. Silence before the roar of fire.

Then Benedictus saw the enemy ahead.

The scourge of Requiem. Their end.

Benedictus let out his breath slowly. Here was his death. The death of these hunted, haunted remains of his kind, the Vir Requis who had once covered the world and now stood, still and silent, behind him.

A tear streamed down Benedictus's cheek. He tasted it on his lips—salty, ashy.

His brother's host dwarfed his own. Fifty thousand men stood ahead: swordsmen, horsemen, archers, all bedecked in the white and gold that Dies Irae had taken for his colors. They carried torches, thousands of fires that raised smoky pillars. Countless griffins flew over these soldiers, shrieking, their wings churning the clouds. The army shimmered like a foul tapestry woven with images of the Abyss.

Benedictus smiled grimly. *They burned our forests. They toppled our cities. They chased us to every corner of the earth. If they force us to fight here, then we will die fighting well.*

He clenched his fists.

War.

War crashed with blood and screams and smoke.

Benedictus, King of Requiem, drew his magic with a howl. Black wings sprouted from his back, unfurling and creaking. Black scales rippled across him, glinting red in the firelight. Fangs sprang from his mouth, dripping drool, and talons grew from his fingers. Soon he was fifty feet long, a black dragon breathing fire. Requiem's magic filled him, the magic of wings and scales and flame, the magic that Dies Irae lacked and loathed. Benedictus took flight, claws tearing the earth. His roar shook the battlefield.

Let them see me. Let them see Benedictus the Black, for one final time under the sky, spreading wings and roaring flame.

Behind him, the Vir Requis he led changed form too. The solemn men, women, and children drew the ancient magic of their race, grew wings, scales, and claws. They too became dragons, as cruel and beautiful as the true dragons of old. Some became elder beasts missing scales, their fangs long fallen. Others were young, supple, their scales still soft, barely old enough to fly. A few were green, others blue, and some blazed red. A handful, like Benedictus, bore the rare black scales of old noble blood. Once the different colors, the different families and noble lines, would fight one another, would mistrust and kill and hate. Today they banded here, joined to fight Dies Irae—the young, the old, the noble and the common.

This night they fought with one roar.

The last Vir Requis, Benedictus thought. *Not humans. Not dragons. Weredragons, the humans call us. Shunned. Today is our last flight.*

War. With steel and flame.

Arrows pelted Benedictus, jabs of agony. Most shattered against his scales, but some sank into his flesh. Their tips were serrated, coated with poison that burned through his veins. He roared and blew fire at the men below, the soldiers his brother had tricked or forced into battle today. They screamed, cursed him, feared him; the Vir Requis were monsters to them. Benedictus swooped, lifted several soldiers in his claws, and tossed them onto their comrades. Spears flew. Flaming arrows whistled. Everywhere was blood, fire, and screaming.

War. With poison and pain.

Around him, the Vir Requis flew as dragons, the forms they always took in battle. They breathed fire and roared. Spears and arrows plucked the young from the skies. Their scales were too soft, their wings too small. They hit the ground, screaming, soon overcome with swordsmen who hacked them. Blood splashed. In death they resumed human forms; battered, bloodied, butchered children.

They take our youth first, Benedictus thought. He slammed into soldiers below, biting, clawing, lashing his tail, ignoring the pain of swordbites. *They let us, the old, see the death of our future before they fell us too from the skies.*

These older Vir Requis—the warriors—fought with fire, claw, and fang. These ones had seen much war, had killed too many, bore too many scars. Soon mounds of bodies covered the battlefield. The Vir Requis howled as they killed and died.

Our race will fall here today, Benedictus thought as spears flew and shattered against his scales. *But we will make a last stand for poets to sing of.*

And then shrieks tore the air, and the griffins were upon him.

They were cruel beasts, as large as dragons, their bodies like great lions, their heads the heads of eagles, their beaks and talons sharp. In the books of men they were noble, warriors of light and righteousness, sent by the Sun God to fight the curse of Requiem, the wickedness of scales and leathery wings. To Requiem they were monsters.

Today Benedictus saw thousands of them, swooping beasts of feathers and talons. Two crashed into him, scratching and biting. One talon slashed his front leg, and Benedictus roared. He swung his tail, hit one's head, and cracked its skull. It tumbled. Benedictus blew fire onto the second. Its fur and feathers burst into flame. Its shrieks nearly deafened him, and it too fell, blazing, to crash into men below.

Panting and grunting with pain, sluggish with poison, Benedictus glanced around. The griffins were swarming; they outnumbered the Vir Requis five to one. Most Vir Requis lay dead upon the bloody field, pierced with arrows and spears and talons. And then more griffins were upon Benedictus, and he could see only their shrieking beaks, their flashing talons. Flaming arrows filled the air.

Has it truly been only five years? Benedictus thought as talons tore into him, shedding blood. Haze covered his thoughts, and the battle almost seemed silent around him. *Five years since my father banished my brother, since a million of us filled the sky? Yes, only five years. Look at us now.* Dragons fell around him like rain, maws open, tears in their eyes.

"No!" Benedictus howled, voice thundering. He blew fire, forcing the haze of death off him. He was not dead yet. He still had some killing in him, some blood to shed, some fire to breathe. *Not until I've killed more. Not until I find the man who destroyed us. Dies Irae. My brother.*

He clawed, bit, and burned as his comrades fell around him, as the tears and blood of Requiem filled the air and earth.

He fought all night, a night of fire, and all next day, fought until the sun again began to set. Its dying rays painted the world red.

Pierced by a hundred arrows, weary and bloody, Benedictus looked around and knew: The others were gone.

He, Benedictus, was the last.

He flew between griffins and spears and arrows. His brethren lay slain all around. In death, they lay as humans. Men. Women. Children. All those he had led to battle; all lay cut and broken, mouths open, limbs strewn, eyes haunted and still.

Benedictus raised his eyes. He stared at the army ahead, the army he now faced alone. Thousands of soldiers and griffins faced him under the roiling clouds. The army of Dies Irae.

He saw his brother there, not a mile away, clad in white and gold. Victorious.

Bleeding, tears in his eyes, Benedictus flew toward him.

Spears clanged against Benedictus. Arrows pierced him. Griffins clawed him. Still he swooped toward Dies Irae. Fire and screams flowed around him, and Benedictus shot like an arrow, roaring, wreathed in flame.

Dies Irae rose from the battlefield upon a griffin, bearing a lance of silver and steel. Gold glistened upon his armor and samite robes. He appeared to Benedictus like a seraph, a figure of light, ablaze like a sun.

Benedictus, of black scales and blood and fire, and Dies Irae, of gold and white upon his griffin. They flew toward each other over the mounds of dead.

Benedictus was hurt and weary. The world blurred. He could barely fly. He was too hurt, too torn, too haunted. Dies Irae crashed into him, a blaze like a comet, so white and righteous and golden. Benedictus howled, hoarse. He felt Dies Irae's silver spear pierce his wing. He heard that wing tearing, a sound like ripping leather. It was the most terrifying sound Benedictus had ever heard, and the pain seemed unreal, too great to truly fill him. He crashed into the griffin that bore his brother. Screaming, mouth bloody, he bit down. His jaws severed Dies Irae's arm. He felt the arm in his mouth, clad in armor, and he spat it out, saw it tumble to the ground.

Dies Irae screamed, cried, and clutched the stump of his arm. Blood covered him. His griffin clawed Benedictus's side, pain blazed, and Benedictus kicked. He hit the griffin's head, crushing it. The griffin fell. Dies Irae fell. His brother hit the ground, screaming. His griffin lay dead beside him.

Benedictus landed on the ground above his brother.

The battle froze.

The soldiers, knights, and griffins all stood still and stared, as if in shock. Benedictus stood panting, blood in his mouth, blood on his scales, and gazed down at his brother. Dies Irae looked so pale. Blood covered his golden armor and samite robe.

"My daughter," Benedictus said, voice low. "Where is Gloriae?"

"Please," Dies Irae whispered, lips pale, face sweaty. "Please, Benedictus. My brother. Please."

Benedictus growled. He spoke through the blood in his maw, voice hoarse and torn. "You destroyed us. You butchered a million souls. How dare you ask for mercy now? Return me my daughter."

Dies Irae trembled. Suddenly he looked so much as he did years ago, a timid and angry child, a scorned brother cast away from his father's court. "Please," he whispered, clutching his stump. "Please."

Benedictus raised a clawed foot, prepared to strike down, to kill the man who had hunted his race to near extinction. Dies Irae shut his eyes and whimpered. His lips prayed silently and his blood flowed.

Benedictus paused.

He looked around him. No more Vir Requis flew. Their war had ended. The time of Requiem had ended.

It is over, Benedictus knew. *No. I will not end it this way, not with killing my brother. It is over already.*

With a grunt, Benedictus kicked off the ground, flapped his wings, and rose into the air.

Men and griffins screamed around him.

"Kill him!" Dies Irae shouted below. "Don't let him flee! I want him dead!"

Benedictus would not look back. He could see only the thousands of bodies below. *I will find you, Gloriae. I won't forget you.*

His wings roiled ash and smoke. Arrows whistled around him, and he rose into the clouds. He flew in darkness. Soon the screams of men and griffins faded into the distance.

Benedictus the Black, King of Requiem, disappeared into the night.

MIRUM

The Lady Mirum was riding her mare by the sea when she saw the griffins. She shivered and cursed.

The morning had begun like any other. She woke in Fort Sanctus to a windy dawn, waves crashing outside, the air scented of sea and moss. Julian packed her a breakfast of bread and kippers wrapped in leather, and she took the meal on her morning ride along the gray, foaming sea. No omens had heralded danger; no thunderstorms, no comets cutting the clouds, no strange pattern to the leaves of her tea the night before. Just another morning of galloping, of the smells of seaweed and salt and horse, of the sounds of gulls and sea and hoofs in sand.

Yet here they flew, maybe a league away, their shrieks clear even over the roar of hoofs and waves. Mirum saw three of them—great beasts, half lions and half eagles, fifty feet long. In the distance, they looked like seraphs, golden and alight.

Griffins. And they were heading to Fort Sanctus. Her home.

Mirum's mare bucked and whinnied.

"Easy, Sol," she said and patted the horse's neck, though she herself trembled. She had not seen griffins in ten years, not since Dies Irae had killed her father, not since she had sworn allegiance to the man at age sixteen, kissed his hand so he'd let her live, let her keep the smallest of her father's forts.

Sol nickered and bucked again. The griffins were flying closer, shrieking their eagle shrieks. Though still a league away, Mirum could see glints of armor, and the stream of golden banners. *Riders.* She felt the blood leave her face.

Dies Irae's men.

Maybe, Mirum thought with a chill, Dies Irae himself rode there.

The wind gusted, howled, and blew Mirum's cloak back to reveal her sword. She placed her palm upon the old pommel, seeking strength in the cold steel. It had been her father's sword, the sword he'd worn the day Dies Irae murdered him. *Please, Father, give me strength today.*

"Come, Sol," she said and dug her heels into the mare. "They're heading to Sanctus. Let's meet them."

Sol was a good horse, well trained, from her father's stables. Most of those stables had burned in the war, their horses slaughtered or stolen, but Sol had remained. She now galloped, kicking up sand and seaweed, the waves showering foam at her side. The morning was cold, too cold for spring. Clouds hid the sun, and the sea was the color of iron. The wind shrieked and cut into Mirum. As she rode, she tightened her woolen cloak, but that could not ease her tremble. Fort Sanctus still lay half a league away, a jutting tower of mossy stone and rusty iron. It rose from an outcrop of rock over the sea like a lighthouse. There was no doubt now; the griffins were flying toward it, and would be there soon. If they found what Mirum hid there....

Even in the biting wind, sweat drenched Mirum. She cursed and kneed Sol. "Hurry, girl," she said. "Hurry."

A wave crashed against a boulder, and water hit Mirum, soaking her hair and riding dress. The gray wool clung to her, salty and cold, and Mirum tasted salt on her lips. In a flash, the memory pounded through her. She remembered herself ten years ago, only sixteen, a youth caught in the war. She remembered Dies Irae murdering her father before her eyes, how the blood had splashed her face.

"He stood against me," Dies Irae had said to her then, bloody sword in hand. "He stood with the weredragons." He spat that last word, the word he'd invented to belittle his foes, as though it tasted foul. He held out a hand heavy with rings. "But you need not suffer the same fate. Kiss this hand, Lady Mirum, and join my ranks. Join me against Requiem, and I will let you keep what remains of your father's lands."

She had been a child. Scared. Innocent and shocked. The blood of her father had still covered her, his body at her feet. She wanted to spit at Dies Irae, to die at his sword, to die at her father's side. But she was too frightened, too young. She kissed his ruby ring, swore allegiance to him, swore to join his quest to destroy the Vir Requis.

"Good, my child," he said and kissed her bloody forehead. He knew her that night, raped her again and again, then left her at dawn in Fort Sanctus, alone and bloody, corpses surrounding her.

She had not seen him since that winter.

Fort Sanctus was close now, casting its shadow over Mirum and her horse. It was but a single tower, mossy and old, topped with iron crenellations brown with rust. Once it had been a proud fort, but its soldiers and servants had perished in the war. Only old Julian remained, loyal steward of her father, and several fishermen in the village that sprawled behind the tower. Mirum had done what she could to maintain the place—cleaning the fireplaces, sweeping the floors, and helping to mend the fishermen's nets. She had no money to hire help, and Julian was getting on in years. And so Sanctus had fallen into disrepair, a sore thumb here on the beach, a crumbling tower of moss, rust, gull droppings, and haunting memories.

The waves now pummeled it, raising fountains of foam. Gulls flew around the fort, cawing. Their cries seemed to warn Mirum. "Go! Go!" they seemed to cry. *Flee!*

Loud as they were, their cries drowned under the shrieks of griffins. The beasts swooped down just as Mirum reined in her horse by the fort.

The griffins were beautiful. Even as horror pounded through her, Mirum recognized this beauty. The fur of their lion bodies shone golden, and the feathers of their eagle heads glowed white as fresh snow. Gilded helmets topped those eagle heads, in the manner of horse armor, glistening with rubies. Their wings, a hundred feet in span, churned the air so powerfully that the sea rippled. When the griffins landed on the outcrop of stone where Fort Sanctus stood, their talons cut grooves into the rock.

Bane of Benedictus, Mirum remembered. *That is what they would call them.*

She sat before them on her horse, sword at her side, the wind streaming her cloak and hair. She placed her right fist on her heart, Dies Irae's salute of loyalty.

Riders sat upon the three griffins, staring down at her. Each wore steel armor filigreed in gold, a sword in a jeweled sheath, and a snowy cape. The man who rode the largest, foremost griffin was especially resplendent. He looked like a god of wealth. Sapphires, rubies, and emeralds encrusted his helmet. Garnets and amber formed a griffin upon his breastplate, and golden weave ran through his samite cloak. His gilded helmet hid his face, the visor shaped as a griffin's beak, but Mirum saw his arm, and she knew him at once.

Mirum had been there that day, the day Dies Irae lost his left arm. She had been sixteen when the battle of Lanburg Fields raged. Her father had been dead for only a moon, and already she, Lady Mirum, rode to war under Dies Irae's banner. He insisted she ride at his side, reveled in the thought of her fighting for him, he who'd murdered her father and raped her. She watched, weeping, as Dies Irae killed the last Vir Requis, the remains of that ancient race. She watched, shivering, as the legendary Benedictus—King of Requiem and brother to Dies Irae—bit off her tormentor's arm. *You wept like a babe at my feet,* Mirum remembered, but she had felt no pity for him. She had not seen Dies Irae since that night... not until this gray morning, until he arrived at her doorstep, arrived with his griffins and soldiers and old, pulsing pain.

Like a body tossed into the sea, you return to my shore, rotten and smelling of old blood. Sol nickered beneath her and cantered sideways as if feeling her pain.

"Go! Go!" the gulls cawed. *Flee!*

But Mirum did not flee. Could not. She would not abandon what she hid here.

"Hail Irae!" she called, as she knew she must.

Upon his griffin, Dies Irae nodded to her, a golden god. He said nothing.

He wore a new arm now, she saw. It was an arm made of steel, encrusted with garnets like beads of blood. Instead of a fist, the arm ended with a mace head, spiked and cruel. It glistened even under the overcast sky.

Mirum dismounted her horse and curtsied before him.

Please, Earth God, she prayed, staring at the stone ground. *Please don't let him find what I hide here.*

She heard the three riders dismount their griffins, heard boots walk toward her. Soon she could see those boots as she curtsied, spurred leather boots tipped with steel. Then the spiked mace—the iron fist of Dies Irae's new arm—thrust itself before her face.

"You may kiss my hand, child," came a voice, the chilly voice Mirum remembered from a decade ago, the voice that had murmured in her ear as he raped her by her father's body.

Though disgust filled her, Mirum kissed the mace head, a hurried peck of her lips. It tasted like coppery blood.

Please, Earth God, please. Don't let Irae find him....

"Your Grace," Mirum said, head still lowered, fingers trembling.

"Rise, child," he said, and she straightened to face him. She could not see his face, only that jeweled visor shaped like an eagle's head, and she shivered. Dies Irae's lieutenants noticed and laughed—cold, cruel laughter like the sound of waves against stone. One was a tall, gaunt man covered in steel, his visor barred like a prisoner's mask. The other was a woman in white leggings, her breastplate molded to fit the curve of her breast, a gilded visor hiding her face. Both bore swords with grips shaped as talons.

Dies Irae turned to face them, those riders bedecked in gold and steel, and clucked his tongue. "Now now, it is impolite to laugh." He turned back to Mirum, standing too close, mere inches away. "You must forgive my riders. They do not often find themselves in the presence of a lady, and they are weary from a long flight. If you do not mind, we would much like to break our fast here, and to drink wine from your cellar. Would you be so kind as to host us at your home, if only for an hour?"

Mirum bowed her head. It was not a request, she knew, but a command. Her stomach roiled. The memories and fear pounded through her. "It would be an honor, my lord."

She led them down the outcrop of stone, her boots confident upon the moss. Waves crashed at their sides. Behind her, she heard the griffin riders struggling and muttering curses. She could walk this damp, mossy stone as though walking across a grassy meadow, but most struggled for balance upon it, and the spraying waves did little to help. Still, Mirum would not turn to offer aid, nor would she slow her pace. *Let them slip upon the moss. Let them fall against the boulders, and drown in the sea at the foot of my tower.*

Her prayers went unanswered. Soon she reached the doors of Fort Sanctus, towering doors of chipped oak, the wood dark with mold, the knobs brown with rust. The griffin riders, still cursing under their breath, came to stand beside her. Ignoring them, Mirum placed her hands on the doors, leaned against them, and they creaked open on rusty hinges.

"By the Sun God, the place still stinks," Dies Irae muttered, though still Mirum would not turn to face him. Her hall might be dusty, its walls mossy, its tapestries tattered... but it did not stink. It smelled like salt, like seaweed, like sand and like horse. This was no stench, but a smell Mirum loved. It had stunk once, that night ten years ago when Dies Irae had slain her soldiers, her servants, and her father.

Mirum dared glance at Dies Irae's neck. She saw a golden chain there, its links thick. Those links disappeared under Dies Irae's breastplate. *Does he wear the amulet, the Griffin Heart?* she wondered, fingers trembling. She imagined leaping forward, tugging the chain, stealing his amulet, stealing his griffins. But of course, armies of Vir Requis had fought to reclaim the Griffin Heart, to reclaim the power to tame and control griffinflesh. Those armies had failed. What chance would she have?

Dies Irae jerked his head to one of his lieutenants, the gaunt man with the barred visor. Hand on the pommel of his sword, the man moved to guard the doors.

God, he knows, Mirum thought. Her heart pounded. *He knows what I hide here, he knows of him, he's blocking his escape. God, why did I let the boy fly? Somebody must have seen him, and now Dies Irae has come here, come to this hall with his sword and his promise of blood.*

Mirum clutched her fingers behind her back to hide their tremble.

"Please sit at my table, my lord," she said. She stared at that chipped old table, not daring to look at Dies Irae. Her heart thrashed. "I will serve you bread and fish."

With a snort, the female griffin rider removed her helmet, and Mirum felt herself pale. She recognized this face, and it sent shivers through her. The woman was beautiful, achingly so, with icy green eyes, red lips, and cascading golden locks. She couldn't have been older than eighteen, yet none of youth's life nor folly seemed to fill her; her face was cold and cruel as a statue.

Gloriae.

Dies Irae's daughter.

As Mirum watched, Gloriae spat onto the floor. Her spit landed at Mirum's feet.

"Bah! Bread and fish," Gloriae said, those perfect red lips curling in disgust. "We've not flown for hours to this place to eat bread and fish. Have you no boar? No deer or fowl? What kind of hall do you run, you seaside waif?"

Mirum felt the blood rush back into her cheeks. She knew the stories. She knew that King Benedictus had believed this young woman to be his own daughter, not the daughter of Dies Irae's rapes. Mirum, however, saw only the cruelty of Dies Irae in this one. She remembered the stories of Gloriae killing her first Vir Requis at age six, of killing ten more when she was but eight.

Trained from childhood in malice and murder, Mirum thought, for a moment rage overpowering her fear.

Disgust filled her mouth, tasting of bile. She forced herself to curtsy before Gloriae. "Forgive me, my lady. This is a but a simple seaside fort, the home of waifs, not the abode of great, illustrious nobles such as yourself." She wondered if Gloriae would detect the sarcasm in her voice. "But if you please, I would be glad to serve fine ale with your meal."

Gloriae stared at her, eyebrows rising over those icy green eyes. Her white cheeks flushed just the slightest. She took a step forward, drew her sword with a hiss, and placed its cold tip against Mirum's neck. Mirum stiffened. The blade was white steel, beautiful and glinting, its base filigreed in gold, and Mirum could imagine Vir Requis blood flowing down its grooves.

"Ale, you say?" Gloriae said softly, regarding her, one eyebrow raised. She tilted her head, her expression almost quizzical. "No fine wine for us great, illustrious nobles? Maybe instead of red wine, I shall content myself with red blood."

Mirum stared back, not tearing her eyes away, and clenched her jaw. They might kill her now, she knew. *Kill me if you must, but don't look in my tower. Please, Earth God, don't let them see what I hide.*

Dies Irae stepped forward. He placed a hand on Gloriae's shoulder. "Now now, sweet daughter," Dies Irae said, voice echoing inside his eagle helm. "This is not the time for blades. Mirum is being the most gracious host she can, for one who lives in a seaside ruin. Let her serve us her bread, her fish and her ale. We are not above the simple pleasures of peasants, are we?"

Mirum felt the rage boil in her, and she swallowed hard. Hers was an old, noble line. Her father had ruled many forts, as had his father, and many past generations of their line. Mirum was descended of great blood, and yet Dies Irae saw her as a waif, a fisherwoman barely worthy to serve him. Still she curtsied again. "I have no fine wine, but my ale is cold, and my bread warm."

Finally Dies Irae removed his helmet, and Mirum saw his face for the first time in ten years. It froze her blood. Here he was, here was this same face, the face that had haunted her for so long. It was ironic, she thought, that he looked so much like the beasts he rode. His face was like the face of an eagle, cold, handsome, his skin a golden hue. His hair was slicked back, blond streaked with gray, and his nose was hooked like a beak. His mouth was a thin line; his lips were so thin and pursed, he seemed almost to have no lips at all. A few more creases marred that face now, and more gray filled his temples, but it was the same face from ten years ago. The cold, golden, griffin face.

He was born to Vir Requis, Mirum remembered suddenly. He had their noble face, their high forehead. But of course, Dies Irae had been born without the gift, without the ancient blessing, without the magic to become a dragon. *It must have been so hard,* she reflected, shocked to find pity fill her. *To be firstborn of Requiem's king, yet lacking the gift. To be cast aside. To grow to hate that gift, to seek to destroy it. So much pain must dwell in him.*

That thin mouth curved into a smile, a cold smile, a smile that made that face even harsher, crueler. "Do you fear me, child?" he asked. "You tremble."

She lowered her head, realizing that she had stared at him. "It's been long since the presence of greatness has entered my hall. Forgive me, my lord. I'll fetch your food and drink."

Dies Irae sat at the chipped oak table. Gloriae removed her white leather gloves, stared at a wooden chair distastefully, and too sat down. The third rider—the gaunt, silent man—stayed to guard the door. His barred helm still hid his face.

Mirum hurried out of the hall. She paced downstairs into the cellar, legs trembling, heart thrashing. The cellar was a dark, dusty place carved into the rock beneath Fort Sanctus. The roar of waves was loud here, as were the smells of moss, dried fish, sausages, bread rolls, and oak barrels of ale. She had thought to find Julian sweeping the cellar floors. When she did not see him, she remembered that he had taken his donkey to town that morning, gone to buy turnips and onions and spices. *He will probably buy me a gift, too; flowers for my room, or a simple necklace of beads. Dear old man.* She was glad that he was gone. He was safe away from this fort. If Julian had been here, Dies Irae would have killed him for sport. Mirum was sure of that.

She collected pewter mugs from a shelf, opened a keg of ale, and began filling the mugs. As she worked, her mind raced. Had the boy in her tower seen the griffins? Surely he had. Surely he knew to fear them. She had rehearsed this day with him many times—every night. She would clutch his shoulders, stare into his eyes, and force him to repeat what she had taught him.

"Stay in the tower," he would say, bored with the words he would recite every night for ten years. "Do not turn into a dragon. Do not fly. Do not try to escape. Stay hidden, stay silent, stay inside my barrel."

Please, Kyrie, Mirum thought as she placed the mugs of ale upon a tray. *Just don't panic. Just don't fly.*

She found some chipped wooden plates and began loading them with smoked fish and bread rolls. Ten years ago, she had found the boy lying in the devastation of Lanburg Fields. Dies Irae had been flown away, armless, pale, near death. Benedictus the Black, King of Requiem, had fled. The other Vir Requis all lay dead upon the field, the last of their kind. Most of Dies Irae's soldiers had left the bodies to rot, but a squad of men, their white cloaks now red, had remained to move among the bodies, to search for the wounded and spear them. When they saw Mirum moving between the bodies too, they laughed, mocked her, called dirty words her way. She was so numb, she barely heard.

When she first saw the boy, she thought him dead. He looked six or seven years old, thin, covered in blood. Many young Vir Requis had come here to fight, flushed out of hiding with their elders, but this one was the youngest she saw. He did not move at first, but when Mirum stood above him, crying over his body, he opened his eyes.

"Mama," he whispered, voice high and soft.

"I... I'm not your mama," Mirum whispered back, glancing behind her, praying the men in bloody cloaks did not hear.

The boy spoke again, tears on his ashy cheeks. "I want my mama."

She had wrapped him in her cloak that night, placed him on the saddle of her horse, her good horse Sol. He was so small, so thin, he could be mistaken for a bundle of clothes or firewood. She sat behind him in the saddle and galloped, galloped harder than she ever had, galloped over bodies and fields drenched in blood, galloped away from the mocking men and the death of an ancient race, galloped home. To Fort Sanctus. To her sanctuary by the sea, to the fresh graves of her men, of her father, of her old life.

Kyrie Eleison was his name. She kept him in her tower, this young Vir Requis, kept him hidden for ten years now. She had stood by Dies Irae that day, stood with his banners as he murdered the last survivors of Requiem. She too was stained with their blood. If she could save one, just the life of one boy, maybe... maybe she would find redemption. Maybe the blood would be washed from her hands. So she had hidden him, and raised him, and prayed every night to forget the sight of all those bodies, the bodies of her men, of her father, of Kyrie's people. She tried to toss those memories into the sea, to let the waves claim them. For ten years she had gazed upon this angry sea, praying to forget.

She stepped back into her hall, tray of ale and food in hands.

Mirum set the table silently, eyes lowered. As she worked, Dies Irae stared at her body, and his eyes told her, *I hunger for you more than for your food.* Feeling blood rise to her cheeks, Mirum was acutely aware of her riding dress, how its wool clung to her, still wet from the waves. She forced herself to suffocate the memory of that night, that endless night of rapes. She had to bite her lip, to shut her eyes, to swallow the anger and continue setting the table. Anger would kill her now. She raised her eyes and glanced at the door, but the gaunt man still guarded it, arms crossed, face hidden. Mirum wanted to flee. Every instinct in her body screamed to run, to escape, to jump out the window if she must, even if jumping meant crashing against the boulders and drowning broken in the sea. Yet she could not. She had to stay here, serve these riders, protect Kyrie. She had vowed ten years ago to protect him. She had done so since. She would do so now... whatever it took.

When she placed the last plate on the table, Dies Irae reached under her skirt to find and squeeze the soft flesh beneath. Mirum's breath froze and her heart leaped. *I still have Father's sword at my waist,* she thought and trembled. *I can still draw it, kill at least one of them, maybe two before they kill me. I'm good with the sword.* But no. She could not die now. Not as Kyrie hid in her tower; she owed him to live, to protect him, no matter what Dies Irae did to her.

"Father, must you while I'm around?" Gloriae said, staring distastefully at Dies Irae's hand up Mirum's skirt. She sipped her ale, wrinkled her nose, and spat it onto the floor. "Honestly, Father, you can be as tasteless as this ale."

Dies Irae laughed, and blessedly, his hand left Mirum's skirt. She exhaled shakily.

Dies Irae sipped his ale and his thin, curved mouth curved even further. He put the mug down, lines of disgust appearing in that golden skin of his. "I certainly would hate to appear as coarse as this drink," he said.

These ones rarely drank cheap ale, Mirum knew, but were used to sipping fine wines. Their tastes had to be as exquisite as their jeweled armor and priceless samite capes. Dies Irae pushed the mug away, his eagle face frowning, and reached out to grab Mirum's arm.

She couldn't help but yelp, which made Gloriae laugh, a cold and beautiful laugh like ice cracking. But Dies Irae did not laugh. His fingers clutched her so painfully, Mirum wanted to scream. It felt like his fingers could tear into her, pull the muscles off her bone. She had not known fingers could cause such pain.

"Mirum... sweetness," Dies Irae said, voice soft, cold, like a slow wave before a storm. His eyes pierced her, steady and dark blue. They bored into her, a stare so cold and sharp, it almost hurt her skin.

"My lord," she whispered, unable to talk any louder. She wanted to scream or faint from the pain.

He tightened his grip on her, fingernails digging, and she bit her lip hard. "Sweetness," he said, "do you know why I am here today? Do you know why I've come to this wretched, seaside ruin of a fort, this pile of moldy stones by this cesspool you call a beach?"

She wanted to hit him, to spit at him, to draw her sword with her free hand and run him through. *Kyrie,* she thought. *I must live for Kyrie. He has nobody else. And neither do I.*

"I don't know, my lord," she whispered.

He rose to his feet so suddenly, she started. He released her arm, shoved her back, and backhanded her face. Pain exploded. For an instant, Mirum saw only white light. She took a ragged breath, wobbling, spots dancing before her eyes. She could barely see, barely breathe. *Draw your sword,* a voice inside her whispered. *Draw Father's blade and finish him now, or he'll rape and kill you, or kill and then rape you. Kill him now and then fall upon your sword.*

Yet she could not... and she didn't know if it was because she was brave, or because she was a coward.

"You're lying," Dies Irae said, voice as hard as his hand.

Mirum's eyes were glazed, and she gazed past him, gazed out the window toward the sea. She could see the waves there, hear their murmur, taste their salt on her lips. So many of her tears, so many of her whispers and mumbles those waves had swallowed. So many of her fears she had spoken into their roaring depths. The promise of hidden realms and seascapes of wonder pulsed beneath them, a world unknown to her, unknown to any human. Standing in this room, blood on her lip, cruelty surrounding her, Mirum wished like never before to dive into those waves, to disappear into their kingdoms of seashells, sunken ruins, twinkling beads of light so far from pain. *From the sea we come, to the sea we return,* were the words of her forefathers, words always murmured at births and deaths. *Who will utter those words for me? Will I be buried too in the kingdom of waterdepth, or burned upon my walls?*

Dies Irae returned to his seat. He leaned back, placed his hand behind his head, and laid his boots upon the table. "There are rumors," he said, voice soft, but Mirum could hear him so loudly, she wanted to cover her ears. "There are rumors in the village. The fishermen whisper of... a shape at night, a shape in the skies. A shape that blocks the stars."

"Could it be a cloud, my lord?" Mirum dared to ask, and Dies Irae laughed mirthlessly.

"You are an endearing creature, are you not?" He placed his boots on the floor and gestured at Gloriae. "Bring her to me."

The young woman was slim, no taller than Mirum and unlikely to be stronger, but still she stepped forward, green eyes flashing with amusement. A slight, crooked smile on her lips, Gloriae shoved Mirum.

Dies Irae caught her and pulled her down, so that Mirum sat in his lap. She tried to rise, to struggle, but Dies Irae held her firmly, his iron arm across her. She turned her face away from his, disgusted, but he clutched her cheek with his good hand and turned her face toward him. Gloriae laughed icily.

"So innocent," Dies Irae whispered to Mirum. His good hand was gloved in moleskin, and he used it to wipe the blood off her lip. "You are still a child, are you not? Like the last time I saw you. A cloud, you say. It is sweet, my child, sweet like your soft cheeks, like your bloodied lips, sweet like all of you." His eyes undressed her. "But no, child. This was no cloud. This was the shape of a dragon, swooping low over the sea at nights, sometimes roaring, scaring fishermen's children, waking them, filling their nightmares. Can you imagine the atrocity, child? A dragon flying at night... here in my lands? Over the sea of Fort Sanctus, which I let you rule?"

Mirum shut her eyes. Looking at his golden, hard face was too painful. "I have seen no dragons here."

Dies Irae squeezed her thigh, and Mirum struggled, but could not free herself. "Nobody has seen dragons, not true dragons, not in a thousand years. The true dragons left these lands long ago. No, child. This was a Vir Requis."

At the sound of that ancient name, the tittering Gloriae fell silent. Mirum froze, her breath dying within her. *Vir Requis.* Nobody spoke those words anymore. They were forbidden words, taboo, words Dies Irae allowed nobody to speak.

Vir Requis. The ancient blood. The men who carried the old magic, the magic that let them take dragon form. They were not true dragons, but nor were they true men. Vir Requis. A proud, ancient race. They were remembered now as weredragons, as if they were monsters, no nobler or prouder than beasts.

"But... but I thought they're all dead," Mirum whispered and opened her eyes.

Dies Irae was looking at her, and Mirum realized that his eyes were the same color as her sea, gray blue, as cold and dangerous as those waves that crashed against her fort.

"I thought so too, child," he whispered, so softly that she read his lips more than she heard his voice. "But they say that one may have survived. One... maybe two. Maybe three. No more. No more out of a million. But a handful might remain, pretending to be decent humans. Like cowards they hide—in basements, in caves. Maybe even, child, in a ruined seaside tower."

There could be no doubt now. He knew of Kyrie. Someone had betrayed them. One of the villagers. One of her friends. Someone had seen Kyrie, had seen him turn into a dragon, and had talked.

A tear rolled down Mirum's cheek.

"Now now, dear child," Dies Irae said and lifted the tear on his finger. "Why do you cry? Is it for your shame, your shame for having betrayed me?"

Mirum tightened her lips. *No! Do not give up now. Not yet. Live a little longer, for Father, for Kyrie.* She swallowed hard, swallowed down all her terror, all her memories. "There is no weredragon here, my lord. You may search this tower if you will. You will find none."

He rose suddenly, shoving her off. She hit the table, then hit the floor, but this time Gloriae did not laugh. There would be no laughter so soon after the forbidden words had been uttered. *Who of them will rape me today?* Mirum thought. *And will Irae kill me after, or before they've had their way?*

"Show us to the tower top," Dies Irae said, all the softness gone from his voice. That voice was now cold, commanding, and sharp as Gloriae's blade. "Let us search this ruin."

Dies Irae left the hall, holding Mirum before him, and they stepped onto the staircase. His lieutenants walked behind: the cold and dainty Gloriae, all in steel and gold, and the gaunt, silent man whose face still hid behind his helm. The staircase wound up the tower, its steps chipped, centuries old. Mirum walked numbly, Irae's fingers digging into her arm. They walked round and round, up and up, and Mirum kept looking out the arrow slits, peering at the roaring sea, wishing again that she could dive under that water, swim away, drown into the world of hidden wonders.

Please, Kyrie, she thought feverishly, lips trembling. *Please hide.*

And if they found him... she still had her sword at her side. She could not hope to kill them all, probably not even kill Dies Irae. Even if she did kill him, that meant torture for her. They would break her spine with hammers, break her limbs and string them through the spokes of a wagon wheel, and hang her outside to slowly die. They would do the same to Kyrie, not caring that he was still a boy, only sixteen. But maybe... maybe if she could draw her sword fast enough, she could still fall upon it.

They reached the tower top. A rotting wooden trapdoor lay above her, leading outside to the crenellations.

"Open it," Dies Irae said.

With numb hands, Mirum pushed open the trapdoor, then stepped outside onto the windy, crumbling crest of Fort Sanctus.

The waves roared below, spraying foam. The wind lashed her, streamed her hair, and flapped her cloak and dress. Old iron bars surrounded the tower top, the vestiges of some ancient armaments, now rusty. The stone they rose from was moldy and chipped. *This tower has been in my family for centuries. Will it fall today?*

Below the tower, Mirum could see the three griffins, those beautiful beasts. She could not see Sol. Had the griffins eaten her, or had her mare escaped? Either fate seemed kinder than what Mirum would endure if they found Kyrie here today.

Mirum could see for leagues from here. On one side, she saw the endless sea, gray water flowing into the horizon. On her other side, saw leagues of boulders, rocky fields, and scraggly deltas. Once all these lands had belonged to her father, and to his father before him, and many forts had risen from them. Dies Irae had taken these lands, toppled these forts, killed her father and his father. All he'd left was this place, this old tower, this old village. When Mirum looked down, she could see the fishing village, this hamlet where somebody had betrayed her, where somebody had seen Kyrie and spoken.

I told you, Kyrie, she thought and tasted tears on her lips. *I told you not to fly. I told you never to use your magic, never to become a dragon.* But he would never listen. A Vir Requis was meant to fly. If they stayed human too long, they grew thin, pale, withered. They needed to breathe fire, to flap wings and taste the firmaments between their jaws.

"There's nobody here," Gloriae said, her sword drawn. The wind streamed her golden hair and turned her cheeks pink.

Dies Irae raised his steel fist, the spiked mace head. "Wait, my daughter. We will look."

A few old chests and barrels littered the tower top. Dies Irae eyed them.

"Old fishing gear," Mirum said, and was surprised to hear no hoarseness to her voice, almost no trace of fear. Her voice sounded dead. Flat.

Dies Irae did not spare her a glance. "We shall see. Molok, the laceleaf, please."

The gaunt man stepped forward, rail-thin, tall and gangly. Finally he lifted his helmet's visor, and Mirum saw his face. The face was cadaverous. His cheekbones jutted and his dark eyes were sunken. Mirum knew this one. Lord Molok—known in whispers as the baby killer, for he had once slaughtered five Vir Requis infants in a village, and probably many more that men did not speak of. As Mirum watched, trembling, Molok opened a leather pouch. He pulled out crumpled leaves and handed them to Dies Irae.

Mirum's knees trembled. *Laceleaf.* The pale, serrated leaves leaked white latex like milk. Laceleaf was what Dies Irae would call it, of course; a mild name, the name of a herb one might find in an old woman's garden. To the Vir Requis it had other names.

"Do you know what this is?" Dies Irae asked. He held the leaves up to Mirum's nose. He crushed one between two fingers, and she smelled it, a smell like vinegar and overripe apples.

"A herb," she whispered.

Dies Irae laughed softly. "To you or me, yes. A harmless herb. My maids often cook my meals with it. But to the weredragons... do you know what they call it, sweetness?" His nostrils flared, inhaling the plant's aroma, and he let out a satisfied sigh. "They call it ilbane, or deathweed, or devil's leaves. In their ancient tongue, which the weredragons spoke in the old days, it was simply called *valber*, which is their word for poison."

"It kills weredragons," Mirum said, hating the taste of that word on her lips. *Weredragons.* A foul word. The name of monsters.

Dies Irae shook his head. "Kills them? Oh no, my dear. It takes more than a herb to kill beasts of such evil. It sickens them. Burns them. When they are in human form, it reveals the monstrosity that lies within them, their reptilian blood. But no, sweetness, it does not *kill* them." He raised his iron fist. The sun finally peeked from the clouds, and the mace head glittered. Dies Irae's thin lips smiled. "*This* kills them."

So swiftly Mirum gasped, Dies Irae swung his iron arm. The mace head hit a rotted chest, showering splinters of wood. Mirum bit her lip, instinctively reaching for her sword, but Lord Molok grabbed her arm with a gauntleted hand, and she could not draw her blade.

Mirum took a ragged breath. Nothing but some old arrowheads, flasks of oil, and rope fell from the shattered chest.

Mirum saw two more chests, both of rotting and cracked wood, and five barrels. Which one hid Kyrie? *Fly, Kyrie,* she thought feverishly, trying to transfer her thoughts to him as by magic. *The time to fly has come. Escape!*

Dies Irae smirked and approached a barrel. Now that the clouds had parted, he truly looked like a seraph, his armor so bright it hurt Mirum's eyes, the jeweled griffin on his breastplate shining like stars. The garnets on his mace appeared like drops of blood.

That iron arm swung again and slammed into a barrel.

Splinters scattered.

Turnips rolled onto the floor.

Fly, Kyrie! Mirum wanted to scream, but she could bring no breath to her lungs. She felt paralyzed, could barely breathe, and would have fallen had Molok not been holding her.

Dies Irae swung his mace into another chest.

Wood shattered.

Splinters flew.

A cry of pain sounded, and there—in the splintered wreck of the chest—huddled a boy.

Kyrie.

"Ah, here we go," Dies Irae said pleasantly, as if he had just found a missing sock.

Mirum stared, mouth open, Molok clutching her. Huddled on the floor, glaring up with burning eyes, Kyrie seemed so young to her. He was sixteen now, but suddenly to Mirum's eyes, he seemed six again, a mere child, like when she'd found him bloodied among corpses at Lanburg Fields. His hair was fair, dusty, wild. His eyes were brown, more pain and anger in them than fear. As always, his parchment map was rolled up and stuffed into his belt. Kyrie always kept the map on him; his bit of hope, bit of memory, bit of anger.

Ice filled Mirum's stomach. Kyrie did not know Dies Irae like she did. If he had seen Dies Irae slaughter her father, rape her all night by the corpse, he would have less anger in his eyes... and more terror.

Cradling his arm—Dies Irae's mace must have bashed it—Kyrie rose to his feet. He was taller than Mirum already, but when he faced Dies Irae, the golden lord towered over him.

"All right, all right, you win," Kyrie said, eyes flashing. "You found me. Now bugger off before I bash your beak nose."

As Mirum gasped, Dies Irae laughed. It was not a cruel laugh, Mirum thought, nor angry; Dies Irae seemed truly amused. "Bold words," he said, "for a worm caught cowering in a barrel like a rat."

Kyrie glared, fists clenched at his sides. "Am I a rat or a worm? You're good at bashing things, but your tongue is as blunt as that freakish iron hand of yours."

"No, Kyrie," Mirum whispered through a clenched jaw. *Fly! Turn into a dragon and fly! Why do you linger here?*

But of course, she knew. If Kyrie flew, he'd prove to Dies Irae that he was Vir Requis. The griffins would chase him, but they would not just kill him; they would torture him, then burn him alive upon the towers of Flammis, Dies Irae's marble palace. *He thinks he can withstand the ilbane*, Mirum realized, feeling faint. Her knees buckled, and she stayed standing only because Molok clutched her arms. *No, Kyrie, you cannot; no Vir Requis can, not even the great Benedictus.*

"What's your name?" Dies Irae asked the boy, still seeming more amused than slighted.

"Kyrie Eleison," he replied, chin raised, fists still clenched.

"Kyrie, I like you," Dies Irae said. "Most weredragons are terrified of me. They tremble in my presence like the sweet Lady Mirum here. But you, Kyrie... you feel no fear, only anger. That is rare for weredragons, who are known for their cowardice."

"Yes, yes," Kyrie said, and Mirum knew that he was scared now, terrified, but letting his anger drown that fear. "I have weredragon features, and Eleison is a weredragon name. I hear that all the time. Why do you think I hide here? People always mistake me for a weredragon. My father was one. But then... so was yours, wasn't he, Irae?"

Mirum gasped. Nobody mentioned Dies Irae's father to him. Nobody who wished to live. Everyone knew that this was Dies Irae's greatest shame.

Dies Irae's thin mouth curved bitterly, and lines ran down his face. His fist clenched the ilbane, and sap dripped. "Yes," he said, "my father was a weredragon. The filthiest, most cowardly among them."

"He was their *king*," Kyrie spat out, eyes aflame. "But you were a disgrace to him, weren't you? His firstborn son... but without the ancient magic, unable to become a dragon. You were a freak in his court, weren't you? So he disowned you. He had another son, Benedictus, to replace you—"

"*Enough!*" Dies Irae shouted, so loudly that Mirum, Irae's lieutenants, and even Kyrie started. Dies Irae shook with fury, fist clenched, face red. His eyes burned. "My lineage is none of your concern, weredragon. That old, royal house of Requiem is gone now. My father is dead. My brother is dead—"

"Benedictus is *not* dead," Kyrie interrupted, and Mirum wept, because she knew that their torture and deaths were now certain. "You never killed Benedictus. You stole his amulet, and you stole his griffins, but you never killed him. Your brother bit off your arm. He could have *killed* you, but he showed you mercy, and he flew away. I know! I was there. I saw it happen—"

Kyrie froze and bit his lip.

Oh, Kyrie..., Mirum thought, tears in her eyes.

Dies Irae stared silently for a moment, a moment that seemed to Mirum to last a lifetime. Finally he broke the silence. "You were... there. Certainly you were too young a decade ago to fight under my banners." Dies Irae raised his fist, bringing the ilbane near Kyrie... and then pressed the leaves to Kyrie's cheek.

Kyrie tried not to scream. His teeth gritted, and sweat washed him, and his eyes moistened. Mirum saw welts rise on his cheek, and his fist clutched his map, that parchment forever at his belt, as if it could save him, give him strength. Mirum struggled to free herself from Molok, but could not. Finally voice found her throat.

"*Fly, Kyrie!*" she shouted at the top of her lungs.

Kyrie too shouted, a cry of pain. He leaped away from Dies Irae, cheek blistering, and suddenly fangs grew from his mouth. Claws sprouted from his fingertips. Dies Irae swung his mace, but Kyrie leaped back, and the mace missed him.

Kyrie leaped off the tower.

In the chaos, Molok's grip loosened. Mirum twisted, freed herself, and drew her blade.

She thrust her sword at Dies Irae. *You killed my father!* she wanted to scream. *You raped me! You murdered millions!* But everything happened so fast, she had time for only a wordless cry of all her rage and tears. Her blade gleamed.

Dies Irae swung his mace, met her blade, and shattered it.

Mirum fell to her knees, clutching her bladeless hilt, and saw a dragon rise over the tower's crenellations, forty feet long and roaring. Blue scales covered Kyrie. Flames rose from his nostrils, and his wings churned the air, blowing the hair back from Mirum's face. Mirum heard the thud of griffin wings, their eagle shrieks.

"Fly, Kyrie!" Mirum shouted. He was reaching toward her. "Leave me! Follow your map, Kyrie, and fly!"

Kyrie's claws almost caught her, but Dies Irae's mace slammed into them, knocking them away. Kyrie howled and blew fire into the sky. One griffin rose behind him, clung to his back, and bit his shoulder.

"*Fly, Kyrie!*"

The last thing Mirum saw was Dies Irae's mace. It swung toward her head.

She felt only an instant of pain.

White light flooded her.

Floating.

Her spirit... flying, gazing down upon her body, her blood upon the mossy old stones of Fort Sanctus, her home, the home of her forefathers.

And then... nothing but light.

Father....

Child....

She could now see nothing, nothing but white, but she could imagine the rolling lands of her realm, their proud towers standing again, the sea that called her home.

I'm going to that world, the kingdom of waterdepths, the land of seaweed and seashells, of beads of light and endless sleep, endless wonder.

It was like falling asleep...

...and she was gone.

KYRIE ELEISON

"Mirum!" Kyrie howled.

The griffin on his back shrieked and dug its talons into him. Kyrie struggled, lashing his tail, and freed himself. Two more griffins flew at him, one from each side.

Mirum....

Tears in his eyes, Kyrie pulled his wings close. He swooped from the tower top to the boulders below, the rocky beach, and the crashing waves. Water sprayed him. He twisted, skimmed across the water, and shot up. The griffins followed, reaching out their talons.

"No... Mirum...," Kyrie wept. He could barely see the waves, the clouds, the fort, the griffins that followed. All he could see was the image of Dies Irae clubbing Lady Mirum, the image of her falling, head cracked. Dead. She could not have survived that blow; Kyrie knew it. And yet... he had to go back. He had to get her body, to bury her at sea.

Fly, Kyrie! Her voice still echoed in his mind. *Leave me!*

A griffin slammed into Kyrie, and its talons ripped off scales. Kyrie screamed, pain blazing. He blew flames, roaring red flames of all his fury, setting the griffin alight. It shrieked so loudly, it hurt Kyrie's ears. It swooped into the sea, then emerged smoking and screaming.

Fly!

"I'll come back for you," Kyrie swore... and he flew.

He flew low and skimmed the water, the wind lashing him. He was soon a league from Fort Sanctus. When he looked back, he saw the griffins following. Dies Irae, Gloriae, and Molok rode them. *Damn.* Dragon eyes were sharp—sharper than his eyes in human form—and Kyrie could see that Dies Irae glared, his thin mouth curving. His mace was raised.

Let's see how fast you bastards can fly, Kyrie thought and narrowed his eyes. He pumped his wings. At night, streaming over fields and seas, he could travel hundreds of leagues in a flight. Now he flew faster than ever. There was no way those griffins could fly half that fast, Kyrie told himself. Not while bearing armored riders.

He rose above the water, moving higher and higher. He crashed through the clouds and emerged into startling blue sky, the sun a blazing disk above, blinding him. Kyrie found an air current and shot forward, body straight as a javelin. He gritted his teeth and flapped his wings madly, pushing himself forward with all his strength. He was moving so fast now, the clouds below him blurred. The sun hit his back, and the icy air bit him. He had never flown faster.

Beat that, Irae, he thought and grinned bitterly.

Then he heard it.

A griffin shriek.

He turned his head and cursed. *Impossible!* The griffins were pursuing, bodies like arrows. How could they fly so fast?

Kyrie grunted. He flapped his wings with all his might. His body ached. The air stung him, icicles covered him, and he could hardly breathe. It was cold up here, freezing, the air so thin his head spun. He would not survive much longer at this altitude. Kyrie lowered himself just a few hundred yards, dipping into the clouds. Moisture clung to him and filled his maw, eyes, and nostrils. When he turned his head again, he could see nothing but cloud, but he heard them. They were moving closer. Gritting his teeth, Kyrie kept flying, aching, moving faster than an arrow. He must have traveled thirty leagues, maybe more, but could not lose them. He pulled his wings close, dived, and emerged from under the clouds.

He saw a land of rock and water. He still flew over the sea, but great stone teeth now rose from the water, some hundreds of feet tall. The jutting rock formed towers, snaking walls, canyons of foaming sea. Rising from crashing waves, the rocks looked like forts, with pillars and bridges and tunnels, battlements of some forgotten water gods. The sea roared between the pillars, through the stone tunnels, moving in and out of crevices like the watery breath of sea monsters. Kyrie had never seen this place, this realm of rock and foam and salt, and he gasped at its beauty and danger.

Shrieks sounded above him. Kyrie raised his head and saw the griffins swooping from the clouds, talons outstretched, beaks open.

Damn it.

Kyrie veered aside, but a griffin clawed his leg, drawing blood. Cursing, Kyrie shot into the clouds again. The griffins followed. He dived to the sea, but another almost clawed him. A third flew from below, and Kyrie swiveled, dodging it, then spun again, just missing another griffin. They surrounded him.

Damn the stars!

Kyrie blew fire. The griffin ahead swerved, dodging the flames. Kyrie swooped, zoomed by it, almost hit the water, then straightened himself to skim over the waves. The boulders rose around him, black and jagged, and one almost hit his shoulder. Waves and foam brushed his belly.

You're fast bastards, he thought, *but let's see you maneuver.*

Stone walls rose ahead, a canyon between them, barely wider than his body. Kyrie flew into the canyon, the walls rushing by his sides. The sea roared below, spraying him with foam, and he could barely see the sky. Screeches came behind him, and when Kyrie glanced over his shoulder, he saw the griffins follow him into the canyon.

Rocks jutted out from the cliff sides, and Kyrie flew up and down, dodging them. He snaked around boulders like liquid silver streaming through a labyrinth. Fire pumped through him, and despite the danger and anguish, Kyrie grinned over gritted teeth. This was what he'd been born for. This was *flying*. In some places, the canyon walls met above him, forming tunnels. One tunnel was so low, Kyrie's belly grazed the sea as he flew. A thud came behind him, followed by a shriek of pain.

"Having fun, girls?" Kyrie shouted over his shoulder, and saw that one griffin was hurt, its shoulder bleeding. Kyrie grinned and kept flapping his wings, which was hard to do in a tunnel this narrow. His heart raced. *I was made for this.*

Suddenly the canyon curved, and Kyrie made a sharp turn. His shoulder grazed the stone wall, and he grunted, but he made the turn with nothing but a scratch. Behind him came a thud, a shriek, and a rider's cry; one griffin at least had not made the turn. Kyrie kept flying. When he glanced over his shoulder, he saw that the wounded griffin was gone. So was its rider, the gaunt Lord Molok. Kyrie hoped he was dead.

The canyon ended, the walls giving way to a network of jagged pillars. Some met above him, crisscrossing, molded together. Kyrie flew up and down, left and right, moving between the pillars at top speed. Around one column, a boulder rose from the waves, and Kyrie shot straight up, under an overhanging stone, left around another column, and quickly down into a tunnel.

Damn, he thought, then heard a crash behind him. A second griffin was gone. Its rider, the beautiful and icy Gloriae, crashed into the water.

One griffin remained now, and one rider.

Dies Irae.

The man who'd killed Mirum.

Kyrie grunted. *Now we're even.*

Flying between the stone boulders, he spun to face Dies Irae on his griffin. He howled and blew fire.

The flames roared, and the griffin rose, dodging the fire, but hit an overhanging arch of stone. The beast screeched, and Kyrie shot forward, claws slashing.

Dies Irae pulled the reins, and his griffin bucked, raising its talons. Kyrie's claws hit the griffin's leg, drawing blood. The griffin reached out to bite, but Kyrie was too fast. He dodged the beast, then lashed his spiked tail.

He hit Dies Irae, cracking his armor. Blood seeped from the steel. More blood flowed down the griffin's flanks. Kyrie growled.

"You're dead now, Irae," he said. Smoke rose from his nostrils. "You killed Mirum. You killed my family. And now I'm going to kill you."

He sucked in air, prepared to blow flames and roast the glittering, one-armed lord.

Dies Irae raised a crossbow.

So fast Kyrie barely saw it, a quarrel flew. It slammed into Kyrie's chest.

Kyrie howled. Pain bloomed, twisting and sizzling. He knew that pain. *Ilbane.* The quarrel was coated with the poison.

Kyrie gritted his teeth. *No! No. This does not end here.* He blew fire.

The flames roared, hit the griffin, and its fur kindled. It screeched, and Kyrie tried to fly toward it, to claw it apart, to crush Dies Irae, but his wings felt stiff. He could barely fly. He dipped several yards.

A second quarrel flew.

Wings aching, pain blazing, Kyrie managed to flap aside. The quarrel scratched his shoulder, tearing off a scale, burning.

Kyrie roared. He felt ready to pass out, but he mustered every last bit of rage, horror, and hatred in him, and he shot forward.

For Mirum. For my father, mother, brothers, and sisters. For ten years of hiding in stinking barrels. He opened his maw, howling, prepared to bite off Dies Irae's head.

For an instant, his eyes locked with Dies Irae's stare. The man's eyes blazed. He seemed full of so much hate, so much pain, that Kyrie nearly faltered. What was it? What caused the man to hate Vir Requis so much?

It happened so fast, Kyrie barely registered it. Dies Irae tugged the reins, and the griffin shot up.

No! Kyrie tried to follow. He flapped his wings, but felt so heavy. The griffin was shooting into the skies. It was getting away.

"Come back here, coward!" Kyrie howled. He blew fire, but his flames felt weak. They could not reach the griffin, who was only a distant spot now.

A third quarrel came zooming down. Kyrie spun aside, and the bolt missed him. He flew higher and higher, and his head exploded with pain.

"Irae, come back here and finish what you started!" he cried, then shut his eyes with pain. He dipped a hundred yards, another hundred. Another quarrel flew. It sank into his shoulder, and he screamed. He fell. He crashed into the sea. His wings would no longer move, and his muscles ached. Waves roared around him, icy cold, and water filled his mouth. He swam toward a boulder that rose from the waves, clutched it, and climbed onto it.

He became human again.

He clung to the rock, shivering. His shoulder and chest bled, and the ilbane coursed through him. It wouldn't kill him, he knew. He remembered what Dies Irae had said; the stuff was not lethal, but it burned. Worse than the pain was his grief.

Dies Irae had gotten away—gone to fetch more griffins, no doubt. The man was a coward. And....

Kyrie lowered his head. He tasted salt on his lips, and didn't know if it was from the sea, or his tears. *Mirum.* His best friend, the light of his life. Mirum was dead.

A wave washed over him, and Kyrie barely held onto the boulder. His clothes, which had shifted with him, now clung to him, cold and wet. His veins felt full of lava, and his head felt ready to crack. The waves kept pounding him. He looked around, but saw only furious water, jagged rocks, and pillars of stone. He was a hundred leagues away from shelter, from civilization, from life. He was stuck here on this jagged rock, shivering, bleeding, maybe dying. More griffins would arrive any moment. The waves roared so loudly, his ears ached.

Kyrie lowered his head against the stone. He closed his eyes. *It cannot end here. I cannot die here like this. Not now.*

He took a deep breath, lungs aching. With trembling fingers, he felt for the parchment map. It was still there, hanging from his belt. It was soaked, but it was still there.

There was only one thing to do now, Kyrie knew. It was a crazy quest, a fool's quest. The chase of a myth. But Kyrie knew it was the only path he could now follow.

He must find him.

He must still live... somewhere.

Kyrie nodded. He would seek Benedictus.

DIES IRAE

Dies Irae could barely hold the reins. His shoulder ached. The armor was dented, and blood seeped through its joints. His griffin, Volucris, was also wounded; his fur smoked and stank, and blood poured down his sides. Dies Irae clenched his jaw and clung to Volucris as he flew. Smoke filled his nostrils, and he grunted and coughed.

It seemed an eternity before he saw land ahead. A beach of black rocks stretched for a hundred yards, giving way to a forest of elms and birches. Gritting his teeth, Dies Irae directed Volucris to the shore. His ears ached as he descended. He landed upon the rocky beach.

Grimacing, Dies Irae alighted from Volucris, then stood before the foaming sea. He removed his pauldron. Beneath the gilded steel, his shoulder was a mess. A bruise was already spreading, and the skin was cracked and bleeding.

Disgusting reptile, Dies Irae thought. Lady Mirum had been hiding him all this time. Dies Irae wished he could club her again, hear the crack of her skull. He should fly back to her body and let Volucris eat it.

He clenched his good fist. Kyrie Eleison. A living weredragon.

Dies Irae spat. How could one of the monsters have escaped him for so long? Dies Irae decided not to kill the boy. No. Once he mustered reinforcement, he would capture the monstrosity, chain him, and display him as a freak for Osanna to jeer at. The last member of a wretched race, Kyrie would become a side show, a curiosity for a menagerie.

Dies Irae sat down with a grunt. *Where is Gloriae?* he wondered. Last he'd seen, she was swimming toward a boulder, bruised and battered. Had she flown back to land, or still remained at sea? Either way, she would live. He'd seek her soon.

Fingers stiff, Dies Irae caressed the amulet that hung around his neck, the amulet that contained the blood of the griffin king. As always, touching the amulet calmed him. The

Griffin Heart. For centuries, it had hung around the necks of his ancestors, a jewel of Requiem's courts.

When Volucris saw the amulet, he bucked and clawed the air.

"Yes, Volucris," Dies Irae whispered. "Yes, it hurts to see, does it not? It burns your eyes."

The griffin growled, and Dies Irae patted him. Volucris mewled and clawed the beach. Dies Irae remembered that day long ago, the day he took the Griffin Heart, took the amulet that should have always been his.

"For one hundred generations, the Griffin Heart went to the firstborn," he had said that day, a younger man, not yet forty and still full of youth's rage and strength. "Father! How dare you deny me this?" Tears had stung his eyes, and his voice had quavered.

His father sat upon Requiem's throne of twisting oak roots, the throne now chopped up and burned. The king looked down upon Dies Irae, his firstborn, the giftless son. His shame. The shame of the court.

"My son," the king said, "I have told you. This court is forbidden to you. How dare you enter it? How dare you demand a gift from me?"

Around the court of Requiem, the lords stared silently, grim, hands on their sword hilts. They wore green and silver, dragons embroidered onto their tunics. Beyond the columns, Dies Irae could see Requiem Forest, the hoary birches that spread for leagues. Birds chirruped and griffins flew above.

Standing below the throne, Dies Irae glared at his father. "I will not hide in my chambers any longer. I will not sit with the women of your court, learning to scribe, learning to count, learning to become some servant to you. I am your firstborn. I demand the—"

"You are a disgrace!" Father shouted, rising to his feet. Dies Irae froze and stared. So did the lords of the court. Even the birds fell silent. The King of Requiem stood, white hair wild, liver-spotted fists clenched.

"Father," Dies Irae whispered, lips trembling.

The king took a step toward him, jaw clenched. "How dare you demand anything from me? I do not know whose son you are, boy. You cannot turn into a dragon. What kind of Vir Requis are you? You think you can lead this people, sit upon this throne, use the Griffin Heart to tame them? You are no son of mine. I do not know what human my wife bedded, or how you were begotten, but—"

Dies Irae shouted, tears falling. "I am no bastard son! I am *your* son. The son of the king. No, I cannot turn into a dragon. I lack the gift. Others do too. Dozens of us were born this way, but you banish us. You make us your servants, but we're not weak. I will take the Griffin Heart. I will wear the amulet. I might not have dragon wings, but I will have griffin ones. And when I control the griffins, you will pay, Father, you will—"

"Brother!" came a voice from behind, and Dies Irae's voice died. Shaking with fury, he spun around to see Benedictus.

His younger brother was entering the hall. He wore green and gray, forest garb. He must have been out hunting, as was his wont. His black curls clung to his brow with sweat.

"Benedictus!" Dies Irae called across the hall. "*Prince* Benedictus, I should say. Heir to our throne. Baby brother." The words tasted vile.

Benedictus. Born to replace him, Dies Irae, the elder son. Benedictus, the second born. The great Vir Requis prince, able to become the great black dragon. Future king. *You too will kneel before me*, Dies Irae swore. *You too will beg for mercy when the Griffin Heart hangs around my neck.*

"Brother," Benedictus said and reached out callused hands. "Father. Please. Do not yell. Perhaps we can give the Griffin Heart to Dies Irae, Father. If I was born to sit upon the throne, he can sit beside me, rule the griffins for me."

Dies Irae spat. "I'll do nothing for you," he said. His hand strayed toward his sword. "I am first born, and I'll not see you sit upon any throne. If I cannot have this throne for myself, and myself only, I will destroy it. I will rule this kingdom, or I will burn it."

With a hiss, he drew his blade.

Bloodlust filled him, painting the world red.

Eyes narrowed, Dies Irae thrust his sword into Father's chest.

"Father!" Benedictus shouted and ran forward, but the hall was long. Long enough for Dies Irae to grab the Griffin Heart, which hung around Father's neck. Father gasped, his blood gushing, and his fingers clawed the air.

"I can't grow fangs," Dies Irae said and snapped the amulet off its chain. "But swords can bite just as deep."

A roar sounded behind. Dies Irae spun to see Benedictus shift into a dragon and leap at him.

Dies Irae snarled and raised the amulet.

With shrieks and thudding wings, a dozen griffins swooped into the hall and crashed into Benedictus. As his brother's blood spilled, Dies Irae smiled.

The griffins were his.

Requiem's greatest servants became her greatest enemies that day. They flew for him. They toppled the columns of this court. They tore down the birches. They burned all the shame and weakness from his heart; he was their master, and the world was his.

The Requiem War began.

Standing on the beach, Dies Irae clutched the Griffin Heart. The amulet bit into his palm. He forced himself to take a deep breath, to release the memories. That had been many years ago. The Vir Requis were nearly extinct now. His father was dead, the Oak Throne destroyed, Requiem in ruin. Benedictus was gone; nobody had seen him in a decade.

He released the amulet and took another deep breath. If he let the pain claim him now, let the memories fill him, he could lose track of time, drown in his rage, spend days in it. He gritted his teeth.

"There's no more time for memories," he whispered to Volucris, the greatest of the griffins, a prince among them. He mounted the beast. "Our war is not over yet. There is a weredragon to find."

As he took flight, Dies Irae imagined crushing Kyrie's bones, like he had crushed Mirum... and he smiled.

KYRIE ELEISON

As Kyrie traveled the land by foot, he learned something new about himself.

He hated walking.

Loathed it.

A blister grew on his right heel, two on his left. He didn't even know which foot to limp on. He had stubbed two toes against a root a league back, and the nails were turning black. *Disgusting*, he thought. His legs ached, and his wounded chest burned. His back also screamed.

He spoke between gritted teeth to the surrounding trees. "I. Hate. Walking."

He wanted to *fly*—to turn into a dragon, flap his wings, feel the rush of air, the power. *That* was the way to travel. But not today. Nor for the past month he'd spent walking in human form.

Flying, he knew, was just too dangerous.

Dies Irae was after him. Kyrie had seen parchments posted upon roadside taverns, crossroad signs, even the occasional oak. "Weredragon at large! Kyrie Eleison, escaped monster, transforms into a blue reptile. Bring dead or alive to the nearest Sun God temple for reward."

Kyrie snorted whenever he saw the posters. The crude drawing of a dragon was laughable; it showed him clutching a maiden in each hand, toppling a house with his tail, and chomping a baby. *Ridiculous.* If anyone ate babies, it was the beautiful and icy Gloriae; the young woman seemed just vicious enough.

Laughable as the poster was, Kyrie still dared not fly. Not with griffins patrolling the skies. An hour did not pass without Kyrie hearing a distant griffin cry. Several times a day, he saw them too, like eagles high above. And he knew they were looking for him.

Indeed, as Kyrie now limped on his blisters, more shrieks sounded above. Griffins. Three or four, by the sound of it. With a grunt, Kyrie dived into a leafy bush. He saw the griffins between the branches, talons like swords. Did Dies Irae ride one? The griffins shrieked again, then were gone, flying into the distance.

Kyrie sighed and climbed out from the leaves. He sat down on a fallen log and gazed around him. The forest was thick, and Kyrie couldn't see more than a few yards in each direction. Oak, birch, and ash trees grew here, and most seemed centuries old, thick and knotty. Their leaves rustled, scattering motes of light. Fallen logs crisscrossed around him, covered with moss and mushrooms.

"What am I even doing here?" he asked aloud.

Nobody answered but chirping birds, pattering squirrels, and rustling leaves. There was nobody here. Nobody in the entire forest.

Benedictus is dead, he told himself. *I'll never find him here. I'm the last Vir Requis. And once those griffins catch me, I too will die.*

Kyrie suddenly felt hot, his blood boiling. He wanted to scream, but dared not. Instead he gritted his teeth and punched a tree trunk. It hurt. *Good.* Physical pain could drown anguish. Pain was easier than anguish.

"That bloody, stupid, cursed map," Kyrie said and spat.

Breathing hard, he pulled the rolled up map from his belt. The parchment was old, cracked, and burned in one corner. The sea had soaked it, leaving it wrinkled. For five years, he'd carried it on his belt, refusing to shelf or box it. For five years, it had been his hope.

But the map couldn't be real. It too was just a child's dream. Wasn't it?

Kyrie unrolled the parchment. The ink was faded and smudged, but Kyrie had examined this map so many times, he could read it with eyes shut. He had found the parchment when he was eleven. An old peddler had ridden his donkey to Fort Sanctus, his cart overflowing with trinkets. Mirum bought a pan, tea leaves, and a necklace of agate stones. Kyrie wanted to buy a knife with a horn handle, but then saw a pile of scrolls. Fort Sanctus had a few scrolls in the basement; some contained prayers to the old Earth God, others epic poems of legends. Kyrie loved reading them, especially the poems. Most of the peddler's scrolls contained prayers to the new, cruel Sun God, but a few featured maps. And one map—the smallest, most tattered one—made Kyrie's heart skip.

The map showed a mountain, a river, and forest. It marked several villages and a cave. A road led between a castle and a port, and several roads led to towns. It was a map for peddlers, but Kyrie didn't care for its trade routes. What caught his eye was the map's corner, where Hostias Forest lay. Above that forest, smaller than his fingertip, appeared a picture of a black dragon. "Beware," was written over the drawing, "the black fangs."

A black dragon. Fangs.

Benedictus.

Kyrie had bought the map, the knife with the horn grip forgotten. Gasping, he'd shown it to Mirum, talked about it all day, told her that this map showed the location of Benedictus, the legend, the king in exile.

"Kyrie," Mirum would say, "it might be only a decoration, a scribble. It might mean nothing. And the map might be old, drawn when many dragons filled the land."

Kyrie would shake his head. "No. It's Benedictus. I know it."

Mirum would sigh, say nothing more, and ignore the parchment that forever hung at Kyrie's side. She let him believe, Kyrie knew, because she wanted him to have hope, to have a dream, to feel he wasn't the only one. For years, Kyrie clung to that dream, knew that Benedictus still lived, that somewhere there were others like him. Others who could turn into dragons. Others who were hunted, who hid, who remembered Requiem. Others who could some day come together, raise their race from hiding, and once more find the skies.

But standing here in the forest, wounded, hungry, hunted... it was hard to believe. Things were so different now. He had followed the map here, to this forest, to this corner where black fangs should bite. And what did he find? Birds. Squirrels. Shattered dreams.

"Damn it!" Kyrie suddenly shouted, not caring if griffins heard. He no longer cared about anything, and he pounded the tree again. Fingers shaking, he tore the map to shreds. "Damn Dies Irae, and damn Benedictus."

He stood panting, leaning against the tree, eyes shut... when a voice spoke.

"And damn loud, bratty kids scaring away deer."

Kyrie froze, then spun around, eyes opening.

A man stood before him.

Kyrie breathed in hard, fighting the urge to become a dragon, to attack or flee. This man was trouble; Kyrie could smell the stink of danger on him.

"What do you want?" Kyrie demanded, eyes narrow.

The man spat and growled. "For you to shut up. I was just about to shoot a stag, and you scared him off. How about you keep your trap shut, or go whine in somebody else's forest?"

The man wore ragged furs and carried a bow. A quiver hung over his back, full of stone-tipped arrows. He looked familiar, though Kyrie couldn't remember where he'd seen him. He seemed to be in his fifties, his face weathered like old leather. His hair was black and shaggy, strewn with gray, and his eyebrows were thick. His eyes were dark and piercing, two burning coals.

"It's not your forest," Kyrie said, anger bubbling in him. "You look like a common woodsman—or outlaw, more likely. You don't own this place, so bugger off."

Kyrie instantly regretted those words. The man took a step forward, and Kyrie suddenly realized how tall and powerful he was. He was perhaps forty years older than Kyrie, but all muscle and grit. A scar ran along his cheek, and another scar peeked from under his collar. In some ways, this ragged man, with his furs and arrows, seemed even more dangerous than Dies Irae with all his armor and griffins.

"If you don't shut your mouth," the man growled, "I'll punch the teeth out of it."

Then Kyrie realized why the man looked familiar. He looked liked Dies Irae, cold and hard and dangerous. *Only Irae is blond and golden like the sun,* Kyrie thought, *and this man is dark as midnight.* They had the same brow. The same strong, straight nose. The same... aura, an aura of pride and power.

Kyrie's heart leaped.

"Benedictus," he whispered. "It's you." His fingers trembled, and he took fast breaths. "You're Dies Irae's brother. Benedictus the Black." His head spun, and words spilled from his mouth. "You can help me! You can fly with me against Dies Irae, steal his Griffin Heart, and defeat him."

The man stared at Kyrie as one would stare at the village idiot. He spat again. "What's wrong with you, kid? I don't know no Irae. Don't know no Benedictus. My name's Rex

Tremendae. Now get out of my forest, or I'll stick one of these arrows in your throat."

GLORIAE

Gloriae cut the sky.

She lashed her riding crop, and her griffin shrieked, flapped her wings, and drove forward. The wind howled, biting Gloriae's face and streaming her samite cape.

"Fly, Aquila," Gloriae called to her griffin over the wind's roar. Her riding crop flew too. "Fly hard."

As Aquila flew, Gloriae narrowed her eyes and scanned the lands below. Hills, copses of trees, and farmlands stretched into the horizons. Hearth smoke plumed from a distant village, and a fortress rose upon a mountain.

"Where are you, Kyrie?" Gloriae whispered, willing her eyes to see through every tree, into every barn, down every road. He was down there somewhere. He would travel north, travel to Hostias Forest where they whispered that Benedictus still roared. He would stay off the roads, sneak into barns for food, and sooner or later she would find him.

"You cannot hide for long," she spoke into the wind, and her lips pulled back from her teeth. Men often called her smile a wolf's grin, and Gloriae felt like a wolf, a huntress, a creature that lunges and kills and digs its fangs into flesh. "I will find you, Kyrie Eleison, and I will not take you alive. No, Kyrie. My father wants to capture you, to parade you as a freak, but not I." She caressed the hilt of Per Ignem, her sword of northern steel, which hung at her side. "I will make you taste my steel."

When Gloriae remembered the last time she saw Kyrie, she snarled. She had nearly drowned that day, but she had pulled herself from the roaring water, had survived, and now she hunted again.

Soon she flew over the village. *If you could call it that,* Gloriae thought. It was merely a scattering of cottages around a square. It was a wretched place, the houses built of mud and cow dung, the roofs mere thatch that no doubt crawled with bugs. Gloriae wrinkled her nose; she imagined that she could smell the place's stench even in the sky.

She turned her head to see the three griffins she led. Lord Molok flew alongside two riders of lower rank, men whose names Gloriae hadn't bothered to learn.

"The village below," she called to them and pointed. "We seek the weredragon there."

They nodded. Gloriae tugged the reins, and her griffin began to descend. The cold air lashed her, and Gloriae pulled down the visor of her helm. Peasants scurried below, fleeing into homes and closing the doors. Gloriae smiled her wolf's grin. Did they think their huts of mud and dung could stop her, Gloriae the Gilded, a maiden of the blade?

She landed her griffin in the village square, sending pigs and chickens fleeing. Gloriae snorted. Pigs and chickens? Truly this was a backwater; just the sort of place a weredragon would hide, cowering in the filth of beasts and the hovels of commoners. Gloriae drew Per Ignem, and its blade caught the light. She craved to dig this blade into Kyrie, to let weredragon blood wash it.

"You reptiles killed my mother," she whispered inside her visor, her jaw tight. "I was only three, but I know the story. You killed her. You *ate* her. You burned our towns, and poisoned our wells, and drank the blood of our children. Now I will wet my steel with your blood, weredragon. I am Gloriae the Gilded. You cannot hide from me."

Her men landed behind her and dismounted. Lord Molok gazed upon the village silently, face hidden behind that black, barred visor. His lieutenants drew blades and awaited orders.

"Into the inn," Gloriae said, gesturing with her chin toward the building, a scraggly place of wattle and daub. "We will ask there."

She walked ahead, leading them, and kicked open the inn's door. Her boots were leather tipped with steel, and the door swung open easily, revealing a dusty, shadowy room where commoners cowered. The air stank of ale, sweat, and grease. If she hadn't been wearing a visor, Gloriae would have covered her nose.

"Who runs this sty?" she demanded.

A wiry man hobbled forward, bowing his head. He wore an apron and held a mug and rag. "Welcome to our town, fine lady! May I offer you some bread and butter, mayhap some ale or—"

Daniel Arenson

"Still your tongue before I cut it from your mouth," Gloriae said, glaring at him. "Do you think I've come for the dung you try to pass off as food, or the piss you serve as ale? I come seeking somebody. A boy."

Three men sat in the back of the tavern. Two were thin peasants, but the third was taller and broader than a peasant, his clothes finer, and he bore a sword. He'd been a knight once, perhaps; maybe a follower of Osanna's old, corrupt kings. This one was trouble, Gloriae knew. She would keep on eye on that shadowy corner.

The barkeep bobbed his head and whined, drawing Gloriae's attention away from the burly man. "Yes, my lady," he said. "I understand. But there is no boy here, as you can see." He tittered. "We are but simple folk, and—"

Gloriae stepped toward him, reached out a gloved hand, and clutched his throat. "You talk too much," she hissed. She raised her sword above him. "A boy with blond hair. A weredragon child. If I find that you've seen him, barkeep, and fed him your gruel, I will have you beg for death."

A chair scraped behind, and Gloriae turned her head to see the burly man rise to his feet. He had not drawn his sword, but his fingers lingered near the hilt

"Sit down, drunkard!" Gloriae told him, her voice filling the hovel.

The man gave her a long, hard look. He did not bow his head nor lower his eyes. "There was no boy," he said, voice low. "And you may refer to me as Taras, not drunkard."

Gloriae shoved the barkeep away, and he fell to the floor, gasping and clutching his neck. Gloriae stepped toward that burly man, that Taras, her sword drawn. Her fellow griffin riders stepped behind her.

Facing Taras, Gloriae pulled off her helmet. She tucked it under her arm and shook her hair so that it cascaded down her back. The barflies gasped, and even Taras narrowed his eyes. Gloriae smiled thinly. Men often gasped when they first gazed upon her green eyes, her golden locks, her legendary beauty.

"Whoever you are," Gloriae said softly, a crooked smile finding her lips, "you will obey me. Sit down."

Taras gave her a long, hard stare... then sat back in his chair.

"Good," she said to him, voice sweet. "Now, you say there was no boy, yet you bear a sword. Why do you need weapons here, if no weredragons terrorize your village?"

Taras still stared into her eyes, something few men dared. He had brown eyes, eyes that were tired but still strong. "I followed Osanna's old kings, and I worshiped her old Earth God. Your griffins killed our king and our monks, stripped our temples bare and crowned them with Sun Disks. Why do I bear a sword, my lady? It is not Vir Requis that I fear, but—"

Gloriae backhanded him, putting all her strength into the blow, and his blood stained her white leather glove. "You will not speak that name here," she hissed, voice trembling with rage. "You will not speak the name they gave themselves. They are weredragons; that is what you will call them. They are murderers. Do you work for them, worm? Did you hide the boy?"

She tried to backhand Taras again. He reached out and caught her wrist.

"I hide nothing," he said, glaring, and rose to his feet. He towered over her. "I know who you are. You are Gloriae. You are the daughter of the usurper, and you are no rightful ruler of Osanna. The old dynasty and monks will return, Gloriae the Gilded, and—"

Gloriae pulled back from him and swung her sword.

He was fast. He had expected this. Eyes still cold, he leaped back, drew his blade, and parried.

Gloriae kicked the chair at him. It hit his chest, tangled against his sword, and Gloriae swung her blade. The steel cut Taras's shoulder. He grunted, fell back, and Gloriae lunged with a snarl. Before he could recover, she shoved her blade into his chest, driving it through him and into the wall behind.

She stepped back, watched him die, then pulled Per Ignem free. Taras slumped to the floor, and Gloriae placed her helmet back on.

"Would anyone else like to cause trouble?" she asked, aware that she was smiling wildly, that her chest rose and fell, that her blood roared. When nobody spoke, she nodded. "I didn't think so." She looked at her men. "Torch the place; it stinks of old piss."

She walked out of the inn, snarling, as her men tossed logs from the hearth onto the floor. When she smelled smoke, she laughed and mounted her griffin.

"Kyrie Eleison was never here," she called to her men; they too were mounting their griffins. "And if he ever does come this way, well... there will be no place left to hide."

She dug her spurs into her griffin, and once more she flew, the wind in her eyes and the sky in her lungs.

KYRIE ELEISON

When the gruff woodsman walked off, Kyrie waited several moments, then followed.

What kind of name is Rex Tremendae? he wondered as he sneaked from tree to tree. *That's a fake name if I've ever heard one. This is him. Benedictus. It must be.* Kyrie's heart thrashed and his fingers trembled.

The man was easy to follow. He tramped through the forest with steps as gruff, hard, and angry as his face. His heavy boots snapped fallen branches, kicked acorns and stones, and raised dirt. *Aren't hunters meant to be stealthy?* Kyrie thought as he followed, branches snagging him and sap smearing him. This man moved as if he owned the forest, as if nothing could harm him.

After a while, when Kyrie was out of breath and dizzy, Rex's voice came from the forest ahead.

"I know you're following me, kid. Go home."

Kyrie could not see the man—the forest was too thick—but his voice sounded about a hundred yards ahead.

"I'm not leaving," he called back. This time he did not speak High Speech, the language of Osanna, but spoke in the older Dragontongue, the language of Requiem. Dragontongue felt odd in his mouth—he hadn't spoken it since childhood—but he knew this man would understand. "I'm sticking with you, so you better get used to the idea. You and I will fly against Dies Irae, reclaim the Griffin Heart, tame the griffins, and rebuild Requiem."

Rex kept walking, and it sounded like he was moving faster, his stomping boots angrier. Kyrie could barely keep up. After weeks of journeying with little food, he was weak. But he bit his lip and kept following. This Rex couldn't just be a simple hunter. The scars. The scowl. The black hair and eyes. It had to be Benedictus.

"Because if it isn't," Kyrie muttered, pushing his way between branches and bushes, "the world is crueler than I can believe."

Kyrie walked for hours, covering at least two leagues. His feet ached. Just when he thought he could walk no further, he spotted a hut between two oaks. Rex's boots left prints in the soft earth, leading to the hut. The door was closed; Rex had to be inside.

The shack was built of crooked, mossy wood bristly with splinters and bent nails. Vines crawled its walls like green snakes. Turnips, peppers, and peas grew nearby in a weedy garden. A smokehouse stood beside the embers of a cooking fire. Kyrie frowned. *The place is a junkyard.* Was this truly the home of Benedictus, the great king? Doubt punched Kyrie's belly, as cold as Gloriae's eyes. Maybe Rex *was* but a woodsman. Maybe Benedictus the Black, the Vir Requis king who'd bitten off Dies Irae's arm, truly was dead.

No. No! He's alive. He is here.

Kyrie pounded on the hut's door.

"Go away, kid," came a growl from inside.

Kyrie pounded the door again. "I want a job."

"What language you speaking, kid? Talk to me in High Speech. I don't understand your gibberish."

Kyrie snorted, but decided to humor Rex. He switched back to the language of Osanna. "I said I want a job."

"Got no money to pay you," replied Rex's voice from inside the hut.

"I don't need money. I'll work for food. I'm a good worker. I can hunt, repair things, cook...."

For a moment there was silence. The moment lasted so long, Kyrie raised his fist to pound again, and then the door swung open. Rex stood there, black hair dusty, eyes dark. He shoved a loaf of bread, a flask, and a shank of meat into Kyrie's hands, then slammed the door shut.

"Eat that," came Rex's voice from inside the hut. "Then go away."

Kyrie considered pounding on the door again, but the food smelled too good. He sat by the fire pit and ate. The bread was homemade, not a day old, grainy but soft. The meat was slow cooked—deer, Kyrie thought—and melted in his mouth. The flask contained good, strong beer. It was the best meal Kyrie could remember eating; definitely the best he'd eaten since fleeing Fort Sanctus. He polished off every crumb and drop, then leaned back on his elbows, sighing. *I needed that. Badly.*

Maybe Rex was just in a bad mood today, but would feel better tomorrow, Kyrie thought. It was getting dark, the sun dipping between the trees, casting long shadows. Kyrie yawned. He curled up outside the hut, hoping no bears or wolves frequented this part of the forest. He closed his eyes and instantly slept.

He did not dream.

He woke at dawn to the sound of the hut door slamming open. Before Kyrie could even open his eyes, he felt a boot prod his side. He heard Rex's gravelly voice.

"I thought I told you to get lost, kid."

Kyrie blinked, rubbed his eyes, and rose to his feet. Rex stood by him, a knife in his belt, a bow in his hands. The scar peeking from his shirt looked red in the dawn.

"I wanted to thank you for the food last night," Kyrie said. "Let me work for breakfast. I can weed your garden, or skin your catch, or—"

"Or get lost," Rex said. "How about you do that for me?"

The hunter walked away, disappearing into the trees.

Kyrie hurried to follow. "You won't get rid of me that easily," he called after Rex, trudging over fallen logs and boulders. "I know who you are."

Rex spoke without turning to look back at Kyrie. "Told you, kid. You've got the wrong guy. Ain't ever heard of no Benedictus or weredragons. You're wasting your time. Go home."

Kyrie struggled to keep up. The forest was thick. Every step he took, branches, thorns, rocks, or vines nearly tripped him. Rex's large boots trod here with ease, but it was all Kyrie could do to keep up.

"I don't have a home," he said. "Not anymore. Nor do you. That hut you've got? You should be living in a palace! Dies Irae destroyed our home. Your brother. He didn't have Vir Requis magic, so your dad hated him. He stole the amulet, he controlled the griffins, he destroyed Requiem—"

Rex spun around. His face was so livid, Kyrie took two steps back. Teeth bared, eyes flashing, Rex's weathered face resembled a dragon's face. "Stories," Rex grumbled. He spat. "Fairytales. I don't know who you think I am, kid. I'm just a hunter. No weredragons. No palaces. Just a hunter, nothing more. Okay?"

Without waiting for a reply, Rex stormed off.

That night Kyrie pounded on the hut's door again. Again Rex shoved food into his hands, then slammed the door in his face, grumbling at Kyrie to go away. Again the next day, Kyrie followed Rex through the trees. Again Rex would answer him only with growls and grunts.

For a week Kyrie spent his nights outside the hut, and spent his days demanding a job. For a week he heard nothing but grumbles, saw nothing but frowns.

On the seventh night, a sound woke Kyrie in the darkness.

He opened his eyes and saw the stars above between the trees. He heard the sound again—the hut's door clanking. Kyrie closed his eyes and pretended to sleep. He heard Rex's boots walking beside him. Normally Rex thumped through the forest, but now he paced softly, as if trying not to wake Kyrie.

What's going on? Kyrie waited until the footsteps moved farther away, then opened his eyes and rose to his feet. He followed in the darkness.

Kyrie walked in his socks, but still had to tiptoe to avoid making noise. Luckily the wind moaned this night, a loud and mournful sound, masking his footfalls. Rex carried a lamp, and Kyrie followed its light, his breath quick. Owls hooted, frogs trilled, and crickets chirped. Soon it began to rain, and still Rex walked through the darkness, Kyrie slinking behind.

Finally the forest gave way to a clearing.

It was a small clearing, circular, sunken in. Kyrie had read that wroth angels sometimes tossed boulders from the sky, and where their heavenly rocks hit, no trees could grow. This looked like such a place. Pines and oaks fringed it, tall and dark, and the clearing's floor danced with pattering raindrops.

As Kyrie watched from the trees, Rex entered the clearing and stood at its center. Kyrie held his breath.

Rex looked to the sky, tossed his head back, and outstretched his arms. Wings sprouted from his back, leathery and black. His arms and legs grew longer, and claws grew from his hands and feet. Scales flowed over him, and fangs grew from his mouth. Before Kyrie's eyes, the rough woodsman became a black dragon with a scar along his chest and a torn wing.

Hiding among the pines, Kyrie tasted tears on his lips.

Benedictus the Black, King of Requiem, stood before him in the night.

LACRIMOSA

The mountain winds howled around Lacrimosa, threatening to topple her. They billowed her cloak, flapped her hair, and stung her eyes with snow. With shivering fingers, she tightened her cloak around her, but its white wool did little to warm her, and her fingers looked pale and thin to her. *My bloodline was never meant for snow and mountains, but for glens and glittering lakes,* she thought. Her family had always had pale skin, pale eyes, silvery hair; they were the color of snow, and brittle like it, but with a constitution for sun and meadows.

"Agnus Dei," she whispered, lips shivering. "Please."

She stared at the cave, but could not see inside. She saw only darkness that fluttered with snow, deep like the chasm that had opened in their family, their home, their people.

"Agnus Dei," she whispered again, voice so soft, she herself could not hear it. "Please."

The mountains rose above the cave, disappearing into cloud—cruel, black mountains covered with ice and snow, bristly with boulders like dragon teeth. The snowy winds danced around their peaks like white demons, and even when Lacrimosa turned to gaze below, she could not see the green of the world she had fled.

She dared take a step toward the cave, but it was a trembling step. She was afraid. Yes, afraid of her daughter, afraid of what Agnus Dei had become. The girl was eighteen now, no longer a child, and she had become like a stranger to Lacrimosa, as wrathful as her father.

Lacrimosa smiled sadly. Yes. Agnus Dei was like her father, was she not? So strong. Proud. Angry. Tough enough to live in forests and snowy peaks, while she, Lacrimosa, withered in these places and missed the warmth of their toppled halls and the song of their shattered harps.

Does Agnus Dei remember those halls, where marble columns stood, where fallen autumn leaves fluttered across tiled floors? Does she remember the song of harps, the poems of minstrels, the chants of our priests? Does she remember that she is Vir Requis, or is she full dragon now, truly no more than a beast of fire and fang?

"Agnus Dei," Lacrimosa tried again. "Let us talk."

From inside the cave came a growl, a puff of smoke, a glint of fire. Yes, she was still in dragon form. Why did she never appear as human anymore? She was such a beautiful child; not pale and fragile like Lacrimosa, but dark and strong like her father. Lacrimosa still remembered the girl's mane of dark hair, her flashing brown eyes, her skin always tanned, her knees and elbows always scraped. A wild one, even in childhood. She had been seven when her uncle destroyed their world, when Dies Irae shattered their halls, and the harps were silenced.

Seven is too young, too young to understand, Lacrimosa thought. *She was too young.*

She felt a tear on her cheek. *And I was too young when I married Benedictus, too young when I had my children, the loves of my life, my Agnus Dei and my Gloriae.* She had been only fifteen when she married Benedictus, twenty years her senior, to become a princess of Requiem. She had been only sixteen when she gave birth to the twins. *We were all too young.*

She sighed. But that had been so long ago. Now this was all that remained. This mountain of boulders and snow, and this cave of darkness, and this husband who hid in exile. One daughter kidnapped. The other lost in darkness and rage.

"Agnus Dei," she said and took another few steps toward the cave. She could see inside now, see the fire that glowed in Agnus Dei's dragon mouth, see the glint of it against red scales. Red—a rare color in their family. Lacrimosa became a silvery dragon, as had her father and forefathers, while Benedictus and his line had forever become black dragons. Yet Agnus Dei's scales glinted red, a special color, the color of fire.

"It means she is blessed," a monk said when Agnus Dei first became a dragon at age two, drawing gasps and whispers at her color. "It means she will forever be as wildfire."

Lacrimosa wanted to believe. She prayed to believe. When she looked at Agnus Dei's dark hair and flashing eyes, she told herself that she saw Benedictus there. Again and again, on darkest nights, she would pray to the Draco constellation. "Let Agnus Dei and Gloriae be the daughters of my husband, the daughters of Benedictus."

Yet in the deepest halls of her soul, Lacrimosa's fears whispered. She would remember the day Dies Irae found her, grabbed her, forced himself upon her. The day she swore to never reveal, to die with her secret. Had this been the day her daughters quickened within her?

Lacrimosa shook her head, banishing those memories, that old pain. *Agnus Dei and Gloriae are the daughters of Benedictus. They are good at heart like him, angry and fiery like him. They are his, and let those whispers of my heart never cast their doubts again.* She tightened her lips, the snow stinging them, and clutched the bluebell pendant she wore around her neck, the pendant Benedictus had given her.

She took another step, so that she stood at the cave's mouth. She felt the warmth of her daughter's flames, and though she feared the wrath and wild ways of Agnus Dei, she could not help but be grateful for the heat. A wry smile tickled her lips. *We silver Vir Requis of the warm glens; we'd welcome the fury of our offspring to escape the snow and winds of banishment.*

"Hello, daughter," she said softly.

Agnus Dei crouched in the cave, smoke rising from her nostrils, flames fluttering around her fangs. Her tail flicked, and her claws glinted. A growl sent ripples across those red scales. The girl spoke in a low, dangerous voice. "I am staying a dragon."

Lacrimosa sighed. She stepped toward her daughter and touched her shoulder, feeling the hot red scales. Agnus Dei growled and pulled away, flames leaving her nostrils. Lacrimosa caught her reflection in her daughter's brown, burning eyes. A slender woman, of long fair hair, of delicate features. Eyes that were haunted, too large, too sad. She was the opposite of Agnus Dei; soft while Agnus Dei was strong, sad while Agnus Dei was dark, reflective while Agnus Dei was angry. But then, she had not seen Agnus Dei for a year now, not in human form at least.

"You'll have to become a girl again sooner or later," Lacrimosa said. Her eyes moistened. "You can't stay like this forever."

Agnus Dei growled. "And why not? The true dragons of Salvandos have no human forms. They live upon great mountains of gold, and they fear no one." She growled and blew flames from her mouth. Lacrimosa stepped aside, heart fluttering, and watched the flames exit the cave to disappear into the snowy winds.

Lacrimosa shook her head, hair swaying. "The true dragons live thousands of leagues from here, and some say they are but a myth. Agnus Dei. Daughter. Beloved. You cannot stay in this cave forever, hidden in darkness, rolled up into this ball of flames and scales. You—"

Agnus Dei roared, a sound so loud, Lacrimosa covered her ears. "If I were pale like you, I could fly outside, is that right, mother? But I am red. Red like fire. And I would burn like fire upon the mountainside, a beacon for our enemies to see, a call for them to hunt us. I say let them come! I fear no man. If Dies Irae arrives, I will burn him." She bared her fangs, and her eyes blazed.

Lacrimosa again placed her hand against Agnus Dei's scales. "You could not fight Irae, my child. With a hundred thousand Vir Requis we fought him, and we died at the talons of his griffins, at the sting of his swords."

Agnus Dei smiled bitterly. "Oh, but we did not die, did we, Mother? No. Not I, the daughter of Benedictus the Black. Not you, his young wife, the girl who married the legend. No. We were the family of royalty. We were kept in safety." Her voice rose to a yell, and her fire filled the cave. "As the multitudes died, as they fought and perished, we remained hidden. As King Benedictus called the hosts to his service, led countless to die under his banners, he hid us. So we lived, Mother. Yes, we lived. We should have died, but we were blessed, were we not? Blessed with royal blood, blessed to be the family of our king, and look at our blessed life now." She gestured at the cave walls. "To live in a hall of royalty."

Lacrimosa had heard this before, had heard her daughter's rage a hundred times in this cave. "Agnus Dei, please—"

The dragon shook off Lacrimosa's hand, rising as tall as she could in the cave, this cave too small for a dragon's body. Tears filled her eyes. "I should have fought with them! I should have died with them, now drink and dine with them in the halls of afterlife."

"You were a child—"

"I am eighteen now, and I am old enough. I will fight Irae now." She growled again, flames shooting, and Lacrimosa had to step back. "I am a dragon. I fear no one."

"You are a Vir Requis—"

"I am a dragon! A true dragon. I have no more human form. I have not taken my human shape in a year, and I never more will. Vir Requis are weak. Vir Requis are gone. Let me be a true dragon—like those of the west—and I will never more hide in caves."

Sometimes Lacrimosa thought that Agnus Dei did not know who she raged against. Was it the Vir Requis? Was it her mother, her father? The color of her scales? Her life while so many others lay dead? Maybe it was all these things, and maybe Agnus Dei was simply like wildfire, and needed kindling to burn, any kindling she could find. And so in this cave she flared.

"The new moon approaches," Lacrimosa tried again, as she did every month. "Let us travel to Hostias Forest. Let us see Father, like we used to. We'll become dragons together for one night. We'll be a family again."

But like every month for years now, Agnus Dei shook her head and roared. "I don't want to see him. He could live with us here if he pleases."

"You know Benedictus cannot live with us," Lacrimosa said. "It's too dangerous. He would place us in danger."

Agnus Dei stretched her wings so that they hit the walls of the cave. She seemed like a caged beast, barely able to move. "I would welcome danger. I would welcome a fight. I would welcome death, even."

Lacrimosa cried. She had lost her parents, her siblings, and her home in the war. She had lost her husband, could see him only one night every new moon. She had lost her daughter Gloriae; Dies Irae had kidnapped her, raised her as his own, raised her to hunt Vir Requis. How had she lost Agnus Dei too? Only a few years ago, Agnus Dei loved her mother, would play with her, listen raptly to her stories, travel with her in human form to visit Benedictus. She had always been a wild child, bruised and dark and angry, but cheerful too, loving and beautiful. How had this happened? How had Agnus Dei become this enraged beast?

Lacrimosa closed her eyes. She took a deep breath, trembling, tears still on her cheeks. Her voice was but a whisper. "As the leaves fall upon our marble tiles, as the breeze rustles the birches beyond our columns, as the sun gilds the mountains above our halls—know, young child of the woods, you are home, you are home."

She hugged herself, trembling. The song of her childhood, of her people, of those marble halls now shattered, covered in earth and burned trees. The whispers of their fallen race. Her voice shook. "Requiem. May our wings forever find your sky."

When she opened her eyes, Lacrimosa saw her daughter regarding her, silent, staring. Finally Agnus Dei spoke.

"There are no more marble tiles; they are shattered and buried, Mother. There is no more breeze to rustle the birches; it stinks now with smoke and death. The halls are gone, and the golden mountains are but a memory. I remember them, Mother. But I wish I did not. I wish I forgot that I am Vir Requis. It is a dead race. You can look to the past. I will not. I will be as a true dragon—wild. Goodbye, Mother." A tear streamed down Agnus Dei's cheek. "I love you."

And then, so fast Lacrimosa could not stop it, could barely react, Agnus Dei leaped out of the cave. She shot into the howling winds, roaring, breathing fire.

"Agnus Dei!" Lacrimosa cried. She raced outside the cave and saw Agnus Dei already aflight, already distant, a comet shooting through snow and wind. Sobs shook Lacrimosa's body. She had already lost one daughter; how could she lose Agnus Dei too?

"Agnus Dei! I love you, daughter. Goodbye! I love you."

She did not know if Agnus Dei could hear. The red dragon flew, churning the clouds, roaring and breathing fire. And then she was gone... gone like the halls of Lacrimosa's youth, gone into memory.

Lacrimosa fell to her knees and wept.

KYRIE ELEISON

Kyrie was collecting firewood when he heard the griffins.

Five days had passed since he saw Benedictus shift, since he saw Black Fang—Benedictus in his dragon form, the beast that had led the Vir Requis to war, to their final stand at Lanburg Fields. Five days had passed in silence. Five days of collecting firewood, of sleeping on the ground, of trying to speak to the gruff man and hearing only silence.

Today shrieks broke this silence—the eagle shrieks that still haunted Kyrie's nightmares, the shrieks he'd heard the day Lady Mirum died.

He squinted, dropped the firewood, and saw them above. They were close.

He had seen many griffins since his chase above the sea, but they had been distant. These ones flew just over the forest canopy. Kyrie could see their talons glint, their beaks snap, their armored riders scan the forest. They swooped, flew into the sky, looped, swooped again. They moved fast, blurred into streaks, wings churning the air. Their cries hurt Kyrie's ears.

"Damn it," he muttered and began to run back toward the hut, boots kicking up moss and dirt. He had to find Benedictus.

He stumbled over a tree root, almost fell, and managed to steady himself. He kept running, branches slapping his face. The griffins swooped. One's talons hit a treetop, and branches crashed behind Kyrie.

What if... I led them here?

A griffin swooped so close, Kyrie dropped down. The beast tore the canopy with its talons. Kyrie leaped up and ran from tree to tree, hiding under the foliage.

Ice filled his stomach. *They could have seen me... last night.*

Tears stung Kyrie's eyes. He couldn't have helped it. He'd had to turn into a dragon. Had to. It had been a month already. A Vir Requis needed to fly once a week; going longer could drive him mad, fill his blood with fire, make his fingers shake, his head ache. So he had shifted. He had flown. He had soared over the

65

trees at night, streamed through the clouds, and let the cold air fill his maw. *Did they see me then?*

Talons tore down the tree before him. Kyrie found himself staring into a griffin's eyes.

He recognized its rider. She was a young woman, her gilded armor molded to the curve of her body. She wore white leggings, white gloves, and leather boots with steel tips. A helmet hid her face, but Kyrie could imagine those icy green eyes.

"Gloriae," he whispered.

For an instant the world froze.

Then Kyrie shouted, leaped up, and shifted.

A tail sprung from his back, wings unfurled, and blue scales flowed across him. His maw opened, full of sharp teeth, shooting flame at Gloriae.

Dragon and griffin soared into the sky, wreathed in fire.

Griffin talons shot out. Kyrie blocked them with his claws. He leaned in to bite, and his teeth closed around the griffin's neck. Gloriae screamed. Her lance stabbed Kyrie's shoulder, and he howled and blew flames.

Talons clutched his back. A second griffin landed on him, biting and clawing. Kyrie felt his blood flow, and he shouted and spewed fire, spinning above the trees, lashing his tail.

He beat off the second griffin, but he was hurt, maybe badly. He blew flames again; they roared around Gloriae's shield, staving her off. A quarrel zoomed. Gloriae was firing a crossbow, and the quarrel scratched Kyrie's belly. It was only a nick, but Kyrie felt the sting of ilbane, and he howled. The sun blinded him.

Talons scratched. Kyrie kicked, lashed his tail, and blew flames in all directions. Through the blinding light, light that shone against Gloriae's armor, Kyrie saw three more griffins swoop toward him.

For a second, Kyrie froze with horror. He saw his life like pictures in a book. His parents. His siblings. His old dog running through autumn leaves. And then his family dead, his house burned, Requiem Forest torched, columns shattered upon the ground. Lanburg Fields, and dead all around, and Lady Mirum lifting him. Fort Sanctus by the sea. Waves, salt, flights under stars over water.

And death.

Lady Mirum broken.

Griffins upon him, and claws, beaks, pain.

He tried to fight them off, but they were too many, and one griffin clutched his neck. Kyrie closed his eyes, prepared to die.

A roar shook the forest.

It was a thundering roar, impossibly deep, a roar like the darkest caves, the deepest tunnels. Kyrie opened his eyes and saw the great dragon, the Black Fang, the beast with the torn wing.

Benedictus crashed into the griffins, biting and clawing, knocking them off Kyrie. The black dragon's eyes blazed red, and fire burned from his maw.

Though bleeding, muzzy, and trembling, Kyrie cried in joy. "Benedictus flies!"

The sight of this legendary creature, its wings spread again, sent lightning through Kyrie. He soared with more passion and strength than he'd felt since Mirum died. He roared, shooting fire at the griffins who flew toward him. "And I fight alongside him!"

They fought. Two dragons. Five griffins and five more joining them from the eastern sky. Among swirling clouds and blazes of fire, the roars and shrieks rippling the air, they fought.

Four griffins latched onto Benedictus, clawing and scratching, their riders lashing spears. He was a large dragon—larger than Kyrie—burly and jagged, a few of his scales missing, a scar rending his breast. He was like Fort Sanctus, Kyrie thought—tough and proud, but old and rundown, years past his glory days. *But he is still great; our greatest warrior, our greatest legend.*

As this gnarled black beast roared and lashed his tail, Kyrie shot up. He crashed between three griffins, knocking them aside, and somersaulted.

"Benedictus, I'm here!" he cried, flew to the sun, then pulled his wings close. He swooped, whooping, and somersaulted again. He crashed into a griffin that clutched Benedictus's neck, knocking it off.

"Get out of here, kid," Benedictus growled, eyes blazing. His wing knocked a rider off a griffin. Blood coated his claws. "I'll take care of them. You go!"

Kyrie grunted and nodded. "I'll take a few off your back."

He swooped and flew over the canopy, letting the leaves
skim his belly. When he turned his head, he glimpsed five
griffins following him. Their riders shot quarrels, but Kyrie flew
up and down, left and right, zipping around like a lightning bolt,
and they could not hit him. When he saw an opening in the
forest canopy, he dived and flew among the trees.

The griffins followed, through the canopy toward the
forest floor. One slammed into an oak's trunk, and Kyrie
whooped. He flew just over the ground, shooting between the
tree trunks, spinning around boulders. Another griffin hit a tree.
Another's talons hit a boulder, sending the griffin tumbling,
tossing off its rider. Kyrie laughed and kept flying, and soon
found himself over a forest pool. Two griffins still flew behind
him, and he heard Benedictus roaring somewhere far behind, still
fighting.

Grinning, Kyrie flew along the pool, and found himself
before a cliff and waterfall. He turned his head, blew fire at the
pursuing griffins, then flapped his wings hard. With a
thundering cry, Kyrie shot toward the waterfall, then flew up the
cascading water like a salmon. He emerged wet above the cliff,
flew toward the sun, then swooped down upon the blinded,
soggy griffins.

"Nobody," he roared, biting and clawing, "messes with
Benedictus and Kyrie."

One griffin crashed dead into the water.

Only one griffin remained. The griffin bearing Gloriae.

Fury filled Kyrie, burning and red. He remembered how
Gloriae had stood upon Fort Sanctus, a small smile on her lips,
watching her father murder the Lady Mirum. He remembered
the stories villagers would tell of her: How she had murdered a
Vir Requis at age six, three more when she was eight. *She's a
demon bred for cruelty.*

"I kill you now, Gloriae," he hissed.

Gloriae tilted her head. She pulled back her griffin, flew
over the water, and landed on the forest floor.

"You kill me?" she cried. "You kill me, weredragon?
Then face me as a human, not as the blue monstrosity you
become." She dismounted her griffin, drew her sword, and
stood golden in her armor.

The sounds of Benedictus's roars were far; he fought
griffins half a league away. Kyrie was alone here, alone with

Gloriae. He flew toward the ground where she stood. He shifted into human form while still flying, then landed on his feet before Gloriae, snarling.

"You want to duel?" he said, eyes narrowed, hair wet. "You got it." He drew his knife from his belt.

Gloriae laughed. He could not see her face—her visor hid it—but he could see her green eyes mocking him.

"Stupid boy," she said. "I will teach you some sense." She thrust her sword.

Kyrie realized that he *was* stupid. Gloriae wore armor and bore a sword. While Kyrie's clothes and knife could magically shift with him, that magic could not turn them into his own armor and sword. Stupid, yes; but the rage and horror made it impossible to think. Kyrie leaped sideways, dodging the sword, and thrust his knife. The knife hit Gloriae's breastplate, sending pain up Kyrie's arm, doing the girl no harm.

Gloriae laughed again, an icy trill. "Having fun, boy?" She swung her sword lazily, forcing Kyrie to duck. *She's toying with me,* Kyrie thought. *She's having fun before she kills me.*

"I'm having a blast," Kyrie said, eyes narrowed. He grabbed a rock and tossed it, but it only bounced off Gloriae's armor, not leaving a dent.

Gloriae took a step toward Kyrie, swiping her sword. The blade scratched Kyrie's arm, drawing blood, and Kyrie grunted. Pain burned.

"What was the girl's name?" Gloriae asked. She took another step toward Kyrie, swinging her sword, making Kyrie leap from side to side. "Lady... Mara? Mira? She was a sweet thing, was she not? Did you ever bed her, boy?" Her sword bit Kyrie's shoulder, a nick to fuel her amusement. "We did, as she lay with a bashed head, still twitching; she died there beneath us. Such a sweet thing, boy. I hope you tasted her. If not, you don't know what you missed."

She's trying to get me mad, Kyrie knew. *She's lying. She's trying to enrage me.* And it worked. Kyrie screamed and leaped forward. "You monster."

He swung his knife. Gloriae laughed and stepped aside, grabbed Kyrie, and shoved him. Kyrie stumbled and hit the ground, and Gloriae kicked his side. She kicked again. Kyrie grunted, pain filling him. Gloriae's sword flew down, and Kyrie rolled, barely dodging the blade.

"You are the monster," Gloriae said, eyes cold. She placed her boot upon Kyrie's neck, her sword on his chest. "Did you think you could beat me like this? As a human? You weredragons—your pride and honor were your undoing. It is so today too." With her free hand, Gloriae removed her helmet and shook her head, letting her hair fall loose. The golden locks shone, and Kyrie saw that angry pink patches spread across her pale cheeks. She gazed down upon him, eyes frozen. "Goodbye, Kyrie Eleison."

Gloriae raised her sword.

Kyrie shifted.

He ballooned in size, shooting up, his head growing scales and horns. Gloriae's sword bit, chipping his scales, scratching his flesh, and Kyrie's head slammed into her. The horn on his head slashed her thigh, and blood covered Kyrie's eyes. He roared and flew into the air. Gloriae's griffin shrieked, but Kyrie blew fire at it. It caught flame and writhed on the ground.

Kyrie plucked Gloriae off his horn and stared at her, disgusted. She was still alive, blood flowing down her leg. Her fists clenched and she grimaced.

"Honor?" Kyrie whispered, flapping his wings. The trees bent and rustled below him. "Pride? What would you know of such things? You'd be nothing but a spoiled girl were your father not Dies Irae. What do you know of the honor and pride of an ancient race, a magic that has flown over the world for millennia? Honor and pride could never undo us, Gloriae. Benedictus is back. We fly again."

He held her in his claws. Though her limbs shook and sweat beaded on her brow, Gloriae fixed him with a stare. Pain filled her eyes, but ice and determination too.

"Kill me then," she said. "Spare me your speeches and kill me. I am a mistress of steel. I am ready for death. I've lived my life to die in battle. Kill me, weredragon; I welcome it."

Suddenly Kyrie realized how young Gloriae was. Only a youth; not much older than him. What lies had Dies Irae told her? What cruelty had he inflicted upon her, to turn her into this heartless killer, this creature of hatred? *She's only a girl,* he thought, shaking his head. *What kind of girl yearns to die in battle?*

Kyrie felt his anger melting, replaced with pity. He had suffered in his childhood, Dies Irae hunting him. What would it be like to have Dies Irae as your father, to grow up in his hall? It sounded to Kyrie like a childhood infinitely worse than his own.

In his moment of hesitation, he barely saw her draw the vial.

She smashed it against his claws.

The glass shards stung him. More painful was the ilbane sap the vial had contained.

Kyrie roared, his claws burned, and he dropped Gloriae. She fell into the water below. Despite her wound, she began swimming away.

Kyrie wanted to follow, but the ilbane was like chains around him. He crashed into the pool, swallowed water, and floundered. His head spun and he could barely swim. Finally he crawled onto the bank, coughing, and looked around.

Gloriae was gone.

Kyrie howled. He tried to take flight, but his wings barely flapped. He spat and cursed. It was long moments before the pain of ilbane faded. When it did, Kyrie crashed through the treetops into the sky.

Where was Gloriae? Kyrie wanted to seek her, but griffins still filled the air. Three were attacking Benedictus in the distance. Three more flew toward Kyrie.

Forget Gloriae for now, he told himself. *Benedictus needs me.* Kyrie shot between clouds, zooming, tumbling, somersaulting. He flew with eyes narrowed, flew like never before, dazzling the griffins, spinning so fast, they barely knew where to follow. As he flew, he roared in pain and pride, for his king had returned.

Benedictus joined him. Together they fought. Blue dragon and black. Kyrie and Benedictus. Together they flew. One dragon slim, fast, dizzying; the other large, slow, his wing torn. Together they killed. Soon three griffins remained, then two, then one.

They killed the last griffin with fang and fire, then landed on the forest floor, wounded, panting, and victorious.

Kyrie shook with excitement. He turned back into human form. His knees wobbled, and the hatred for Gloriae, the thrill of the battle, and the pain of his wounds all throbbed in his head.

He faced Benedictus, who shifted back into human form too. The gruff man spat, breath heavy. Sweat drenched his graying curls, and his eyes seemed darker than ever.

"You were amazing," Kyrie said. "I've seen you fly before, at Lanburg Fields, but that was from a distance. To fight beside you... it was an honor." Before he realized what he was doing, Kyrie knelt; it felt right. "My king. You have returned, and you fly again."

Benedictus grunted. He grabbed Kyrie's shoulder and pulled him to his feet. "Get up," he said in disgust. For the first time, Kyrie heard him speaking Dragontongue. "I'm no king. That was a long time ago. Honor? Honor is dead, kid. I was amazing? I was slow. I was clumsy. I could barely fly with my torn wing. I probably would have died were you not here."

Kyrie felt himself glow. Pride welled up in him, like a torrent of water rising throughout his body. "Thank you." He wanted to say more, but found no words. His throat was tight.

Benedictus turned and walked toward a fallen log, rubbing his shoulder blade, the shoulder blade where his torn wing grew in dragon form. He sat down with a grunt. For the first time, Kyrie realized that Benedictus was aging. He was still closer to fifty than sixty perhaps, but not by much. Lines covered his brow, gray hairs filled his stubble, and his joints creaked. It had been ten years since Lanburg Fields, and those years had not been kind to Benedictus. The great King of Requiem moved slowly, grunted when he sat down on the log, and still panted and wiped sweat from his brow. *He's four decades older than me,* Kyrie realized, *and he thinks his time is over. But it's not over yet. He still has some fight in him.*

Kyrie sat down beside him, and for long moments, the two said nothing. Finally, when his breath had slowed and his sweat dried, Benedictus spoke in his low, gruff voice.

"I knew your parents, kid."

Kyrie spun his head toward him so fast, his neck hurt. "My parents?"

Benedictus nodded. "Aye. Your father was a bellator in my court. Do you know what that means? In our forests of Requiem, the bellators were our warriors of noble blood, commanders of our wings; like knights in the armies of Osanna. Your father was among the best I knew. I knew your mother too. I courted her once, but she chose your father instead." He chuckled—a deep, sad sound, lost in memories. He gazed into the trees, as if again seeing those marble tiles and columns that grew between the birches in Requiem's old courts.

"I... I didn't know. They died when I was six. I remember little. I never met another Vir Requis until I met you, not since Lanburg."

Benedictus rubbed his shoulder again and grimaced. His scar, peeking from under his shirt, seemed livid. "He was a proud warrior, your father. I fought with him. When Dies Irae killed your parents, I... that's when I gathered the last of us, that's when I marched to Lanburg Fields, to our final stand."

Kyrie felt his fingers tremble. He buried them in his pockets. "I thought my parents died at Lanburg Fields. I was there, but I don't remember much."

"They died a month before. Dies Irae murdered them. He torched their house and shot them when they fled. I'm sorry, kid. They were friends of mine. You survived. You were but a little one. We took you with us to Lanburg. We took all the orphans. There was nowhere to hide you, nowhere safe left in the burning world. You flew as warriors. I thought all the children had died." Benedictus's eyes were suddenly moist. "But you lived."

Kyrie bit his lip. His eyes were moist too, and he took short breaths, struggling to curb his tears. He could not cry before Benedictus, before his king. For the first time, Benedictus was talking about the past, speaking to him as an equal, and Kyrie's head spun.

Through clenched teeth, Kyrie said, "I will kill Dies Irae some day." He clutched Benedictus's shoulder and stared at him. "Fight with me, Benedictus. Fly with me again. Let us seek more Vir Requis. There are more. There must be more. Let us raise our banners, fly one more time, fight Dies Irae again. If we can grab the Griffin Heart, the griffins will fly with us. We can rebuild Requiem. We will speak the old words. I remember them." His voice shook, his body trembled, and tears flowed down his cheeks. "Requiem! May our wings forever find your sky."

The softness in Benedictus's eyes, that sadness of memory, died. At once his eyes were cold again, his face hard. He rose to his feet, shoving off Kyrie's arm. Once more he was Rex Tremendae, the hunter, the gruff man who knew nothing of "weredragons".

"Go home, Kyrie," he said and started walking away.

Kyrie leaped to his feet and began to follow. Griffin blood and feathers covered the forest floor. "I have no home."

Benedictus did not turn to look at him as he walked, boots crunching leaves. "So just go away."

Kyrie shook his head, eyes stinging, heart thrashing. "How can you still say this? After what just happened? I want to fight!"

Finally Benedictus looked at him, eyes blazing, deep and dangerous like demon caves. "You need to know how to fly, kid, if you want to fight Dies Irae."

Kyrie bristled. "I'm a great flier. Did you not just see that? Did you not see me shake off three griffins between the trees, shoot among them in the skies, blind them with sunlight, claw them as they wobbled around me?"

Benedictus spat again. His boots kept thumping, and he seemed not to notice the branches snagging him as he walked. "I saw a stunt show. You're a great showman, you are. Doing loops. Flying up and down like a bird. Are you a dragon, or are you a sparrow? You want to fight Irae, you better straighten out, lose your hotshot attitude, and learn to fly straight."

Kyrie felt mad enough to catch flame. He forced himself to take a deep breath, to calm his anger. "Will you teach me?" he said.

Benedictus grunted. "You will learn nothing. I've known young Vir Requis like you. Showoffs. Hotshots. We had a lot like you in the war. They fall from the sky faster than raindrops."

Kyrie struggled to keep up with Benedictus's long strides. Branches slapped him, smearing him with sap. "I won't fall so easily. Fly again, Benedictus. Fly against Dies Irae like in the old days."

Benedictus stopped walking and reeled on Kyrie. "The old days are gone," he growled, voice so loud that birds fled. "My wing is torn. I can barely fly straight these days. I could barely beat those griffins. I'm old and wounded, and I'm tired. It's over, kid."

Kyrie shook his head in disbelief. How could Benedictus say this? How could their great king, the Vir Requis who had killed so many griffins, speak this way?

"But don't you hate Irae?"

In a flash, so fast Kyrie could not react, Benedictus grabbed Kyrie's throat and slammed him against a tree. Kyrie could not breathe, could not struggle, could not move, could only stare at Benedictus's burning eyes. Stars floated around him, and he thought he would die.

"Dies Irae kidnapped my daughter," Benedictus said, voice cold, his fingers tight around Kyrie's throat. "I hate him more than you can imagine. You cannot know how I feel."

Kyrie could not breathe. He could barely speak. Sure he would pass out any second, he managed to whisper hoarsely. "He murdered my family. I know exactly how you feel."

Benedictus let go. Kyrie fell to the ground, clutching his throat, taking ragged breaths. Stars still floated before his eyes.

"I want you gone by tomorrow," Benedictus said, walking away into the trees, leaving Kyrie gasping and coughing on the ground. "I told you. The war is over."

DIES IRAE

When his hall's doors slammed open, and Gloriae limped in bloody and bruised, Dies Irae did not need to be told.

He knew at once.

Benedictus still lived.

"Daughter," he said, rising from his throne.

Dirt and blood covered Gloriae's breastplate. She dragged her left leg, which was a bloody mess. She carried her helmet under her arm, and her face was ashy, her hair tangled. As she limped across the marble tiles, her blood trickled. The lords and ladies of the court gasped and stared.

"Father," she said, limping toward his throne. "I would not rest. I come bearing news. Benedictus— he— he's—"

"He's alive," Dies Irae said, voice icy.

Gloriae nodded, panting. "He slew us all. My men. Our griffins. The boy Kyrie Eleison flies with him. Let us go. Now! On the hunt." She drew her sword, then wobbled. Dies Irae dashed forward and grabbed her, holding her up.

"Daughter," he said and caressed her cheek. She looked up at him, green eyes so large and beautiful. Dies Irae kissed her bloody forehead. "You are hurt. Come sit by my throne."

She nodded, and they walked across the hall. The nobles of the court stared silently, the light from the stained-glass windows glinting in their jewels.

Light filled his court this day, glistening upon these jewels, upon golden statues of his likeness, upon filigreed columns and chandeliers. This court was a place of beauty, of light and truth, of righteousness and splendor... but today it seemed dark to Dies Irae. All the gold and jewels in Osanna, his empire, could not light his eyes today.

He sat Gloriae on the stairs by Osanna's Ivory Throne. Servants rushed forward to bandage her leg, to pour wine into her mouth, to remove her bloodied armor. Dies Irae watched them work, then turned his gaze to his left arm, the deformity Benedictus had given him. And now... now Benedictus was back.

With sudden rage, Dies Irae grabbed his crystal goblet and tossed it with a howl.

The lord and ladies of his court, a hundred jeweled nobles, started and stared at their feet. Only Gloriae, the servants bandaging her leg, did not flinch. Blood speckled the marble stairs beneath her, and her eyes burned.

"You failed me," Dies Irae said to her. "You failed to kill him."

Her cheeks flushed, and for a moment Gloriae looked ready to scream. Then she lowered her eyes. "Forgive me, Father. I have failed you once, but I will not fail again. Let us fly on the hunt. I know where he is. We will find him. We will kill him. I will kill Kyrie Eleison, and you will kill Benedictus." She drew her sword with a hiss.

Dies Irae began to pace the hall. Around him the nobles spoke in hushed tones, daring not meet his eyes; a wrong glance now could kill them, they knew. Gloriae shoved away the servants tending to her, rose to her feet, and limped beside him. Pink splotches spread across her cheeks, and fire blazed in her eyes. Her hand trembled around the hilt of her sword.

"Is he plotting a return?" Dies Irae wondered aloud.

Gloriae spat onto the marble tiles. "He flies with the boy. The weredragons plan an attack against us, Father. They will gather more. They will fly upon this city."

Dies Irae nodded, the conviction growing in him, festering like a wound. "Yes, he will return now. If he found the boy, that will embolden him. Two weredragons? He will think it an army." He stared at his daughter. "Can you find the way back, Gloriae? We will kill him."

Gloriae snarled and placed her helmet on her head. "Yes, Father. Let us fly together. The boy gave me this wound. He is mine. You will kill the Black Fang."

Dies Irae nodded, fire growing in his belly. He clenched his good fist. *Yes, I will find you, brother, and I will kill you. You have hidden from me for ten years. But you cannot hide any longer.*

"There are more," Dies Irae said. "More weredragons. There have been sightings of a red one—a young dragon, female they think, slim and the color of blood. Villagers spotted her flying over the Fidelium mountains. And in the north, they speak of a silvery dragon, female too. Females can breed,

Gloriae. They can fill Osanna with their spawn. I will not have my empire infested with new broods of these creatures."

Gloriae snarled and swung her sword. "I have killed their spawn before. If they breed, I will do so again."

Suddenly a lord burst forward, abandoning a group of ladies he had been courting. Dies Irae could not remember his name, but he was a pudgy man, balding, bluff and drunk. He wore a billowy fur coat and tunic to cover his girth, and wore a ruby ring on each finger.

"Bah, they cannot hurt you!" the lord blustered, cheeks red with wine. Sweat glistened on his brow. "My lord Dies Irae! You are powerful beyond measure. How can a handful of Vir Requis harm you?"

Gloriae gasped.

Silence filled the hall.

Dies Irae's jaw twitched.

For a long moment nobody spoke, and the lord stood teetering, nearly falling over drunk.

Finally Dies Irae broke the silence. He stared at this corpulent lord, fist clenched. "What did you call them?"

"Vir Requis, Vir Requis! Weredragons, whatever. Who cares? Call them what you like. They cannot harm us! Osanna is bold and strong." He drew his sword, swiped it so wide that Dies Irae had to leap back, and began singing a drunken war song.

When a guard stepped forward to grab him, the lord stumbled back, sputtering. "Unhand me, man!" he cried, grabbed a bottle of wine from a table, and drank deeply. "I am no woman for you to fondle. Let go!"

The guard shoved the man down, more guards stepped forward, and soon the large lord stood chained to a column. The other lords and ladies looked aside, too fearful to speak, to even look upon Dies Irae. They had seen too many chained to this column stained with old blood.

"Sun God," Gloriae said, blanching. She returned to the marble stairs leading to Dies Irae's throne, faced that throne, and clenched her fists.

A smile spreading across his lips, Dies Irae sat back on his throne. He watched as handlers brought in the griffin cubs. The young beasts—each the size of a horse—whimpered and screeched, claws clanking against the floor, beaks open in hunger. Their handlers kept them always famished, caged, dreaming of tearing their beaks into flesh.

"Watch, Gloriae," Dies Irae said softly. "I want you to see this."

Gloriae still faced the other way. "I do not wish to look upon this."

Dies Irae glared at her. "I command it. Watch, daughter. Watch every bite."

Gloriae turned, and when she saw the snapping griffin cubs, she shuddered. The chained drunkard was thrashing and screaming. His screams of terror soon turned to screams of pain. The lords and ladies watched, silent, as the griffin cubs feasted, as new blood stained the column.

"Sun God," Gloriae whispered again, staring with narrowed eyes. Her skin was ghostly white.

When the griffin cubs had finished their meal, gulping down the last bites, their handlers led them away. The drunk lord was now nothing but bones, skin, and blood against the column.

"These cubs will grow," Dies Irae said softly to Gloriae. His daughter looked ready to throw up. "In a few years, they will be fifty feet long, and fine fliers. And they will fly in a world without weredragons."

Gloriae nodded but said nothing. She was a fierce warrior, Dies Irae thought; he had raised her for fierceness, for cruelty. But he had not finished the job. He had not finished molding her. Some of life's harshness still frightened Gloriae, harshness like the justice he dealt in his court. But she would learn. He was a good teacher, and he would teach her, would kill all softness and mercy within her.

He rose from his throne, caressed Gloriae's hair, and kissed her head.

"Come, Gloriae," he said and began to walk across the hall, heading toward its doors. "My brother awaits. We head to the griffin stables. We fly."

KYRIE ELEISON

"Benedictus," Kyrie said, "you can't go back to your hut."

Benedictus stopped walking.

Slow as sunset, he turned to face Kyrie. His face seemed harder than a mountainside, and his eyes burned. Words left his mouth slowly.

"Why not?"

Kyrie took a deep breath. His fingers tingled. He knew he had to tell Benedictus the truth, but he was afraid. What would Benedictus do to him? Would he beat him? Kill him, even? He took another deep breath, then spoke with a wince.

"I let one get away, Benedictus. I'm sorry. Dies Irae will know we're here. He might be on his way already."

Kyrie had expected Benedictus to be angry. The fury that suffused the man's face, however, still managed to surprise him. Benedictus's lips peeled back from his teeth. It was a wolf's snarl. He stomped toward Kyrie, eyes blazing. Kyrie tried to flee, but Benedictus caught his shoulders and shook him.

"You... did... what?" Benedictus demanded.

Kyrie lowered his eyes. "I'm sorry, Benedictus. I know I should have killed her. I wanted to. But... she's only a girl. I hesitated, and she escaped me. I was stupid. I realize now that she probably flew for reinforcements. I should have killed her right away, but I couldn't, Benedictus. I couldn't."

Benedictus seemed ready to howl and beat him, but then his eyes narrowed. He sucked in his breath. "Who, Kyrie? Who couldn't you kill?"

At the memory of those green eyes and golden locks, Kyrie shuddered. "Gloriae. Dies Irae's daughter."

Benedictus's fingers dug into Kyrie's shoulders. "Gloriae? You saw her? She lives? Did you wound her?"

What was going on? Kyrie felt dizzy. Benedictus seemed almost concerned about Gloriae, but that was impossible. "Yes, I saw her. I wounded her, but she's alive. I... what's wrong, Benedictus?"

The man was suddenly pale. He released Kyrie and turned aside. For a long moment, Benedictus stared away from Kyrie, silent. Finally he spoke again. "Don't worry about it, kid. You did fine. But she'll be back here before long, and Dies Irae will fly with her. We pack our things. We go."

Kyrie rubbed his shoulders where Benedictus had grabbed him. "Go where?"

Benedictus lowered his head. "I don't know. But we can't stay here. This forest is no longer safe. We leave tonight."

"Tonight?" Kyrie remembered Gloriae's boot on his neck, choking him, and the bite of her sword. He shook his head. "Gloriae might be back by then. Let's leave now! We can... we can go to Gilnor's swamps in the south and hide there. Or we can travel to Salvandos in the west; few griffins venture that far. Wherever we go, we have to leave now."

Benedictus said nothing for a long moment. Finally he sighed and said, "I have nothing of value in my hut. A hammer and axe. A few bowstrings and arrows. Nothing more. But there is a treasure I must save from this forest. I go there tonight. We leave at midnight." He lifted a fallen branch and tossed it at Kyrie, who caught it. "Start building a fire. We'll hide half a league from it. If griffins arrive, they'll head to the smoke, and we'll see them."

As Kyrie built the fire, he tried to ask Benedictus more questions. A treasure? Something to save tonight? What was the man talking about? And why, for stars' sake, did he seem so concerned about Gloriae's well being? But Benedictus only stood silently, staring into the forest, until the fire burned. They left the flames between stones, and walked north through the forest. Sunset began to toss shadows.

"Where are we going?" Kyrie said.

Benedictus grumbled. "You talk too much, kid."

They walked for a long time through the darkness. It began to rain, and soon Kyrie was soaked and shivering. It was a cold night, starless, and Kyrie imagined that he could hear griffins in every gust of wind. How Benedictus could navigate in this darkness, Kyrie didn't know. He tried to ask more questions, but heard only growls in reply.

Finally Benedictus stopped by an oak tree. He said to Kyrie, "Wait here."

"Wait for what?" Kyrie said. His teeth chattered, and raindrops dripped down his nose.

But Benedictus did not answer. He walked past the oak, disappearing into darkness. Just then the clouds parted, the rain stopped, and the stars shone. Kyrie saw that they had reached the crater. He remembered. This was where he'd first seen Benedictus shift. Starlight fell upon the clearing. It seemed to Kyrie like a holy place, almost like the old courts of Requiem. The crickets fell silent and the wind died.

Kyrie stared, silent, and saw Benedictus walk to the center of the crater. The moonlight limned his form. As Kyrie watched, a woman stepped into the crater and stood before Benedictus.

Kyrie froze.

A woman?

Silent, hidden between the oak leaves, Kyrie stared. His breath caught. The woman was beautiful, the most enchanting creature he'd ever seen. His body tingled to view her. Mirum had been beautiful too, but in an earthy way, a beauty of sand and salt. This woman's beauty was ethereal, a beauty of starlight and magic. Her hair was long and fine, a blond so pale it was almost silvery. Her skin was milky, and she was tall and slender, clad in white silk. Kyrie gaped.

"Lacrimosa," Benedictus said to her. His voice was softer than Kyrie had ever heard it. "You shouldn't have come."

Lacrimosa smiled sadly. "You say that every new moon, yet every new moon I'm here." Her voice was soft and high. *If moonlight could speak,* Kyrie thought, *it would sound like her.*

"It's dangerous," Benedictus said and held her hands.

Lacrimosa nodded. "You say this every new moon too, yet I still live."

She took a step back, releasing Benedictus's hands, and shifted.

Kyrie gasped. She was Vir Requis! Like a butterfly emerging from the cocoon, she grew white wings, silvery scales, and a slender tail. Soon she stood as a dragon, tall and lithe, glistening in the stars.

A third living Vir Requis! Kyrie watched, eyes moist, as Benedictus too turned into a dragon, the great black dragon, chest scarred. The two dragons, the black and the silver, flew through the night as in a dance. They coiled under the stars, whispering to each other, a dance of sad beauty. Kyrie could no longer hear their words, but their dance spoke of old love and lost dreams.

Finally the dragons landed, one woven of darkness, the other of starlight. In the crater under the stars, they shifted back into human form: one man gruff and dark, one woman pale and glowing. They began walking toward the trees, toward Kyrie. He could only gape, awed.

"Close your mouth, kid," Benedictus said when he reached Kyrie. "A griffin might fly into it." He turned to the woman. "Lacrimosa, meet the kid I told you about."

Not sure how to react, Kyrie knelt before Lacrimosa. He tried to kiss her hand, but stumbled in the mud and fell. He pushed himself to his feet, stammering apologies, and tried to introduce himself.

"My lady! I'm Kyrie Eleison. It's good to meet you, my lady. How are you? I mean... I hope you are well. Are you?"

He realized how he sounded, winced, and cursed himself silently. But Lacrimosa seemed not to mind. She smiled, her teeth white, a smile that filled Kyrie with peace and angelic warmth.

"Hello, Kyrie," she said. "I'm Lacrimosa. I'm so happy to meet you."

Her eyes were large and lavender, and Kyrie was surprised to see tears fill them.

The three Vir Requis walked together, silent in the darkness. Kyrie had so many questions. He felt as if ants raced inside him. Who was Lacrimosa? Where had she been hiding? Were there even more Vir Requis survivors? Kyrie ached to ask, but something about the night's silence seemed holy. He dared not break it. Fireflies emerged to dance lazily like tiny dragons, as if they came to witness a sacred night, a night that would forever change Kyrie's life and his people's fate.

Kyrie noticed that more light glowed. Not the starlight, nor the light of fireflies, but a red, flickering light. He stopped in his tracks, and his nostrils flared.

"Smoke," he said.

Lacrimosa's eyes widened. "Fire," she whispered.

Kyrie stiffened. Yes, fire; he could smell it. Suddenly a crackle rose, and the trees ahead burst into flame. Sparks flew like the fireflies. Memories flooded Kyrie. He could almost see them in the darkness: the burning of Requiem, and the flames of war upon Lanburg Fields.

"Run!" Kyrie said. He turned and began fleeing the fire. Benedictus and Lacrimosa ran beside him. The flames roared behind, and smoke filled Kyrie's mouth. The heat burned his back.

"I should have killed Gloriae," he said as he ran, eyes stinging. "I should never have let her flee. It's my fault." Tears filled his eyes.

He saw the griffins before he heard them. He looked up and they filled the sky. There were hundreds.

Kyrie jumped and shifted. "Fly!" he shouted as he grew a tail and scales, as his wings sprouted and flapped. He crashed through the canopy, branches snapping against his scales. "Benedictus, Lacrimosa, fly!"

With light and fury, they flew.

They flew as griffins followed. They flew as arrows fired through the night, aflame, whistling comets in the darkness. They flew as the trees burned, as flames howled, as smoke blinded them. Into the darkness they fled, crying in the night. Below them the forests burned, and all around them griffins filled the skies.

"Benedictus!" Kyrie cried. Three griffins fell upon Black Fang, and Kyrie shot forward, screaming, and knocked them off. He turned to fight them, to claw and bite and burn, but Benedictus growled at him.

"We do not fight tonight. Fly!"

The three Vir Requis kept flying. Kyrie could barely see, and the night swirled around him, smoke and flame stinging his eyes. Stars spun and flaming arrows whistled. One clanked against his scales. A griffin talon hit him, tossing him into a spin, and he howled, lashed his tail, and hit something. He flapped his wings. He kept fleeing. Where were Benedictus and Lacrimosa? He couldn't see them.

"Fly east!" he shouted. "Fly to the sea!"

Had they heard him? Did they still live? Kyrie could barely see for the smoke and fire, and ten griffins flew toward him. Kyrie flew, spun, swooped to the treetops, shot up again. A griffin slashed Kyrie's leg, and a flaming arrow slammed against his scales. He grunted.

A cry rose over the thud of wings and roaring flames, a cry of pain and terror. *Lacrimosa!* Kyrie flew toward the sound, eyes narrowed in the smoke, knocking griffins aside. He saw Gloriae upon her griffin, clad in her gilded armor, driving a lance toward Lacrimosa. The lance glinted red in the firelight and hit Lacrimosa's shoulder, drawing blood.

"No!" Kyrie cried.

"Gloriae!" Lacrimosa called out, eyes narrowed, voice nearly lost beneath the roar of griffins and fire. "I—" Griffins shrieked and fires blazed, drowning her words. "—your mother!"

Gloriae seemed ready to attack again. She drew back her lance, but hesitated. Before she could recover, Kyrie flew toward her, clawed her griffin, and it pulled back howling. More griffins flew toward them, and Benedictus too joined the fray, biting and clawing. Kyrie looked around wildly, searching for Gloriae, but the girl was gone.

"Lacrimosa!" Benedictus said, eyes burning, smoke rising from his nostrils. She leaned against him, bloody, barely able to fly.

"Fly, get out of here!" Kyrie shouted, spreading his wings wide. A hundred more griffins came shooting toward them, their riders firing arrows. "I'll hold them off. Benedictus, get her to safety."

Benedictus paused. "Ky—"

"GO!" Kyrie shouted and blew flames at a hundred storming griffins. Behind him he heard dragon wings thud. Benedictus flew off, holding Lacrimosa.

Kyrie hovered in midair, eyes narrowed, wings churning the smoke. The hundred griffins would be upon him in seconds. Kyrie snarled.

"Come on, you bastards," he hissed. "Let's see what you've got."

He knew he would die. He was ready. He would hold them back. He would let Benedictus and Lacrimosa flee. She could be the last female of their race, the last hope of Requiem. He would not let her die.

"*Come on!*" he shouted to the griffins, hoarse, and rose higher into the air, shooting flames.

And they were upon him.

Kyrie fought like he had never fought, and he flew like had never flown. Like a comet he shot through the sky, spinning, falling, shooting up, rising from flame. He shot fire and the griffins burned. He bit, clawed, fled and charged. Talons lashed at him, beaks bit, and Kyrie roared with fury even as his blood fell.

"You will not reach them," he cried. "You will not touch them."

There were a hundred, and more were joining them. How long did he hold them off? Was it only a minute? Was it an hour? Kyrie did not know. It was a timeless eternity. But he held them off. He let Lacrimosa flee. With fang and claw and fire, he held them.

And then, with a roar that rocked the night, with a blast of flame that blinded Kyrie, the Black Fang charged into the ranks of griffins, scattering them.

"Get out of here, kid," Benedictus growled, glaring at Kyrie.

"Not without you!" Kyrie slashed at three griffins and knocked a fourth back with his tail.

"I'm right behind you, kid. Now fly!"

They turned to flee, the griffins screeching behind. Benedictus was wounded, Kyrie saw. Blood covered his left leg, and three arrows stuck out from his back. He wobbled as he flew with his torn wing.

"Where's Lacrimosa?" Kyrie shouted as they flew, the burning arrows zooming around them.

"She's safe." An arrow glanced off Benedictus's scales. He grunted. "Follow me."

They turned east. The sea spread out beyond the forest, a sheet of black in the night. Benedictus flew toward it, wobbly, and Kyrie followed. The griffins shrieked behind. The trees burned below.

When the sea was beneath them, Benedictus swooped and crashed into the water, disappearing into the depths. Kyrie took a deep breath and followed. The water so cold, he grunted. The salt stung his wounds. He forced his eyes open, though they stung too, and saw Benedictus swimming in the darkness. Kyrie could barely make out the great dragon; he only glimpsed glints on black scales. He heard several griffins dive into the water, and Kyrie swam as fast as he could. In the darkness, he felt fish and seaweed slap him.

Where was Benedictus? Kyrie could barely see. The world was but murky ink. *Wait. There!* Kyrie saw a tail. Benedictus seemed to swim into an underwater cave, and Kyrie followed.

Worry gnawed him. As a dragon, he had large lungs, but he'd been swimming for a while now. He couldn't hold his breath much longer. He swam through an underwater tunnel, seeing nothing but darkness. He felt stone walls against his sides, smooth, brushing against him. Where was Benedictus going? How had he found this underwater place?

A shriek shook the water behind him. A griffin. Kyrie slapped his tail, and it hit a griffin's head. He slapped his tail again, knocking it against the wall. It seemed to fall; he no longer heard it, and when he glanced over his shoulder, he saw only black.

Kyrie's lungs screamed. If he didn't breathe soon, this mad flight would have been for nothing; he'd die here underwater. *Damn,* Kyrie thought. Benedictus had led them to a watery death. Stars floated before Kyrie's eyes, and his limbs ached. His head spun.

The tunnel opened up, and Kyrie found himself in open water again. Not looking for Benedictus, not caring if griffins still followed, Kyrie shot straight up. He thought he saw starlight above, but it could have just been the stars in his eyes. How deep was he? He kicked and flapped his tail, shooting up as fast as he could. Was this sea endless?

And then—*thank the stars!*—he burst onto the surface. Kyrie took a huge breath, a breath that could suck in the world. He savored it. Air had never tasted sweeter. He coughed, breathed ragged breaths, and laughed.

"Benedictus," he called when he could speak again.

The black dragon was coughing beside him, head sticking out of the water. His breath wheezed. "Quiet, kid," he managed. "We might not be out of the woods yet."

"Oh, we're out of the woods all right," Kyrie said. He looked toward the forested shore; it lay half a league away, rising in flame. It was hard to believe they had swum so far. Griffins still fluttered over the trees. More griffins were diving into the waters by the shore, seeking them.

"Let's go," Benedictus said. "Best we swim underwater."

"Where's Lacrimosa?" Kyrie asked.

Benedictus grunted. "I'll take you to her. Follow me."

They dived underwater again and swam, close to the surface, and soon reached an islet. It was only several yards wide, not large enough for dragons. They shifted into human forms and climbed onto the rocky shore.

"Lacrimosa!" Kyrie cried. He saw her there. She lay between the rocks, cradling a bloodied arm. Moonlight glinted on her wet hair, and her eyes were huge and haunted.

"Keep down," Benedictus said. "Keep behind the boulders. And keep your voices low. Griffins have sharp ears. We're not safe yet."

Benedictus tore a strip from his tunic and bound Lacrimosa's wound. He touched her hair, kissed her cheek, and whispered in her ear. She embraced him. He held her, and she laid her head on his shoulder. Kyrie watched them silently.

"We have to go," Kyrie finally said, glancing nervously back at the griffins. "They'll scan these waters. They'll find us."

Benedictus glared at him. "When Lacrimosa is ready."

Lacrimosa touched Benedictus's shoulder, her eyes soft. "I can swim. Let's go."

They swam in the darkness, remaining in their human forms. They were slower that way, but smaller and harder for griffins to see. When they were far enough, they shifted into dragons again and swam faster, swam all night, until at dawn they climbed onto a distant shore.

They collapsed onto the sand as the sun rose around them. Kyrie had never felt so tired. Everything hurt. Bruises and cuts covered him, his muscles screamed, his lungs burned, and his head pounded. Blood beaded on wounds on his shoulders and left leg. On the sandy beach, he took ragged breaths and fell onto his back, shifting into human form. Dawn rose before him.

Benedictus and Lacrimosa collapsed beside him, also becoming humans. If Kyrie felt so exhausted, he could only imagine how tired Lacrimosa was, being so dainty, or Benedictus with his old wounds. For a long time, they only lay on the shore, watching the dawn. They had not heard griffins in hours, and could see none in the new light. Only gulls fluttered across the skies. No more fire, no more griffins, no more armored riders with flaming arrows.

For a long time, they just lay.

When Kyrie could move again, he sat up and finally saw Lacrimosa in daylight. She looked more beautiful than ever. Her hair was like gossamer, her skin fair, her lips full and her eyes large. Her body was slender and long. Kyrie could not guess her age. She was not young; not young like him, at least. Her eyes were too wise for youth. Neither was she old. No wrinkles marred her face, and her skin looked soft and pure. She seemed ageless. She wore a silver pendant shaped as a bluebell; it glowed purple in the dawn.

A third Vir Requis. A woman. Kyrie had never known, had never dreamed of another....

He turned to look at Benedictus. The gruff man stared back, face inscrutable, eyes dark. Sand filled his rough curls and stubble covered his face, salt and pepper.

Kyrie spoke to him. "Dies Irae will return. He will never stop hunting us."

Benedictus stared back, eyes boring into him. "I know."

Kyrie stood up and stepped toward him. "Fight with me, Benedictus. Help me reclaim the Griffin Heart. Rebuild Requiem with me."

Grunting, Benedictus struggled to his feet. He stood before Kyrie in the sand, glaring. His eyes were so dark, coal black. If Lacrimosa's face was pale silk, Benedictus had a face like beaten leather. For a long time, the man just stared silently.

Finally he spat into the sand, then stared at Kyrie. "Will you fly silently? No whooping or shouting?"

Kyrie nodded.

Benedictus gritted his teeth. "And will you fly straight? No loops? No somersaults? No showing off?"

Kyrie nodded again.

Benedictus took a step toward him, so that he stood so close, he could have reached out and throttled Kyrie. "And will you do exactly as I tell you?"

Kyrie nodded a third time.

Benedictus growled. "Look, kid. I don't like this. I don't like you. But I'm old, and my wing is torn, and I can't fight alone. You learn how to fly fast, you learn how to fly deadly, and you can fly with me. But you obey my orders. No questions, no talking back, no attitude. You show me lip, I'll bash your mouth in. Deal?"

Kyrie reached out his hand. "You got a deal, old man."

Benedictus glared for a moment, as if staring at a rotted carcass on a roadside. Then, with a grunt, he grabbed Kyrie's hand and shook it.

GLORIAE

They were gone.

Once more they had escaped her. Once more she had failed.

Gloriae stood over the smoldering hut, staring at its embers, and her eyes burned. Whether they burned from smoke or tears, she did not know.

She kicked the embers with her boot, searching for something, some clue, some answer... to what? Gloriae didn't know. There was a riddle here, a secret, but she knew neither the answer nor question.

A wind blew, streaming her hair, a hot wind smelling of smoke and blood. She stood alone; she had sent her griffins to scour the beaches, islands, and forests, to burn and destroy whatever they could not search. Her father had joined them, trembling with rage.

"What did she say, Aquila?" Gloriae asked her griffin. The beast stood beside her, lion body singed, feathered breast cut with Kyrie's claws. Aquila cawed and scratched the burned earth.

"The silver one, the female," Gloriae said. "She spoke words."

Suddenly Gloriae was trembling, and she clutched her lance and gazed at its bloodied tip. She had wounded that silvery beast, driven her lance into its flesh, and it had opened its evil maw and spoken in a voice too soft, too delicate, too... *familiar.* Those words still echoed in Gloriae's mind.

"Gloriae, I—" it had called, and here griffin shrieks and fire had drowned its words. "—your mother!"

Gloriae closed her eyes, the wind stinging her face, the smoke stinging her nostrils. A tremble took her, and she had to lean against Aquila. A dream came unbidden to her mind, but not a dream as those which invaded her sleep; it filled her like a spell. She was a child. She walked between pillars in a birch forest, and the leaves were golden like her hair, gliding around her, scuttling against marble tiles. She held her mother's hand and wore no armor, only silk.

"Mother!" she spoke in her dream, and she saw her mother's eyes gaze down upon her, lavender eyes, loving, and Gloriae played with her mother's hair and laughed.

Gloriae opened her eyes and stared back at the burned forest. She trembled and clutched Per Ignem's hilt.

"A memory," she mumbled. "A memory, no more."

She knew not its place, nor its time. Her mother had died when Gloriae was only three. Gloriae had thought that no memories of the woman remained, but here this vision had come to her, and Gloriae knew it to be from those first three, joyous years of her life.

She looked at her bloodied lance and tossed it down in disgust.

"Gloriae!" the weredragon had spoken. How dared it speak her name? What kind of devil spoke with such a soft, beautiful voice? Only the greatest evil would mask its true nature with such a voice, Gloriae knew. And what did it mean?

"I—" Shrieks and fire. "—your mother!"

"The weredragons killed my mother," Gloriae whispered, jaw clenched, staring at the hut's embers. "I know the story. My father told me. They kidnapped her, tortured her, and ate her." She screamed, drew Per Ignem, and stabbed the ashes. "How dared one speak of my mother?"

Then Gloriae knew. With trembling fury, fury more white and burning than the embers, she knew the answer. That silvery dragon, that *Lacrimosa* as the others called it, had been the one. It had killed Gloriae's mother. It had taunted her mother with that soft voice, had ripped into her with claws.

"'I *killed* your mother,' it tried to say." Gloriae spoke in icy hatred, and Aquila cawed and retreated several steps, wincing as if expecting a blow. "Come, Aquila. We fly."

Aquila was wounded, but Gloriae drove her hard that day. If the griffin whimpered or slowed, Gloriae whipped her with her riding crop, and dug her spurs into her sides, and drove her onward. Today was important. Today she would fly faster than ever. They flew over the burning forest, and over lakes, and over more trees and farmlands. They flew until night, and slept in a field, and flew again with dawn.

For three days Gloriae flew upon her griffin, eyes narrowed, clutching her lance, the wind streaming her hair.

On the fourth morning, Gloriae saw the place she had sought. It lay ahead in the distance, a great stretch of ash and rubble, a patch of death upon the land. Once this land had been called Requiem, she knew—the evil land of the Vir Requis. Today it was a mere stain upon her beautiful empire of Osanna.

Lashing her crop, Gloriae directed her griffin to fly over the desolation. Aquila whimpered, but Gloriae drove her on with crop and spur. This was a strange land, a silent land. No birds chirped here, nor did any leaf sprout. Ash, rubble, smashed columns, and skeletons littered the ground.

"We will build a palace here, a great temple to your glory, and to the glory of the Sun God," the gaunt Lord Molok had once told Dies Irae.

But Gloriae's father had only shaken his head. "No. Forever shall the lands of the weredragons lay barren and ugly; that will be their legacy."

That legacy now stretched below Gloriae, and she imagined that she could still smell the blood and fire from Requiem's destruction ten years ago. A force seemed to guide her, like those whispers of her dream. She had never been to these lands, but somehow she knew what she sought. Somehow she knew where to fly. Gloriae flew north over the burned lands, scanning the ruins below, until she found the place she knew would be there.

She landed by toppled, shattered columns.

They were carved of marble, and must have risen a hundred feet tall in the days when Requiem still stood. The columns lay smashed now, each segment no longer than several feet. Their capitals had once been shaped as dragons; hammers, maces, and time had taken to them, beaten them down into shapes Gloriae could barely recognize. But Gloriae knew these columns; she could still see them standing among the birches.

"How... how could this be?" she whispered, clutching her sword. Cold wind blew, invading her armor, and she shivered. Bones, cloven shields, and shattered blades littered the ground. A mosaic lay cracked at Gloriae's feet, half buried in mud. The place was a ruin, but... she had been here before, seen this hall when it had still stood. She had walked here with her mother, had—

"You should not have come here," spoke a voice behind.

Gloriae spun, drew Per Ignem with a hiss, and snarled. Her heart burst into a gallop, and she tightened her lips.

Upon toppled bricks, stood a red dragon.

Sucking in her breath, Gloriae pointed her sword to the beast. Aquila stood cawing at Gloriae's side, and Gloriae mounted the griffin, never removing her eyes from the dragon's.

"These are the lands of my father's empire," she spoke, eyes narrowed, and placed her helmet on her head. She sheathed her sword and grabbed her lance. "It is you who should not have come. The weredragons' age has passed. You will join their bones here upon their toppled columns."

The red dragon sneered, smoke rising between her teeth. It was female, Gloriae knew; the dragon was too slim to be male, too graceful. Her scales were red like the fire leaving her nostrils. She looked young, only a youth.

"The only fresh bones here will be yours, Gloriae the Gilded," the dragon said. Her voice was that of a young woman. "Yes, Gloriae, slayer of Vir Requis children, I know your name. I am Agnus Dei, daughter of King Benedictus, heir to Requiem. I am the one who will kill you today."

The dragon leaped toward her.

Gloriae drove her griffin forward, steadying her lance.

Agnus Dei growled and blew fire, and Gloriae raised her shield. The flames burned around her, lapping at Gloriae's breastplate and helmet. Her lance scratched Agnus Dei's side, and the dragon grunted. Gloriae tugged the reins, spun around, and saw Agnus Dei leaping toward her again.

Narrowing her eyes, Gloriae pointed her lance. She gritted her teeth, and Agnus Dei blew fire again. The fire enveloped her shield, and Gloriae cried in pain; a tongue of flame found its way around her shield to burn her gloved hand. The leather protected her skin, but turned hot enough to blaze with pain.

"You will die, lizard!" she screamed and drove Aquila forward. The two had risen and now flew high over the ruins. Aquila too wore gilded armor. The fire had not kindled her fur or feathers, but that steel now burned hot, and the griffin screeched.

Agnus Dei was laughing. Blood seeped down her side, but still she laughed, smoke pluming from her maw. She charged, swooped, and before Gloriae could right her spear's thrust, Agnus Dei bit Aquila's leg.

The griffin shrieked and tried to bite, but Agnus Dei pulled back. Gloriae wished she could reach for her crossbow—its quarrels were coated with ilbane—but dared not drop her lance. She could not lose a second. As her griffin cried, Gloriae dug her spurs deep.

"Fly, Aquila! Fly at her."

Agnus Dei flew toward the sun, then dived down, the sunrays blinding Gloriae. Cursing, Gloriae raised her lance and shield, and felt a great weight land upon her. She saw nothing but scales, fire, and light. Her lance clanged. Agnus Dei was clawing, pushing her down. A claw scratched Gloriae's breastplate. She dropped her lance, drew her sword, and swung it. The steel cut scaled flesh, and Agnus Dei howled.

"Weredragon!" Gloriae cried. "I spit on your forefathers' graves. I will kill you upon their bones."

Agnus Dei drove her down, pushing Gloriae onto the ground. The claws lashed again, and Gloriae leaped off her saddle and rolled across the earth. Agnus Dei's claws slammed down, missing Gloriae by an inch, and she lashed her sword. The steel hit Agnus Dei's leg, spouting fresh blood. The red dragon roared.

"I will kill you even without my griffin," Gloriae said and snarled. She charged at the dragon, screaming, sword raised.

Agnus Dei flew up, and Gloriae screamed. "Coward! Come back here, girl, and face your death."

Gloriae ran toward the fallen griffin, not caring if Aquila lived or died; she cared only for the crossbow on the saddle. She grabbed it, aimed, and fired.

She caught Agnus Dei as the dragon swooped. The bolt hit the dragon's neck, and the scream of pain thudded against Gloriae, knocking her down. Agnus Dei kicked, and her leg hit Gloriae's breastplate. Gloriae saw nothing but white light. She flew, breath knocked out of her, and crashed against a smashed column. Armor covered her, but this blow still ached. For a moment, Gloriae could not breathe, and tears streamed down her cheeks as she struggled to her feet. Shakily, she raised her crossbow.

Agnus Dei was lumbering toward her, snarling, limping, unable to fly. She blew fire.

Gloriae ducked, rolled, and raised her shield. The flames burned around her shield, and Gloriae squinted. When the fire died, she aimed her crossbow and fired again.

The bolt hit Agnus Dei's shoulder, and the dragon screamed. She fell upon the ruins, cracking a fallen statue of an old king.

"Yes," Gloriae said, smiling through her snarl. "The ilbane on my quarrels is strong and thick. It burns, doesn't it? I finish you now." She stepped toward the dragon, the wind blasting her, Per Ignem raised.

Agnus Dei struggled to rise, but could not. She glared at Gloriae, and her eyes seemed so human—brown, pained eyes—that Gloriae faltered.

"Gloriae...," Agnus Dei spoke, blood seeping down her sides, squinting in pain. There was something about that voice, those eyes.... Gloriae shook her head. *Finish her!* cried a voice inside her. *Bring down your sword, chop off her head, kill the beast!*

"Requiem," Agnus Dei whispered at Gloriae's feet. "May our wings forever find your sky."

Those words! Gloriae knew them! But how could she? Tears filled her eyes, and her arm trembled. Her sword wavered. Gloriae could not breathe. Standing over the wounded Agnus Dei, she tore off her helmet, shook her hair loose, and took deep, desperate breaths.

Agnus Dei, staring up from the ground, gasped. Those eyes—those brown, almost human eyes—widened. "I... I know you, Gloriae. I've seen you before, I...."

Gloriae trembled. She walked between columns, the birches rustling, holding her mother's hand. She heard old songs on harps, and played with a girl her age, a girl with brown eyes, and—

"No!" Gloriae screamed, a scream so loud, that Agnus Dei started. "I do not know you, lizard! I— I know only your evil. You cast spells upon me. You cast evil magic. I will not let you invade my mind. I will not!" Her eyes swam with tears.

She could no longer bear to look into those brown eyes. She saw lies and dreams within them, trees that still rustled, and songs that still played, and smiles from... what? A different life? A different world?

No! Spells! Lies! Black magic of beasts.

Gloriae fled, boots kicking up ash, leaving the creature there. The weredragons were more dangerous and evil than she had imagined.

"Aquila!" she cried. The griffin still lived, through she was wounded, maybe badly. Gloriae climbed onto the saddle and urged the beast up. "Fly, Aquila. Fly far from here. This land is cursed."

The wind streamed her hair, stung her eyes, and blew the tears off her cheeks. Clutching her wounds, Gloriae flew, trembling, vowing to never more return to the ruins of Requiem.

LACRIMOSA

Lacrimosa walked along the beach, her shoulder bandaged, tears on her cheeks.

She walked alone. She needed to be alone. She needed to think, to breathe, to shed her tears in silence and solitude. She had left her husband behind with the boy; the two tended to a campfire she could just see in the distance, its smoke unfurling. It was dangerous to light a fire, to cast smoke into the sky like a dragon's tail, but Lacrimosa had lived her life in danger. She had been running for ten years, hiding in forests, in snowy mountaintops, in caves and along beaches of ruins such as this one.

Old bricks lay in the sand around her feet, and Lacrimosa saw the ruins of a fort toppled across a hill ahead. Its scattered bricks and broken walls had settled years ago, and the water had smoothed them, and covered them with moss. Gulls picked between the stones, and crabs scuttled along toppled battlements. What fort was this? Lacrimosa did not know. She had once known the names of many forts, but in the past ten years, memories of the old world had fled her. She could no longer remember Osanna's castles, those castles the Vir Requis had once fought and died against. She could no longer remember a time when the men of Osanna lived alongside her race, would visit their courts, would treat with them. Sometimes Lacrimosa could barely remember Requiem, the autumn leaves that scuttled along mosaic floors, the columns that rose in the forest like so many birch boles, Requiem's elders walking in green velvet embroidered in gold. Those memories were fleeting too. They emerged now only in dreams or in the moments of her greatest loneliness and fear.

Lacrimosa stepped among the ruins of the fort. Water pooled between the stones, and the waves whispered, entering and leaving the homes these stones formed for fish and crabs. Salt and seashells glistened in the sand. Lacrimosa knelt to lift a conch, pink and large as her fist, and beneath it she saw a bone emerging from the sand. A human bone.

She dropped the shell and walked on, a tear on her cheek. Thus it was these days, she thought. Whatever beauty she found hid darkness.

"Like my daughters?" she whispered.

No. She hated those whispers. Hated the doubts. Agnus Dei was beautiful, forever good and right, a future for their race, a hope. She could not conceal darkness. She could not have quickened that day, that day that hid beneath her memories of beauty. And yet the memories flooded her.

Lacrimosa had been fifteen, a wispy youth of marble skin, of hair that Benedictus said was woven of moonlight. Her father was a great lord, and her coming of age was a grand party, among the grandest Vir Requis girls had known, for she was among their fairest. She glistened in white silk inlaid with diamonds, and apple blossoms lay strewn through her hair. She had felt shy, but beautiful too, fearful yet joyous in the beauty of Requiem. She walked among lords and ladies in jewels.

Among the lords stood Prince Benedictus, the younger of the princes. He wore green velvet embroidered with gold, a sword upon his hip, and a crown atop his black curls. Lacrimosa thought him handsome, but she feared him. He was twenty years her senior, from a different world, destined to someday be her king.

Her lord father presented Lacrimosa to Benedictus that day, and they danced to the song of flutes, and drank wine. Benedictus was a clumsy dancer, and he did not speak much, but he was courteous and sober, holding her hand gently, praising her gown and beauty. She knew she would marry him; they all knew. Perhaps they had known for years, these noble families of their courts.

That evening she walked alone, leaving the palace for some solitude, some reflection in the woods. She often walked here alone among the birches, to speak with the birds and deer, to pray, to escape the lords and ladies and servants that forever fussed around her. She would find treasures here most days: acorns, or pretty stones, and once a golden coin lost two hundred years before. But this day, the day of her fifteenth birthday, her coming of age, she found something else in the forest. She found pain, and darkness, and a secret that would forever haunt her.

Dies Irae stood leaning against a birch, dressed in white. He looked much like Benedictus—the straight nose, strong jaw, tall brow. Yet his hair was golden, not black, and his eyes were not solemn but cruel, calculating.

"Hello, my lord," she said to him and curtsied, and he only stared with those cruel eyes, blue and hungry.

He spent many days in these woods, she knew, for his father scorned him. Dies Irae had been born without the magic. He could not shift, could not become a dragon. All her life, Lacrimosa had pitied him. How horrible it must be, to be forever in human form! How painful to be the elder brother, yet not heir to the throne—an outcast, a sad child.

"Let us return to the court," she said and smiled, hoping to soothe his pain. "There are honey cakes and wine."

But he wanted more than honey cakes and wine. He wanted the Griffin Heart, revenge against his family, revenge against the race that had outcast him. And he wanted her.

He took all those things.

Between the birches, he stuffed ilbane into her mouth, and muffled her screams with his palm. The pain stunned her, dazed her so she couldn't shift. He knew her there, pinning her down. With a clenched jaw, he made her swear to secrecy, to swear by their stars, on the honor of her forefathers. And she swore, vowed to never speak of how he'd hurt her, planted his seed inside her. When she cried that night, back in her home, all assumed that she was overcome by her party, by meeting Benedictus whom she would wed. She never spoke of what happened in that forest, not even a week later when she married her lord Benedictus, not even nine moons later when she gave birth to her daughters.

They were twins, one dark, the other fair.

"Agnus Dei, I name you," she whispered to the babe with dark curls. Lamb of God, the name meant, for the child's hair was soft and curly as lamb's fleece, and she was holy.

"And I name you Gloriae," she whispered to the fair child, for this babe seemed a being of light, angelic and pure, a golden child.

One dark babe, one fair. One child of fire, the other of gold. One child Lacrimosa kept; the other Dies Irae stole from her. Agnus Dei and Gloriae; the chambers of her heart.

They are Benedictus's daughters, Lacrimosa told herself when they were born, and she told this to herself today too, walking among the ruins of this seaside fort. *They are like him. They are his. They could never be the children of Dies Irae; they are too noble, too good at heart, even Gloriae whom Dies Irae has raised. They are ours.*

Tears were salty on her lips like the waves that whispered. Lacrimosa turned and walked back to their camp, to the fire Benedictus and Kyrie were tending. She approached her husband, a trembling smile found her lips, and she kissed him. He held her by the fire and water. She laid her head against his shoulder, shut her eyes, and felt safe in his arms.

That was when she heard the whistles.

Lacrimosa opened her eyes, and she saw thousands of slivers in the sky, shadowing the world.

"Arrows!" Kyrie shouted. "Fly!"

Lacrimosa ran and shifted. Arrows peppered the beach around her. Two hit her back, but snapped against her scales. Ilbane sizzled over her, and she yelped.

"Fly over the water!" she cried and flapped her wings. She saw Benedictus and Kyrie flying beside her; they too had shifted. She heard more whistles. When she peeked over her shoulder, she saw a thousand archers in the trees above the beach. Their arrows flew, and more clanked against the fleeing Vir Requis. This time, an arrow broke Lacrimosa's scales and pierced her. She cried in pain; ilbane coated the arrowhead, sending fire through her.

"Fly faster!" she cried. They were far from the shore now, and when more arrows flew, they fell into the water. Lacrimosa exhaled in relief. *We made it.*

That was when she heard the griffins.

When Lacrimosa looked over her shoulder, she saw them there: Three griffins, their armor gilded and their wings wide. She recognized the leader. A woman sat atop that griffin, aiming a lance, her armor golden.

Gloriae. My daughter.

The sight of Gloriae sent more pain through Lacrimosa than the arrows. She wanted to fly toward her, to embrace her, to tell her who she was, to save her from Dies Irae. But how could she? How could she reveal this shattering truth to Gloriae? How would this girl raised to loath, hunt, and kill Vir Requis ever believe it?

You are Vir Requis too, Gloriae! she wanted to cry out. *You have our magic within you. You can shift, become a dragon. I know it. You are not Dies Irae's. You cannot be his. You are the daughter of Benedictus.*

All these things Lacrimosa ached to cry out, and tears filled her eyes, but she could bring no words to her lips. Gloriae and the riders she led were firing crossbows. The bolts whizzed by Lacrimosa, and one hit Kyrie's tail. The boy yelped, dipped several feet, but kept flying.

"That's it!" Kyrie said. He snarled, and suddenly he spun around to face the griffins. Lacrimosa's heart froze, and she cried out. Eyes narrowed and grin tight, Kyrie began flying toward Gloriae.

"Kyrie!" Lacrimosa cried.

Quarrels flew across the young Vir Requis. One hit his shoulder, and he grunted, but kept flying.

"Hello again, sweetheart," Kyrie said and drove his head into Gloriae's griffin.

Gloriae screamed and lashed her lance, but her griffin was bucking, and she could not aim. Kyrie clawed the beast, bit its shoulder, and shoved it. The two other griffins were clawing, but Kyrie's lashing tail kept them at bay.

Gloriae and her griffin fell and crashed into the sea. Kyrie blew fire at the other two griffins, holding them back.

"You die now, blondie," Kyrie said, growled, and swooped at Gloriae with open claws.

"No!" Lacrimosa cried and flew. Ice seemed to encase her. She was about to watch Kyrie kill her daughter. "Kyrie, no, she's my—"

The words froze on her lips. She could not reveal the secret, not like this, not here. Instead, she grabbed Kyrie and pulled him back. He struggled, and then Benedictus was flying there too, pulling the boy away.

A griffin flew at Lacrimosa. She blew fire, and it caught flame. Screeching, it dived into the water. The third griffin attacked Benedictus, and he swatted away with his tail, cutting its side.

"Fly!" Lacrimosa said, still struggling to pull Kyrie back. Gloriae was swimming away, tossing off her armor. Kyrie was trying to reach her, to claw her, but Lacrimosa would not let him.

"I'll explain later, just fly now, fly away, there are more griffins coming."

She could see them on the horizon. A hundred more flew their way, maybe two hundred. They would be on them within seconds.

Kyrie saw them too. He grunted and began to fly away. The three dragons were soon flying into the clouds, fleeing as fast as they could.

"Swim back to shore, Gloriae," Lacrimosa whispered as she flew, breath aching in her lungs. "Leave this place, and travel far, and forget about us. I love you, my lost daughter. I love you."

KYRIE ELEISON

They flew all day and into night, until they lost the griffins over a forest of oaks and pines.

Under rainclouds and trees, they ran in human form, small and cloaked in darkness. They ran for a league, maybe two, ran until Kyrie's side ached and his lungs felt ready to burst. They ran until they heard no more griffins, and then ran some more.

Lost, wounded, and exhausted, they finally collapsed in the forest.

Kyrie sat on the wet ground, leaned against an oak, and shut his eyes. Everything hurt. Lacrimosa and Benedictus collapsed beside him. Benedictus breathed ragged, creaky breaths like a saw. Lacrimosa's chest rose and fell, and she seemed paler than ever.

It was long moments before Kyrie could speak again. Finally he turned to Lacrimosa and said, "Why? Why wouldn't you let me kill her?"

She looked at him, pain in her eyes. "She is a sad child."

Kyrie shook his head in disbelief. Gloriae? Sad? He snorted. He saw rage in Gloriae. He saw cruelty. He saw a killer. There was no sadness in those icy eyes, in those cruel lips.

Lacrimosa began crying. Kyrie felt guilt like a rock in his belly.

"Lacrimosa, I—" He couldn't understand. It seemed almost like Lacrimosa loved Gloriae, loved this killer, the daughter of Dies Irae. But how could that be? "I'm sorry, I don't understand."

"Drop it, kid," Benedictus said, still wheezing. "Gloriae's tale is a sad one. Dies Irae kidnapped her when she was three, raised her to hate Vir Requis, raised her to kill. The girl is not evil at heart; she's simply ignorant."

Kyrie doubted that. He had looked into Gloriae's eyes. He had seen something cold, cruel, and calculating there. If that wasn't evil, he didn't know what was. Lacrimosa, however, was still crying, and Benedictus's eyes were shooting daggers. Kyrie decided to drop the subject.

He rubbed his aching shoulder. "All right," he said. "I'll drop it. But I'm not done asking questions. I have many. And I want answers to some at least. In the past few days, I've been shot at, clawed at, bitten, burned, and hit with about a field's worth of ilbane. My wounds ache, this rain is bloody cold, I'm famished, and I stubbed my toes about fifteen times on these roots. I think I've earned some answers." His voice was hoarse and his eyes stung. "So tell me this at least: Are there more Vir Requis? Or are we the last?"

Before anyone could answer, a griffin shrieked in the distance. Kyrie stiffened. He sat still, daring not breathe. Beside him, Benedictus and Lacrimosa also froze. An old oak rose above them, twisted and leafy. No griffins would see through its boughs, but still Kyrie's fingers trembled. He scanned the clouds for griffins. He saw a glint above—a rider carrying a torch. *Is that Dies Irae who rides there? Or Gloriae?* Then the griffin flew by, its shrieks fading into the distance.

When they could no longer hear the griffin, Benedictus turned to face him. At least, Kyrie thought he did; in the darkness, Benedictus appeared as but a shadow, burly and stiff like the oaks around them.

"There is another," spoke his gruff voice in the night.

Kyrie's heart leaped. Another! Another Vir Requis! He wanted to leap up and dance, and only the memory of the last griffin kept him still. "Who?" he breathed. "A girl Vir Requis?"

In the darkness, he heard Lacrimosa laugh softly, and Kyrie felt blood rise to his cheeks. *Nice one, Kyrie,* he scolded himself. *You sound like a lonely, love-starved boy.*

But maybe it wasn't so foolish a question, he decided. A female Vir Requis meant hope. A female could bear children. And if Kyrie himself was the father.... He felt even more blood rush to his cheeks, and he was grateful for the darkness that hid his fluster. Suddenly he was no longer cold.

"I know what you're thinking," Benedictus said. "And you can forget it right now. Yes, she's a girl. But she's not for you."

Why is he so angry? Kyrie wondered. Had he somehow offended the old warrior? It was hard to know; Benedictus was angry more often than not.

"Who is she?" Kyrie said. His fingers tingled. All his life, he'd been sure no other Vir Requis lived, except perhaps for the legendary Benedictus. And now, within a moon's cycle, he had met not just Benedictus, but Lacrimosa too. And there was a fourth! A second female! For ten years since Lanburg Fields, the world had seemed so grim, a world of hiding in Fort Sanctus, a world of pain and loneliness. Now things were different. To be sure, he still lived in hiding, and danger and loneliness were still his companions, but promise filled this night, and hope, and wonders. These were new feelings to Kyrie, and they made him feel drunk. He wanted to become a dragon and fly to find this new Vir Requis right away. Had she too been hiding all this time, alone in some fort? Had she too been dreaming of finding others, of finding Benedictus? Why wouldn't the old king speak? The burly shadow merely stood silently. It boiled Kyrie's blood.

"Well, why don't you speak?" he demanded, then bit his tongue. "I'm sorry, but— can't you tell me?"

Benedictus only growled again, a sound like a bear in its den. "I told you, kid, forget about her."

A griffin shriek sounded, but it was a league away. Kyrie ignored it. He stood up, boots crunching the leaves that carpeted the forest floor. Rising so quickly made his wounds hurt, but he ignored the pain. "How can I forget her?" he said. He knew his voice was too loud, but couldn't help it. His fists clenched. "I've spent ten years thinking I'm alone, thinking all the others died. Now I learn there's another—a girl!—and you tell me to forget her? Why, Benedictus?"

The shadow also stood up. Kyrie was tall, but Benedictus towered over him. That growl sounded again, louder this time. "Watch your mouth, kid, unless you want it bashed in."

Now it was Lacrimosa's turn to rise. A slender shadow in the darkness, she leaped forward. If Benedictus was gnarled, tough, and wide as an oak, Lacrimosa was like a sapling. She came between them and placed one hand on Kyrie's chest, the other on Benedictus's chest. Kyrie marveled at how small and soft her hand felt, and how her hair, only inches from his face, smelled like jasmine.

"Please don't fight," she said. Though the night was starless, and they had no fire or lamp, Kyrie could see her hair glitter like moonlight. "Ben, we must tell him."

Benedictus regarded her for a moment, then turned away. He faced the oak and stood silent for a long time, fists at his sides. Finally his voice came in the darkness, low, almost sad, a voice drenched in memory and regret.

"Her name is Agnus Dei," said Benedictus. "And she will not join us. She will not fly with us."

"Why not?" Kyrie said, stepping forward, heart leaping. Fire blazed through him.

Benedictus still did not face him. "Agnus Dei is a wild one. She spends all her time in dragon form. Forgets she's a Vir Requis. Thinks she's a true dragon, forgets her human side, forgets her humanity. More dragon than woman, that one is. I don't think she's been in her human form in a year."

Kyrie shook his head. "How is that possible? How has she survived? How do you know her? Where is she?" He had so many questions, he could have asked a hundred more, but Benedictus turned to face him. Kyrie could see but two blazing eyes in the shadowy form, and something in those eyes silenced him.

"She's my daughter," Benedictus said.

Kyrie took a step back. "Your... daughter?"

He did not know how to feel. Elated? Heart-warmed? But more than any other emotion, Kyrie felt sudden rage. His daughter! Kyrie clenched his fists. He had seen Requiem burn, had seen her courts topple. He had been to Lanburg Fields where the last of their kind perished, even the children. Yet Benedictus's family had been safe! His wife, Lacrimosa. His daughter, Agnus Dei. Where had he kept them? Had he hidden them underground while leading the others to die? Kyrie felt as if dragonfire consumed him. He wanted to pummel the old man. He wanted to shout, to accuse Benedictus of cowardice, but could bring none of it to his lips. So many emotions swirled through him, spinning his head, that he could barely speak. He could only manage two more words: "Your daughter."

Benedictus stared at him. "Yes, kid. I have a daughter. And I know what you're thinking. Yes, I kept her safe. Yes, I kept my child and wife away from Lanburg Fields." He took a step toward Kyrie; they stood only a foot apart. "Yes, I lead the rest of you to die. I lead thousands to die, but I kept my family safe. Even in the darkness, I can see that you hate me. And you're right to hate me. I've spent ten years hating myself, so a little more hate ain't gonna make a difference."

Silence filled the night. Not even crickets chirped. Lacrimosa stood by them, staring, and Kyrie did not know what to say. Finally he just turned around, walked toward the oak tree, and placed a hand against the trunk. Leaning against the tree, he lowered his head. His eyes stung.

"Kyrie," came Lacrimosa's voice behind him, soft and entreating. He felt her hand, so small and light, on his shoulder.

He turned around. He stared at Lacrimosa and Benedictus. "I want to find her."

"Forget her," said Benedictus.

"No!" Kyrie yelled, and Benedictus growled. Yelling could alert the griffins, but Kyrie didn't care. He preferred a fight to hiding. "No," he repeated. "She's your daughter, Benedictus. And she might be the only other Vir Requis who lives. The time for hiding has ended. Let's find her. We can't live scattered like this, in caves, in towers, in forests." Kyrie gritted his teeth. "We fly again, Benedictus. We fly like in the old days. And we fly with Agnus Dei."

Benedictus glowered. "She will not fly with us."

"I will get her to fly." He smiled mirthlessly. "We both saw our childhoods cut short. We will understand each other. Benedictus. Lacrimosa. Please. Let me speak with your daughter. Will you take me to her?"

He noticed suddenly, with a wrench of his heart, that Lacrimosa was weeping. Her tears glistened in the night, and her body shook. Such guilt filled Kyrie, that he felt like somebody had punched his stomach.

"Lacrimosa," he said, voice soft. "I'm sorry. I didn't mean to hurt you, I...."

She shook his head. "No, you don't hurt me. You're right, Kyrie. We'll seek her. I want her to meet you." Her voice shook and her tears fell. "I've wanted her to meet other Vir Requis for so long, others her age, of her kind. Maybe you can help her. Maybe you can help heal the pain within her." She smiled a trembling smile. "You're right. We're all in this together. Benedictus is no forest hunter. Agnus Dei is no wild dragon. We are Vir Requis. Tomorrow morning, I'll take you to her."

Kyrie was about to speak when shouts filled the forest. He heard creaking armor, swords being drawn, and thumping boots. Dogs barked.

"Actually, I think we better go now," Kyrie said and started running. "Tomorrow morning? Too late."

Benedictus and Lacrimosa ran beside him. They fled through the forest, panting, aching. *We're going to need to find more than one Vir Requis,* Kyrie thought as branches slapped him and the rain pelted him. *We're going to need to find a hidden army.* He suddenly missed Fort Sanctus; even hiding in that dank fort seemed heavenly compared to this, to running scared through the rain and darkness. Soon griffins flew above.

"They haven't seen us yet," Benedictus whispered as they ran. "Do not shift! Keep running, and keep quiet, and keep hidden. It's the dogs I'm worried about."

"Me too," Lacrimosa said, "I—"

She fell, twisted her ankle, and bit down on a yelp. His heart racing, Kyrie helped her up, glancing behind him. He could see steel blades and torchlight. Benedictus lifted Lacrimosa over his shoulder, and they kept running. Thunder rolled and the rain hammered them.

Kyrie clenched his fists. He had never harmed Dies Irae or Gloriae. Why were they so desperate to murder him? He wanted to shift, to roar, to fight them, but he just kept running. Lightning flashed, the dogs howled, and suddenly Kyrie doubted that he'd ever see Agnus Dei. He doubted that he'd live through the night.

Through rain and darkness, the Vir Requis ran.

DIES IRAE

Dies Irae slapped the girl's face, not hard enough to cut her, but hard enough to knock her to the floor. "You looked into my eyes," he said, voice icy. "Never look into my eyes."

She lay at his feet, trembling, hair covering her face. When he'd seen her that afternoon in the village, a peasant girl hawking eggs, he knew he must have her. A girl not yet twenty, slender, her hair fair and soft... she looked so much like Lacrimosa, that Dies Irae knew he would take her. Hurt her. Punish her for what Lacrimosa had done to him all those years ago.

"Please, my lord," the girl whispered, voice shaking. "My husband. Is he—"

"Be silent," Dies Irae said, staring down upon her. "Do not speak unless you are spoken to."

Her husband! Dies Irae barked a laugh. He had dealt with the farmer. The man had put up a fight, trying to protect his wife; he had even dared punch Lord Molok. Dies Irae smiled when he remembered how Molok had grabbed the man, then dragged him away screaming. If griffins had not eaten the peasant yet, it was only because Molok was still torturing him.

Dies Irae sighed. These backwater villages taxed him, with their crude peasants, impudent girls, and cold stone forts. He hated Benedictus for drawing him away from Confutatis, his Marble City of splendor and comfort. He hated Benedictus for eluding him this long, for leading him on a chase that seemed to never end. Dies Irae stared out the window of the fortress, gazing over the filthy village below, the field and forest, and the distant mountains.

"My lord, please, I beg you—" the peasant girl began, rising to her feet. Dies Irae hit her again, a punch that knocked her to the ground. Blood gushed from her lips.

"Silence," he said. These peasants lived so far from Confutatis, from his glory and statues and palaces. They forgot his power, his holiness. He would beat respect into them.

The girl was weeping at his feet.   With his iron fist, the mace he now wore for an arm, Dies Irae caressed her hair. She shivered at his boots. *So young, soft, pale. So much like Lacrimosa.*

Dies Irae smiled when he remembered that day, eighteen years ago, when he'd found Lacrimosa in the forest. She had been only fifteen, fresh like an autumn fruit, and he had enjoyed hurting her, hurting his brother's prize. Yes, Benedictus had inherited the Oak Throne, Benedictus had gotten Lacrimosa to be his bride. But Dies Irae was the elder brother; if he could not inherit his birthright, he could destroy it.

"So I burned your throne, brother," he said softly. "And I broke your wife."

The girl at his feet looked up, then quickly looked away. Blood covered her mouth. The sight of her blood stirred Dies Irae's own blood.

"I will hurt you now, girl," he said, grabbed the girl's hair, and pulled her up. "And I will hurt Lacrimosa still. And I will hurt Benedictus, and that boy who flies with them. You all tried to cast me aside, to exile me, to hurt me. Look at you now."

The girl screamed, and he covered her mouth with his good hand. From outside his window, from the village stables, came more screams—the sounds of her husband, and the shrieks of feasting griffins. As the screams rose across the village, and across his empire of Osanna, Dies Irae smiled.

Soon, Benedictus, he thought as he shoved the girl down and tore off her dress. *Soon, Lacrimosa. Soon you will scream too.*

When he was done with the girl, he pulled her to the window, shoved her outside, and watched her crash to the cobblestones below. She convulsed, kicked, and lay still. Blood spread below her.

She was too skinny, Dies Irae thought.

He turned away from the window and stared into the mirror. He was old, he saw. Lines ran down the sides of his mouth, and gray streaked his golden hair. Wrinkles surrounded his eyes. But he still stood straight and strong, and he could still defeat men half his age in combat. *I still have my strength, and my rage, and the light of the Sun God.*

He left the room, stepped downstairs, and exited the fort. He walked across the courtyard, where his men were dragging the dead girl away. A cold wind blew, ruffling his robe, and Dies Irae looked up to see crows gliding under gray clouds. *Winter is coming,* he thought. *The weredragons will freeze in the snow and winds, but I will burn with the Sun God's flame.*

He walked down the hill, hand on the hilt of his sword. The stones were rough beneath his feet, and the grass and trees moved in the whistling winds. Below in the village, he saw his soldiers move from house to house, plundering food and grabbing peasant girls. When Dies Irae reached the stables, he stepped inside to find ten griffins. Gloriae stood there too, tending to her mount.

"She's hurt... badly," Gloriae said, not turning to look at him. A tin lamp hung over her, its light warm against her golden hair, her soft cheek, and her white tunic. Her griffin lay on her side, bandages covering her leg, side, and neck. She mewled.

"Kill the beast," Dies Irae said, not bothering to hide the irritation in his voice. "She's useless now."

Gloriae reeled on him, eyes flashing. Golden flecks danced in those green eyes, as ever when fury filled her. "How dare you say this? I've had Aquila since I was a child." She patted the griffin's head. "Hush, princess of the sky. You are strong. You will heal."

Dies Irae looked down at his daughter and her griffin, and couldn't decide what emotion he felt more strongly: disgust at her weakness, or admiration for her passion. The latter won, and Dies Irae sighed.

"Gloriae, I have spoiled you. I should have been harder on you, taught you to see griffins as tools, no more; not living creatures to love. But how could I? I admit it; I too have fond feelings for my griffin Volucris, and would rage should a weredragon wound him." He took her hands in his. "We will heal dear Aquila, and we will kill the weredragons who hurt her."

Gloriae looked at the griffin, chewed her lip, and said, "The blue weredragon hurt her. He'd have killed her and me, but... the silver dragon stopped him. I can't understand it. Kyrie Eleison had me; I was his to kill. The one they call Lacrimosa pulled him back." She shook her head as if to clear it. Her locks of golden hair swayed. "I don't understand, Father. I'm confused. Lacrimosa said something to me in the forest. Something about my mother." She looked back at her griffin, worry clouding her eyes.

Dies Irae winced inwardly. Of course Lacrimosa still recognized Gloriae. Of course she would stop Kyrie from killing her daughter. *Gloriae must never know,* he told himself, as he'd been telling himself for fifteen years, since that day he took one sister for his own, and left the other for the weredragons.

"Daughter," he said, "have I told you about your mother?"

"Of course. You told me that the weredragons killed her."

He nodded. "When you were three years old. Of course Lacrimosa wanted to pull Kyrie back. She wanted to kill you herself. Lacrimosa, you see, is the weredragon who murdered your mother."

Gloriae's face changed. All worry and doubt left her, and hatred suffused her expression. She whispered through a tight jaw. "I knew it."

Dies Irae stepped toward his griffin, the great Volucris, who stood at the back of the stable. He mounted the beast. "Come, Gloriae. Sit before me on the saddle. We go hunting weredragons."

Within minutes, they were flying over the countryside, a hundred griffins behind them. As the wind streamed through his hair, Dies Irae allowed himself a small, tight smile.

KYRIE ELEISON

They flew through the night. In the darkness they streamed forward, three Vir Requis—one young and blue, fire in his nostrils; one black and burly, scarred and limp; one slender and silvery, her eyes like stars. Cloaked in night and clouds, they flew like the great herds of old.

It feels good to fly, Kyrie thought. They had run for leagues on human feet, until finally shaking off the pursuit in hills of thick pines. The griffins could still return, he knew, and he kept both eyes wide open—but for a moment, he allowed himself to breathe easy.

"Are you sure she'll be there?" Benedictus called over the roaring winds. They flew hidden in cloud. Their scales glistened in the firelight from their mouths and nostrils.

Lacrimosa nodded. "She loved that cave as a child, that summer we hid there. In the snowy Fidelium, she always spoke of returning someday. She'll be there."

Kyrie watched the two Vir Requis fly side by side. He could not help but envy them. They shared a past and memories. They had a family. Kyrie had nobody to reminisce with. His family had perished. His home lay in ruins. Dies Irae had killed Lady Mirum. Kyrie had nobody who also remembered his childhood, remembered his home among the trees, and then his home in Fort Sanctus. He would never have what those two had, and it filled him with both fire and ice.

Dawn was rising, he saw. He could see Benedictus and Lacrimosa more clearly now. He could not yet see the sun, but its pink tendrils touched the clouds where they flew, kindling them. Soon the clouds blazed like dragonfire.

They had flown for hundreds of leagues. They were far now from the Marble City of Confutatis, from Dies Irae's center of power, from his armies and griffin stables... but not beyond the length of his arm. *His griffins fly far,* Kyrie knew. *They fly across this land too, and the distant lands beyond it. Maybe they fly until the end of the world.*

"We're close now," Lacrimosa said, the dawn glittering on her scales like sunlight on morning sea. The three dragons pulled their wings closer and descended, tails snaking behind them, until the clouds parted and they saw green land. Grassy hills rolled for leagues, cradling valleys of bindweed and goldenrod, leading to chalk mountains under yellow sunrise. Kyrie scanned the land, but saw only wild sheep, starlings and robins, and a fox running across a hill to disappear into a burrow. No griffins. No Dies Irae or Gloriae. No people at all.

"What is this place?" Kyrie asked.

"It's called Sequestra," Lacrimosa said. "Our kind used to herd here before—"

A roar pierced the land, cutting her off. Lacrimosa narrowed her eyes, Benedictus grunted, and Kyrie stared to the mountains. The roar had come from there. That was no griffin shriek. That was the sound of a dragon. *An angry dragon*, Kyrie thought.

The three Vir Requis kept flying, gliding lower, until they were near the mountains. Pines grew across the mountainsides, clinging with gangly roots and looking as if a sparrow could topple them. The smell of pines, chalk, and grass filled Kyrie's nostrils, and he savored it. He'd spent a decade by the sea, smelling the salt and waves and fish. He loved the seaside smells, but this place had a new scent, invigorating, healthy, and he imagined the ages long ago when herds of Vir Requis—thousands of them—filled the skies over Sequestra.

Lacrimosa was leading them toward a cave upon the mountain. Ash covered the mountainside here, the pines were burned, and great claw marks dug into the chalk and earth. A roar sounded again, coming from the cave. It echoed across the mountains and valleys, so loud that birds fled. Smoke and flames flew from the cave, and Kyrie tensed. Would a dragon attack a dragon? Kyrie knew that in the old days, Vir Requis houses would sometimes battle one another, but would Vir Requis fight even now, near extinction? He growled, gearing for a fight should it come.

Kyrie soon reached the cave and flapped his wings, hovering before it. Lacrimosa and Benedictus hovered beside him.

Lacrimosa called out, voice loud and clear across the mountainside. "Agnus Dei! Come and see us."

More fire emerged from the cave, and that roar sounded again, so loud that stones rolled down the mountainside. Then, with a puff of smoke, a red dragon burst out from the cave.

Kyrie couldn't help but retreat a dozen feet. He had never seen a dragon look so fierce, so wild. Agnus Dei looked like a creature woven of flame, her scales burning red. Her fangs and claws glinted, white and sharp. She was a long dragon, lithe but strong, her wings wide and blood red. She howled to the skies and blew more flames.

No wonder the humans think us monsters, Kyrie thought. *They must have seen Agnus Dei.*

"Hello, my daughter," Lacrimosa said. Her eyes were stern, but compassion and love filled them too. "Your leg. You're hurt."

Kyrie noticed that a long cut, as from a sword, ran along Agnus Dei's leg. The red dragon seemed not to mind. She snorted. "It's nothing, Mother. When will you stop worrying?"

"When you stop getting into fights!" Lacrimosa said.

Agnus Dei rolled her eyes, and smoke rose from her nostrils. She groaned, then seemed to notice Kyrie for the first time. The annoyance left her eyes, and amusement filled them instead. She raised an eyebrow and smirked. She looked like a girl who, in the midst of a heated argument, saw a silly dog and couldn't help but laugh. She studied Kyrie for a moment, then turned to Benedictus.

"Who's the pup?" she asked her father.

Kyrie bristled, and Benedictus snickered.

"The pup's with me," Benedictus said. "Thinks he's a hot shot."

Agnus Dei looked at Kyrie again, the sunlight glinting on her red scales. "Cute pup," she said to Benedictus. "Can he fly?"

Benedictus snorted. "Barely."

Kyrie had heard enough. He felt like roaring and blowing flames. "I can fly better than you any day," he said to Agnus Dei, baring his fangs. He spread his wings wide, trying to appear as large, wild, and intimidating as possible.

Agnus Dei laughed. She gestured with her head to a valley below the mountain. "Race you. First one to grab a deer wins."

"You're o—" Kyrie began when Agnus Dei took off, blazing over his head toward the valley.

Cursing, Kyrie spun around and shot after her. He saw her flying ahead, already distant, her tail swishing. Kyrie narrowed his eyes and flew like an arrow, diving toward the valley, wind whistling around him. His eyes scanned the grass and trees for deer. Agnus Dei was flying five hundred yards ahead, heading to a copse of trees, and Kyrie followed. Deer had to gather there. If he could just—

There! He saw one. A doe was racing across the grass, and Kyrie grinned and dived, snarling. The doe raced, fleeing to the trees. Kyrie swooped. He reached out his claws, and—

With a flash of red, Agnus Dei came swooping. She slammed into him, shoving him aside, and Kyrie howled. She drove him into a hill, and they slid across it, tearing up dirt and grass.

"Let go!" Kyrie cried, struggling to throw her off, but she clung to him, pinning him down.

"That deer was mine," Agnus Dei growled, her maw inches from his face. Her fangs glistened.

Kyrie struggled, freed a leg, and tried to push her off. She wriggled, clutching him with her legs and tail, refusing to release him. They wrestled in the grass, and Kyrie growled. He could not free himself; not without tearing into her flesh with claws and teeth, which he was not prepared to do. Not yet, at least.

"Get off," he grunted. Grass and dirt covered him.

Pinning him down, her knee in his side, she laughed and twisted his front leg. "Pup," she said.

Kyrie growled, smoke rising from his nostrils. "Benedictus warned me about you. He said you're more dragon than woman. He said you forgot what your human form is like. You must be a hideous freak, if you just stay in dragon form."

Agnus Dei laughed again, leaped off him, and shifted. Her wings pulled into her back, her scales vanished, and her claws and fangs retracted. She stood before him in human form.

Kyrie stared. Her hair was curly and black, her eyes brown and mocking, her skin tanned. She was tall and lithe, clad in tattered black leggings and a brown bodice. When he'd met Lacrimosa, Kyrie had thought her the most beautiful woman he'd seen, and he still thought so, but *this* woman.... If Lacrimosa was beautiful as moonlight, Agnus Dei had a beauty of fire, and that fire boiled Kyrie's blood.

"Stick your tongue back in," Agnus Dei said, her smile just as mocking as her eyes. "You might trip on it."

Kyrie frowned and shifted into human form too. He stood before her, covered in grass and dirt.

"I do not forget," Agnus Dei said. She drew a dagger from her belt and pointed it at him. "I merely do not fear. Others fear their dragon forms. They spend all their time as humans. I have no fear." She growled. "You are a pup." Then she shifted back into a dragon and leaped into the air, kicking up grass. She flew, heading back to the mountainside.

Kyrie too shifted back to dragon. He leaped and flew as fast as he could. He wanted to beat Agnus Dei back to her cave, to show her his speed, but he reached the cave just behind her. She looked at him with those mocking eyes and barked a laugh, and Kyrie felt his cheeks grow hot, and smoke rose from his nostrils.

Agnus Dei, he knew, would be a lot of trouble.

AGNUS DEI

Agnus Dei sat on her haunches, the cave dark around her, and growled at her parents. Smoke rose from her nostrils to sting her eyes.

"Agnus Dei, please," Mother said, soft silver in the darkness. "We've talked about the growling."

Agnus Dei shot flames from her nostrils. The fire glinted on Mother's silver scales, Father's black scales, and the pup's blue ones.

"Agnus Dei!" Mother said, rising to her feet, though the cave was too low for her to stretch to full height. "Will you *please* stop that?"

Agnus Dei turned to Father. The black dragon sat beside her, watching her with dark eyes.

"Do you see what I've had to put up with?" Agnus Dei asked him. "Do you see, Father?" She mimicked her mother. "Do not growl, do not blow fire, do not act like a dragon. Be a lady, Agnus Dei. Be like me, the noble and beautiful Lacrimosa."

"I never told you to be a lady," Mother interjected, eyes flashing.

"But you want it, don't you?" Agnus Dei said and growled, just to annoy Mother. "You want me to be like you. Delicate and fair, walking around in human form, all pretty." Agnus Dei thrust out her chest and let fire glow in her mouth. "But I'm like Father. I'm like the Great Benedictus, a wild thing."

Still Father said nothing, and that pup Kyrie also only watched from the shadows, eyes burning. *He doesn't care for me much, that pup,* Agnus Dei thought. *Or maybe he cares for me too much, and can't stand it.* She gave him a crooked smile, but he only bared his fangs at her.

"Pup," she said to him, and he growled.

"Now don't you start growling too, Kyrie," Lacrimosa said to him. "Don't let my daughter spoil you. I knew your parents, Kyrie Eleison; you are a child of nobility. Noble children do not growl."

Grinning now, Agnus Dei gave the loudest, longest growl of her life, a growl that shook the cave. Kyrie couldn't help but smile, the menace leaving his eyes, and he joined her, growling so that his whole body shook and his scales clanked. Even Father, always so stern and angry, began to growl deeply, eyes glinting with mischief. Birds fled outside, and Mother covered her ears.

"All right, all right!" Mother said. "I get the point. Benedictus, really. I expect this behavior from the young ones, but not from you. So stop it."

For the first time in her life, Agnus Dei saw her father look sheepish. He let his growl die, and Agnus Dei laughed. Father, cowed into silence! Her laughter seized her and she rolled around on the cave floor, tail lashing in all directions, slamming into the walls and several times into the pup.

"Cut it out," Kyrie said, rubbing his side where her tail had struck. "The spikes on your tail are huge. Stars. Your parents warned me about you."

"Did they, pup?" she asked.

"Stop calling me that!" he demanded, smoke rising from his nostrils.

Agnus Dei laughed at the sight of him bristling; he reminded her of a baby porcupine. "Okay, pup. Pup pup puppy pup."

He objected some more, as did Mother, but Agnus Dei could not hear. She was laughing too hard. It felt good to laugh. For so long, she had hidden alone in this cave. She had not spoken to anyone in days. After a year upon the snowy mountains, she had fled to this place, this green land on the far side of the world, this land where few men and griffins ventured. This land near the fabled kingdom of the salvanae, the true dragons.

I fled here to escape Mother, but... I missed her, Agnus Dei thought. She hated to admit it, even to herself, and would never tell Mother. But Agnus Dei knew it was true. Though she clashed horns with Mother whenever they spoke, figuratively and sometimes literally, she did love her. She had missed her. She had missed Father. Her laughter died, and she regarded her parents in silence for a moment.

"You two always said it was dangerous being together," Agnus Dei finally said. "You said we must live separately; Father in the forest, Mother and I in the snowy mountains, that we could not risk the griffins killing us all together. So why are you here? Why are we together? Why did you bring the pup?"

"I'm not a—" Kyrie began, flames leaving his nostrils, but Mother touched his shoulder, hushing him.

"I'll tell you," Mother said. "It begins with Kyrie on a seaside fort...."

For a long time, Mother spoke and Agnus Dei listened. She lowered her head as Mother told of Dies Irae arriving at Fort Sanctus and killing the Lady Mirum. She gasped when Mother spoke of Kyrie and Benedictus fighting off griffins in Hostias Forest. She shook her head in wonder as Mother talked of their flight from the woods, their plunge underwater, their journey here to Sequestra Mountains. When Mother finally fell silent, Agnus Dei rose to her feet, head brushing the cave's ceiling, and nodded.

"Well," she said, "there's only one thing to do now."

They all looked at her: Father with his dark eyes; Mother, her eyes sad; Kyrie, eyes gleaming and curious and fiery. Agnus Dei looked back at each one, took a deep breath, and struggled for the courage to speak what she thought. *Yes,* she told herself. It was the only way. The only hope they had, if they were to fight back, if they were to fly again. She was surprised to find tears in her eyes. *I will not hide again, I will not spend my life in caves. We are Vir Requis. Once more, our wings will find the sky.*

She spread out her wings and snarled. "We will find the true dragons. We will have them join us."

Agnus Dei watched their reactions. Benedictus lowered his head and let out a long, tired breath. Mother sighed and shook her head softly. Kyrie, however, widened his eyes and nodded, teeth bared. "Yes," he whispered, voice eager like fire seeking kindling.

"No." Father spoke for the first time, voice deep and gruff. "And that's that."

Agnus Dei reeled on him. "Why not?" she demanded, flames tickling her teeth.

"Because I said so," Father said, baring his fangs, fangs twice the size of Agnus Dei's. "We will not seek any of these salvanae, these 'true dragons'. As far as anyone knows, no such creatures even exist."

Agnus Dei could not believe it. The fire burned inside her belly, and she blew it at the ceiling, lighting the cave in red and yellow. Her roar echoed. "How can you say that?" she demanded. "Father! They are real. I know it."

Agnus Dei expected Mother to rage, but the silvery dragon only looked at her with sad eyes and touched her shoulder. "My daughter. Sweetheart. Those are only stories. Stories I told you when you were a child. There are no salvanae in real life. They are only legends humans told, mistaking us Vir Requis for creatures with no human form."

Agnus Dei did not know if to feel more foolish or more angry. She glared, fangs bared, all eyes on her. Could Mother be right? Had she simply believed fairytales from her childhood? *No, impossible!* Salvanae did exist, flying serpents with no human forms, creatures who could join them, fly with them, breathe fire across the skies. The legends were true. The salvanae simply lived far away, far over mountains and lakes and forests, hiding in the fabled land of Salvandos, a land where no griffin dared fly.

Agnus Dei turned to Kyrie. She grabbed his shoulders. "You believe, don't you?" she said. "I can see you do! Don't deny it. You too know the stories are real. Imagine, pup!" She shook him. "Imagine... a mountain covered with dragons, *real* dragons, not Vir Requis. Wild, untamed beasts who have no human forms, who live for fire and wings and battle." Agnus Dei growled. "We can find them. You and I. We can have them join us, fight with us against Dies Irae."

Kyrie's eyes shone. He believed her; Agnus Dei could see it. He turned toward Benedictus, as if seeking permission from the old king. Agnus Dei grabbed Kyrie's face and pulled it back toward her.

"Don't look at him!" she said. "He is old and tired. He does not believe. Look at me. I'm young and hungry like you, and I want to fight. I want to fly. I want to fly with the true dragons like in the legends. Come with me to find them, pup. Kyrie, I mean. Come with me. I remember the stories of Salvandos, of this distant land of golden trees and misty mountains. A land so far, not even griffins fly there. But I can fly there."

Father stepped toward Agnus Dei, kneeling under the cave ceiling. He glared at her, and she stared back, refusing to look away though his gaze burned.

"Daughter, if you remember the stories, you will remember this too," Father said, voice grave, that cold voice of the Black Fang, King of Requiem. "You will remember that the salvanae were treacherous, untameable. Beastly. In the stories, they hate Vir Requis. They see us as demonic shape shifters, as profane, an insult to their kind. If humans hate us for having dragon forms, the salvanae hate us for having human forms."

Agnus Dei growled. "I am like a true dragon. I do not have to take human form again. They hate Vir Requis? I will remain a dragon. I will tell them I am a dragon true, that I need their aid." She grabbed Kyrie. "Kyrie and I are going. What else could we do? Stay in this cave until Irae finds us? I want to fight. Fly with me to the west, Father, Mother."

Not waiting for a response, not caring if she was reckless, not caring that griffins might be flocking outside, Agnus Dei ran to the cave opening. She burst outside into the wilderness and sunlight, spread her wings, shot up toward the sky, and roared. Her fire flew, raining sparks.

She heard a roar behind her and saw Kyrie flying toward her, also breathing fire. His blue scales shimmered, blinding her. "I'm with you," he said. "Kitten."

She lashed her tail at him, but he ducked, narrowly escaping it.

"Who are you calling kitten?" she demanded and blew fire at him.

He swerved, dodging the flames, and grinned at her. Mother and Father were flying toward them too, and Agnus Dei looked at them, and saw in their eyes that they would join her, would fly west with her, fly to seek that land of legend. Land of the salvanae. The true dragons.

As Agnus Dei roared and flapped her wings, she was surprised to feel icy fear trickle down her spine.

The war, she knew, would flare again.

DIES IRAE

Dies Irae stood in the courtyard of another fort on another cold, dreary hill, and gazed down upon the lashed body of a shepherd.

He admired the bruises and welts covering the man and smiled.

"Gloriae, your work is beautiful," he said.

His daughter stood by him. The wind streamed her hair and rustled the weeds between the cobblestones. Ice filled her eyes. She stared at the moaning peasant and spoke, her face blank. "He was hiding information about the weredragons. He got what he deserved. There is no beauty to this, Father. I took my information with my lash and my boots. There is beauty to the white towers of Confutatis, and to her banners that fly golden. This?" She nodded her head at the tortured man. "This is no art; it is justice, harsh and unforgiving."

The shepherd groaned at her feet, blood trickling across the cobblestones. Dies Irae caressed his daughter's cheek, so soft and cold. "I've taught you well, Gloriae."

He nodded at his guards, and they dragged the man away, leaving a trail of blood. Dies Irae caressed his mace, this new left arm. Benedictus had eluded him for too long, but he could not hide forever. When shepherds saw the monstrous shapes against the stars, they would speak, or they would die.

"They fly to Sequestra Mountains in the west, and they're hurt," Gloriae said, staring at those stains of blood. Her face was blank. "Soon we'll be upon them.

Dies Irae nodded. "Benedictus, Kyrie Eleison... and Lacrimosa."

Lacrimosa. Dies Irae loathed displays of emotion, but now he twisted his lips into a small, thin smile. Lacrimosa—of pale skin, lavender eyes, and moonlit hair. He remembered how he'd bruised that skin, filled those eyes with tears, pulled that hair. His blood boiled at the memory. He wanted to hurt her again, to tear her clothes, grab her breasts, hear her scream.

Gloriae looked to the west, over the crumbling fort to the distant mountains and forests. Dark clouds covered the sky, elk herded in the distance, and the grassy plains undulated in the wind. "There are those three... and there is a fourth," she said. "A red one. A female."

Dies Irae stared at his daughter and frowned. A red dragon. A female. Could it be? Dies Irae clenched his jaw. There was only one such living weredragon.

"The shepherd spoke of her?" Dies Irae asked, struggling to keep the rage from his voice.

Gloriae nodded. "He did, and I saw her myself. Her name is Agnus Dei."

Dies Irae turned from his daughter and stared into the distance. Vultures were circling under the clouds. A cold wind chilled him. *Yes, Agnus Dei.*

Two girls, one dark and wild, one fair and cold. One could shift, become a red monster. The other had no curse; she would remain forever beautiful and pure. Agnus Dei and Gloriae. Daughters of Lacrimosa. Benedictus believed they were his own; Dies Irae knew better.

Does Gloriae know? Dies Irae thought in sudden fear. *Does she know the truth, know that Agnus Dei is her sister, that Lacrimosa is her mother?* He stared at his daughter, seeking the answer in her eyes, and saw only steel. No, Gloriae did not know. That was good. Dies Irae loved her more than anything; he would shield this horrible truth from her. If she knew, it would crush her.

Agnus Dei, he thought, staring at his iron fist. *The cursed, monstrous twin. You I will not kill, no. You will serve as my mount, daughter. You are fairer even than Volucris, the king of griffins. I will ride the last living weredragon, conqueror of the race.*

Dies Irae turned and walked away. He carefully avoided the blood on the cobblestones; his boots were priceless, those boots made from the golden scales of a Vir Requis child. Two of his men stepped forward, eyes lowered, and placed his samite robe around his shoulders.

"Come, Gloriae," Dies Irae said. He walked down a crumbling staircase, past saluting soldiers, weedy walls, and tethered griffins. "We have lingered in this fort long enough. We resume the hunt."

He was surprised to find a smile still on his lips, twitching, and his gut felt like ants raced through it. Dies Irae prided himself on controlling his emotions, but this chase thrilled him.

I destroyed the weredragons who shunned me. I killed the father who disowned me. But you, Benedictus... you are the one who stole my throne, who took my arm, who turned Father against me. Now, finally, I will hurt you like you hurt me. Now I will punish you for what you did.

Dies Irae clenched his good fist. Fury flooded him, turning the world red, and he licked his lips. When the fire burned inside him, that was when he felt alive. This was what he lived for.

Because fire and anger, whispered a voice inside him, *are better than pain.* Hatred was better than fear. Dies Irae hated the pain that surfaced at nights, hated the nightmares that haunted him. All the statues, all the women, all the gold in the world could not drive that pain away, the shunned child inside him. But anger could. Hatred could.

I am no longer a frightened, lonely boy, an outcast, a freak. You are the freak now, Benedictus. You are the outcast, and you now cower. You fear like I have feared. I am a terror and light to the world. You will see this, Benedictus.

The passion blinded him. Dies Irae barely noticed time pass. He found himself on his griffin, taking flight from the stables, soaring into the sky. Gloriae flew behind him, and behind her flew a hundred more armored riders upon a hundred griffins. The fort disappeared in the distance, and cold wind slapped Dies Irae's face. He lowered the visor of his helmet, the visor shaped as a beak, and reached around his neck to clutch the golden amulet. When he remembered how he'd taken the Griffin Heart, Dies Irae felt a heady mix of fear, joy, and power. He snarled.

They flew for a long time.

They flew over forests of oaks and mist, and over fields of wheat and barley, and over lakes. They flew over farms where peasants labored and fields where shepherds roamed. *A beautiful land,* Dies Irae thought. *My land.* They flew over cities of stone towers, statues, murals, and Sun God temples. They flew over toppled cities too, now only ruins covered with moss and ash, piles of shattered columns and burned trees. Dies Irae smiled when he saw them; they were the most beautiful sight in this land. Here were the ruins of weredragon cities, great cemeteries to his enemy. He would let them lie forever ruined, a reminder of the weredragons' evil and his conquest of it.

"The weredragons will be lost to memory," Lord Molok had said to him once, on a day they burned a weredragon town and cleansed it of the beasts. The man's black eyes had burned.

Dies Irae had shaken his head and stared at the thousands of weredragon bodies littering the ruins. "No. I want all to remember the weredragons. History must remember their evil, and remember it was we, men of light, who defeated them."

That had been years ago, and still those ruins remained. Still weredragon bones lay among them.

"Look what you did, Benedictus," Dies Irae whispered as they flew over the ruins of Requiem. His griffin heard him and looked back, but Dies Irae barely noticed the beast. He was seeing his brother in his mind. "See what you did when you stole my birthright, took Requiem's throne, took the woman who should have been mine."

The griffins were soon tired, eyes rolling, fur matted with sweat, but Dies Irae refused them rest. How could they rest when they were so close, maybe moments away from killing Benedictus? Night was falling when they finally saw Sequestra Mountains ahead, deep purple veiled in shadows.

Dies Irae snarled a grin. He scanned the darkness. This was the place the shepherds had spoken of. Where were the weredragons? *Where are you, brother?*

"Fan out!" Dies Irae barked and gave a few signals with his good arm. The griffins split into five squads, twenty griffins in each. They began scanning the mountain and valley. Dies Irae led his squad to a piney mountainside. He narrowed his eyes, searching for caves. Weredragons liked cowering in caves, hiding their shame in the darkness.

They searched the mountains for a long time.   The sun set, and the moon shone. *Where are you, Lacrimosa?*

"Father!" came Gloriae's voice beside him. She flew toward him, moonlight on her armor. Her griffin panted, eyes rolling back. "Father, the griffins must rest. They are weary enough to fall."

Dies Irae shook his head. "No, daughter. We must find the weredragons." His own griffin panted, but Dies Irae knew he could push the beast a while longer.

To his right, one griffin faltered and crashed to the ground. Dies Irae snorted; that one was a weakling. If any griffin could not survive this flight, they did not deserve to fly in his herd.

"Father, I—" Gloriae began again, but Dies Irae interrupted her.

"Look, Gloriae. There."

A cave yawned open in the mountainside ahead. Dies Irae led his griffin toward it. His heart raced and his fingers tingled. He imagined that he could feel his missing hand tingle too, as if fingers still moved there instead of an iron mace. He landed his griffin outside the cave and dismounted.

"Men, join me," he called and waved to the others. Soon twenty griffins covered the mountainside, panting, collapsing. The riders dismounted and joined Dies Irae outside the cave.

Dies Irae grabbed a torch from his griffin's saddle and lit it. His men too lit torches, drew swords, and Dies Irae led them into the cave. He gritted his teeth and raised his iron arm, prepared for a fight.

Inside the cave, he slowly exhaled. The place was empty, and Dies Irae lowered his mace, pulled up his visor, and spat. So the cowards had fled him. They had camped here. Ash covered the walls and ceiling, speaking of recent dragonfire. Claw marks covered the floor, and the place stank of them. Dies Irae could recognize that stench anywhere, a smell like smoke and oil.

Where are you, sweet Agnus Dei, sweet daughter? Dies Irae narrowed his eyes. He spun around, shoved his way past his men, and stepped outside into the night. He gazed up at the sky, sniffing the air. *Where did you fly to, weredragons?*

Dies Irae shut his eyes. He could imagine that he smelled their trail through the sky. They would not fly east, no. They would not fly north into the cold, nor south into the deserts. They could flee west, hoping to fly beyond his arm, but Dies Irae's arm was long enough to hunt weredragons anywhere.

Dies Irae opened his eyes and turned to his men. They stood behind him, torches and swords still raised. "Feed and water your griffins. You have ten minutes. Then we fly west... and hunt weredragons."

LACRIMOSA

As the four dragons streamed between the clouds, Lacrimosa shook her head. *We're on a fool's quest,* she thought. *Chasing a legend, a dream.*

The clouds filled her nostrils, tickled her cheeks, and stung her eyes. She could see Agnus Dei's red tail ahead, lashing from side to side. Benedictus and Kyrie flew by her, but the clouds hid them; she glimpsed only flashes of sunlight on their scales.

We're safe here, she thought. No griffins would see them in these clouds. Still Lacrimosa shivered as she flew. She wished she were in human form, walking upon the land; it was safer that way. Griffins could fly far, and Dies Irae would never stop hunting her, Lacrimosa knew.

We're risking our lives. And why? For a bedtime story I'd tell Agnus Dei years ago. A story, that's all. And for hope.

Lacrimosa sighed. The clouds darkened and moisture covered her. *Maybe that is enough. Maybe Agnus Dei needs some hope, a journey, a future to cling to. There might be no true dragons, but if I can give Agnus Dei hope, even fools' hope, maybe that will help her. Maybe that will soothe the pain inside her.*

As if to answer her thoughts, Agnus Dei turned her head. The clouds veiled her, but Lacrimosa could see her daughter's blazing eyes and the fire in her mouth. "Come on, catch up!" she said. Excitement, even joy, filled her voice. It had been years since Lacrimosa had seen her daughter happy, and she felt droplets on her cheeks, and knew it was not the clouds, but her tears.

"We're flying as fast as we can," Lacrimosa called back, and couldn't help but laugh and cry. "I'm old and slow, Agnus Dei."

That was a lie, of course; Lacrimosa was neither old nor slow. But Benedictus was, and his wing was torn, and he was too proud to admit weakness. Lacrimosa looked at her husband and smiled. He looked at her with one eye and grunted. The clouds flowed around him.

Kyrie, a stream of blue scales through the clouds, gazed anxiously at Agnus Dei. His claws flexed, and Lacrimosa knew he was aching to fly ahead by Agnus Dei, to spend time alone with her among the clouds. But the young Vir Requis looked at Benedictus, tightened his lips, and kept flying by the black dragon.

As much as my daughter's charmed him, he worships my husband more, Lacrimosa thought with a sad smile. He was like so many young Vir Requis in the war, so many who had fought for Benedictus. *I myself once worshiped him thus; he was a being of legend to me. Maybe he still is.*

Lacrimosa sighed and turned her gaze to her husband. He flew solemnly, staring ahead, his torn wing wobbly. *The wing Dies Irae tore with his spear.* Lacrimosa closed her eyes as she remembered that day so long ago, that day more terrible than any other. Benedictus had returned from Lanburg Fields, bleeding. He was half dead, and he only said to her, "It is over." Then he collapsed and slept for days, and Lacrimosa thought he would die, and she wept so many tears. Their race had died then, its last remnants fallen upon the fields, the elderly and the children. Only her family had remained: her husband, her daughters, and herself.

But no, Lacrimosa thought as she flew through these clouds. Kyrie Eleison survived. *Our leader, Benedictus the Black, still flies. We still fly by him. And one day Gloriae will return to us, and fly with us too.*

Lacrimosa tightened her lips and blinked tears out of her eyes. Sometimes she felt like a youth again, a youth in love with her prince.

"I still fly with you, my lord, my love," she whispered.

When night fell, the Vir Requis flew down under the clouds, cloaked in darkness. Agnus Dei's nostrils glowed with fire, and Lacrimosa nudged her until the girl sniffed back the flames.

"Do not blow fire, do not growl, fly like a shadow," Lacrimosa whispered, and Agnus Dei nodded.

Lacrimosa scanned the darkness. In the distance she saw the lights of human fires; it looked like a town, but it still lay leagues away. Below them Lacrimosa saw no lights, no sign of life. She glided down, silent, and landed in a field of wheat. The others landed by her. The youths landed silently and gracefully, but Benedictus hit the ground with a thud and muffled grunt.

Lacrimosa glanced around, hoping nobody heard. In dragon form, her eyes were sharp, but she could see nothing but wheat and a farmhouse half a league away.

"Mmm, a barn!" Agnus Dei whispered, drooling. "I'm going to get us some sheep."

"Go in your human form," Lacrimosa whispered. "All of you—shift now. It's safer."

Lacrimosa let her magic fill her, tickling all over, and shifted. Her scales vanished, her claws and fangs retracted, and soon she stood on human feet. It was suddenly cold, and she shivered in her thin, white dress and hugged herself. Around her, the others too shifted, even—with a grumble—Agnus Dei.

Lacrimosa walked toward her daughter and embraced her. Agnus Dei grunted and tried to shove her off, but finally capitulated and just sighed. Lacrimosa didn't care. It felt so good to see her daughter in human form again, taming her wild side. It had been so long.

"You flew well today," Lacrimosa whispered into her daughter's mop of curls. "I'm proud of you. I love you."

Agnus Dei wriggled out of the embrace. "Mother, really. I'm not a child."

She was right, Lacrimosa knew. Agnus Dei was no longer a child. The girl was eighteen now, and as tall as Lacrimosa. *When I was eighteen, I was already married and had two daughters. Agnus Dei, I'm so sorry I raised you in this world, that you grew up in caves and tunnels. I'm so sorry we couldn't give you a better world.*

"Mother, will you stop looking at me like that?" Agnus Dei demanded, eyes fiery. "Wipe your tears away. Stars above, I'm fine, okay? You're always worrying. Even when you say nothing, your eyes are nagging me."

Lacrimosa laughed. "Okay, Agnus Dei, okay. Go grab us some chickens or sheep. And here, take this." She pulled a silver coin from her pocket. "Don't let the farmers see you, but leave this in place of the animals you take."

Agnus Dei's eyes flashed, and she seemed ready to complain, but Lacrimosa glowered at her so severely, that her daughter only sighed, snatched the coin, and stormed off.

"I'll go with you," Kyrie offered and followed her. "You'll need help carrying back the grub."

When the young ones vanished into the shadows, Benedictus and Lacrimosa sat down. She leaned her head against his shoulder, and he placed an arm around her, kissed her hair, and sighed. For a long time they sat together, staring into the night. The clouds thickened and a drizzle fell, so light it barely wet them, but cold enough that Lacrimosa trembled. Stalks of wheat rustled around them, and Lacrimosa wrapped her arms around Benedictus, seeking warmth from his body. He was all muscle, bones, and scars, but there was warmth and softness to him too.

"How are you, Ben?" she finally asked.

He stared ahead into the night and said nothing. Lacrimosa waited. She knew that he needed time to gather his thoughts, to form his words. Benedictus rarely spoke freely. When he spoke, it was because he had considered every word and meant it. After a long moment, he spoke into the darkness.

"I'm scared," he said.

Lacrimosa looked at him and bit her lip. Benedictus the Great, the Black Fang, the King of Requiem—scared? Lacrimosa touched his dark curls lined with gray, and her hand seemed so small and soft against his gruff, tousled head.

"I'm scared too," she whispered.

Benedictus ran his hand against her thigh, a rough hand, the hand of a hunter and fighter, calloused. "The kid, he... he believes in me, Lacrimosa. He looks up to me; worships me, even. I used to demand that from young Vir Requis. I used to expect it. They died under my command, Lacrimosa. Thousands of kids like Kyrie died under my banners. If anything should happen to Kyrie, or to our daughters...."

Our daughters. Lacrimosa closed her eyes, the secret of her shame burning within her. *Yes, Agnus Dei and Gloriae are ours, mine and Ben's, and not grown from Dies Irae's seed.*

Sometimes Lacrimosa ached to tell him, could almost speak her secret. Tonight she wanted to whisper to her husband, to hold him, touch his hair, speak of that night long ago. Tell him what Dies Irae had done. But she could not. Not yet. The pain still burned too strongly, even after all these years.

She kissed his stubbly cheek. "They may die," she whispered. "I know that. And I want to protect them. But how much longer can we hide, Ben? We've hidden for years, but they keep hunting us, sending us fleeing. You know how Agnus Dei was. Half mad with cabin fever and pain. I watched her and I wept and feared. I thought she would become wild, untameable, that she would become fully mad with rage. I thought that she would fly with fire and let the griffins find her. You sent men to die, Ben, yes. And you sent women to die, and children, and I know, my lord, I know how much blood covers your hands, and how it haunts you. But you are a hero to Kyrie. And you are a hero to Agnus Dei; she will not admit it, but I know it's true." Tears filled her eyes, and Lacrimosa smiled. "She always tells me: I am not fair and graceful like you, Mother, I am strong and proud like Father. That is how she loves you. You are brave, and noble, and you are doing right. If you were not scared, you would be heartless. Your fear speaks of your goodness."

He smiled in the dark, one of those rare, soft smiles of his. "You were always better at words, my love," he said, and she leaned her head back against his shoulder.

The sounds of stomping feet and crackling wheat filled the darkness, and Lacrimosa stiffened, suddenly sure that Dies Irae had found them... but it was only Kyrie and Agnus Dei walking back toward them.

"Pup, you are wrong as always," Agnus Dei's voice carried through the night. "The word for sheep meat is mutton; lamb is what you call a baby sheep."

Kyrie grunted. "So why do you call them lamb chops, not mutton chops? Lamb is the meat; the child sheep is called a kid."

"You're thinking of goats, pup," she said.

"Stop calling me that!"

Lacrimosa rose to her feet and shushed them. They were a dozen feet away, and when they saw her, they closed their mouths and approached silently. They carried lambs under their arms. Lacrimosa found herself again smiling with teary eyes. *Are you going soft, Lacrimosa?* she asked herself, but she couldn't help it. For the first time in years, she saw two Vir Requis, a boy and girl, walking together through a field, talking, happy. Memories of the old days, of her own youth among her kind, flooded her so that she could barely breathe.

They dared not make a fire, so after scanning the field again for unfriendly eyes, they shifted into dragons and ate the meat raw. They then lay on their backs, digesting, letting the drizzle fall upon their bellies. Lacrimosa nestled against

Benedictus, while the young ones whispered to each other. Lacrimosa could not hear them, but she smiled because she knew that, for the first time in years, Agnus Dei had a friend.

"I'll guard first," Lacrimosa said. "Best we sleep as dragons tonight, at least until we digest those lambs. But stay low, and try to look like haystacks."

"I'll guard second," Agnus Dei said, licking her lips. "If any griffins show up, I'll pound them!" She clawed the air and snarled.

Kyrie agreed to guard third, and Benedictus last. When they all slept, Lacrimosa watched them, smiling softly. The drizzle fell upon them, and their scales glinted wet, but they seemed not to notice. All three slept soundly, and Lacrimosa felt warm even on this cold, wet night. *We are family,* she thought, *and we are together again. Kyrie too is part of our family now.*

The Eleisons had been a proud line, and close to her own blood, Lacrimosa remembered. Kyrie's parents had been blue too, fiery like their son. *They are gone now, gone like so many others, bones and ash in our burned forests. But we will look after you, Kyrie. We will protect you like a son.*

She thought, too, of her lost daughter, of Gloriae. The fair twin. The babe who rarely cried, who stared, who seemed lost in thought even in her cradle. *I will find you, Gloriae. I will bring you back to our family.*

Weariness tugged Lacrimosa. She wanted to stand up and walk to keep awake, but dared not. She would not walk in dragon form, not so close to a human farm, not even on a starless night. Nor did she dare turn human again, not until she digested the meat in her belly. So Lacrimosa bit her tongue, twisted her tail, and tried to recite old poems to ward off sleep.

Then she saw something that made the poems die on her lips.

Lacrimosa stiffened, frowned, and stared.

A shadow in the sky. No, only her imagination. Or maybe.... Lacrimosa raised her head and her claws. There! She saw it again. A snarl came to Lacrimosa's lips, and she wanted to wake up Benedictus. She nudged him.

"Ben," she whispered.

He moaned but did not wake. Lacrimosa stared into the sky, seeking that shadow, that black patch against the clouds. She saw nothing. It was gone.

It was just a shadow in my mind, a fear in the night. She kept watching the sky for a moment longer, then blew out her breath.

Nothing.

Then—

Griffin wings spread open above. A bolt of metal shot down, and pain stung Lacrimosa's neck. She opened her mouth to scream, but could not utter a sound. Ilbane flowed through her, and her eyes rolled back.

"Ben!" she tried to call, but no voice found her lips. She fell back, trembling, and griffin talons clutched her.

DIES IRAE

Dies Irae flew, the wind biting his cheeks, his griffin clutching Lacrimosa.

"Fly, damn you," he hissed. "Faster, Volucris!"

Volucris was large and heavy, twice Lacrimosa's size, but the chase had wearied him, and he flew slowly. Dies Irae dug his spurs into his flanks.

"Fly!"

Already the sounds of the other Vir Requis, roused from sleep, sounded behind him. "Lacrimosa!" one howled, and soon the others joined the howling. "What happened? Lacrimosa!" and "Mother! Mother, where are you?"

Dies Irae cursed under his breath. This night was not going as planned. He had hoped to catch the Vir Requis with a hundred griffins at his back. After finding the cave deserted, he had broken up his herd, then sent individual griffins to scan the fields and forests. Now he flew alone.

"Lacrimosa!" came a deep cry in the distance. It had to be Benedictus.

I should have killed him in his sleep, Dies Irae thought. *I should have killed them all as they slept.* But of course, that had been impossible. He'd arrived alone, and in the second he had before Lacrimosa could raise the alarm, he'd done what he must.

She squirmed in Volucris's talons, voice weak. "Ben... Benedi..." Her voice faded and she fell limp.

"Lacrimosa!" came the howls behind, and Dies Irae heard flapping dragon wings. "Lacrimosa, where are you?"

Dies Irae laughed. He turned in his saddle and gazed into the darkness. He could see nothing under the dark, raining clouds, but he could hear them, smell them.

"Do you want her back, Benedictus?" he shouted. "Do you want your Lacrimosa? I have her, Benedictus! I have the creature. If you want her, you'll follow."

Howls of pain and rage filled the night, widening Dies Irae's grin. So he was alone. So he could not kill them all. So Benedictus still lived. But this night was still proving useful.

They would follow, Dies Irae knew; their pathetic weredragon "code of honor" demanded it. They would follow Lacrimosa, try to rescue her, and fly into his camp.

"Where are you, Benedictus?" he cried over his shoulder, the wind whipping him. They were blowing fire behind him, still distant, trying to see him. "Is that the fastest you can fly?"

He turned back forward and spurred his griffin. "Fly, Volucris. Faster."

The griffin grunted. His talons tightened around Lacrimosa's slender body. She was still mumbling, but Dies Irae could not make out the words. He had coated his quarrels with potent ilbane; the stuff would keep her dazed for hours. Despite the howling behind him, the thud of wings, and the roaring flames, Dies Irae felt his blood boil at the thought of Lacrimosa. True, she was in dragon form now, a hideous beast of scales, but he would force her to take human form later. He had ways to force her. In the night, the memories resurfaced, the sweet memories of that night in the woods, the night he caught her alone, the night he pulled off her dress and—

"I see him!" came a cry behind. It was the young blue weredragon from Fort Sanctus, Dies Irae realized; the Eleison kid. "I see him—there, follow me!"

Dies Irae turned in his saddle, aimed his crossbow, and fired at Kyrie. The weredragon was easy to spot; he was blowing fire and burning in the darkness. The crossbow shot true, and Kyrie cried and fell back. Dies Irae loaded another quarrel and shot again. Again he hit Kyrie, and again the weredragon yelped. He tumbled from the sky.

Dies Irae smirked. *One gone, two to go.* Benedictus and Agnus Dei still followed him, blowing flames. *Pathetic,* he thought. *They reveal themselves with fire, while I fly hidden in darkness.* He was tempted to turn and charge them head on, but dared not with his griffin's talons clutching Lacrimosa, unavailable for battle. He kept flying.

"Faster, Volucris, faster."

Benedictus was falling behind. When Dies Irae glanced over his shoulder, he could not see the great black beast. But Agnus Dei still flew there, moving closer and closer, gaining on him. Her red scales glinted in her firelight.

"Hello, my daughter," Dies Irae whispered and shot his crossbow.

Agnus Dei cried. The quarrel hit her neck, coated in ilbane. Her wings wobbled and she fell, crashing from the sky like a comet, flaming and howling.

"Join me in Confutatis, Benedictus!" Dies Irae shouted back into the night. "Join me in my palace, if you wish to see Lacrimosa again. You know where I live." His voice was hoarse, and he laughed. "I will see you there, weredragon, or I will torture this silver beast until she breaks. Goodbye for now, Benedictus! I will see you soon."

They howled in the distance, and Dies Irae spurred his griffin onward. They shot through the night, the howls of the weredragons fading behind.

BENEDICTUS

Benedictus flew as fast as he could, cursing, fear an iceberg in his gut.

"Lacrimosa!" he howled, voice hoarse. "Lacrimosa!"

He could see nothing but blackness, and the rain and wind whipped him. He blew fire, but could not see Dies Irae ahead. Benedictus cursed his brother, and cursed himself for sparing Dies Irae that day, for biting off an arm but not finishing the job. *I spared your life, brother. I let you live then. I will not let you live today.*

"Lacrimosa!"

He heard Volucris's shriek ahead, and Benedictus narrowed his eyes and flew in that direction. *Damn this torn wing.* In the old days, he could fly faster than any griffin, but now he lagged behind. Where was Kyrie? Had he survived? Where was Agnus Dei?

Benedictus blew fire again, and it glinted against red scales half a league ahead. Agnus Dei! Benedictus flew toward her, his wings churning the clouds. Darkness cloaked her, and he blew fire again, saw the red glint again.

"Agnus Dei!"

Soon she was only feet away, and Benedictus felt his heart tighten. She was hurt. Her wings flapped weakly, and her head lolled. She barely stayed in the sky. Blood trickled down her neck.

His fire died in his mouth, and Benedictus could see nothing again. He grabbed Agnus Dei in the darkness.

"Get out of here," he said. "You're hurt. Fly back. Find Kyrie. He was hit."

She shook her head, struggling to free herself from his grasp. "Mother!" she whispered, tears in her eyes. Her voice was hoarse, heavy, thick with the pain of ilbane. When lightning flashed, Benedictus saw that her eyes were glazed. "Mother is ahead, I have to save her, I have to...." Her voice died, drowning in pain.

"I'll save Mother," Benedictus said, pulling Agnus Dei to the ground. She was too weak to resist, and Benedictus knew he must hurry. Every second he lingered here, Dies Irae was flying farther away. He reached the ground and laid Agnus Dei on the grass. He blew fire, lighting the world, and examined her wound. It was not lethal, but the ilbane would hurt for hours. With a quick tug, he removed the quarrel that had pierced her. Her blood dripped.

"Find the salvanae," he said to her. "Fly west and find them with Kyrie. I'll go after Mother."

Her eyes stared at him, pleading. "I want to go with you. Let's hunt Dies Irae together, we'll save Mother—"

"No!" Benedictus rose to fly again. "Find the salvanae; that's what I need you to do. Fly west. With Kyrie. Fly as far as you can—to the end of the world. That is your mission now."

With that Benedictus took off, leaving her below, heading into the eastern sky. Clouds and rain and wind lashed him. There were no salvanae, of course. Dragons with no human form? That was a myth. A bedtime story. But it was a myth that would send Agnus Dei and Kyrie flying west, far from Dies Irae, far from all this war and blood. If there was safety for them, it lay in the distant lands where perhaps Dies Irae's arm could not reach.

I might never see them again, Benedictus thought as he flew. *But maybe that's safest for them. I put my daughter in danger. I put Kyrie in danger. May they fly far, and fly well, and may they find safety on their quest.*

Where was Dies Irae? Benedictus could not see the man nor his griffin, could no longer hear griffin shrieks. But he knew where Dies Irae headed. He was taking Lacrimosa to Confutatis, to chain her, to torture her, to lure him—Benedictus—into danger. *It's me you want, Dies Irae. It's me you'll get. We'll face each other again in battle, and this time, one of us will die.*

As Benedictus flew, piercing the night, a chill ran through him. He knew that he most likely flew toward his death.

Fly west, Agnus Dei. Fly west with Kyrie. You two are the last hope for our race.

Benedictus howled in the night.

KYRIE ELEISON

Kyrie struggled to rise from the ground. Everything ached, and lava seemed to flow through his veins. He strained his muscles, but the pain flared, and he collapsed. Mud and moss squelched around him.

"Lacri... Lacrimosa—" he managed, gasping for breath. The pain was worst on his chest, where the quarrel had struck. The bolt burned, and blood seeped around it. The ilbane sent sluggish ache through Kyrie from horns to tail.

"Agnus Dei—" he said, struggling to utter each word through clenched teeth. He wanted to shout, but his voice was so hoarse and soft. "Benedictus—"

He coughed and struggled to breathe. With blazing agony, he raised his head and stared into the sky, but saw only blackness. Rain pattered against him. Kyrie heard nothing but wind, thunder, and creaking trees.

I have to save them. I have to fly. Gritting his teeth, he managed to push up one shoulder, then the other. With a grunt, he pushed himself to his feet, though the ilbane felt like shackles tugging him to the ground.

Lightning flashed, and Kyrie saw a dozen eyes blazing, staring at him from shaggy black forms. *Wolves.*

"Stay back!" he warned, but his voice was weak. He tried to breathe fire, but only a small puff of flame left his mouth. Lightning flashed again, growls rose, and the wolves were upon him.

Kyrie cried in pain. The wolves covered him, biting and clawing. Though ilbane burned, Kyrie rolled around, struggling to shake them off, but they moved like devils. The wolves on his back could not break his scales, but no scales covered his belly, and one wolf bit him there.

The new pain made Kyrie buck, and in his rage, he blew fire at the wolf. The beast caught flame and fell off his belly, howling. Kyrie swiped his claws at the blazing wolf, tossing it into the grass. Soon the grass too caught fire and burned around Kyrie. The other wolves howled and fled.

The pain and fear were enough to let Kyrie limp forward, flap his wings, and fly a hundred feet. He landed, aching, wings stiff, and kept limping.

"Agnus Dei!" he cried hoarsely. "Benedictus!"

Where were they? Were they dead? Had more griffins arrived? Kyrie cursed himself; he had fallen first, had flown clumsily, had let Dies Irae shoot him down. He clenched his jaw, wanting nothing more than to find Dies Irae and kill him. *If I catch him, I'm going to rip off his other arm, then beat him to death with it.*

"Agnus Dei!" he called out in the night. Wolf howls answered him. Thunder boomed and the rain grew even stronger, pattering against him. Hail rattled against his scales. He wanted to blow fire, a beacon for the others, but could bring none to his breath. When lightning flashed, he saw only clouds. No dragons, no griffins.

"Agnus Dei!" His voice was only a hoarse call; he doubted it carried a hundred yards.

The wind slammed against him, carrying a whimper.

Kyrie stiffened and gazed into the darkness.

The whimper sounded again. He thought he heard a voice calling, distant and weak.

"Who's there?" Kyrie cried, but his voice was only a whisper. He began to trudge forward, slipped into the mud, shoved himself up, and kept limping. His wings hung uselessly at his sides. "Benedictus? Agnus Dei?"

"Pup!" came a cry from ahead.

Kyrie felt his eyes moisten. He laughed, as horrible as everything was. "Agnus Dei!"

He tried to run toward her voice, fell, and groaned in pain. He struggled to rise, fell again, and reached out into the darkness.

Dragon claws reached out and clutched him.

"Agnus Dei!"

"Pup!"

And then she was upon him, embracing him, weeping. She was hurt, and Kyrie felt his anger bubble. Fire burned in her nostrils, and in its light, he saw blood trickle down her neck.

"Where's Benedictus?" Kyrie asked, hoarse.

Agnus Dei trembled. "He went after Mother. We have to find the salvanae, Kyrie! We have to. Only they can help us now. Only they can help us save Mother and Father. We must find them. We must!"

She struggled to her feet and kicked off the ground. Her wings flapped, she flew a few yards, then crashed to the ground. She raised her head weakly, looked at him with pained eyes, and whispered, "We have to."

Her eyes rolled back, and she collapsed.

Kyrie crawled toward her and embraced her. She still lived; he could feel her chest rise and fall. The rain fell upon them. Kyrie managed to pull himself above her, shielding her from the rain. In a few hours, he knew, the ilbane's pain would die, and they would fly again.

It would be a long, cold night.

AGNUS DEI

Strange dreams filled Agnus Dei's sleep.

She walked on human legs, but had a dragon's head. The heavy, scaly head wobbled on her human body, the thin body of a child, a child lost in a burning forest. Ash flew around her like the ghosts of butterflies, and shattered columns littered the forest floor. Though the trees were burned, dry leaves fell from them, gold and orange and rufous, gliding to fizzle into steam upon hitting the ground.

"Mother!" Agnus Dei cried, but her voice was hoarse, beastly, the shriek of a dragon. She clutched her scaly head with soft hands, tears in her eyes. "Mother!"

Ahead she saw a ruined palace—the palace of Father, the Vir Requis King. Its columns and walls had fallen, and scattered fires burned where statues had stood. Skeletons littered the ruins, all with human bodies and dragon heads, the skulls glaring at her, turning to follow as she walked.

"Mother!" she cried again, a twisted shriek. *I am a creature, a freak, a thing not human nor dragon.* She tried to turn all dragon, or all human, but could not.

"Look at the monster!" came voices from ahead, and Agnus Dei started. A group of Osanna's soldiers stood ahead atop a fallen column, clad in steel, their capes billowing though there was no breeze. Above in the skies, countless griffins streamed, row by row of them, silent, flying without flapping their wings.

"I'm not a monster!" she replied, but her words came out a horrible shriek, a sound like a dying hawk. As the soldiers laughed, a scream came from the sky, and Agnus Dei looked up to see a griffin clutching her mother. The griffin was the size of the whole sky, casting a shadow across the ruins. Mother seemed so small in its talons, like a house lizard in the clutches of an owl.

"Mother!" Agnus Dei tried to cry, but again only a screech left her mouth. The griffin holding Mother turned and flew away, vanishing into the distance. Agnus Dei tried to follow, but the soldiers shot flaming arrows at her, and she caught fire.

"Mother!" she cried, burning, and fell into wet grass.

"Agnus Dei," spoke a voice in her ear, and she felt a hand on her head.

She rolled around, trying to extinguish the flames. Wet grass squelched beneath her. "No, no. Please no! Leave me alone, I'm burning." Tears flowed down her cheeks, and she wondered if they could put out the flames.

"Agnus Dei, wake up. You're having a nightmare."

She opened her eyes, panting, and saw Kyrie above her. He had taken human form, and looked like a drowned cat, muddy and bloody and wet. The sun was rising, casting pink and red light across a soggy field.

Agnus Dei leaped to her feet. She realized that she had taken human form in her sleep, possibly when trying to shift in her nightmare. She looked to the sky, seeking Mother or Father, seeking griffins. Nothing but clouds and sunbeams filled the sky. She spun to face Kyrie.

"What happened?" She heard anger in her voice, and she narrowed her eyes. She pushed muddy hair back from her face. Her clothes too were caked with mud, grass, and blood.

Kyrie stared to the east, eyes dark. "Dies Irae flew east, taking Lacrimosa. Benedictus followed." He tightened his fists. "I tried to follow too, but... the ilbane. It was too much. I... I passed out. You did too." He trembled and his face was red.

Agnus Dei jumped into the air, shifted into a dragon so quickly that her head spun, and flapped her wings. Hovering, she turned to look at Kyrie. "Come! We fly."

Kyrie hesitated, standing below in human form.

"Come on!" She growled. "What are you waiting for?"

"I...." He frowned. "Agnus Dei, are you sure we can catch Dies Irae? Free Lacrimosa? He has armies, Agnus Dei. Armies. Tens of thousands of griffins. I want to rescue Lacrimosa." His eyes were suddenly moist. "More than anything. But how could we? If we fly east, aren't we flying to death?"

Agnus Dei growled and blew flames toward the clouds. "You pup. We're not flying east. I know I can't save Mother by dying. We're flying *west*, pup. We're flying to get the salvanae. And then we too will have armies." She snarled. "We fly."

She flapped her wings, shooting into the west. She heard a roar behind her, a dragon's roar, and soon Kyrie flew beside her, a great beast of blue scales. They left the ground far below and flew hidden between the clouds. The clouds were sparse this morning, dispersing after the stormy night, and Agnus Dei found herself flying in and out of blue skies. Anyone could see them here, she knew, but she narrowed her eyes and kept flying. She dared not walk in human form, not as Mother and Father were in danger. Walking was slow; as a dragon, she could fly hundreds of leagues a day.

She looked at Kyrie. He seemed to be thinking the same thing. Whenever they emerged from cloud cover, he narrowed his eyes, tightened his jaw, scanned the ground and sky, but kept flying.

I'm glad you're here with me, Kyrie, she thought. The thought surprised her. She was a loner. She needed nobody else. For years, she had prided herself on fierceness, strength, independence. *Are you growing soft?* she asked herself, but when she looked at Kyrie again, she understood. *Kyrie is like me; young, fiery, the last youth of an endangered species.*

Kyrie noticed she was staring and met her gaze. Concern filled his eyes. "Do you think there really are salvanae?" he said, the wind whipping his words. "That it's not just a legend?"

She bared her fangs. "Of course there are salvanae." She growled, blew fire, and clawed the sky, because inside her dread swirled. Ice filled her belly, and a shiver ran along her spine. If there were no salvanae, there was no hope. She would never save her parents. She would never defeat Dies Irae.

At the thought of Mother in prison, Agnus Dei felt a lump in her throat. She could imagine griffin talons scratching Mother, spears piercing her, ilbane burning her. Would Dies Irae kill her? Torture her? Agnus Dei couldn't help it—tears fled her eyes and flew back across her cheeks.

"Agnus Dei," Kyrie said, voice almost drowned under the wind. "Agnus Dei, I... I'm sorry about what happened. But Benedictus... I've seen him fight, Agnus Dei. He is amazing. I've never seen such a warrior. And he's after Dies Irae. He's flying to save Lacrimosa. If anyone in the world can do it, it's your old man."

She looked at him, tears still in her eyes. Clouds and sunbeams streamed between them. "If he's still alive."

"He is," Kyrie said, but uncertainty filled his voice.

The final clouds vanished, and they flew in clear skies. The land was wild below, covered with brambles and twisted oaks. Boulders jutted like teeth from tall grass. Rivulets glistened, and Agnus Dei saw a herd of deer raise their heads from the water, look up at them, and begin to flee. Agnus Dei was hungry, and her stomach growled, but she dared not swoop to hunt. Eating would delay her, and Agnus Dei wanted to fly, to cross thousands of leagues far into the misty realms of the west, lands beyond the maps of men and Vir Requis.

"Let's fly higher," Kyrie said. "We're too easy to spot here. If we fly high enough, we might appear as great birds."

She snorted. "You maybe, pup. I would never pass for a bird."

Still she flew upward. Kyrie flew by her, eyes narrowed, jaw clenched. They shot up in a straight line so fast, her stomach churned, her head ached, and spots danced before her eyes. But she kept flying. Soon they were so far up, she could barely breathe, and the thin air chilled her. When she looked down, the land was so distant, she could make out no trees or boulders or bushes, only patches of green and brown in all shades: bright green like fresh leaves, and deep gray-green like old forests, and brown like the barks of oaks, and pale green like the leaves of birches back in Requiem. The streams and rivers were but strands of silver, glinting. She had never flown so high.

Kyrie slapped her with his tail. "Fly straight," he called over the roaring wind, "and breathe well. If your head spins, or your eyes go dark, we'll go lower."

She growled at him. "I don't need flying lessons from a pup. Come on. See if you can catch up."

Agnus Dei flew as fast as she could, like she would as a girl when fleeing her scolding parents. As a child, none could keep up with her, not even the bigger kids, but Kyrie flew beside her the whole time. She tried to fly faster, to beat him, but could not. *Hot shot,* she thought with a snort. *Hot pup.*

Osanna moved beneath them, endless lands of wilderness, an empire stretching across the known world. *But there is a land beyond Osanna,* Agnus Dei thought. There had to be more lands. Had to! The world could not be just Osanna, just the realms of Dies Irae and his griffins. Once there had been other lands—Gilnor in the south, snowy Fidelium the north, and

Leonis across the sea. Once there had been a land called Requiem, too, a land of marble columns among birch trees, a land where dragons flew. Requiem lay in ruins now, forgotten, her glow drowned under Osanna's fire. But she had once stood; Agnus Dei remembered. She would never forget the courts of Requiem.

Like there was a Requiem, there is a Salvandos too, a land far in the western mists of legend. Agnus Dei nodded as she flew. Salvandos was real. She knew it with every heartbeat, every breath. This land would not have fallen under Osanna's rule.

They flew for hundreds of leagues before Agnus Dei's head began to spin, and they had to dive down. She saw no towns, only a forest and grasslands where deer grazed. She and Kyrie landed in the grass, caught a deer, and ate silently. They drank from a stream. Agnus Dei's wings, lungs, and heart ached, but she dared not rest for more than a few moments. Then she was flying again, Kyrie at her side.

"You look tired, pup," she said to him.

He grunted, flapping stiff wings beside her. "I can keep up with you." He snorted fire at her. "Kitten."

"We'll see, little puppy."

They flew until nightfall, the most Agnus Dei had ever flown in one day. They must have crossed a thousand leagues, moving so far from Sequestra Mountains, so far from the marble city of Confutatis where Dies Irae lived. In the darkness, they found a forest and shifted into human form.

"It's best we sleep as humans," Agnus Dei said. "Just in case Dies Irae has dragon hunters roaming the woods."

Oaks, elms, and birches rustled around them like ghosts in the night. The air smelled like mold and earth, cold in her lungs. They had no blankets, so they curled up on the ground, holding each other for warmth. Kyrie smelled like grass and wind and clouds, and she clung to him in the darkness, her face against his chest. He began to stroke her hair, but then his hand stilled, and he snored softly.

I miss you, Mother, Agnus Dei thought and tears fled her eyes. *I miss you, Father.* She shivered against Kyrie, more lost and lonely than she'd ever felt. Flying all day had left her stiff, sore, and exhausted, but she couldn't sleep. In the darkness, she kept seeing Dies Irae chaining, stabbing, and torturing her mother.

"I'll save you, Mother," she whispered. "I'll find the salvanae, you'll see."

The trees rustled and wind moaned. An owl hooted. Agnus Dei wondered if wolves or bears filled these woods, or worse—men. She shivered and wept for a long time, grateful that Kyrie slept and couldn't see her weakness. When he peeked at her, then closed his eyes again, she realized that he feigned sleep to spare her embarrassment, and that soothed her. Finally, nestled against him, she fell into slumber.

LACRIMOSA

Lacrimosa did not remember losing consciousness. She did not remember the sun rising. She did not remember landing in this rocky field. Last thing she remembered was a starless night, her husband and daughter beside her, then—she grimaced to recall it—searing pain and griffin talons.

Where am I?

She gazed around, eyes blurry. She was still in dragon form, and everything hurt. Boots stomped around her head, spurred leather boots with steel tips. Lacrimosa tried to raise her head from the ground, but could not. A chain bound her neck down, she realized, and more chains bound her body. The boots stirred up dust, and she coughed and blinked.

"The creature!" called a voice, the voice of a young man, a soldier. "The creature is waking up."

She could see only his boots; their steel tips had skulls engraved upon them. He sounded like a youth, and Lacrimosa felt a deep sadness that Dies Irae should infect youth with his hatred. More boots raced toward her, and Lacrimosa cried out. Several pointy objects, spears or sticks, jabbed her sides, her back, her tail. She roared and tried to raise her head, but could not, and her roar was muffled. She tried to blow fire, but an iron muzzle held her mouth closed.

"The creature is struggling, yeah?" said one soldier and laughed, and more laughter sounded. Boots kicked Lacrimosa, their steel jabbing, and tears filled her eyes.

"Please," she tried to whisper, but could not speak through the muzzle. The soldiers laughed and kept kicking and jabbing her.

She wanted to shift, to take human form, to try and escape her chains, but dared not. As a dragon, her scales offered some protection. If she became human, the boots and spears could kill her. She remained chained, beaten, spat on. The torture seemed to last forever, an eternity of pain, leaving her squirming and unable to beg for mercy. Finally—it must have been ages before it happened—a voice spoke over the soldiers' laughter.

"Enough."

It was only a cold word, spoken softly, but at once the boots and spears ceased their torture. The boots backed off, slammed together in attention, and one soldier cried out, "The Commander, his lordship Dies Irae, Light of Osanna!"

As the dust settled, Lacrimosa moaned and blinked feebly. She could still not raise her head, and saw only the men's boots and dust, and droplets of her blood upon the ground. A new pair of boots strode between the soldiers, but these boots were not leather. They were made of golden Vir Requis scales—the rarest color—and steel claws grew from their tips, like the claws of a dragon. *Dies Irae's boots,* Lacrimosa knew.

For a long time, Dies Irae merely stood above her, and though she could not see his face, she felt his eyes boring into her. Then he turned to face his men. "All right, men, you've had your fun. This beast must reach Confutatis alive. If we reach my city, and the weredragon is dead, it will be your hides. Understood?"

"Yes, Commander!" a dozen voices shouted together.

"Leave us," Dies Irae said, and the boots marched away.

For a long time, Lacrimosa lay on the ground, struggling not to whimper. His boots faced away from her, as if he still watched his men depart, or maybe gazed upon his camp in reflection. Finally he turned back toward her, placed his boot under her chin, and forced her head back painfully. Lacrimosa grimaced, the muscles in her neck creaking, and found herself staring up at Dies Irae.

He looked down upon her, cloaked in samite, his armor bearing the jeweled likeness of a griffin. His visor was raised, and Lacrimosa could see his face—a hard face, golden and cruel, so much like the face of Benedictus, but colder. His eyes stared at her, ice blue, and she shivered under his gaze.

"Hello, Lacrimosa," he said. "Hello, sister-in-law."

She could not speak for the muzzle around her mouth, nor had she any words to say to him.

"How is Agnus Dei?" he asked, his boot still under her chin, its steel claws painfully close to piercing her. "How is my daughter?"

Lacrimosa growled, and smoke rose from her nostrils. How dared he? Fury and pain bloomed inside her, a hundred times more powerful than when the men tortured her. She struggled against her chains, but could not free herself, and only froze when she felt the claws of his boots press closer against her. She froze but fumed, a growl in her throat. *Agnus Dei is not your daughter, snake,* she thought. *She is everything like Benedictus and nothing like you. There is nothing pathetic, base, and cruel to her, and you are all pathetic cruelty. I will kill you, Dies Irae, or my husband will.*

It was as if he heard her thoughts. "She is my daughter, sweetness. I remember that day in the woods. That day you surrendered to me. You want to kill me now. I see that in your eyes. You may think, even, that you *can* kill me, or that your husband can. Yes, I imagine that he will emerge from hiding now, that he will fly to Confutatis on some bold rescue mission. I am sure he is flying now in pursuit. I will kill him, Lacrimosa. I will kill him, but I will not kill you, and I will not kill our daughter. No. You two will live."

The way he said it, Lacrimosa knew: Benedictus was getting the sweeter deal.

She growled again, and blew flames from her nostrils, but Dies Irae only laughed. He pulled back his boot, letting her head hit the ground with a thud. He marched away. Soon Lacrimosa heard the cries of griffins, the thud of their wings and the scratching of their talons, and the scurrying of soldiers as they gathered their camp.

Griffin wings fluttered above, a shadow covered her, and talons grabbed her. Dies Irae cried "Fly!" above her, and the griffin lifted her. The ground grew far below her, and a hundred griffins flapped wings.

They flew over fields and forests, and over marble cities where statues of Dies Irae glittered. They flew over mountains and lakes. They flew over Requiem Forest, where the ruins of the Vir Requis courts lay burned and toppled, and when Lacrimosa saw her homeland below, she shed tears.

They flew, a hundred griffins, a bound Vir Requis, crossing hundreds of leagues, heading to the Marble City, to Confutatis, to Dies Irae's home.

Fly west, Agnus Dei, Lacrimosa thought, willing the words into her daughter's mind. *Fly away from here, fly to find your true dragons, fly with Kyrie into distant lands. And my sweet husband, I pray that you too flee, that you too fly west, though I know you're coming here, that you're following.*

That last thought made fear wash over her, colder and crueler than any fear she'd ever known. As the talons clutched her, and Dies Irae barked commands above, Lacrimosa shut her eyes and trembled.

BENEDICTUS

Benedictus cursed as he flew.

He cursed such foul words, he thought birds might fall dead from the sky, and the clouds themselves wilt. He cursed his old bones, and the wound on his chest that ached in this high, cold air above the clouds. He cursed himself for sleeping while Dies Irae had kidnapped Lacrimosa. Most of all, he cursed his torn wing; it meant he flew so much slower than griffins, flew so slowly as Dies Irae bore Lacrimosa to imprisonment and torture.

"You got what you wanted, brother," he said as he flapped that wobbly, torn wing. The clouds streamed around him. "You got me out of hiding. I'm flying to meet you again."

He knew what he must do. He knew what he should have done years ago. He would meet Dies Irae, kill the man, and steal back the Griffin Heart. With the amulet, he could reclaim the griffins. With the amulet, he could topple Confutatis, that city of marble and gold and malice. With the amulet, he could save Lacrimosa, save his children, create a world safe for Vir Requis.

"I will face you again, brother, and kill you. I spared you last time. No more."

Benedictus sighed, a deep sigh that felt close to a sob. Were these but fantasies? In his mind, he saw himself biting his brother, spilling his blood, killing him for all the evil he'd done. He saw himself with the Griffin Heart, the old hero, King Benedictus risen to reclaim his glory.

He sighed again. *Fantasies.* Deep inside his old heart, he knew that he flew to his death, a death at Lacrimosa's side. *I will die with you in the Marble City, Lacrimosa, but in our hearts, we will be in Requiem.*

He thought of his daughters—of Agnus Dei, who grew hunted, and of Gloriae, who grew molded into evil—and a tear fled Benedictus's eye. It had been so long since he'd cried, and when he looked down to see where his tear fell, he saw the ruins of Requiem. Once those forests had rustled with countless birch trees, and Vir Requis children raced between statues, and wise elders walked in robes upon cobblestones. Now the birches were burned, still blackened, and ivy grew over smashed columns. So many lay dead there—a million skeletons burned and broken. His parents, his wise old uncles, his fussy aunts, the cousins he would wrestle and hunt with, his friends... all dead now, all bones and ash.

Benedictus forced his gaze away. He narrowed his eyes and stared east. Confutatis lay beyond that horizon.

Dawn was rising, the sky was clear, and this was griffin country. *It's too dangerous to fly in the open,* Benedictus thought.

As if to answer his thought, shrieks sounded below. Benedictus stared down to see three griffins upon a fortress.

Benedictus cursed. He tried to fly faster, but could not. As he watched, riders leaped onto the griffins, and they flew toward him.

Benedictus flapped his wings as powerfully as he could, but his left wing blazed with pain, and he grunted. "So much for out-flying them," he muttered.

He roared, reached out his claws, and then the griffins were upon him.

He took out the first one with a blaze of flame. As it fell burning, the other two griffins attacked, one at each side. Benedictus slammed his tail into the right griffin. He hit its rider, sending the man tumbling to the ground. The left griffin bit Benedictus's shoulder, and he roared.

He clawed the griffin, etching red lines down its flank. The right griffin was riderless, but still attacked, and Benedictus howled as its talons scratched him. He lashed his tail, bit, and clawed. He hit one griffin, and it tumbled. The second bit again, and Benedictus roared and blew fire. It caught flame, and Benedictus bit into its roasting flesh, spat out a chunk, and kicked.

The griffin's rider thrust his lance. It dug into Benedictus's shoulder, and he growled, clawed, and snapped the man's head. The body slumped in the saddle. Benedictus clawed again, and the griffin fell dead from the sky.

Benedictus looked around. Were the griffins all dead?

No. The first griffin he'd burned was still alive, fur and feathers blazing. It shot toward him, screeching, its rider also burning and screaming. The man had removed his armor, and his skin peeled and blazed. His eyes had melted, but his mouth was still open and screaming. Still the griffin flew at Benedictus, talons outstretched.

Benedictus blew more fire. The blaze hit the griffin, pushing it back. It tumbled a few feet, then again flew at Benedictus. It looked like some roasted animal now, smoking and furless, its skin red and black and blistering. The beak was open and screeching, the rider writhing and screaming, a ball of fire and blood.

Benedictus howled and lashed his tail, driving its spikes into the griffin, and finally it tumbled toward the ground. It fell like a comet, still screeching, until it hit the ground and was silent.

Benedictus turned and kept flying after Lacrimosa.

"Damn the fire, and damn the blood," he said, jaw tight. He had seen so many burned this way, so many dying in agony. What was one more to the weight already on his soul? His wounds ached, blood dripped down his shoulder, but Benedictus ignored the pain. What were more scars to those he already bore, and what was more pain to the weight of his memories?

He gritted his teeth and flew.

Distant figures flew a league ahead, mere specks. Benedictus narrowed his eyes. More griffins, he knew. He didn't have to get any closer to know these were no birds, but riders Dies Irae had sent after him. Benedictus cursed under his breath and turned south. Storm clouds gathered there, maybe two leagues away. They would serve as cover. It was out of his way, but clear skies swarmed with griffins. If Benedictus wanted to reach Confutatis alive, he'd have to take the long route.

"I'm sorry, Lacrimosa," he whispered. He flew south toward those storm clouds, glancing east toward the griffins until he no longer saw them. "I'm sorry, love of my life. You'll have to hold on a little longer, but I'm coming for you. I'll be there soon."

His wing ached more than ever, a searing pain that drove down his entire left side. Soon Benedictus flew through rain and thunder. He told himself that the drops on his cheeks were only rain, not tears. Again, as with his hope of defeating Dies Irae and saving his family, he knew that he was lying to himself.

DIES IRAE

As they flew, Dies Irae couldn't help it. He kept looking over his shoulder, scanning the distance for Benedictus. At times he thought he saw the beast, but it was only a distant vulture, or another griffin on patrol, and once—Dies Irae shook his head to remember it—even a crow had made him squint and stare and hope.

Soon twilight fell, and Benedictus had not caught up. *Of course not,* Dies Irae told himself with a grunt. His brother still had a torn wing; he could not fly as fast as these griffins. It was pathetic. Benedictus, great King of Requiem, was but a slow, lumbering beast.

Should I send griffins after him, hunt him down? No. He will come to me. He will follow.

The setting sun gilded the mountains below. Their western slopes, snowy and undulating, glimmered like beaten gold. Their eastern slopes melted into mist, deep blue and purple strewn with black lines where rocks broke the snow. Yellow and orange wisps ran across the sky, and the clouds burned. *The glory of Osanna,* Dies Irae thought, admiring the masterpiece that was his empire. *My land, beautiful, no longer tainted by the scaled beasts that once covered its skies.*

But of course, some weredragons remained. A moan sounded below, and Dies Irae looked down. Volucris still clutched Lacrimosa in his talons. Her scales were dented, and blood seeped from nicks and scratches that covered her. *Why does she not take human form?* Dies Irae wondered. *Why does she remain this beastly lizard?* Dies Irae wanted to see her human shape again—ached for it. He remembered that night in Requiem Forest, how he'd pressed his body against hers, grabbed it, squeezed it. His blood boiled at the thought. He wanted that human body again, to clutch it, crush it, hurt it. He'd wanted this for years.

"Down, Volucris," Dies Irae said and tugged the reins. The sun dipped behind a western peak, and though Dies Irae was tempted to fly through the night, he would not. His griffins needed rest. So did his men. And Dies Irae wanted something this night, wanted it now. He looked back down at Lacrimosa, imagined her human form, and licked his lips.

He found a snowy valley and began to descend. His men followed, leading their griffins down in spirals, until talons kicked snow and men dismounted with creaking armor. Volucris tossed Lacrimosa down, and she rolled in the snow, hit a boulder, and moaned. Chains still bound her limbs and wings, and a muzzle clutched her mouth.

"Set camp," Dies Irae told his men. "We spend the night."

His men scurried to raise tents, tether and feed griffins, kindle campfires, and distribute rations. As they bustled across the valley, and griffins gulped chunks of raw cattle, Dies Irae walked toward Lacrimosa. His boots crunched the snow, their golden scales glinting. A cold wind blew, rattling the tents and rustling Dies Irae's cape. He smiled thinly when Lacrimosa saw him approach and whimpered. Snow whitened her chains, and droplets of blood speckled the snow around her. Dies Irae saw the lines of Volucris's claws across her flanks, and his smile widened.

"Hello, Lacrimosa," he said when he reached her.

She stared up and said nothing. A tear streamed down her cheek.

"Darling," Dies Irae said. He placed his good hand upon her head. Her scales were cold, surprisingly smooth, shimmering like mother-of-pearl. "Will you not take human form? I've waited long years to see you again."

She stared up at him. Still she said nothing.

Dies Irae pursed his lips, looked aside, then with a sudden movement, he kicked Lacrimosa's head. She cried out and fresh tears sprung into her eyes. Blood dripped between the iron bars of her muzzle.

"Turn into a human," he said.

She snarled, smoke leaving her muzzle. Finally she spoke, voice muffled behind the iron. "I know what you'll do if you see my human form. I will not allow it. I will not let you rape—"

"I will not rape you," Dies Irae interrupted her. He snorted. "Look at you. Bloody. Covered in ash, snow, and mud. What kind of unclean creature do you think I am? I have my standards, Lacrimosa. Once you were fair; a princess in silk and jewels, young and beautiful, and yes, I took you then. Look at you now. Old. Filthy. What man would touch you?"

She stared at him, eyes blazing, and fire glowed inside her muzzle. Her tears dried, and her stare blazed with such hatred, that Dies Irae snickered. He raised his foot to kick her again.

Lacrimosa flinched, looked away, and shifted.

Her wings pulled into her back, her scales vanished, and she shrunk in size. Her chains and muzzle, shaped to fit a dragon, fell into the snow. She lay before him, bloody and wet, her silvery dress tattered. Her hair like moonlight covered her face.

Dies Irae was surprised by the force of his memories. They hit him so hard, he took a step back. Requiem rushed back into him, not Requiem today of ruins and ash, but the Requiem where he'd lusted for Lacrimosa, a land of passion and anger.

"Stand up," he said softly.

Lacrimosa raised her head to look at him, and Dies Irae saw that she was still beautiful. He hadn't seen her in... what was it? Fifteen years? And yet her beauty had only grown, even as blood and dirt caked her, even as her hair was tangled and her dress torn. He stared at the tatters of that dress, and at the flesh he could see through it. Her left thigh was bare, and he could see the tops of her breasts, pale and small. Yes, she was filthy, bloody, deplorable, but he wanted to renege on his promise, to grab her, hurt her, take her right there.

"You promised," she whispered to him.

He spat. "Stand up."

Legs trembling, she struggled to rise, and finally stood in the snow. She glared at him, chin raised, snowflakes in her hair. Her body shook; from fear or cold, Dies Irae did not know.

"You promised," she whispered again.

He grabbed her arm, digging his fingers into her white skin. "I lied," he said.

She glared and bared her teeth, as if she were still a dragon with fangs to flaunt. "If you touch me," she said, voice strained, "I will turn into a dragon. I will become one as you're in your passion, as you're inside me, and I will kill you."

Dies Irae hesitated. He hadn't considered that. It was possible, he conceded; she had nothing to lose. If he dragged her into his tent, and took her there, he'd be vulnerable. If she became a beast, her claws and fangs could tear him apart.

"Not if I drug you with ilbane," he said. "I'll fill your mouth with it, like I did that day."

She barked a laugh. "Try it then. I'm no longer fifteen, Irae. I've suffered enough ilbane to shift though its pain. You've given me this strength."

Damn it. Anger flared in Dies Irae, and he shouted and slapped her, knocking her down. Fresh blood speckled the snow. He stormed off, leaving her there, bloody.

"Chain her," he ordered his men. "And keep guard, three griffins around her at every moment. If she escapes, I kill every one of you."

Men and griffins rushed toward Lacrimosa, and Dies Irae entered the tent his men had raised for him. Inside the embroidered walls, he fumed and paced.

"You made a mistake, Lacrimosa," he said, though none were there to hear. "You will pay for it. You will suffer. Once we reach Confutatis, you will suffer more than any weredragon ever has."

Outside he heard her cry in pain, and he smiled, a mirthless smile.

The tent flaps flew open, and Gloriae stormed inside. She carried her helmet under her arm, and her cheeks were flushed—from anger or cold, Dies Irae did not know. *Probably both,* he thought.

"Let me kill her," Gloriae demanded, eyes flashing. "Let me kill the weredragon." Her chest rose and fell, and her hand trembled around the hilt of her drawn sword.

"In time," Dies Irae said.

"Now. She killed Mother. I will avenge her." Tears filled Gloriae's eyes. "Please, Father. I will kill her like you've taught me to kill."

She must never know, Dies Irae told himself. *She must never know that Lacrimosa did not kill her mother... but is her mother.* The truth would crush her, Dies Irae knew. If Gloriae learned she was descended from monsters, it would be a pain too great to bear. He would spare her this. He would keep Lacrimosa gagged, he decided, to stop her from speaking the truth.

He gestured at an upholstered chair in the corner. "Gloriae, sit down."

She shook her head wildly. "I will not. Father, I—"

"Sit down, Gloriae," he said again, a little more firmly.

She held her breath, bit her lip, seemed about to scream, then finally stormed to the chair and sat down. She still held her sword raised.

Dies Irae sat beside her in a second chair. "Daughter, you know that I love you."

"And I love you, Father." Her voice was ice over fire.

"If you love me, you'll stay away from Lacrimosa. You will not kill her. You will not remove her muzzle to speak with her. You will not even approach her."

Gloriae rose so quickly, she knocked back her chair. It hit the tent wall, and a flurry of snow blew in. "I refuse."

"Gloriae. Sit down." This time his voice was cold, and he raised his mace. When she was a child, he would never beat her. Instead, he would whip her handmaiden, bloodying the girl as Gloriae watched and bit her lip, stifling tears. The handmaiden's back still bore scars, and Gloriae still harbored a fear of him. Face pale as the snow, Gloriae righted her chair and sat again.

Dies Irae touched a strand of her hair. So golden, so beautiful. It was like his own hair. Inwardly, Dies Irae snorted. And Benedictus thought he was her father? That a beast like him could beget a child as fair as Gloriae? Benedictus could keep Agnus Dei, that beastly child of scales and flame. Gloriae was pure.

"You are beautiful, my child, and your spirit is still soft."

Gloriae glared. "My spirit is cold and strong as my blade."

"It is still soft. The weredragon would ensorcell you. She might even inflict her disease upon you, so that you too grow scales, wings, and turn into a lizard."

Gloriae narrowed her eyes and gasped. "They can spread their curse?"

Dies Irae nodded, forcing a sad expression to his face. "Most cannot, but Lacrimosa is fouler than her kin. She killed your mother, and so your soul is vulnerable to her black magic. I fear for you, daughter."

Gloriae snarled. "I don't fear her." She raised her blade. "She will fear my sword."

"Do it for my own fear, then," Dies Irae said. "I confess that I'm afraid. Please, Daughter. I grow old. In only several winters, I will be sixty, did you know? An old man. You are the light of my life, Gloriae. All that I do, all the wars I fight, all the cities I build... it is for you. I try to clean this world, to turn it into a empire of light and goodness, so that when I die—"

"Father!"

"Hear me out, Gloriae. I will die someday, maybe in a year, maybe in twenty years, but I will die. And then you will sit upon the Ivory Throne. I want to leave this a good world for you to rule. If you should fall to Lacrimosa's magic, I... I could not bear it."

"I will not fall to her curse."

Dies Irae caressed her hair with his mace. "You are brave, Gloriae, but I am not. Not when it comes to your safety. So do an old man a favor. Don't kill Lacrimosa; not until she lures Benedictus to us. Don't speak to her. Leave my men to hurt her."

"But *I* want to hurt her."

"If you do, you will hurt me. Do you want to hurt me, daughter?"

Gloriae stared at him, green eyes icy, face expressionless, and Dies Irae saw the answer in her eyes. *Yes. She does.*

"I will not kill her yet," Gloriae finally said, staring into his eyes, not blinking. "I will let her live until Benedictus flies to rescue her, until we catch and kill him, and Kyrie Eleison, and Agnus Dei. I will keep our bait alive. But once we kill the others, then, Father... then I will hurt her like she hurt me. Then I will kill her like she killed Mother."

Not waiting for him to reply, Gloriae rose to her feet and stormed out of the tent. Snow flurried in, and Dies Irae stared at the embroidered cloth walls for a long time. Finally he spoke, as if she were still there to hear.

"Very well, Gloriae." He sighed, remembering that day in the forest, Lacrimosa's soft skin, her screams, her hair in his hands. "Very well. Then you may kill her."

KYRIE ELEISON

Kyrie had never felt more pain.

He and Agnus Dei had not touched ground in a day and night. Through darkness and hail, and sunlight over burning cloudscapes, they flew faster than wind, higher than mountains. Again the sun was setting, blazing orange and red over a sea of clouds, casting rays between the Vir Requis. How far had they flown since that night Lacrimosa fell captive? It must be close to three thousand leagues, Kyrie thought. Maybe more. He had never flown so fast, so far.

His wings ached. His lungs burned. His joints felt like rusty metal hinges. He looked at Agnus Dei. She flew beside him, her scales blazing red in the sunset. Her eyes stared forward, narrowed and fiery. Her fangs were bared. Yet Agnus Dei too needed rest, Kyrie knew. Pain lived on her face alongside her anger, and her wings looked stiff and aching.

"Let's rest!" he called to her over the wind.

She glowered. "Not until we find the salvanae."

"Maybe they're below the clouds," Kyrie said. "Let's land and look for them on the ground."

She gave him a look that said, *Nice try, pup, but no cookie.*

Kyrie attempted to think of another argument, found none, and resigned himself to grabbing Agnus Dei and pulling her down.

"Let go!" she cried as they tumbled through the clouds.

But Kyrie would not let go. He wrapped himself around her and swooped through the clouds, into clear sky, and toward the earth. She wriggled in his grasp, and he tightened his grip, eyes narrowed and teeth clenched. Luckily she was too weary to break free.

No trees covered the land, and the grass was thin and yellow. Hills rose from the earth, round like upside down bowls on a tabletop. A stream ran between them, gray under the clouds, and deer drank from it. Still pulling Agnus Dei, Kyrie landed by the water. The deer snorted and fled, hoofs kicking up dirt and grass.

"Let go, pup," Agnus Dei said, panting. She finally shook herself free from Kyrie. She looked to the sky, as if considering to take flight again, then shook her head and approached the stream. She drank deeply.

Kyrie joined her. He dipped his head underwater and drank. The water was icy, and it filled him with such goodness that he sighed. He drank until his belly bulged, then raised his dripping head from the water.

"I needed that," he said.

Agnus Dei gestured toward the next hill, which lay nearby. More deer stood there in the dusk, promising a meal. "I'm hungry," Agnus Dei said. "Feel like mutton?"

"Their meat is called venison," Kyrie said.

Agnus Dei rolled her eyes. "Now don't start that again."

They flew toward the hill where the deer grazed, and caught one before the others escaped. It was mostly skin and bones, and its meat was tough. After a day of no food, however, Kyrie wasn't complaining.

Agnus Dei swallowed her last bite and licked her lips. "Let's fly. Ready, pup?"

Lying on the ground, Kyrie turned his head toward her. He wanted to be ready. He wanted to fly, to find help, to find the salvanae. In his dreams, he saw himself leading an army of dragons to Confutatis, saving Lacrimosa, and avenging all those whom Dies Irae had killed. But were those only dreams? Kyrie sighed.

"What if there are no salvanae?" he whispered. "What if we're only chasing a myth?"

Agnus Dei's nostrils flared. Her eyes blazed, and flames escaped her lips. "Kyrie, you know how I feel. You know I believe."

Kyrie nodded. He wanted to believe too. After flying all of last night, however, he also ached for sleep. The thought of flying another night and day made his head, body, and soul hurt. Of course, that pain was nothing compared to what Lacrimosa must be enduring. Dies Irae would torture her; Kyrie knew that. He had to do something, anything, even if it was just chasing a dream.

"All right," he said. "Let's fly."

He struggled to his feet and stretched, his joints and wings aching. He looked at the setting sun; it would soon disappear behind the horizon. Kyrie sighed. It would be a long night.

Before he could take flight, however, a herd of deer upon a distant hill bugled. They began to run together, wailing. They fled toward Kyrie and Agnus Dei, as if mere dragons—hungry dragons who had just eaten one of them—were gentle compared to what chased them.

"What the—" Agnus Dei began, then her voice died and she stared.

Kyrie stared too. Four creatures emerged from behind a hill, dragon-sized and covered in bloodred fur. Bat wings grew from their backs, and their claws tore grass and earth. The beasts stared at Kyrie and Agnus Dei. Flames crackled in their eyes, and their fangs oozed drool. Their stench carried upon the wind, a stench like corpses. Lanburg Fields had smelled the same.

Kyrie growled and bared his fangs. Agnus Dei snorted a blast of fire. They stood side by side, silent and watching.

"Ugly buggers," Agnus Dei muttered to Kyrie.

"And smelly ones," Kyrie muttered back.

One of the four red beasts was larger than the others. A crest of black hair ran along its head and back, and three serrated horns grew from its brow. It took three steps forward, smoke rising from its nostrils. Saliva dripped from its maw.

"Are you griffins?" it asked, voice low, a growl like broken rocks.

"Not too bright, are they?" Agnus Dei whispered to Kyrie from the corner of her mouth. She then stared at the creature and raised her voice. "Griffins? Do we look like griffins? We hate those things. What are you?"

The creatures ignored her. The beast with the black crest, apparently their leader, snorted smoke. It licked its lips with two slobbery tongues.

"Are you dragons?" it asked with that low, crackling growl. The other three beasts growled too and scratched the ground, their claws red in the sunset.

"Dragons?" Kyrie said, narrowing his eyes. "We're Vir Requis. We seek the salvanae. Do you know where we can find them?"

The black-crested beast snarled and snapped its teeth. "You are Osanna stock. You may not pass the Divide. You may not enter Salvandos. We are dividers. We guard the Divide; it is holy. You have touched the Divide. Flee now, or you will die."

Kyrie took a step closer to the creature, this *divider*. Its stench was so powerful, he nearly gagged, but Kyrie forced himself to stare into its eyes.

"We must pass the Divide," he said. "We must enter Salvandos."

The dividers howled, a sound that shook the hills. Lightning slashed the sky, and dark clouds gathered. The chief divider snarled, eyes blazing, and took another step toward Kyrie. It now stood so close, it could claw Kyrie.

"No griffins may pass the Divide."

Kyrie gulped. The divider was sixty feet long; a good twenty feet longer than Kyrie. Muscles moved beneath its fur, and its claws glistened when lightning struck. Its tongues licked its chops again, dripping drool that burned the grass and sizzled, eating holes into the earth.

"I told you ugly buggers!" Agnus Dei said and stepped up beside Kyrie, flames leaving her nostrils. Her eyes blazed nearly as angrily as the divider's. "We're not griffins."

The dividers considered her. Their chief said, "You are dragons. No dragons or griffins may pass the Divide. We are dividers. The Divide is holy. Leave now, or we will feast upon you."

All four dividers licked their chops.

Agnus Dei rolled her eyes. She flapped her wings and said, "Oh, give me a break."

Then she took off and began to fly over the dividers' heads.

"Agnus Dei, no!" Kyrie shouted, ice flowing through him.

The dividers howled and leaped toward Agnus Dei, bat wings flapping.

Agnus Dei blew fire at them.

Kyrie cursed, kicked off the ground, and flew toward her.

The fire roared. It flowed over the dividers above, and then covered Kyrie. He shut his eyes, grunted, and veered left and out of the flames. The fire blackened the scales across his right side.

The dividers were blazing. If Kyrie's scales protected him from fire, the dividers' fur now crackled and burned. Kyrie expected them to die, or at least flee, but the fire seemed only to enrage them. They screamed, horrible sounds like slaughtered animals, and flew toward Agnus Dei. Their claws scratched and their teeth snapped.

"Hey!" Kyrie called. "Leave her! Take me on."

He swiped his tail at one blazing divider. He knocked it aside. The others were clawing at Agnus Dei, who was lashing her tail and snapping her teeth.

"Oh sure, save the damsel in distress, my hero pup," Agnus Dei called to him over the shrieking dividers. She lashed her tail and hit one divider, knocking it into a spin.

Two dividers turned toward Kyrie, maws open. Fire raced across them, raising sparks, but seemed not to slow them. They flew toward Kyrie. Kyrie lashed his tail and hit one, driving his tail's spikes deep into its side. The other bit Kyrie's shoulder. He howled. The divider's fangs pushed through his scales and into his flesh, and its fire blazed against Kyrie.

"Get off!" Kyrie grunted and shook, but the divider kept its fangs in his shoulder, shaking its head like a dog biting a bird. Kyrie shoved his claws into its side, grunting as its flaming fur burned him, and kept clawing until its innards spilled. Even in death, it kept its jaw locked on his shoulder. Kyrie could barely keep above the ground. The dead divider weighed more than him. Its entrails dangled.

"Agnus Dei!" he called. She was fighting above him. Scratches covered her, and five dividers surrounded her. *Five dividers?* Kyrie grunted. Where had more come from? Then he noticed that a dozen dividers now surrounded him.

"Damn it," Kyrie muttered. One flew toward him. Kyrie lashed his tail at it. The dead divider clung to his shoulder, jaw locked in its death bite, tugging him closer and closer to the ground. Kyrie growled, pulled its jaw open with all his might, and sent the body crashing down. Fresh blood spurted from his shoulder.

Kyrie was close to the ground now. Agnus Dei fought a good thousand feet above. Kyrie flapped his wings, shooting straight up, knocking through a crowd of dividers. They clawed and bit, and Kyrie clawed and bit back, shoving his way through them. Twenty flew around him. In the distance, he saw a hundred more flying toward the fray.

"Agnus Dei!" he shouted. "Let's get out of here!"

She was fighting above, scratching and biting and blowing fire. Her eyes blazed. Scratches covered her, and several of her scales were missing. A gash ran along her tail.

"Agnus Dei!" Kyrie cried. He blew fire at one divider, clawed another's face, and flew beside her. A hundred dividers surrounded them, a sea of red fur, fangs, and fire. Thunder boomed and lightning rent the sky.

"Hello, pup," Agnus Dei said as she fought. Blood trickled from her mouth. "What were you doing down there—taking a nap?"

Kyrie blocked a swipe of claws from a divider, clawed back, and grabbed Agnus Dei's shoulder. "Agnus Dei, this is no time for jokes. Come with me."

The dividers screamed around them, lashing their tails, and Kyrie grunted when one hit him. He wanted to blow fire, a Vir Requis's best weapon, but flames only enraged the dividers.

Agnus Dei shook him off. "We must enter Salvandos! I won't back down." She slashed at a divider, sending it crashing down, but one scratched her back. Her blood poured, and she cried in pain.

"Agnus Dei, come on!" Kyrie shouted, grabbed her again, and pulled her back. Maybe the pain of her wound changed her mind. She flew with him. They crashed through a dozen dividers, heading back toward Osanna.

The dividers followed, howling, bat wings flapping.

"We're back in Osanna!" Kyrie cried over his shoulder. "Leave us."

The black-crested divider leered. Its fur had burned off, revealing scraggly, blackened flesh covered with scratches and blood. Blood filled its mouth, and smoke rose from it. "You have touched the Divide," it said. "You will die."

The hundred dividers, eyes like raging stars, stormed forward.

Kyrie cursed under his breath, grabbed Agnus Dei, and pulled her with him. They flew east and down, moving close to the grass.

"Let go!" Agnus Dei demanded, squirming as she flew, trying to release his grasp. "I flee from no fight."

"I have an idea," Kyrie said. "Just do what I do."

Lightning crashed, and the clouds roiled. The dividers screamed, their bat wings churning the air. Kyrie flew behind a hill crowned with boulders. For a moment, he couldn't see the dividers behind him. The boulders shielded him and Agnus Dei from view.

Kyrie landed by a stream and turned human. His wounds ached even worse this way, and the deer meat grumbled in his belly.

Agnus Dei glared at him, still in dragon form. "What are you doing? They'll eat you."

"Agnus Dei, shift now!" he shouted.

She grunted, blew flames to the sky, and shifted into human form. She stood by him, her clothes tattered, her black hair a knotty mess.

A hundred dividers came roaring over the hill, flying east. They glanced down at the humans, barely registered them, and looked around in puzzlement.

"They went that way!" Kyrie shouted, pointing east.

The dividers howled. "Who are you?" their chief asked, its last patches of fur still burning.

"We're neither dragons nor griffins," Kyrie cried up to them. "We're only two-legged travelers. The dragons you seek fled east. You can still catch them. Fly, fly after them!"

The dividers hovered above them for a moment. It seemed like an eternity to Kyrie. Then they howled and flew east, a few still flaming.

Kyrie and Agnus Dei stood panting, watching them disappear into the distance.

"They're mean bastards, but they're dumb as dung beetles," she said. She sat down hard and took deep breaths. Blood dripped down her shoulder.

Kyrie collapsed onto the ground. His head spun, and his wounds ached.

Agnus Dei tore strips off her shirt, including both sleeves, and bound their wounds. Though Kyrie ached, and felt more weary than ever before, he couldn't help but notice Agnus Dei's exposed flesh. With her shirt mostly torn off, and her leggings tattered, only thin strips of cloth covered her. Her body was bloodied, bruised, and cut... but also tanned, lithe, and intoxicating. As Agnus Dei leaned over him, bandaging his shoulder, Kyrie's blood boiled. He gulped and looked away quickly.

"Cool it, pup," Agnus Dei said wryly. She tightened the cloth around his wound painfully enough that he winced. "Put your tongue back in your mouth before it hits the dirt."

Kyrie shut his mouth and muttered under his breath, face hot. He forced himself to stare at the ground rather than at Agnus Dei, but could still sense the mocking smile on her lips and in her eyes. Strangely, that look of hers, and that crooked smile, only boiled his blood hotter.

What was it about Agnus Dei? Kyrie had seen beautiful women before. Lacrimosa was beautiful, her beauty like starlight. Lady Mirum had been beautiful, a beauty like the sea. Gloriae was beautiful, a beauty of ice and snow. Yet Agnus Dei... she stirred something new inside Kyrie. She was no starlight nor sea nor snow; she was *fire*. And Kyrie liked fire.

"You're done," Agnus Dei said, bandaging his last wound. She punched his shoulder. "You okay?"

He nodded and looked back at her. "And you? You took a beating up there." Bruises and cuts covered her. The worst wound was behind her shoulder; it was a bleeding mess. "Let me help you with that."

He cleaned her wound with water from the stream, then bound it with cloth he tore from his shirt. Sweat covered her brow, and her jaw tightened when he bound her wound, but she made not a sound. When he was done, he wiped the sweat off her brow... and found himself smoothing her tangled hair. Despite its knots, her hair was soft, damp, and—

"What," she asked him, "do you think you're doing?"

He pulled his hand away, muttering. "You have blood in your hair."

She stared at him, eyes flashing. He stared back, jaw tightened. *Why should I look away? Let her stare at me with that fiery stare; it won't cow me.* She leaned forward, still staring, and grabbed the back of his head, painfully tugging a fistful of his hair. He grunted.

"You do too," she said, pulled his head toward her, and kissed him.

Her lips were soft and full, and her hand still clutched his hair, pulling it. Kyrie closed his eyes. He kissed her, head spinning, and placed his hand on the small of her back. She pushed him to the ground, and he grunted at the pain of his wounds, and then Agnus Dei was atop him, kissing him deeply, her tongue seeking.

The sun sank behind the hills, and the distant cries of beasts still carried on the wind, but Kyrie knew nothing but Agnus Dei, and fire, and her lips and body against him. Darkness and flame covered his world.

BENEDICTUS

Benedictus trudged through the snow, his hands pale and numb, his feet icy in his boots. He pulled his cloak close around him, shook snow out of his hair, and cursed again. He'd never felt such chill, both the chill that filled his body and the ice that filled his gut.

He wished he could fly. Walking like this was so slow, and every hour he delayed was an hour Lacrimosa suffered. But he dared not fly. Not with the griffins that filled the skies, the eyes in every town that watched for him.

"Lacrimosa," he whispered, plowing through the snow, his fists trembling from anger and cold. "I'm going to find you. Just hang in there, and I'll—"

Shrieks tore through his words. Griffins. Benedictus cursed and dived down, pulled his cloak over his head, and lay still. His cloak was coarse charcoal wool, now covered in snow. Benedictus knew that lying here, he could look like just another boulder. The snow filled his mouth, stung his face, and the griffins shrieked. They flew above every hour, their riders scanning the mountains, bearing crossbows and lances. Benedictus lay still, not even daring to breathe.

The griffins' cries came closer. Benedictus cursed again. *They're going to find me this time,* he thought and clenched his jaw. How many were there? He hadn't had time to look. A dozen? Twenty? Last time they flew above, he had counted seventeen. He could not beat that many. Not these days, old and lame. Not without Kyrie and Agnus Dei at his side.

The shrieks were so close now, they loosened snow from the mountainside. Chunks of the stuff hit Benedictus's back, heavy and icy. Benedictus tightened his fists. What if the falling snow became an avalanche, burying him? Lacrimosa would remain in captivity, Dies Irae torturing her for sport—

No. Benedictus shoved the thought away. *I'm going to live. I'm going to save Lacrimosa. And I'm going to save Gloriae too. I'm finally going to bring my daughter back.*

Griffin wings thudded above. Benedictus heard talons landing, kicking up snow. It wasn't fifty yards away. More talons landed, scraping snow and rocks. There were many griffins this time; at least twenty, maybe thirty. They cawed and scratched the ground.

Get up and fight, spoke a voice inside Benedictus. *You are King of Requiem, Benedictus the Black. You do not cower. You do not hide under a cloak. Get up and kill these bastards.*

"I saw something," spoke a voice ahead—one of the riders. "A man walking through the snow."

A griffin shrieked. Leather and metal moaned and chinked—saddles and armor. Scabbards clanged against cuisses. Benedictus heard the sound of a crossbow being drawn.

"Bah!" came another voice, deeper than the first. "I see nobody here. No man can survive these mountains. You saw a goat, that's all."

Rise up and fight them, spoke the voice in Benedictus's head. *I will not be caught cowering like a dog.* He gritted his teeth. *No. Stay still. You can't save Lacrimosa if you're dead.*

A griffin walked toward him; he could hear the talons sinking into the snow and scratching the stone beneath. It took all of Benedictus's willpower to stay still. He could feel the rider's gaze upon him, and Benedictus thanked the gods that their shrieks had loosened the snow on the mountainside. That snow now buried him.

The griffin's talons hit the ground inches from him. One talon, long and sharp as a sword, pierced the snow near his eye. Old blood coated it.

"I told you," came the deep voice from farther away. "There's nobody here. Come on, we're wanted back by nightfall."

The griffin above Benedictus lingered a moment longer. Then its rider spat noisily, Benedictus heard jingling spurs, and the griffin's talon pulled out from the snow, missing Benedictus's face by a hair's length. The griffins took off, wings thudding.

Benedictus breathed a sigh of relief. He remained under the snow for several long moments, then dug himself out. He was now drenched and colder than ever. He watched the griffins disappear into the horizon.

Benedictus hugged himself, but found no warmth. He craved a fire, but dared not light one, and he doubted he'd find firewood here anyway. More than anything, he wanted to fly. In dragon form, he could be in Confutatis within a week, could storm the city and save Lacrimosa. But no. He dared fly no more; during his last flight griffins had attacked within moments. The beasts filled these skies, tens of thousands watching the world.

"Be strong, Lacrimosa," he whispered. He knew she was still alive. Dies Irae would not kill her, not when he could torture her, use her to lure Benedictus to him. *It's me he wants most.*

Benedictus kept walking, shoving aside snow with his arms. He thought of Agnus Dei and Kyrie. Where were they? Were they safe in the west? Were they flying out of Osanna, heading into the realms of myth where no griffins flew? Benedictus did not know. They could be dead.

He lowered his head, grief and fear pulsing through him. With clenched teeth, he kept moving.

LACRIMOSA

She saw Confutatis at dawn, rising from the east, shining like a rising sun.

Lacrimosa blinked feebly. She struggled to raise her head, but could not. Volucris's talons clutched her, and the winds lashed her. She was in human form today, limbs bound and mouth gagged. Her dress was tattered, her body bruised and bloody, and her hair streamed behind her like the banners Dies Irae and his men bore. The other griffins flew around her, shrieking at the sight of their home.

Gloriae too flew there, Lacrimosa saw, but her daughter never approached her. The other men mocked and beat her. Gloriae remained at a distance, and Lacrimosa thought she knew why. *Dies Irae ordered her away from me. He fears she'll learn the truth... that she's my daughter, and that I love her.*

"Ben," Lacrimosa whispered, lips cracked. Though her hand was so weak she could barely move it, she clutched the pendant that hung around her neck, a silver pendant shaped like a bluebell, their flower. "Fly away, Ben. Fly away from this place."

Confutatis glittered, growing closer, a city of white spires, marble columns, and statues of Dies Irae with his fist upon his chest. A city of a million souls, cobbled streets snaking between proud buildings and temples, a city swarming with countless griffins—griffins atop every wall and tower and fortress. The Marble City. City of the Sun. Jewel of Osanna. Confutatis had many names, but to Lacrimosa, it was one thing: a prison.

"Turn into your reptilian form," Dies Irae's voice spoke above, colder than the wind. "I will have the city see your monstrosity."

She considered disobeying him, but dared not; that would only mean more cuts from the spears, more pain, more ilbane rubbed into her wounds. She shifted into a dragon. Volucris grunted at the greater weight, tightened his talons around her, and flapped his wings harder. A tear fled Lacrimosa's eye and fell to the fields of barley and wheat below.

When they flew above the first walls, Dies Irae's men blew trumpets, and the griffins cried in triumph. *Heroes returning in glory,* Lacrimosa thought. *I am their prize.*

Confutatis rose upon hills of granite and grass. Three towering walls surrounded the city, moats between them. Guards covered the walls, armed with arrows and catapults and leashed griffins. When they saw their emperor, they slammed fists against their breastplates and called his name. Behind the walls, the city folk saw the banners of Dies Irae, and they bowed. All looked upon her, soldiers and commoners, fear and disgust in their eyes.

"Weredragon," she heard them whisper, a vile word. "Weredragon."

Once a wise king had ruled Confutatis, she remembered, a kindly old man with a long white beard. She would visit here as a child, tug that white beard, run along the cobbled streets. Once Requiem and Confutatis had shone together—proud, ancient allies. But that had been years ago, before darkness had covered Lacrimosa's world.

Clutched in Volucris's talons, she watched the city below. They flew over courtyards where soldiers drilled with swords and spears, forts where great walls rose, towers where archers stood, stables of griffins. She saw catapults and chariots, armored horses, gold and steel everywhere. Statues of Dies Irae stood at every corner, statues of him raising a sword, or swinging a mace, or riding a griffin. Banners of war fluttered from every roof, white and gold and red, swords and spears embroidered upon them.

So many soldiers, she thought. *So many things of war.* And yet the war had ended, had it not? Dies Irae had destroyed the Vir Requis, killed every one other than a handful. Why did steel and military might still fill these streets? Why did she see more swords and shields than flowers or trees? What enemy did Dies Irae fight now, and what peril could justify this city? No, not a city; Confutatis was a huge fortress now, a barracks of a million people all taught to worship their emperor and hate their enemies.

A palace rose upon the highest point of Confutatis. Golden roofs topped its white towers. A hundred marble statues stood upon its battlements.

A square stretched out before the palace, five hundred yards wide and twice as long, marble columns lining it. The palace's greatest statue stood here, a hundred feet tall and gilded—a statue of Dies Irae in armor, holding aloft a sword. The statue's cold gaze stared upon the city, proud and judging.

Dies Irae and his griffins flew over the palace towers, and Lacrimosa saw a cobbled courtyard below. The griffins descended, and Volucris tossed her down. She slammed into the cobblestones, banging her shoulder, and bit back a cry of pain. Walls surrounded her, archers and griffins atop their battlements. A statue of Dies Irae stood upon a column, glaring down at her.

"Collar her," the real Dies Irae said, dismounting his griffin. He marched across the courtyard toward a gateway. "Muzzle her and chain her to the column."

She raised her head and tried to stand up. A dozen men rushed forward, kicked her, and slammed shields against her, knocking her head to the ground. They closed an iron collar around her neck, muzzled her, and chained her to a column.

"Gloriae, help me," Lacrimosa tried to say, but could not speak with the muzzle. Her daughter stood across the courtyard, eyes cold and arms crossed, staring at her. *She hates me,* Lacrimosa knew.

Dies Irae approached Gloriae and spoke to her. The two walked through the gateway, leaving the courtyard, capes fluttering. The gates slammed shut behind them, leaving Lacrimosa at the mercy of their soldiers. Those soldiers leered, and several kicked her, spat at her, and mocked her.

Lacrimosa mewled and tried to free herself, but could not. The collar hurt her neck, and she dared not become human; those kicking boots would kill her without her scales offering their meager protection. She weakly flapped her tail at the men, but they only laughed and kicked her harder.

She lowered her head. *Fly away from here, Ben,* she thought. *I cannot bear this fate to be yours too. I cannot live if I see you too chained and beaten. Fly away, Ben, fly and be with Kyrie and Agnus Dei. Never return here.*

Finally the soldiers tired and left the courtyard. The archers above kept their arrows pointed at her, staring down with narrowed eyes.

They all think I'm a beast, a monster.

She closed her eyes and tried to remember Requiem, the golden leaves upon the birches, the marble columns, the courtyards where she would walk with Benedictus, dressed in gowns and jewels. As night fell, she let those memories fill her, and her tears fell like jewels in the starlight.

KYRIE ELEISON

"How long has it been?" Kyrie asked Agnus Dei, wings flapping. The sun rose over the horizon, a disk like a burnished, bronze shield from Lanburg Fields. Snowy mountaintops peaked from clouds below. Where the cloud cover broke, Kyrie saw piney mountainsides. Rivers roared between boulders, feeding pools of mist. He saw no game, and his belly grumbled.

"Seventh morning since the Divide," Agnus Dei said, flying beside him. She looked at him, and Kyrie thought that her eyes had lost something of their rage. A week ago, fire and pain had filled them, but now he saw weariness and fear there. Her eyes, normally brown, appeared golden in the sunrise. Dawn danced on her scales.

"Is this all Salvandos is?" he asked. "Mountains, and rivers, and lakes, and...."

His voice died off. During the past week, they'd flown over more landscapes than he'd thought the world held: hills of jasmines that rolled for a hundred leagues, lakes full of leaping trout, plains of jagged boulders like armies of rock, and many realms his weary mind could no longer recall. But no humans. No griffins. And no salvanae. Salvandos—fabled realm beyond Osanna, beyond the dividers. A realm of great beauty that, at times, brought tears to Kyrie's eyes... and, it seemed, a realm of great loneliness.

"There are salvanae here," Agnus Dei said, though her voice had lost its former conviction. She was reciting. "We'll find them soon. Maybe today."

The clouds parted below, and Kyrie eyed a stream. "Let's grab some breakfast," he said, watching the silhouettes of salmon in the water. Without waiting for an answer, he dived toward the river. Cold winds and mist hit him, and soon he reached the river and crashed into the water. He swam, then rose into flight again, three salmon in his jaws. He swallowed them, dived, and caught two more.

His hunger sated, he landed on the river bank. Agnus Dei swooped and crashed into the water too, spraying Kyrie. Soon she stood beside him, chewing a mouthful of salmon. Kyrie watched her as she ate. She was beautiful in dragon form, her scales brilliant, her eyes glittering, her fangs sharp... but Kyrie couldn't stop thinking of her human shape. He hadn't seen her human form since that day, that horrible and wonderful day on the border. He remembered her bruised, hot body pressed against him, her lips against his lips, her—

No. Kyrie pushed the thought away. She had lost blood that day, had been confused and frightened. Whenever he tried to speak of their love making, she glared at him with dragon eyes, fangs bared, and he shut his mouth. He knew that he better forget it soon, or she'd beat the memory out of his mind.

But... spirits of Requiem, how could he forget the most intoxicating and wonderful night of his life?

"I love sardines for breakfast," Agnus Dei said. She dunked her head into the river, then pulled back with spray of water, another salmon in her jaws. She gulped it, then drank from the river.

Kyrie drank too, remembering those breakfasts of porridge and bacon back at Fort Sanctus, and he thought of the Lady Mirum, his heart heavy. When he finished drinking, he licked his chops and said, "Where now, Agnus Dei? How much longer can we fly? Maybe there is no golden mountain. Maybe there are no salvanae."

He looked around at the clear waters, the mountains covered in snow and pines, the valleys of grass and boulders. He wished he could stay here forever with Agnus Dei. No griffins filled these skies. They could rebuild the Vir Requis race here—him, her, their children. This land could promise a future for the Vir Requis, and... Kyrie felt his blood boil again. It could mean many more nights with Agnus Dei.

He sighed. No. He could not just hide here, not when Lacrimosa and Benedictus needed him. He would not abandon his friends.

Agnus Dei too looked around the valleys and mountains, lost in thought. She also sighed, then said, "Maybe you're right, pup, maybe—"

A roar pierced the air, sending birds fluttering.

Kyrie and Agnus Dei stared up and froze.

Nothing.

Nothing there.

The roar had sounded above them, maybe a league away. Griffins? No, that was no birdlike shriek, it was—

Again the roar shook the world. And there—a serpentine shadow above the clouds.

Agnus Dei burst into flight. Kyrie followed, wind whipping him. They crashed through the clouds and looked around.

"Where is it?" Agnus Dei demanded, looking from side to side. Kyrie looked. He saw nothing but leagues of clouds, mountain peaks, and the sun above.

"Where did it go?" Agnus Dei roared and blew fire. "True dragons! Hear me. Answer my call."

Kyrie heard nothing but the wind and, below him, the distant calls of birds. But he had seen the silhouette of that serpentine creature, had heard that roar. That had been no griffin nor divider; it had no wings, and yet it flew, a hundred feet long and coiling.

Kyrie scanned the clouds. He saw a wisp in a field of white fluff; something had dived through those clouds.

"There!" he said and flew. He reached the place where the clouds were disturbed, pulled his wings close to his body, and dived. Agnus Dei followed. Under the clouds, the mountains and rivers spread into the horizons, and again Kyrie saw no dragon. But....

"Look!" he said. Birds were fleeing a distant mountaintop. Something had disturbed them. Kyrie flew toward that mountaintop, Agnus Dei by him. He was tired, but he had never flown faster. Could it be? Had they found the true dragons of old, the lords of Salvandos?

They flew around the mountaintop, a tower of stone and snow. *There!* He saw a green, scaly tail disappear around a cliff. He narrowed his eyes and followed, Agnus Dei at his side.

A flash of brilliant green. The dragon ahead soared into the clouds.

"Wow," Kyrie said. He could think of nothing more to say. He glimpsed the dragon for only a second, but it was beautiful, the most beautiful creature he'd ever seen. This was definitely no Vir Requis. The creature was half as slim and twice as long. It had no wings, but moved like a snake in the sky, coiling and uncoiling. Emerald scales covered its body, and its horns and claws glowed. It sported a flowing mustache and beard, snowy white and flapping in the wind.

In a flash, it was gone into the clouds, leaving a wake of glittering blue.

"Come on, Kyrie!" Agnus Dei shouted, and Kyrie realized he was hovering in place. He blinked, shook his head, and flew hard. He broke through the clouds and saw the salvana in the distance, already a league away, undulating as it flew. It dived under the clouds again, disappearing from view, like a snake diving under water.

"Come back here," Kyrie cried, but doubted the salvana could hear him. It was such a strange creature, Kyrie wondered if he'd just gone mad with weariness. Flying green serpents with golden horns and white beards? What was next, pink elephants with swan wings?

Kyrie and Agnus Dei kept racing, chasing the coiling green dragon. It was fast—faster than them, growing smaller and smaller in the distance. Kyrie knew that on a good day, well rested and well fed, he could catch up, but he was too tired now. He could barely keep his wings flapping, but he pushed himself as far as he could go.

After an hour of flight, the salvana—now just a speck on the horizon—dived under the clouds again.

Kyrie and Agnus Dei, both so weary they could barely fly, followed. They too dived under the clouds... and their breath died.

Tears filled Kyrie's eyes.

"It's real," Agnus Dei whispered, eyes moist.

A mountain of gold rose before them. Kyrie had seen gold before—Dies Irae certainly wore enough of it—but here was an entire mountain of the stuff, a league high and blinding in the sun. Rings of mist surrounded the golden mountain. Snow capped its peaks. It dwarfed the smaller, jagged mountains that surrounded it. Most beautiful of all, however, was not the gold and mist and sunbeams, but the thousands of salvanae who flew here. Some were blue and silver, others green and gold, and some were white. Their eyes were like crystal balls, large and spinning. They bugled songs like trumpets, and flowed in and out of round caves in the mountainsides.

"Har Zahav," Kyrie whispered in awe. "The Golden Mountain of Salvandos." He looked at Agnus Dei and saw that she was weeping.

Three salvanae flew toward them. Two had green scales, golden horns, and long fangs. The third was golden and seemed elderly; his beard was white and flowing, his eyes pale blue with long white lashes. He flew first, leading the others, like a stream of gold.

The salvanae flew up to hover before them. Their eyes glittered, large as watermelons. They blinked, lashes sweeping, and said nothing.

"Hello," Kyrie said, then paused and cleared his throat. What did one say when meeting legendary creatures? He doubted they would understand Osanna's High Speech, but would they speak Requiem's older Dragontongue? Kyrie decided to speak the latter. "My name is Kyrie Eleison of Requiem," he said in that ancient, rolling language. "This is my companion, Agnus Dei, daughter of Benedictus and Lacrimosa. We flee danger and suffering. We come seeking your aid."

The old dragon listened, the wind in his beard. Sparks like lightning rose between his teeth. He looked at Kyrie and Agnus Dei with crystal ball eyes. He spoke then with an old, crinkly voice, heavily accented but definitely speaking Dragontongue. "Greeting, travelers and strange things. I am Nehushtan, High Priest of Draco's stars. May they bless you. I welcome you to Har Zahav. You are fellow things of flight and fang. The light of Draco shines upon you, though it glimmers oddly. You may spend the darkness, and pray to the Draco constellation, and return to your lands when the sun wakes."

Kyrie opened his mouth, then closed it again, dumbfounded. Agnus Dei's eyes flared, and smoke rose from her nostrils.

"No!" Agnus Dei said to Nehushtan. "We do not come to rest. We need help! Our people are hunted. We're nearly extinct. The griffins have killed all but four of us. They captured my mother. Please help us." Tears filled her eyes.

The salvana guards growled. Nehushtan only nodded slowly. He blinked, his great eyelashes like fans. He puffed out several rings of smoke. Finally he spoke again, turning his eyes from Agnus Dei, to Kyrie, and back again.

"We of Har Zahav convey our grief. We weep to hear your tragedy, and we pray that the spirits of your dead find peace in the afterlife. You may stay three darknesses and recover your strength. Then you may fly to your home, and we will pray that the Draco constellation glows upon you there, and protects you in the afterlife should you perish."

Kyrie shook his head and grunted. Were these salvanae daft? He blurted out his words, anger boiling his blood. "Is that all you can offer us? Three nights' stay? Then you'll send us back to die? Won't you help us? Don't you care that griffins are slaughtering fellow dragons?"

Nehushtan puffed out more smoke, seeming lost in thought. The smoke formed tiny, dancing salvanae.

"You are not fellow dragons," he finally said, "though you speak our tongue. You are the Vir Requis, creatures of old stories in our land. Yet our light shines with you, for many years ago we were allies, and fought together against the griffins, when the griffins were still wild, and no amulet could tame them. This was many seasons ago. Today we dragons of Salvandos no longer fight the wars of Requiem. Like the snow upon the mountains, we live through sunshine and rain, and thrive both in light and shadows. Ours is a peaceful life, a life of prayer and meditation, of stargazing. We cannot fight the wars of griffins and Vir Requis. You may stay here for seven darknesses, but then you must leave, and I can offer no more."

Agnus Dei roared so loudly, the salvana soldiers growled and blew smoke, and their eyes flared. "If you don't help us, we'll die," Agnus Dei cried. "Our race will vanish."

Nehushtan blinked and nodded. He puffed more smoke, which now looked like a Vir Requis dragon, wings spread, mouth blowing fire. "As fire may rise in smoke, so may the life of a dragon rise as a spirit; it does not vanish, but joins the winds and the rain that falls. Fear not, Vir Requis, for your spirit is strong. When its time to rise comes, it will find its way to the temples of your forefathers." He turned around. "Follow me, and I will lead you to rest, food, and meditation."

Agnus Dei panted with anger, eyes flaring, flames dancing between her teeth. The salvana soldiers eyed her, fangs bared. Kyrie trembled with rage, but forced himself to take deep breaths. He wasn't ready to give up yet. So long as they remained here at Har Zahav, there was hope.

"Come, Agnus Dei," he said to her. "Let's go with them. We might convince them yet."

The salvanae began flying toward the golden mountain. Kyrie and Agnus Dei followed. Watching how the salvanae coiled through the air with no wings, Kyrie felt clumsy as he flew. He marveled at how long, thin, and glittering these air serpents were, with their glowing horns, fluttering mustaches, and eyes like orbs of colored glass.

As they flew closer to the mountain, Kyrie saw many other salvanae flying around him. They flew in every color, from the deepest black flecked in silver, to bright reds and greens. Some tossed bolts of lighting from their maws. The light blinded Kyrie.

Nehushtan led them higher, moving toward the crest of Har Zahav. Flying so high, the mountains surrounding Har Zahav seemed small as hills, their pines mere specks. When they flew above Har Zahav's crest, Kyrie gasped. The golden mountain ended not with a peak, but with a gaping hole.

"It's a volcano," he whispered.

He saw darkness and stars inside the volcano, as if gazing into night sky. The salvanae coiled down toward the volcano's mouth, straightened their bodies, and entered the hole. They disappeared into the darkness.

Kyrie and Agnus Dei hovered over the volcano's mouth. The opening was five feet wide, suited for the slim body of a salvana. How would Vir Requis—with their bulky frame and wings—enter?

Kyrie and Agnus Dei landed on the mountain beside the opening. Winds lashed them, and snow flurried around their feet. Nehushtan and his soldiers were gone, and the only other salvanae flew far below.

"Well," Kyrie said, struggling to speak as snow flew into his mouth. "I guess it's time to reveal our human forms, if we're to fit through this hole."

The two shifted into humans. Though wind lashed him and he shivered, being human again felt good. Kyrie had flown for so long, he'd missed the feeling of ground beneath human feet. In his smaller form, the mountaintop seemed even more colossal, the winds wilder, the height more dizzying. He could barely breathe the thin air.

Kyrie looked at Agnus Dei. Again he realized how much he loved her human form. As beautiful as Har Zahav was, with its golden slopes, coiling salvanae, and snowy peaks, Kyrie thought that Agnus Dei was the most beautiful thing around. She was a mess, her clothes tattered and muddy, her skin bruised and battered, her hair a great tangle of knots. But she couldn't have been more beautiful to Kyrie, not if she wore gowns and perfumes and jewels.

"Kyrie," she said, "they're... not happy."

Kyrie tore his eyes away from her. Salvanae were flying up toward them from the mountainsides. They roared and blew lightning from their maws. "Demons!" they called. "Shape shifters invade Har Zahav."

Before Kyrie and Agnus Dei could react, the High Priest Nehushtan reemerged from the volcano, body flowing out from the narrow opening. He faced the charging salvanae, blew lightning, and called out, "Starlight be upon you! They are my wards."

The charging salvanae paused, tongues lolling, sparks rising from their nostrils. Kyrie released his breath slowly, fingers trembling.

"These are Vir Requis," the priest said, "our allies of old. They are strange things, but bring no evil into Har Zahav." He turned to Kyrie and Agnus Dei. "I offer sorrow; they do not remember the ancient songs. The Inner Realm is wide and warm. You may enter in your small forms, and regain your dragon beings inside."

Nehushtan reentered the hole, once more disappeared into darkness.

Kyrie peered into the volcano. He saw only inky darkness strewn with floating orbs of light. He turned his head back to Agnus Dei.

"Should we just jump in?" he asked.

Agnus Dei rolled her eyes. "Oh, pup, don't tell me you're afraid of the dark."

Before he could respond, she shoved him into the volcano.

Kyrie bit down on a yelp. He fell through darkness, the lights streaming around him. He glimpsed countless salvanae around him. With a groan, he shifted back into dragon form, flapped his wings, and steadied himself.

"Hey pup!" Agnus Dei said. She was falling in her human form. She shifted, then hovered beside him. "That wasn't too bad, was it?"

They gazed around. Thousands of orbs floated around them, glowing white and yellow and gold. Salvanae flowed between them, moving so fast, they appeared as glimmering streaks. This Inner Realm seemed endless, a universe. Kyrie had expected to see golden walls—the inner mountainsides—but the darkness and light seemed to spread forever.

"Where is Nehushtan?" Kyrie asked. "Do you see him?"

Agnus Dei pointed. "Down there."

Kyrie looked below. The orbs clustered there, glowing more brightly, a nexus of light. The Inner Realm seemed to Kyrie like some great flower, its glowing center casting pollen into the darkness. Many salvanae coiled among the cluster of orbs below, and Kyrie glimpsed Nehushtan's tail.

He flew down, Agnus Dei beside him. Salvanae stared from all directions, eyes spinning. Soon the Vir Requis crashed through hundreds of orbs, scattering them, and emerged into a bubble of light the size of a cathedral. The orbs resettled behind them, sealing them in this glowing chamber. Hundreds of salvanae flew here. Great rings of lightning spun upon the floor like an electrical storm. Every second, another salvana dipped toward the rings of lightning and blew upon it, feeding it sparks. As they coiled, the salvanae sang wordless songs like the sound of flutes and harps.

Nehushtan saw them and flew toward them. "Here is the Light of Har Zahav, which we guard with our spirits. Here is the heart of our land. Welcome, Kyrie Eleison and Agnus Dei, to our Inner Realm. Warm yourself by the Draco Light, pray, and rest."

He gestured toward a hollowed bowl in the stone floor, like a small crater. It lay a hundred feet from the electrical rings. A thousand other holes covered the floor, Kyrie noticed, and salvanae slept inside them.

Kyrie and Agnus Dei landed in the depression. It was a tight squeeze for their dragons forms, so they shifted into humans again, and sat side by side. The electrical rings rose to their right, warming them.

Salvanae flew down, bearing glowing bubbles, which they lay by Kyrie and Agnus Dei. Some bubbles held water, some held nuts, and others held pomegranates.

"Eat, drink, and meditate," said Nehushtan, floating above them. With a nod and blink, he turned and disappeared into the lights above.

"What a place," Kyrie said, watching the electrical rings and the coiling salvanae above. "Have you ever imagined such a thing? Agnus Dei?"

He looked at her, and saw that she wasn't listening. She was popping the bubbles and devouring the food inside. Kyrie joined her, wolfing down the nuts and fruits.

The bubbles were the size of pots, meant to feed dragons. Even in their human forms, however, Kyrie and Agnus Dei put serious dents into the meal. When they could eat no more, they lay on their backs, the hollowed stone smooth and warm. They patted their bellies and sighed. Bowl-shaped, the depression forced them to lay pressed together. Agnus Dei's body was warm against his.

"You were right, Agnus Dei," he said. "The salvanae are real. You were right all along."

But Agnus Dei was already snoring, her head against his chest, her tangle of curls tickling his face. She tossed an arm over him.

"Good night," he whispered and kissed her head. He closed his eyes, just for a moment, marveling at how her hair smelled like flowers and trees even after all the fire, pain, and blood they'd flown through. He wanted to wake her. He wanted to find Nehushtan again, to demand aid at once, to demand they flew now to save Benedictus and Lacrimosa. But sleep grabbed him too powerfully to resist. Before he knew it, he was asleep, his arms around Agnus Dei.

LACRIMOSA

Dreams whispered in the darkness.

"Lacrimosa!" her mother called, voice a whisper, a flutter. "Come hear the harpists, daughter, come hear the song."

She ran, bare feet upon fallen petals, laughter like ice drops on glass, frozen in time, frozen in memory. Her mother stood before her all in white, smiling, arms open, skin like alabaster and blond hair streaked with white, drowned in light, forever out of reach.

"Mother!" she called, but her voice floated in the air, more ice drops that hung, floated, whispered and echoed.

The harpists walked between the columns of Requiem, bleached, white robes fluttering and silent, eyes a startling blue, peering through her. The birch leaves glided among them, silver, and only their harps seemed real. She could see every leaf of gold upon them, every line and knot in the wood, and the strings cut through her vision, sharper than claw or fang. They played among the columns in their courts, but she could not hear them. Not anymore. Not here, not now.

Darkness.

Darkness and pain.

She gasped, and her fingers clawed the stone ground.

"Mother." A whisper. She tried to clutch the memory, but it fled; it was not real, nothing but a wisp. She could not enter it. She could not find it. Never again, not from this darkness, not from this silence.

"It is a world," she whispered. "We were a world entire, and we are gone. Who will remember us? Who will remember the courts of Requiem when ivy grows over our ruins, and our shattered statues turn smooth under the rain of too many springs? We will be vanished then; we will be lost. Whispers. Then silence. And darkness."

But this darkness was not silent, not hers, not anymore. A rumble sounded in the black, a distant roar of a hundred thousand voices. A crowd chanting, Lacrimosa realized. She had heard crowds in Requiem, clapping people gathered in woodland theaters to see minstrels play. This was different. This crowd roared, clamored, and called for blood. They were angry, they were thrilled, and they were hungry.

She opened her eyes, but saw only shadows. Chains bound her to the floor, and stone walls surrounded her. How long had she been in this prison cell? She had drifted in and out of sleep for days, it seemed. She was in her human form, her dress mere tatters, her head spinning and her arms weak. A bowl of water lay before her, but her arms were bound behind her. She drank like a dog. Outside the stone walls, the crowds roared and thumped feet. Trumpets blew.

A door behind her clanked, and torchlight spilled into the room, blinding her. Lacrimosa squinted and moaned.

"Come on," spoke a deep voice, a voice like death. It sounded familiar, and sent fear through her, but she could not place it. Hands grabbed her, pulled her to her feet, and dragged her to the door. Others walked around her, but she could still not see in the blinding torchlight. She thought they moved down a hall of stone, and the crowd's cheering grew. Soon they entered a towering room. The chanting roared behind bronze doors.

Hands grabbed her arms, and with a clack, somebody removed the shackles from her wrists. She gasped with pain and moved her arms, rubbing them, letting the blood flow through them.

"Turn into the beast," spoke that cold voice, a voice like cracking wood in the heart of winter. Lacrimosa blinked, her eyes adjusting to the light, and then she saw him. She knew him at once.

Molok.

Gaunt and tall, the man looked like a torture device. His armor looked like an iron maiden, spiked and black. His helmet looked like a prisoner's mask, its bars like the bars of a cell. He raised that visor now, revealing a cadaverous face and sunken eyes.

"I know you," Lacrimosa hissed. "I saw you murder five infants in Requiem. I saw you r—"

He backhanded her, knocking her down. Her cheek burned, and her knee banged against the stone floor. She gasped in pain and tears filled her eyes. She glared up at Molok between strands of her hair. He'd always been Dies Irae's foulest pet—a murderer of children, a rapist and torturer. *Someday I will kill you,* she vowed silently.

"Turn into the beast," he repeated and raised his sword. His blade was black and spiked.

"I—" she hissed, and he kicked her. His boot drove into her stomach. She gasped and new tears filled her eyes.

"Turn into the beast."

Tears on her cheeks, pain saturating her, she shifted. Scales covered her, a tail and wings grew from her, and soon she crouched in the chamber, a dragon, smoke leaving her nostrils. Molok seemed so small now, a fraction of her size, and she wanted to tear her fangs into him. But that would mean death for her. That would mean she'd never see Benedictus, Kyrie, and her daughters again.

Molok collared her, then pulled her on a chain toward the bronze doors. When the doors opened, the cheering hit Lacrimosa so heavily, her head spun. Molok dragged her into a sandy arena. Tens of thousands of people cheered around her. It was an amphitheater, Lacrimosa realized, but not like the small theaters in Requiem where her kind would gather to hear minstrels or storytellers among the trees. This was a colossus, a great ring of stone. How many of Osanna's sons and daughters howled and jeered her? There were fifty thousand at least, maybe twice as many, an army of people hating her. They pelted her with rotten vegetables and cursed her. The colors and sound swirled around her, deafening, overwhelming.

Molok attached her chain to a metal post in the center of the ring. He backed away, leaving her in the middle of the amphitheater, alone, the crowd cheering. When Lacrimosa looked up, squinting in the sunlight, she saw a gilded boxed seat high upon the stone tiers. Purple curtains draped it, and griffin statues guarded its flanks. Dies Irae sat there upon a throne of ivory and jewels, wearing samite and gemstones, a crown atop his head. He gazed down at her, face blank.

What's the point of this show? Lacrimosa wondered, glaring up at Dies Irae. *Why does he chain me here? Just so Confutatis can see me, mock me, throw their rotten vegetables at me?* She growled, smoke leaving her nostrils, incurring wild cries from the crowd. *Why does he do this?*

Dies Irae rose from his seat. He raised his arms, and the crowd fell silent. For long moments, Dies Irae passed his gaze over the crowd, as if he would stare at every man, woman, and child. The sudden silence was eerie to Lacrimosa; silence before a storm. Nobody in the crowd so much as whispered. Lacrimosa could hear distant birds chirp. Finally Dies Irae spoke.

"Behold our enemy," he called out, voice loud in the silence. "Behold the beast, the weredragon. These are the creatures that threaten your children."

The crowd hissed and glared. Dies Irae spoke louder.

"These weredragons bring evil into our city. When plagues strike, it is because the weredragons poisoned our wells. When fires burn our homes, weredragon breath kindled them."

The crowd jeered so loudly now, the amphitheater seemed to shake. Dies Irae shouted to be heard.

"When rain does not fall, and crops die, it is because weredragons moved the clouds with their wings. When earthquakes tremble, it is weredragons shaking the earth. When there is not enough bread, or fruit, or milk, it is because the weredragons stole them."

The crowed howled. Several men tried to run down the tiers, into the arena, and attack Lacrimosa. The guards held them back, but the guards' eyes too burned with hatred.

Lacrimosa understood. This city was no heaven of splendor and riches; only its palaces were, only the courts of Dies Irae. The rest of Confutatis was a hive of poverty, a simmering pool of fear and misery.

"And we're the scapegoats," Lacrimosa whispered, tears in her eyes. This was how Dies Irae raised his armies, earned their loyalty, convinced them to burn Requiem, to murder babes in the cradle.

Lacrimosa glared at Dies Irae. She called out, her voice barely heard over the crowd, but she knew Dies Irae would hear. "Is this because of your father?" she cried. "Is this because he hated you for lacking the magic of Requiem, because he chose Benedictus to be his heir? Dies Irae! You have betrayed your home, you will...."

Her voice trailed off.

Bronze doors were opening behind her, and she heard grunting.

Three beasts burst into the arena.

At first she thought they were bulls. They had shaggy bodies, bull horns, and golden rings in their noses. But these were no ordinary bulls; instead of hooves, they had clawed feet, and fangs grew from their mouths. Smoke and fire left their nostrils.

They charged toward her.

Lacrimosa's heart leaped. She tried to escape, but the chain ran from her collar to the metal post, barely fifty feet long. She blew fire toward the charging bulls, and they scattered, howling.

The crowd cheered.

One bull skirted the flames and nearly gored her. Lacrimosa lashed her tail, hit it, and knocked it ten feet back. Another bull charged toward her other side. Lacrimosa pulled back, nearly choking as the chain tugged her collar. She blew more fire, hitting the bull in the face. It howled and fell, burning.

The third bull charged. Lacrimosa moved aside as best she could, the chain restricting her movements, and the bull's horns grazed her leg. Her blood flowed.

Lacrimosa howled in pain. She kicked the bull, sending it flying. The beast crashed into two guards, knocking them down, and the crowd cheered louder than ever.

The wounded bulls struggled to their feet and surrounded her. They growled, blew smoke from their nostrils, and clawed the earth. They realized her strength now, and they began pacing around her, judging her with narrowed eyes, waiting for an opening to attack.

Lacrimosa wanted to weep. She wanted to die. She missed her husband and daughter so badly. But she could allow no despair to overcome her. She had to live for her family. She kept lashing her tail, glaring at the bulls, keeping them back. If one seemed ready to charge, she blew fire until it retreated. Still they walked in circles around her.

"I love you, Benedictus," Lacrimosa whispered when the bulls charged together. She blew fire, kicked, and screamed. Pain and flames covered her world.

GLORIAE

She walked through the dungeon, hand on Per Ignem's hilt. She wore her gilded breastplate and helmet. Her boots clanked against the stone floor, tipped with steel, and a dagger hung at her side. Gloriae wondered why she brought arms and armor here today. The beast was chained. The beast was hurt. It could not harm Gloriae, and yet she felt naked without her armor, vulnerable, only a girl, a princess with soft cheeks and golden hair.

But I am a lady of steel, she thought, gloved hand tightening around her sword's hilt. *This blade is steel, and so is my heart, and so is my resolve, and so is the punishment I deal to those who hurt me.*

Soon she reached the doorway. The guards recognized her, blanched, and slammed their fists against their hearts. Gloriae did not bother returning the salute.

"Open the door," she said. The guards glanced at one another, and Gloriae drew her sword. "Do as I say, or I'll have you flayed and hung upon the palace walls."

They obeyed. Gloriae grabbed a torch from the wall and stepped into the chamber, sword drawn. She blinked as light and shadows swirled, and then she saw the beast.

Lacrimosa lay on the floor. She was in human form today, and Gloriae's breath died. She had come here expecting a reptile, a monster. On the floor lay a beautiful woman. Lacrimosa was slender, and her hair shone like moonlight, a blond so pale it was almost white. She seemed ageless to Gloriae. Lacrimosa was not young like her; when those lavender eyes looked up, Gloriae saw the wisdom of age in them. And yet no lines marred Lacrimosa's face, and her beauty seemed eternal, the beauty of a flower coated in frost.

Gloriae took a step back, raising the torch. She wanted to hate Lacrimosa, but how could she hate a creature that took such a delicate, beautiful form? It was a spell, Gloriae told herself; an illusion to hide lurking evil.

"Hello, Gloriae," Lacrimosa said, and tears filled her eyes. She rose to her feet.

Rage flared in Gloriae, nearly blinding her. She reminded herself why she had come here. She had wanted to see the creature that had murdered her mother... and to hurt it. She walked toward Lacrimosa, sword raised, and was surprised to find tears in her own eyes. She let her anger sear them away.

"You murdered my mother," Gloriae said, voice little more than a whisper.

Lacrimosa wept. Her slender body trembled and she shook her head. "Gloriae... my beloved. Is that what they told you?" Lacrimosa reached out toward her. "Gloriae, I am your mother."

"You lie!" Gloriae screamed.

Lacrimosa shook her head, tears streaming down to wet her dress. "I gave birth to you in the courts of Requiem. You are Vir Requis, child. You're one of us. I don't know who your father is, whether he is Benedictus or Dies Irae. But I know that I gave birth to you, that I nursed you, that I raised you for three years before Dies Irae took you."

Gloriae trembled. *No... no! It can't be.* Images slammed against her. She saw herself as a toddler among marble columns, heard harps, saw light and leaves and—

"Liar!" Gloriae screamed, shaking her head so wildly, that her hair covered her eyes. She trembled. "No. No, beast. I am not one of you." She snarled. "You are cursed, you are evil and you trick and you lie and you kill. You murdered my mother. You try to enchant me now. I see those images you place in my head. I laugh at them. You think you can fool me, lizard?" She raised her sword, laughing and crying and shouting. "You will die, Lacrimosa. You will die like the vermin that you are. My father will torture you. He will break you until you pray for death. And then, when that time comes, I will be the one who kills you, who lands this sword upon you."

Lacrimosa reached out toward her, eyes entreating. "Daughter, Gloriae—"

"Do not speak my name. All your words are spells. I killed a Vir Requis child when I was only six. I killed three more when I was eight. Do you think I don't know your kind? That I don't know your evil and your magic?"

"Listen to me, please!" Sobs racked Lacrimosa's body. "They have hurt you, lied to you, but I love you. I love you, daughter. You can shift too. You can become a dragon like us. I know it, you—"

"Silence!"

"I will not be silent. You must know the truth, Gloriae. Dies Irae never taught you your magic. He is Vir Requis too, but he was born without the gift. You have it! I know you do. It's deep within you, hidden, repressed. You are scared and ashamed of it. They taught you to hate it, to hide it. But the light of Requiem glows within you. It's buried but still lives. Try it, Gloriae! Shift here in this chamber. Look into your soul, find your dragon light, and you can—"

Gloriae shoved Lacrimosa, and she fell, weeping, finally ceasing to speak. Gloriae stared down at her. Her heart thrashed, her fingers trembled, and she longed to bring Per Ignem down upon this creature. "You will not cast your curse upon me," she said, voice cold. "You will beg me for death before I grant it."

With that, Gloriae spun and left the chamber. She slammed the door behind her.

She marched down the hallway, up onto the surface of the world, and to the stables. She mounted Aquila and flew to the Palace Flammis, this jewel of marble and gold that rose upon the highest hill in the Marble City of Confutatis. After tethering Aquila, she marched across the gardens and into the palace. She marched down hallways past lords and ladies, suits of burnished armor, and scuttling servants. The people she passed saluted her, fear in their eyes. Gloriae did not need a mirror to know that her cheeks were flushed, her eyes enraged, her lips tightened into a cruel line. She carried Per Ignem drawn, prepared to slay anyone who spoke to her. None did.

She reached her chamber, stepped in, and closed the door behind her. Finally she allowed herself to close her eyes, lean against a wall, and take a deep breath.

"My lady?" came a voice, and Gloriae opened her eyes to see May, her handmaiden. The girl was her age, and had been with her since childhood. Her hair was long and auburn, her skin pale, her brown eyes soft with worry. "My lady, are you all right?"

Gloriae sheathed her sword. "Come to me, May."

Her handmaiden stepped forward, and Gloriae embraced the girl, leaned her head against her shoulder, and closed her eyes. "When will the pain leave, May?" she whispered.

May caressed her hair, untangling a knot in its curls. "Shall I draw you a bath? Bring you wine or food, my lady?"

Gloriae shook her head, opened her eyes, and looked at May. The girl smiled at her, and that smile soothed Gloriae. There was still some loyalty in the world, some goodness. "May, you've always been my friend. You always will be. No matter what. No matter what you may ever learn about me, promise that you'll remain mine."

"Of course, my lady."

Gloriae nodded. "Leave me."

May curtsied and left the chamber, dress rustling. When she was gone, Gloriae surveyed her room. This was not the room of a princess. She had no lap dogs, no dolls, no jeweled mirrors and gowns. Swords hung over Gloriae's fireplace, and daggers and crossbows lay upon her tables. Instead of bottles of perfumes, bottles of ilbane lined her shelves. Instead of gowns, suits of armor filled her room. She had dedicated her life to this war, to hunting weredragons. That was all she knew, all she'd ever lived for.

She sat on her bed, head spinning. She thought back to Lacrimosa's words. *I love you, daughter. You can shift too. You can become a dragon like us.*

Gloriae snorted. Now that she was back home, those words seemed less frightening, and more ridiculous. Lacrimosa must have been desperate. Her lies were feeble. Turn into a dragon? Her, the greatest hunter of weredragons?

Gloriae closed her eyes. "I'll prove you wrong, beast. Want me to try it?" She snorted again. "Fine." She would prove the weredragon a liar.

With a deep breath, Gloriae tried to imagine herself as a dragon. She pictured herself with scales golden like her hair, like the golden scales of Father's boots. She imagined herself with glinting claws, fangs, leathery wings. In her mind, she flapped her wings, flying over mountains and forests, tail swishing. Wind streamed around her. Cold air filled her nostrils. She roared, and fire left her maw. She could feel it, hot and wonderful, stinging her lips. The light of the Draco constellation filled her eyes, and she could hear the harps of Requiem calling, see the glint of her towers and—

Stop.

Stop it.

Gloriae snarled and tried to open her eyes, but could not. The light tugged at her. "No!" she cried.

Clouds and winds flowed across her. She could see her mother flying ahead, silvery, glinting in the sunlight. She could see her sister, a red dragon flowing on air. She could see her father, a black dragon, and—

Gloriae was weeping now. "No, no," she pleaded. She opened her eyes... and screamed.

Scales covered her arms, small and golden. Claws were growing from her fingertips. She wanted to stop it. She wanted to resist. But she also needed this, she craved it, loved it. She wanted to fly, to roar, to breathe fire. It claimed her, better than wine, better than anything. The magic flowed through her, and she both fought and welcomed it.

With a gush, wings sprouted from her back. She felt a tail beneath her, and she was huge, no longer a slim girl, but a great creature that filled her chamber. Her tail crashed against her table, knocking over the arrows, crossbows, and daggers. Her limbs were so long now, they knocked over her wardrobe. Her head hit the ceiling, no longer the head of a girl. She could see herself in a fallen, burnished breastplate. Her head was a dragon's head, golden, its eyes green as emeralds.

Gloriae froze.

She wanted to roar. She wanted to flee. But no. She must remain silent. She must alert no one. Had anyone heard her tables falling over? Would anyone burst into this room, see her like this, see the monster she'd become?

Silence, Gloriae, she told herself. *Breathe. Think. Calm yourself. Do not panic.*

She shut her eyes, forced deep breaths, and imagined herself as a girl again. She forced the image of her human form into her mind. A girl, slender but strong, of golden locks, of green eyes, of marble skin. She took deep breaths and opened her eyes.

Once more she was a girl.

"Was it all a dream?" she whispered. No. She could see claw marks on the floor, and her room was a mess. Gloriae trembled. Cold sweat drenched her, soaking the shirt under her breastplate. She had never known such terror, not in all her battles.

A thought struck her. She tugged open a drawer and grabbed a leather pouch. Inside were crumbled ilbane leaves. Fingers shaking, Gloriae reached into the pouch and touched the leaves. She yelped, dropped the pouch, and pulled back her hand. She stared at her fingers. They were red and blazed as if she'd touched open flame.

Sun God... I'm infected.

Gloriae clutched her head. She understood what had happened. Lacrimosa had given her the disease, the curse. Gloriae now carried that evil within her.

She too had become a weredragon.

Gloriae began to weep. She curled up on her bed, hugged her knees, and sobbed. She had never cried so much in her life. She was a freak now, diseased and monstrous. How would she continue? How could she face her father again? How would she ever get married, have children, raise a family? Would her children inherit this curse? She wanted to scream, to call for help, but dared not.

A knock sounded on the door. "My lady?" came May's voice. "My lady, are you well?"

"Leave me!" Gloriae cried. She rose to her feet, frantic, hair wild. *I must hide this mess,* she thought. *Nobody must know. Nobody must ever know.*

Gloriae nodded. *Yes, yes.* She would keep it secret. She would tell nobody. How would they know? If she never shifted again, they could not. It was simple.

She allowed herself a wild, weepy smile. "I can hide this."

She placed a rug over the claw marks on the floor, righted her furniture, and arranged everything as it had been. *Perfect.* Finally she spent a few moments fixing herself. She removed her sweaty clothes and brushed her hair. She pulled on leggings, a cotton shirt, a leather belt, tall boots—her clothes of battle. She owned no gowns or dresses. She had never been much of a girl, she thought, but now she wanted to be nothing more.

"May!" she called.

Her handmaiden stepped into the chamber, and Gloriae pulled her into an embrace.

"Hold me," she whispered, trembling. "Tell me it'll be all right. Please." Tears filled her eyes.

They sat on the divan, and May held her and smoothed her hair, and Gloriae slept in her arms.

She woke up to discover that night had fallen. May slept against her, her arms around her. Gloriae gazed upon the girl, her best friend since childhood, her only friend. *I won't let you down, May,* she thought. *I won't let evil fill this world. You're my friend. You're pure and good. How can I let you live in a world so dangerous, so cruel?*

Gloriae knew what to do. She had known for years perhaps, but never dared. Tonight she would dare.

Moving slowly, she wriggled out of May's embrace and placed a blanket upon the girl. Eyes narrowed, she silently put on her armor: her breastplate of steel, molded to the curve of her body, gilded and jeweled; her helmet, its visor a golden mask of her face; her greaves and vambraces, their steel bright. Finally she donned Per Ignem, lifted her shield, strapped her crossbow to her side, and left her chamber.

She found her father in his hall. He sat upon the Ivory Throne, talking to the gaunt Lord Molok. When Gloriae entered the hall and walked across it, the two men turned to face her. Molok wore no helmet today, and she could see his ashen face, sunken eyes, and slit of a mouth. Her father was frowning.

"Father," Gloriae said when she reached his throne. She slammed her fist against her breastplate.

He nodded. "Daughter."

"Take me to the Well of Night."

Dies Irae rose to his feet, his face reddened, and for a moment Gloriae thought that he would strike her. But he only stared at her, eyes harder than his fists. "No."

Gloriae took a step closer to him. She snarled. "I saw Lacrimosa, Father. I spoke to the beast. They are fully evil creatures, more than I knew. They die this night. No more ilbane. No more griffins. No more games. We release the nightshades. We wipe them out."

Dies Irae bared his teeth, and his eyes looked ready to gore her. He grabbed her arm, fingers digging into her flesh. He leaned forward and whispered through clenched teeth. "You disobeyed me, Gloriae. You do not know what you ask."

"I do, Father. I know very well. I know their power is greater than—"

"You have not seen the nightshades," Dies Irae said, grinding his teeth. His fingers sent such pain through Gloriae, that she wanted to cry out, but held her voice. "I will show you. You think weredragons are evil? You think they are strong? You haven't seen these creatures."

He began to drag her across the hall. She struggled to free herself from his grip, but could not. He dragged her through the doorway, down stairs, and along more halls. They walked for a long time. They moved down more stairwells, and down dark corridors, and finally into dungeons and tunnels.

"You've never seen the darkness that lies beneath this city," Dies Irae said, still clutching her arm, still dragging her. "I raised you in light and beauty, surrounded with gold and jewels and goodness. You haven't seen what lurks beneath this place, far from the light of the Sun God."

Gloriae gazed around, her father's digging fingers almost forgotten. She'd heard whispers of dungeons beneath Flammis Palace, but never seen them. The walls were roughly hewn, the floor raw stone, the ceiling dripping mold. It seemed that they traveled for leagues. The air was cold and clammy, the ground slippery. They plunged deeper and deeper underground, until Gloriae thought they would reach the end of the world.

Finally a tunnel lead into a chamber where a hundred soldiers stood. They wore plate armor and carried battle axes. They slammed fists against breastplates, saluting their lords.

"Soldiers, here underground?" Gloriae asked. "Father, wha—"

"They are guards, Gloriae," he said. "They guard the terror that dwells behind these doors." He gestured at towering doors set into the stone wall.

Gloriae looked at those doors and shivered. They were made of iron. Golden skulls were embedded into them, twice the size of men's skulls, soft light in their eye sockets. The skulls seemed to watch her, and Gloriae knew; the nightshades dwelled behind these doors.

She shivered. *Nightshades.* In her childhood, she would fear them, see them in shadows under her bed, dream nightmares of them.

"These creatures cannot be tamed like griffins," Dies Irae said. "They cannot be killed like weredragons. And you want to wake them?"

Gloriae stared at that door. She thought back to her secret, her shame. *I'm infested with the weredragon curse. I have the evil within me. I must make this land pure. For May. For all the other innocents. I cannot let anyone else catch their disease.*

"I want to see them."

Dies Irae nodded to the guards, and several grabbed chains that hung from the doors. They began to pull, and the doors creaked open, inch by inch. Lights flickered in the eye sockets of the doors' skulls.

Cold wind blew from beyond, sneaking under Gloriae's armor, and she shivered. She saw only blackness. When the doors were open, Dies Irae dragged her through the doorway, into the cold and darkness.

She found herself in a chamber lined with torches. It was a great chamber, round and large as the amphitheater where Lacrimosa fought. It looked like a cave, its walls and floor rough, its ceiling hidden in shadows. In the center, Gloriae saw the well. She had always imagined a normal well, maybe three feet wide. This well was a hundred feet wide—more a pool than a well, Gloriae thought—and not built of bricks, but carved of solid stone. Mist hovered over it.

"Step up to the well, child," Dies Irae said, finally releasing her. "Gaze into the abyss."

Suddenly Gloriae was fearful. Suddenly she wanted to flee back to her chambers, back to May. But she would not show her father any weakness. He had beaten this strength into her as a blacksmith beats strength into steel. She was a maiden of steel. She would face this. Whatever lay in the abyss, she would stare it down.

She walked forward, knelt over the well, and gazed into the darkness.

At first she saw nothing but black smoke, inky and swirling. She wanted to laugh. Had she been so frightened of nothing but this—smoke and shadows? She was about to turn away, but could not. The darkness seemed... endless, of a size unimaginable to her. Gloriae clutched the well's rim, fingers pushing against the stone. She thought that she gazed into the night sky. Was she gazing below into the earth, or above into the stars? This abyss had the same depth, endless, leading into realms unknown and light that did not shine. This was the opposite of light. Not darkness, no. Darkness was merely the lack of light. This... this was its antithesis, and it was greater, deeper, tugging at her soul.

"What evil is this?" she whispered. It seemed to pull her soul downward, out of her body, so that her consciousness ballooned and filled the well like spreading ink. All her life, she had seen the world from the confines of her skull. Such a small enclosure. Now she knew that the world was larger, infinitely so, not only of three dimensions, but of endless layers and eternal time. The enormity made her grimace, fall to her knees, and cry.

Then she saw them.

They coiled in the darkness—maybe yards away, maybe millions of leagues away. They were long, murky black, not made of solid matter, but of darkness and smoke and lightning. Their eyes shone like stars, their teeth dripped smoke, and they stared at her, and spoke to her, and filled her mind and body, and *enough, enough, please— Please, Father, enough! I cannot bear them. I cannot stand them inside me, cannot stand the size, the darkness, the dimensions, I want to leap into the abyss, I want to become one of them, to expand and fill the universe, and... God... Sun God, please, if you have power here, save me, I—*

Hands clutched her. Someone pulled her back.

"Where... where am I?" she mumbled. She was lying on a rough stone floor. She gazed up and saw a man there, a man with a face like a griffin, his nose hooked like a beak, his skin golden, his hair slicked back. Who was he? He'd been her father once, a thousand lifetimes ago, but what did that mean?

"Do you understand, Gloriae? Do you understand why we must never release them?"

Gloriae blinked. "I... the world is so large, Father. It is larger than this place, I... we can fill it. We can see it!" Tears streamed down her cheeks. "It's horrible, please, save me, make it stop, make them stop pulling me." She curled up and wept.

Dies Irae pulled her to her feet. He slapped her face. The pain shot through her, and suddenly she felt herself... sucked up, pulled back, drawn inside her body. Her soul slammed into her skull, and she wobbled. It felt like smoke retreating back into a jar.

"I..." She blinked, looked around, and saw that they no longer stood in the chamber of the nightshades. They were back in the room with the guards. She had not even noticed herself returning to this place.

"Come, daughter, we return to the air and light and music of the world."

She followed him in a daze, climbing endless stairs, and neither spoke. It was not until she stood in the gardens of the palace, breathing the sweet night air, watching lords and ladies travel paths between cypresses, that Gloriae shook her head and blew out her breath. She had returned to herself; the nightshades were gone from her mind.

"They cannot be tamed," Dies Irae said, and Gloriae started, for she hadn't realized that he still stood by her. "And you cannot release them. Only the one who sits upon Osanna's throne can open the Well of Night, and I will not. I will not release the terror that lurks there. One day you will sit upon the Ivory Throne, daughter. You will have the power to guard or release these creatures. When that day comes, remember this night. Remember what you saw there. Remember to keep it forever sealed."

Gloriae nodded. "The abyss will remain sealed, today and always."

Dies Irae nodded. He left her there in the garden. She spent a long time walking its paths, gazing up at the stars, lost in thought.

BENEDICTUS

Benedictus trudged toward the gates of Confutatis, cloak wrapped around him, two daggers at his belt.

Other travelers covered the roads around him. Benedictus saw pilgrims in robes and sandals; Sun God priests in samite riding white horses; merchants in purple silk riding in carriages; shaggy peddlers riding mules, leading wagons of wares; thin peasants and farmers, their tunics muddy and patched; and many armored soldiers, their shields emblazoned with griffin heads.

Benedictus scowled under his hood. He remembered days years ago, before Dies Irae, when he'd visit Confutatis with his father to meet its wise king. Few soldiers had marched these roads then, and the farmers were not bedraggled, but healthy and bearing wheelbarrows of crops. Monks had worn homespun robes and worshiped the benevolent Earth God, not this vengeful Sun God who cloaked his priests in gold and jewels. Now the priests were wealthy, the soldiers many, the peasants hungry, the Vir Requis dead. *Sad days,* Benedictus thought, staring at his boots so as not to gaze upon these processions of might and vicious piety. *Cruel days.*

The sound of hooves came behind him, and Benedictus turned to see a knight on horseback leading twenty marching soldiers. The knight wore plate armor and bore a banner with a red, two-headed griffin upon a yellow field. The peasants on the road leaped into the muddy gutters and knelt. Benedictus stepped to the roadside and kept walking, refusing to cower in the mud.

"You there!" came a voice. "Peasant."

Benedictus stared from inside his hood. The knight reined his courser and stared down upon him. "Into the gutter with you," he said.

Benedictus forced his growl down. He bowed his head. "The road is wide, and you have room to pass. I don't disturb you."

The soldiers clinked in their armor, reaching for their swords. The knight raised an gauntleted fist. "I said into the gutter. I want you kneeling in the mud as I ride by."

This time Benedictus did growl. He wanted to shift. He wanted to turn into a dragon and kill these men. He recognized this knight's banner. A two-headed griffin upon a yellow field—this was the banner of House Crudelis, a banner of foul memories. Ten years ago, Benedictus had flown to aid a burning village in Requiem. When he'd arrived, all the villagers were already dead, their bodies tortured and raped. The griffins and soldiers of Osanna had come, destroyed, and left. Only the banner of Crudelis remained, flapping over a pile of dead Vir Requis children.

"Ride by, Crudelis," Benedictus said from the roadside. He reached into his cloak and grabbed a dagger's hilt. "Ride by and let me be. I don't want trouble."

The soldiers stood at attention, but sneaked glances at one another. Crudelis stared down, silent for a long moment. Then he dismounted, walked toward Benedictus, and reached for his sword.

Benedictus thrust his dagger into the knight's visor, deep into his head, spurting blood.

As the knight fell, the soldiers charged. Benedictus ran into the forest. He dared not shift. If they knew a Vir Requis was here, garrisons would storm this forest. Benedictus ran, his old wounds aching, his fists pumping. The soldiers clanked behind him in their armor.

Benedictus grunted. He might just escape them. He was thirty years older than these soldiers, but their armor slowed them. Just as he began to feel safe, something whizzed by his ear. A quarrel hit a tree ahead. More quarrels flew.

"Great," Benedictus muttered as he ran. "They have crossbows."

One quarrel scratched his shoulder, tearing his cloak and drawing blood. Two more hit a tree before him. Benedictus ran from tree to tree, cursing. He saw a declivity ahead, leaped down, and fell. He rolled over roots and rocks, hit a fallen bole at the bottom, and pushed himself up with a grunt. The soldiers stood above, firing down. One quarrel scratched Benedictus's leg. He ran behind more trees, kicking up mud.

"Damn," he muttered. He was too old for this. His lungs ached. He kept running until he reached a cliff, thirty feet tall and covered with vines.

Benedictus spun around, his back to the cliff, and faced the soldiers. Boulders and brambles rose at his sides. He was trapped.

As the soldiers approached, Benedictus raised his hands.

One of the soldiers had a red griffin inlaid into his helmet. With Crudelis dead, this one seemed to have taken command. He grinned at Benedictus, a wolf's grin.

"Are you surrendering, old man?" the soldier said with a sneer. "You do not surrender to us. We are soldiers of Dies Irae. We take no prisoners." His grin widened and he stepped toward Benedictus.

"I'll have to kill all of you," Benedictus said. "I can't let any escape to call for help. If you do this, you will all die."

The soldiers laughed. Their leader raised his sword.

Benedictus shifted.

He did as he'd promised. A few tried to flee, calling for help. Benedictus crashed through the trees toward them, claws outstretched, and tore them down. They were too far from the road; if anyone heard their cries, they wouldn't know where to look. It only took a few moments. It was like stomping on bugs.

Benedictus shifted back into his human form. The soldiers lay dead around him, armor broken, blood feeding the earth.

As he walked back through the forest, seeking the road, Benedictus lowered his head. He hated killing. What he'd just done lay sour in his belly like rotten meat. He knew these men were no innocents; their leader had murdered many Vir Requis, and even the younger soldiers, those who'd not fought in the war, had been brainwashed into malice, tools of death for Dies Irae. Still Benedictus hated the blood on his hands.

"I will never forgive you for this, brother," he whispered. "I will never forgive you for forcing me to kill, for turning me into this. You have called me a monster. You have made me one."

Soon he found the road, and he kept walking. By evening he stood before the white walls of Confutatis. Lacrimosa and Gloriae waited for him there... and Dies Irae.

AGNUS DEI

"But you must help us!" Agnus Dei demanded, eyes teary. "Please."

Her claws dug into the cave floor, a floor made of gold and diamonds. The cave walls were golden too, and gems sparkled in them, reflecting the fire in Agnus Dei's nostrils. On any other day, Agnus Dei would find this vast, glittering chamber inside Har Zahav a place of beauty and wonder. Today she cared little for beauty; she was ready to blow fire, lash her tail, and topple the golden mountain.

"Won't you help us?" she asked again, smoke leaving her nostrils.

The council of salvanae hovered before her and Kyrie, undulating. Sparks of electricity danced between their teeth. The high priest, Nehushtan, hovered at the head of the council. Six other salvanae, their mustaches long and white, hovered behind him. All their eyes—those large, round eyes like glass orbs—stared at the two Vir Requis.

"Agnus Dei," Kyrie whispered from the side of his mouth, "maybe it's a lost cause. They're peaceful creatures. I'm not sure they can help us fight." He too stood in dragon form, claws upon the golden floor.

Angus Dei looked back at Nehushtan. "Please," she said. "They'll kill my parents. They've killed so many Vir Requis already. Fly with us! Bring your warriors. Their fangs are sharp. Their lightning is hot. Fight with us. Fight Dies Irae."

Nehushtan regarded her silently for long moments. He puffed rings of smoke from his mouth, then spoke in his creaky voice. His words were slow and calm. "We of the land of Salvandos, of the holy Har Zahav mountain, do not concern ourselves with the ways of humans, or of griffinflesh. We are salvanae, the true dragons of ancient times. We concern ourselves only with dragonkind. The way of the dragon is our way, and it is a good way. A way of peace. Of meditation. Of reflection and prayer."

"But we're dragons too," Agnus Dei said, eyes stinging. She bucked and clawed the air. Her tail lashed, hit a wall, and knocked down a shower of gems. The priests winced.

"Agnus D—" Kyrie began, but she ignored him.

"Look at these wings!" Agnus Dei said. "Look at these fangs." She blew fire against the cave ceiling, blackening its gold and incurring more winces. "Look at these flames. These are dragon flames. I am a dragon maiden. And my way is the way of honor. Of helping friends. Of fighting for life and goodness." Tears rolled down her cheeks. "We are dragons too, so fly with us. Shoot your lightning with our fire."

Nehushtan raised his tufted white eyebrows. "But you have human forms. How could you be dragons? We have seen you walking upon two legs."

As Agnus Dei fumed, Kyrie touched her shoulder and answered for her. "The smoke rings you blow also change form. They sometimes looks like dragons, sometimes like men, sometimes like, well... nothing at all. But it's always the same substance. Same with us Vir Requis."

Nehushtan blinked, blew smoke rings, and watched them take the shape of coiling dragons. He thought for a long time, moving his eyes from Agnus Dei to Kyrie. The other priests did the same. Finally Nehushtan spoke again.

"You have spoken well, Kyrie Eleison of Requiem, so I will offer you this. Beyond Har Zahav, and the mists of Arafel Canyons, rise the Stone Rings. There do young dragons prove their worth. There you too must fly. If you survive the Stone Rings, you'll have proven yourselves worthy dragons, that your blood and soul shine under the Draco stars. We will then fly with you."

"And if we fail?" Agnus Dei asked.

Nehushtan blinked sadly. "If you fail... you will die."

Agnus Dei growled. "Let's go."

The salvanae took flight, bodies snaking into a tunnel. Agnus Dei followed, growling. Kyrie flew behind her. The tunnel was just wide enough for their dragon forms, and it led them past gems, subterranean waterfalls, caverns of golden stalactites and stalagmites, and finally out a cave onto the mountainside. They flew into the cold air, following the salvanae. Soon the mountain of Har Zahav was far behind, a golden triangle, and then it was only a glint in the distance.

Clouds streamed around Agnus Dei, cold against her face, filling her mouth and nostrils and eyes. She blew fire and roared. Whatever these salvanae had in store, she would face it. She would overcome.

"For you, Mother," she whispered, and her eyes stung with tears. "For you, Father. I love you so much."

She sniffed, shook her head to clear her tears, and glanced at Kyrie. *I hope he didn't see me cry. He is a pup, and I am a creature of fire, and he must never see my weakness.* If he saw, however, Kyrie had the grace—and good sense—to pretend he hadn't.

"Pup," she said, "what do you reckon these salvanae have planned for us?"

Kyrie looked at her, fangs bared. He looked ready to fight an army. The salvanae flew far ahead, too far to hear.

"A test of courage," he said. "A test of strength. A rite of passage for salvana warriors. Whatever this challenge is, we're going to beat it. I'm a good flier. You're not bad, either."

She bristled and blew flames. "I can beat you at any challenge they give, pup. But this time we're not competing against each other. We're going to prove that we Vir Requis have just as much strength, speed, and spirit as they do."

She tried not to think of Mother in captivity, or of Father flying into battle. Today she would think only of proving her worth, of flying to save them.

They flew for hours, following the salvanae who snaked ahead. They flew over canyons of stone, and over forests of pines, and over grassy fields and rushing rivers. Finally they reached a land of towering stone columns, each column a league high, carved into the shape of great faces. Eyes the size of palaces glared at them, and mouths larger than cathedrals gaped in silent screams. The columns—and the faces carved into them—seemed ancient. They were smooth and mossy. It seemed that centuries of rain and wind had pummeled them into weary, grotesque figures. The salvanae flew between the columns, seeming as small as dragonflies around men.

"What is this place?" Agnus Dei asked Kyrie. "Those faces are strange."

Kyrie nodded. "Feels like they're staring at you." He flew before one face's eye. It was larger than him. They couldn't even see the ground; the columns disappeared into darkness leagues below.

The salvanae led them toward an empty space of mist and shadows. Though it had been day only minutes before, night cloaked this place. Agnus Dei saw stars above, and three purple moons. They were strange stars, and strange moons, things of a different sky, too close, too large, and Agnus Dei had to look away. She felt like that sky could swallow her.

"Look!" Kyrie said. Agnus Dei followed his stare and gasped. Ahead in darkness, distant but growing larger as they flew, hovered three stone rings. No columns held them; they floated on air. One ring was large, a dozen feet wide; the next was half the size, and the third half again. When Agnus Dei flew closer, she saw that blades filled the rings, rusty and bloodied.

"What are those?" she asked and hissed. Smoke rose between her teeth.

"I don't know," Kyrie said, "but look below them."

Agnus Dei looked and growled. Jagged rock and metal rose below the floating rings, and upon them lay the skeletons of a hundred salvanae. Some bones were ancient, bleached white like dragon teeth. Others were newer and bloodstained. Some bones looked fresh; bits of skin and scales covered them, rotting in the mist.

"What is this place?" Agnus Dei demanded of the salvanae. They hovered ahead, bodies coiling beneath them, eyes blinking at her. "Answer me! What graveyard have you brought us to?"

Nehushtan regarded her. After a long silence, he spoke. "This is our gauntlet. This is the blood of dragons. Here we prove our worth, and here you will prove you are true dragons, worthy of the name, worthy of your wings. If you are demons cloaked in dragon flesh, you will die here. If your forms are true, and if Draco starlight shines upon you, you will survive. We will fight with you then."

Agnus Dei roared and lashed her tail. "What do we do?"

Nehushtan gazed at the bloody blades that filled the stone rings. "Fly through the stone rings, from largest to smallest. The blades inside the rings are poisoned; a scrape is lethal. If you fly too clumsily, the blades will kill you. The blades will lengthen as you fly, blooming like steel flowers. If you fly slowly, they will kill you. Fly straight. Fly fast. Or you will die."

Agnus Dei and Kyrie stared at the stone rings. Those rusty, bloody blades seemed to stare back. Fly through the rings? *It's impossible*, Agnus Dei thought. *Impossible!* The first hoop was twelve feet wide. That was large enough for a slim, serpentine salvana to clear. They had no wings, no limbs, and a body lithe and long. But how would she, a Vir Requis with long wings and limbs, fly through this ring of death? And even if she cleared the first ring, the second was only six feet wide, and the third—only three.

"Impossible," Agnus Dei said. "These hoops were built to test slim salvanae, not bulky Vir Requis. Give us another test."

Nehushtan shook his head. "This is the gauntlet of the dragon. If you cannot pass this test, you are weak, or you are demons in dragon form. A soul of Draco stars, worthy of our help, will fly through the Stone Rings. Fly now! Or leave our land and return to Osanna."

Agnus Dei stared at Nehushtan, the smoke from her maw obscuring her vision. Rage flared inside her. She wanted to fly at the priest and rip him to shreds. But she needed him. She needed his warriors. Agnus Dei closed her eyes, took deep breaths, and thought about her mother.

Mother has always loved me, she thought. *Even when I yelled, or rebelled, or hated her—she loved me. She raised me, protected me, kept me alive as Dies Irae hunted us across the world.* And now Lacrimosa was captured, maybe dead, maybe tortured. Father had gone to save her, but even the great Benedictus, the Black Fang, could not fight the might of Dies Irae and his hosts. *Only I can save them,* Agnus Dei knew.

She opened her eyes. "You're on," she said to Nehushtan. She flapped her wings.

"Wait!"

Kyrie grabbed her tail, holding her back. Agnus Dei howled and snapped her teeth at him, new fire filling her. "Let go, pup."

"No!" he said, eyes pained. "Agnus Dei, you'll die. Please. This is not the way."

She shook her head wildly, struggling to free herself. "If we cannot pass this gauntlet, we'll all die. You, me, Mother, Father, the memory of Requiem, the blood of Vir Requis. This is the only way, Kyrie. I can do this." She stopped struggling, flew toward him, and nuzzled his cheek. "I can do this," she whispered into his ear. "I love you, Kyrie. Believe in me."

His grip on her tail loosened. Agnus Dei flew toward the stone rings.

BENEDICTUS

Benedictus stood outside the city gates. People crowded around him—beggars in rags, peddlers riding wagons of trinkets, peasants leading oxen laden with grains and vegetables, merchants in fur coats, and pilgrims bearing coins for Sun God temples. Guards stood at the gates, golden griffins embroidered onto their red tunics, their armor burnished and their swords at their sides. They were searching everyone for weapons, collecting the gate tolls, and letting people into Confutatis one by one.

Benedictus grumbled, bent his head, and tugged his hood lower. Few people would recognize him in his human form—most knew him only as the black dragon—but he'd take no chances. He reached into his pocket and felt his coins—enough to bribe the guards should they become suspicious. He then felt at his side, where his dagger hung. The guards would confiscate this dagger if they let him in. If they caused trouble, he might bury it in their throats. Under his cloak, his fist clutched the hilt.

The people shuffled closer to the gates. Benedictus could hear the guards now. "Right, what's that then? No staffs. Give me that, old man. Nothing that can be used as a weapon. What's this here? I'll take that knife. Hand it over. All right, that's good copper; two coins a head. In you go. You there, two coppers toll, no blades, no arrows, no sticks or stones. Two coppers, you're good."

Benedictus scowled under his hood. Once he would fly into this city bearing banners, dine with the king in palaces, hear music in gardens between statues of angels. So much had changed. This city. Himself. The world. Benedictus ached for his daughters. *My daughters will never know the world I did as a youth, a world of peace and beauty.* To his daughters, it was this: a world of violence, hatred, and fear.

He shuffled closer in the crowd, one hand clutching his coins, the other his dagger. When he was ten people away, a chill ran through him. The guards held leaves, which they pressed against the chests of all who passed.

Benedictus growled.

Ilbane.

Benedictus wanted to turn away, to push back through the crowd, to find another gate. But he dared not. Too many people had seen him. To flee after seeing the ilbane would look suspicious. A few whispers in the crowd, and the guards would chase him. No. He'd enter these gates.

Ilbane burned hotter than fire, Benedictus knew. He could still feel that fire, all these years after Lanburg Fields where ilbane-coated arrows had pierced him. If the ilbane touched him, he would sweat, grunt, even scream. No Vir Requis could withstand its torture and remain composed; not even him, the great Benedictus the Black, the King of Requiem.

"Move along, come on, maggots. Move, damn you!" Two old peasants, possibly a husband and wife, were shuffling into the city. The guards had seized their canes, and they moved on shaky legs.

The guards growled, and one shouted. "Move it, peasants. We haven't got all day." Two guards shoved the old couple. They laughed as the peasants fell onto the cobblestones.

Grunting, Benedictus shoved his way through the last people in line. He tried to go help the peasants who lay on the ground beyond the gates.

"Hold there!" shouted a guard, and rough hands grabbed Benedictus's shoulders. He turned his head, scowling, to see two guards clutching him. Their faces were unshaven and their eyes red.

"I'm going to help them," Benedictus said in a low, dangerous growl.

The guards laughed, showing rotting teeth. Their breath stank. "No you're not, worm," one said. "Toll's two coppers. Pay up and open that cloak of yours. No weapons. No sticks or stones. And no lip."

One guard held ilbane a foot away from Benedictus. Even at this distance, Benedictus felt the heat and pain of those leaves. Sweat beaded on his brow.

"All right," he said, speaking slowly and carefully. He wanted nothing more than to kill these men, but then the entire city guard would fall upon him. Then he would let down Lacrimosa. *Control your temper,* he told himself. *Be careful.*

He grabbed three silver coins from his pockets. It was more than these guards would earn in a month. His teeth clenched, Benedictus slammed the three silvers against a guard's chest.   "Your birthday present is early this year," he said in a low voice. "Now let me through, no questions asked, and you'll get another gift when I leave tonight."

The guard stared at the coins, and his eyes widened. He bit one and raised an eyebrow. "Who are you, peasant?" he asked, voice low.

"A private man," Benedictus said. "Now let me through."

Without waiting for a reply, he took a step toward the gate. He took a second step. A third. He forced himself to move slowly, to breathe calmly.

A hand clutched his shoulder.

"All right, stranger, no questions," spoke the guard who'd taken the coins. "You like your privacy, and you can pay for it. But we must do one thing."

The guard shoved the ilbane against Benedictus's chest.

AGNUS DEI

Agnus Dei shot toward the first stone ring, eyes narrowed. She could still hear Nehushtan's voice echoing in her mind: *The blades will lengthen as you fly, blooming like steel flowers. If you fly slow, they will kill you. Fly straight. Fly fast. Or you will die.* Agnus Dei snarled, pulled her limbs and wings close, and became a long, thin shape.

The ring's blades creaked.

Agnus Dei shot forward.

The bloody blades began to extend.

Agnus Dei screamed, shooting into the hoop. A blade scratched one of her scales, and Agnus Dei howled, but she was safe; it had not touched her blood, had not infested her with poison.

"I made it!" she cried.

"Quick, the other ring!" Kyrie shouted.

The blades in the second, smaller ring were also extending; the opening was barely four feet wide now. Agnus Dei snarled and shot forward, knowing it was too narrow for her dragon body. The ring was close now, inches away. Agnus Dei screamed as she shifted. In midair, she became human and somersaulted through the hoop. A rusty blade sliced a strand of her hair. She was through! She shifted back into a dragon and howled.

"The third ring, hurry!" Kyrie cried, and Agnus Dei grunted and flew. *No, impossible!* The third ring was so small, three feet wide, and its blades were extending inward. There were barely two feet between the blades now.

"Hurry!"

Agnus Dei sucked in her breath, flew, and shifted again. She was human, tumbling through the air. Instead of somersaulting through this hoop, she dived. She held out her arms, and pulled her legs together, and held her breath.

She shot through the last hoop, the blades shredding her clothes.

She fell through air.

"I'm through!" she cried, falling toward the skeletons below. Before she could hit them, she shifted into a dragon again, and shot into the sky with a roar and shower of flame. "I'm through!"

The salvanae began bugling, heads tossed back. Agnus Dei panted, hovering in midair. The blades in the rings pulled back into the stone, leaving just their rusty tips. *I made it. I'm going to save you, Mother.* Tears stung her eyes.

Kyrie roared and flew toward the stone rings. He too flew through the first, wide ring in dragon form. He then shifted in midair and tumbled through the second, smaller ring in human form. He shifted into dragon shape, flapped his wings, shifted again. He dived through the last, smallest ring. The blades ripped his cloak, tore off his left boot, and sliced strands of his hair.

Once through the third ring, he became a dragon again and flew beside Agnus Dei, panting. The salvanae cried to the sky, their roars shaking the world. Three pillars cracked and tumbled into the darkness.

"We did it!" Agnus Dei roared to the salvanae. "We passed your test. We proved our dragon worth. Now fly with us. Tonight! Fly with us to war."

The salvanae blew lightning into the skies. They looked at one another, at Agnus Dei and Kyrie, at one another again. They spoke rapidly, some shouting, some whispering, some spitting lightning.

"Well?" Agnus Dei said and roared. "Stay true to your word! Fly with us. Or are you cowards and liars?"

The dragons roared, and blew more lightning, and spoke louder. Finally Nehushtan shouted above them, and the others silenced. The High Priest turned toward Agnus Dei. His eyes were narrowed, and smoke left his nostrils. He coiled through the sky, flying toward her, and stared into her eyes. Angus Dei saw lightning in those eyes.

"Tonight," he said, "the salvanae fly to war."

As the salvanae flew, and the Vir Requis followed, Agnus Dei tightened her lips and shivered. Confutatis lay many days away. She was bringing help... and she prayed that she wasn't too late.

"Hang in there, Mother," she whispered. "I'll be there soon."

BENEDICTUS

Pain like shattered glass filled him.

The guard held the ilbane against his chest, and Benedictus wanted to die. The fire spread across his ribs, into his heart, down his spine, and scorched his fingertips. He had not felt such agony since Lanburg Fields.

"How does it feel, old man?" the guard asked, eyes narrowed.

With every last drop of will, Benedictus forced himself to remain silent, to keep his face calm. He even tried to will sweat from appearing on his brow.

"Fine," he whispered. He could speak no louder. He wanted to fall to his knees. He wanted to kill the guard. He wanted anything but to remain standing, casual, the ilbane against him. *Take it off!* he wanted to scream. *I've stood my ground. Remove the leaves!*

But the guard held them against Benedictus. "Are you sure?" he asked, frowning. "You look pale. And there's sweat on your brow."

Benedictus growled, though he wanted to scream in pain. *The fire!* The fire filled him. It was too much, too much. *This must be how women feel at childbirth,* he thought, almost blind with pain. Stars and mist flooded his vision.

"It's been a long journey," he somehow managed to say, mustering all his will to stop his voice from cracking. "If I were a bloody weredragon, this stuff would kill me, not just bring sweat to my brow."

The guard's frown deepened. *Take it off, take it off!* Benedictus did not think he could last a second longer. He was just about to shift into a dragon, to kill every guard he saw, to storm the city, when....

"All right," the guard said and pulled the ilbane back. "Sorry to trouble you, and I know you pay well. In you go."

Benedictus turned around quickly, and once the guard was behind him, he grimaced. His knees trembled, but he forced himself to keep walking. Once in the city, he knelt by the fallen old man and woman, who were still struggling to rise from the cobblestones. He knelt not only to help them; he could no longer stand upright.

"Here," he said to the old peasants when he'd caught his breath, "let me help you up."

He took several more deep breaths, assisted the peasants to their feet, and walked deeper into Confutatis, leaving the gates behind.

"I'm almost there, Lacrimosa," he whispered. "Almost there to save you, my love." He clenched his fists. "And I'll find you too, Gloriae. I'll find you, daughter, and I'll free you too from Dies Irae."

He moved through the city, cloak pulled tight around him, hood low. His old wound ached with new fire, his joints burned, and his head pounded. The ilbane had taken so much of his strength. Benedictus could barely walk. If soldiers attacked him now, he would not fight well. He grunted, leaned against a wall, and clutched his chest.

Some hero, he thought as he stood, catching his breath. *Look at the great king now. Just a gruff old man sneaking through alleys, grunting in pain.*

As he took ragged breaths, Benedictus noticed people rushing down the cobbled streets. Kids were jostling one another as they ran, smashing dragon dolls with wooden swords. Adults were placing bets and talking about "the beast" fighting new creatures today, "something truly deadly; lions I hear, or elephants in armor." Most of those hurrying down the street were commoners, but Benedictus also saw two wealthy merchants in a carriage, and even a noblewoman on a palanquin.

The beast.

Benedictus steadied himself and kept walking. He stumbled down the cobbled road among the commoners, nobles, and horses. Crenellations and towers rose at his sides, laden with guards sporting the golden griffin upon their shields. Real griffins stood atop towers and walls, armored, staring down at the crowd.

At every square he passed, Benedictus saw a marble statue of Dies Irae. The statues all stared toward the heavens, one fist against the heart, the other around a sword hilt. In the statues, Dies Irae still had both his hands. But Benedictus remembered biting off the left one, spitting it out, then taking pity on his brother. *I left you alive, Irae. If I meet you again, you will find that my mercy has left me.*

Benedictus did not want to meet his brother. He wanted only to find Lacrimosa and Gloriae, to steal them back, to flee with them into the west. He'd had enough of fighting, of killing, of his monstrous brother. And yet, another part of him did want to meet Dies Irae here. Craved it. That part felt like a shark in bloodlust, wanting only to bite, to kill. Benedictus hated that part of him, and hated Dies Irae for placing it within him.

The streets of Confutatis widened as he walked, clutching his chest. The crowds thickened, some chanting "Blood for the beast!" Fortresses towered here, and griffins circled in the skies. Soldiers stood at every street corner, and monoliths of Dies Irae gazed down from hills, jeweled eyes watching the crowds. Troops patrolled between the commoners, armor chinking.

The Marble City—once a place of gardens, of peace, of poets and artists. Now a city of sword and shield, of beak and talon.

Soon he beheld the amphitheater of Confutatis, a ring of white marble. Its walls rose two hundred feet, set with alcoves that held statues. Years ago, solemn stone statues of kings had filled these alcoves; today he saw figures of Dies Irae holding the Sun Disk. A golden idol stood outside the amphitheater's gates, a hundred feet tall, hands raised. It was carved as a young Dies Irae, cherubic, a halo encircling his brow.

"The beast is hungry today, I hear," said a bearded man beside Benedictus, speaking to his friends. "Whatever Dies Irae has in store for her today, it ain't gonna be enough. I bet a bronze coin on her."

One of his friends snickered. "That beast ain't nothing but a tired old lizard. Irae's been feeding her dust, I hear, and whipping her. The creature's too thin and weak to win another fight. I'll take your bronze."

The first man laughed. "Torture makes that one hungry and mean. Who else? Bronze on the weredragon!"

Weredragon.

Inside his hood, Benedictus growled. That was a cruel word, a slur that should never be uttered, least of all by scraggly men who bet on misery and blood. He stepped toward them.

"A fool bets against a proud, dying race," he said, voice low. "And a greater fool stages fights for fools' bets."

The men laughed. "What are you, a poet or something?" the first man said, scratching his beard. Fleas filled it.

"You know me," Benedictus rasped. "You know my name. Your lord wants me forgotten, but it will not be so. You will hear our roar again."

With that he left them, stepping toward the amphitheater's gates. *Foolish thing to say,* he knew. Why did he risk his cover for these men? He forced himself to focus, to forget these cruel crowds, to remember his task. *I will save you, Lacrimosa,* he thought. *Soon you'll be flying west with me to find our children.* Kyrie too was his child now, by adoption if not by blood. All the last Vir Requis were his children, his torch to keep aflame.

And I have not forgotten you, Gloriae. In the deepest corners of his heart, Benedictus knew that Gloriae was evil now, corrupted and cruel. She might be unreachable to him, a maiden of steel in her palace, but Benedictus dared to dream, dared to pray that he could save her.

He paid to enter the amphitheater, stepped inside, and found himself dizzy. Tens of thousands of people surrounded him, cheering from a hundred tiers of marble seats. Slave girls danced in the arena, chains binding their necks, raising sand under their feet. They were nude, their bodies painted red and gold. Benedictus knew that their heavy makeup hid bruises, and one's nose was bandaged. Guards watched the dancers from the sidelines, clutching whips.

Benedictus imagined those whips cutting Lacrimosa, and he clenched his fists and ground his teeth. Below the lowest tier of seats, Benedictus saw doorways and stairwells leading underground. *Which leads to Lacrimosa?* Benedictus wanted to bash down every door, storm down every passageway, and save his wife. He forced himself to wait. There were many doorways here, and many guards, and he would not find her. If he charged brazenly, like Kyrie might, he'd only get himself killed, and probably earn torture for Lacrimosa.

"Patience," he told himself. "You're not a rash, hot-headed youth like Kyrie or Agnus Dei. You can wait. Bide your time. Learn where she is."

Nobody noticed him talking to himself. The crowds were too busy cheering, stamping their feet, and leering at the dancers. Benedictus found his seat on the thirtieth row and sat on the cold stone. A father with two children sat to his left. To his right sat two young maidens, henna on their eyelids and perfume on their fair skin. Both wore white silk that revealed more flesh than it hid.

Families with children, Benedictus thought in disgust. *Young women on a day out. The blood of Requiem is sport for them.*

The dancers finished their dance, bowed to the crowd, and disappeared into an underground passageway. Silence fell upon the crowd, and everyone leaned forward, waiting for the beast to emerge. Only Benedictus did not stare at the arena. He scanned the crowds until he found the man he sought.

Dies Irae.

His brother sat across the amphitheater, a palanquin of samite shading him. Two griffin statues guarded his sides, and a slave girl lay collared at his feet. Dies Irae wore his white, jeweled armor. Sun God warriors stood at his sides, his elite guard, their helmets shaped as sunbursts, their swords shaped as sunbeams.

"Hello, brother," Benedictus whispered. "It's been a long time."

Three hundred feet away, Dies Irae raised his eyes and stared at Benedictus.

Ice shot through Benedictus. He froze, unable to look away. How could it be? How could Dies Irae have heard him? Benedictus was about to run, but then Dies Irae looked away. Heart racing, Benedictus took a deep breath. *He couldn't have seen me. My face is hidden in my hood. It was only chance.*

His heart was still thrashing when Sun God priests stepped onto the arena, saluted Dies Irae, and began to sing a hymn. The crowd rose to their feet. Benedictus did not want to rise, but forced himself to. The priests were clad in white, and white masks hid their faces. They sang for the Sun God to bless Dies Irae, the favored child of the heavens, and to grant death to his enemies.

"Child of the heavens," Benedictus grumbled. "He's calling himself the son of gods now."

When the song ended, the priests pulled forward a child in silk, her face also masked. The priests cried for the glory of the Sun God, and before Benedictus realized what would happen, they had set the girl on fire.

"No!" Benedictus cried, jumping to his feet. Nobody heard him. The crowd was cheering for the Sun God, crying out for his glory and blessings. The girl was still alive; she thrashed and screamed, a ball of fire, before falling dead to the ground.

The priests extinguished the flames with sand, then raised the small, smoldering body over their heads. They sang, calling for the Sun God to accept this offering, to grant them triumph, and to curse the weredragons who tainted the world. The crowd cheered.

The burned girl twitched and moaned.

She's alive! Benedictus wanted to retch. The small figure, blistered and smoldering, was whimpering. The priests placed her down and stabbed her dead.

Benedictus sat down, shaken. He'd seen much cruelty during the war against Dies Irae years ago. He'd seen people burn to death. He'd seen Dies Irae murder children. But this... this was different. The war had ended. Dies Irae had won his glory, his throne. Why this killing? Why still the torture and murder of innocents? Benedictus had always known his brother was evil, but for the first time, he realized how truly insane the man was.

The entire city seemed just as insane, Benedictus thought. Dies Irae and his god had turned these people into... what? Monsters? Demons? Benedictus had no name for it. In their eyes, he was the monster. Benedictus was no scholar. He could not explain this. He only knew he had to end it.

I can't just take Lacrimosa and Gloriae and flee, he realized. *I have to stop my brother. Not only for the memory of Requiem, but for the fate of the world.*

Before he could wonder how, gates opened below, and guards dragged out a chained, beaten Lacrimosa.

LACRIMOSA

Lacrimosa limped when the guards pulled her chains. They had sent strange creatures to fight her yesterday—furry beasts wielding hammers—and she had killed them, but not before one hammered her leg. What would Dies Irae unleash against her today? Creatures of horn, or talons, or fangs? More slaves with swords, or bears in spiked armor? How long before one of these creatures killed her, ending her pain?

As the crowds cheered around her, and the sunlight blinded her, Lacrimosa lowered her head. Today she would not fight. Whatever beasts attacked her, she would let them. She would endure their horns, claws, or fangs, let them tear her apart and end her misery.

"I'm sorry, Ben," she whispered, tears in her eyes. "I'm sorry I wasn't strong enough, that I couldn't hold on. I love you. Find our children. Fly away from here. My time is ended, and I will soon join the spirits of Requiem, and see those halls among the birches once more." She smiled through her tears. The spirits of her forefathers awaited her, and she would drink wine in their halls.

When she'd reached the arena's center, the guards attached her leash to a post. They left her there. The crowds jeered and pelted her with rotten fruit.

A trapdoor on the floor opened. Three red tigers emerged, blew flames from their maws, and raced toward her.

Lacrimosa lowered her head. "Goodbye, Ben," she whispered, waiting for the tigers. "Goodbye."

And then she heard a voice.

"Lacrimosa."

She opened her eyes.

"My love."

The tigers reached her, and Lacrimosa lashed her tail, sending them flying. She looked around wildly. Who had spoken? She could see nobody. The voice had not come from the crowds; it seemed to have spoken within her. A tiger leaped at her. She clawed it, kicked it aside, and lashed her horns against another tiger.

"Lacrimosa, of moonlit hair and eyes of stars. Lacrimosa, daughter of Requiem. You do not die today."

Light broke through the clouds, falling upon her, and she felt Benedictus with her. She couldn't see him, but she knew he was near. She knew these were the whispers of his soul, his ancient magic, flowing through her.

The tigers leaped and bit, but they could not hurt her today. Today the light of her ancestors, and love of her king, filled her with more strength than Dies Irae could conquer. She slew these tigers of fire upon the sand, and roared to the city of Confutatis, and flapped her wings, and watched them cower.

"For Benedictus, and for Requiem," she whispered, tears on her cheeks. "Let this city see our pride one last day."

The guards dragged her back into her cell underground, and chained her to the wall, and slammed the door shut, but even in the darkness Lacrimosa could see that light, feel that warmth.

"Benedictus is here," she whispered.

BENEDICTUS

Benedictus walked through the shadows. It was a starless night, a black night of the soul, and he held his breath as he padded across the cobblestones. The amphitheater was deserted now. Only three soldiers had guarded it; he had knocked them out with barely a sound. The arena now held nothing but silence, sand, and him—King Benedictus.

Once he had led armies in war. Once he had led men, women, and children to die under his banners. Once, years ago, he'd have stormed this place with fang and fire and fury, would have brought the might of Requiem upon its walls and shattered them. Tonight he lurked, a shadow, alone in darkness and pain.

He'd seen where they kept her. He crept to that old, iron trapdoor in the arena's floor. He tugged at it. It was locked, but Benedictus had taken the keys from those guards he sent to sleep. He tried the keys now, one by one, until one fit. The lock clicked, and Benedictus opened the trapdoor.

Cold air blew from below. At first Benedictus saw only darkness, but soon he discerned soft light, like a glint from silver scales.

"Lacrimosa," he whispered.

Before he could enter the dungeon, a caw sounded behind Benedictus. He spun around, eyes narrowed. A shadow darted, then vanished. Benedictus stared, heart racing, but saw nothing. *An owl,* he decided. Nothing more. He turned back to the door.

"Lacrimosa," he whispered again.

For a moment there was only silence. Then he heard a voice from below, a voice soft and pure as moonlight. "Ben?"

Tears filled his eyes. He shivered and could barely breathe. "Hang on, my love. I'm coming down, I—"

Something creaked behind him.

Benedictus spun around, and then he saw him.

Upon the seats of the amphitheater, high above and watching him, stood Volucris, the King of Griffins. Dies Irae sat upon the beast, clad in armor.

"Hello, brother," Dies Irae called down. "Hello, Benedictus, King of Weredragons, Lord of Lizards. Welcome to my home."

With a growl, Benedictus shifted.

Volucris swooped.

A black dragon blowing fire, Benedictus leaped toward the griffin.

His joints still ached from the ilbane. His heart was still heavy. But tonight Benedictus ignored the pain. With a howl, he slammed against Volucris, crashing with a ball of fire, his roars shaking the world. Volucris shrieked, clawed, and bit. They broke apart. They leaped again.

"Tonight you're mine, brother!" Dies Irae called from atop Volucris, aiming a lance. "Did you truly think that I didn't see you earlier today?"

Benedictus roared and snapped his teeth. Volucris pulled back. Benedictus's teeth clanged against Dies Irae's shield.

"I saw you, brother," Dies Irae laughed. "I saw you today, and I have seen you for years in my mind. I saw you whenever I crushed a bug under my foot, or cut the head off a serpent that crawled through dust."

Volucris bit, Benedictus pulled back, and the beak scratched him. Benedictus howled, raised his claws, and blew fire. Volucris soared and prepared to swoop. Benedictus shot up, crashed into the griffin, and sent it tumbling.

Dies Irae spurred Volucris and flew high. Benedictus followed. The amphitheater was soon distant below, and Volucris swooped toward Benedictus. He met the griffin head on, crashing into him with biting teeth and scratching claws. Feathers and scales flew. Blood rained. They pulled apart, roared, and crashed again. Fire crackled.

"You've slowed down, brother!" Dies Irae howled, laughing, mad. Volucris burned but still fought. Dies Irae's cape caught fire, but still the madman cackled. "You have slowed, you have aged, and now I will kill you. Tonight you die."

They were high above the city now. The marble streets and forts of Confutatis seemed like toys below, small fires burning among them. Benedictus swiped his claws, but his brother was right. He was slow now. His torn wing screamed. Volucris pulled back, dodging the blow, and scratched. More scales fell, and blood seeped down Benedictus's leg.

He shouted with fire and pain. "Return the Griffin Heart, brother. Return the amulet that you stole. These beasts are not yours to tame. This throne is not yours to—"

Dies Irae pulled a crossbow from his saddle and shot. The quarrel hit Benedictus in the shoulder.

Pain flowed through him, the pain of ilbane, not old leaves like the guards had used, but the pure juice of the plant. It coated the dart, spreading fire through him. Benedictus howled. The city spun below. The statues and temples and streets all blurred. More griffins lurked there, but Benedictus could barely see them. Tears filled his eyes.

With all his will, he flapped his wings and lunged at his brother. "It ends tonight, Irae. Tonight you—"

Dies Irae fired his crossbow again. A quarrel hit Benedictus's chest. He howled, blood in his eyes, blood in his mouth.

"Oh dear, brother," Dies Irae said. He raised his visor, and through squinting eyes, Benedictus saw that he was smiling. "Oh dear indeed. All these years you've hidden, Benedictus. All these years you've dreamed of revenge. Only to fail like this... an old man, tired, Lacrimosa now my slave and—"

"You will not say her name!" Benedictus said. He did not know how he still flew. He'd never taken so much ilbane, had never felt such agony, but Lacrimosa's name on Dies Irae's tongue tore him with more anguish than the poison.

Somehow, impossibly, he flew against his brother. He bit and he clawed.

Dies Irae shot a third time.

The quarrel hit Benedictus's neck.

He tried to scream. He tried to blow fire. He tried to bite, to claw, to kill his brother. But he could not even flap his wings. He could not even breathe.

I'm sorry, Lacrimosa, he thought, tears falling, before darkness spread across his eyes. *I'm so sorry.*

Benedictus the Black, King of Requiem, closed his eyes and fell from the sky.

DIES IRAE

Dies Irae stood, arms crossed, and watched his brother wake up.

Of course, his arms were not crossed, not really. You could not cross your arms if you had only one. That groggy, bloody man below him—no, not a man, a *creature*—had bitten off his left arm. Now he had but an iron mace, a freak thing, a deformity. It was a deadly deformity, to be sure, and one that he enjoyed flaunting, intimidating with, killing with... but a deformity nonetheless.

"You crippled me, Benedictus," he said softly, so softly the sound did not carry past his griffin-head visor. "You made me what I am."

Knocked into human form, Benedictus groaned on the cobblestones. Blood covered him, and his eyes blinked feebly, struggling to stay open. Red lines stretched across his chest, lines of infection from the ilbane. Dies Irae spat at him.

"You turned me into this. Yes, Benedictus. You and our father. You drove me into shame, into pain and rage. I am a year your senior. I was to be Requiem's heir, even without the dragon curse. But you stole my place. You sweet-talked Father into casting me aside. You forced me to become this man, Benedictus. To kill Father, to raze Requiem. You have suffered for it, brother. Today I end your suffering."

Benedictus struggled to rise, but chains held him down. Dies Irae wanted to spit on him again, but his mouth had gone dry. It only curled bitterly. "Today I show you final mercy. I will not torture you, Benedictus. I have tortured you for many years, but you're still my brother. Despite all you've done, all your sins, you're still my brother. I will kill you painlessly. I give you that last gift."

Finally Benedictus managed to focus his gaze and speak. "I go to the halls of my ancestors, of the spirits of Requiem. When you die—and all men must die, Dies Irae, even those who style themselves deities—may the Sun God burn your soul in eternal fire."

Dies Irae kicked him in the stomach, and Benedictus doubled over. Dies Irae kicked him again in the back, driving his steel-tipped boot into him. "You die tonight, weredragon."

He kicked Benedictus a third time, then turned and marched across the courtyard. His boots sloshed through Benedictus's blood, which had fallen from the sky. *Fitting,* he thought. His boots were made of a weredragon child; let them now walk upon the blood of the Weredragon King.

Walls and towers rose around him, the fortifications of Confutatis. Griffins manned their battlements. Soldiers stood at attention and saluted as he walked by. Dies Irae ignored them. He walked past his hosts, past the courtyards and forts, until he reached Volucris. The griffin was feeding upon the bones of a prisoner, blood staining his beak.

"Come, Volucris", Dies Irae said. He placed a hand upon the griffin's head. Volucris cawed, and Dies Irae mounted him. His body ached from the fight—bruises were probably spreading under his armor—but he ignored the pain. "To the palace."

They flew over the forts and streets, and Dies Irae watched his palace from above. He gazed upon his statues that stood, shadows in the night, with two arms. He gazed upon his menagerie of caged tigers, elephants, and other beasts. He gazed upon his banners flapping from a dozen towers. It was a palace of splendor, of endless lavishness and power. But it wasn't enough. Nothing would be enough until he killed Benedictus, killed him a million times, profaned his memory. Fire filled Dies Irae, for he realized that even in death, Benedictus would taunt him, realized that even the destruction of the last Vir Requis could not calm the shame, the rage.

"Damn you, brother," he whispered.

The anger pulsed through him, hot and red like blood. He clenched his fist and watched it shake. When his griffin landed, Dies Irae marched through the halls of his palace, lips tight. He passed a maid, a girl no older than his daughter, and grabbed her arm so painfully, tears filled her eyes.

"My— my lord—" she began to mumble, and he slapped her.

"Silence."

He dragged her up one of his towers, slammed the door behind him, and shoved her prostrate onto a divan. He took her there, his palm covering her mouth to stifle her screams. When he was done, he removed his palm, and found that she no longer breathed. That only enraged him further. He tossed her body out the window.

"How?" he asked himself, staring out that window into the night sky. "How do I kill him?"

In the amphitheater? No. That was a place for games, not for this, not for such a victory. In his palace gardens? No; he'd never get the stench out. In a dark alley, in a fortress, upon the city walls? *No, no, no.* Dies Irae slammed his mace against a table, shattering it. Benedictus deserved a special place to die, a place more ghastly, more humiliating than—

Dies Irae froze.

Of course.

He burst out of the room and marched down the hallway, scowling, ignoring the terrified servants who saluted him.

"Of course," he muttered between clenched teeth.

Within an hour, Dies Irae had mustered ten thousand griffin riders. He would bring an army to see this. He flew at their lead under grumbling black clouds, his bannermen flying behind him. Volucris held Lacrimosa in his left talons, Benedictus in his right. The two were in human form, wrapped in chains that would crush them should they shift. Their mouths were gagged, their backs lashed, their spirits broken.

"Tonight, I do what I should have done years ago," Dies Irae spoke into the wind, though he knew none could hear. A smile spread across his face.

He hadn't woken Gloriae to see this; she still slept in her chambers. *Why?* Dies Irae wondered. He'd spent years raising her to hate, to hurt, to hunt weredragons. Why on this night should he leave her to her dreams? Was it because Lacrimosa was her mother, and no child should witness the death of her mother? Was it because he feared for her, even with Benedictus and Lacrimosa gagged—feared that they'd hurt her, or tell her the truth of her parentage?

No, Dies Irae decided. It was not those things. It was because of something he saw in Gloriae's eyes of late. A fear and rage that burned above... what? Compassion? No. It was more like *recognition.* It had begun when they captured Lacrimosa, that strange glow in Gloriae's eyes.

Could it be that Gloriae had the curse too? Could she also shift? She had never done so before, at least not within his sight.

But the possibility had begun to gnaw on Dies Irae. So he had left her in the palace. He would keep her away from these weredragons, away from their curses and magic.

Clouds still hid the stars, grumbling. Dies Irae flew over hills and farms, leaving Confutatis behind. When he looked over his shoulder, he could see his army there, thousands of riders upon thousands of griffins, their torches blazing, their armor and swords glittering. Smoke rose from their torches, trails of black and red like rivers of blood. Dies Irae snarled a grin. He wanted to see Vir Requis blood again, smell it, taste it. He spurred Volucris, and the griffin flew faster, and the wind whipped Dies Irae's face. His grin grew, his lips peeling back from his teeth.

It began to rain when he saw the place ahead. Darkness cloaked the land, a sea of tar, but Dies Irae knew this was the place. He could feel it, smell it on the wind.

"We're here," he said to Volucris, pulled the reins, and the griffin began to descend in circles. The ten thousand griffins behind him followed, wings thudding. Soon they were close enough to the ground that their torches lit the place, and Dies Irae snarled again and laughed. The torchlight flickered against bones, some the bones of men, others of women and children. The skeletons of five thousand weredragons littered the place, half-buried in dirt, a graveyard of victory and blood. There were no bones of dragons, of course; in death, these creatures returned to their human forms, fragile.

When they were several feet above the ground, Volucris tossed down Benedictus and Lacrimosa. They hit the earth with grunts and rolled, still chained. Volucris landed beside the skeletons of two weredragons—a mother huddling over her child. Dies Irae dismounted and inhaled deeply. It still smelled like fire, old blood, and metal.

They had reached Lanburg Fields.

Dies Irae walked toward Benedictus and Lacrimosa, this couple of "eternal love" that sickened him. His boots scattered bones. Dies Irae wondered if the bones came from the same Vir Requis child whose scales made his boots. The thought tickled him. When he reached Benedictus, he stood staring down upon him. The man was filthy. Wretched. His hair was unkempt, his face scruffy, his skin like old leather. His clothes were torn and muddy.

"Look at yourself," Dies Irae said, disgusted. His own raiment glinted, a masterpiece of white steel, gold, and jewels. This was how a king looked, he knew; not like that maggot at his feet. "You are disgusting."

Benedictus stared up between strands of black hair streaked with gray. Hatred burned in his stare. The man said nothing.

"Good," Dies Irae said. "Hate me. I've hated you for a long time, Benedictus. When you sat by Father, and I wandered the forests in shame, I hated you. When you married Lacrimosa, and I was left alone, I hated you. I do not hate you now, brother. I pity you. But I will still kill you. I will cut off your arm, the way you cut off mine, and then I will cut off your head."

Benedictus tried to say something, but he was gagged, and his voice was but a moan. Dies Irae kicked him in the chest. Benedictus coughed and moaned, and Lacrimosa screamed behind her gag.

"What is it, Benedictus?" Dies Irae asked. He ripped off his brother's gag. "There is nothing more for you to say. Look around you, brother. Look at the bones that lie strewn like a playground for ghosts. Do you know this place, Benedictus? Do you remember all those you led to die here? Women. Children. You led them here to their deaths. You chose not to flee with them. You chose to bring them here to me, to die at my sword, and the talons of my griffins, and the heels of my boots. You kept your wife safe, Benedictus, and you kept your daughter in hiding. And you led the rest to die upon the fields. You are a coward. You are a hypocrite. You fled me that day; you yourself dared not die with the women and children you killed. Today I kill you for those sins. Today it ends, here at the place where you lost your soul to blood and cowardice."

Benedictus stared up, saying nothing. Tears streamed down his cheeks. Dies Irae spun around and cried out to his men. "Gather here! Gather to see the great Lord of Lizards die."

The griffins shrieked, and their riders gathered around. They covered the land and circled above. The Griffin Heart was hot under Dies Irae's armor, nearly burning his chest. The amulet of his father.

Dies Irae raised his mace over Benedictus's head—this arm of steel where once a true arm had lived. "You die now with the weapon you gave me."

Benedictus mouthed something, but it was impossible to hear over the roar of fire and griffins.

Dies Irae laughed. "What is that? You wish to speak last words? I cannot hear your croaks. Speak loudly. I will give you these last words, for you are my brother."

Benedictus spat and spoke again, and this time Dies Irae heard his voice, and the words made him frown.

"Fight me."

Dies Irae raised his mace higher. "Fight you? Why should I fight you, brother? Why should I not bash in your skull now and be done with?"

Benedictus's lips were dry, his face bruised, his chin bloody. "We should have fought to the death ten years ago. That's how it should have ended. Let us end this now. Fight me, great and courageous Lord of Light. To the death."

Dies Irae laughed. "As it should have been? A fight to the death? Ten years ago, Benedictus, you faced my army alone. We had slain all the women and children you brought to fight your war. You faced an army of men, and you fled."

Benedictus growled. "I showed you mercy. I left you to live. I will not repeat that mistake again."

Dies Irae shook his head and sighed. "Very well, brother. You want to turn back time, to return ten years ago? I will grant you that. You will fight to death. But you will fight not only me, brother." He swept the mace head around, displaying his army. "You will fight all of us... like you fought ten years ago. We turn back time tonight."

BENEDICTUS

"Requiem... may our wings forever find your sky."

As Dies Irae's men unlocked his shackles, Benedictus closed his eyes and whispered the Old Words. His voice was hoarse, his throat aching, and his limbs burned as he stretched them. When they had bound him, they had beaten him, covered his body with bruises. Yet through the pain, he remembered. He could still speak those ancient words, the prayer of his people. He struggled to his feet with eyes closed, the courts of Requiem resplendent in his mind.

He heard Dies Irae laughing scornfully; as a child, no doubt Dies Irae had hated the Old Words, those words every child in Requiem must speak in mornings. Dies Irae had never had the magic, never had wings; for him Requiem's sky had been unreachable.

"Are you ready, brother? Are you ready to die here?" Dies Irae's voice was icy with hatred and fiery with rage.

Behind closed eyes, Benedictus gazed upon those courts of Requiem, the marble columns that rose from the forest floor, the birch trees that grew beyond them, the rustling leaves. He could see autumn leaves skittering across the tiles of their forest courts, could see Father's throne of twisted oak roots, could see his friends, his family, his love Lacrimosa wearing silks and jewels, could see them ruling wisely under skies of blue and gold and white. *Let me die with this memory,* he thought. *I go now to to the halls of my ancestors, to drink from their wine in our courts among the stars. I now take my greatest flight.*

He opened his eyes. Around him spread the ruin of his people, the ribs rising like the teeth of dragons, the bashed skulls like so many rocks. But bones, ash, and blood could not make him forget the beauty of those old courts.

He stared at Dies Irae. His older brother. The shadow that would lurk beyond those courts, hiding and hating in its forests, planning revenge. Dies Irae was no longer a shadow; he was now a Lord of Light, a beacon of cruelty and fire to the world. Usurper of Osanna, destroyer of Requiem. Strangely,

Benedictus no longer hated his brother. Neither did he fear him. As he looked upon Dies Irae, this glittering deity of steel and gold, he felt only sadness.

"We made you into this," he said quietly. "We created you. We scorned you. We turned you into this monster."

Dies Irae mounted his griffin. "Shift, brother. Turn into the dragon. Show us who the true monster is. You will die in the lizard's form."

Benedictus looked at Lacrimosa. She lay on the ground, still chained, blood trickling down her lip. The rain soaked her hair and tattered dress, and she gazed up at him with tragic, haunted eyes.

Benedictus looked back to Dies Irae. "She fights with me."

Dies Irae barked a laugh. "Are you trying to redeem yourself on this last night? Ten years ago, you would not let her fight. You hid her then, while letting the other females of your kind perish. Very well; she too will die here at my griffin's talons. Men, free the lizard whore."

When they unchained her, Benedictus helped her to her feet, and held her, and kissed her brow, and told her of his love.

"I love you, Ben," she whispered back, eyes teary, the rain streaming through her hair, hair like molten moonlight. Her eyes were the most beautiful he'd ever seen. He kissed her lips, and remembered kissing her in Requiem so long ago.

Dies Irae scoffed from atop his griffin. "You love the whore, do you?" he said.

Benedictus turned toward him, his rage finding him. He clenched his fists. "You will not call her that."

Dies Irae laughed. "But it's true, brother. That's what she is. Do you know that I broke her in for you? Yes, Benedictus. Eighteen years ago, before she married you. I took her in the forests, I placed Agnus Dei and Gloriae within her womb, I—"

"You will speak no such lies!" Benedictus shouted. He took a step toward Dies Irae, raising his fists.

Dies Irae only laughed again. "I speak the truth, brother. I raped your wife. Though to be honest, I think the whore enjoyed it. Yes, Benedictus. Agnus Dei and Gloriae are my daughters, not yours. If you do not believe me, look in the whore's eyes, and you'll see the truth."

Benedictus's head spun. His fingers trembled and his heart thrashed. He turned to look at Lacrimosa, and saw tears in her eyes. Her body trembled.

It was true.

He wanted to howl. To kill. To destroy.

Instead, Benedictus embraced his wife.

"You should have told me," he whispered, tears filling his own eyes.

She shook her head and hugged him. "I could not."

"I love you, Lacrimosa, now and forever. We go now to our courts in the sky. We will be together there. Goodbye, daughter of Requiem."

He released her gently, then turned around, shifted into a dragon, and leaped at Dies Irae.

LACRIMOSA

Tears in her eyes, Lacrimosa shifted too. Dies Irae had beaten her, tortured her, unleashed unspeakable horrors against her. *He made me strong.*

She had learned to fight in his arena, learned to kill. Tonight, upon this field of death, under this rain of fire, she would kill again before they took her down. She saw Benedictus roaring beside her, blowing flame. He slammed into Dies Irae's griffin, and more griffins mobbed him.

Lacrimosa shouted and flew skyward.

Hundreds of griffins attacked. She lashed her tail, blew fire, snapped her teeth, and clawed them. Blows rained upon her. Talons scratched her. Beaks stabbed her.

"Requiem!" she cried, weeping, and blew fire. The griffins' fur blazed around her, lighting the night, lighting the thousands of Vir Requis skeletons.

She could no longer see Benedictus. She could no longer see the skeletons below. She saw only griffins, and light that rolled over them, drowning them, not light of fire but the good light of death, the light of her courts in the heavens. Starlight.

I am flying to them, she thought, *to the Requiem beyond the stars.* She whispered last words.

"Requiem! May our wings forever find your sky. I love you, Benedictus. I love you, Gloriae. I love you, Agnus Dei and Kyrie. Goodbye."

And from the west, they answered her voice.

"Mother!" came the voice of Agnus Dei, choked with tears. "Mother, I'm here!"

Lacrimosa smiled in the light of death, the pain that was numbing. Agnus Dei had died too; she was waiting for her in the stars.

"Lacrimosa!" cried Kyrie, and Lacrimosa wept that they had died so young.

Agnus Dei's howl filled her ears. A figure of red scales and flames shot before her, rending the mists of death, crashing into griffins. "Mother, fly!"

Lacrimosa could not believe her eyes. Agnus Dei flew before her. Not a ghostly daughter of starlight, but a living, howling dragon, blowing flame, biting and clawing. Kyrie flew there too, and all around them flew serpents of lightning.

"Agnus Dei!" Lacrimosa cried, weeping, and bit a griffin that was clawing her daughter. "Agnus Dei, you're alive!"

Agnus Dei blew fire at three griffins and lashed her tail at a fourth. "No time for teary reunions now, Mother. Fight!"

Lacrimosa fought, head spinning. She could barely believe her eyes. Thousands of wingless, limbless dragons flew around her. Salvanae! True dragons from Salvandos! Agnus Dei and Kyrie had found them. The creatures howled, swarming around the griffins, biting and setting them aflame.

A griffin flew toward Lacrimosa. She blew fire at it, then clawed its neck. Its rider tumbled to the distant ground, screaming.

"Ben!" Lacrimosa called. She saw him half a league away, battling Dies Irae in the sky, fires lighting them. The other griffins were battling the salvanae. Every second, a griffin or salvana fell dead from the sky to slam against Vir Requis skeletons.

A shriek tore the air, and a large griffin flew toward her, ablaze. Its rider burned too, but still wielded a lance, driving it toward her.

Lacrimosa recognized the man's armor at once, armor like an iron maiden, the helmet like a prisoner's mask.

Lord Molok.

Lacrimosa narrowed her eyes, snarled, and flew toward him.

She screamed, ducked, and cried as his lance scratched her shoulder. She clawed his griffin, drawing blood. They flew in opposite directions, turned, and charged again.

Lacrimosa snarled. She remembered that night ten years ago, when she had seen Molok murder a dozen Vir Requis children. She remembered him beating her in Confutatis, laughing at her pain.

"For all those you tortured, murdered, and raped, I kill you now," she said, smoke rising from her nostrils.

He drove his lance again. Lacrimosa dived low, but still his lance hit her shoulder. She cried, tumbled, and struggled to keep flapping her wings. Molok cackled above her, blazing.

He pointed his lance and swooped. Lacrimosa blew fire, but nothing could stop him. She saw death driving toward her with steel and flame.

A flash of red scales.

Agnus Dei slammed into the fireball that was Molok and his griffin. They tumbled aside, Agnus Dei screaming and clawing. Molok swung his sword and sliced Agnus Dei's leg. She cried.

Rage claimed Lacrimosa, rage as she'd never felt. *No. You will not hurt her.* She screamed hoarsely, so loud that men and griffins turned to stare. Lacrimosa flapped her wings, dazed and pained, burning with fury. She flew toward Molok and drove her claws into his griffin's belly. Guts spilled like bloody serpents.

Molok's griffin tumbled, but Lacrimosa was not done. No. She would not let the ground kill Molok; he was hers. As the griffin fell, Lacrimosa bit, tearing Molok off the saddle. He struggled in her jaws, burning, and Lacrimosa bit into his armor, bending it, pushing it into his flesh. He screamed, and she tasted his blood, and she kept grinding her teeth until he struggled no more.

She spat out his body. It tumbled to the ground and thudded against his dead griffin.

Lacrimosa stared down at Molok's corpse, eyes dry and burning.

"Nobody," she said, "hurts my daughter."

Agnus Dei flew toward her, and the two shared a quick embrace. There was no time for words, no time for tears. The battle still raged around them. The salvanae were terrible to behold. They streamed like rivers, roaring, tearing into griffins with their teeth. They shot thunderbolts from their mouths, setting griffins afire. The griffins fought with equal vigor, biting serpents in half, clawing out their innards. Half the griffins now rose in flame, but still they fought; the fire only seemed to enrage them. Everywhere she looked, Lacrimosa saw griffins, roaring serpents, blood, swords, arrows, and lances. The clouds themselves seemed alight, grumbling and raining ash. Thunder boomed and lightning rent the sky. Bodies kept falling.

"Where is Father?" Agnus Dei shouted over the din, and Lacrimosa winced. *Father.* It could mean Benedictus or Dies Irae. In either case, the answer was the same.

"There," she shouted and pointed.

They looked to the east. Over a hill, griffins and salvanae surrounding them, the brothers battled. Dies Irae fought atop Volucris, driving his lance forward. Benedictus howled, the firelight shimmering on his scales. His wings churned the smoke that rose all around.

"The Great King fights again!" Kyrie said, voice awed, flying toward them. Wounds covered him, but still his eyes flashed. A tear flowed down his cheek. "King Benedictus is sounding his roar."

Lacrimosa wanted to fly to her husband. Griffins and salvanae surrounded her, and when she tried to fly forward, beaks and talons attacked. They held her back, held her from Benedictus. As Lacrimosa fought, she watched the duel, anguish gnawing her.

BENEDICTUS

War.

War rolled over the world with fire and wings.

No Vir Requis marched today under his banners. No armies mustered to his call. They lay below him now, skeletons ten years dry, fresh blood raining upon them. As fires blazed, smoke billowed, and salvanae and griffins fought, Benedictus saw but one thing.

Dies Irae.

"You should have killed me ten years ago," Dies Irae shouted over the roar of battle. His voice was maniacal, emerging like an echo from his griffin-head helm. "Your serpents cannot save you now."

Benedictus narrowed his eyes. His torn wing ached; he could barely flap it. Wounds covered him, and ilbane stiffened his joints. He didn't care. Tonight his pain ended, with death or with vengeance. Tonight all this pain—of wounds, of genocide, of haunting memory—would burn in fire. Tonight he came full circle, defeated his demons or died trying. Tonight was a blood night.

Volucris flew toward him. Dies Irae leaned forward in the saddle, aiming his lance. Benedictus charged, blowing fire, refusing to back down. The lance drove toward him. Benedictus roared.

The lance grazed his shoulder, and he shouted. His claws swung and hit Dies Irae in the chest.

Benedictus kept shooting forward, howled, and turned to face Dies Irae again. His brother had been knocked back, but pulled himself back into the saddle. Scratches ran along his breastplate, peeling back the gold and jewels to show steel.

War.

With claws and metal.

Dies Irae charged again, lance red in the firelight. Benedictus too charged, flapping that aching, torn wing. He blew fire, and Volucris caught flame, and the lance drove forward. Pain filled Benedictus's good wing. The lance pierced it, then pulled back, widening the wound. Blood fell and Benedictus roared.

"Look at you!" Dies Irae screamed and cackled. "The great Benedictus. After all these years, to die like this!"

Volucris swooped. The lance hit Benedictus's shoulder, tossing him into a spin. He tried to flap his wings, but barely could. He couldn't right himself. Talons scratched him, and a beak bit his wounded shoulder, and the lance struck again.

Benedictus howled in rage and pain.

Then, in the darkness rolling over him, he saw the Griffin Heart.

In the battle, the amulet had emerged from Dies Irae's armor. It hung around his neck on a golden chain, glowing and humming, binding the griffins to its power.

The amulet of their father.

"You stole that from Requiem," Benedictus said, finally managing to steady his tumble. Though pain filled them, he flapped his wings, flying up toward Dies Irae. He felt weak, weaker than he'd ever been, but kept flying. "I take it back from you today."

Dies Irae swooped on his griffin, lance glinting.

Benedictus was slow and wounded, but he was fast enough. He swerved, and as Volucris flew by him, he swung his claw. He hit Volucris in the head.

The griffin screamed, bloodied, and flapped his wings madly. The wings hit Benedictus, blinding him, but he no longer needed to see. He bit and clawed, digging into griffin flesh. Volucris thrashed above him, and Benedictus clutched the griffin, refusing to release him. He bit again, tearing into Volucris's chest. Blood covered him, and he drove his head up, goring the griffin with his horns.

Dies Irae screamed.

Benedictus tossed Volucris off him. The griffin and Dies Irae tumbled to the ground.

Suddenly Benedictus could see the battle again. Thousands of griffins and salvanae howled around him, staring at him and the fallen Dies Irae. Thousands more lay dead or dying upon the ground. The skeletons of the war ten years ago were red with fresh blood and fire. Below, Dies Irae still lived. He pushed himself off Volucris.

Benedictus landed before his brother and blew fire. Dies
Irae ran through the flames, swinging his mace. The mace
slammed into Benedictus's leg, so hard it nearly broke his bone.
Benedictus kicked his brother, knocked him down, and placed a
foot upon him. Dies Irae struggled, but could not free himself.

The battle froze around them.

Everyone watched silently: salvanae, griffins, men, Vir
Requis. The only sounds now were the moans of the dying, the
wind and rain, and the fire.

"So we end up here," Benedictus said to his brother, "the
same as we were. This is how you lay ten years ago. On your
back in this field. Me with my claws against you."

Dies Irae's visor had been knocked back, revealing his
face. Blood trickled from his lip, and ash covered his skin. He
spat out a tooth, then laughed with blood in his mouth. "You're
a coward."

Benedictus growled. "And you're a dead man."

Dies Irae shook his head. "No, Benedictus. You will not
crush me to death. I know you. I unchained you; I let you fight
me to the death. You want to kill me? Do it as a man, not a
lizard. Shift, Benedictus. Face me as a man, or forever be
known as a coward."

Growling, Benedictus kicked Dies Irae aside, then shifted
into human form.

"Swords!" Dies Irae cried. Two soldiers leaped off their
griffins and ran forward. They gave one sword to Dies Irae, the
other to Benedictus.

Benedictus drew the blade. It was heavy, well balanced,
with a grip wrapped in leather. A good sword.

Dies Irae drew his own blade and swiped it, testing it. It
whistled.

"Father!" came an anguished cry above. Benedictus
looked up, and his heart leaped. Agnus Dei! Agnus Dei flew
there! And Kyrie flew by her.

"Agn—" he began, but then she screamed. Benedictus
looked back down to see Dies Irae lunging at him.

Dies Irae's sword flew. Benedictus parried. The blades
clanged and raised sparks.

The blades drew apart, clanged again. Around them the
fires burned, the armies watched, the winds howled, and the rain
fell. Benedictus had not dueled with blades for years, not since

Requiem had fallen. His shoulders ached, his wounds burned, and he felt sluggish as he swung his blade.

Dies Irae thrust his sword, and Benedictus grunted as he parried. Dies Irae thrust again. Benedictus parried again, but barely. His boot slipped, and he fell to one knee.

The armies gasped. Agnus Dei screamed.

Dies Irae's blade came swinging down, reflecting the fires. Benedictus parried and punched, hitting Dies Irae's helmet. His knuckles ached; he might have broken them. Dies Irae fell into the mud. Benedictus leaped up and swung his sword.

His blade hit Dies Irae's helmet.

Dies Irae, grinning with blood in his mouth, pushed himself up and swung his sword.

Benedictus blocked, thrust, and hit Dies Irae's breastplate. His blow sent jewels flying, but could not break the steel. Dies Irae thrust, and his blade sliced Benedictus's arm. Blood flew, and Agnus Dei screamed again.

Benedictus howled and charged in fury, swinging his sword. Dies Irae blocked the blade with his mace, that left arm of steel.

Benedictus's blade shattered. Shards flew, leaving only a hilt and jagged steel in Benedictus's hand.

"It's over, Benedictus!" Dies Irae cackled and swung his blade. Benedictus parried with his broken sword. He managed to divert the bulk of the blow, but the sword still sliced his shoulder, and Benedictus fell to his knees.

Dies Irae swung his sword again.

Benedictus rolled aside, grabbed a shard of broken blade from the mud, and thrust it up.

The metal drove deep into Dies Irae's left eye.

Dies Irae screamed. It was a horrible scream, a shriek like a dying horse. He clawed at his face, but could not pull out the shard in his eye.

"Damn you, Benedictus!" he screamed, a high pitched sound, inhuman. Blood spurted. He fell to his knees, hand covering his wound. Suddenly he was blubbering, blood and mucus and tears flowing down him.

Benedictus rose slowly to his feet. Blood covered him, and he could barely feel his arm. He limped toward his brother. Dies Irae had dropped his sword, and Benedictus lifted it. He held the blade over his brother's head. Everyone watched around them, but dared not move or speak. The rain pattered.

"It *is* over now, brother," Benedictus said and raised the sword. Dies Irae was weeping. "Goodbye."

Dies Irae shook his head and held out his hands, one hand of flesh, the other a fist of steel. "Please, please, brother," he said. "Spare me, please. I beg you." He bowed, covering his samite and jeweled armor with mud and blood. He wept. "I beg you, Benedictus. Spare me. Show me mercy. I am your brother."

Benedictus stared down. The rain kept falling, steaming against burning bodies. Benedictus looked at those bodies, thousands of them, and around them thousands of old skeletons from the war years ago. So many had died already. So many deaths because of these struggles between him and his brother.

"What are you waiting for?" Kyrie shouted somewhere above. "Kill him!"

But Benedictus could not. He could not ten years ago, and he could not now. Not after all this blood, all this death. His brother was a monster. A murderer. A despot who had committed horrible crimes. But he was still Benedictus's blood, still a man who begged for life, a man who was surrendering to him.

Benedictus looked down at this groveling, pathetic creature. Disgust filled him.

"You will return with me to the ruins of Requiem," Benedictus said, tears choking his voice. "We will stand among the columns which you toppled, among the graves of the children you murdered, and there you will stand trial. No, I will not kill you, Dies Irae. But I will judge you. For the rest of your life, you will live imprisoned to me. You will watch as I return Osanna to its old kings. You will watch as I show the world the crimes you've committed."

Benedictus, King of Requiem, lowered his sword.

Sobbing on his knees, Dies Irae crawled toward him in the mud. "Thank you, thank you," he blubbered, blood covering him, and reached out as if to kiss Benedictus's boots.

But instead, so quickly Benedictus barely saw it, Dies Irae drew a hidden dagger.

The blade flashed.

Agnus Dei screamed.

The dagger buried itself into Benedictus's gut, and Dies Irae turned the blade, grinning a bloody, insane grin.

The birch leaves rustled around him, bright green, and dapples of light danced upon the marble tiles. The columns rose around him, white marble, and he saw Lacrimosa walking among them, clad in white silks, her hair braided. Agnus Dei ran toward him, so small, her hair a tangle of black curls, and he lifted her and laughed. Gloriae ran to him too, hair golden, laughing, and he lifted her with his other arm. It was spring in Requiem, and it was beautiful, so beautiful that he wept.

Benedictus fell to his knees. Dies Irae grinned in the mud, twisting the blade. Benedictus looked up, eyelids fluttering, and saw his family there, and he smiled. "I love you," his lips uttered silently.

"I will rape Lacrimosa again," Dies Irae whispered into Benedictus's ear, blood dripping from his lips. "A thousand more times. I want you to die knowing that."

With blurry eyes, Benedictus saw Kyrie swooping toward them. He saw Dies Irae crawl through the mud. He saw Volucris stir, still alive. Then Benedictus could see no more. He fell into the mud, and rain pattered against him. He turned his head, and he beheld a sight so beautiful, that he wept.

Before him stretched the halls of his fathers, all in silver and mist, columns rising among the stars.

KYRIE ELEISON

Kyrie saw Benedictus fall. His heart shattered. That day ten years ago returned to him, the day King Benedictus had led him to this field.

Kyrie wanted to rush to Benedictus, to his king.

Instead he flew to Dies Irae.

The destroyer of Requiem, the man who'd murdered Kyrie's family, was dragging himself through the mud toward Volucris. The griffin was cut and burned, but still alive.

He's going to get away with the amulet! Kyrie thought. He could not allow that. He leaped onto Dies Irae, who squirmed beneath him. Dies Irae's armor was slick with blood. His visor had opened, revealing a shattered face, a shard of steel deep in his eye. The man was cackling, mucus and tears and blood flowing down his face. Kyrie nearly gagged.

"You murdered my parents," Kyrie said. "You murdered Lady Mirum. Benedictus showed you mercy. I will not."

Dies Irae was struggling, but growing weaker, his face paler. He looked moments from death. Kyrie shifted into human form. He placed his boot against Dies Irae's neck, reached down, and grabbed the Griffin Heart.

"It's over, Irae," he said. He pulled the amulet back, snapping it off its chain. "I have the Griffin Heart. The griffins are mine. I want you to die knowing that. I...."

Kyrie wanted to say more, but could not. The amulet blazed in his hand, sizzling hot, cutting off his words. Kyrie cried in pain and almost dropped it.

The griffins screeched.

Dies Irae shouted.

The amulet vibrated and hummed in Kyrie's hand. The griffins went mad; they were flying to and fro, and their riders could not control them. Kyrie felt their fury. They hated him, hated the amulet; Kyrie had never known such hatred. They wanted to tear him apart. Volucris, wounded in the mud, seemed to gain new strength and took flight.

"Men!" Dies Irae cried. He began crawling away from Kyrie, and soldiers rushed to him. A few men lifted him, and others surrounded him with drawn swords.

"Irae!" Kyrie shouted. He wanted to stop him, to kill him, but could not. The amulet claimed him, spinning his head, burning his fist. He could barely stay standing.

Gritting his teeth, Kyrie held the amulet over his head. He shut his eyes, ignoring the pain in his hand. The griffins began to swoop toward him, talons outstretched, blood in their eyes.

How did the amulet work? How could he tame the griffins? He felt the magic burning down his arm, flowing up his spine...

...and then he felt a million griffins in his mind, flapping wings inside his skull.

They were his.

LACRIMOSA

"Benedictus!" Lacrimosa cried, tears blurring her vision.

The griffins were flying around her, enraged and confused. Dies Irae had vanished in the shadows and chaos. The salvanae stared with their golden orbs. Lacrimosa flew, shoved her way through them, and crashed to the ground by her husband.

"My king," she wept. She shifted into human form and grabbed him. She held Benedictus in her arms, and she saw the dagger in his belly, and a sob racked her body. "Do not die today, my love."

He blinked and soft breath left his lungs. He tried to speak, but could not. Blood soaked his shirt. His fingers moved weakly.

"I need a healer!" Lacrimosa cried.

Agnus Dei landed beside her, shifted into human form, and knelt by her father. She held him and gazed upon him with huge, haunted eyes.

Kyrie too stood by them in human form, but seemed not to see them. He held the Griffin Heart over his head. The amulet vibrated and hummed and glowed. The griffins screeched above and clawed the air. For a moment it seemed they would attack. Kyrie snarled, holding the amulet to the skies, and pointed to the south, back to Confutatis. With shrieks, the griffins flew away, their riders powerless to stop them.

"A healer, quickly!" Lacrimosa cried. Benedictus moaned in her arms, blood still flowing, eyes glazed.

A bugle sounded among the clouds, and a great salvana came coiling down, furling and unfurling like a snake in water. His golden scales shimmered in the firelight. His eyes like crystal balls blinked, and wind whipped his white beard. He was larger than the other salvanae, and older, and Lacrimosa guessed that he was their leader.

Agnus Dei seemed to recognize him. She leaped to her feet and waved to the salvana. "Nehushtan!" she called. "Nehushtan, please help us!"

The salvana kept coiling down. The firelight glinted against him so brightly, it nearly blinded Lacrimosa. When he was near, Nehushtan hovered above them, his head lowered over Benedictus. The head seemed so large next to Benedictus's human form, all golden scales and white hair.

"Nehushtan," Agnus Dei said between sobs. She placed her hands on his head. "You are a great priest. Can you heal him? Please. He's my father."

Benedictus was barely breathing, barely moaning. Nehushtan sniffed him. As he inhaled, Lacrimosa saw golden powder and wisps of light. The priest's eyelashes, each like an ostrich feather, fanned her as he blinked. The rain streamed down his scales.

"Please, Your Highness," Lacrimosa said to him, not sure if the title was appropriate, but not caring. Her husband's blood soaked her hands. She could not live without him. Without Benedictus, life was meaningless for her. *Don't leave me now, my love. Please. Stay with me.*

Nehushtan sniffed again, inhaling wispy light that floated from Benedictus, as if he were smelling the king's soul. Finally he turned that great, golden head to Lacrimosa. He blinked again, eyelashes fanning the ash, and spoke in an old voice like flowing water.

"The Draco Stars shine bright in him." Nehushtan nodded. "I have rarely seen such bright light, such powerful dragon spirit. He is a mighty king."

"Can you save him?" Lacrimosa pleaded. She placed a bloody hand against Nehushtan's scales. They felt warm against her palm.

Nehushtan blinked again, turned his orbs to Benedictus, then back to her. "The stars of the dragon shine forever upon all who follow their light. Such light cannot be extinguished; it flows forever in our wake, from birth, to life, and to the great journey to those stars. Do not grieve for those who join the constellation, daughter of dragons, for his light will shine bright among them."

Benedictus's eyes fluttered, then closed. His breath was so shallow now, Lacrimosa was not sure that he breathed at all. Agnus Dei sobbed, and even Kyrie was crying.

Lacrimosa shook her head, her hair covering her face. Tears and raindrops streamed down her cheeks. She placed her second hand against Nehushtan's head. "Not yet. Please, Your Highness. I'm not ready to lose him."

Nehushtan lowered his head to Benedictus, blinked several times, and sniffed again. "Yes, his dragon force still pulses, and starlight flows through him. But his human body, this one that lies before me, is dying. This body I cannot heal."

Agnus Dei looked at the salvana desperately. "But can you save his dragon form? If he shifted, could you heal him?"

Nehushtan looked at her. "I do not know, daughter of dragons, but I can try. His human body is beyond my skill; its form is made of ash, and to ash it will return. I can pray for his dragon form. Whether his human body survives, I do not know."

Lacrimosa wept. To lose Benedictus's human body forever? To lose his kisses, his embraces, the stubble on his cheeks, his calloused hands, the crow feet that grew around his eyes during his rare smiles? How could she lose this, to sleep at nights without his form by her side, to walk without his hand in hers? Yet she nodded, trembling. "Please, Nehushtan. Do what you can."

For the first time, Lacrimosa noticed that all the other salvanae—thousands of them—were watching from above. Their bodies were as strands of gold, and as Lacrimosa watched them, she gasped. The salvanae flowed to form a ring in the sky, and in the center of that ring, the clouds parted and no rain fell. It was like the eye of a storm. Through her tears, Lacrimosa saw that stars shone between the salvanae. *The constellation Draco. Light of dragons.* The beams of light fell upon her and Benedictus.

Nehushtan began to sing, a song in an old language, a tune that sounded ancient beyond knowing. His voice was a deep rumble, beautiful like crystals in deep caves, and the starlight moved to the notes he sang. Lacrimosa could see chords of light flowing through the air, notes descending, spinning, and landing upon Benedictus. The music lived around her in light and ancient piety. The other salvanae began to sing too, some in bass, others in a high, angelic choir of light. Lacrimosa wept, for she had never heard anything more beautiful.

The notes of light lifted Benedictus from the mud, and cleaned the dirt and blood from him. Lacrimosa wanted to hold onto him, to clutch him in her embrace, but she had to trust the music. She released her grip, and let the dragon song lift him on its light. He hovered above her, and soon he floated high under starlight, and he was no longer a man, but a dragon, a great dragon with midnight scales, with wings that were no longer torn. Benedictus the Black, King of Requiem, opened his jaws and roared, and the roar shook the land. No fire left his mouth, but starlight that flowed, danced, and sang.

"Hear the Black Fang sound his roar," Kyrie whispered, watching with moist eyes, the amulet clutched in his fist. "Hear the song of Requiem."

Strands of starlight woven around him, Benedictus descended to the earth, and stood by Lacrimosa, healed. His wing was whole now, and his scars gone. He looked so much like the old Benedictus, the great dragon who had led them to war so many years ago. He lowered his head to Lacrimosa, who stood in the mud in human form, and she embraced him.

"Benedictus," she whispered, and she smiled a teary smile, and then she was weeping. There was so much she wanted to say to him. She wanted to speak of Dies Irae torturing her, forcing her to fight in his arena. She wanted to speak of her years in hiding, raising Agnus Dei in the snowy mountains of Fidelium. She wanted to speak of Dies Irae raping her all those years ago, how she did not know who fathered Agnus Dei and Gloriae. Lacrimosa wanted to speak of two decades of horror, of pain and of longing, but she could bring none of it to her lips. Benedictus knew. She did not need to speak, and her smile widened as she cried. She leaned her head against him, and for the first time in years Lacrimosa felt that beautiful light lay in her future, and great love and timeless music.

"Is... your human body dead?" she whispered to him, embracing his dragon head. "Can you feel it within you?"

Benedictus nodded gently. "I can feel it. It's hurt, and it's weak. It will be many days before I dare shift. But my human form lives, Lacrimosa. We can heal it."

Lacrimosa closed her eyes and wept against him.

And then Agnus Dei and Kyrie were embracing Benedictus too, and jumping onto his back, and climbing his neck, and laughing and playing as if they were still children. Benedictus too laughed, a deep rumbling dragon's laugh. *Dies Irae took their childhood,* Lacrimosa thought, looking at the young ones. *Let them be as children now.*

Nehushtan watched, and it seemed to Lacrimosa that the old priest smiled. She turned to him and bowed her head.

"Thank you."

Nehushtan too bowed his head. His body hovered several feet above the ground. "Will you return with us to Salvandos, and dwell with us in Har Zahav, the mountain of gold?" he asked. "We have learned today that Vir Requis are noble, and great followers of the Draco stars. Return with us to Har Zahav, and fly with us there in golden clouds."

Benedictus bowed to the priest. "I thank you, Lord of Salvandos. But I must decline. Our home is Requiem, and that home now lies in ruin. I am still king of that land, though it is burned to ash, and I still lead my people, though only five remain. I must stay true to my fathers, and to the courts of Requiem." His eyes glimmered in the starlight. "I do not know if I can rebuild the halls of my fathers. I do not know if our race can survive. Many dangers still await us. Dies Irae will still hunt us. The men and women who live across Osanna, and over the ruins of Requiem our motherland, still fear and hate us. Our song does not end today, great priest, nor does our quest. I remain in the east. If more Vir Requis still live in hiding, I must find them, and for the memory of my forefathers, I will rebuild our kingdom among the birches. Goodbye, dear friend. Forever will Requiem be an ally to Salvandos, and forever be in its debt." He bowed again to the High Priest, and he uttered the Old Words. "May our wings forever find your sky."

Nehushtan smiled, a deep smile that sparkled in his eyes. And then the priest was flying away, and the other salvanae were coiling behind him and bugling. Within moments they were gone into the west.

KYRIE ELEISON

Kyrie watched the salvanae leave, and he felt a sadness in him, a deep sadness that he could not explain, a sadness of beauty and music. He turned toward Agnus Dei. She stood by him in human form, her clothes tattered, blood and mud smearing her skin. Ash covered her face, and her hair was a mess of tangles. Yet still she was beautiful to Kyrie, more beautiful than the salvanae or their song.

"Will you go live in Salvandos now?" he asked her, suddenly fearful. "You've often spoken of wanting to be a true dragon, to forget your human form." Strangely Kyrie wanted to cry again, and he hated his weakness. For so many years, fire and pain had blazed within him, but this day was a day of tears.

Agnus Dei snorted so loudly, it blew back a strand of her hair. "Pup," she said, hands on her hips, "there are some things dragons can't do."

"Like what?" Kyrie asked.

She walked toward him in the mud, grasped his head with both hands, and kissed him deeply. The kiss lasted for long moments, and Kyrie shut his eyes. Her lips were soft and full, her fingers grasping in his hair. When finally she broke away, leaving him breathless, she said, "This. And I intend to do a lot of it with you."

Kyrie laughed. His placed an arm around her waist, pulled her close, and kissed her hair. "I love you, Agnus Dei," he said, and suddenly tears filled his eyes again, and he turned away lest she saw them.

She smiled and pulled his face back to hers. "Right back at you, pup."

When they looked back to Benedictus, they saw that Lacrimosa had become a silvery dragon, and stood by her husband. She was only half his size, so delicate and lithe by his bulky form, her scales like starlight.

"Do you really think we can do it?" Kyrie asked her and Benedictus. "Can we rebuild Requiem?"

Benedictus looked at the horizon, beyond which Requiem lay, then at Kyrie. "I don't know, Kyrie. But we're going to try."

Kyrie raised the amulet. It felt hot in his hand, still humming and trembling. "We have the griffins with us. I sent them to Confutatis, but I can bring them back. With their help, we can—"

"No," Benedictus said, shaking his head. "The servitude of griffins to Osanna or Requiem ends today. Hand me the amulet, Kyrie, so that I can destroy it."

Kyrie gasped. He shook his head wildly. "No! Benedictus! I mean, Your Highness. I mean... I don't know what I'm supposed to call you now, but we can't release the griffins. Dies Irae still has armies that can hunt us. You yourself said so. The people of Osanna hate us, and—" Kyrie blew out his breath, exasperated. "I can't believe this. We need the griffins." He clutched the amulet so tightly, it hurt his palm. "With their power, we can reclaim our land, and reclaim our glory."

Benedictus only gazed at him, waiting for Kyrie to end his speech. When finally Kyrie could think of nothing more to say, Benedictus spoke softly.

"We cannot rebuild our land with the slavery of others, Kyrie. We have seen where that can lead. Enslaving the griffins was the downfall of my father; once Dies Irae stole the amulet, his rule crumbled. No, Kyrie. Griffins cannot speak, but they are wise beasts. They can be as wise as men, when they are free. If we can rebuild Requiem, it will be with justice and light, not as overlords of another race."

Kyrie took deep, fiery breaths. Anger pulsed through him, tingling his fingers, but he forced himself to clench his teeth. Benedictus was right, he knew. He hated that it was so. Hated it! But he knew the king spoke truth.

Wordlessly, lips tight, he held out the amulet in his open palm.

Benedictus lifted it with his mouth, smashed it between his teeth, and spat out the pieces. Somewhere in the distance, a league away, rose the cries of ten thousand griffins.

"They're free now," Lacrimosa said quietly. "They will no longer serve us, nor will they hunt us. May they find their way back to Leonis, their fabled land across the sea, and prosper there."

Kyrie stood with arms limp, not sure how to feel. Without the griffins, the road ahead seemed impossible to travel. How could they rebuild Requiem now, just the four of them? Could they truly find more Vir Requis survivors? Did any even exist? Would Dies Irae heal and resume his hunt, or was he dead already? Kyrie did not know, and the world seemed darker and more confusing than ever.

He thought of Lady Mirum, how she'd protected him for ten years in her fort, and knew the first thing he would do now. He would find her body. He would give her a proper burial. He would rededicate the fort in her name.

"We return to Fort Sanctus," he said, and did not need to say more. The others understood and nodded. There his journey had begun; there it would end.

Agnus Dei kissed his cheek, ruffled his hair, and said, "You are a pup." Then she shifted into a red dragon, all fire and fang, and took flight.

Kyrie shifted too, and soon the four Vir Requis, perhaps the last of their kind, flew together. The clouds parted, and the dawn rose, and they flew into that good, golden light. The sunrise gilded the clouds, spreading pink and orange wisps across the land, and the stars still shone overhead.

As they flew into that sunrise, Kyrie dared to hope, to imagine. The world was still dangerous for the Vir Requis. Many still feared them. Many would still hunt them. But as he flew now, his new family at his side, he breathed the cold air and smiled. He imagined flocks of thousands of Vir Requis flying, the glory of their magic. He would help rebuild that race with Agnus Dei, whom he loved more than life, and maybe someday, years from now, many dragons would fly again.

"Requiem," he whispered into the dawn. "May our wings forever find your sky."

AGNUS DEI

As Agnus Dei flew beside her parents, a thought kept rattling in her mind. She chewed her lip, but could not rid herself of it. The wind blew around her, scented of morning and dew, and sunlight filled the sky, but Agnus Dei did not see this beauty. She thought back to the ruins of Requiem, where she had fought Gloriae the Gilded, and ice filled her belly.

Father had spoken words to Nehushtan, words that kept echoing. "I still lead my people, though only five remain."

Kyrie had not noticed, but Agnus Dei had.

Five.

Five Vir Requis.

She looked at Mother and Father, and at Kyrie, and tears filled her eyes.

"Mother," she whispered. Her whisper barely carried in the wind, but Lacrimosa still heard. She turned to face Agnus Dei, eyes soft.

"Mother," Agnus Dei said. She hated that her voice trembled, that tears filled her eyes, but could not help it. "Mother, Father said that— He—" She trembled. "Mother, who is the fifth?"

Lacrimosa was crying too. She smiled through her tears. "Agnus Dei," she said, "you have a sister."

GLORIAE

Gloriae was pacing the throne room when Dies Irae stumbled in, a shard of sword in his eye.

Gloriae's jaw unhinged. For a moment she could do nothing but stare. Blood, mud, and ash covered her father. Fresh blood spurted from his eye and filled his mouth. He cackled as he limped into the throne room, stunned guards at his sides. Blood trailed behind him.

"Benedictus!" Dies Irae shouted, mouth full of blood, and laughed madly. "He lives. He lives! He killed me. Daughter!" He collapsed at her feet.

Blood spattered Gloriae's leggings, snapping her out of her shock. She raised her eyes to the guards. "Fetch priests!" she said. "And ready the griffins."

Dies Irae laughed at her feet. He stared up at her with one eye. The other eye too seemed to stare up, if a shard of steel could stare. "The griffins abandoned us, Gloriae. Look what they did to me. Look what the weredragons did." He was weeping now.

Priests burst into the room. Their servants carried a litter.

"Take him to the temple," Gloriae ordered them. She allowed no tremble to fill her voice, no emotion to show on her face. She ruled Osanna now; she would rule with steel. "Pray for him. Let the Sun God heal him. If he dies, so will you."

For an instant, hatred blazed across the priests' faces. Gloriae knew they were not used to hearing threats, not even from emperors. Yet they only nodded, placed the cackling Dies Irae on the litter, and carried him away.

Gloriae stared at the blood smearing the marble tiles. Splotches of it stained her clothes. Finally her head began to spin. She wanted to follow the priests, to be with her father, but her feet would not support her. The closest seat was Father's throne, and she fell into it. For the first time in her life, she sat upon the Ivory Throne of Osanna.

The lords and ladies of her hall gazed at her, shocked. Fury filled Gloriae, and she let her stare pierce them. "My father is hurt. Until he's healed, I rule in his stead. Now leave this place."

As they left the hall, Gloriae shut her eyes. Blood pounded in her head. She clutched the throne's arms, and felt its power flow through her. Osanna. A realm of endless forests, towering mountains, great armies. Hers. From here flowed her dominion over the empire.

Her eyes snapped open. She left the throne and strode across the hall. She did not walk to the temple. She would be of no use there. But there was something she could do now, something Father should have done years ago.

Gloriae left her hall, walked down stairs, marched down tunnels, climbed down and down into the belly of the world. She walked for hours perhaps, lips tightened, eyes dry. She walked until she reached the chamber with the guards, where golden skulls bedecked iron doors, gazing upon her with glowing eye sockets.

Gloriae stepped through that doorway and approached the Well of Night.

She stood over the abyss and hesitated. *The nightshades.* Gloriae could not forget the time she saw them, how they had sucked her soul into their endless cavern, turned her to smoke and darkness. Then Gloriae remembered the steel shard in Father's head, the blood on his face, and the blood on her leggings. She remembered, too, the curse she carried now, the lizard curse Lacrimosa had given her.

Gloriae took a deep breath, tightened her fists, and jumped into the well.

She floated through darkness. It was calm, soothing, an inky blackness that caressed her.

Then she screamed.

The nightshades appeared around her, creatures that were the opposite of light, creatures of smoke and fear and blackness. Their eyes shone as diamonds, and she felt them tugging her spirit, pulling it from her body, as if it were wisps of steam.

"Hear me!" Gloriae shouted. "I sit upon the Ivory Throne. I have the power to free you. I release you from this well! Emerge from the abyss and serve me."

They swirled so fast, Gloriae was tossed in all directions, spun like a top, and shot into the air. She screamed and laughed and spread out her arms.

"Fly into the world, creatures of night. I am your ruler now. I tame you now. Kill the weredragons! That is my order to you, the price I charge for your freedom. Hunt them until the last one begs for death."

The creatures swirled around her, disappearing and appearing, teeth like shards of glass, bodies like clouds, eyes crackling. They laughed, a sound of storms. Gloriae's body was like a coin rattling in a cup. They flowed out of the well, raising her upon them, and swirled through the chamber. They howled and laughed and ballooned. Gloriae floated among them, high above the well. She tilted her head back, laughing, arms spread to her sides.

I will kill them, she promised herself. *I will do what Father could not. I will rid the world of the weredragon curse.*

"I will lead you there," Gloriae said, a smile tingling the corners of her mouth. "I will lead you to Benedictus and Lacrimosa, and we will kill them."

They flowed out of the chamber, down tunnels, up stairs... and into a world of dying daylight.

BOOK TWO:
TEARS OF REQUIEM

KYRIE ELEISON

Kyrie was collecting firewood when he heard thunder, shivered, and saw the smoke creature.

The smoke was distant, a league away, but Kyrie could see there was something wrong about it. It coiled through the sunset, serpentine, moving toward him. A wisp of some campfire? A cloud? No. Whatever this was, it moved like a living creature. Kyrie's fingers went numb, and he dropped the branches he'd collected.

"Agnus Dei!" he whispered through clenched teeth. "Where are you?

She didn't answer. Kyrie tore his eyes away from the smoke and scanned the woods for her. In the twilight, he saw rustling oaks, birches, and elms. He saw fleeing animals: birds, squirrels, and a deer. But he could not see his companion.

"Agnus Dei, where are you?" he whispered again. He dared not speak louder. "There's something coming over, and it doesn't look friendly."

Still she did not appear, and Kyrie cursed and returned his eyes to the smoke. It was so close now, Kyrie could see that it was indeed alive. Arms and legs grew from it, and its eyes glinted like diamonds. Teeth filled its maw. Whatever this creature was, it was no wisp of smoke. It seemed to see Kyrie and approached him, soon five hundred feet away, then only a hundred, then a dozen.

Kyrie considered shifting into dragon form. Like all Vir Requis—or at least, the five that remained after the war—he could become a dragon. He could blow fire, slash with claws, bite with fangs. But as the creature approached, Kyrie remained human. Turning into a dragon was dangerous; men hated dragons and hunted them. And besides, Kyrie doubted even dragonfire and fangs could kill this smoky being.

Instead, he addressed the creature. "What are you? Turn back!"

The creature seemed to laugh. Its laughter was like thunder, shaking the trees. It floated above Kyrie, thirty feet long and undulating. It wasn't made of smoke, Kyrie realized. It seemed woven of darkness, but even that was inaccurate. Darkness was merely the lack of light. This creature was the opposite of light, deeper and blacker than mere darkness.

"Leave this place!" Kyrie demanded. He glanced around the forest. Where was Agnus Dei? He would not let this creature harm her. He had to protect her. He loved Agnus Dei more than anything; he would beat this creature to death with his fists, if he had to.

"You...," the creature whispered. Its voice made trees wilt, turn gray, and fall to the forest floor. "...are... Vir Requis...."

Kyrie wanted to attack. He wanted to flee. He wanted to find Agnus Dei. He wanted to do anything but just stand there, hearing that voice—no, not a voice, but merely an echo—a sound that made his insides shrivel up.

"I...," he began. With fumbling fingers, he managed to draw his dagger. "You will...."

He could say no more. All he saw was that creature of blackness, its diamond eyes, its teeth like wisps of white smoke. He felt as if he too became smoke. His soul seemed to leave his body, flowing from his nostrils and mouth. He could see his body below, wobbling on the forest floor—just a kid, seventeen years old with a shock of yellow hair and too many battle scars.

And then he could see too much.

He screamed. He saw the universe. Not only the three dimensions of his world, but endless others. His spirit was no longer confined to his skull. It spread through the forest, through the empire of Osanna, through the multitudes of dimensions beyond. So much space! So much pain. So much fear. Kyrie whimpered. He wanted to hide, to weep, but had no eyes for tears.

"Please," he whispered. "Please, it's so... open. So much space. So much pain."

The creature laughed, and Kyrie knew he would soon join it, become smoke and blackness and flow through the endless, empty spaces.

"Agnus Dei," he managed to whisper. "I love you...."

A voice, worlds distant, answered him.

"This is no time for romance, pup. Get out of here, run!"

Hands clutched his shoulders. Shoulders! Yes, he had shoulders, and a body, and a physical form. He had tears, he had a voice, had—

"Pup, snap out of it!" said the voice. He felt a hand slap his face. He could feel! He could feel his body again. His soul coalesced, and his body sucked it back in. It felt like water flowing back into a jug. His spirit slammed into his skull, and he convulsed, and jumped to his feet. He hadn't realized he had fallen.

"Agnus Dei!" he said. Tears filled his eyes. His beloved knelt above him, her tanned face so beautiful to him, her curls of black hair tickling his cheeks. "What, where—"

She hoisted him to his feet. "Run, pup. Run!"

She pulled him up, and they ran through the forest. When Kyrie glanced over his shoulder, he saw the black creature. It was chasing them, flowing between the trees. Every tree it passed wilted and fell.

"What is that thing?" Agnus Dei cried as they ran.

"I don't know," Kyrie said, boots kicking up leaves and dirt. He almost fell over a root, steadied himself, and kept running. "Don't look into its eyes, Agnus Dei. It did something to me. I'm not sure what. But don't look at it. Just run."

"I am running, pup. And I'm a lot faster than you."

"Agnus Dei, this is not the time for another race." He panted. "Everything is a competition with you, even who can flee faster from a flying smoke demon."

The creature shrieked behind them. It was a sound like fingernails on glass. Kyrie and Agnus Dei covered their ears and grimaced while running. Birds fell dead from the sky. Bugs burst open on the ground, spraying blood. The creature shrieked again, and Kyrie screamed in pain; his eardrums felt close to tearing.

It was dark now. The sun disappeared behind the horizon, leaving only red and orange wisps across the forest. The creature grew in darkness. When Kyrie looked at it again, it was twice the size.

"I think it likes darkness," Kyrie shouted. It was rumbling and cackling behind him, and trees kept wilting. The boles crashed around them, maggoty and gray and crumbling.

"Then we'll roast the bastard with dragonfire," Agnus Dei said. She leaped over a fallen tree, spun around, and shifted.

Leathern wings grew from her back. Red scales flowed across her. Fangs and claws sprouted from her. Within seconds, she was a dragon. With a howl, she blew white-hot fire at the smoky creature.

Kyrie ducked and rolled, the fire flowing over his head. He shifted too. Blue scales covered him, he ballooned in size, and soon he too was a dragon. He blew the hottest, whitest fire he could, hitting the creature head on.

It screamed. Trees cracked. Boulders shattered. Kyrie too screamed, his ears thudding, but kept breathing fire. Agnus Dei blew fire too. And yet the creature lived, swirling and crying. Kyrie felt its tug, felt his soul being sucked out, drawn into those empty spaces. He shook his head and gritted his teeth, clinging onto himself.

"We need light!" Kyrie shouted. "The light bothers it, not the heat. Let's light this forest."

Agnus Dei nodded, and they began blowing fire in all directions. The trees, moments before lush and green, had wilted around the creature. They were now dry and caught fire easily. They crackled, blazing, and the creature howled. A crack ran along the earth, and sparks rained from the sky. The creature seemed to suck in the light. Wisps of light flowed into it, and it howled.

"Leave this place!" Kyrie shouted to it. "There is light here, light that will burn you. Fly away into darkness."

It howled, surrounded by firelight, and gave Kyrie a last glare. Its eyes were so mean, small, and glittering, that Kyrie shuddered.

Finally it coiled, spun around, and fled into the night.

Kyrie watched it flee, then turned to Agnus Dei, who still stood in dragon form. "Let's contain this fire," he said.

She nodded, and they shoved the burning trees into a great pyre. With dragon claws, they dug ruts around it, so it would not spread, and tossed the dirt onto the burning boles. They worked silently until the fire died to embers.

Their work done, they shifted back into human forms and collapsed into the ash and dirt. Kyrie was bone tired. Blowing so much fire had taken a lot out of him, and he shivered to remember what the creature had done. Out of his body, his soul had glimpsed something... something Kyrie shuddered to remember. He pushed it out of his mind. He had seen a horror beyond the world he did not want to ponder.

"You all right?" he asked Agnus Dei.

She lay beside him, chest rising and falling as she panted. Ash smeared her cheeks and filled her mane of curls. He reached out, touched those curls, and kissed her cheek.

She shoved him back. "Am *I* all right?" she said. "Oh, thank you for asking, brave hero, defender of distressed damsels. But if I recall correctly, you're the one who almost died. I had to show up to save your backside. So the question is, pup: Are *you* all right?"

He grumbled and rose to his feet. "I'm fine, and I've told you a million times. You might be a couple years older than me, but don't call me pup."

She stood up, brushed ash off her leggings, and smirked. "Okay, puppy pup." When he scowled, she walked up to him, mussed his hair, and kissed his cheek. "For what it's worth, I'm glad you're all right. But you're still a pup."

Kyrie looked to the night sky. The creature was gone, but he could still imagine it, and his belly knotted. "Have you ever seen anything like that? What was it?"

Agnus Dei scrunched her lips and tapped her cheek. "I think it was a nightshade."

Kyrie raised an eyebrow. "A nightshade? I've never heard of them."

"I don't know much about them," Agnus Dei said. She too looked to the sky, as if scanning for its return. "But my mother used to tell me stories of them. She said they were made of unlight."

"Unlight?"

Agnus Dei nodded. "The opposite of light. Did you see how our firelight disappeared into it, as if the creature and light cancelled each other out? That's unlight."

"Scary stuff." Kyrie hugged himself. He remembered the firelight flowing into the nightshade, like wisps of cloud. Had his soul looked the same when the creature pulled it? "Do you reckon Lacrimosa knows more about them?"

"Maybe. Mother knows a lot. You and I never read much growing up, but Mother was raised in Requiem before it was destroyed. She spent her childhood in libraries. Let's find her. I hope Mother and Father didn't meet that nightshade too."

They walked through the forest, heading south toward their camp. The Draco constellation shone above between the boughs, the stars of Requiem, guiding them. Crickets chirped, and Kyrie held Agnus Dei's hand. Her hand was slender and warm. It was hard to believe that, only a week ago, they'd been fighting Dies Irae. It seemed a lifetime ago that they'd stolen the tyrant's amulet, freed his griffins, and found sanctuary in this forest. A chapter in Kyrie's life had ended when he'd sent Dies Irae fleeing, wounded, back to Confutatis. A new chapter had begun now, it seemed, and Kyrie didn't like how it started. Not one bit.

They were still far from camp when they heard boots trudging toward them. At first, Kyrie wanted to flee. He was used to footfalls heralding pursuit—Dies Irae's soldiers with swords and crossbows. But then he heard Lacrimosa's voice calling, "Agnus Dei! Daughter, do you hear me?"

Agnus Dei cried, "Mother! I'm here."

Soon Lacrimosa emerged from between the trees, carrying a tin lantern. Kyrie couldn't help himself. Whenever he saw Agnus Dei's mother, the queen of fallen Requiem, he paused and stared. Lacrimosa, pale and dainty, seemed woven of moonlight. Her hair was a gold so fair, it was almost white. Her eyes were pools of lavender, and she wore a pendant shaped as a bluebell.

"Agnus Dei, are you all right?" Lacrimosa said. "We heard fire and howls, and I heard you scream."

Agnus Dei hugged her mother. The two looked nothing alike, Kyrie reflected. Agnus Dei had tanned skin, curly black hair, and blazing brown eyes. Lacrimosa was starlight; Agnus Dei was fire.

"We saw a nightshade," Kyrie said to the two women. "Well, we did more than see it. The bloody thing nearly killed us before we blinded it. Do you know much about nightshades, Lacrimosa?"

Lacrimosa grew even paler than usual.

"Nightshades," she whispered.

A voice spoke ahead between the trees, deep and gruff. "Impossible."

With snapping twigs and ragged breathing, Benedictus—King of Requiem and father to Agnus Dei—emerged from the trees. He held a torch and walked up to them. His chest rose and fell. Sweat soaked his leathery face and matted his graying black hair. He glared at Kyrie, fists clenched.

"I'm telling you, we saw a nightshade," Kyrie said to his king. At least, Benedictus had once been his king, back when Requiem still stood and a million Vir Requis still flew. "Tell him, Agnus Dei."

Agnus Dei spent a moment describing their ordeal to her parents. When she was done, even Benedictus looked pale. The king closed his eyes and seemed lost in old, painful memories. For a long time, the others stood in silence, waiting for Benedictus to speak.

Finally Benedictus opened his eyes and said, "We leave this forest. It's no longer safe."

He began trudging through the woods. The others hurried to keep up.

"Why?" Kyrie demanded. "What do you know of these creatures? Speak, Benedictus!"

The older man, a good four decades Kyrie's senior, scowled. "You don't want to know, kid."

They continued walking through the night. Their boots rustled fallen leaves and damp twigs, and the wind moaned. Kyrie tightened his cloak around him, but found no warmth. He tried to speak a few times, but Benedictus scowled and silenced him, saying these woods were full of ears. And so Kyrie walked silently, thoughts rattling in his skull. He remembered floating over his body. The nightshade had tugged his soul, and was taking it... where? To a place colder and darker than this night, than any night. Kyrie shivered. He didn't know how long they walked through the forest. It seemed like hours, but time felt lost to Kyrie. Finally he could bear it no longer.

He grabbed Benedictus's shoulder. "That thing did something to me, Benedictus. I don't know what, but it scared me."

Benedictus grumbled. "The night is no time to speak of these things."

"I don't care. It seemed to... pull me, Benedictus. Not my body, but whatever's inside my body. My soul, if you'd believe it. And I saw things. Well, I didn't see them, but I felt them. Dimensions, and space, and other worlds. My soul seemed to balloon to fill them, like smoke in a jar, and...." His stomach knotted. He took a deep breath. "I think I've earned the right to learn more. Tell us what you know."

Benedictus growled, still stomping through the dark woods. "You want to know about nightshades, kid?" He pointed his torch to his left. "Look."

Kyrie looked, and saw that they had chanced upon a road that ran downhill, cut through a farm, and ended at a village. The village burned. Kyrie saw bodies between the buildings. A dozen nightshades swarmed above them, coiling, their eyes glittering. The creatures laughed, their voices like thunder.

"Stars," Agnus Dei whispered. She placed a hand on Kyrie's shoulder. "Are those people all dead?"

Benedictus shook his head, staring at the village below. "Not dead. Something worse. Their souls are with the nightshades now, lost in the worlds beyond this world, in lands of darkness and fear. They will remain there forever. They are already praying for death, but no death will release them."

For a long moment, the companions—the last surviving Vir Requis—stared down at the village. Finally Kyrie nodded.

"Great!" he said. "Just great. We finally defeat the griffins, and now these guys show up. As much as I'd love to fight them too, and start a whole new war, I think I'll pass. Not our problem. Osanna is infested with nightshades? Let Dies Irae handle them. Come on, Benedictus. Let's return to Requiem, or at least, what's left of it. This is not our war."

"But it is our war," Lacrimosa answered for her husband, voice haunted. "I remember tales of these nightshades. They were sealed centuries ago. Only the one who sits upon Osanna's throne could release them. That means these creatures work for Dies Irae now. And that means...."

Kyrie clutched his head and finished the sentence for her. "They're hunting us."

The nightshades below shrieked as one. Though they were a league away, and the companions were hidden in the trees, the nightshades saw them. Their eyes blazed, and they abandoned the village. They came flowing up the declivity, heading to the Vir Requis.

"Fly!" Benedictus shouted. He shifted into a black dragon, flapped his wings, and flew into the night. "Only light can stop them. Fly after me, we seek sunrise!"

The others shifted too, and the four Vir Requis flew in dragon form.

Dozens of nightshades howled behind them, chasing in the night.

GLORIAE

Gloriae the Gilded, Steel Maiden of Osanna, stood upon the walls of her palace and watched the city crumble.

Confutatis was known by many names. The Marble City. The Jewel of Osanna. The Cradle of Light. It was a sprawling city of a million souls. A city of forts, snaking walls, and gilded statues of Dies Irae. A city known for a military might that cowed the world. Today, as Gloriae stood upon the battlements of Confutatis, she did not recognize it. She saw no military might, no Sun God light, no glory for the poets to sing of.

She saw death, darkness, and cracking stone.

"Nightshades!" she cried, standing atop the tallest steeple of her palace, overlooking the city. "I have summoned you. I am your mistress. I sit upon Osanna's throne as my father lies dying, and you will obey me."

They swirled across the city, like wisps of black smoke with diamond eyes. Their teeth appeared as but mist, but they toppled towers, statues, and temples of the Sun God. Thousands of people ran through the streets. The nightshades dipped into every road, square, and alley, shrieking. People fell before them, and even from here upon her palace, Gloriae knew that nightshades were sucking up their souls. Bodies littered the streets, not dead but mindless, soulless.

"Nightshades!" Gloriae cried again. "I am the one who freed you. I sit on the throne. You will cease this destruction and obey me."

They laughed at her. A dozen flew toward her, eyes mocking, and swirled around her. They lifted her into the air, flapping her hair like storm winds, seeping under her armor to caress her skin.

"Gloriae the Gilded," they whispered in her mind. "Our mistress."

They laughed, a sound like thunder. She felt them tugging her soul, side to side, toying with her, like dogs fighting over a steak. They pulled wisps of her left and right, snapping her out and into her body.

"Stop this!" she screamed, burning with fury. "You will obey me. You will hunt the Vir Requis."

They hissed like water on a frying pan. "Oh, yes, great mistress. We will destroy the Vir Requis, yes. We will destroy all souls who live entombed in flesh. We will free them. We will free you."

They bore her into her palace, past halls and chambers, knocking down pictures and candlesticks and suits of armor. Servants fled before them. Guards attacked them with swords, only to fall soulless. The nightshades carried Gloriae into her court, and placed her upon her father's throne. They swirled around her, draped around her neck, and wrapped around her legs.

"Sit upon your throne, mistress," their voices mocked. "Rule us from here, oh mighty empress."

Gloriae's belly ached with fear. She had made a mistake, she knew. A horrible, shattering, tragic mistake for her and her empire. Father had warned her. Why hadn't she listened? Why had she freed these creatures?

She clenched her fists and snarled. "Release me, beasts. I gave you one task, and one task only. Hunt the Vir Requis."

They laughed. "Should we hunt you too then, Gloriae of Requiem?"

"I am not from Requiem," she said, but heard the doubt in her voice. Tears stung her eyes. She remembered what Lacrimosa said. *I am your mother.* She remembered shifting into a golden dragon in her chamber, of swearing to hide her shame. "Lacrimosa lied to me. She gave me her illness, the lizard's curse. I hate the Vir Requis. I will kill them all."

"Then will you kill yourself?" the nightshades asked.

They swirled around her like a hurricane, tugging her soul. She screamed. She felt herself split into a hundred pieces, then a thousand, then a million. The tiles of her court cracked. A column fell. And then Gloriae was inside the nightshades, not just the dozens around her, but the thousands that filled the world. Her soul had scattered and flew within them.

She saw Confutatis from their eyes. She saw temples fall, buildings collapse, streets rise and crash, raining cobblestones. She saw the multitudes dying, the rivers boiling, children crushed with stones. Other parts of Gloriae flew in the east. She saw nightshades attack the griffins, those griffins Dies Irae had once ruled, but now lost. She saw the griffins shriek, bite and claw, try to attack, but fall lifeless in the night. Their souls too had been claimed and tossed into darkness. Gloriae flew in the west, countless pieces of her soul within each nightshade. She saw them attack the salvanae, the true dragons of legend, and fell so many of those ancient, proud creatures.

And she saw herself.

In the shards of her soul, she saw a broken woman. She saw a woman broken in childhood, stolen. A woman raised in lies, in light that blinded her. She saw the old courts of Requiem, before her father had destroyed them. She walked there with Lacrimosa, her mother, in the halls of the Vir Requis. She heard their harps, and saw their birches, and—

No! Lies, all of it. These were the images Lacrimosa had planted within her, false memories.

"Where are the Vir Requis?" Gloriae said, speaking from every shattered part of her, into the mind of every nightshade. They laughed and hissed, and her soul dispersed and collected within them. She found the nightshades who chased the Vir Requis, and she gazed upon them from countless eyes.

They fled through the night, four dragons. Benedictus, their king, black and cruel. Lacrimosa, his wife of silver scales, beautiful and deceiving. Agnus Dei, the red dragon who'd attacked her in the ruins of Requiem. Kyrie Eleison, the cub, the boy who'd gored her leg with his horn.

"I will kill them," Gloriae vowed, urging the nightshades onward. "Destroy the world if you must. But destroy them with it. I command you."

As they hissed and howled, Gloriae sensed that she commanded nothing of their actions. They were humoring her. *So be it,* she managed to think even with her soul splintered across countless of these beings. *So be it.*

"So long as the Vir Requis die, I've done my job."

Slumped in the throne back at Confutatis, the body of Gloriae twitched, clenched its fists, and smiled.

DIES IRAE

Dies Irae awoke to pain.

He tried to open his eyes, but only one would open. His left eye blazed in agony, and when Dies Irae brought his fingers to it, they touched bandages. More bandages covered his arm, which hurt too—the pain of fire.

What had happened? He could not remember. He could barely remember his name. Grunting, he moved his head, though it shot stabs of pain through him, and looked around. He lay in a Sun God temple. Candles covered the floors and walls, a golden disk shimmered behind an altar, and priests in white masks moved about, chanting.

"Lord Irae," spoke one priest, kneeling above him. The man wore all white—white robes, a white hood, and a white mask. "The Sun God has woken you."

Dies Irae struggled to push himself up on his elbows. The priests had placed him upon white marble tiles. Dies Irae grunted. Couldn't they have given him a bed? But Sun clerics had always been an odd lot; powerful, yes, but strange of ways.

"How long was I unconscious?" Dies Irae asked. It felt like a long time. His memories were still fuzzy. He remembered riding out on Volucris, the prince of griffins, but little else.

The priest bowed his head. "Seven days of glory, your lordship, and seven nights of tribulation."

"Seven days!" Dies Irae said, feeling the blood leave his face. He struggled to his feet. The cleric watched silently. When he was standing, Dies Irae found that his knees shook. He had to lean against a column. A servant brought him a bowl of soup, and Dies Irae wanted to wave it aside, then changed his mind and took the bowl. He drank deeply. Hot beef broth.

"Seven days," he repeated softly. What in the Sun God's name had knocked him out so soundly? He frowned, and the movement made his left eye scream in pain. He felt blood trickle down his cheek, and he tasted it on his lips.

The taste brought the memories back. They hit him like a blow, so hard he dropped the bowl. It cracked, spreading broth across the floor like blood.

Benedictus.

His brother.

"Yes, you did this to me, brother," Dies Irae whispered. "You thrust jagged metal into my eye. You burned me. You—"

Dies Irae froze.

He reached for the amulet that would always hang around his neck. The Griffin Heart. The tamer of griffins.

It was gone.

The weredragons had taken it.

Rage blazed in Dies Irae, stronger than the pain. Dies Irae swung his left arm, the iron mace arm. He knocked down a candlestick. When a servant ran to lift the candle, Dies Irae swung the mace at him too. The mace hit the boy's head. Dies Irae heard the crack of the skull, a beautiful sound. He had missed that sound. The boy fell to the floor, head caved in and bleeding.

"They took the Griffin Heart," Dies Irae said, turning to stare at the priest.

The priest nodded.

Dies Irae stared silently, trembling. Then he marched to the doorways and burst outside. He was barefoot and clad in temple robes, but he didn't care. He had to see Gloriae. He had to see his daughter.

Outside the temple, more pain awaited.

The city lay crumbled and burning around him. In the twilight, Dies Irae saw nightshades flowing across the skies, toppling forts and towers. Three nightshades flew toward a towering, gilded statue of himself, of a young Dies Irae with two arms and both eyes. As he watched, the nightshades toppled the statue. It fell and crushed a house beneath it.

Dies Irae laughed.

He wanted to rage, to scream, to kill. But he only laughed.

The priest stood behind him, silent. Dies Irae addressed the man. "I'm wounded in battle. One week later, my griffins are gone, the weredragons have escaped, and the nightshades have fled the Well of Night to destroy my city. Am I missing anything?"

The priest lowered his head and said nothing.

Ice flowed down Dies Irae's spine. He grabbed the priest's shoulders. "What else? Tell me. By the Sun God, speak."

The priest raised his eyes. Behind his mask, they were black, deep set, aching. "Your daughter, my lord. The lady Gloriae the Gilded. You... you must see her."

Dies Irae began marching through the city, leaving the priest behind. Nightshades howled around him, toppling buildings. The streets were deserted. Only stray cats and dogs, a few beggars, and some soldiers remained; they were fleeing the nightshades, scuttling from ruin to ruin. A nightshade swooped toward him, mouth of smoke opening, revealing white teeth. It shrieked, then seemed to recognize Dies Irae. It spun around and fled. Dies Irae allowed himself a small smile and kept walking.

He hadn't seen such ruin since Requiem's fall. Confutatis, the Marble City, was utterly destroyed. A few buildings remained standing, but nightshades swarmed over them. Bodies littered the roads, both of soldiers and civilians. They were not dead, but neither were they alive. Their hearts pulsed, and their lungs pumped air, but no souls filled the shells. Those souls, Dies Irae knew, now screamed in the realms of night.

Finally Dies Irae reached the palace grounds. The Palace Flammis still stood, though one of its towers and its western wall had collapsed. Bricks and dust covered the courtyards and gardens. Dies Irae stepped around the ruins, entered the main hall, and found bodies inside. Servants, lords, ladies, and soldiers all huddled on the floor, lips mumbling, eyes blinking, but no other life filled them.

Dies Irae walked through this devastation until he reached the throne room. His daughter would be there, he knew. She would have sat upon the throne while he lay wounded. Only one who sat upon Osanna's Ivory Throne could free the nightshades.

Dies Irae pushed open the oak doors and stepped into his throne room.

He was a strong man. He prided himself on his strength. But now, a cry fled his lips.

A hundred nightshades filled the throne room. They swirled above the Ivory Throne, a cocoon of blackness and smoke. Gloriae hovered within them, her eyes closed, a butterfly inside that cocoon of night. She was nude, her body white. Her golden hair flowed around her, as if she floated underwater.

Dies Irae snarled and marched forward. He reached into the cocoon of nightshades, grabbed Gloriae's foot, and pulled her down. The nightshades resisted, tugging her, but Dies Irae kept pulling until she fell into his arms.

"Mother," the girl whispered. She was nineteen, but she seemed so young now, a child. "Mother, may our wings find the sky."

The nightshades howled, eyes blazing. The room shook. Cracks ran along the walls. One nightshade lunged at him, and Dies Irae felt his soul being tugged from his body. Ignoring the feeling, he placed Gloriae on the floor, walked to his throne, and sat upon it.

The nightshades shrieked. Chunks of rock fell from the ceiling, one narrowly missing Gloriae. Dies Irae shut his eyes, clenched his good fist, and tightened his lips. He could feel the nightshades now. The throne gave him power to tame them, the way the Griffin Heart had allowed him to tame the griffins.

Dies Irae had never tried to tame nightshades. Nobody had in two thousand years. They were more powerful than griffins; he felt that at once. Their minds were like furnaces, their hatred exploding stars.

Dies Irae growled. "I am the true ruler of Osanna!" he called out. The throne rattled. "You have claimed my daughter. You will obey me."

They fought him.

They fought him well.

Thousands of them shrieked across the empire, coiled in the night sky, and sent their fire and hatred into him. They tugged at his soul, threatening to rip it into a million pieces.

Dies Irae refused them.

They lifted his throne. They flowed around him. They hurt him. They lifted Gloriae and tossed her against the floor, again and again.

Dies Irae refused to release them. "The old kings bound you to this throne. You still owe it your fealty, beasts of unlight. *You will obey me.*"

With a shriek that shook the city, the throne room shattered. A wall came down. Through the nightshades' eyes, Dies Irae saw the north tower of his palace falling.

Still he clung to them.

He wrestled them into darkness, until they bowed before him, a sea of smoke and shadows.

Dies Irae rose to his feet. His eye no longer hurt, and when he raised his arm, it was no longer burned. Black light flowed in his wounds, powerful, intoxicating. Through the eyes of the nightshades, he could see his face. His bandage had fallen off, revealing a gaping hole where his eye had been. His hair had gone white, and his good eye blazed a bright blue.

Dies Irae laughed. "You are mine now."

Across the empire, the nightshades hissed and bowed to him.

Dies Irae walked across the cracked floor toward his daughter. Gloriae lay there, nude and battered, her hair covering her face. She looked up at him, eyes huge, deep green, haunted.

"Father," she whispered.

Dies Irae removed his robe, leaving himself in a tunic and leggings, and tossed it at her. She draped it around her nakedness and stared at him, cheeks flushed. Her lips trembled.

"Father, I— I thought that—"

Dies Irae had never hit his daughter. When she'd been a child, and misbehaved, he would beat her handmaiden, forcing Gloriae to watch. For years, he had spared her pain. For years, he had coddled her.

Today he hit her. His fist knocked her to the floor, spattering blood.

"Gloriae, daughter of Osanna," Dies Irae said, staring down upon her. Nightshades flowed above him. One draped across his shoulders. "I banish you from this city, and from Osanna. You have a day and night to run. Then I hunt you. If I catch you, your life is forfeit."

Her eyes widened. Rage bloomed across her cheeks.

"Father," she said and took a step toward him. Blood filled her mouth.

Dies Irae raised his fist again, and Gloriae froze.

"I will hear no excuses," Dies Irae said. The nightshades shrieked above him, and he pointed at the door. "Leave this place. You are banished from this kingdom. You are disowned. You are cast out in shame. Leave, Gloriae the Gilded, and never return. Today I have no daughter."

She stared at him, bared her teeth, and clenched her fists. She seemed ready to speak, and Dies Irae kept staring at her, driving his stare into her green eyes.

Finally Gloriae spun around, tightened the robes around her, and marched out of the shattered court.

LACRIMOSA

They flew east, wings churning clouds, breath hot in their lungs. Moonlight glinted on their scales. When Lacrimosa looked over her shoulder, she saw the nightshades. They were darker than the night sky, and their eyes burned, red stars.

"They're getting closer!" she cried, and heard the pain and fear in her voice. She blew fire back at the nightshades, as bright as she could make it. The other Vir Requis—her husband, daughter, and Kyrie—roared flames too.

The nightshades shrieked. The light hurt them. But they kept flying.

"I don't get it," Agnus Dei said. The young red dragon flew by Lacrimosa. "When a nightshade attacked Kyrie and me, firelight sent it fleeing. We had to nearly burn down the forest, but eventually it fled. Why don't these ones flee?"

Benedictus, a great black shadow in the night, grumbled. "You and Kyrie saw one nightshade, a scout, when twilight still filled the world. Nightshades are stronger in the night, and stronger in numbers. Firelight will no longer stop them. Sunrise burns behind the horizon. Fly! Faster!"

The nightshades shrieked again, and Lacrimosa could feel them. They tugged at her soul, as if trying to pull stuffing out of upholstery. She gritted her teeth, flapped her wings harder, and fought them. *You will not claim me. You cannot.*

She scanned the eastern horizon. Where was the sun? They flew so fast, faster than she'd ever flown. Lacrimosa felt ready to collapse, and the nightshades gave her soul a tug so powerful, she cried in pain. She left her body and floated a foot behind it. Benedictus grabbed her shoulder, and the pain jolted her soul back in.

"Fly, my love," Benedictus said to her. "We're almost there."

Tears streamed down her cheeks. Her wings burned. Her lungs felt ready to collapse. "I fly for you."

Hadn't she always flown seeking sunrise? For nearly two decades—since Dies Irae had raped her, toppled the courts of

Requiem, and stole her daughter Gloriae—she had flown seeking light. Darkness had chased her for years.

Screeches rose around her, cutting off her thoughts. They were so loud she had to cover her ears. Ten more nightshades took flight, left and right, and flew at them. The nightshades behind shrieked too, welcoming their companions. The world shook. Lacrimosa screamed.

"Fly!" Benedictus shouted. "Fly fast, the sun shines behind the mountains."

Lacrimosa flew hard. Tears streamed down her cheeks, her wings screamed, but she flew. The nightshades tugged at her. One flew only a foot away, grinning, showing its smoky teeth.

"Lacrimosa...," it hissed, and she couldn't help but stare into its eyes. They were two stars, glittering. Beckoning. There were worlds beyond those stars, dimensions that swirled and spun, a space so much wider for her soul to travel. She would be free there. In darkness. In pain.

She could see her body flying below her. A silvery dragon, so delicate, so small. The worlds in those eyes were endless. Her dragon wings stilled. She began to fall. She saw Benedictus fly toward her, grab her, dig his claws into her shoulders.

"Lacrimosa!" he cried, shaking her in midair. Kyrie and Agnus Dei flew by him, nightshades wreathing them.

"You should not struggle," Lacrimosa tried to say, but she had no voice. "Join the unlight. Join the worlds. There is loneliness here. There is pain. There is darkness to fill. Join."

"Lacrimosa!" Benedictus shouted, and he slapped her face.

Pain. She felt pain. She felt her body. *No!* It sucked her back in. It pulled her. She slammed back into her body, and that pain filled her, and she saw the world through her eyes again.

She wept.

"I'm here, Benedictus. I'm here. I'm back. Fly!"

She could see hints of dawn now. It was only a pink wisp ahead, but it filled her with hope. Benedictus saw it too, and he howled and blew fire, and flew with more vigor. The nightshades swarmed around them, hissing and laughing.

"Mother!" came Agnus Dei's voice, frightened, almost childlike.

Lacrimosa saw that a dozen nightshades swarmed around her daughter, forming a shell of smoke and shadow. She struggled between them, as if floundering in water, and screamed.

"Agnus Dei!" Lacrimosa called and flew toward her daughter. She blew fire at the nightshades. They shrieked. Benedictus and Kyrie shot flames at others. Agnus Dei screamed, the horrible sound of a wounded animal.

"Mother!" she cried, tears falling.

Lacrimosa blew more fire, but the nightshades would not leave her daughter. *No. No! I already lost one daughter. I will not lose the other.*

"Take me!" she said to the nightshades. "Leave her and take me."

They laughed their hissing laughter. Their voices were only an echo. "We will take both, Lacrimosa. We will torture you both in the worlds beyond."

Lacrimosa saw them inhale around Agnus Dei. Silvery wisps rose from the girl's body, entering the nightshades' nostrils and mouths.

"No!" Lacrimosa screamed and blew fire.

Agnus Dei went limp. She began to tumble from the sky.

As Kyrie blew fire at the nightshades, Lacrimosa and Benedictus swooped and caught Agnus Dei. Her eyes stared blankly. In their grasp, she returned to human form. She seemed so small. A youth, that was all, only nineteen. A girl with a mane of black curls and scraped knees. She lay limply in Lacrimosa's grip, eyes unblinking.

"The sun!" Kyrie called. Tears flowed down his cheeks. "Let's get her into light."

They flew eastward, blowing fire at the nightshades that mobbed them. With a great flap of their wings, they cleared a river, and sunrise broke over a cover of mountain. Light drenched them.

The nightshades howled. Their screams made the river below boil. Trees wilted and fell, and a chunk of mountain collapsed. A barn burst into flame.

"Agnus Dei!" Kyrie cried, flying toward Lacrimosa. "Is she dead?"

Lacrimosa was weeping. "No." *She is something worse.*

The nightshades tried to swipe at them, to bite and claw, but they sizzled in the light. Howling, they turned and fled back into darkness.

"Yeah, you better run!" Kyrie called after them and shot flames in their direction. Then he looked at Agnus Dei, eyes haunted. "Let's get her on the ground."

Lacrimosa nodded and descended to a valley. She landed by a willow and placed Agnus Dei on the ground. The girl lay on her back, eyes staring, not blinking, mouth moving silently. They all shifted into human form.

"Agnus Dei," Kyrie said, kneeling by her. He clutched her hand. "Are you here? It's me, Kyrie."

She said nothing. Her eyes seemed not to see him. Her hand hung limply in his grasp.

Tears ran down Kyrie's face, drawing white lines down his ashy cheeks. He kissed Agnus Dei's forehead, and shook her, but she wouldn't recover.

"Agnus Dei, you wake up right now," Kyrie demanded. "Do it, or I'm going to kick your butt so hard, it'll fall off."

Normally, Lacrimosa knew, the taunt would rile Agnus Dei into a fury, and she would be wrestling Kyrie to the ground and calling him a worthless pup. Today she only stared blankly over his shoulder. Lacrimosa also wept. She knew that Agnus Dei was not here, not in this body. Her soul was shattered and lost in the night worlds.

She and Benedictus both held Agnus Dei's other hand. The sunlight fell upon them, but would not find their daughter. She seemed cloaked in shadows. They tried shaking her, slapping her face, pinching her, singing to her, pleading with her. Nothing helped.

Kyrie looked up, eyes huge and haunted. "What do we do?" he whispered.

He looked so young to Lacrimosa. Sometimes she forgot he was only seventeen, still a youth despite all the battles and fire he'd been through.

"I don't know," she said and hugged Agnus Dei.

Her daughter was cold and limp in her arms.

GLORIAE

She rode across the countryside, eyes narrowed. She had taken little from Confutatis: Her horse, a white courser named Celeritas; her sword, crossbow, and dagger; her gilded armor, the breastplate curved to the shape of her body, the helmet a golden mask shaped as her face. Celeritas's hooves tore up grass and dirt, and Gloriae spurred the beast and lashed it with her crop.

"Faster, damn you," she said. Once she had ridden griffins, could cross a hundred leagues in a flight. Horses were slow and stupid, needed more rest than griffins, and frayed her nerves.

"Move your hooves, you mindless beast," Gloriae said and lashed her crop. Celeritas whinnied, and her eyes rolled, but she kept galloping.

Mindless beast. That was what she herself had been only yesterday, was it not? Yes. She had floated, naked and mindless, among the nightshades. Her soul had been broken, had filled thousands of nightshades across Osanna. She'd seen through their eyes, travelled through their planes. She had seen the weredragons fleeing into the east. She had seen Lacrimosa, the silver dragon who had infested her with the reptilian curse. She had seen Kyrie and Agnus Dei, the youths she had fought. And she had seen Benedictus, the Lord of Lizards, the man who claimed to be her true father, the man she had sworn to kill.

"I know where you are," Gloriae hissed through clenched teeth, the wind claiming her words. "I will find you, weredragons. I will slay you with my crossbow, and sever your heads with my sword. I will drag your heads back to Dies Irae, to my real father, and he will forgive me."

Gloriae nodded and tasted tears on her lips. Shame burned within her. Dies Irae, her real father, had trained her from birth to hate and hunt Vir Requis. She had killed many for him, but failed him now. She had failed to set the nightshades on them, had allowed the creatures to destroy the empire.

"But I will make amends," Gloriae vowed into the wind. "I do not need the nightshades. I will kill the weredragons with crossbow and blade."

Dies Irae's men hunted them too, Gloriae knew. Those who'd survived the nightshades would be patrolling every corner of the empire, armed with blades and ilbane. Whoever killed them would become a hero, a favorite son of Osanna, a lieutenant to Dies Irae. But they did not know where the weredragons cowered. She, Gloriae, had seen them through the nightshades' eyes. She had felt the nightshades tug Agnus Dei's soul, bite it, and rip it apart. Dies Irae might control the nightshades now, but Gloriae had seen enough.

As she rode, spurring Celeritas, she gazed upon the ruin of Osanna. It was daytime now, and no nightshades crawled the empire, but she saw signs of them everywhere. Forts lay toppled upon hill and mountain, blackened with nightshade smoke. Cattle lay dead and stinking in the fields. Farmhouses smoldered and bodies lay outside roadside inns.

I did this. The thought came unbidden to Gloriae's mind. She forced it down, refusing to acknowledge it.

"No," she whispered. "I will feel no guilt. The weredragons made me do it. I will redeem myself when I kill them."

She drove Celeritas out of the fields and down a forest road. The leaves were red and gold. Autumn was here, and cold winds blew, biting Gloriae's cheeks. Other than her armor—a breastplate, helmet, greaves, and vambraces—she wore little. White riding pants. A thin woolen shirt. She had brought no cloak in her haste, and she regretted that now. It was cold, colder than autumn should be. She saw frost on grass and leaf, and even Celeritas's hot body could not warm her. She shivered.

"The light and heat of the Sun God are leaving the world," she whispered. "Nightshades and weredragons have filled it, but my heart still blazes with the Sun God's fire. I will light the world with it, even if I must burn it down."

She let Celeritas rest, eat grass, and drink from a stream. Gloriae dismounted and stretched, ate dried meat and crackers from her pack, and drank ale from her skin. She dipped her head into the stream, scrubbed her face, and looked at her reflection. She was thinner than she'd ever been. Her eyes looked huge in her pale face, too large and green. Her hair was long, cascading gold, like a lion's mane. She was still beautiful, Gloriae thought, but sadder now. Haunted.

She thought back to that day in her chamber. The day she had met Lacrimosa, contracted the disease, and shifted into a dragon. With a shiver, Gloriae pushed that memory aside. She might be cursed now, but she would hide it. She would never become a dragon again. She would remain Gloriae the Gilded, human and healthy, a slayer of weredragons and never one of their number.

She was riding Celeritas again, and heading around a bend in the road, when the outlaws emerged.

They stepped out from behind trees, dressed in brown leather and patches of armor. There were three—tall and thin men, a hungry look to them. One bore a chipped sword. A second outlaw hefted an axe. The third pointed a bow and arrow at her.

Gloriae halted her horse. She raised her shield, raised an eyebrow, and stared at the outlaws from behind her visor.

"So," she said. "A swordsman, an axeman, and an archer. You must be mad. I'm on horseback and wearing armor. You don't stand a chance, so scurry along and find easier prey. You might find children you could steal sweets from."

The archer laughed, an ugly sound. "Aye, but there's three of us, and we're hungry."

He loosed his arrow.

Celeritas whinnied and bucked. The arrow hit her neck, spurting blood. Gloriae fell from the saddle and hit the ground hard. The outlaws rushed at her.

Gloriae could barely breathe, and pain filled her, but she wasted no time. She rolled, dodging the axe; it slammed down by her head. She kicked, and her steel-tipped boot hit the axeman's shin. A sword came down, and she rolled again and raised her shield. The blade hit the shield, chipping the wood and driving pain down Gloriae's arm.

She leaped to her feet, swinging Per Ignem, her sword of northern steel. It clanged against the swordsman's blade. She heard the axe swing behind her, and she ducked. The axehead grazed the top of her helmet. An arrow flew and hit her breastplate; it dented the steel, drove pain into Gloriae's side, but did not cut her.

"Who's mad now?" the swordsman said, grinning to reveal yellow teeth.

Gloriae feigned an attack, but jumped back and over Celeritas. The horse was dead. Gloriae crouched behind the body, as if hiding there, and grabbed her crossbow from the saddle. She rose to her feet to see the outlaws bounding toward her. She shot her crossbow, hitting the archer in the face. He stumbled back, screaming a gurgling scream, and hit the axeman.

Gloriae leaped over the horse, swung Per Ignem, and met the swordsman's blade. She thrust, parried, and riposted. The axeman attacked at her left; she blocked him with her shield, thrust her sword, and slew the swordsman.

The archer had fallen and was screaming, clutching the quarrel in his face. Gloriae faced the axeman. He paled and turned to flee.

Gloriae would not let him escape.

She placed a foot on her crossbow, pulled back, and loaded a new quarrel. She aimed, one eye closed, and shot. Her quarrel hit the fleeing axeman in the back, and he fell.

Gloriae walked between the trees, Per Ignem in hand, its blade dripping blood. She had fallen hard off her horse, and her side hurt, but she was otherwise unharmed. When she reached the axeman, she stood above him. He writhed at her feet, blood spreading down his shirt, and rolled onto his back.

"Please," he said, trembling. "Mercy."

Gloriae stabbed him through the chest. Blood filled his mouth and dripped from his wound. Gloriae twisted the blade, then pulled it out and walked away.

She returned to the road. The swordsman was already dead, but the archer was alive. He sat against a tree. He had managed to pull the quarrel from his face, revealing a gushing wound. When he saw Gloriae, he struggled to his feet and threw a rock at her.

The stone hit Gloriae's breastplate, doing no harm. She walked toward the man, her sword raised. He rose to flee. She chased him down and slew him between the trees. His blood soaked the bluebells that carpeted the forest floor.

Bluebells. The flower brought memories to her. She remembered seeing Lacrimosa wear a bluebell pendant, even as the creature had cowered in the dungeons of Confutatis. Gloriae had been shocked at Lacrimosa's beauty, fragility, the moonlight of her hair. How could a creature so evil seem so beautiful?

"I am your mother," Lacrimosa had said. "You have our magic, you can shift too, become a dragon."

Yes, Gloriae had shifted that night, become a golden dragon of scales, fangs, and claws. But she knew this was no gift, as the weredragons claimed, no lofty magic passed down from kings. It was a curse. Dies Irae was her father, and Lacrimosa had infested her with disease.

Jaw clenched, Gloriae again stabbed the body at her feet, as if stabbing the memory of that day.

She took what supplies she could carry from her slain horse: a rolled up blanket, a cast iron pot, three skins of ale, and a pack of battle rations. In the outlaws' pockets, she found a few coins and took those too. She slung her shield and sword over her back, and continued down the path with her crossbow in hand. She kept a quarrel loaded. Should more outlaws attack, she would shoot them. She left her horse behind, bloodied on the road; the wolves would dispose of it.

The road was long, overgrown with weeds and burrs, and rocky. Soon Gloriae's feet ached. A thistle snagged at her leggings, tearing them at the knee. Blood and mud stained her leather boots. Gloriae was bone-tired, and evening began to fall, but she refused to rest. She had to find the weredragons. She had to kill them. Had to.

"I will regain your trust, Father," she whispered through shivering lips. A cold wind blew, sneaking under her armor like the icy hands of a ghost.

When darkness fell, Gloriae wished she had brought her tin lamp and tinderbox. She had forgotten it upon her horse's body, and she cursed herself. How would she light a fire? Her horse was too far behind now, so Gloriae trudged on. Owls hooted around her, and jackals howled, but Gloriae did not fear them. Worse creatures emerged in the night.

The trees soon parted, and Gloriae found herself walking in open country. Clouds cloaked the sky, but once when they parted, revealing the moon, Gloriae saw hills and a stream. She recognized this place. The weredragons had flown here before Dies Irae had taken the nightshades from her, stealing their eyes.

"Where are you, weredragons?" Gloriae whispered, clutching her crossbow. The quarrel was coated with ilbane—weredragon poison.

A screech above answered her.

A nightshade.

Gloriae ran. Her shield and sword clanked over her back, and her boots squelched through mud. The nightshade saw her. It dived toward her, eyes blazing. She loosed her quarrel, but it passed through the creature, barely dispersing its smoky body. Gloriae cursed and kept running. The nightshade chased.

"Father!" she shouted. "Call it off!"

The nightshade only shrieked. Was Father controlling it? Was he watching through its eyes and could stop it? If so, he did not. The nightshade swooped and flowed across her. She shivered; the nightshade was so icy, it made the night winds seem warm. She swung Per Ignem at it, dispersing some of its smoke, but it only laughed.

Light. I need light! Why had she forgotten her lamp? Gloriae ran. She felt the nightshade tugging her soul, felt her spirit being torn, tugged from her body. She screamed and swung Per Ignem, but the nightshade only laughed and kept tugging. She no longer sat upon the Ivory Throne; a nightshade would show her no quarter now.

Then she saw light ahead.

It was still distant, but burned bright. A ring of fire in the valley. Gloriae ran toward it, swinging her sword and shouting. She had never run faster. With a great tug, the nightshade pulled her soul clear from her body. For a second, she saw herself from above. But the jolt of her body tripping on a root pulled her back in, and she kept running.

She reached the fire. She leaped over the flames, ignoring the pain, and spun around, panting. The nightshade hovered outside the ring of fire, ten feet above the ground. It glared at her, drooling wisps of smoke.

Gloriae grabbed a burning branch and held it before her. She stared at the nightshade, daring not remove her eyes from it.

That was when she noticed, from the corner of her eyes, that others stood in the ring of fire.

The weredragons.

Gloriae gasped, spun to face them, then spun back to the nightshade. She didn't know who posed a greater threat, but she knew that she would die. She could not defeat both these enemies.

All four weredragons were there—Benedictus, their king, a gruff man with a tangle of black curls; Lacrimosa, his wife, a dainty and pale woman; Kyrie Eleison, the boy who had wounded Gloriae's leg. Agnus Dei was there too, but she lay on the ground, eyes open but unseeing, and Gloriae knew what that meant. The nightshades had gotten her.

In a flash, Gloriae realized that she herself had claimed Agnus Dei's soul—or at least, lived in the nightshade that had done so. A shard of that soul still pulsed within Gloriae, weak but crying inside her. Now that she gazed upon Agnus Dei, she could feel it inside her, weeping, crying for release.

She had no time to ponder it further. The three standing weredragons looked at her, then shifted. Soon three dragons blew fire beside her. Gloriae ducked and hid behind her shield, but the dragons were not burning her. They were shooting fire at the nightshade. It screeched, and Gloriae watched, mouth hanging open. The creature seemed to suck in the light, to cancel it out. The dragons kept blowing fire at it, white hot fire that drenched Gloriae with sweat.

I can shift too, she thought. *I can help them. I can also blow fire. I shifted once.*

But no. She dared not, would not. She had vowed never again to shift. She would not allow the curse to claim her.

The fire kept burning, and finally the nightshade shrieked and flew away. Gloriae watched it disappear into the night, fleeing into the forest.

The weredragons shifted back into human forms. For a moment, they all stared at one another.

Then Gloriae raised Per Ignem. She would have shot them, but had no quarrel in her crossbow, nor time to load one. She pointed her blade at Benedictus.

"You will not touch me," she hissed. The ring of fire crackled around them. "Take one step forward, lizard, and your head will be my trophy."

Benedictus scowled, Lacrimosa shed a tear, and Kyrie rolled his eyes.

"Oh, give it a rest!" said the boy. He pointed his dagger at her. "Gloriae, you are denser than a mule's backside, and just about as pleasant. Even I figured out Benedictus and Lacrimosa are your parents by now, and I'm not even related. Can you really be so dumb?" He spoke slowly, as if spelling out a truth to a child. "Benedictus is your father, not Dies Irae. Lacrimosa is your mother. Dies Irae lied to you. You are a Vir Requis. Get it? Good. Now sheathe your sword, before I clobber some sense into your pretty head."

Gloriae gasped. Nobody had ever insulted her like that. If anyone ever had, they'd be broken, slung through a wagon wheel, and left to die atop her city. She took a step toward Kyrie, sword raised.

"I will cut your lying tongue from your mouth."

He gave her a crooked smile. "I'd like to see you try, sweetheart."

Benedictus stepped toward them, fists clenched. "Stop this," he demanded.

Gloriae swung Per Ignem at him.

So fast she barely saw him move, Benedictus raised a dagger and parried. With his other hand, he shoved her back. She fell two paces, snarled, and prepared to attack again... but Kyrie reached out a foot, tripping her.

She fell. Benedictus placed a boot on her wrist and yanked her sword free. Kyrie leaped onto her back and held her down, pressing her head into the mud.

"Take her crossbow too," Benedictus said. "And there's a dagger on her thigh. Grab it."

As Gloriae struggled, Lacrimosa took her weapons. She screamed and floundered, but Kyrie and Benedictus held her down. Mud and hair filled her mouth, but she managed to scream.

"Cowards! Fight like men. I will kill you, weredragons."

"Stars, she's dumb," Kyrie said, his forearm on the back of her neck, holding her head down. "Are you sure she's your daughter, Lacrimosa? Maybe she was actually born to a warthog. She does smell like one."

Gloria screamed into the mud. She felt Kyrie pull her arms back and bind her wrists. She kicked, but Benedictus grabbed her legs and tied them too.

No, no! I cannot fall prisoner to weredragons. Cannot. Tears burned in her eyes. First she had failed to kill them. Then Lacrimosa had infested her with the curse. Now the nightshades she had freed were destroying the empire, and the weredragons had captured her. Her world crumbled around her, and she screamed and wept and shouted curses.

Once she was tied up, they placed her on her back beside Agnus Dei. Kyrie stuffed an old sock into her mouth and smirked.

"I've been wearing this sock for two days," he said. "It should be nice and stinky now, and perfect for keeping you quiet."

Gloriae ceased struggling. It was pointless. The sock tasted foul in her mouth, and she glared at Kyrie with a look that swore she would kill him. Most men would cower under that glare; she had killed men after staring at them thus. Kyrie, however, only snorted and rolled his eyes again.

What will they do to me? Gloriae wondered. Would they torture her, or would the death they gave her be quick? She suspected the former, but she was ready for it. She could endure it.

Lacrimosa knelt over her, and Gloriae clenched her jaw, prepared for whatever torture the weredragon planned. But Lacrimosa only held out her bluebell pendant, clicked a hidden clasp, and it swung open. The insides of the locket were painted with a delicate hand. The right side held a painting of a brown-eyed baby with black curls. The left side featured a baby with green eyes and golden locks.

"The black-haired baby is Agnus Dei," Lacrimosa said, voice soft and sad. A tear ran down her cheek. "The golden baby is you, Gloriae. That's how you looked before Dies Irae kidnapped you."

She tried to speak, but could not. The sock still filled her mouth. Lacrimosa reached for the sock, but paused and said, "You must promise not to scream if I remove it. Do you promise?"

Gloriae glared at the weredragon woman and nodded. Lacrimosa removed the sock from Gloriae's mouth, but left her arms and legs tied.

"Dies Irae is my father," Gloriae said, letting all her fire and pain fill her voice.

Lacrimosa nodded. "Maybe. Maybe not. He raped me, Gloriae. I don't know who your father is, Benedictus or Dies Irae. But I know that I gave birth to you and Agnus Dei." She gestured at the girl, who stared unblinking into space. "She's your sister."

Gloriae looked from weredragon to weredragon. "I... I remember harps. And... columns among birch trees. I remember walking with my mother and sister through courts of marble."

Lacrimosa nodded. "You remember the courts of Requiem. Dies Irae toppled them with his griffins, and burned the birches, and stole you from me. You were only three years old. He left Agnus Dei, because she could shift into a dragon already; Dies Irae thought her cursed."

"I can shift t—" Gloriae began, then bit her lip. Suddenly she was crying and trembling. "You cursed me," she said, tears on her lips. "You infected me. The day I met you in the dungeon, when you told me I could shift, I... I turned into a dragon that day. A golden dragon. I'm horrible now, diseased."

Lacrimosa leaned down and hugged her. Gloriae squirmed, but Lacrimosa would not release her. "Gloriae, my beloved. My sweetness. You are not cursed. You are blessed with beautiful, ancient magic that flows from starlight. I knew you could shift too. You bloomed into this magic late, but the Draco stars shine bright in you. Do not fear your magic, or be ashamed of it. It is beautiful. You are not diseased, Gloriae. You are perfect and beautiful and blessed."

Gloriae wept onto Lacrimosa's shoulder. She wanted to scream, to bite, to struggle, but only trembled. Her head spun. She was not cursed? Not diseased?

"I'm so confused," she said, speaking into Lacrimosa's hair. "Dies Irae told me that you murdered my mother."

Lacrimosa nodded, weeping too. "I know, child. But I am your mother. Don't you remember me? Do you remember nothing of your first three years?"

Gloriae sniffed back tears. "I remember you, but... I thought you had planted those memories in me. With foul magic."

Lacrimosa shook her head. "Those are your real memories, Gloriae. That is who you are. Do not doubt it, and do not fear it. I love you."

Gloriae shook her head too. "It makes no sense! Why would Dies Irae lie to me? He loves me. He... he's my father."

Benedictus knelt beside them. He placed a large, calloused hand on her shoulder. "Dies Irae is my brother, and he hates me. He hates our father. He is Vir Requis too, and mostly he hates that he lacks our magic. So he killed our father, destroyed Requiem, and hunts us. He trained you to kill us, but he cannot hide the truth from you. Not any longer." Benedictus seemed overcome with emotion. His eyes were moist. "Welcome home, daughter. Welcome back to our family."

Gloriae gazed at him, this rough man, her tears blurring his hard lines. "You are my real father?"

He touched her cheek. "I don't know. But I think so. I'm almost certain." He smiled, and Gloriae could see from the lines on his face that he smiled rarely. But it was a warm smile. A good smile.

He does not hate me, Gloriae realized. *He does not try to kill me. He truly loves me.* How could he? He was a weredragon! He was evil! Wasn't he?

A twinge yanked her heart.

Gloriae froze.

Again, something tugged her chest. It felt like a demon had wrapped a noose around her heart, and was pulling it tight.

"What are you doing to me?" she demanded, breathing heavily. Were the weredragons casting a spell upon her? Her head spun. She had heard of warriors stepping into battle, then clutching their chests and dying without a scratch, their hearts stilled. Was this happening to her? Again something tugged inside her, invisible hands.

"What are you talking about?" Kyrie said. "We haven't touched you."

Gloriae clenched her jaw. Something was crawling inside her chest, pulling, whispering, calling to her.

"Sister," it spoke. "Sister, hear me."

Gloriae thrashed in her bounds. "You cast a spell upon me! Stop this black magic."

The invisible hands wrapped around her heart, her soul, her mind... and tugged. It felt like a nightshade, but nightshades pulled souls out of the body. Whatever spell infested her, it was pulling her soul inward, deeper into her body, into a world that pulsed far in memory. Gloriae resisted, gritting her teeth, clenching her fists, and kicking.

"You will not—" Gloriae began to shout... and her breath died.

"Sister, hear me!" the voice inside her cried, and pulled harder. White light flooded Gloriae.

That was it, she thought. She was dead. This black, weredragon magic was killing her. She tried to scream, to roll around, to fight it, but could not. She drowned in the light. The force pulled her. She felt herself sucked into a tunnel, and she tumbled down, deep, far, streaming into nothing. She flowed like water down a drain.

Nothing but white light.

She floated.

Sunlight fell upon her eyelids.

Gloriae opened her eyes, and saw birch leaves. They rustled above her, kissed with sunlight, the green of spring. Their shadows danced upon her, and Gloriae saw that she wore a white dress. She no longer had the body of a woman. Her body was small now, the body of a toddler, no more than two or three years old. She wore no leather boots, but soft shoes. She wore no armor, but a cotton dress.

"Where am I?" she whispered. Her voice was that of a child.

She was lying on her back, and pushed herself onto her elbows. Marble columns stood before her, their capitals shaped as dragons. *A temple,* she thought. But not a temple to the Sun God. No golden dome topped this temple. It had no ceiling, and birch leaves scuttled along its floor.

Roars sounded above her. Gloriae raised her eyes and gasped. Dragons! Dragons flew there! Not scattered refugees, but a herd. There were hundreds. Green dragons, and blue, and silver, and red, and black. They did not fly in war. They did not burn or bare fangs. They would not hurt her, Gloriae knew. She felt only warmth and love from them.

"Do you remember, Gloriae?" somebody spoke beside her. "Do you remember this place?"

Gloriae turned her head, and saw a ghost sitting beside her. It seemed the ghost of a girl her age, but Gloriae could not be sure. The ghost was near transparent, flickering in and out of sight.

"Who are you?" Gloriae whispered.

The ghost smiled. Her hair was like black smoke, a mop of curls. "I'm your sister. I'm Agnus Dei. A part of her, at least. A whisper and a speck."

"Are you a ghost?"

Agnus Dei shook her head. "I'm a figment. A shard of a soul. I live inside you now, Gloriae."

Gloriae rose to her feet. It felt strange to stand this way. She was used to standing tall and strong, powerful in her steel-tipped boots, a warrior. She was so short now, her limbs so soft, her voice so high.

"What do you mean? Why am I a child here? Is this a spell?"

Agnus Dei shook her head. "It's a memory. A memory that still lives inside me, and inside you. Do you remember being inside the nightshades?"

Gloriae nodded. "I... I flew with them, yes. I saw through their eyes. I smelled through their nostrils of smoke. My body sat upon the Ivory Throne, but my soul was scattered, hunting with a thousand nightshades."

Pollen glided through the ghostly girl. "And now my soul is shattered. The nightshades broke me into a hundred pieces. Ninety-nine of those pieces are trapped now. Nightshades devoured them. But one piece, Gloriae... the hundredth piece... that piece went into you. When you flew inside the nightshades, you claimed that piece for yourself. Maybe you didn't mean to. Maybe you didn't even know it. But that piece of my soul is trapped inside you. That piece is me, who speaks to you here."

Gloriae shook her head. Her hair whipped side to side, slapping her face. "I don't understand."

"Neither do I. But I've looked inside you, Gloriae. I've seen our past together." The ghostly Agnus Dei spread her arms around her. "Look at this place, Gloriae. This is a memory I found within you. It's no spell. It's no trick. This place is yours."

Gloriae looked around her, at the marble columns, the birches, the herds of dragons.

"It is Requiem."

Agnus Dei nodded. "Requiem sixteen years ago—when you and I lived here, twin girls."

Dapples of sunlight played across the grass. The air smelled of bluebells, trees, and life. Robins, starlings, and finches chirped in the trees. Home. Was this truly her home? Gloriae had always lived in Flammis Palace, in a room full of swords, lances, and armor. She had never lived among flowers, trees, and birds. And yet... this felt real to her. Agnus Dei spoke truth. Gloriae could feel it. This was no spell, but a memory that filled her nostrils, her ears, her eyes, and her soul.

"I remember," she whispered. "I had a cat here, a gray cat with green eyes. We lived beyond that hill, in a palace of marble. You and I shared a room. There was a fireplace for the winters, and flowers on the walls, purple ones." Her eyes moistened. "This is where I'm from. This is where I was born. But... how did I leave this place? What happened to me?"

Agnus Dei smiled sadly. She flickered more weakly now, appearing and disappearing.

"Look," she whispered and pointed skyward.

Gloriae looked, and ice flowed through her.

Griffins.

Hundreds of the beasts swooped upon Requiem. They shrieked, lashed claws, and their wings bent the trees. Riders rode them, clad in white and gold. Dies Irae rode at their lead, bearing a lance of silver and gold. His banners flapped around him, the red griffin upon a golden field. A jewel glowed red around his neck. The Griffin Heart.

"Run, Agnus Dei!" Gloriae said. She tried to grab her sister, but her hands passed through the ghostly girl.

Agnus Dei smiled sadly. "Watch, Gloriae. They cannot hurt you now."

Gloriae stood and watched the skies. The dragons crashed against the griffins, blowing fire. The griffin riders attacked with crossbows, lances, and bows. Flame and blood filled the sky. The trees burned. Feathers and scales rained. The war was like a painting of red, gold, and black, the colors swirling, mixing together, and tearing the canvas.

Gloriae wanted to fly, to fight, to kill. But... who was her enemy now? This was her home, and the griffins were destroying it. Their talons tore down trees. They crashed into columns, toppling them. Were they her warriors, or her enemy?

"Agnus Dei, what's happening?" she demanded, but she knew the answer.

Dies Irae had stolen the Griffin Heart. The war of Requiem had begun.

Flame and tears covered Gloriae's world. She fell onto her back, her eyes closed, and ash fell onto her like snowflakes.

She lay for a long time.

When she opened her eyes, it seemed like many days had passed. The griffins and dragons were gone. The fires had burned away. Requiem lay in ruin around her. The trees smoldered. The columns lay smashed. Bloodied bodies covered the field, vultures and crows gnawing on them. Requiem stank of rot, blood, and fire. Gloriae couldn't help it. She rolled over and threw up, then lay trembling.

For a moment she could only lie there, hugging herself.

"Agnus Dei?" she finally whispered. "Is this a memory too?"

Her ghostly sister still sat beside her. She nodded.

"Look, Gloriae. Stand up and look around you."

Gloriae stood on shaky legs. The ruin spread around her. She saw nothing but blood, ash, and destruction. She should be happy, she knew. Requiem was defeated! The evil of weredragons was wiped clean!

But Gloriae could not rejoice. Nothing seemed clean here. There was no Sun God light, only ash and smoke in the sky. There was no good, clean earth, only bodies and blood.

But no. Not all were dead. A group of dragons crouched behind the toppled columns. A few were warriors, tough male dragons with sharp claws and dented scales. A few were females. Some were children.

"Dragons of Requiem!" cried a burly black dragon. "Fly! Fly from here."

It was King Benedictus, Gloriae realized, but he was younger here, stronger, his voice clearer. Blood and ash covered him. He flapped his leathern wings and took flight, leading the other dragons into battle.

As Gloriae watched them fly away, she heard a new voice.

"Daughters."

She turned toward the voice, and tears filled her eyes.

It was her mother.

Mother was beautiful, her hair silvery-gold, her skin pale, her eyes deep lavender. She wore a gown of white silk. Blood and ash covered her.

"Girls, come, we must leave," Mother said. She ran toward them, feet silent on the bloody earth.

Wings flapped.

A griffin landed before Mother.

Volucris. King of Griffins. And Dies Irae rode him.

"You will not touch them!" Mother screamed and shifted into a silver dragon. She lunged at Dies Irae, blowing fire.

Volucris leaped back. Dies Irae shot his crossbow, and the quarrel hit Mother. The silver dragon screamed, lashed her claws, and hit Dies Irae's armor. Dies Irae fell from his griffin, hit the ground, and swung his sword. Mother tried to bite him, but Dies Irae held her back with his blade. Volucris leapt onto the silver dragon. Shrieks tore the air. Fire rose. Blood splashed.

Gloved hands grabbed Gloriae. Somebody hoisted her into the air.

"Mother!" she screamed. Dies Irae had grabbed her, she realized. His fingers dug into her, so painful she could barely breathe.

"No!" Mother cried. "Not my daughter. Leave her, Irae!"

Dies Irae only laughed and shot his crossbow again. He hit Mother in the neck, and the silver dragon screamed and fell.

"She's my daughter too, lizard whore," Dies Irae said. "You can keep the dark one, the freak who shifts into a red dragon. Gloriae is pure. Gloriae is not cursed. She is mine."

Mother tried to rise, but Volucris kicked her down.

Gloriae screamed and cried and twisted. "Mother!" she cried. "Sister! Help me!"

Dies Irae's gloved hand covered her mouth. She could not scream. She could not breathe. Stars floated before her eyes. She was so small, so weak, her arms so soft.

She thought she would die, and then a dozen dragons swooped upon them.

Fire. Claws. Pain and heat and blood.

Gloriae kicked and felt faint. Her lungs felt ready to burst. Her eyelids fluttered.

The world went black, then red, then blue. The next thing she knew, they were airborne. She sat in a griffin's saddle. Dies Irae sat behind her, his arm wrapped around her. Dragons chased them through the sky, and a thousand griffins screeched and flowed around them. The griffins and dragons clashed, and blood rained. The screams nearly deafened Gloriae.

"Daughter!" Mother cried somewhere in the distance. Gloriae could not see her through the smoke and fire. "Gloriae! Stay strong, daughter! I will save you."

Gloriae cried, and screamed, and kicked, but Dies Irae held her tight.

They flew from the battle. They flew from the smoke and fire, from her mother's cries. They flew over leagues of ruin, toppled temples, fallen palaces, burned forests, a million bodies. They flew to the east.

The world of ruin blurred.

She slept.

When she awoke, she saw a world of light and beauty. Forests and rivers. Farms of gold. Castles and walls. Dawn, sunset, stars, and dawn again. Still they flew, Dies Irae clutching her in the saddle. Finally she saw a city ahead, a great city of white stone, its towers touching the clouds, its banners white and gold.

"Our new home," Dies Irae said. "Behold the city of Confutatis." He stroked her hair. "I will raise you here, Gloriae. Away from the weredragons. I will raise you to be pure, and strong, and cruel. I will raise you in the light of the Sun God, to be a huntress of evil."

"I want to go home," she whispered, tears on her cheeks.

He kissed her head. "We are home, daughter."

"Where is Mother? Where is Agnus Dei?" She trembled.

Dies Irae caressed her cheek. "The weredragons killed your mother. They killed your entire family. All but me, your father. I will teach you to fight back, to kill those who hurt us. Do you understand?"

She did not, but said nothing. He took her to this city, to a palace of light and gold. He took her to a room of blades, shields, and poison. She trained. She hated. She fought and she killed. She wore gold, steel, and fury.

"I am Gloriae the Gilded," she cried to the city, a woman, a huntress, a ruler. "The weredragons cannot hide from me."

She ruled, and she warred, and she killed. She freed the nightshades, and she lived inside them, and her soul shattered. She tore into the soul of the red weredragon, this Agnus Dei. She scattered the pieces into the worlds beyond this world... all but one shard, a whisper inside her, a voice and memories.

"Do you see?" Agnus Dei whispered, a ghostly child. She was fading fast, dispersing like smoke.

"I don't understand," Gloriae whispered.

But she did. She trembled, shook her head, and wanted to scream.

She understood. She remembered.

"Now you must help me, Gloriae," Agnus Dei said. She was nothing but smoke, her voice an echo. "Return this shard of me, this bit of soul, into my body. Breathe this smoke into my lips. Return me to my body, so that I may wake, and hold you, and see you in life."

Gloriae shook her head wildly. "How can I? You are but one piece. One of a hundred."

"I will find the other ninety-nine. I will reclaim them. Please, Gloriae! Please, sister. I love you. Please. Only you can save me now. Open your eyes. My body lies here beside you. Only you can wake it."

Agnus Dei flickered like a guttering candle. Her voice faded into nothing.

"Please, Gloriae. Please...."

Gloriae's eyes snapped open.

She took a deep, desperate breath like a woman saved from drowning.

"Agnus Dei!" she cried.

The weredragons crowded around her. She was back in the true world. She was captive in the night, her limbs bound.

"Mother!" she said. Her arms trembled. "Mother, help me. He's taking me with him. He's taking me from you. Mother!"

Above her, Lacrimosa and Benedictus looked at each other, and their eyes softened. Kyrie's eyes filled with confusion.

"She's lost her mind," the boy said. "I didn't think I hit her that hard."

Gloriae turned her head, and saw Agnus Dei, not the ghostly child, but the soulless woman. Her empty body still breathed, but her breath was shallow.

Please, the voice whispered inside her. *Please.*

Gloriae took a deep, shaky breath, then looked at Benedictus.

"I think I can cure her," she said to him.

"How?" the three Vir Requis asked together.

Gloriae lowered her eyes. "I was in... inside the nightshades. When they attacked Agnus Dei." She took a deep breath, prepared for a storm of anger. "I was controlling them. Well, not truly. Mostly they controlled me, but I could see through their eyes. I know where they hid Agnus Dei's soul. They did not claim all of it. They wanted to. I wanted to. But a piece still remains inside me."

Kyrie took a threatening step toward her, fists raised. "I'm going to kill you if she dies."

Lacrimosa placed a hand on Kyrie's shoulder, holding him back, and looked at Gloriae.

"What can you do to help her?"

Gloriae shuddered. "I don't know. I understand little of it. Agnus Dei fought well; I felt it inside the nightshade. She is strong. Her soul still remembers its name. When the nightshades sucked her soul, part of it went into them, and part into me. I think I can give it back. The jolt might cure her, suck in the rest of her soul, and wake her up."

Kyrie blew out his breath loudly. It fluttered his hair. "Fighting griffins was easy. You bit, you clawed, you blew fire. These nightshades... none of it makes any sense to me."

"I understand little too," Gloriae confessed. Her head still spun from the memories. "I feel more than I understand. Their world is so different from ours. It's not a world our language has words for. It's not a world of objects or flesh. It's of endless dimensions, of emotions rather than thoughts, of smoke and shadow and darkness, not material things. They don't understand our bodies. They only see our minds. Let me go to Agnus Dei. Can you free my hands?"

The Vir Requis glanced at one another, and Gloriae knew they didn't trust her. She herself wasn't sure what she'd do with free hands. Would she try to attack them? She had spent years wanting to kill them. But... her memory was true. She knew that.

This was a piece of her twin.

Benedictus untied her hands, and Gloriae knelt by Agnus Dei. She placed her hands on her sister's cheeks. Her flesh was cold, but she still breathed. Her eyes stared blankly. They looked alike, Gloriae realized, almost shocked. Their faces were identical. Agnus Dei had a mane of black curls, and Gloriae had a mane of gold. Agnus Dei had tanned skin and brown eyes, while Gloriae had pale skin and eyes of green. But otherwise they had the same face—the same full lips, high cheeks, straight nose.

"Agnus Dei," Gloriae whispered. "Once we were together. We were one being in the womb. We are one again and need to separate. Take your spirit, Agnus Dei. Sister. It is yours."

Gloriae leaned down and kissed her sister's lips. Mist fled from her mouth into Agnus Dei's mouth. A light glowed. Agnus Dei coughed.

"Agnus Dei!" Lacrimosa called.

Gloriae looked into her sister's eyes, still holding her cheeks. "Do you hear me, sister? You have a piece of yourself now. Call your other pieces. Summon them; they are there in the worlds, you can find them, grasp them. Wake up, Agnus Dei. Your time has not yet come. Return to your body and speak to me."

Agnus Dei's mouth opened wide, and she called out, wordless. Her eyes moved. Her body floundered, but still Gloriae held her cheeks, keeping her head still.

"Sister, can you hear me?" Tears streamed down Gloriae's cheeks to land on Agnus Dei. "I was lost from you for so long. For years I wandered the world without you. I didn't know. I was torn and broken. Now I'm back, and you are lost. You are torn. You must return too. You must return and be with me, with us. I love you, Agnus Dei." Her own words shocked her, but Gloriae could not stop them; they flowed from a deep, hidden place inside her, a place now broken and spilling its secrets. "I remember you, sister. I love you."

The tears fell onto Agnus Dei's face.

The girl took a deep, ragged breath.

"Gloriae!" she called. She hugged her sister. "Gloriae, I remember you too. I saw you in the worlds. I saw us as children. I loved you once. I remember. I love you again. You've returned to us."

And then the others were embracing them too. Lacrimosa wept, and even Benedictus and Kyrie shed tears. The five hugged one another, the fire burning around them. The Draco constellation shone above.

The nightshades could return any moment, Gloriae knew. The next time, she would not be able to heal the bodies they emptied. Dies Irae would lead them upon the Vir Requis with all his wrath and pain. But Gloriae could not fear nightshades, not tonight.

Tonight her world crashed around her. Tonight memories flooded her, making her fingers tremble, her eyes water, and her head spin. Dies Irae had banished her; the weredragons had welcomed her. Who was her family? Who was she now? Gloriae looked to the sky, swallowed, and closed her eyes.

BENEDICTUS

"Get up," Benedictus said to the others. "We move."

The twins still lay on the ground, embracing. Lacrimosa and Kyrie were hovering around them, hugging and laughing and crying. Benedictus too wanted to cry, to laugh, to hug them, but forced himself to his feet. He pulled a burning branch from the ring of fire, and held it as a torch.

"What do you mean 'move'?" Kyrie asked, tearing himself away from the twins. "It took us three hours to build this ring of fire. We're safe here for the night."

Benedictus grunted. He drew his dagger and pointed at the sky. "Safe from a scout nightshade, maybe. We have enough light to send one fleeing. But you heard Gloriae. Dies Irae controls the nightshades now, and whoever controls them can see through their eyes. Dies Irae knows we're here. There's likely an army of those creatures heading our way as we speak. Up! On your feet, everyone. Agnus Dei, you too. We move."

"Where will we go?" Kyrie demanded, clutching his own dagger. "Where can we flee that's safer than here?"

"Anywhere is safer," Benedictus replied, glaring at the boy. "We move until sunrise. There will be no safety this night."

They collected their things with numb fingers. They didn't have much—a few blankets, a pot and pan, some ale and bread and salted beef. Gloriae gave her dagger to Agnus Dei, and her crossbow to Lacrimosa. She kept her sword, holding it drawn.

"We should all be armed," she explained. Still, she kept eyeing her crossbow as if she missed it, or didn't trust Lacrimosa fully, or perhaps both.

"Grab torches from the fire," Benedictus told the others. "These will serve you better than weapons tonight."

Soon they were walking along the valleys and hills, burning branches in hand. They wrapped tattered bits of a blanket around the branches' tops, fashioning torches. Benedictus kept glancing around for nightshades, but it was hard to see in the dark. Once he thought he saw one, but it was only a pair of stars behind a cloud.

As he walked, he also kept looking at Gloriae. The others did too. They all walked near her, surrounding her, glancing at her. For so many years, Gloriae had hunted them. To have Gloriae the Gilded, the Terror of Osanna, walk among them.... It was surreal, Benedictus thought.

My lost daughter. Benedictus felt a lump in his throat. *She's back.*

She saw him gazing at her, and turned to look at him. Her eyes were quizzical. Little emotion showed on her face, and Benedictus guessed that she often looked this way. It was the look of a warrior, a killer trained to feel no compassion or pain.

"When you were three years old," he said to her, "you argued with Agnus Dei over a rag doll. You pulled one end of the doll, Agnus Dei the other, until it split. Agnus Dei ran to her room, crying. That evening you brought all your dolls to Agnus Dei, ten of them or more. You gave them to her. I was proud of you."

Gloriae's eyebrows rose. "I played with dolls? I was raised on swords, arrows, and shields. I don't remember playing with dolls."

Benedictus felt an ache in his chest. "I'm sorry, Gloriae. I'm sorry for how my brother raised you. To fight. To hate. To kill. For many years, I wanted to storm Confutatis, to steal you back, but... I knew that was impossible. I knew Dies Irae was raising you, looking after you. Not as I would, no. And cruelly perhaps. But you were alive. You were well. That comforted me. I'm sorry we couldn't save you, return you to us earlier."

Gloriae stared into the distance, and for a long time, she said nothing. Finally she spoke. "Let's not talk of my childhood yet. I'm still confused. I still don't know what to think of Dies Irae. Is he my father? Are you my father? I don't know." She looked at him. "I was raised to kill you, Benedictus. That was my purpose. Give me time."

He nodded. "I will. When you're ready to talk, we'll talk. For now, you're safe here, Gloriae. At least, as safe as I can make this world for you. That perhaps is not saying much, but know that we love you. Fully. Forever."

She nodded but said nothing more. She walked staring blankly into the night, the starlight in her hair.

They saw wisps of pink dawn in the east when the nightshades shrieked.

Benedictus spun around and stared to the west. An army of nightshades flew there. There must have been thousands—tens of thousands.

"Oh great," Kyrie muttered beside him.

Benedictus shifted into Black Fang, the great dragon. "Fly!" he said. "It's almost dawn. Fly to the sun!"

The others shifted too. Lacrimosa became a silver dragon, Agnus Dei a red one, and Kyrie blue. Gloriae, however, remained standing in the field, arms limp at her sides.

"Gloriae, can you shift too?" Benedictus asked. "Or should I carry you?"

The nightshades screeched. The world trembled. They were getting closer, crackling with thunder and lightning. Gloria stared at them, shivered, then looked at Benedictus.

"I shifted once," she said. "I didn't fly then, but... I can do it. I think so. I'll try."

"Well, you better get a move on, sweetheart," Kyrie said, tapping his claws. "We haven't got all night."

Gloriae nodded, clenched her jaw, and shifted. She did so slowly, hesitantly. Golden scales grew across her. Wings unfurled from her back, trembling, growing larger and larger. Fangs grew from her mouth, then claws from her fingertips. Finally a beautiful, golden dragon stood in the grass, her eyes emerald green.

"Now fly!" Benedictus bellowed as nightshades howled behind. "All of you."

They began flying to the east, even Gloriae. The girl flew slowly, wobbling, and Benedictus kept tapping her with his tail to guide her. The nightshades were gaining on them. When Benedictus looked over his shoulder, he saw them like a puddle of oil, covering the land. Countless eyes burned in their darkness.

"We're almost there," Benedictus said to Gloriae. She was growling and flapping her wings mightily. Her jaw was clenched. "You fly very well."

She snickered. "I spent my life on griffinback. This is surprisingly similar."

When they reached the dawn and flew into sunbeams, the nightshades screamed behind. A few flew into the light, then screeched and turned back. The Vir Requis turned to watch. The nightshades bellowed. Lightning flashed between them, and stars swirled. Finally they turned to flee, and soon disappeared into the west, back to darkness.

"Yeah, keep running!" Agnus Dei shouted after them. She blew fire.

The land here was rocky, strewn with pines and mint bushes. Benedictus led the others to a hilltop. They landed by an ancient oak tree and shifted back into human forms. Kyrie and Agnus Dei began arguing about who had flown faster. Lacrimosa busied herself dividing their meager food. Gloriae stood by the oak, one hand upon its trunk, and stared silently into the west.

Benedictus approached Lacrimosa.

"Both our daughters returned to us today," he said to her softly. "Our family is whole."

His wife smiled at him. "I knew it would be so some day." She lowered her eyes. "I just wish it were on safer days."

After long moments, Gloriae left the tree and approached her parents. Finally Benedictus saw her in daylight. Her leggings were torn, her boots were bloody, and ash covered her cheeks. And yet she walked with the stately, powerful stride of a warrior. Her armor still shone. Her eyes were steel, her face beautiful but cold and deadly. Gloriae the Gilded.

"Benedictus," she said to him. "I... I am to blame for this. The nightshades were entombed in the Well of Night, in a dungeon below Confutatis, and... I freed them. I thought I could control them, use them to... well, to kill you. I'm sorry. I will leave now, and return to Confutatis, and reseal these creatures in the Well of Night."

Benedictus lowered his head. *My daughter destroyed the world in an attempt to kill me; how could such darkness have befallen our family?* He sighed, her words stinging. "Daughter, you cannot control these creatures. Not anymore. How would you seal them in the Well?"

Gloriae lowered her head too. "I don't know." She looked up again, eyes flashing, pleading. "But I must do something. I caused this. I must fix it."

The others stood around them, watching silently. Lacrimosa gazed with moist eyes. Agnus Dei and Kyrie stood holding hands, silent. Benedictus looked over them, then back to Gloriae.

"How were they originally sealed?" he asked. "Do you know?"

Gloriae shook her head. "Father— I mean, Dies Irae spoke of heroes sealing them in the Well of Night thousands of years ago. It sounded like there was a great struggle, that sealing them was a great triumph. But I don't know how it was done. Irae might be able to reseal them; he controls them now. But how are we to do it? I don't know."

Benedictus turned to the west. He gazed past the hills and valleys, as if seeking Confutatis and his brother. Finally he turned back to the others.

"It's time," he said, "that we hold council, and decide what to do. Sit down, we'll build a fire, and we'll talk."

Once they were seated around a campfire, eating the last of their rations, Benedictus spoke again.

"We must rebuild Requiem, our home among the birches. We must rebuild the Vir Requis race. But we cannot do so while these nightshades hunt us, as we could not while griffins hunted us. We freed the griffins, and now we must seal the nightshades in the Well of Night, as Gloriae said. First we must learn more about them. We know they steal souls. We know they fear light. But where are they from? How were they first sealed? How can one reseal them?"

Kyrie rolled his eyes. "So we're on a quest for knowledge now? I prefer a straight fight, like with the griffins. Bite, scratch, kill. That's my kind of mission."

Benedictus glowered at him. "Quiet, kid. Don't speak unless you have something smart to say. In other words, don't speak at all." He sighed and his voice softened. "When I was prince of Requiem, and the old kings still ruled in Confutatis, I would visit the city. I especially liked exploring the city library. I recall great chambers full of scrolls and books. Dies Irae has no use for books, but the kings he usurped had collected them. Gloriae, does the library still stand?"

She nodded. "Yes, I've seen it. The books are still there. Irae does not read them. Nor would I, or anyone else. But the library is a beautiful building, of marble columns and gilded ceilings, so Irae left it standing."

Benedictus grumbled. "Maybe if Irae spent more time reading books, and less time polishing swords, his empire would prosper. The library might contain books about nightshades.

We might find the answers we need there." He placed a hand on Gloriae's shoulder. "Daughter, you know Confutatis better than we do. You know its alleys and secret halls. You will travel there, in disguise, and seek books about nightshades. We must learn how the elders sealed them."

"Great!" Kyrie said, rising to his feet. He seemed thrilled to get rid of Gloriae. "Gloriae will go read some books, and meanwhile, the rest of us will fight the nightshades. Right? Right, Benedictus?"

Benedictus shook his head. "Sorry, kid, but no. You're going with Gloriae—to protect her on her way."

Both Kyrie and Gloriae began to protest, voices raised and hands waving.

"I don't need some callow boy to protect me!" Gloriae said.

"I don't want to go to some dusty library, especially not with *her*!" Kyrie said.

Benedictus scowled. "I haven't asked what you want, or what you need. I tell you what to do. You obey. This isn't a request, this is a command." Then his voice softened. "Gloriae, you are strong and brave. But you sleep at night, don't you? You'll need a companion to guard while you sleep, at least."

"I am not a bodyguard," Kyrie said.

"No," Benedictus agreed. "You are a strong fighter. I've seen you fight, and I can tell you: You fight as well as the greatest warriors I've commanded. I need a good fighter like you for this quest."

Kyrie beamed with pride. His cheeks turned red, his chest puffed out, and he seemed to grow an inch taller. "Very well. When you put it that way, I suppose it makes sense. We'll go to Confutatis. We'll find books for you. But if I see Dies Irae, I'm going to kill him."

Benedictus nodded. "If you see him, you have my blessing to do so."

Agnus Dei had sat silently throughout the meeting, chewing a piece of dried meat. Now she stood up, shook her black curls, and snorted. "So Kyrie and Gloriae go on a quest. What about the rest of us? What, we just wait here and hope the nightshades don't kill us?" She shuddered. "I don't want to meet those nightshades again. Not after what they did to me."

Benedictus shook his head. "You have a task too, Agnus Dei. You will join me. We go to Requiem."

The others gasped.

"Requiem?" Agnus Dei whispered. "Dies Irae will know to seek us there among the ruins. He knows we want to rebuild our courts. The place will be swarming with his men, and probably with nightshades too."

"Maybe," Benedictus said. "But we must seek knowledge there too. Not only Osanna has books. The Vir Requis elders were wise. They wrote much of their wisdom onto scrolls. They did not keep the scrolls in libraries, but in underground tunnels. Those tunnels might have survived the fall of Requiem. They might still contain scrolls. We will seek knowledge of nightshades there."

Agnus Dei shuddered again. "Tunnels beneath ruins, in a land swarming with nightshades. Lovely."

For the first time, Lacrimosa spoke. The dainty woman, Queen of Requiem, stood up. She wrapped her cloak around her, shivered in the wind, and said, "And I will fly to seek the griffins."

They all gaped at her. Kyrie rubbed his eyes.

"It's official now," the boy said. "Lacrimosa has gone mad."

"My love," Benedictus said to her. He walked to his wife and held her hands. "Are you sure? The griffins still hate us. They no longer serve Dies Irae, but they remember centuries of servitude to Requiem's kings. They were slaves to my father, as they were slaves to Dies Irae. They hold no love for Requiem, even now."

Lacrimosa nodded. The wind played with her pale hair. "I know. But we need them, Benedictus. Not to be our slaves. To be our allies." Wind blew, and she shivered again. "If we're to rebuild Requiem, to raise her from the ruins, we'll need allies. We cannot face Dies Irae alone, just the five of us. Even if we seal his nightshades, he'll still have men, horses, armies. The salvanae are our allies, but they live far in the west, and might not readily fight with us again. The griffins hate us? Maybe. But they will hate Dies Irae more. I will speak to Volucris, the prince of griffins. He served as Irae's mount. He will hate the man. I will have him join our war."

Benedictus embraced her and kissed her forehead. "The griffins live many leagues beyond the sea. They dwell on islands no Vir Requis has visited in centuries, maybe millennia."

Lacrimosa nodded, staring into the east. Geese flying south for winter reflected in her eyes. "I know. I will find them."

Benedictus pulled Agnus Dei into the embrace. After a moment's hesitation, Kyrie and Gloriae joined too. The five Vir Requis, the last of their race, held one another, huddling together in the cold. The grass and trees moved in the cold autumn winds.

"The moon is full tonight," Benedictus said. "In two more moons, we meet in Fidelium Mountains. We meet in the cave where Agnus Dei and Lacrimosa hid throughout the summer."

They nodded, embraced again, and whispered teary goodbyes. Benedictus hugged and kissed Lacrimosa.

"Come back to me," he whispered.

She nodded and caressed his rough, stubbly cheeks. "Now and always."

Kyrie and Agnus Dei embraced too, and when they thought nobody was looking, they shared a kiss. Benedictus pretended not to see. He wanted to grumble and throttle the boy, but he only grunted and looked away. Agnus Dei had found a good man, he knew. Kyrie was a man now, seventeen this autumn. As much as Kyrie irked him, Benedictus knew his heart was true.

"It's time," he said softly after the goodbyes were said. "We go. Keep to human forms. Shift into dragons only when nobody can see, and only when you must. The skies are watched. The ground is safer. Remember that."

They nodded. Everyone but Gloriae had moist eyes; hers were cold, almost dead.

Kyrie and Gloriae began moving downhill, armed with dagger and sword. Lacrimosa, holding the crossbow, headed east.

Benedictus held Agnus Dei's hand. "We go north, daughter. We go to the ruins of Requiem."

They began walking. The winds moaned, ice cold. Winter was coming.

KYRIE ELEISON

"First thing we'll need is a good horse," Gloriae said.

Kyrie rolled his eyes. They were only minutes away from the hill they'd camped on, and already she was complaining.

"Walking not good enough for you, princess?" he asked.

Gloriae glared at him. Her eyes flashed with green fire, and blood rushed into her cheeks. "Watch your tongue, boy. You are not my family. I owe you no fealty, and if you speak out of line, I will bash respect into you."

Kyrie snorted. "Spare me. You might have been high and mighty in Osanna. But if I recall correctly, Dies Irae banished your backside. Out here on the run, you're no more important than me."

She gritted her teeth. "I am the daughter of King Benedictus, Lord of Requiem, am I not? You are Vir Requis. I am your princess. You will show me respect, and you will obey me."

Kyrie couldn't help it. He burst out laughing, which seemed to only further infuriate Gloriae. Her cheeks were deep pink now.

"My princess? Oh, pardon me, Your Majesty," Kyrie said. He sketched an elaborate bow. "How shall I serve the princess? Shall I fetch thee thy slippers? Perhaps some tea and pastries?"

She tried to slap his cheek. Kyrie caught her wrist, blocking the blow. They stared at each other. Gloriae was thinner than him, but almost as tall, and her eyes blazed. Golden flecks filled her green eyes, he noticed, like sparks from fire.

"Release my wrist," she said.

Kyrie shook his head. "Depends. Will you slap me again?"

"Maybe."

"Then I'm not letting go."

She kicked his shin. Kyrie yelped and released her arm, and she punched his chest. He couldn't breathe. She kicked him again, and he fell to the ground.

He grabbed her leg and pulled.

Gloriae fell, and before she could recover, Kyrie was atop her. He pinned her arms down and snarled.

"Do I have to tie you up again, princess?"

She tried to bite him. He pulled his head back, narrowly missing her teeth. She spat at him instead, hitting his eye.

He grunted, rolled off her, and rose to his feet. She stood up too, eyes now icy, fists raised.

"Had enough, boy?" she asked. A crooked smile found her lips.

Kyrie wiped her spit off his face. "I think I'm going to be sick."

Gloriae shook her mane of golden hair. "Look, kid. I don't like walking. I don't like blisters. I like riding. If I can't ride a griffin, and if Benedictus said we can't shift into dragons, I want a horse." She pointed to a town a league away. "They'll have horses."

Kyrie looked at the town. He couldn't see much from here, only stone walls and chimney smoke. "And I suppose you'll walk in and demand they give you one, because you are Gloriae the Gilded, Maiden of Confutatis?"

She shook her head and sighed. "Those days are behind me. But I have gold in my pouch. Not much, but enough to buy a horse and some food. We'll buy disguises too. Come, Kyrie. We go to town."

Kyrie grunted. He doffed his cloak and handed it to her. "Wear this. You don't want people seeing that gilded, jewelled armor of yours. You'll stick out like a golden thumb."

Gloriae took the cloak and sniffed it. "This thing stinks, and there are moth holes in it. God, don't you ever wash it?"

"Sorry, princess, but when you're on the run from griffins and nightshades, laundry isn't exactly a priority."

Wrinkling her nose and groaning, Gloriae donned the cloak. She coughed. "Now I think *I'm* going to be sick."

"Just don't throw up on my cloak."

"Not that it would make it any dirtier or smellier."

They walked downhill toward the town, pebbles crackling beneath their feet. Ant hives and mole burrows littered the earth. Crows and geese flew above. The wind kept blowing, rustling the sparse grass and mint bushes. When they were closer to town, Kyrie noticed that something was wrong.

"That smoke... it doesn't look like chimney fire."

Gloriae shook her head. "This place is burning."

They found a dirt road leading to the town walls. They followed it to the gates, which were open. The guards lay slumped by them, eyes staring blankly, chests rising and falling, mouths open and drooling.

"Nightshades were here," Kyrie whispered.

Gloriae rolled her eyes. "Sir Obvious saves the day again."

Kyrie glared. "Why don't you show some respect? People died here."

Gloriae shook her head and hitched the cloak around her. The wind moaned, scattering ash. "No, they're not dead. They probably wish they were, though."

They entered the town and walked along its streets. Many of the buildings had burned down. Some still smoldered, flames crackling within them. Bodies littered the streets. Some were burned. Some had fallen upon swords. Most were still alive, but soulless.

"They must have realized the nightshades hate light," Gloriae said, walking down a cobbled street between smoldering shops. She coughed and waved smoke away. "They knew firelight scares them. They ended up burning down the town."

Kyrie shuddered. "Lovely creatures, the nightshades. Let's get out of here."

Gloriae shook her head. "We came for horses. We'll find them."

Kyrie wanted to throttle her. "Horses? How can you think of stealing horses from this place? This is a graveyard, Gloriae. I don't like it here. Let's leave."

Her eyes flashed with rage. "If there are horses here, they'd die alone. Would you leave them to starve? Let's find a stable."

They kept walking. The devastation worsened as they walked deeper into town. When they reached town square, they found a hundred bodies on the cobblestones, twisting and drooling. The shops surrounding the square smoldered. Many had shattered windows and doors; people had looted them.

Kyrie pointed with his dagger. "That temple is still standing."

It looked like an old building, round and crumbling. Kyrie guessed it had once been an Earth God temple, now converted to Dies Irae's new religion. A bronze Sun God disk crowned its dome.

"Do you think the priests are alive inside?" Gloriae asked.

"I don't know, but I have an idea. Follow me."

They entered the temple and winced. Hundreds of people were crammed inside. Many were dead and stinking. Others were alive, but soulless. Ash and smoke clung to the walls, as if nightshades had rubbed against them.

Gloriae covered her nose. "God, it's awful."

Kyrie pointed at two priests, a man and woman, who lay slumped upon a stone altar. "White cloaks. White masks. Disguises."

Gloriae glared at him. "Stealing from dead Sun God priests? You're mad, Kyrie."

He snorted. "The Sun God can go kiss Dies Irae's wrinkled old backside. And besides, those priests aren't dead. They're just... missing their souls. Look, Gloriae. We can't just saunter into Confutatis as we are. Dies Irae knows my face. He'd recognize you too, even in that smelly old cloak. But if we enter with the robes and masks of priests, well... the city will be ours. Nobody would try and stop us."

Gloriae sighed. "Fine, but I hope the Sun God forgives us." She closed her eyes and muttered a prayer.

Kyrie groaned, rolled his eyes, and went to the priests. Soon he and Gloriae were walking down the town streets, clad in white silk. They kept the white masks in their backpacks; there was no point wearing them now, not with the whole town soulless. They walked until they found stables by a manor. Half the stables were burned and smoking.

"Think there are any horses alive in there?" Kyrie asked.

"Let's see," Gloriae said.

They stepped into the stables to another ugly scene. Many horses had burned. Others had died in the smoke, or maybe the nightshades had attacked them too. The beasts lay on the ground, buzzing with flies. Only one horse lived, a chestnut mare with a white mane.

"There there, girl," Gloriae whispered to the horse. It whinnied and bucked, but Gloriae kept patting its nose and whispering soothing words into its ears. Finally it calmed, and Gloriae kissed its forehead. "Good girl, good girl."

"If only you were so sweet with people," Kyrie muttered. As Gloriae kept patting the horse, Kyrie couldn't help but stare at her. She looked so much like Agnus Dei, the girl he loved, and it confused him. True, Agnus Dei had tanned skin and black curls, while Gloriae was all paleness and golden locks, but otherwise, the two were identical. Even their tempers and the fires in their eyes were the same.

Kyrie shook his head to clear it. *Cool it, Kyrie,* he told himself. Gloriae might be beautiful, achingly so, but she was Agnus Dei's sister. And he loved Agnus Dei more than anything. He didn't want anyone else. *So stop thinking about Gloriae like that right now,* he told himself. He didn't care if she was the most beautiful woman in the world; she was a snake, and he didn't trust her. For all Kyrie knew, Gloriae still worked for Dies Irae.

Kyrie remembered that day at Fort Sanctus. The Lady Mirum had raised him there since Dies Irae had murdered his parents. For ten years he had lived with her at the seaside fort... until Dies Irae and Gloriae arrived. Until they murdered Lady Mirum. To be fair, Kyrie told himself, Dies Irae had landed the killing blow. But Gloriae had been there. She had watched, smirking. Kyrie vowed to never forgive her for that. Benedictus and Lacrimosa might have forgiven Gloriae, but they had to; they were her parents. Kyrie, however, was unrelated. He knew that once a killer, always a killer; he would always hate Gloriae.

"All right, stop cooing to that horse, and let's go," he said. He ached to leave this town. The whole place stank of blood and fire.

Gloriae saddled the horse and mounted it. She patted the half of the saddle behind her. "Well, come on, little boy. I thought you wanted to leave. Up you go."

Kyrie raised an eyebrow. "I'm not riding that thing. I'll walk."

She snorted. "I intend to gallop today. You would not keep up walking. Into the saddle. You're not afraid, are you?"

Kyrie had never ridden a horse, and in truth, he was a little afraid. But he refused to show it. "All right, all right," he muttered. He tried to mount the saddle, slipped, fell, cursed, and tried again. Gloriae watched, silent, eyes never leaving him. Kyrie cursed and grumbled and struggled. Finally he pulled himself into the saddle and sat behind Gloriae.

"Comfortable?" she asked.

He wasn't. His legs felt stretched, and the saddle pushed him against Gloriae. His torso was pressed against her back, and her hair covered his face.

"I'm fine," he said.

"Then we ride."

Her boots were spurred, and she nudged the horse. Soon they were riding through the town. Kyrie had never felt more uncomfortable. The saddle hurt his legs. He felt ready to fall off any moment. He kept sliding around, and had to wrap his arms around Gloriae's waist to steady himself. The vertigo and wide saddle were bad enough. Worse was feeling Gloriae's body. To have her bouncing up and down against him, her hair in his nostrils, was just... wrong. It felt intoxicating and horrible.

"You okay back there, kid?" she asked, leading the horse out of town and into the countryside.

"I wish we could just fly," he muttered.

"You heard Benedictus. Too dangerous. Irae's men would see us for leagues."

He snorted. "I'd prefer they saw us. I'd prefer a fight to this slinking around. Can you please take your hair out of my face?" He spat out a lock of the stuff.

"I could wear my helmet, but it would bash your nose in. I think you would prefer my hair."

Kyrie moaned. The horse clipped down a road, wilted willows and elms at their sides; the nightshades had flown here too. "Why did I have to go with you?" he lamented.

Gloriae looked over her shoulder at him. Her cheeks were pink with wind. "Because Benedictus doesn't want two young female Vir Requis together. He wants me and Agnus Dei apart."

Kyrie glared. He hated those green eyes of hers. He hated every freckle on her nose. "Why? You two are sisters. Doesn't your dad want you two to bond or something?"

"Kyrie," she said, "you really are dense. I hope your dagger is sharper than your mind."

Kyrie bristled. He opened his mouth to speak, but Gloriae cut him off.

"There are only three Vir Requis females left," she said. "We can bear children. We can continue the race. You think Benedictus wants to place all our eggs in one basket? What if only death awaits in Confutatis? Then Agnus Dei and Lacrimosa can still bear more children. What if the underground below Requiem collapses, killing Agnus Dei? Well, then maybe you and I will survive, and can have children."

Kyrie felt hot in the face. He was keenly aware of Gloriae's body pressed against him, bouncing in the saddle, and of the smell of her hair in his nostrils. He cleared his throat. "Well, why didn't he send Agnus Dei with me, then?"

"You know why. Agnus Dei doesn't know Confutatis. She wouldn't find the library. I know the city."

Kyrie wanted to say more, but could not. To bear children with Gloriae? He hated himself for it, but couldn't help imagining Gloriae naked, lying against him, her breasts in his hands, and—

No. He pushed the thought aside. He loved Agnus Dei. And he hated Gloriae. Didn't he?

"Do you think we'll find anything in Confutatis Library about how the elders sealed the nightshades?" he asked. "Lady Mirum had a library too, at Fort Sanctus, but it was all prayer scrolls and—"

He bit his words back, realizing what he'd said.

Gloriae looked over her shoulder at him. Then she halted her horse and dismounted. She stood in a patch of grass under an elm. Hills rolled around them.

"Off the horse," she said to Kyrie. "Talk time."

"Look, Gloriae. Forget it. All right? We both know what happened, and—"

"Off. The. Horse."

He dismounted, fingers shaking slightly, and stood before her. Gloriae stared at him, eyes icy, cheeks pinched. The wind streamed her golden locks. What she did next shocked Kyrie so badly, he lost his breath.

Gloriae the Gilded, the Light of Osanna, the Killer of Vir Requis... hugged him.

"Kyrie," she whispered into his ear, "I know you're always going to hate me. Maybe someday I will hate myself too. You were an enemy to me. You and the Lady Mirum. I was raised to hate my enemies. To crush them. That is what we did at Fort Sanctus. I show no mercy; you already know that about me. That was true then, and it's true now."

"Gloriae, forget it, really," Kyrie said. He squirmed out of her embrace. "Can we not talk about this now?"

"Fine, Kyrie. Just remember that I didn't know I was Vir Requis then. I thought the Vir Requis were monsters, that they killed my mother. That's what Dies Irae told me. You may hate me and judge me harshly. I just ask that you remember that. Do I regret what I did? I don't know. I'm still confused. Just promise me I won't wake up one night with a knife in my throat."

He groaned. "I was going to make you promise the same."

"I promise. I won't kill you, Kyrie."

Her words sounded both comical and chilling. He nodded. "I won't kill you either. And... I understand. About Dies Irae. At least, I'm trying to. That doesn't mean I don't hate you. I'll always hate you, Gloriae. But I won't kill you in the night. Deal?"

She shook his hand. "Deal. Now back on the horse."

They kept riding, soon moving into a forest of old oaks. Kyrie felt hopelessly lost, but Gloriae seemed to know the way. "I would normally fly over these lands on griffinback, but I can find my way on horseback too," she explained.

In the evening, they reached a crossroads, a tavern, and a well. They heard no sounds of life, but smoke rose from the chimney. The tavern's iron sign read "Oak Cross"; it swung in the wind, creaking.

Kyrie sniffed the air. "I smell beef stew." His mouth watered and his stomach grumbled. "Think there's anyone alive in there?"

"What do you think, Kyrie?"

He sighed. "You know what I think. But I don't care. I'm hungry enough to dine among bodies."

They dismounted, led their horse to the tavern stables, and found no stableboy or horses. They tethered their horse, fed it hay, then stepped toward the tavern.

Gloriae drew her sword, Kyrie drew his dagger, and they stepped inside.

Kyrie grunted.

"I knew it," he said.

Bodies lay slumped against the tables and bar. They were not dead, merely soulless, but that didn't stop two rats from gnawing on one's face. The man had only a bit of cheek and forehead left. The rats screeched, teeth bloody, and fled. Kyrie covered his mouth, nauseous.

"Lovely," Gloriae said, looking a little green. She gestured with her sword to a doorway. "The kitchen would be back there. Let's eat."

Kyrie hesitated. "It's almost night. Do you think the nightshades will return?"

Gloriae shrugged. "They might. But I'd rather face them here, with a burning fireplace and food in my belly."

Kyrie wanted to argue, but he could smell beef stew and bread, and that overcame all other thoughts. They stepped into the kitchen to find a cook slumped on the ground. They propped him up against a wall, found a pot of simmering stew and bowls, and returned to the common room to eat. They filled mugs from a casket of ale at the bar. As they ate, Kyrie kept looking outside the windows. It was getting darker. Soon night fell.

"Let's add some logs to the fire," he said.

Gloriae nodded. Soon the fireplace blazed. They found oil and lit the tin lamps around the common room. Wind rattled the shutters, and the lamps swung on their chains, swirling shadows like demons.

"It's still not very bright in here," Kyrie said. He clutched his dagger, as if that could stop the nightshades. *As if anything could stop them,* he thought.

"No," Gloriae whispered. She was pale. The firelight danced against her face.

They returned to their table and sat silently, weapons drawn.

"At least we had one good, last meal, huh?" Kyrie said.

Gloriae regarded him with eyes that were clearly not amused.

A log in the fireplace crackled.

Lamps swung.

Outside, nightshades shrieked.

Gloriae stiffened, and her hand tightened around the hilt of her sword. Kyrie bit his lip and struggled not to shiver. It was a horrible sound, so high pitched it raised his hackles. Even the bodies on the floor and tables shivered, as if they could still hear.

"Glor—" Kyrie began.

"Shh!" she hushed him. Her face was a mask of pain and rage.

The nightshades kept shrieking, and soon Kyrie could see them out the windows. They swirled around the inn, rustling the trees, creaking the walls. *Please, Draco stars, send them away,* Kyrie prayed. *Let them leave this place.*

Had nightshades found Agnus Dei too? What about Lacrimosa? Kyrie clenched his jaw. Would they all die this night?

A window smashed open in the kitchen.

A nightshade shrieked, its shadow spilling into the common room.

Gloriae slumped onto the tabletop, her arms sprawled at her sides.

No! Kyrie thought. *The nightshades got her.*

"Gloriae," he whispered and clutched her.

She glared at him. "Down, you idiot!" she whispered. "Play dead."

Kyrie slumped across the table too, closing his eyes to slits. Just then the nightshade burst from the kitchen into the common room. It was a huge thing, twenty feet long, maybe thirty. It snaked around the room, sniffing at the bodies. When it neared the fireplace, it shrieked so loudly, the casket of ale rattled and shattered. Ale spilled across the floors.

Kyrie wanted to shift. He wanted to blow fire. He wanted to flee. But a thousand nightshades filled the forest outside. He knew that if they attacked too, he would die. He kept lying against the tabletop, not moving, peeking beneath his eyelids. Gloriae was slumped against him, her hair once more tickling his face, her hand under his.

The nightshade moved from body to body, sniffing. It cackled, a sound like the fireplace. It then moved its great, wispy head of smoke to Kyrie and Gloriae.

The head hovered over them. Kyrie had never seen one so close. He had often thought them made of smoke, but he saw that was false. They were made of black, inky material that swirled. Stars seemed to shine inside them. Their eyes were glittering stars, so bright they burned him.

Go away, he prayed. *Leave this place.*

The nightshade sniffed him and Gloriae and seemed to be considering. It had passed over the other bodies quickly, but it paused over them.

It knows we're alive, Kyrie thought. *Stars, it knows.*

The sound of hooves sounded outside.

"Back, demons!" cried a voice outside. Several other voices screamed. "Back!"

The nightshade over Kyrie and Gloriae screamed. It was so loud, Kyrie's ears thrummed. With a jerk, the nightshade left them and flowed outside the window.

Kyrie raised his head an inch. Gloriae did the same, staring at him. Her eyes were ice, as if she felt no fear.

"Is it gone?" Gloriae whispered.

Kyrie nodded. "For now. But they'll return. It smelled a ruse. Let's move upstairs, it might be safer there."

They hurried to the tavern's second floor and entered a bedroom. They found a single bed, two bodies within it.

"Under the bed," Kyrie whispered. "They might not find us there."

"Kyrie, these are nightshades. They're smart enough to look under a bed."

Kyrie glared. "If you have any other ideas, I'd like to hear them. I don't think they're that smart. If they were smart, they'd have caught us in the common room. We leave the bodies in the bed. We hide beneath them. If a nightshade enters the room, it'll see the bodies and leave."

Gloriae sighed. "Well, I don't have any better ideas, so we'll try it."

They crawled under the bed. It was dusty, dark, and cold. They crept into the middle and huddled together. The nightshades shrieked outside, and soon the screams of men died. Kyrie could hear the nightshades smash tables and plates in the common room below. He pushed himself deeper into the shadows under the bed, close to Gloriae.

As Gloriae huddled against him, Kyrie found himself cursing the endless circumstances he found himself pressed against her. First there was the horse, then the table, now this. He tried not to think about her. He tried to ignore the smell of her hair, the curve of her body, the beauty of her eyes. But damn it, how could he ignore all that when he kept finding himself huddled against her?

Cool it, Kyrie, he told himself again. *This is hardly the time or place. And it's Agnus Dei you love. Only her. Not Gloriae.*

As the nightshades screamed downstairs, Kyrie thought of Agnus Dei. He remembered the softness of her lips against his, the warmth of her hands, her mocking eyes. He missed her so much, he ached. He couldn't wait to get back to her, to get away from Gloriae.

Someday you and I will live together in a reborn Requiem, he thought, willing his thoughts to travel into her mind. *We'll be together forever, Agnus Dei. I love you.*

The door burst open, and two nightshades flowed into the bedroom. Kyrie froze, not daring to breathe. Gloriae clutched his hand so tightly, it hurt.

The nightshades screamed and swirled across the room. The curtains swung, and the lamp on the bedside table guttered. The nightshades sniffed the bodies on the beds, screeched, and then they were gone.

"It worked!" Gloriae whispered.

Kyrie nodded. "Let's stay under here for tonight. We might be safe here if they return. You sleep for a few hours, and I'll watch. I'll wake you for your watch."

He had barely finished his sentence before she was asleep, her face on her hands. Kyrie could barely see her in the darkness. Once, when the moonlight flowed through the window, it touched her cheek. Kyrie marvelled at how soft and white it looked.

Then shadows covered the moon, and the night fell into long, cold darkness.

LACRIMOSA

She walked through the country, watching leaves fall from wilted trees. They glided before her, danced around her feet, and reminded her of the birch leaves that would fall in Requiem. *My home.*

She smiled sadly as she recalled the light that had shone between Requiem's columns, and the harpists who walked in white silk, and the birches she would play among as a girl. Those columns were smashed now, and the birches burned, and so did Osanna now lie in ruin.

Everywhere she looked, Lacrimosa saw the nightshades' work. Smoldering houses. Fallen temples. Bodies lying along the roads. When she saw these empty shells, she wiped the sweat and dirt off their faces, and closed their eyes lest flies nest within them, and prayed for them. She no longer knew if the stars heard her prayers, if they still lit the world. How could such horrors exist in realms where stars still shone? Perhaps their light was not holy, but mere memories of old gods, dying flames.

Icy wind blew, ash fluttered, and Lacrimosa felt coldness spread inside her.

"All the world has fallen. Can I still find starlight under the sky? Can I still find joy here for my family?"

Two more leagues down the road of ruin, and Lacrimosa came upon the soulless body of a knight. He was middle aged, his face weathered, his beard rustling with insects. A swooping vulture was emblazoned on his shield. House Veras, she knew, and lowered her eyes. Her heart felt colder, the world darker. She had seen this coat of arms before. Griffin riders bearing these banners had descended upon her home once; it seemed a lifetime ago. The blood of her parents and siblings had splashed these vulture shields.

"Are you the man who killed my family?" she asked the body.

For once, no tears found her eyes. The pain seemed too great for tears; it froze them dry. Had her stars truly abandoned her? Or worse, did they mock her by showing her this knight, this murderer?

A glint caught her eye, and she stared down. The knight bore a jewelled sword. Sapphires shone upon its hilt, arranged as the Draco constellation. The scabbard was filigreed with silver birches. This was no sword of Osanna. Now tears did fill Lacrimosa's eyes, and streamed down her cheeks. She smiled through them. She fell to her knees and raised her eyes to the sky. She laughed and trembled.

"You have not abandoned me, my stars," she whispered. She laughed again and clasped her hands together. "I will never more lose hope in your glow."

She reached gingerly toward the sword, as if reaching for a holy relic. It hissed as she drew it, and its blade caught the light. It shone upon her face like the Draco stars, like the souls of her slain family. This had been her father's sword.

"I will never more lose faith, Father," she whispered. She took the scabbard and hung it from her belt. "I will never more fear, not with your sword on my waist. I will never more walk in darkness, for I know that your light shines upon me. Thank you for this gift."

Vir Requis fought as dragons; their swords were beacons of honor, of ceremony, of beauty. Stella Lumen, her father had named this blade. The light of stars. The light of her soul.

"I will carry your honor. I still fight, Father. For your memory. For your grandchildren. For our lost home. I love you forever."

She kept walking through swirling ash and dead leaves, her hand on the hilt of her sword.

That evening, she found a farmhouse among burned fields. *The peasants burned their crops to ward off the nightshades,* she thought. The sunset red around her, Lacrimosa entered the farmhouse, and found a family there. The nightshades had robbed them of their spirits. The parents huddled over three children, eyes still wincing, mouths still open as if in screams.

Silently, Lacrimosa moved the bodies away from the hearth, and laid them side by side. She gave them water from her wineskin, closed their eyes, and covered them with blankets.

Night was falling. Lacrimosa scanned the room and saw a chest by the wall. She hid inside, closed the door, and waited.

She did not have to wait long.

The nightshades emerged as the sun set, howled, rattled the house, and shook the chest. Lacrimosa shivered inside, hugging her knees, prepared to leap out if she must, to shift into a dragon and breathe fire. But the nightshades did not sense her. Perhaps they saw the soulless farmers, and knew they had already claimed this house, and moved on.

She slept fitfully inside the chest, and emerged at dawn with stiff muscles.

She missed her family. It ached in her belly. Hunger ached there too, but there was no food in this house. If there had been any before the nightshades, looters had taken it. Lacrimosa moved on. Once more she walked through desolation. She wore her father's sword on her hip, and kept her hand on its pommel.

In the afternoon, she saw the place she sought. The sea, and the port of Altus Mare, lay before her.

She had never been to Altus Mare, but she knew it from stories. Poets sang of its crystal towers that gazed upon the sea; its thousand ships of wood, rope, and canvas; its wharfs where sailors, peddlers, and buskers crowded for space. In the stories, it was a place of exotic spices; shrimps cooked on seaside grills and served hot in fresh bread; dancers from distant lands, clad in motley; and a hundred bars where patrons told ten thousand stories of pirates, sea monsters, and adventure.

Today Lacrimosa saw no life here. Smoke rose from the city, and vultures circled above it.

She walked the road toward Altus Mare, and found that its walls had fallen, and no guards defended it. She walked in and saw looted shops, children cowering in a gutter, boarded windows, and everywhere—soulless bodies.

She walked through the narrow streets, hiding her sword under her cloak. There were survivors here, but they huddled indoors. Lacrimosa could see them peeking between shutters, daring not speak to her. She kept walking, found a tavern, and stepped inside. It was empty, and she ate and drank from the pantry, then resumed her walk to the sea.

When she reached the wharfs, she found that most ships were gone. The poets had spoken of a thousand ships here. Lacrimosa saw only four, and between them—row after row of empty wharfs.

"They fled this city," came a voice behind her.

Lacrimosa spun around, drawing her sword.

She found herself facing a man with rough stubble, a shock of brown hair, and dark eyes. He appeared to be her age—somewhere between thirty to forty—and his weathered face spoke of years at sea.

He nodded at her sword. "A fine weapon," he said, "but it won't help you here. Not against the creatures who sent these ships fleeing."

Lacrimosa nodded, fingers trembling, and sheathed her sword. "Forgive me," she said. "I startle easily these days."

The man squinted and gazed over the empty wharfs. The soulless bodies of several sailors lay there. Vultures were eating them alive.

"This place is a graveyard, my lady," the man said. "Flee into the countryside. Hide in the hills. Or better yet, fall upon that pretty sword of yours. The death it will give you is kinder than the vultures." He gestured his chin at the birds, then lifted a rock at tossed it at them. They scattered, hissed, then returned to feast.

Lacrimosa gave the man a closer look. He was dressed as a sailor, she saw, in canvas pants and a leather tunic. A short, broad sword hung from his belt.

"Why do you not flee then?" she asked. "Why don't you fall upon your sword?"

He drew that sword, and pointed the blade to one of the remaining ships. She was a small cog, smaller than Lacrimosa's dragon form, with a single mast. She sported the wooden figurehead of a griffin, its paint faded.

"My ship," the man said. "I sail east today, seeking lands where no nightshades fly. Her name is Leo, after the star." He bowed his head to her. "And my name is Marcus."

She examined the ship. She creaked as the wind rocked her. Lacrimosa turned back to Marcus and raised her eyebrows.

"Marcus," she said, "the stars shine upon us. I have five copper coins, and one of good silver. Would you accept this payment? I would sail with you."

"When ruin covers the world, what could coins buy?" Marcus said. "Smile for me instead; smiles are worth more these days."

An hour later, they sailed the sea.

A ship bearing a griffin figurehead, to sail to the land of the griffins. A ship named Leo, to sail to Leonis. Surely she was star blessed, Lacrimosa knew, standing on the ship's bow, gazing into the horizon. The wind whipped her hair and caught Leo's sails.

She did not know much about sailing, but she learned, and she followed Marcus's orders, and the ship cut through the waters. They sailed east. East to Leonis. East to hope. East where the sun rose, and griffins dwelled, and perhaps Lacrimosa could find aid.

Marcus joined her at the prow, and placed a calloused hand on her shoulder, and gazed into the sea.

"You think the griffins can truly fight nightshades?" he asked, squinting.

Lacrimosa saw old pain in his eyes. For so many years, she had lived the pain of Requiem's loss. Did Marcus feel the same now, his own home destroyed?

"Do you have a family?" she asked him softly.

He scratched his cheek. "A wife," he said, voice low. "Once."

He turned away, entered the ship's belly, and soon returned with a bottle of wine. He opened it, drank, and passed the bottle to Lacrimosa. She drank too. It was strong and thick, and only several sips made her head fuzzy.

"I'll teach you a song," he said, and began to sing a song about randy sailors, and buxom maidens, and unholy deeds that made Lacrimosa laugh and feel her cheeks burn.

"You should not sing such songs to a lady!" she said, but could not stop laughing. The song got ruder and ruder as they drank, and soon Lacrimosa sang along, voice loud, singing words she'd normally blush to utter.

She had not laughed in so long.

When the bottle was empty, and Marcus had taught her several more songs, she finally fell silent. She gazed into the sea, wrapped her cloak around her, and whispered.

"The sun is setting."

Marcus's eyes darkened. "Would nightshades fly this far out to sea?"

Lacrimosa clutched the hilt of her sword, remembering Marcus's advice. *Fall upon it.* She shivered. "I don't know."

Soon they sailed in darkness. It was a quiet night. Lacrimosa heard nothing but the water, gently lapping against Leo, and the creaking of wood and rope. The breeze was soft, and the stars shone above. She saw the Draco constellation in the north, and smiled sadly. Requiem lay beneath those stars.

Marcus stood beside her, hand on his sword's hilt. For a long time he was silent. Finally he spoke, voice soft.

"My wife's name was Aula." He stared into the night. "I buried her at sea with my unborn child. I loved her. I don't know why I tell you this. I want to tell someone before...."

He froze.

He spun around.

Lacrimosa followed his gaze and felt her insides wilt.

Two stars moved toward them from the night. Eyes. Nightshade eyes.

The creature screeched, and the ship rocked, and Lacrimosa bit down on a scream.

"Did it see us?" she whispered.

Ten more pairs of eyes opened in the dark. Screeches jostled the boat, and this time Lacrimosa did scream. Marcus drew his sword, grabbed her arm, and pulled her.

"Into the hull!" he whispered, pulling her downstairs. "We hide."

They raced into the shadows, and leaped behind caskets and a roll of canvas. A lamp hung from the ceiling, swaying madly. Lacrimosa's heart pounded and cold sweat drenched her. The shrieks grew louder, and the ship rocked, nearly capsizing. Barrels, rope, and jugs rolled across the floor.

Marcus gripped his sword. "I won't let them take us alive." His eyes were dark, his jaw tight.

The ship jolted.

Splinters flew.

Lacrimosa screamed, and the ship swayed, and something slammed into it again. More splinters flew. The lamp fell and shattered, and the floor began to burn. A third time, something crashed into the ship, and wood shattered. The head of a nightshade burst into the hull, screaming, eyes blazing. Water followed it, crashing into the ship. A second nightshade slammed into the hull, and the world became fire, water, and smoke.

The nightshades began tugging her soul, and Lacrimosa howled and fought them. Through the fire and darkness, she saw Marcus draw his sword. He was burning.

"You will not take us alive!" he shouted.

He thrust his sword into his chest.

Lacrimosa screamed.

Tears filled her eyes.

With a howl, she shifted.

Her body ballooned, until she was forty feet long, and the ship shattered around her. Tears in her eyes, anguish in her chest, she dived into darkness. She swam into the black water, seeing nothing, trembling, Marcus's cry echoing in her mind. Her tail flapped behind her, driving her deeper and deeper.

The nightshades screamed behind her.

Lacrimosa swam until her lungs ached, and she hit the seabed. She would need to breathe soon. When she looked above, she saw nightshade eyes scanning the darkness, a dozen pairs.

Do I die here, at the bottom of the sea? Do I die alongside Marcus?

Her lungs screamed. She trembled. The nightshades swarmed above, and in the light of their eyes, Lacrimosa saw Marcus's sword. It sank slowly, hit the sand beside her, and was still.

AGNUS DEI

"Father, please, will you *stop* doing that?" Agnus Dei said. She snorted, blowing back a curl of her hair.

Father growled. "Doing what?"

"Humming. You've been humming for days."

He scowled at her, the legendary scowl of King Benedictus. "I do not sing. I do not dance. And I definitely do not *hum*."

Agnus Dei shook her fist. "Stars, are you stubborn!"

They walked in silence for long moments. Their boots rustled weeds that grew from the road. A stream gurgled at their side, and oaks swayed around them, their leaves red and yellow. Blue mountains soared to the east.

"There!" she suddenly said, wheeling toward Father. "What was that?"

Benedictus raised his eyebrows. "What?"

"That sound! That sound that left your throat. That hum."

He snorted. "That was no hum. That was just me clearing my throat."

"You clear your throat to the tune of Old Requiem Woods?"

He sighed and shook his head. "Agnus Dei, do you have something against Old Requiem Woods?"

She jumped up and down in rage and kicked a rock. "Oh, it is a lovely tune... if you're eighty years old. And you have a lovely humming voice... that is, if you're a toad. But since I'm nineteen, and not a toad, I would dearly appreciate it if you *stopped* humming. Okay? You've been humming Old Requiem Woods for three days. Three days. I've had enough of Old... Requiem... Woods. For a lifetime."

His eyes twinkled, and King Benedictus, the Black Fang himself, began to sing. "Old Requiem Woods, where do thy harpists play, in Old Requiem Woods, where do thy dragons—"

Agnus Dei gave the longest, loudest groan of her life. "Father!"

He laughed, a sound like stones rolling. "Okay, Agnus Dei, but tell me one thing. How did your Mother ever handle you?"

She stared at him. "Maybe you'd know, if you were with us."

He sighed. "Daughter, we've been over this. You know it was dangerous. You know we had to stay separate. I wanted to see you more often, but—"

"But yes, we couldn't keep all our eggs in one basket, griffins were hunting us, this and that. I've heard it all before. Let's just walk in silence, okay? I don't want to talk. I don't want singing or humming. I just want some silence."

Father winced. *Good*, Agnus Dei thought. She wanted to hurt him. The man might be the King of Requiem, a warrior and leader of legend, but he was intolerable. Agnus Dei couldn't understand how Mother could love him so much, or how Kyrie could worship him. He scowled all the time. He hummed. He snored. When she did try to talk to him, he was about as interesting as a log. He looked a bit like a log too, if you asked Agnus Dei.

She sighed. Though she'd never admit it aloud, she missed Kyrie. He was a pup, of course, but a cute pup. She missed seeing the anger in his eyes when she taunted him. She missed kissing him, and.... Blood rushed into her cheeks. Yes, she even missed those things they did in darkness, when nobody was there to see. Lovemaking. Loud, fiery, sweaty and—

Agnus Dei shoved the thought aside. This was no time for such thoughts. They would soon be in the ruins of Requiem and delve underground. Agnus Dei shuddered.

"Father," she said, "what do you know of the tunnels under Requiem? Where the scrolls are?"

Benedictus seemed to be looking inward, and a soft smile touched his lips. "They are where Requiem began. Before we learned how to build homes of stone, we lived in those tunnels. We painted murals on their walls, and carved doorways and smooth floors. After we moved overground, they remained holy to us, dry and dark. I loved them as a child. I would explore them with lamps and candles, and read all day."

"What did you like to read?" she asked. It was hard to imagine Father as a child. The man was so gruff, all stubble and muscle and leathery skin, his hair like iron. What would he have looked like as a child?

"I read everything I could find, from prayer books to stories of trolls and maidens and heroes."

Agnus Dei sighed. Maybe Father wasn't so bad after all. She slipped her hand into his. "What happened to the tunnels after... after Dies Irae?"

Benedictus looked to the sky and rubbed his chest, where Dies Irae's spear had cut him in Lanburg Fields. "We fled there at first. We sought safety from griffins underground. But Dies Irae sent poison into the tunnels."

"Ilbane?" Agnus Dei asked. Dies Irae had attacked her with ilbane once; the stuff burned like fire.

"Worse," Benedictus said.

"Worse than ilbane?" She shuddered.

"Evil smoke, sickly green. I don't know where he found the magic. Thousands of Vir Requis fell ill in the tunnels, and... changed. Scales grew on them."

"You mean they shifted into dragons?"

He shook his head, eyes dark. "No, they stayed in human form. And these were no dragon scales, but clammy scales, gray and white, like those of a fish. People's eyes bulged from their heads, bloated and yellow, and their fingers became webbed."

Agnus Dei shivered and felt ill. "What happened then? Did they die?"

Benedictus lowered his head. His voice was low. "No. They lived. But they hated daylight, hated life. We burned them. We killed them for mercy. Some escaped deep into the tunnels, and we couldn't find them. But before we fled into the skies, and to Lanburg Fields, we made fires and—"

"Stop," Agnus Dei whispered. She felt the blood leave her face, and cold sweat trickled down her back. Her fingers trembled.

Benedictus nodded. "Those were dark days."

They walked in silence for several hours, first down cobbled roads, and then down dirt roads, and finally through open country. At first trees rustled around them, but as they walked, the trees dwindled and vanished. Burned logs and ash littered the ground. Soon they saw toppled columns, strewn bricks, broken statues, and scattered bones.

They had arrived in Requiem.

They walked silently through the ruins, daggers drawn. Vultures flew under the overcast sky, and bugs scurried around their boots. Nothing else lived here. A cold wind ruffled their cloaks. As they kept walking, more bones littered the earth, thousands of Requiem's skeletons. *Once this place rustled with birch trees, and marble halls rose here, filled with laughter and harp songs,* Agnus Dei thought. *Once we sang here in temples and played in forests. And once we died here; all of us but five.*

She wanted to talk to Father. She wanted to ask about the old life here. Her memories were vague; she had been only three when Dies Irae destroyed this place. But she dared not speak. This place was holy, the graveyard of their kind. Any words would defile it, she thought. She looked around at the skeletons and wondered if any were her cousins, uncles and aunts, childhood friends. The skeleton of a mother huddled the skeleton of her baby. The spines were broken.

Tears filled Agnus Dei's eyes. She hugged herself, and Father placed an arm around her. Finally she dared speak.

"I want to be angry," she whispered, tears in her eyes. "I want to hate Dies Irae. And I do, but... I don't feel hatred or anger now. I feel sadness."

Benedictus held her as they walked, but said nothing. She continued speaking.

"I'm sad to see the bones, and the broken columns, and the ash. All the ruin. But mostly, I'm sad to see the living Vir Requis. I can see them in my mind. The columns still stand, and the trees still rustle. I can hear the songs and harps, the prayers to the Draco stars. It is those visions that make me sad, the lost life more than this death. Does that make sense, Father?"

He nodded and kissed her head.

She looked up to the western horizon. The sun was low, a blob of red like blood. "Night is almost here," she whispered.

They found three columns that had fallen over one another, forming a huddle between them. They sat there in the shadows, hugged their knees, and waited for darkness.

When the sun vanished, the nightshades emerged.

Agnus Dei shivered and hugged her father. He held her and whispered, "Do not move, do not speak. We will be safe. Same as last night. I'll watch first."

She nodded silently, shivering. She could not sleep. The nightshades screamed above, and several times, she saw them dip to swirl among the ruins, then fly into the sky again. Agnus Dei hated those creatures. Hated them with such fire, she wanted to fly at them and torch them all.

"Do you think we'll find answers in the tunnels?" she whispered to Father. "Instructions for how to reseal them?"

He stared grimly out of their huddle, where nightshades swarmed and screeched. "I don't know."

Finally Agnus Dei found fitful sleep, her head against Father's shoulder. Whenever a nightshade shrieked, she started and woke, then slept again. Benedictus watched all night; he let her sleep as best she could.

Finally dawn rose—cold, gray, scented of fire and death.

They continued to walk, cloaks wrapped tight around them. The wind blew, scattering ash. Agnus Dei wondered if the dead Vir Requis had become this ash that stained her clothes, covered her face, and filled her hair. They passed communal graves, some which hadn't been covered. Hundreds of skeletons filled them. Bugs scuttled between the bones. Once they stepped over marble tiles, smashed and crooked, half-buried in dirt. This had once been the floor of a temple or palace. One wall still stood, three skeletons propped against it, staring with empty sockets.

"Why were they not buried?" Agnus Dei whispered, fiery tears in her eyes. "They were just... left here."

Benedictus nodded. "We fled. Griffins and men chased us. We fled into the fields, but died there too. We buried most, whoever we could. We burned others. For every skeleton you see above the earth, we buried a hundred, maybe a thousand."

Agnus Dei covered her mouth. She felt sick. "But there are thousands of skeletons here. That means... Dies Irae must have killed...." She tried to do the math, and felt the blood leave her face.

Benedictus nodded, his own face pale. "A million Vir Requis once lived here, maybe more. Dies Irae murdered all but five. You, me, your sister, your mother. And Kyrie."

Agnus Dei shivered. She had been to Requiem once before, stopping here in dragon form. It was the place she had fought Gloriae. But this was the first time she explored it on foot, seeing all this death, this loss.

"Did we fight well?" she asked. "How many of Osanna's men did we kill?"

"We fought well. We killed many. We toppled their walls, and crashed their forts, and tore into their armies with fangs and claws and fire. We killed countless of Osanna's sons. But they outnumbered us. Twenty to one, or more. They had griffins and ilbane. We could not win."

"But we will win," Agnus Dei said. "The war is not over yet. Not while I draw breath." She clutched Father's hand. "We're going to find scrolls here, and they'll tell us how to seal the nightshades. And Mother will align us with the griffins. And then Dies Irae will fall. Then we'll rebuild this place, and bury the dead, and Requiem will shine again." Tears ran down her cheeks.

Benedictus pointed to a pile of scattered bricks, a fallen gateway, and cracked tiles. "There, Agnus Dei. It's an entrance to the tunnels."

They approached, and pushed aside a burned bole, and saw stairs leading underground. Agnus Dei shivered. Icy wind blew from below, and she could see only ten or fifteen steps down, before the stairs disappeared into darkness.

"What do you think is down there now?" she asked and tightened her grip on her dagger.

"Hopefully some information."

Agnus Dei shivered to remember the stories of the poisoned Vir Requis, the fish scales that grew across them, and their eyes that bulged. "Do you think... do you think the Poisoned are still down there?"

"I don't think so, Agnus Dei."

She took a deep breath. *I don't think so. Not no. Not of course not, don't be foolish, Agnus Dei.* Only... *I don't think so.* It wasn't comforting.

"Let's go," she said. "We'll grab scrolls about nightshades and get out of here. I don't like this place."

She grabbed a broken lance from the ground, tore a strip off her cloak, and fashioned a torch. Benedictus did the same, then lit the torches with his tinderbox.

Daggers and torches held before them, they stepped down into darkness.

LACRIMOSA

She hid underwater in dragon form, lungs ready to burst. Nightshades swarmed above, dipping their heads into the sea, screeching, then emerging into the air again. Lacrimosa felt ready to faint. Stars glided before her eyes.

She flapped her tail, forcing herself through the water. When she thought no nightshades saw, she peeked her nostrils over the water, took a breath, and dived again. She kept swimming.

It's almost day, she thought. *Please, stars, make it be almost day.*

But it was not. The night was still long, a night of nightshades over water, of aching lungs, of stolen breaths. Several times the nightshades saw her. They swooped at her, screaming, sending her deep underwater. There she would swim, rise to the surface as far away as she could, and breathe again.

It was perhaps the longest night of Lacrimosa's life.

When finally dawn rose, the nightshades fled. Lacrimosa rose to the surface, lay floating on her dragon back, and wept. She wept so many tears, she could fill another sea.

She was thirsty, hungry, and bone tired. But she saw no islands, no place to rest. She took flight, wings aching. She flew over the sea, travelling east. How far was Leonis, the realm of griffins? It was a place of legend. Perhaps Leonis did not exist at all.

At noon, Lacrimosa could fly no longer. She floated on her back. She dived into the water several times, caught fish, and ate them. She was still thirsty, but there was nothing to drink but seawater. Then she flew again.

When evening began to fall, she saw an island in the distance. She hoped it was an island of Leonis, but it was only a desolate rock. Fatigued, she climbed onto the island and collapsed.

As she waited for nightfall, it began to rain. Lacrimosa drank from the rain puddles. She shivered in the cold and watched the thunder and lightning. No nightshades emerged this night. Perhaps Lacrimosa was too far now from Osanna. Was there any end to this sea, or was it only water and rocks? Thunder rolled and the rain intensified. Lacrimosa huddled against a boulder, wrapped her wings around her, and shivered until dawn.

She flew again over the sea. She flew into the east.

"I will find the griffins," she whispered into the wind. "I will find Volucris, their king. I will bring them back as allies. We will rebuild our home, Ben. We will rebuild our life and love among the birches."

Her wings stirred clouds. She could see nothing but sea on all horizons.

GLORIAE

Gloriae rode into the city of Confutatis, her sword drawn, her eyes narrowed.

The place lay in ruin.

"Stars," Kyrie muttered. He sat behind her in the saddle, arms wrapped around her waist. "This place is a graveyard."

Gloriae nodded, riding the horse at a light clip. The city gates were smashed open. Guards lay strewn around them, dead or empty shells. Their swords were drawn in their hands, but clean of blood. Past the gates, bodies littered the streets. Vultures, crows, and rats were feasting upon them, tearing off skin, fingers, faces. Blood and sewage flowed across the street. Stray dogs slunk in shadows, growling.

"I hope the library still stands," Gloriae said. Many buildings had fallen. Others burned. Wind shrieked through the streets, billowing smoke.

Kyrie pointed his dagger to a statue of Dies Irae, twenty feet tall and gilded, that stood in a square. "If that statue still stands, the library better too."

Gloriae gestured with her chin toward a distant wall. Soldiers moved there, crossbows in hands.

"Not all here are dead," she said. "Masks on."

She placed her priestess mask on. It was a blank mask, expressionless, formed of white wood. Kyrie did the same. With the white robes they already wore, she hoped nobody would recognize or trouble them.

A child came running toward them. Gloriae raised her sword.

"Halt!" she said. "Do not approach us, or you'll meet my blade."

The child, his clothes tattered and his face ashy, froze.

"Gloriae!" Kyrie said. "He's only a boy. Lower your blade." He looked at the child. "Are you hungry, kid?"

The child—he looked eight or nine years old—nodded. "There is no food here," he said meekly. "The people took what they could. They left the city." He had a black eye and was

missing a tooth. "The ink monsters drove them away. They'll be
here soon. They'll kill you too. The Light of the Sun God does
not shine on them."

Kyrie rummaged through his things, found walnuts and an
apple, and tossed them to the boy. The child caught the food,
turned, and ran into an alley.

"You shouldn't have done that," Gloriae said, watching the
dark alley. She wondered how many more children hid there.
"This city must be swarming with beggars, and beggars are like
stray cats; feed one, and they'll pester you in numbers. We need
our food."

"You are sweet and caring as always, Gloriae. Your reign
must have been a fabulous time for the city. Dies Irae the
Benevolent and Gloriae the Kindhearted, they must have called
you two." He snorted.

Gloriae frowned. "The reign of Dies Irae has not ended
yet, Kyrie Eleison. I may be banished from his favor, but he
rules still."

Kyrie snorted again. "Rules what, a pile of rocks, bodies,
and looters? Aside from a few soldiers on those walls ahead, I
see nobody. And in case you forgot, I freed the griffins."

Gloriae turned to face him. She gave him a blank, cold
stare. "Dies Irae rules the nightshades now, and they are greater
than any soldiers or griffins. Their worlds are greater than any
cities of stone."

Kyrie stared back at her, eyes flashing. Then he turned his
head, spat, and grunted. "Let's find this library."

Gloriae kneed her horse, leading it up the cobbled street,
past the statue of Dies Irae, and up Market Lane. She wasn't
used to travelling the city this way. Usually she flew over these
streets on Aquila, her griffin, or rode in a procession, surrounded
by guards and banners and horses clad in splendor. Riding alone
with Kyrie, robes hiding the gold and jewels of her armor, she
felt like a commoner.

As they rode deeper into the city, they saw more people.
Most were beggars and outlaws and other commoners, those too
poor to have fled the city. Gloriae wrinkled her nose at their
filth and stench. There were soldiers too, their faces gaunt and
their eyes sunken. All who saw Gloriae and Kyrie bowed,
reached out dirty hands, and begged for prayer and favor. Even
the soldiers dropped to their knees and pleaded.

"Pray for us, Sun God priests. Bless us. Shine your light on these dark days."

Behind her mask, Gloriae gritted her teeth. Soldiers bending the knee, forgetting their post? She was half tempted to pull back her cloaks, reveal her identity, and send them to the stocks. She forced herself to keep riding, shoving through them.

Kyrie muttered impromptu blessings to them. He obviously knew nothing about the Sun God; his blessings were probably botched translations of Dragontongue prayers.

Once they had moved through the people, and were riding down Blacksmith Road, Gloriae turned in the saddle to regard him.

"Kyrie," she said, "teach me to speak Dragontongue."

He raised an eyebrow. "Gloriae, this is hardly the time to request tutoring in dead languages."

"Firstly, I am not requesting; I am telling you. Secondly, it's not a dead language. It's what you speak with the other Vir Requis. I just realized that. You were all speaking High Speech for my benefit, but you probably speak Dragontongue amongst yourselves."

"Well, yes," Kyrie said. "But you probably used to speak it too. When you were three. Before Dies Irae kidnapped you from Requiem and took you to Osanna."

"I want to learn again."

Kyrie sighed. "Gloriae, first let's learn how to defeat these nightshades, or ink monsters as folk here seem to call them. All right? Now where's that library?"

"I'm taking us there. Be patient."

They kept riding deeper into the city. Gloriae couldn't help but frown at the devastation. Statues of Dies Irae lay toppled in every square. Most of the buildings were nothing but rubble, and blood seeped from beneath them. Several times, Gloriae saw hands, heads, and legs peeking from the rubble. They were rotting and raising a stench. Around one fallen column, she saw several survivors huddling around a fire, eating what seemed to be a dog. Gloriae covered her mouth, looked away, and rode by.

Soon they rode by the palace. A colossus of Dies Irae had stood here once, marble and gold, gazing over the city. Today the statue's head lay on the road, ten feet tall. As Gloriae rode around it, she wondered where the real Dies Irae was. Did he still sit on the Ivory Throne, encased in nightshades?

She looked up to the palace. Several of its towers had fallen. The main hall's walls were cracked, but still stood. Gloriae stared, feeling a chill.

"Dies Irae is in there," Kyrie whispered, echoing her thoughts.

Gloriae nodded. "Yes. How did you know?"

"I can feel it. Let's not go there. I don't want to get anywhere near Irae. At least, not until we figure out how to hurt his nightshades."

"Agreed. The library is behind the palace. We're almost there."

As they rode around the palace, they saw guards manning the walls and remaining tower. More guards patrolled the streets, crossbows in hand. Kyrie and Gloriae muttered prayers at them, raising their hands as if to bless them. The guards bowed their heads, whispering prayers in return. Their eyes swam with fear.

What has happened to my home? Gloriae thought. She felt close to tears. She had spent years in this palace, since she was only three. Here she had trained with blade, arrow, and fist. Here she had lived with May, her handmaiden and sweet friend. Where was May now? Did she still live in this palace, or had she fled the city? Gloriae had never had a friend but May.

"We must enter the palace," Gloriae whispered.

Kyrie groaned. "What? You're crazy, Gloriae. There's no way I'm going in there."

"So stay here. I... I must look for somebody."

"Who, Dies Irae? I thought we were going to avoid him."

"No. My... friend."

Kyrie snorted. "*You* have a friend? What, your favorite sword? A man-eating tiger? An iron maiden? Forget it, Gloriae. Benedictus sent us to the library."

"We'll go to the library. It'll only take a moment."

Kyrie moaned but said nothing more. Gloriae led her horse under a gateway, nodding to the guards.

"We've come to bless the palace with the light of the Sun God," Gloriae said to them.

They nodded and bowed their heads, and Gloriae and Kyrie rode through. They drew rein in a courtyard. Gloriae remembered that Dies Irae had once chained Lacrimosa here and tortured her. Pushing the memory aside, Gloriae dismounted, helped Kyrie off the horse, and they entered a back door into the palace.

The palace interior had fared scarcely better than its exterior. Suits of armor, tapestries, and swords had fallen. Bloodied prints covered the floor, and ash coated the walls. A servant lay soulless by a doorway, drooling, eyes staring.

"Not the best house guests, nightshades," Kyrie muttered.

Gloriae stared at the servant, a chill claiming her. Would she find May like this too, mindless and drooling?

"Come, Kyrie. Quickly."

They walked down several hallways and up three sets of stairs. Here, the third floor of the eastern wing, was Gloriae's domain, the place she had ruled for fifteen years. Almost running now, her boots clacking, Gloriae headed to the corner by the tower staircase, where May had a small room.

The door was closed. Gloriae paused outside it. She placed her hand on the knob, but dared not open it.

Kyrie caught up with her, muttering and glancing around nervously. When he saw her hand on the doorknob, his eyes softened. He sighed.

"Do you want me to look?" he said quietly.

Gloriae looked at him. His eyes, normally angry, now seemed concerned for her. Caring. Gloriae gritted her teeth. She needed nobody to care for her. She could do this. Whatever she found behind this door, she would deal with it.

She opened the door to May's room and stepped inside.

May lay nude on her bed. Her skull was broken; the wound looked like a mace's work. Her arms were bound.

"Stars," Kyrie whispered.

Gloriae stared at the scene, eyes dry. "She was raped," she said. Her voice sounded dead to her ears. She examined the wound on May's head. "A mace did this. My father's mace."

Kyrie placed a hand on her shoulder. "Gloriae, I'm sorry. Was this girl close to you?"

Gloriae spun to face him. He had removed his white mask. She saw herself reflected in his eyes.

"She was my best friend. My only friend. She... she was with me since childhood."

Kyrie tried to embrace her, but Gloriae shoved him back.

"No," she said. "Spare me your pity. I need no pity. I am Gloriae the Gilded, even now." She drew Per Ignem. "My father did this to her. When I was a child, and did poorly at a lesson of daggers, or at target practice, Dies Irae would be furious at me. He never beat me, though. He would beat May and make me watch. I watched. And I cried. And I knew that he desired May. I could see him staring at her, especially when we grew older." She looked back to the girl, and her voice softened. "But he can't hurt you anymore, May. Wherever you are now, you are safe from him."

Kyrie covered May with a blanket and looked at Gloriae, his eyes haunted. "I'm going to kill Dies Irae," he said.

Gloriae shook her head. "No, Kyrie. You will not. I will kill him."

They took May out of the palace, and built a pyre in the courtyard using firewood from the kitchens. They watched as the pyre burned, the fire drying her tears. *You're with the Sun God now,* Gloriae thought, staring into the flames. Pain like she had never felt filled her. The world entire was on fire. *I'll avenge you, May. I swear. I love you.*

She turned from the fire and lowered her head. Her fists clenched at her sides.

"Come," she said to Kyrie. "The library is near."

They walked silently around the palace, past a cobbled yard, around several toppled statues, and across a bridge. Gloriae breathed out in relief. The library still stood. It was an ancient building, three stories tall and round, topped with a bronze dome. She and Kyrie climbed the stairs, opened the doors, and stepped into a shadowy chamber.

For a moment they froze, gaping.

"Wow," Kyrie finally said, finding his voice.

Gloriae nodded. "Indeed."

She had never been inside the library. Only monks and priests would go here, not maidens of sword and shield. Gloriae had always imagined some dusty chamber full of moldy parchments. What she saw spun her head. Rows and rows of shelves lined the walls, rising all the way to the domed ceiling. Tens of thousands, maybe millions of books covered the shelves, all bound in leather. Gloriae's head spun. Dies Irae never read, but the old kings of Osanna must have loved the written word. She had never imagined so many books could exist.

"Look at the ceiling," Kyrie said, pointing with his dagger.

Gloriae raised her head, and a gasp fled her lips. That ceiling was painted with scenes of stars, clouds, and griffins. Filigree and jewels made the figures glitter.

One part of the ceiling was chipped away. It looked like somebody had painstakingly chiseled at the artwork, as if to efface a scene. The chisel-work resembled the shape of a dragon.

"A Vir Requis was once painted there," Gloriae said. "I'd bet anything. Dies Irae must have ordered it chiseled off, but you can still see the shape."

"I'd like to chisel something of his off," Kyrie muttered. He shook his head, as if to clear it. "So, Gloriae my dear. How in the name of the Draco stars are we going to read all these books?"

She looked at him, placed her hands on her hips, and raised an eyebrow. "Never learned how to read, little boy?"

He groaned. "I can read faster than you."

She gave him a crooked smile. "You're on."

They began attacking the books, and soon realized the shelves were organized by category. One shelf was devoted to herbalism; they felt that shelf safe to ignore. Same for the shelf on astrology and theology. That left an entire wall of books on history, magical creatures, black magic, and warfare. Gloriae figured that information on nightshades might exist in one or all of these sections.

"I'll search the magical creatures shelves," she said to Kyrie. "You peruse the history section; there might be books about how the nightshades were sealed."

Kyrie nodded. They began pulling down books, opening them on the floor, and turning the pages. The books were heavy, ancient tomes, two feet long and often ten inches thick. Bound in leather, their pages sported delicate calligraphy. The scribes had treated these codexes as works of art not inferior to the ceiling. Every letter was a masterpiece, and every page featured colorful illustrations.

"Look at this book," Kyrie said. He sat cross-legged beside her, frowning into a dusty tome. "It's called *Early Kings of Osanna* by a monk named Lodinium." He scratched his chin. "Somebody's tampered with this book."

"What do you mean?" Gloriae asked. She looked up from a book called *Elder Beasts*, which was open to an illustration of a warty roc.

He pushed the book closer to her and sat beside her. "Take a look at this. See these pages at the front? They're frail, tattered, crumbling. Now look. Around the middle of the book, the pages are new. This parchment isn't ten years old, I'd wager."

Sitting on her knees, Gloriae leaned down and scrutinized the book. Kyrie was right. Some pages looked a thousand years old, the others new. "Could it be the author, this Lodinium, added older pages into his book?"

Kyrie shook his head. "No. The binding is old too. It's falling apart. And Lodinium lived over seven-hundred years ago; his date of birth appears on the first page." He looked up at her over the pages. "Somebody changed this book. Recently."

"Why would anyone do that?" Gloriae asked.

Kyrie shrugged. "I reckon there was information they didn't want people to find. Here, look. The first pages tell of Osanna's early days, before there were kings. There were just ten tribes here then. Look how old these pages are—tattered with faded ink. Now look." Kyrie flipped the pages. "Just around the time the first king is crowned...."

"New pages," Gloriae whispered. The parchment was flawless, the ink dark and clear. The handwriting was different too. She read aloud. "In the year 606, Taras Irae built the Ivory Throne of Osanna, and founded the Irae dynasty. The old tribes united under his wise rule." She flipped more pages, tracing the ancestry of the kings. They led from Taras Irae, to Theron Irae, and to many more kings, until finally the last page featured Dies Irae. She looked back to Kyrie and shrugged. "So what? I know this story already. I had to study the Irae dynasty as a child; I myself am... *was* heir to it."

Kyrie snorted so loudly, it blew dust off the pages. "Don't you get it, Gloriae? Dies Irae, the man who claims to be your father, is the first emperor of his line. I mean, the man's a Vir Requis. Sure, he lacks the magic. He can't shift into a dragon. But he's still from Requiem. He's still Benedictus's brother. He killed Osanna's old kings and only pretends to be her son."

Gloriae understood. "He doesn't want people to know he's Vir Requis. Of course. He hates the Vir Requis. He wants people to think his family has always ruled here." She slammed the book shut. "The bastard rewrote history."

"Or threatened the scribes to rewrite it, to be more exact," Kyrie said grimly. He shoved the book aside. "*Early Kings of Osanna* is useless now. Let's keep looking."

Kyrie drew another book off a shelf, and Gloriae returned to *Elder Beasts*, which still lay open on the floor. As she flipped the pages, searching for nightshades, she noticed oddities with this codex too. There were no replaced pages, but some existing pages seemed modified. When she reached a page featuring the Vir Requis, she narrowed her eyes and leaned down, so that her nose almost touched the parchment.

Gloriae gasped. Some words had been scraped off, it seemed. The parchment was thinner and rougher here. New words, their ink deeper, overwrote the old ones.

The weredragons are hideous beasts, the book read. But it seemed like the words "weredragons" and "hideous" were new, replacing older words, which had been scraped off. For all Gloriae knew, it could have once read, *The Vir Requis are noble beasts.*

She read the next line. *They murdered the sons and daughters of Osanna, and destroyed their halls.* Only it seemed like "murdered" and "destroyed" were new words. When Gloriae leaned close and squinted, she could see scratches where the older words had been effaced.

Meanwhile, an entirely new sentence was scrawled in the bottom margin. The ink was darker, the calligraphy similar but not identical. *Dies Irae, noble king of Osanna, defeated the weredragons and banished their darkness from his kingdom of light.*

"Well," Gloriae said, pushing the book aside in disgust, "*Elder Beasts* is useless too. Dies Irae rewrote this one too."

Kyrie groaned. "Stars. Will we find nothing useful here? Was the whole library rewritten to glorify Irae?"

Gloriae sighed. "The entire city was remade to glorify him. Maybe the entire empire. What's one library? But let's keep looking. We've come all the way here. I don't want to give up yet."

The afternoon sun cast long shadows into the library. They found candles between the shelves, lit them on the floor, and rummaged for new books. In every book, they found similar alterations. Some books had pages torn out. Others had new pages sewn in. Some were like *Elder Beasts*; their original pages still existed, but somebody had carefully scraped away some words, then replaced them with others. Gloriae and Kyrie read all afternoon, but found nothing about nightshades. The entire library painted a picture of a heroic Dies Irae, the defeater of weredragons, a noble hero whose line had ruled Osanna for two thousand years.

Finally Kyrie tossed aside a book in disgust. It crashed into a corner, raising a shower of dust. "Great," he said. "Just great. You know, that Dies Irae of yours is a real griffin's backside."

Gloriae scrunched her lips and stared at the Magical Creatures shelves. She tapped her fingers against her thigh. "He is, but we can still find information here."

Kyrie clutched his head. "How? We can't trust anything these books say. Even if we do find a book about nightshades, what's the use? It would probably just tell us that Dies Irae, ten feet tall with muscles of steel, single-handedly tamed the nightshades over breakfast, using nothing but his butter knife."

Gloriae allowed herself a small smile. "Funny, Kyrie. But one can still read between the lines."

They searched the books until they found one called *Mythic Creatures of the Gray Age*. Gloriae wasn't sure what the Gray Age was, but she was certain it was not during Dies Irae's reign; his reign was nothing but white, gold, and blood red.

"Let's try this one," Gloriae said. She opened the book and began reading.

This book, like the others, had been modified. For the first time, however, Gloriae found a chapter speaking of nightshades.

"Look, Kyrie!" she said. She grabbed his arm and pulled him over. They leaned over the book. On the parchment, a drawing of three nightshades stared up at them. The artist had skillfully captured the smokiness of their bodies, and the glint in their burning eyes. Bodies were drawn beneath them, mouths open, eyes blank, limbs limp.

"Those are our boys, all right," Kyrie said.

Calligraphy appeared on the opposite page. The text wasn't far off from what Kyrie had imagined. It didn't quite speak of Dies Irae taming the nightshades with a butter knife, but it did describe a fictional ancestor of his—Lir Irae—taming the nightshades with something called "The Beams".

Gloriae frowned over the calligraphy. "See here, Kyrie. Some of these words are old—the original text. Others are new."

In some areas, the ink looked old, cracked, fading. In other places, bits of parchment had been scraped clean, and new letters appeared here. These letters weren't as cracked and faded. It was truly a masterwork; Gloriae had to turn the pages in the light, squint, and touch the parchment to distinguish the old words from the new.

"This part about these Beams is the original text," Kyrie said. "But what are they?"

"Great rays of light, it seems," Gloriae said. They turned the page to see another illustration. It showed a man holding something—what, they could not see, for drops of ink had fallen there, obscuring the drawing. Whatever the man held, a ray of light shot out from it, and seemed to slay a nightshade. The hero's original face had been scraped away, and replaced with a face that resembled that of Dies Irae's.

"Great!" Kyrie said. He rose to his feet. "So all we need to do is find these Beams, and point them at the nightshades, and kill them. Seems easy enough. So where do we find them?"

Gloriae sighed. "That's the complicated part. Look what it says here. According to this text, the Sun God created the Beams. Which is utter nonsense. The Sun God didn't even exist back in those days; the religion is only a hundred years old. According to the cover, this book is a thousand years old."

"So who did make the Beams?" Kyrie asked. "If we can find whoever made them, they can make us new ones."

Gloriae groaned. "Think, Kyrie! The book is a *thousand years old*, remember? Whoever made the Beams must be long dead."

"Fine, fine! Well, does it say how to make new Beams?"

Gloriae glared at him. She wanted to throttle him. "I'm trying to read, but it's hard with you talking so much. Do shut up. Honestly, I don't know how my sister puts up with you."

Kyrie grumbled, but otherwise remained silent and let her read. *Mythic Creatures of the Gray Age* spoke more about the nightshades and their powers, and offered gory illustrations of nightshades devouring people's severed heads, but didn't explain more about the Beams.

"The Beams are definitely the key," she muttered. "It speaks of them again here." She read aloud. "'Lir Irae rode against the nightshades, wielding the Beams of power, and he blinded the nightshades, and drove them into the Well of Night, and sealed them there.'" She scratched her cheek. "But it says nothing about who made the Beams, or how they're used."

She slammed the book shut, stood up, and went to the Black Magic section of the library. She climbed a ladder to the tallest, dustiest shelf. It lay cloaked in shadows and cobwebs. She blew the dust away, brushed the cobwebs aside, and rummaged through the shadows. Soon she found an ancient codex, bound in red leather, titled *Artifacts of Wizardry and Power*.

She returned with the book to the floor by the window. The sunlight was fading outside. Soon it would be dark and the nightshades would emerge.

"We better hurry," Kyrie said, looking out the window. He clutched his dagger.

"I know, Kyrie. One last book." Gloriae opened *Artifacts of Wizardry and Power* on the floor, blew more dust away, and began reading. The first chapter spoke of glowing "Animating Stones", which could let statues, suits of armor, and even corpses walk. The second chapter was titled "Summoning Stick"; it showed a golden candlestick decorated with emeralds, which when lit could summon others to aid. The third chapter described the Griffin Heart—"we already know about that one," Gloriae muttered—and the fourth chapter made her gasp and slap the page.

"Here," she said. "The Beams. We found what we need."

Kyrie turned from the window, face pale. "Great, Gloriae. But I think reading time is over."

Outside, the nightshades screeched. Night had fallen.

Gloriae tucked *Artifacts of Wizardry and Power* under her arm, then looked around.

"Where can we hide here?" she whispered. Her eyes narrowed as she scanned the library.

"The fireplace," Kyrie suggested and pointed. "You'd reckon nightshades would hate fireplaces. Firelight and all."

Gloriae considered. If cornered, they'd be stuck there. Then the nightshades screamed closer, and she saw them swirling outside the window, and she nodded.

They raced to the fireplace and climbed inside. The chimney led into darkness above, two feet wide.

"Into the chimney," she whispered. "Side by side. We'll be hidden there."

She and Kyrie wiggled into the chimney. Soot covered Gloriae's white robes, filled her hair, and tickled her nostrils. Kyrie coughed beside her, pressed against her, and she elbowed him.

"Shh!" she whispered. "No coughing. And keep your feet inside the chimney. They're dangling into the hearth."

He grumbled and pulled his feet up. It was a tight squeeze. Gloriae's back was flat against the chimney bricks. She was pressed against Kyrie, his nose against her cheek, his breath against her mouth.

"Gloriae," he whispered.

"Shh!" She elbowed his stomach—hard—and he grunted and fell silent. *Artifacts of Wizardry and Power* almost slipped from under her arm, and she tightened her grip on it.

For a moment there was silence. Then Gloriae heard the library doors swing open, and the nightshades swarmed in.

Their shadows danced even inside the chimney. The candles she and Kyrie had lit blew out, leaving them in darkness. The nightshades screamed, the sound echoing in the chimney, making them wince. Gloriae shut her eyes and prayed to the Sun God to save her... though she suspected the book under her arm would provide more succor.

Kyrie slipped an inch.

His foot dangled into the hearth.

The nightshades froze, then shrieked so loudly, the library shook. Gloriae heard books fall off the shelves.

She grabbed Kyrie and pulled him up. The nightshades howled and swirled.

"Climb!" she whispered to Kyrie. "Quickly."

They scurried up the chimney, wriggling into the darkness.

A nightshade's head emerged into the fireplace beneath them.

Gloriae froze. Were they high enough? Were they dark enough?

She peeked down. The nightshade's head was huge; it filled the fireplace. It looked left, right, and then up into the darkness. Its glittering eyes narrowed, as if it tried to peer into the shadows.

It can't see us, Gloriae thought. *It may hate light, but it needs some light to see.*

The nightshade began to sniff. Its head wasn't solid, merely wisps of darkness and stars, but it seemed to have nostrils. Gloriae scratched the chimney wall, so that ash fell down the chimney. The nightshade sniffed the ash, snorted, and shook its head wildly.

It left the fireplace.

Gloriae and Kyrie breathed out shakily. They dared not speak or move, not until the nightshades gave a final screech, swirled, and seemed to leave the library. Finally, when they were sure the library was empty, they crawled back into the fireplace and onto the floor.

Nightshades still swirled and screeched outside, but the library seemed safe for now.

"I'd wager they do a nightly patrol," Kyrie said, "scanning the buildings they haven't toppled yet. That's probably why we found no people in the library. Nobody wants to hide here, not if the nightshades come here at night."

Gloriae nodded. "I hope they only scan the place once a night. We better stay near the fireplace, just in case we have to scurry in again. And this time please do not cough in my face, Kyrie."

He bristled. "Well, don't elbow my stomach. I don't wear a breastplate like you do, and your elbows are bonier than a skeleton's backside."

Gloriae lit one candle—she would risk no more light—and sat cross-legged at the hearth. She opened *Artifacts of Wizardry and Power*, flipped to the chapter on the Beams, and sighed.

"Wonderful," she said. "We finally find the right book, and Dies Irae modified this one too."

In the candlelight, she could see that more words had been effaced, new words replacing them. She read out loud. "'Lir Irae prayed to his father, the Sun God, for light to tame the nightshades. The Sun God, of infinite wisdom and power, created the Beams and filled them with his light and fire, so that Lir Irae might tame the nightshades in his name.'" She scrunched her lips and pointed at words. "'Lir Irae' is new; there used to be another name written here. The stuff about the Sun God is also new. But some of these words, such as 'created the Beams' and 'tame the nightshades', are the original text. You can see how the parchment is thicker, and the ink more faded."

"So let's get this straight," Kyrie said. "We've spent hours in this library, and what have we learned? That thousands of years ago, somebody used something to tame the nightshades." He groaned. "Gloriae, we knew all this already."

She glared at him. "Not *something*. We learned we must seek the Beams. We know there is an artifact that can help us, or was one. We know somebody created it, and it wasn't the Sun God."

Kyrie sighed. He looked out the window at the nightshades that still swirled outside. "We'll learn nothing more here. Let's get some sleep, Gloriae. We'll head to Fidelium Mountains tomorrow, and see if the others learned anything better."

Gloriae sighed too and closed the book. "All right, Kyrie. Good night."

They huddled into the fireplace, under the chimney should they need to climb, and Kyrie took first watch. Gloriae leaned against the cold bricks, but could find no rest. She was cold, and the bricks hurt her head. Finally, silently, she shifted so that her head lay against Kyrie's shoulder, and so his arm draped over her. She did this as if in sleep, so he wouldn't object. She heard him sigh, but he let her nestle against him. His body was warm, and Gloriae felt safe against him.

Visions of sunrise over clouds filled her mind, and the flapping of wings, and Gloriae slept.

LACRIMOSA

After seven days of flying over the ocean, Lacrimosa saw islands ahead.

Tears sprung into her eyes. Her wings ached, but she forced herself to keep going. It had been days since she'd seen land—endless days of flying, floating on her back when she rested, drinking rain when it fell, eating fish when she could catch them. Lacrimosa had not felt such weariness since fleeing the griffins last summer.

So do the fates taunt us, she thought. *I drove myself to agony fleeing the griffins; now I do the same seeking them.*

The islands were still distant, mere specks on the horizon. As Lacrimosa flew closer, she saw that cliffs drove the islands up from the water, dangling with vines. Trees crowned the islands like bushy green hair. Gulls and hawks flocked among those trees, calling over the water.

She saw dozens of islands. She flew to the nearest one. Palm trees grew from it, and a waterfall cascaded down its western facade. Lacrimosa was a league from the island when griffins shrieked, took flight from the trees, and began flying toward her.

The sound made her start. For so many years, the shrieks of griffins had meant running, hiding, praying for life. For so many years, Dies Irae had ruled the griffins, driving them against the Vir Requis, destroying the world with their talons and beaks.

But I no longer need fear them, Lacrimosa thought, watching three griffins approach. *They no longer serve Dies Irae. They no longer hunt Vir Requis.*

Still her heart hammered. The griffins flying toward her were young, burly, twice her size. They shrieked and reached out their talons.

"Griffins of Leonis!" Lacrimosa called. "I come as ambassador of Requiem. I come in peace. Will you let me land on the islands of Leonis, and speak with your king?"

The griffins flew around her, cawing. Lacrimosa shivered. Golden fur covered their lion bodies. White feathers covered their eagle heads. Their beaks were large and sharp; Lacrimosa had seen such beaks kill so many dragons. Memories of the war assaulted her; Dies Irae and his men riding griffins, swooping upon Vir Requis children, cutting them down—

She forced the thought away. "Requiem will be reborn," she said to the griffins. They were circling around her, shrieking. "I am Lacrimosa, Requiem's queen. I seek Volucris, your king."

They shrieked with new vigor. They clutched her limbs, and Lacrimosa cried and thought they would bite her. But they began to fly to the island, dragging her with them.

"Let go," she said, frowning. "I can fly myself."

They cried and kept dragging her forward. Lacrimosa remembered how Volucris had once carried her to Confutatis. She felt a prisoner again.

Soon they flew over the island. The foliage was so thick, she couldn't see the ground. Mist hovered over the trees. Pillars of stone thrust out from the greenery, bedecked with vines. Griffins covered these pillars, nesting in eyries. For leagues in the eastern ocean, Lacrimosa saw other islands—hundreds of them—griffins flying above them.

Lacrimosa wriggled in the griffins' grasp. "Where are you taking me?"

Of course, griffins could not utter the language of men or Vir Requis; they only shrieked, cawed, and squawked. They flew with her to a jagged stone pillar. It seemed a league high, towering over the island, taller than the highest steeple in Osanna. A nest crested the tower, shaking in the winds.

The griffins flew to that nest, and placed Lacrimosa upon the branches, grass, and leaves. They tilted their heads at her, cooed, and one took flight.

"Does he go to call Volucris?" Lacrimosa asked the remaining two griffins. They nodded.

She waited. The winds blew, and the nest shook, teetering on the pillar. She remained in dragon form, should she fall and need to fly. Once she tried to stand up, to peer down the pillar, but the griffins shoved her back down.

"Am I your prisoner?" she asked, baring her fangs. "I am Queen of Requiem. Do not hold me down if I wish to rise."

They shrieked and tilted their heads, and when Lacrimosa tried to rise again, they pushed her down a second time.

Lacrimosa swallowed her pride. She would let them win this battle. She would have to impress Volucris, king of these islands, not these griffins.

An hour passed, maybe two, and finally Lacrimosa saw ten griffins fly toward her. Volucris flew at their lead.

The King of Leonis landed before her. He was the largest of the griffins, fifty feet long and burly. Lacrimosa stared into his eyes, ice in her heart. She remembered Dies Irae riding this griffin. She remembered Volucris hurting her, biting her, carrying her to pain and torture. She bowed her head to him.

"Your Majesty."

Volucris walked toward her, and at first Lacrimosa feared he'd hurt her again. Once more she could feel that old pain, his talons that cut her.

Volucris bowed to her, and nuzzled his beak against her head. He cooed.

Lacrimosa touched his cheek, its soft feathers, the tear that flowed down them. "I'm sorry, Volucris," she whispered. "I'm sorry for what Dies Irae did to you, how he enslaved you with his amulet. I'm sorry for what he forced you to do."

Volucris nodded, and his tear fell into the nest.

"And I'm sorry for what the Vir Requis elders did," she whispered. "We created the amulet with the blood of griffins. We enslaved you too. We forced you to guard our skies, before Dies Irae stole the Griffin Heart."

Volucris stared at her, silent.

Lacrimosa too was crying now. "Requiem was punished for her sins, mighty Volucris. We enslaved you. We paid for that. Dies Irae made us pay. He turned you against us, turned our slaves into our destroyers. But we are reborn now. We rise from our sins and destruction with purer hearts, kinder souls, stronger spirits. Will you forgive us? Will you befriend our new nation?"

Volucris looked to the west, as if he could see over oceans to the distant realms of Osanna, where he was slave to Dies Irae, or to the lands of Requiem, where the Vir Requis kings had bound him. He looked at her and said nothing. Then, so fast that she gasped, he took flight.

His wings flapped, rattling the nest. He gestured with his head for her to follow.

She took flight too. Surrounded by griffins, they flew across the waters, over the islands, heading further east. Lacrimosa gazed in wonder below her. The islands were beautiful; waterfalls cascaded from them, trees rustled upon them, and griffins flocked in all directions.

They flew for an hour, over many islands, until Lacrimosa saw a great island ahead, three times larger than the others. A mountain grew atop it, all stone and vines. Many griffins flew there, and nested in alcoves across the mountainsides.

Volucris led the group to the mountaintop, where Lacrimosa saw a great nest, a hundred yards wide. A harem of two dozen females brooded there. Lacrimosa saw many griffin eggs. Among the eggs lay a golden candlestick decorated with emeralds.

Volucris gestured with his head to the back of the nest. Lacrimosa looked, and saw a griffin cub lying on his side. He was so small, the size of a pony. His eyes fluttered, and his breath was shallow. Sweat matted his fur.

"Your son," Lacrimosa whispered to Volucris. "He is ill."

Volucris nodded. With his beak, he nudged Lacrimosa toward the cub.

Lacrimosa stepped forward, still in dragon form. Two female griffins were tending to the child. They backed away, and Lacrimosa knelt before him.

"Hey there," she whispered. "Good morning, sweetness."

The cub blinked at her. He tried to coo, but the sound was weak. His leg was wounded, Lacrimosa saw, sliced from heel to knee. Maggots and pus filled the wound, and lines of infection ran from it. Lacrimosa winced.

She turned to Volucris. "I'm sorry," she whispered. "How can I help him?"

Volucris gestured back at the cub. He lowered his head, raised it again, and pointed at the child with his talons. *He's trying to tell me something,* Lacrimosa knew. But what?

"Do you want me to do something to him?" she asked.

Volucris nodded.

"Do you think I can heal him?"

Volucris nodded again.

Lacrimosa returned her gaze to the child. How could she heal this? She knew some herbalism, some home remedies. But even if she had herbs, alcohol, and bandages, this wound was beyond her. This wound meant death. Lacrimosa had seen many such wounds during the war. They ended with fever and a grave.

She whispered into Volucris's ear. "His leg is beyond me. We could try to amputate it, but... I don't think that would help. The infection runs through his whole body now." A tear rolled down her cheek. "I cannot heal this."

Volucris cawed and gestured at the cub. He nudged her back to him.

Lacrimosa looked at the child again. She shook her head, and another tear fell. "I'm sorry. I cannot heal him."

Volucris nudged her again, mewling. He pushed her toward the child, almost violently. Lacrimosa wanted to object. She wanted to flee.

"Please," she said. "Don't shove me. I can't heal him."

He placed his foot on her head, and pushed it toward the child. He forced her face near the wound. It stank of rot. The maggots in the blood swirled. Lacrimosa grimaced and tried to pull away, but Volucris held her face up to the wound.

"Please, release me," she said.

The child was shifting, trying to caw. His eyes fluttered. "Ma," he seemed to say. "Ma. Caw! Ma."

Lacrimosa closed her eyes, the stench of the wound in her nostrils. The child would die, she knew. Son of Volucris, prince of griffins, heir to these islands. An innocent child, perhaps the first griffin born in freedom. Lacrimosa thought of all those griffins born into slavery—first in Requiem, then in Osanna. How could she let this one die? She bore responsibility to them. As she wanted to rebuild Requiem, she owed Leonis a debt too.

"Ma," the cub cawed again. "*Caw*. Ma. Ma."

He was in pain. He was weeping. Suddenly it no longer mattered that he was a prince, that Lacrimosa's fathers had enslaved his people. All that mattered was that he was a child. A child in pain, a child dying. Wasn't that the entire gravity of it?

She felt tears gather once more in her eyes. One tear fell, splashed into the wound, and raised steam.

Volucris and the other griffins all cried. The cub yelped and tried to move, but was too weak. Another tear fell from Lacrimosa, hit the wound, and more steam rose. *My tears hurt him,* she thought, but she could not curb them. They fell into the wound, hissing and steaming, as the griffins shrieked.

And then Lacrimosa noticed that when the steam cleared, the wound looked better. The pus drained from it. New blood filled the wound, and then it scabbed over.

"Ma," the griffin cub said, and his voice was relieved, some of the pain cleared from it.

Volucris released her, and Lacrimosa raised her head. She looked at the cub in amazement. The infection had left him! He looked up at her, his eyes clear.

"Dragon tears," Lacrimosa whispered. "They heal griffins."

Volucris nodded. Then he tossed back his head and cried in joy. The other griffins did the same. The young prince rose to his feet, limped, and then flapped his wings. He flew a few feet, landed, and squeaked.

Lacrimosa laughed and cried. *Requiem enslaved you,* she thought. *With our tears we find some salvation.*

The cub embraced his parents. Then Volucris moved toward Lacrimosa. He knelt before her, bowed his head, and looked into her eyes.

Lacrimosa smiled.

"Will Leonis be our ally? Will Requiem and Leonis fight together, fight against Dies Irae?"

Volucris gave her a long stare. He looked to the west. He looked at his son. Then he walked to the eggs, and retrieved from between them the candlestick. He placed it at Lacrimosa's feet.

She shifted into human form and lifted the candlestick. It seemed made of pure gold, and when she turned it in the sun, its emeralds glinted.

"It's beautiful," she said. "Is this a gift for saving your son?"

He squawked and pawed the nest. There was more he wanted to tell her. Lacrimosa examined the candlestick more closely. When she turned it over, she saw words engraved into its base. *Summoning Stick.* Lacrimosa gasped.

"I've heard of the Summoning Stick," she said. "Only two were ever made, one of silver, one of gold. When lit, they call for aid."

Volucris nodded. Lacrimosa embraced his great, downy head.

"Thank you, Volucris, King of Griffins," she said. "When I need your aid, I will light the candlestick." She drew back and gave him a solemn stare. "When we rebuild Requiem, there will be war with Irae. We will need your wings."

Volucris nodded, staring at her, and she saw the answer in his eyes.

Our wings are yours.

AGNUS DEI

At the bottom of the staircase, Agnus Dei froze. The tunnels under Requiem stretched before her, all darkness and moaning wind. She held her dagger with one hand, her makeshift torch in the other.

"How deep are the scrolls?" she whispered. She wasn't sure why she whispered. Surely the Poisoned—those Vir Requis turned scaly and webbed with Dies Irae's black magic—no longer dwelled here. But Agnus Dei found it difficult to speak any louder. *Just in case.*

"They were buried deep in the darkness," Father said, "to protect them from snow, fire, rain... or war."

Agnus Dei glanced at him. She reminded herself that Father was more than just an annoying, gruff old man who hummed and creaked and scolded her whenever she growled. He was King Benedictus, the Black Fang. He had once ruled these lands and worn fine silk and steel. He had once led this land to war and seen it destroyed. He had once fought in these tunnels and watched as others burned, and drowned, and became creatures of fish scales and bulging eyes and—

Enough, Agnus Dei told herself. *Don't dwell on it. Get the scrolls. Get out. Learn about the nightshades. Let the past remain in this darkness.*

She took a step deeper into the tunnels.

The winds from below moaned, rustling her cloak. She clenched her jaw and kept walking, Father at her side. Their torches crackled, and shadows danced like demons. The walls were black stone, hard and smooth, too close to her. Agnus Dei hated enclosed spaces. There was no room to shift into dragons here. What if creatures attacked—ghosts, or... the Poisoned? Could she fight them in human form, with only her dagger? Agnus Dei growled.

Her feet hit something. A clattering sound echoed. Agnus Dei lowered her torch and grimaced. She had kicked a skeleton, scattering its bones. Several more skeletons lay within the sphere of light, covered in dust and cobwebs and tatters of leather. The flickering torch made them seem to shiver.

"Irae's men," she said. They bore chipped, wide blades in the style of Osanna, and one wore a breastplate engraved with a griffin.

Father nodded. "Many of them died here too."

They walked over the skeletons, careful not to further disturb their bones. The tunnel plunged deeper, its slope steep. Shattered swords, arrowheads, and helmets littered the floor. At one point, the skeleton of a griffin cub blocked their way, and they had to walk between its ribs. A rusty helmet topped its skull. The air grew colder and the wind moaned. Once, Agnus Dei thought she heard a cackle from deep below, but when she froze and listened, she heard nothing more.

Around a bend, she saw a new skeleton. She paused and grunted. This skeleton was strange. It was shaped like a man, but the skull was too long, the eye sockets too small. Its fingers were twice the normal length, and its femurs were twisted like ram's horns. At first Agnus Dei thought it an animal—an ape, like those drawn in picture books—but this skeleton held a sword, and wisps of a tunic clung to its ribs.

"A Poisoned," she whispered.

Father nodded.

As they walked around the Poisoned, Agnus Dei couldn't help but stare into its eye sockets. Even in death, it seemed in agony. She could imagine it being a Vir Requis like her once, maybe a girl, poisoned until her bones twisted, and her eyes popped, and—

No. No! Don't think of it. Agnus Dei gritted her teeth and kept walking.

Soon she and Father reached a staircase. The steps were chipped and narrow. Agnus Dei's boots stepped on old arrowheads, a dagger's blade, and a skeleton's hand. Once she kicked a helmet. It clattered down the stairs, echoing. She winced, and Father grumbled, and they froze until the clacking stopped.

Past the staircase, they found a crossroads of three tunnels, and Father led them down the left one. Their torches guttered. Agnus Dei tore fresh strips off her cloak, and wrapped them around the stick she carried, so that it blazed with new light.

In the firelight, she saw many more skeletons. The main battles must have been fought here. Bones covered the floor. Shattered shields, swords, crossbows, and arrowheads lay everywhere, threatening to cut her boots. The air here was so cold and dry, skin and hair remained on the bodies, shriveled and white. Their fingernails were yellow and cracked like rotten teeth.

"How much farther are the scrolls?" she whispered.

"Not far," Father said, his voice low, his eyes watery. Agnus Dei looked at him, and all her irritation and anger at her father faded. She realized that he'd known many of these fallen Vir Requis. Some had been soldiers under his command. Others must have been his friends, cousins, uncles.

They stepped gingerly over the skeletons, and plunged deeper into the darkness. The tunnels kept sloping down; Agnus Dei could not guess how far underground they were. As horrid as the burned forests of Requiem were, with their ash and bones and fallen columns, she longed to return there now, to see the sun, and to see life, even if life meant only vultures and bugs.

Soon they reached the remains of a doorway in the tunnel. Once it had sealed the passageway beyond; today it was but splinters of wood and old hinges. They stepped through it, and found themselves in a towering chamber.

Father pointed with his torch. "There, in the alcoves."

It was hard to see in the darkness, but it seemed like hundreds of alcoves covered the walls, maybe thousands. Rolled up scrolls nested in them.

"Here lies the wisdom and knowledge of Requiem," Father whispered.

They walked deeper into the chamber. Agnus Dei tried to walk lightly, but her boots clanked and echoed despite her best efforts. The walls rose thirty feet tall. *So many scrolls!* She thought it must have taken a thousand years to write them all, and would take a thousand more to read them. She moved her torch left and right, scattering shadows.

"Which scrolls do we need?" she asked.

"In the back, near that tunnel," Father said. "You see where—"

A cry pierced the darkness.

Agnus Dei and Father froze. The only movement was the fire of their torches.

The cry sounded again, coming from the second tunnel, the tunnel that led beyond the chamber of scrolls. It sounded hurt, mournful.

"What—" Agnus Dei began, and then a shadow leaped at her from the ceiling.

She cried, thrust her dagger, and heard a scream. Blood splashed her hand. She had cut something, something of dangling eyeballs, of webbed fingers with cracked nails, of clammy pale flesh. And then it was gone, scurrying into the shadows.

"The Poisoned!" she said. She raised her torch, hand sticky with blood. The firelight reflected in a thousand eyes and fangs.

"Friends!" Father said, voice trembling slightly. "We can end your pain. Do not—"

The Poisoned lunged at them.

"Stay back!" Agnus Dei shouted. She waved her torch and dagger before her. A hundred Poisoned reached with cracked claws. Some of them stared with eyeballs that bulged, bloodshot. Others had eyes that dangled down their cheeks, but even those eyes stared with hatred. Agnus Dei slammed her torch into one; it screamed and fell back, burning. She cut another with her dagger. One cut her, slicing claws down her arm. The cuts blazed and raised green smoke.

"Back, friends!" Father called, slamming at them with his torch. Their scales flew. "We can help you."

But they could not, Agnus Dei knew. There was no cure for these Vir Requis. With a growl, she shifted into a dragon. The Poisoned shrieked, strings of saliva quivering between their teeth. A dozen raced at her, and Agnus Dei blew fire.

"No, Agnus Dei!" Father cried. "You'll burn the scrolls."

Agnus Dei was beyond caring. Blood roared in her ears. She blew flames again. A dozen Poisoned caught fire. They fled into the tunnels, blazing.

Father shifted too. Soon the burly black dragon was kicking Poisoned, biting them, clawing. Tears sparkled in his eyes as he fought. "You'll feel no more pain, friends," he said.

Suddenly, in her mind, Agnus Dei didn't see creatures of scales and claws. She saw men, women, children. Her cousins, her schoolyard friends, her uncles and aunts. How many of these Vir Requis had she known before Dies Irae malformed them? How many had Father known? She blew fire, weeping now, until the Poisoned all burned. They writhed on the floor, screaming, clawing the air. The sound was like steam from a kettle. The stench of their burning flesh filled the air, the stench of rotten fish.

"The scrolls!" Father said. Agnus Dei saw that they too burned. Across the chamber, fires filled the alcoves. The scrolls were curling, smoking, and burning away.

Still in dragon form, Agnus Dei began pulling the burning scrolls from the alcoves. She dropped them to the floor and stepped on them. But the fire was spreading. Smoke filled the chamber. A thousand Poisoned blazed; some dead, others screaming and dying. Father too was collecting scrolls, but soon there was no place to extinguish them. The entire chamber became an inferno, all flame and smoke and screams.

"Let's get out of here!" Agnus Dei cried.

"We must save the scrolls," Father shouted back. She couldn't even see him behind the fire and smoke.

Agnus Dei coughed. "We'll die in here! It's time to go!"

She scooped up what scrolls she could, shifted into human form, and raced into the tunnel they had entered from. A moment later, Father joined her, also in human form, also carrying smoldering scrolls. Smoke and ash covered him.

They raced through the tunnel, smoke and fire and screams chasing them. One Poisoned, who had somehow survived the inferno, ran behind them. He rose in flame, screamed, and reached out crumbling fingers. Agnus Dei stabbed him with her dagger, weeping, and kept running.

When they finally reached daylight and burst into the ruins of Requiem, Agnus Dei fell to her knees. The scrolls fell from her arms, rolled across cracked cobblestones, and sizzled in the rain. Agnus Dei lowered her head, sobbing. Thunder rolled, and mud flowed around her.

Father knelt beside her, breath ragged. The rain streamed down his face. He embraced her, and Agnus Dei clung to him, weeping against his shoulder. He smoothed her hair.

"Their torture is over now," he whispered to her. "They are now among our forefathers in our halls beyond the stars."

Agnus Dei trembled. "There were so many. So many remained...."

Father nodded. "They bred in the tunnels."

Agnus Dei pulled her head back from his shoulder. She stared into his eyes, still holding him. "Papa, are they all dead now?"

He nodded. "They are. I promise."

It was long moments before she could stop trembling. She could still imagine those screams, the hisses, the eyeballs. Finally the rain softened, and she saw a rainbow over the ruins. Even here, in this land of ruins, skeletons, old curses and pain... even here there was beauty. She looked at the rainbow, and calmed her breath, and pulled herself free from Father's embrace.

"I burned most of the scrolls," she said quietly. "I'm sorry."

He squeezed her shoulder. "But we recovered a few scrolls. Let's look at them."

They pulled the scrolls from the mud and cleaned them as best they could. Several yards away, they found a mosaic floor. Most of the floor lay buried in mud. Bones, ash, and dragon teeth covered the rest. They brushed an area clean, revealing part of the mosaic; it showed a scene of dragons flying in sunset. Agnus Dei and Father unrolled the scrolls there and examined them.

They were badly burned. Several crumbed in their fingers. Others were burned beyond reading. A few had survived the fire, but they contained no knowledge of nightshades; one was a prayer scroll, three others contained musical notes, and another two traced the lineage of Requiem's kings and queens.

"We might have come all this way for nothing," Agnus Dei said, head hung low. She hugged herself in the cold and stared, eyes finally dry, at a broken statue of a maiden holding an urn.

"Here, daughter. Look at this." Father brushed off one scroll and unrolled it. At the very top, in delicate ink, appeared a drawing of a nightshade.

Agnus Dei gasped. "You found it, Father! You found the right scroll."

He gave her a wan smile. She wanted to jump onto him, to hug and kiss him, but froze. Father looked so tired. His eyes were sunken, his cheeks stubbly and haggard. For the first time, Agnus Dei realized that Father was growing old. He was no longer the young man who'd led Requiem to war. Gray filled his black curls, wrinkles appeared on his brow, and the cares of the world and a fallen race filled his eyes. She gave him a small kiss on that rough, prickly cheek.

"Let's see what it says," she said.

When they unrolled the scroll further, revealing its calligraphy, Agnus Dei frowned. Burn marks covered the parchment. Some bits had burned away completely. The scroll had more holes than a suit of chain mail. She groaned.

"There's not much left," Father said with a sigh.

They huddled over it, blowing ash and dirt away, brows furrowed. Only one paragraph was legible, and even that one was missing half its text. Agnus Dei read it over and over, but it made little sense as it was.

"In the days of the Night Horrors, King T_____ite journeyed to the southern realms of G____nd sought the Loomers o_____olden pools. The Night Horrors stole the souls of Osanna, and cast them into the d___ness, and Ta_____omers, who were wise above all others in the land. He spoke with the Loomers, and prayed with them, and they crafted him th_____e returned with th_____anna, an_____m upon the Night Horrors. He tamed them, and drove them into Well of Night in the Marble City, and sealed it. He placed guards around it, armed wit_____cape."

"What do you make of it, Father?" Agnus Dei asked, raising her eyes from the scroll. After reading it several times, it still made little sense to her.

He scratched his chin. The wind blew his cloak, which bore as many burn marks as the scrolls. "I think you'll agree that Night Horrors refers to nightshades."

Agnus Dei nodded. "That must be how the ancient Vir Requis called them."

"And Marble City refers to Confutatis," Father said. "That one is easy enough. Even today we sometimes call it that."

"So we know that some king, whose name began with T, tamed the nightshades, and sealed them in Confutatis. Which king began with T?"

Father sighed deeply. He rubbed his neck, joints creaking. "Most of Osanna's kings had names that began with T. There were several kings named Tanith, and two named Talin. There was a King Talon too, I believe, and a few named Thoranor. Before Dies Irae took over, the letter T denoted royalty."

"So we have no idea which king tamed the nightshades."

"No," Father agreed.

Agnus Dei also sighed. "So this scroll isn't much help. I'm sorry, Father. I burned it. Now it's useless."

Father shook his head. "Not useless. Some information is missing, yes, but we have clues. The scroll tells us to seek the Loomers of these 'olden pools'. The Loomers crafted something for the king. What was it? Great weapons?"

Agnus Dei bit her lip. "Probably. Weapons that could defeat nightshades. The scroll says the olden pools are in a southern realm that starts with a G. What place is that?"

Benedictus said, "Well, for one thing, we know it's in the south."

Agnus Dei raised an eyebrow. "Father, did you make a joke? That's a first."

Father watched two crows that flew above. "Let us go to Fidelium Mountains. We'll meet Mother, Gloriae, and Kyrie there. Maybe they'll have found better information."

Kyrie. The word sent fire through Agnus Dei. Her mind flashed back to that day at the Divide, the border with Salvandos, where they had first made love. A day of fire, heat, and sweat. Agnus Dei bit her lip to quell the thought. It was ridiculous. Did she miss Kyrie now? She snorted. The boy was a mere pup.

She rolled up the scroll, rose to her feet, and nodded. "Let's go."

They walked through the wet ruins, between the bones, cracked statues, fallen columns, and old weapons. The rainbow stretched before them across the horizon.

KYRIE ELEISON

After riding all day behind Gloriae, Kyrie was ready to throttle her.

"Gloriae, for pity's sake, my legs feel like they were dipped into lava. Can you please stop that horse of yours?"

Gloriae didn't bother turning to face him. She kept directing the horse down the dirt road, bouncing before Kyrie in the saddle. "Not until we cross the Alarath River. If we're to reach Fidelium by the new moon, we have a schedule to keep."

Kyrie groaned. "Gloriae, seriously. My thighs and backside have blisters growing on their blisters. How can you ride so much? The horse is exhausted, and so am I." He pointed east. "I see a village. Let's go find an inn, eat, and rest."

Gloriae nodded. "You're right, Kyrie. Let's go to town."

Kyrie raised his arms in triumph, then wobbled in the saddle, and wrapped them around Gloriae again. "Great. Finally you're seeing some sense."

They rode toward the village. A small fort rose upon a hill—merely a tower, wall, and stables. A score of cottages nestled below the hill by a temple and tavern. Fields of wheat and barley surrounded the village, fluttering with birds.

"Do you think anyone's alive in this one?" Kyrie asked. At the last few towns they'd passed, everyone was dead, soulless, or hiding.

Gloriae nodded. "I bet we can find a new, living horse." She rode past the cottages, heading toward the fort and stables.

"What? Gloriae! Stop it. Stop it! Turn this horse around right now, and take us to that tavern." He moaned. "Oh stars. I can smell beef stew from here, and bread, and beer."

Gloriae sniffed the air. "I can smell fresh horses ahead. You were right, Kyrie. This horse is exhausted. We'll find a fresh one."

Kyrie cursed to high heavens, and would have jumped off the horse, were he not terrified of breaking his neck. Gloriae was deaf to him, and Kyrie could do nothing but cling to her, arms around her waist, as she rode past the village. Once they reached the fort and stables, Gloriae finally stopped the horse and dismounted.

"Now you may get off the horse," she said.

Kyrie dismounted and moaned. His thighs were so chaffed and stiff, he could barely walk. He rubbed them.

"I'm going to that tavern," he said. He began limping downhill, leaving Gloriae behind. After a few yards, he regretted walking. Walking now hurt just as much as riding. Kyrie sighed. He wished they could have flown. Flying was the way to travel. But how could they? At daytime, anyone would see two flying dragons. And at night, well... he wasn't going anywhere in the open at night, not anymore.

He reached the tavern, stepped inside, and found more soulless people. They lay on the tables and floors, drooling. Kyrie tried not to look at them and stepped into the pantry. His eyes widened, his nostrils flared, and he sighed contentedly.

"Lovely," he said to himself, admiring the smoked hams, biscuits, jars of preserves, turnips, and best of all—caskets of ale. He licked his lips, prepared for a solid few hours of dining and drinking.

Hooves sounded outside. "Kyrie Eleison!" came Gloriae's voice from outside the tavern. "Are you in there? Come. I have a fresh horse. We ride."

Kyrie snorted. "You ride, I eat."

Her voice darkened. "Don't make me come in there to get you."

Kyrie took a bite of ham, chewed lustfully, and called out with his mouth full. "I'd like to see you try."

Not a minute later, Gloriae was dragging him by the hair out of the tavern.

"Ow!" he cried, sausages and bread rolls falling from his arms. "Let go, I'm carrying food and drink here, for stars' sake."

She glared and gave his hair a twist. He groaned. "You're lucky I'm dragging you by the hair, not your ears... or worse. On the horse. Now."

She finally released him. Muttering, Kyrie collected the fallen food. He hadn't grabbed much—the sausages, the rolls, two jars of jam, and a skin of ale. He stuffed them into the saddle's side bags.

"Gloriae, this new horse stinks," he said. "Hasn't anybody washed it?"

Gloriae mounted the horse and settled herself in the saddle. "No, Kyrie. The stable boys were gone. I reckon they fled into the countryside when the nightshades arrived. The horse is dirty, but it's rested, and has been eating leftover hay. I released our old horse into the farms; it's too weary to keep journeying."

Kyrie muttered and climbed onto the saddle behind Gloriae. His thighs protested, but he drowned the pain in curses and grumbles. Gloriae kneed the horse, and they left the village and resumed journeying north.

"So how many more horses are you going to break today?" he asked.

Gloriae shrugged. "As many as it takes. Benedictus gave us a time and place to meet him. I expect to be there."

"Benedictus can go eat a toad's warts," Kyrie said. He sighed. "I wonder if the old man found anything. Stars know we haven't found much at Confutatis. Unless you count the fact that Dies Irae is obsessed with glorifying himself, which I think everyone has sort of figured out by now."

Gloriae turned in the saddle and glared at him. "Kyrie, do you mind not whining and complaining so much? Do I have to hurt you again?"

Kyrie rubbed his neck. He sighed deeply. "You're right, Gloriae. It's just... I miss your sister. And I'm worried about her, and Lacrimosa, and yes, even Benedictus. I know I've been snapping at you a lot. I also haven't been sleeping much, what with those nightshades shrieking all night, which isn't helping."

As Gloriae bounced in the saddle, pressing against him, Kyrie knew he was speaking only half-truth. True, the nightshades kept him up a lot. But half the time, maybe *most* of the time, it was Gloriae who kept him awake. Gloriae's hair in his nostrils. Her body close to his, sometimes pressed against him. Her green eyes, cruel and mocking, and those freckles on her cheeks, and the curve of her—

Kyrie gritted his teeth. *Stop that,* he told himself. It was bad enough that thoughts of Gloriae filled his mind all night. He didn't need to think of her—not like *that*—during the daytime too. He forced himself to think of Agnus Dei again, and his heart melted like butter on hot bread.

Agnus Dei. As beautiful and tempting as Gloriae was, Kyrie knew that Agnus Dei was his true love. He thought of her brown eyes, her mane of bouncing curls, the softness and fullness of her lips. He thought of her pride, her strength, and the softness she showed only to him. Her heart was pure and good, even if she kept it wrapped in fire. Kyrie missed her. Badly. It ached more than his blisters.

"Are *you* okay, Gloriae?" he asked her. "You seem so strong. As if you feel no pain. If you ever want to talk, we can—"

"Kyrie, save it for my sister. I'm Gloriae the Gilded. I feel no pain."

Kyrie nodded. He remembered how Gloriae had wept over May's body. How much pain that one must carry... to have grown up in Confutatis, under the iron fist of Dies Irae.... Kyrie couldn't even begin to imagine it. He suddenly felt such pity for Gloriae, that his arms around her felt less like an attempt to keep from falling, and more like an embrace. If she felt the change in his grasp, she gave no note of it.

They rode silently for a while, Gloriae's curls bouncing as always against Kyrie's face. He occupied himself by looking at the landscapes—hills dotted with oaks, deer, and the occasional fort and village. Every once in a while, peasants, beggars, soldiers, or other motley travellers greeted them on the road. A few seemed hungry enough to attack, but Gloriae and Kyrie merely flashed their blades, and the hungry folk moved on.

"Come nightfall, most of them will be with the nightshades," Gloriae said.

Kyrie nodded. Every day, they saw fewer people on the roads, and more bodies in the gutters.

"At this rate, Osanna won't be much better than Requiem within a week," he said.

Gloriae turned her head and snarled. "Don't say that," she said. She clenched her fists. "Never say that again."

Kyrie glared back at her. "Why not? It's true. You released the nightshades, Gloriae. Take a long, hard look around you. The bloody things are turning the world into a—"

Suddenly she was crying. Kyrie stopped speaking. He had expected her to fume, scream, maybe even attack him. He had not expected this. She turned to face him. Her tears flowed down her cheeks, her lips trembled, and her eyes turned red.

"Kyrie," she whispered.

He didn't know how to react. He hated Gloriae. He wanted her to feel pain. Didn't he? Yet somehow—Kyrie couldn't figure out how—they found themselves standing on the roadside, embracing. She wept against him.

He patted her head awkwardly. "Gloriae, it's okay. We're going to trap the nightshades, and bring things back to normal."

She spoke into his shirt. "I'm scared, Kyrie. I'm so scared all the time. During the days, during the nights. I did this. I know it. I tried to kill you, and I destroyed the world instead. I'm so sorry." Her fingers dug into him. "I want to go home, Kyrie. I want to ride my griffin again, and live in my palace, and be strong. Be brave. Be certain of my way. I hate being so lost, so confused."

Her body trembled against him. She leaned back and looked at him with watery eyes, her lips quivering. Strands of her hair covered her face, and Kyrie drew them back, and tucked them behind her ears.

"Gloriae, have I ever told you about Requiem?" he asked. She shook her head.

"I don't remember much of it," Kyrie continued. "But I know it was beautiful. I remember a stone temple, where chandeliers hung, and monks played harps and sang. The place glowed at night with candles."

The memories flowed back into him, so real he could almost see them. Gloriae clung to him, staring with those moist eyes.

"Keep going," she whispered.

"I would sneak outside of services with my brothers. There were these trees outside the temple. I don't know their name, but they grew hard, green berries. We'd collect the fruit, and have wars, pelting one another from behind logs and benches." He laughed softly. "Requiem is still there. It's ruined now. That temple is gone. The people who prayed there are dead. But you and I are still here, and we have our memories. Once we defeat the nightshades, we'll go back there. We'll rebuild." He held Gloriae's hands. "And then we won't be lost anymore. We'll have our home. We'll have our purpose. We'll have Requiem again. You, me, and the others."

Gloriae looked to the west, as if imagining those old temples. "That doesn't sound so bad," she said, voice almost a whisper.

"Not at all," Kyrie said. But he wondered. Was it an empty dream? Could they truly defeat the nightshades? Even if they did, could they stop Dies Irae and his men? He sighed.

"Let's ride," Gloriae said. "We'll be at Fidelium soon."

They hid that night in a hollowed out log, which they first emptied of mud, twigs, and mice. The log was just wide enough for them, its bark rough and sticky. The nightshades screeched outside all night, and they could see their shadows and lightning, but they remained hidden and safe.

In the morning, they emerged from the log with stiff muscles, and found that the nightshades had claimed their horse. The beast lay on its side, mouth foaming.

"Look away, Kyrie," Gloriae said and drew her sword.

"Gloriae, what are you— Stop tha—"

Gloriae thrust down her sword, piercing the horse's brain. It died instantly, gushing blood. Kyrie covered his mouth, feeling sick.

Gloriae removed her sword, cleaned it with a handkerchief, and stared at Kyrie. Her eyes were emotionless.

"I put it out of its misery," she said. "Crows and jackals would've been eating it alive within the hour."

Kyrie couldn't help but stare at the blood, which was now trickling between his boots. He looked back up at Gloriae, and found no pity, no compassion in her eyes. Gloriae the Gilded. The Light of Osanna.

"Let's go," he said.

They walked down the road, weapons drawn. Their robes, once white and pure, were now grimy with dirt and blood. Mud covered their boots. They walked all morning, their supplies slung over their backs. At noon they saw Fidelium Mountains in the distance, capped with snow. Kyrie's heart leaped. *Agnus Dei will be there.* He ached to hold her, kiss her, never leave her again.

"We travel cross-country from here," Gloriae said. They left the dirt road and walked through a forest of elms, oaks, and birches. Ferns and bushes grew everywhere. Kyrie slashed at them with his dagger. Everywhere were roots to trip him and branches to slap him.

They emerged from the trees in the afternoon, stepped into a field, and moaned. Kyrie felt like a deflated bellows.

"The bastard," he said. "How did he know?"

The mountain was still distant, but they were close enough to see Dies Irae's banners flapping across it. Archers covered the mountainsides, crouching in the snow. Below the mountain, thousands of soldiers drilled, kicking up snow as they marched and clashed swords. Knights on horseback rode among them, armor glinting.

"Back into the forest, Kyrie," Gloriae whispered.

They stepped back and hid behind an oak. They peered between the leaves, watching silently as the armies ahead drilled.

Hundreds of tents spread below the mountain, Kyrie saw. Most were the simple, squat tents of soldiers. One tent was large as a manor, its walls made of embroidered, golden cloth; Dies Irae would be in that one. Three other tents were even larger, their walls black. Those last tents bulged and fluttered, as if beasts swarmed inside them. Kyrie could hear nightshades shriek, and he shuddered.

"Agnus Dei hid here for a year once," he said. "And you and Dies Irae never thought of seeking her here. How did he know to come here now?"

Gloriae bit her lip, considering. "Remember when the nightshades claimed Agnus Dei?"

"Of course."

"They must have seen her memories. They must have learned of this hideout. And they told Irae. Now he's here, waiting for us."

A thought struck Kyrie, and he shivered. "You don't suppose that... the others got here before us? That Irae caught them?"

Gloriae looked at him. Fear filled her eyes. "I don't know."

Kyrie looked back at the mountain. He watched the golden tent's door open, and saw Dies Irae emerge. He wore his gilded, jewelled armor; it glinted like a small sun. As Kyrie and Gloriae watched from the trees, Dies Irae walked toward the dark, fluttering tent and stepped inside. The tent fluttered more wildly, and the nightshades inside screeched.

"Dies Irae is having fun with his new pets," Kyrie muttered. "Now we know where he keeps them during the daytime."

When he looked at Gloriae, he took a step back. She was pale, trembling, her fists clenched. She bared her teeth. She looked like a cornered wolf.

"I'm going to kill him," she said and took a step out of the trees.

Kyrie grabbed her shoulder. She spun toward him, snarling.

"Let go!" she hissed.

He pulled her back into the brush. "Gloriae, Irae banished you. He disowned you. If you walk up to him now, he'll kill you."

She snorted, sword drawn. "He won't kill his daughter."

"You're not his daughter. You know that now, don't you? And Irae must know it too, or suspect it. Gloriae, please. We'll find a better way."

Her eyes narrowed, and blood rushed into her cheeks. Suddenly she was the old Gloriae, horrible and merciless. "What other way?"

Kyrie thought fast. "Look at that camp. Irae has been here for a while, I'd wager; at least a couple days. The full moon is tonight. If your family already arrived here—your real family—they'd have seen Irae and backtracked."

Gloriae's freckles seemed to flash with rage. Golden flecks danced in her eyes like flames. "Where would they go?"

"To Requiem," Kyrie said. He didn't know if that was true. He knew, however, that he had to get Gloriae away from here—as far as possible. If they lingered, she'd march to Dies Irae, confront him, and die. "We've talked of rebuilding Requiem; they'd know to go there, realizing we'd think the same thing."

Gloriae considered him, head tilted, as if she were a bird of prey deciding when to swoop. Kyrie wasn't sure why he cared about her welfare. He hated Gloriae almost as much as he hated Dies Irae, didn't he? So what if she confronted Dies Irae and he killed her? And yet... Kyrie didn't want her to die. She was a Vir Requis. She was his companion. And she was Agnus Dei's sister. He would do what he could to save her.

"Why don't we hide in these woods?" she asked. "We might have a better chance of finding the others here, if they're still on their way."

A gruff voice answered behind them. "This is why."

Kyrie and Gloriae spun around to see five soldiers charging at them, swinging swords.

Kyrie snarled and raised his dagger. He deflected the sword of a sallow-faced soldier with a missing tooth. The soldier grunted and swung his sword again. Kyrie ducked. The sword whistled over his head. Kyrie thrust his dagger and hit the soldier's chain mail; his blade did the armor no damage.

He leaped back. From the corner of his eye, he saw that Gloriae had killed one man, and was battling the others. The soldier swung his sword at Kyrie again. He parried with his dagger, grabbed a branch, and yanked it. He ducked, and the branch slapped the soldier's face.

Kyrie thrust his dagger. It sank into the soldier's cheek, scraped along his skull, and entered his eye. The man screamed. Kyrie pushed the dagger deep, twisted it, and pulled. It came free with blood and eyeball juices.

A second soldier swung his sword at Kyrie. Kyrie jumped back, tripped over a root, and fell. The soldier raised his sword. Kyrie threw a rock at his face. The sword came down. Kyrie rolled and buried his dagger in the soldier's thigh. He twisted and pulled the blade. The man fell, and Gloriae's sword slammed into his head.

Kyrie panted, glancing around. The five soldiers were dead.

"Stars," he muttered, heart pounding and fingers trembling. "I only killed one, and you killed four, Gloriae. And you're not even out of breath."

She pointed her bloody sword to the mountains. "But I can't kill four thousand."

The sounds of battle had alerted the army. Soldiers were leaving the camp and running toward the trees.

Gloriae wrenched a sword out of a dead soldier's hands. "Ever use one of these?" she asked Kyrie.

"Of course," he lied.

Gloriae shoved the hilt into his hand.

"Good," she said. "Now run!"

They ran between the trees, branches lashing their faces, roots and pebbles threatening to trip them. The sounds of soldiers came behind—clanking armor, shouts, hissing swords.

"We go to Requiem, you say?" Gloriae asked as they ran.

Kyrie nodded. "To the old palace, where Benedictus and Lacrimosa lived. Where you were born."

They ran, sap on their faces, until night fell, and the shrieks of nightshades shook the forest. They hid in darkness, huddled in an abandoned wolf's den, under a hill behind the dangling roots of an oak. As nightshades screeched, Kyrie and Gloriae held each other and shivered.

BENEDICTUS

"Well, here's a pretty sight," said the soldier. He reached for his sword. "A father and daughter weredragon out for a stroll."

Ten other soldiers stepped out from the forest. They wore helmets and chain mail, and carried shields emblazoned with Dies Irae's coat of arms. They stepped onto the road, eyes narrowed.

Benedictus grunted. "We're simple travellers," he said to the soldiers. He took Agnus Dei's hand. "Let us be."

The soldiers surrounded them. They drew their swords as one, the blades hissing.

Benedictus glanced at Agnus Dei and nodded.

She nodded back; she knew the signal.

Together, they shifted into dragons and swung their tails.

Benedictus hit one soldier. He drove the spikes of his tail through the man's armor, and slammed him against another man. Agnus Dei took down two more men.

The remaining soldiers charged, blades swinging. Benedictus blew fire. The flames hit three men. They screamed and fell. Agnus Dei shot flames too, hitting two more soldiers.

Three soldiers remained. They were foolish enough to attack. Benedictus lashed his tail and knocked two down. Agnus Dei clawed another. With a few more swipes of their claws, the soldiers all lay dead.

Panting, Benedictus and Agnus Dei shifted back into human forms. They stood staring at the bodies.

"We made a bloody racket," Benedictus said. He panted and wiped sweat off his brow.

Agnus Dei nodded. "And raised smoke and fire." She spat onto the roadside. "If there are more soldiers a league around, they'll know we're here."

Benedictus glared at her. "Agnus Dei, you are a princess of Requiem. Do not spit."

She rolled her eyes. "Father, spare me. Let's go. Off the road."

They stepped into the forest just as the sound of boots came around the bend. Benedictus raced between the trees, Agnus Dei at his side. Grunts and curses sounded behind them, and soon the boots were thumping through the forest in pursuit.

"This whole forest is swarming with Irae's men," Benedictus said. He pointed his sword ahead, where between the trees, they could see an army mustered beneath Fidelium Mountain.

Agnus Dei uttered a curse that could make a sailor blush. "There were no soldiers when Mother and I hid here. Irae discovered our hideout."

They rushed around a boulder and shoved their way between brambles. The sounds of pursuit came between the trees.

"Wait," Benedictus said. "Let's load our crossbows. I want us to fight as humans—for as long as we can. We'd be tougher to find."

They stopped, panting, and loaded quarrels into their crossbows. Benedictus's lungs burned, and his heart thrashed

"Okay, go, quickly."

He heard a stream ahead and headed toward it. Curses and shouts came behind.

"I see prints," a soldier shouted. "That way."

Benedictus and Agnus Dei splashed into the stream. They walked through the water until they reached a boulder on the bank. They left the water, climbed over the boulder, and kept moving.

"You think they'll lose our trail?" Agnus Dei asked. "I—"

Her voice died. Two soldiers stood ahead. They seemed surprised; Benedictus guessed they hadn't expected to find anyone during their patrol. The men barely had time to draw their swords before he and Agnus Dei shot quarrels into their chests.

"Do you think Mother is here?" Agnus Dei said after they reloaded and kept trudging through the forest. "What about Kyrie and Gloriae?"

Benedictus frowned. He stared between the trees at the mountain, at Dies Irae's banners upon it, at the army that camped below.

"I don't know," he said. "We're supposed to meet them today in the cave, but... I don't know how they'd get there. There's an army guarding the place."

They kept running. The sounds of pursuit gradually faded behind. But it wouldn't be long, Benedictus knew, before thousands of soldiers were combing the woods.

Agnus Dei pointed at the mountainside, where archers surrounded the opening of a cave. "That's the cave Mother and I would hide in. Irae is guarding the entrance. But there's a back entrance too. If you go behind the mountain, a small cave leads into a tunnel. You can travel through the mountain, and reach the main cave from there."

Benedictus grunted. "You think the others are inside the tunnels?"

A soldier burst from between the trees, sword raised. Agnus Dei shot him with her crossbow. "I don't know," she said. "If they were waiting in the cave, and Irae arrived, they might have crawled deep into the tunnels, and hid there. We should look for them."

Benedictus stepped toward the soldier Agnus Dei had shot. He was lying in the mud, clutching his chest, whimpering. Benedictus knelt and gave the man water from his canteen.

"Your comrades will be here soon," he said to the soldier. He turned back to Agnus Dei. "More tunnels. I hate tunnels. But fine. Let's go."

They raced between the trees, crossbows and swords in hand, and cut west. They travelled for several hours through the forest. The sounds of soldiers faded behind them.

In late afternoon, the land became hilly, and pines replaced the elms and oaks. They found themselves climbing slopes, moving higher with every step. Old bricks, smoothed by centuries of rain, lay scattered around them. Once they saw the head of a statue, smoothed to bare features, emerging from the dirt. The remains of a wall and aqueduct nestled between a hill, overgrown with moss and vines.

"What is this place?" Agnus Dei asked. "These ruins are older than the ones in Requiem."

Benedictus nodded. "Fidelium Mountain is named after an old kingdom named Fidelium. Two thousand years ago, it fought a war against Osanna, and lost. These are its remains." He pointed at a column's capital rising from leaves and earth. "Most of Fidelium is now buried."

It was evening when they emerged onto a rocky terrain, finding themselves on the north side of Fidelium Mountain. The mountainside soared above them, green with pines. Higher up, they saw snow and jagged black boulders.

"We'll stay here for the night," Benedictus said.

Agnus Dei surveyed their surroundings in the sunset. "Where will we hide?"

Benedictus pointed at a mossy, rain-smoothed pile of stones. "This was a mausoleum once," he said. "The kings of Fidelium would rest in these tombs, in the shade of their mountain. We'll find rest there too, at least for tonight."

Agnus Dei grunted. "You want us to sleep in a mausoleum?" she asked and spat again.

"I told you, Agnus Dei, do not spit. Where did you pick up the habit? And yes, we're going to sleep there. Unless you prefer to sleep outdoors and face the nightshades?"

Agnus Dei grumbled curses so foul, Benedictus thought the pines would wilt. She began tramping toward the mausoleum.

"And where did you learn such language?" he said. "Do not speak that way."

Agnus Dei made a sound like an enraged boar. "Father, really. Must you?"

Benedictus grumbled, and the two knelt by the mausoleum. Most of it was buried. Only the top of its entrance was clear, and they spent some time digging. Finally the entrance was large enough, and they crawled inside. Dirt and dust filled the mausoleum, and they coughed and waved to clear the air. The sunset slanted through the narrow opening, lighting old bricks and shattered pottery. They pulled branches and bricks against the entrance, concealing it.

A second doorway led underground to a dark, clammy chamber. They climbed down to find two old skeletons, perhaps an ancient king and queen, lying by coffins. The grave must have been robbed years ago; the coffins were smashed, the skeletons denuded of jewels.

"Lovely place to spend the night," Agnus Dei said. She sat down with a groan. "If I get cold or lonely, I can cuddle with skeletons."

Benedictus stood, sword raised. "Sleep, daughter. I'll take the first watch."

He had barely finished his sentence, and Agnus Dei was snoring. The skeletons lay beside her, glaring with empty eye sockets at the intruders. Benedictus watched her sleep for a while, and he felt his face soften, the scowl that usually adorned it melting off. During waking hours, Agnus Dei was a firestorm—cursing, spitting, shouting, arguing, or crying. In sleep, she looked peaceful, even with the dirt and blood that still covered her.

Benedictus knelt and kissed her forehead. "You're still my baby," he whispered. "Even if you were cuter as an actual baby."

She stirred, her lips scrunched, but she did not wake.

Benedictus turned to face the doorway they had crawled through. The last light faded, and soon Benedictus heard nightshades screeching outside. The air became icy, and he grunted and rubbed his joints. Lately they always ached in the cold. He held his sword drawn, as if that could harm a nightshade. As if his sword could win any of his battles.

The vision of the Poisoned return to him, and he lowered his head and clenched his jaw.

"It wasn't her," he whispered. "It couldn't have been."

And yet the Poisoned that had scratched his shoulder, the creature he'd killed with claw and fire, had worn his sister's pendant. The golden turtle with emerald eyes.

Benedictus clenched his fists. "No. It wasn't her. She died years ago."

Still the memory floated before him in the darkness—her hissing, toothless mouth; her green claws; her left eyeball that dangled against her cheek, spraying blood....

"No," he said, jaw tight. The nightshades screeched so loudly now, he couldn't hear his own words. "Don't think of her. It's over. It's over now."

Agnus Dei was alive and pure. Protecting her was what mattered now, Benedictus told himself. He turned to look at her... and felt the blood leave his face.

Agnus Dei was gone.

Benedictus stared, frozen for a moment.

He raised his sword.

Gone!

He peered into the corners and coffins, but could not see her. A chill ran through him; the skeletons were gone too.

"Agnus Dei!" he called.

A scream answered somewhere below, distant.

Benedictus searched for a door, but found none. Where had she gone? Then he noticed that the dust had moved by one of the coffins, and he shoved it. It was heavy. Benedictus grunted, strained, and managed to shove it aside.

A tunnel gaped open beneath it.

"Let go!" came Agnus Dei's voice from below.

Cursing, Benedictus leaped into the tunnel.

He fell ten feet and crashed onto bones. He couldn't see them in the darkness, but Benedictus had heard enough snapping bones in his life to recognize the sound. He pushed himself up, fumbled for his oil lamp, and lit it. The light flickered to life, illuminating a pile of skeletons.

"This isn't a mausoleum," he muttered. "It's a mass grave."

A scream sounded down the tunnel, maybe two hundred yards away, followed by the sound of more snapping bones. Benedictus began to run over the bones, moving down dark tunnels. He held his sword in one hand, the lamp in the other. The bones crunched beneath his boots. Spirals and skulls were drawn onto the walls with what looked like blood.

"Agnus Dei!" he called. He heard distant laughter, a chorus of it, cruel laughter. He kept running, the shadows dancing.

He was nearing the echoing laughter when three skeletons rose from the bones on the floor. Dust and cobwebs covered them. They swung rusty blades.

Benedictus parried. The blade he blocked disintegrated into a shower of rust. He swung his sword, decapitating the skeleton. The other two skeletons clawed at him, tugged his clothes, and snapped their teeth. Benedictus slammed the hilt of his sword against them, crushing their skulls. He kicked them when they fell, and slammed his sword down, until they were nothing but shattered bones. The bones moved at his feet, as if trying to regroup. Benedictus stepped over them and kept running.

He raced down the tunnel until he reached an archway. Its stones glowed with golden runes, and Benedictus saw mist and darkness beyond. The laughter came from there. He ran through the gateway, sword and lamp raised.

He found an ancient, dilapidated throne room. The chamber was wide but low, and columns filled it; there was no room here to shift into a dragon. Old candlesticks filled alcoves in the walls, burning with green fire. A hundred skeletons stood between the columns, wearing patches of rusty iron, holding chipped swords.

"Agnus Dei!" Benedictus called.

His daughter stood at the back of the chamber. Two armored skeletons held her arms. Another skeleton stood facing her. This one looked like the king; he wore a crown and still had wisps of a long, white beard. He shoved Agnus Dei into a dusty throne, and tried to force a necklace of jewels around her neck.

"Leave me alone!" Agnus Dei said. She was struggling and kicking, but the skeletons held her down in the throne. "Find yourself a skeleton wife, not me."

Benedictus ran toward them, but a dozen skeletons leaped at him. He hacked at them, but his sword did little damage; it kept entangling itself in their ribs. One of the skeletons wielded a mace. Benedictus grabbed it, wrenched it free, and began to swing. Bones shattered and flew in all directions. For every skeleton he bashed dead, new ones appeared. They surrounded him, scratching and biting. One sunk its teeth into his shoulder, and he shouted and clubbed it off.

"Agnus Dei, I'm here!" he called.

In the chaos, she had broken free from the skeletons holding her. She held an old iron candlestick, and was swinging it left and right, breaking skulls.

Benedictus clubbed several more skeletons, drove his shoulder into two more, and barrelled his way toward his daughter. Finally he reached her. She was still battling skeletons. Scratches covered her shoulder and thigh.

"I'm here, Agnus Dei, it's all right now," he said.

Agnus Dei groaned and kicked a skeleton's face, snapping its neck. "I do not...." She clubbed a skeleton with her candlestick. "Need you...." She kicked another's ribs. "To save me!" She sliced a skeleton in half with her sword.

The king skeleton leaped at them, snarling. His beard fluttered, and fires blazed in his eyes.

"You looked like you needed some help," Benedictus said to his daughter, swung the club, and bashed the king's ribs.

"I was fine," Agnus Dei said with a snarl. She swung her sword, shattering the king's shoulder.

"You were fine like I'm a nightshade," Benedictus said, clubbed the king's face, and watched the skeleton fall.

The king's bones collapsed into moldy heaps. As if signalled by some unseen banner, the other skeletons fell where they stood. They crashed to the floor, their bones disintegrating. Dust flew and the columns shook.

Benedictus and Agnus Dei stood facing each other, panting. For a moment, Benedictus had to place his hands on his knees, lean forward, and breathe.

"Are you all right?" he asked Agnus Dei, raising his head to stare at her. His hair was damp with sweat.

"I'm fine, Father. You worry too much."

"Worry too much? There was an army of skeletons after you."

She snorted, blowing back a curl of her hair. "I was handling them. I've always handled myself fine, Father. Good thing you finally remembered to look after me."

"What are you talking about?" He straightened and tried to examine her wounds, but she shoved him back.

"You don't even know, do you?" she asked. She snarled, but her eyes were red, as if she were about to cry.

"No!" he said. "I never know anything about you, Agnus Dei. I don't know why sometimes you're happy, and sometimes you're sad, and sometimes you're angry at me. I don't know why one moment, you're noble and proud, and the next moment, you spit and curse. And I don't know why you look like you want to kill me now."

Tears flowed down her cheeks, drawing lines through the dirt. "Of course you don't know!" she shouted. She clenched her fists. "You don't know me at all. You never bothered to get to know me. I grew up with Mother in caves, in tunnels, in hovels. You were off in your forest. I saw you maybe once a month, for only a few hours—"

Benedictus growled. "You know why. I've told you many times."

She rolled her eyes, sniffing. "Yes, yes. We were safer away from you. You know what? That's griffin dung. I think you just enjoyed being away from us. Being away from the memories. Not having to remember how you saved us, while everyone else died, and—"

"Agnus Dei!" he roared, voice so loud the chamber trembled, and dust rained from the ceiling. She froze, fell silent, and glared at him. Her hair was damp, and she panted.

"Agnus Dei," he said again, softly this time. "I love you. More than anything. More than life."

She stared at him silently. Slowly her fists unclenched. "You never tell me that," she said. "You never told me growing up."

He embraced her. She squirmed and struggled, but finally capitulated.

"I'm telling you now," he said. "I love you, daughter. I love you and Gloriae more than anything. I've always only wanted to protect you."

She sighed. "I hate you sometimes, Father."

"I know. That's all right. I hate myself sometimes."

She raised her eyes. "Really? You shouldn't." She sighed. "You snore, and you hum, and you make an annoying sound when you eat. You grumble way too much, and you don't shave nearly often enough. But you're not that bad, Dada. I'm sorry."

He scratched his stubble. "I do need a shave, don't I?"

She nodded. "Let's get out of here," she said. "We have a mountain to climb in the morning."

GLORIAE

The road was long, winding, and full of sadness.

Gloriae saw the sadness of the land—the bodies in the gutters, the toppled temples, the burning towns. She saw hungry children peeking from logs, from trees, from holes in the ground. She saw the blood and mud that covered them, the hunger in their eyes. Wilted trees filled the forests; nightshades had flown by them. Forts lay as scattered bricks. The horror she had unleashed from the Well of Night covered the world.

She looked at Kyrie, who walked beside her. He was staring at the wilted trees, eyes dark. Gloriae slipped her hand into his. He tried to pull his hand back, but she held him tight.

"Don't let me go," she said to him. He sighed and let her hold his hand.

"I have a memory of Requiem," she said. "From when I was three. I remember our home. I think it was our house. I remember marble tiles, and birches, and harps. Kyrie, what do you remember?"

He looked at the wilted trees, lost in thought. Finally he said, "I remember the temple with the fruit trees outside. I remember the harps too. And... I remember seeing many dragons in the skies. Thousands of them, entire herds."

Gloriae tried to imagine it—thousands of dragons, the sun on their scales, the sky in their nostrils. She imagined herself among them, a golden dragon, gliding through the clouds, her true people around her.

She looked at the ruins around her, and thought of the ruins of Requiem, and Gloriae made a decision. She squeezed Kyrie's hand, and smiled to herself, but said nothing.

In the afternoon, the forest recovered. The trees were not wilted, but alive with golden, red, and yellow leaves. Birds flew and deer grazed. A sign on the road pointed to a town, and promised a tavern and bathhouse.

Kyrie sighed. "I supposed this is another town you want to avoid. Too dangerous, huh."

"Actually, I'd like to visit that tavern," Gloriae said. "I've had enough of sleeping in logs and burrows, haven't you?"

Kyrie raised his eyebrows. "Didn't you say just the other day, how nightshades are smart enough to search inns now, and how Dies Irae has informants in them, and how you're a maiden of steel or something like that, and don't mind sleeping outside?"

Gloriae wanted to glare and hurt him, but not today. Today she'd have to be nice, if her plan was to work. She forced herself to smile. She knew that she had a beautiful smile, a smile to melt men's hearts. "I think we've earned a rest."

He nodded and whistled. "All right! Tavern it is. Beer, stew, bread, and a soft bed."

He walked with new vigor, and Gloriae smiled. Soon they approached the town. A score of cottages with thatch roofs nestled in the hills. A temple and tower rose above them, and farms rolled around them. The tavern stood closer to the road, its sign showing a turtledove sitting upon a firkin. Gloriae saw no movement in the windows, and two peasants lay slumped in the yard, drooling. The nightshades had been here too. She and Kyrie entered the tavern, and found the usual scene of soulless travellers.

"Not only nightshades have been here," she said. "Outlaws too."

The soulless were missing shoes and jackets. When she stepped into the pantry, Gloriae saw that most of the food had been taken. Only a handful of turnips, onions, apples, and sausages remained.

"I was hoping for some bread," Kyrie said, "but I'll make do with what we have. We'll cook a stew of it."

Gloriae left the pantry and searched the bar. Luckily, the caskets of ale were attached to the walls; the outlaws had left them. Most of the other drinks had been taken.

"And I was hoping for some wine or spirits," she said, scrunching her lips. "Something stronger than ale."

She could see marks on the floor where barrels of wine must have stood. She rummaged behind the bar and found a small, hidden door. When she swung it open, she smiled.

"Ah, good rye," she said. She lifted a bottle. "In a glass bottle too. These things cost a fortune, you know. Must be good stuff."

"I didn't know you're a drinker," Kyrie said, already eating an apple.

"There are many things you don't know about me. But you'll find them out."

They cooked a stew of turnips, onions, and sausages. Gloriae kept pouring ale into Kyrie's mug, though she drank little herself. They ate well, and then Gloriae opened the bottle of rye. She stood up, solemn, and raised the bottle.

"To Requiem," she said. "May our wings forever find her sky."

Kyrie too stood up. He nodded and repeated the Old Words.

Gloriae feigned a deep draft from the bottle, but only allowed several drops into her mouth. The spirits were strong, so strong they burned. She handed Kyrie the bottle.

"Drink deep," she said. "Drink well. For our home and forefathers."

He nodded and drank deeply. His cheeks flushed, he coughed, and he slammed down the bottle. "Good stuff."

Gloriae realized that she still wore her white cloak, and her armor beneath it. She removed the cloak and placed it on her chair. Her helmet followed. Gloriae shook her hair free, and the golden locks danced. She saw Kyrie staring, and she smiled crookedly.

"Drink, Kyrie," she said. "Drink for Requiem."

"For Requiem," he said and drank again. He passed Gloriae the bottle, and she feigned another draft.

When Kyrie had drunk a third time, Gloriae removed her breastplate. She placed it on a table, and stood before Kyrie in her undershirt. The cloth was thin, white cotton, damp with the sweat of their journey. Gloriae knew it clung to her, that it showed the curve of her breasts. She undid the laces at its top, opening her shirt halfway down her chest, and shook her hair again.

"It feels good to finally take off my armor," she said. She moved near Kyrie, took the bottle from him, and this time she truly did drink. The spirits burned down her throat. She shoved the bottle at Kyrie, placed her hand on his thigh, and told him, "Drink."

He drank, and she played with his hair and whispered into his ear. "It tastes good, doesn't it?"

Kyrie looked at her. His eyes were watery, his cheeks flushed. "Gloriae. What are you doing?"

She trailed her fingers along his thigh, and saw his flush deepen. Smiling crookedly, she brought the bottle to his lips. "Drink, Kyrie. For Requiem."

When the bottle was half empty, Kyrie was wobbling in his chair. "I'm tired," he said.

She nodded. "Me too. Let's find a bed and get some sleep."

She led him upstairs, helping him climb. They found a room, and Gloriae laid him in a bed. It was not yet evening; she still had time.

"Gloriae," he said groggily. "What are you doing?"

"I'm taking my clothes off," she said. "They're sweaty and dirty, and I want them off me."

"You shouldn't," he said from the bed.

But Gloriae was already naked. She stretched by the window, the sun on her skin. It felt good to be free of her clothes; she felt like a nymph. She ran her hands through her golden locks, smiled at Kyrie, and stepped toward him.

"Gloriae," he said, frowning.

He tried to rise from the bed, but she pushed him back down. With deft movements, she unlaced his pants and straddled him.

"Don't move, Kyrie," she said. "Just lie still. I'll do everything."

He tried to push her off, but he was too drunk. She held his hands, leaned forward, and kissed his forehead.   "It's all right, Kyrie," she said. "I know what I'm doing. It's for the best."

"I can't," he said, though she could feel his eyes on her breasts, feel his desire beneath her. Gloriae had never done this before, but she knew how to. She had grown up among soldiers; she was no innocent. She did the deed quickly, gasping and digging her fingernails into Kyrie, her head back. It didn't take long. He was done. She left him. She pulled on her clothes, leaned over him, and kissed his lips.

"Thank you, Kyrie," she said. "Now sleep. I'll take the first watch."

He confronted her in the morning. Gloriae was in the common room, setting bowls of porridge on the table. Kyrie came stumbling downstairs. He had sacks beneath his eyes, and a sallow look, and winced in the sunlight.

"Good morning, Kyrie," she said. "I found some oatmeal in the pantry and made breakfast."

He trudged to the table, sat down, and lifted a spoon. His eyes never left hers. He began to eat, frowning at her suspiciously. She sat down beside him and began to eat too. For a moment they were silent.

Then Kyrie slammed down his spoon. "Gloriae," he began, "you—"

"Hush, Kyrie," she said and took a spoonful of porridge. She swallowed. "I don't want to hear it."

He rose to his feet so suddenly, his chair crashed to the floor. He winced and rubbed his temples. "Last night, you—"

Gloriae stood up too and slapped his face, hard enough to knock him back two steps.

"Kyrie," she said, glaring at him, "I have killed Vir Requis. Many of them."

He stared at her silently, his cheek red with the print of her hand. He said nothing.

"I killed my first Vir Requis when I was six years old," she said. "I've killed more since, many more. Now there are only five left. Maybe fewer now; we don't know if the others survived."

"They sur—"

"Quiet, Kyrie!" She grabbed his cheeks and stared into his eyes. "I am Vir Requis too. I know that now. And I need a child. We all need one, a new life for our race. So yes. I will have your child. You might not like it. I don't care. I will have it. Remember what we drank for last night? For Requiem. For her will I bear new life."

He tore free from her. "I promised my love to Agnus Dei," he said.

She snorted. "Promised your love? Are you a poet now? Well, good for you and Agnus Dei. I'm happy for you two. And I know that once we all reunite, you'll marry her. When we rebuild Requiem, you'll build a house with her, and have children with her, and then my chance will be gone. I need your child before then. So I made one with you last night."

Kyrie glared at her, eyes red. For a moment it seemed he would yell, but then he simply righted his chair and sat down with a sigh. He placed his elbows on the tabletop and leaned his head down. "You don't know that you're pregnant. It can take more than one try."

She nodded and placed her hand on his head. "That's why we're going to repeat last night. Again and again, until we reach Requiem and you're reunited with my sister."

He looked up at her. "Gloriae, you're her twin sister. It's wrong."

"The whole world is wrong. We do what we can to right it. Don't we?"

He took her hands. "Gloriae, look. You're beautiful. Achingly beautiful; a goddess. You're strong, and intelligent, and... everything a man could want. But I love Agnus Dei."

"I'm not asking you to love me, Kyrie. I'm not asking you anything. I'm telling you. We need more Vir Requis. I did my part hunting the race to near extinction. I'll do what I must to rebuild it, to redeem myself. Even if it hurts you and Agnus Dei. The future of our race is more important than your pain." She shoved the porridge close to him and patted his cheek. "Now eat, darling. You're going to need your strength."

After breakfast, they left the tavern with fresh supplies, and walked down dirt roads. In the distance, they saw mountains of burned trees.

The ruins of Requiem were near.

AGNUS DEI

She climbed through the snow, fingers stinging, the wind whipping her face. Snow filled her clothes, hair, and mouth. She spat it out.

"Have I mentioned already that I hate snow?" she said.

Father grunted. He was climbing beside her, snow covering him. It clung to his stubble like a white beard.

"Once or twice," he said. "Or a million times."

Agnus Dei looked behind her. They'd been climbing all morning, and the mausoleum of skeletons lay a league below, piny hills surrounding it. When she turned her head and looked above her, she saw Fidelium soaring, all black boulders and swirling snow. The wind howled.

"We're close," she said. "We'll reach the cave within an hour."

Father nodded and they kept climbing, shivering in the cold and wind.

Agnus Dei thought of Kyrie as she climbed. The thought of him made her feel warmer. What was the pup up to now? Was he tolerating Gloriae? Agnus Dei knew the two held no love for each other. *I hope they made it to the caves,* Agnus Dei thought. *I hope they're huddling inside, waiting for us. Maybe I'll see them again soon, in only an hour or two.* She promised herself that she'd give her sister a hug, and the pup a kiss that would knock his boots off.

And what of Mother? Had she found the griffins? Would she be waiting here too? Suddenly Agnus Dei felt fear, colder than the snow. What if they weren't here? What if the nightshades had caught them, or Dies Irae's crossbow, or the griffins had attacked, or—

Agnus Dei shook her head to clear it. There was no use worrying now. Soon enough, she would know.

The wind howled, and a strange sound—a twang—sounded above.

Agnus Dei froze and frowned.

"Did you hear that?" she said to Father.

He nodded and drew his sword. "Yeah, and I don't like it."

The twang sounded again, closer now. It sounded like a wobbling saw, metallic. Agnus Dei narrowed her eyes, staring up the mountain. Snow cascaded.

"What—" she began.

Something leaped above, emitted that wobbling twang of a cry, and disappeared behind snow.

"Griffin balls," Agnus Dei swore, narrowed her eyes, and aimed her crossbow. "What the abyss was that?"

"Don't curse!" Father said.

The creature had seemed large, the size of a horse. Agnus Dei had only glimpsed long limbs, white skin draped over long bones, and three eyes. Where was it now?

The creature burst from behind a mound of snow, flying toward them. Its mouth opened, revealing teeth like swords, and its eyes blazed.

Agnus Dei shot her crossbow into its head.

It crashed a hundred yards away, squealed, and came sliding down the snow toward her. Agnus Dei snarled. *It's hideous.* It had a knobby spine and six legs, bony, with large joints. White, wrinkly skin draped over it. Agnus Dei had once seen a hairless cat; this creature looked like a cross between that poor critter and a giant spider.

It squealed at her feet, black blood squirting from its wound. It snapped claws and teeth at her. Father shot his own crossbow, sending the quarrel into the creature's brain. It made a mewling, high-pitched sound that sent snow cascading down the mountainside, then lay still.

Agnus Dei looked down at it. She shivered. "Ugly bastard. And new to this mountain. These things weren't here in the summer."

"Dies Irae must have new pets," Father said grimly. "This is a snowbeast, a creature from the far north."

"Let's shift and fly the rest of the way up," Agnus Dei said. "I don't want to meet any more of these creatures."

Father shook his head. "No shifting, Agnus Dei. Your scales are red. Irae's men would see you from the forests leagues away. Let's keep climbing." He pointed his sword. "I see the back cave. We're almost there."

They stepped around the dead snowbeast and began climbing again.

With a chorus of twangs, a dozen snowbeasts appeared and leaped toward them.

Agnus Dei and Father shot their crossbows. Two snowbeasts crashed and slid down the snow, screaming. The others screeched, scurried on six legs, and jumped at them.

Agnus Dei swung her sword. The blade sliced through a bony, wrinkly limb. The limb flew, the snowbeast screeched, and its blood spurted. It snapped its teeth at her, and Agnus Dei fell onto her back. Snarling, she drove her sword up. It hit the snowbeast's teeth, knocked one out, and drove into its head.

The snowbeast fell onto her, drool and blood dripping. One of its remaining teeth scratched her cheek. Agnus Dei grunted and shoved it aside. She rose to her feet to see two more snowbeasts leaping at her.

She swung her sword left and right. Bony limbs flew. Black blood covered the snow, smelling like oil. All around, from behind boulders and snow, more snowbeasts were appearing.

"We can't kill them all," Father cried over their screams. Black blood covered his blade and arms. "Run to the cave!"

They began running uphill, swords swinging. The snowbeasts' limbs littered the mountainside, but new ones kept swarming. Even the wounded came crawling at them, screeching. One scratched Father's calf, tearing through his pants and skin. Agnus Dei ran screaming, sword and arms sticky with blood. A snowbeast jumped off a boulder, swooping toward her. She tossed her dagger at it, burying it in its head, and kept running.

When she reached the cave, she dashed in. Father was a few paces behind. Hurriedly, Agnus Dei loaded her crossbow. She shot over Father's head, hitting the snowbeast behind him.

"Hurry up, old man!" she said.

He dashed into the cave, breath ragged, the snowbeasts in hot pursuit. Father and daughter stood at the cave entrance, swinging swords. Creatures' limbs and heads piled at their feet.

"Get lost!" Agnus Dei shouted at them. "Away, find food elsewhere!"

Finally, her shouts and their blades convinced the snowbeasts to leave. They scurried away on their bony limbs, their white skin flapping in the wind.

Agnus Dei and Father leaned against the cave walls, breathing heavily. Her heart thrashed, and even in the cold, sweat drenched her.

"Nothing's ever easy," Father muttered, and she nodded.

When they had caught their breath, Agnus Dei said, "The tunnel passes through the mountain. It's dark, and it's narrow, but I've travelled it before. It's safe. After an hour's walk, we'll reach the south cave."

She checked her tin lamp, which she'd pilfered from an abandoned inn three nights ago. She still had some oil left; maybe an hour's worth. She lit the wick, narrowed her eyes, and stepped into the darkness. Father walked beside her, his sword raised.

A hundred yards into the cave, Agnus Dei grimaced. Her lamplight flickered across hundreds of eggs. The eggs were the size of watermelons, translucent and gooey. She could see snowbeast maggots inside, their limbs twisting, their mouths opening and closing. Mewls left their throats, the sound muffled inside the eggs.

"They're even uglier as babies," she muttered. "I'd hate to be here when they hatch."

Benedictus nodded. "We won't be. Let's keep walking."

As they walked down the tunnel, Agnus Dei tightened her grip on her sword. She hated narrow places like these. It meant she couldn't shift. She had mostly resisted shifting outside the tunnel, but at least the option had existed. Here, if she shifted into a dragon, the narrow tunnel would crush her. Her lamp swung in her hand, swirling shadows, dancing against clammy walls. She imagined that she saw small nightshades in the shadows, and Agnus Dei shivered. Would she find Mother, Gloriae, and Kyrie here, or would she find their bodies?

The tunnel twisted and narrowed. At times they had to walk slouched over, or even crawl. After an hour, Agnus Dei was sure they must be close to the southern mountainside. Where was the cave? She should see it by now. Her lamp guttered, and the shadows darkened.

"We're running out of oil," she said. "Father, do you have any oil in your lamp?"

He shook his head, and Agnus Dei cursed. She quickened her step, her boots clacking. Within moments, her lamp gave a final flicker and died.

Darkness enveloped them.

"We continue," Father said. His voice was a low growl. "Walk carefully. Crossbows raised."

Agnus Dei nodded and kept walking. She kept one hand on the clammy wall. She gripped her crossbow with the other. The south cave couldn't be far now. The sound of water dripping echoed, and wind moaned.

A screech shook the tunnels.

Agnus Dei screamed and shot her crossbow. She heard Father do the same.

The screech rose, so high pitched, Agnus Dei's hackles rose. The tunnel trembled. Two eyes opened ahead, burning like stars. Their light illuminated a swirling, inky head and white teeth.

"A nightshade!" Agnus Dei cried. "Run, Father!"

They spun around to flee, but another nightshade shrieked there too. Its eyes blazed, and it flowed toward them like smoke. Its maw opened, and it screamed so loudly, Agnus Dei had to cover her ears.

She moved her head from side to side. *Surrounded!* She could see more nightshades behind those closest to her. They filled the tunnels.

"Light, we need light," she said, but they had no oil, no torches, and the tunnel was too narrow to become dragons and blow fire.

Father slipped his hand into hers. "Agnus Dei," he said, "I'm sorry. I love you."

She felt the nightshades begin to tug her soul. Wisps of it tore free from her, like feathers plucked from a chicken. She closed her eyes, tears stinging.

"Goodbye, Dada. I love you too."

The nightshades shrieked, and Agnus Dei saw the darkness beyond them. She saw the endless worlds, the dimensions that spun her head, the space, eternal, the caverns. She prayed with trembling lips. *Goodbye, Mother, Father, sister. Goodbye, Kyrie.*

She fell to her knees, and her eyes rolled back.

Then a voice spoke.

"Enough."

The nightshades howled. Agnus Dei's soul slammed back into her body. She opened her eyes, trembling. She squeezed Father's hand. She could see now, she realized. Firelight blazed.

"Who spoke?" she demanded and rose to her feet.

Her heart thrashed.

Agnus Dei snarled and drew her sword.

"You."

Carrying a torch, Dies Irae stood before them in the tunnel.

Agnus Dei charged at him, screaming, sword raised.

Dies Irae waved his hand, and nightshades swarmed. They slammed into Agnus Dei, knocking her down. She fell, cursing. She leaped up and charged again, sword swinging. Dies Irae waved his hand again, and again nightshades knocked Agnus Dei to the ground.

"We can keep doing this all day, sweetness," Dies Irae said, voice soft. He spoke from within his helmet, the steel monstrosity that looked like a griffin's head. "You would tire of it sooner than I would, I promise you."

Agnus Dei pushed herself up, sword in hand, snarling. Father stood beside her, eyes dark, silent. Agnus Dei made to charge again, but Dies Irae clucked his tongue, wagged his finger at her, and she paused.

"I'm going to kill you," she said, snarling.

He laughed and lifted his visor. Agnus Dei couldn't help but gasp. Dies Irae had changed. His face had once been tanned gold. It was now white streaked with black lines, as if oil coursed through his wrinkles. His left eye was gone. An empty socket gaped there, blazing. Starlight and darkness filled the wound, as if nightshade maggots nested there. His good eye blazed, milky white and swivelling. He looked, Agnus Dei thought, like a man possessed by demons. Which, she decided, he was.

"I think not, my daughter," Dies Irae said.

"Silence," Father said and took a step forward, raising his sword.

Dies Irae laughed. "But I am her father, Benedictus. When I raped Lacrimosa, that little whore of yours, I created two smaller whores—Gloriae and Agnus Dei."

While he spoke, Agnus Dei loaded her crossbow. She fired.

Dies Irae had only to stare in her direction. Sparks and black smoke flowed from his empty eye socket, and the quarrel shattered. Steel shards flew, hit the walls, and fell to the floor.

"My my, daughter," Dies Irae said. "You are almost as feisty as your sister, are you not? I spared Gloriae's life. Yes. I let her flee into exile. Do you know why I let her live, Agnus Dei? I let her live because she killed many Vir Requis in my service. She killed children, did you know? Maybe some had been your friends." He raised his left arm, the prosthetic arm made of steel, ending with a mace head like a fist. "But you were never in my service, second daughter. I will kill you... and that pathetic brother of mine who claims to be your true father."

Dies Irae ran forward, mace swinging.

Agnus Dei dropped down and slid forward. The floor was wet, and she flew past the charging Dies Irae. She swung her sword. The blade clanged against Dies Irae's armor, doing him no harm. Jewels flew from it, and its gilt peeled, but the steel beneath stood.

Dies Irae spun, swinging his mace. Agnus Dei ducked, and the mace whooshed over her head.

Father slammed his sword, hitting Dies Irae's helmet. The helmet dented. Dies Irae's head tilted, and Agnus Dei dared to hope that his neck was broken... but he only laughed and punched Father with his good fist, a fist covered in a steel gauntlet. The blow hit Father's chest, knocking him back.

Agnus Dei screamed. She swung her sword and hit Dies Irae's neck. The sword rebounded, sending pain up her arms. It didn't even dent Dies Irae's armor.

The mace swung again. Agnus Dei leaped back, and the tip of the mace grazed her arm. She grunted. The mace had not hit her bone, but it would leave an ugly bruise. The pain burned. She thrust her sword, aiming for Dies Irae's face, but he had managed to lower his visor. The blade hit the metal and bounced back.

The mace swung. Agnus Dei raised her sword and parried with its pommel. The mace hit with incredible force. The blow knocked back her arm, and the sword flew from her hand. It clanked behind her.

Dies Irae swung the mace again.

Father barrelled into Dies Irae, shoving him forward. Agnus Dei scurried back and retrieved her sword. She swung at Dies Irae and hit his breastplate. More jewels flew from the armor, scattering across the floor. The steel, however, remained strong.

Father swung his sword, but Dies Irae parried, almost lazily. He swung his mace toward Father's head.

Agnus Dei lunged and grabbed Dies Irae's legs. She tugged and he fell.

Father slammed his sword against Dies Irae's helmet. Agnus Dei slammed against his back. Their blows could not dent the armor, but they were dazing him, hurting him. Agnus Dei drove her sword down hard behind Dies Irae's knee, where the armor was weak. Blood spurted, and Dies Irae screamed.

"Nightshades!" he cried. "Kill them."

The nightshades, who until then had merely watched the fight, screeched. They rushed at Father and Agnus Dei, swirled around them, and howled.

"No!" Agnus Dei screamed. Once more they were tugging her soul, and her sword fell from her hand.

Red light filled the tunnel.

Heat blazed.

Fire burned.

"Leave this place!" came a dragon's roar. The fire died, and Agnus Dei saw a dragon's head in the darkness ahead, where the tunnel was wide.

"Mother!" she cried.

Lacrimosa, lying in the tunnel in dragon form, blew fire again. Agnus Dei and Father ducked and covered their heads. The firelight blackened the ceiling, and the nightshades screamed. The creatures began to flee.

Mother shifted into human form and ran toward them.

"Up, run!" she cried. "The firelight won't frighten them for long. Out of the tunnel!"

Agnus Dei looked for Dies Irae, but he was gone. She grabbed Mother.

"You're running to the south cave, Mother! Irae's got men covering that side of the mountain."

The nightshades were recovering, collecting their wisps of smoke and howling.

"It's our only way out!" Mother shouted and began to run. "Come on!"

They raced through the tunnels, nightshades howling around them, tugging at them, and snapping their teeth. Soon sunlight washed the tunnels, and they burst into the old cave, the same cave Agnus Dei had once spent a year in. Archers stood there, firing arrows.

Agnus Dei howled, shifted, and blew fire. Arrows flew around her, and once pierced her wing. She screamed, and her fire roared, and the archers fell burning.

She flew into the sunlight. The nightshades shrieked in the caves and cowered. Below her, Agnus Dei saw dozens of swordsmen and archers. She swooped at them, took another arrow to the wing, and blew fire. Her talons tore into swordsmen. Her flames burned the archers. Blood splashed the snow. Thousands of soldiers were leaving the camp below and racing up the mountain. Hundreds of crossbowmen ran with them.

"Let's get out of here," Father said, shifting into a dragon. He roared and blew fire at ten soldiers who charged at him. Mother shifted too, and the three flew. Arrows zoomed around them. One scratched Agnus Dei's side, and another cut Father's leg.

"Fly!" he roared.

They flew west, arrows zooming around them. More arrows flew, but soon the dragons were out of range.

"I thought you said we're not allowed to shift!" Agnus Dei cried over the roaring wind. Her wounds ached and blood seeped down her wing.

"Case by case basis," he called back. The forests streamed below them, and clouds gathered above.

"Why, by the stars, would you two enter that mountain?" Mother demanded. She glared at her husband and daughter. An arrow had grazed her flank, drawing blood. "Irae has thousands of men there. He was waiting for us. And you two go marching right in, like sheep into a butcher shop."

Father glanced at his wife, indeed seeming almost sheepish. "We were seeking Kyrie and Gloriae."

"We all agreed we'd meet there," Agnus Dei added, flames dancing between her teeth. "Remember, Mother?"

Mother rolled her eyes. Smoke left her nostrils. "Kyrie and Gloriae are not knuckleheads like you two. Of course they wouldn't march into a cave full of nightshades, with Dies Irae's army camped outside. They'll have returned to Requiem. I wager that if we fly there now, we'll find them."

Agnus Dei blew fire in rage. The flames lit the clouds. "If Father and I are such knuckleheads, then so are you, Mother. You also entered the cave."

Mother gave her a stare so withering, that Agnus Dei growled and bared her fangs.

"I entered the cave to save you, Agnus Dei," Mother said. "I had just arrived, saw Irae dash into the cave, and heard you scream."

Agnus Dei growled. "I don't need you to save me. I'm a grown woman now."

Mother glared. "You're a grown woman like I'm a griffin."

"You're one ugly griffin then."

Father roared. "Silence! The griffins are free now, Agnus Dei, and you will show them respect. You are a princess of Requiem."

"I am a warrior of Requiem," she said. "I'm no spoiled princess."

"You are my daughter, and I am the king, therefore you are a princess. And now kindly shut your maw. We fly to find Kyrie and Gloriae."

He roared fire, and his wings churned the clouds. He rose higher into the air, until they burst over the clouds, and flew under a shimmering sun. Mountain peaks rose below them, gold and indigo. Benedictus gave a roar that seemed to shake the skies.

"We fly to Requiem."

DIES IRAE

He pushed himself to his feet.

He stared at the blood seeping down his leg.

Jaws clenched, he walked out of the cave, stood upon the mountainside, and saw the weredragons disappear into the distance.

Bodies lay around him, blood painting the snow. Some of the men were burned, their skin peeling, their flesh red and black. Thousands of living soldiers stood there too. They froze when they saw Dies Irae, stood at attention, and slammed their fists against their chests.

He surveyed the scene for a long time, silent. Then Dies Irae left the cave, and walked through the snow to the body of a wounded soldier. The man was missing a leg. The wound looked like a dragon bite. Clutching the stump, the man stared up at Dies Irae.

"My lord," he whispered.

"Give me your sword," Dies Irae said.

The man raised his sword with a bloody, trembling hand. Dies Irae took the weapon, then drove the blade into the man's chest.

He raised his eyes and stared around him. The men still stood at attention, stiff, pale.

Dies Irae approached another wounded soldier. This man lay curled up in red snow, weeping and whispering for his mother. He clutched his spilling entrails, as if he could force them back into his belly. *Dragon claws,* Dies Irae knew.

"A weredragon attacked you," Dies Irae said.

The soldier wept and nodded.

"And you failed to kill it," Dies Irae said.

The soldier looked up with teary eyes, and Dies Irae drove his sword into the man's chest, pushing him into the snow.

The mountain was silent now. The weeping stopped. The only sound was the wind and swirling snow. Dies Irae looked over his men, the dozens of wounded, the dozens of dead, and the thousands that still stood.

"Has anyone else failed to kill a weredragon today?" he asked.

They stared, silent.

"All who killed a weredragon, raise your hands."

The men stood stiffly, pale, a few trembling.

Dies Irae called forward his captains, the commanders of the ten companies he'd brought to Fidelium. The captains stepped toward him, clad in plate armor, and slammed gauntleted fists against their chests.

"Hail Irae!" they said.

Dies Irae barely acknowledged them. He moved his eyes over the rows of soldiers in the snow. "My men disappointed me today. Decimate them."

The captains breathed in sharply.

"Decimation, my lord?" whispered one, a burly man with a battle axe. "That punishment has not been handed out since the Gray Age."

Dies Irae slowly turned his head, his armor creaking, and examined the man. "You are displeased with my command?"

The captain shook his head and saluted again, fist on breastplate. "Decimation, my lord. As in the days of old."

As Dies Irae watched, the captains arranged their companies into formation. The men stood in rows, ten men deep, fists against their chests. The captains raised their eyes to Dies Irae.

He frowned, thought a moment, and said, "The seventh row."

The soldiers in the seventh rows shifted uneasily. Sweat appeared on their brows. The captains pulled the first men from each seventh row, placed them in the snow, and swung their axes.

Blood splashed, and heads rolled.

The captains pulled the next men from formation.

Dies Irae stood, silent and still, watching as it continued. Some men of the seventh rows tried to flee. The captains shot them with crossbows. It took two hours of blood, grunts, but no screams. Not one man screamed. Dies Irae had taught them well.

When it was over, three-hundred heads were collected into a pile. Three-hundred bodies were stacked by them.

"Leave them here for the snowbeasts," Dies Irae said. "They will provide fresh meat for a while." He began walking down the mountainside, heading to the camp below. "We go to the ruins of Requiem, and we march hard. The weredragons will be heading there. I can feel it."

Soon his army snaked across the land, silent and bloody, leaving the bodies behind. Dies Irae rode at their lead on his courser. They bore the nightshades in shadowed wagons; the beasts screeched and fluttered inside them, rattling the wagon walls. When they were a half a league down the road, Dies Irae looked over his shoulder, back to the mountains.

Snowbeasts were feasting.

Dies Irae smiled thinly.

KYRIE ELEISON

As they collected firewood, Kyrie couldn't stop glancing at Gloriae. She would notice his glances, raise her eyes, and give him a stare so deep, so meaningful, that he had to look away. He knew what her eyes were saying. *Today. Again.*

He muttered and leaned down to collect twigs and branches. There wasn't much kindling here in the ruins of Requiem. Most of the trees had burned to ash. What branches they found were old, blackened, and would probably only burn for seconds.

"What we need are logs, an axe, and some rabbits to roast," Kyrie said. He tried to imagine the heat of a roaring fire, and the smell of dripping meat. It wasn't because he missed those things—though he did—so much as it beat thinking about Gloriae. And he was thinking a lot about her. About her naked body in the sun, her lips against him, her—

"Kyrie, you've dropped your sticks," she said. She was standing only a step away. He hadn't even noticed her approach, and he started, muttered under his breath, and leaned down to collect the wood.

"I think we have enough firewood now," he said, not bothering to mask the gruffness in his voice. "At least, all the firewood we'll find in this place. The whole kingdom is a wasteland."

She placed a hand on his shoulder. "Kyrie—" she began.

He walked away, ignoring her. He pointed at three fallen columns, a smashed statue of a dragon, and bits of a wall. Ash, bones, and mud littered the place. If there had been a floor, the dirt now covered it.

"This is the place," Kyrie said. "The hall of Requiem's kings. At least, I think it is. To be honest, all of Requiem looks more or less the same to me now."

She walked up behind him and placed her hands on his shoulders. When he turned to face her, she cupped his cheek and kissed him. "It's time," she said. "Now."

Roughly, he removed her hand and held her wrist. "Gloriae, no."

Her eyes flashed with sudden anger, and her jaw tightened. But then she calmed, leaned close, and kissed his lips again. "You know we must."

"But—"

She pressed a finger to his lips. "No buts. Down, Kyrie. Here by the columns."

She began to remove her clothes, staring into Kyrie's eyes all the while. First she doffed her priestess robes. Then she removed her breastplate and dropped it to her side. It clanged against old tiles. Still staring at Kyrie, she unlaced her shirt, her lips parting. She had begun unlacing her pants, too, when footfalls sounded behind.

Agnus Dei stepped toward them.

Kyrie's heart galloped.

"Agnus Dei!" he said. He gasped and his cheeks burned. He wanted to rush to her, but something in her eyes held him back.

Agnus Dei stood still, mouth open. She held a sword in one hand, and a crossbow in the other. She held the crossbow aimed at them, and it was a moment before she lowered it.

"What's going on here?" she asked, eyes narrowing.

Gloriae turned to face her sister. Her hair was down. Her shirt was unlaced to reveal most of her breasts. She removed her hands from the lacing on her pants, which she had begun to undo, and took a step toward Agnus Dei.

"Sister!" Gloriae said. She reached out to embrace Agnus Dei, who still stood frozen.

Kyrie too stepped toward her, arms outreached. "We're so glad you're alive, Agnus Dei. Thank goodness you're here."

She turned to look at him, but said nothing. Her eyes remained narrowed.

More footfalls sounded, and Lacrimosa and Benedictus stepped around a smashed wall toward them. Lacrimosa called out, and ran to them, and embraced Kyrie and Gloriae. Tears filled her eyes. Benedictus too joined the embrace, and for a moment everyone was talking at once, and sharing their stories, and mumbling their relief.

All but Agnus Dei, that was. She stood apart from them, staring from Kyrie to Gloriae and back again. Her black curls cascaded down her back, and ash covered her bodice and leggings. Scratches and bruises ran along her arms. She looked so beautiful to Kyrie; even more than he'd remembered. He walked toward her.

"Agnus Dei," he said. He wanted to take her hands, or embrace her, or kiss her, but she still held her sword and crossbow before her.

She nodded and gave him a small, mirthless smile. "Kyrie."

Kyrie cursed himself. He cursed Gloriae. This was not the reunion he'd imagined. In a thousand dreams, he'd imagined him and Agnus Dei running to each other, embracing, kissing. She'd call him pup and muss his hair, and then he'd kiss her again, and they'd be as they'd always been. Now Agnus Dei seemed icier than Gloriae.

"I... I've missed you," he said to her. "I love you."

She nodded curtly, then turned to her parents, and began talking to them about firewood and sharpening stones and unpacking their food.

Kyrie stared at her, aching. *She knows,* he thought, his cheeks growing hot. She knew he had slept with Gloriae. She knew everything; she had seen it in his eyes. Guilt filled him, suffocating. He could have stopped Gloriae. Even drunk on spirits, he could have stopped her, pushed her off him, stormed downstairs. And yet... he had stared at Gloriae's naked body in the sun. He had desired it. He had let her kiss him, let her undress him, let her lie with him.

"It's my fault," he whispered to himself. "I'm sorry, Agnus Dei."

Nobody heard him, and Kyrie felt anguish tearing inside him like griffin claws.

They stacked what kindling they had. Benedictus had carried firewood in his backpack all the way from Osanna, and soon a campfire crackled. They warmed themselves by the flames, ate old bread and turnips, and talked of their journeys.

Kyrie opened his backpack and pulled out the books *Mythic Creatures of the Gray Age* and *Artifacts of Wizardry and Power*.

"We borrowed these from Confutatis Library," he said. "Our friend Dies Irae edited them a bit."

He showed the others how the original parchments had been tweaked, some words scraped away and overwritten. When

Agnus Dei saw the illustration of the hero taming the nightshades, his head replaced with the likeness of Dies Irae, she snorted. Kyrie looked up at her over the fire, hoping she'd laugh and smile at him, but she wouldn't meet his eyes.

Kyrie finished by reading from *Artifacts*. "'Lir Irae prayed to his father, the Sun God, for light to tame the nightshades. The Sun God, of infinite wisdom and power, created the Beams and filled them with his light and fire, so that Lir Irae might tame the nightshades in his name.'" Kyrie cleared his throat and slammed the book shut. "In short, we don't know much. The part about the Beams is the original text. The words 'Sun God' and 'Lir Irae' are new, overwriting the original text. Who actually created the Beams, and who used them? We don't know."

For the first time, Agnus Dei spoke. "We do know."

She met Kyrie's eyes over the fire, but there was no emotion in them. They were colder and sharper than her sword. She tore her eyes away and unrolled a burned, tattered scroll. She showed them the text, which was badly damaged, missing many words.

"In the days of the Night Horrors, King T_____ite journeyed to the southern realms of G____nd sought the Loomers o_____olden pools. The Night Horrors stole the souls of Osanna, and cast them into the d___ness, and Ta_____omers, who were wise above all others in the land. He spoke with the Loomers, and prayed with them, and they crafted him th_____e returned with th_____anna, an_____m upon the Night Horrors. He tamed them, and drove them into Well of Night in the Marble City, and sealed it. He placed guards around it, armed wit_____cape."

Kyrie thought for long moments, staring at the scroll, and trying not to stare at Agnus Dei and Gloriae. He could feel both girls watching him, and his cheeks burned, and he forced his mind away.

Instead of looking at them, he looked over the fire at Benedictus and Lacrimosa. The two sat holding each other, the firelight orange against them.

"So we know who created the Beams," Kyrie said. "The Loomers of the olden pools, in some realm that starts with a G."

Benedictus nodded. "And we know that a king of Osanna used the Beams. We know his name started with 'T', and ended with 'ite'." He scratched his chin. "We should visit the tombs of Osanna's kings; they stand in a valley a few leagues from Confutatis. We might find answers there."

Kyrie rose to his feet. He could no longer stand sitting there, feeling Gloriae and Agnus Dei staring at him. He could imagine their thoughts: Gloriae thinking of lying with him and having his child, Agnus Dei suspecting and simmering. Kyrie didn't think he could stand their eyes on him one moment longer.

"Great," he said, brushing dust off his pants. "We go back to Osanna. I'm up for a journey. We'll find out who this king is, and research him, and see how he found the Beams."

Benedictus gave Kyrie a long, hard stare, eyes narrowed. "Kid, you okay? You look like a scorpion bit your backside."

"I'm hot by the fire," Kyrie said. "I'm going for a walk."

Without waiting for a reply, he turned and left the campfire. He walked past toppled bricks and earth, and felt the others looking at him. He didn't care. His eyes burned, and he wanted to be alone. Dust rose under his boots, and he clutched the hilt of his dagger. Soon he entered a copse of burned birches. Most had fallen, but some still stood, blackened. Kyrie's boots stepped around arrowheads, shattered blades, and a helmet with a skull still inside. He knew that the ash and dirt hid many more memories of the war.

Soon he came to an old wall and tower. Only about ten feet of the tower remained; the top part had fallen over, and its bricks lay among the burned trees. The wall too had crumbled, leaving a stretch only several feet long. Around the wall, Kyrie saw the skeleton of a griffin, half buried in earth. Its ribs rose like the teeth of dragons, and Kyrie stared at it. He thought of his childhood in this land, when it had still bloomed with life. He thought of Lanburg Fields, where so many had died around him, where he lay wounded in his blood. He thought of the Lady Mirum finding him, raising him in Fort Sanctus, dying at the hands of Dies Irae and Gloriae.

And he thought of Agnus Dei. When he'd met her, his life seemed good again, full of promise. In her eyes, he found a future, a meaning to his survival.

"I love you, Agnus Dei," he said softly. "I'm sorry."

Her voice spoke behind him. "I love you too, Kyrie."

He turned to see her standing by the toppled wall, her sword sheathed. Her eyes were moist, her hair dishevelled. He walked toward her, but she raised her hand, as if to hold him back.

"Agnus Dei, I—"

"Tell me it's not true," she said. "Tell me what I suspect is wrong."

Kyrie wanted to lie. It would be so easy to. He could tell her how he'd never slept with Gloriae, tell her it was only a misunderstanding. She would believe him, he knew. And yet he could not bring the words to his lips.

Agnus Dei lowered her head, and a tear streamed down her cheek. "Why, Kyrie? She's my sister."

As Kyrie searched for an answer, Gloriae too stepped from behind the wall. Her golden hair was still down, but she wore her gilded breastplate now, and rested her hand on the hilt of her sword. Her leggings were tattered, her left boot torn, and her cloak muddy.

"Because I forced him to," Gloriae said to her sister.

Agnus Dei snarled, drew her sword, and charged.

Gloriae drew her own sword and parried. The blades clanged and locked.

"You slept with him," Agnus Dei said and snarled.

Gloriae nodded, still holding her blade against the blade of her sister. "Yes."

Agnus Dei pulled her sword back, then attacked again. Gloriae parried. Sparks rose.

Kyrie ran toward them.

"Don't fight!" he said and placed himself between them. He held his hands out, one against Agnus Dei, the other against Gloriae. Both girls shoved him aside, barely acknowledging him. He tripped on a brick, fell, and banged his elbow against a rock.

"I knew you wouldn't change, Gloriae," Agnus Dei said. Tears filled her eyes. "We should have killed you long ago. I will kill you now."

The blades clanged a third time. Gloriae narrowed her eyes, and her cheeks flushed. "Agnus Dei, listen to me. Kyrie loves you. I knew it when I lay with him. And it's still true."

The blades clashed. "So why did you two... you two...." Agnus Dei grunted and sobbed. "It's disgusting."

The blades clanged, raised sparks, and Gloriae kicked. Her foot hit Agnus Dei's shin.

Agnus Dei fell into the dirt, and Gloriae stepped on her wrist, holding the sword down. Agnus Dei tried to kick and struggle, but Gloriae pressed a knee into her chest, pinning her down.

Kyrie stood up and watched them, rubbing his elbow. He wanted to intervene, but knew he shouldn't. He knew he must only watch now, and let the sisters battle it out.

"I seduced him," Gloriae said to her sister, face blank, eyes cold. "I got him drunk, and I seduced him. He had little say in the matter."

"Why?" Agnus Dei demanded, lying pinned below her sister.

"Because he loves you," Gloriae said. "That's why. Because he missed you. Because he talked about you all the time. Because I knew that, as soon as you two reunited, you'd be together forever, you'd get married, you'd have children. I needed his child before that happened."

Agnus Dei snarled. "His child?"

Gloriae nodded. "We need more Vir Requis. There are only three females left, and we need to bear children. All of us. Lacrimosa, you, and me. I saw my chance. I took it. It only happened once, Agnus Dei, and against his will. I wanted to lie with him more times, but he wouldn't let me. If you must hate somebody, hate me, not him. He loves you. He doesn't care for me; you are all he wants."

Agnus Dei's eyes softened, and she loosened the grip on her sword. It fell from her hand.

"Get off me," she said to Gloriae. "I won't hurt you."

Gloriae removed her knee from Agnus Dei's chest and stood up. Agnus Dei also stood and stared at Gloriae, her eyes red and watery.

"Are you pregnant?" she asked.

"I don't know," Gloriae said.

Agnus Dei gave her sister a long, searching stare. Her face was hard. Gloriae stared back, face blank, ash darkening her hair. Finally Agnus Dei spoke again.

"Leave us."

Gloriae nodded, sheathed her sword, and turned to leave. Soon she disappeared behind the ruins.

Agnus Dei turned to Kyrie. His heart pounded when her eyes met his. Those brown eyes seemed full of so many emotions: Kyrie saw love, hate, rage, and fear there. Agnus Dei trembled. He walked toward her and embraced her.

"I'm sorry," he said.

She squirmed, trying to free herself. "Don't touch me. I can only imagine you touching her."

He kissed a tear off her cheek. "I know. I hate myself for it. I was stupid. I was wrong. Please forgive me."

She slapped his face. Hard. White light flashed, and stars flew before his eyes.

"Don't you dare kiss me," she said.

He held his burning cheek.

"Agnus Dei—" he began, reaching out toward her.

She brought her knee into his stomach. He doubled over, and she punched him. Pain exploded. He fell to the ground, moaning, the stars swirling before him.

"Agnus Dei, stop—" he said, but felt her grab his hair. She pulled him up, and he groaned, and stood again before her. She backhanded him, knocking him back two steps.

"Kyrie," she said, "if you hurt me again, I'm going to hurt you badly. This was nothing. This was only a taste. If you ever touch another girl, I swear by the stars, I'm going to give you the beating of a lifetime. It would make this one look like a caress."

He cursed, voice hoarse. He felt blood tickle down his chin and a bruise spread under his eye.

"Bloody stars," he managed to say. "Deal, all right? Now do you forgive me?"

She grabbed his face, digging her fingers into his cheeks. Kyrie thought she would hit him again. She snarled, eyes blazing.

"I will never forgive you," she said, "but I still love you."

She kissed him on the lips. He kissed her back, and wrapped his arms around her. She embraced him, and they kissed for a long time among the ruins. Finally they broke apart.

Kyrie took her hand.

"Marry me, Agnus Dei," he said.

She snorted. "Pup, go marry a nightshade."

They walked back to camp, hand in hand.

DIES IRAE

He stood, hands on hips, staring at the wagons. They were large wagons, twenty feet tall and a hundred feet long. Bulls with clawed feet and fire in their nostrils stood tethered to them, backs whipped and maws muzzled. The bulls were impressive beasts—Dies Irae had once sicced them on Lacrimosa—but today he cared not for the creatures who pulled the wagons. Today he cared for the creatures inside.

"My pets," he whispered and heard them shriek. "My lovelies."

Black cloth draped the wagons, and that cloth fluttered now, and bulged with strange shapes. The shrieks inside the wagons made grass and trees wilt. The nightshades were angry. They would get angrier. A smile spread across Dies Irae's lips. He stepped toward one wagon, grabbed the black curtains, and pulled them open.

Sunlight drenched the nightshades. They screamed. Steam rose from them. They spun and swirled in the wagon, slamming against its steel bars.

"You will stay in the wagon," he told them. He knew they could break the bars if they pleased, or flow between them. His power over them—the power of Osanna's throne—kept them trapped. "You will suffer the light."

They snapped teeth, howling, and began to eat one another. A few began to eat themselves, wispy teeth of mist tearing into their inky bodies. They had blood like steam.

"Had enough?" he asked them.

They screeched, begging for mercy. Dies Irae watched them for several long moments, savoring their pain. Then he closed the curtains. The nightshades squirmed and hissed inside the wagon, hating him but serving him.

"You will learn, my pets, to tolerate sunlight," Dies Irae said. "You will learn to hunt the weredragons by day as by night. You will learn that I am your master, the giver of pain and mercy. You will fly into the sun should I ask it of you."

Dies Irae moved to the next wagon. He drew its curtains and watched, smiling thinly, as these nightshades screeched and hissed too.

"You will soak up the sunlight," he said, "until it is like moonlight upon you."

Dies Irae nodded, waiting long moments before closing the curtains. Sunlight burned them like fire against men, Dies Irae knew. But it would not kill them. It would not stop them. There was only one light, he knew, that could harm these creatures. Only one light that could truly tame them.

And that light Dies Irae kept buried and forever extinguished.

As he watched the third wagon of nightshades rattle, he thought of his daughter.

"Thank you, Gloriae," he whispered, gazing into the west, to Requiem. She flew with the weredragons now. She had betrayed him, stabbed his heart, gone to evil. But she had given him the nightshades. She had done that. "Thank you for my lovelies."

If he ever met Gloriae again, he decided that he would not kill her. He would lock her in the wagons with the nightshades, and allow them to bite her, to rip her soul to shreds, to play with her.

"Then you too, Gloriae, will beg me for mercy. But I will give you none."

He left the wagon and walked between rows of soldiers who stood at attention, fists on their chests. One man, he saw, had a nervous tic. His left eye kept winking. Dies Irae approached him.

"Is that involuntary?" he asked.

"Yes, Comma—" the man began.

Dies Irae swung his left arm, his iron arm, and shattered the man's head. He fell. The other soldiers stood still, not daring to breathe.

"I don't care," Dies Irae said to the body.

He stepped into his tent and shut the curtains behind him. Golden vases, jewelled statues of eagles, and other fineries filled his tent. The girl was there too, sitting on a divan, eyes pleading.

"Please, my lord," she began, tears filling her eyes. "Please, is my brother—"

"Your brother is dead. You'll be dead soon too."

She wept, covering her face with her hands. He grabbed her wrist and pulled her hands free.

"I want to see your face," he said. He leaned down and stared at her. She looked back, trembling. He had found her in the nearby ruins of a village, cowering with her brother in a barn.

"Yes, you look just like her... just like my Gloriae."

She shivered. "My lord, I don't know Gloriae, I—"

He backhanded her. She fell to the floor, bleeding.

"You will suffer, Gloriae, for betraying me," Dies Irae said. "You disobeyed me. You freed the nightshades. You fly with the weredragons."

The girl trembled on the floor. "Please, my lord, I don't know who Gloriae is. My name is Alendra, I... I...." She wept. "I'm only a peasant girl, my lord."

"You are a betrayer, Gloriae," he told her, and when she tried to rise, he beat her down. "You will suffer now."

The nightshades screamed inside him. He could feel their maggots squirm in his wound, the gaping hole of his left eye, the eye Benedictus had taken from him. The light of the maggot eyes burned, painting the girl a blood red. She whimpered and cowered, and Dies Irae laughed. The smoke of nightshades danced around his fingertips as he grabbed her, shook her, hurt her.

He soon stood above her dead body. Blackness like ink coiled in the air around him, and he laughed.

LACRIMOSA

From the distance, Lacrimosa could hear the youths fighting. She could not make out the words—only raised voices, clanking steel, and shouts. She stood up to rush over, to find the young ones and break them up.   Benedictus also stood up and put a hand on her shoulder.

"Let them settle their conflicts," he said, voice soft. The firelight painted his face orange and gold.

Lacrimosa shook her head in frustration. "They're fighting, Ben."

He nodded. "Let them fight. They're young, angry, and strong. All three of them are. They need to clash and lock horns; that's their way. They'll blow off steam, even if they bash one another around a bit."

Lacrimosa sighed. "Maybe you're right. Were you and I ever so young and angry?"

They sat down again by the fire. Lacrimosa leaned against her husband, and Benedictus placed his arm around her. They watched the firelight crackle among the ruins, lighting the smashed statues and burned trees.

"We were that young once, yes," he said. "But you were never angry. You were strong too, and you're strong now. But yours is the strength of water. Kyrie and Agnus Dei are fire. Gloriae is ice."

"And what are you, Ben?" she asked him.

He let out a long, deep sigh and stared into the flames in silence. Finally he said, "I am nothing now but old memories and pain."

She played with his hair, black streaked with gray. "Something weighs heavy on you," she said.

He nodded but said nothing. Lacrimosa wished she could ease his pain; she saw it every day in his eyes. She saw the burning of Requiem there, as she saw it around her. She saw Lanburg Fields, and the mountains of bodies, and all those who'd died under his banners. And she saw new pain there today; he had seen something during the past moon, but

Lacrimosa knew he needed time to reflect upon it. Maybe he would never speak of it. She kissed his cheek.

"You are strong, my lord, and brave and noble. You are my husband, my king. You are a hero to the young ones; even to Gloriae."

She ran her fingers across his cheek, his skin rough and stubbly. He pulled her closer to him.

"They would fight even as toddlers, the twins," he said. "Do you remember?"

She smiled. "I do. They would fight over dolls, over candies...." She laughed softly. "Do they fight over Kyrie now?"

"That boy was trouble from day one. Do you know, I spoke to him in Lanburg Fields. I blessed him before the battle." Benedictus sighed. "I thought they had all died, Kyrie too. I thought Gloriae was gone from us forever. I thought Agnus Dei would die under the mountain. We've cheated death for so long, Lacrimosa. How much longer can we flee?"

She took his hands in hers. His hands were so large and rough; hers looked tiny and white atop them.

"We're done fleeing," she said. "The griffins are our allies; they'll fight with us when the time comes. And we'll find the Beams. We'll seal the nightshades and defeat Dies Irae."

"And what then?" he asked. "Even with Irae dead, another will replace him. One of his lieutenants will inherit the throne, and be as cruel, as heartless, as ceaseless as Irae was in hunting us."

A voice came from across the fire.

"No," spoke Gloriae. "I will sit upon the Ivory Throne then."

Lacrimosa saw her daughter step from behind burned trees. The girl's golden hair cascaded across her shoulders, strewn with ash. Her leggings were torn, her boots muddy, her armor's glint dulled. And yet she walked nobly, and her eyes stared with green ice.

"Daughter," Lacrimosa said. "We cannot ask this of you. You belong with us now, here in Requiem."

Gloriae stood by the fire, hand on the hilt of her sword. "I am Vir Requis, yes. My loyalty is now to my true father, King Benedictus. We will rebuild this land. I promise it. And I will not watch an heir to Dies Irae destroy it again. The people of Osanna know me. They have known me for years as Dies Irae's daughter, as second-in-command of their empire. If we kill Dies Irae, they will accept me as their ruler. As empress of Osanna, I will forge peace with Requiem, and help her grow."

Lacrimosa felt a twist in her heart, and she winced. For so many years, Gloriae had lived away from her, a ruler of Osanna in marble palaces. Had she finally reclaimed her daughter only to lose her again? She stood up, walked to Gloriae, and hugged her. At first Gloriae only stood stiffly. Finally, hesitantly, she placed her arms around her mother.

A shriek rose.

Lacrimosa and Gloriae broke apart and drew their blades. Benedictus leaped up, raising his crossbow.

The shriek sounded again.

A nightshade.

"But it's not night yet," Lacrimosa whispered, looking from side to side.

Kyrie and Agnus Dei came running toward them, weapons drawn. Their eyes were wide with fear.

"Behind us!" Agnus Dei cried. "Ten nightshades in the daylight. They saw us." She jumped over a fallen column, shifted into a red dragon, and flew. Kyrie became a blue dragon and took flight beside her.

Lacrimosa touched Gloriae's cheek. "Shift now; you can do it. I'll help you fly."

Soon the five Vir Requis flew as dragons, the ruins far beneath them. When Lacrimosa looked over her shoulder, she saw ten nightshades rise from the ruins like pillars of smoke. The beasts screamed and chased them.

"I thought nightshades only came out at night!" Lacrimosa shouted in the roaring wind.

Gloriae, now a golden dragon, narrowed her eyes and snarled. "Dies Irae changed them—bred them with other beasts, or tortured them to overcome their fear of sunlight."

When Lacrimosa looked again, the nightshades were closer. They swirled, dispersed, collected themselves again, and moved like ink in water. Their eyes glinted and mocked her. Their howls rose, and Lacrimosa realized that she could hear voices in those howls.

"Lacrimosa...," they screeched. "Lacrimosa, return to me...."

She realized it was Dies Irae speaking through them, his voice broken into a million hisses rising together. She shivered.

"Let's see if they still like dragonfire," she said, turned her head, and blew flames at them.

They howled. The other Vir Requis also turned to blow fire, and the flames covered the nightshades.

The nightshades screamed so loudly, what ruins remained standing below collapsed. They emerged from the inferno, teeth drawn, as if the fire only enraged them. The Vir Requis kept flying.

"Into those storm clouds!" Benedictus said, pointing. The clouds were leagues away, a tornado spinning beneath them. Lacrimosa didn't know if they'd reach them in time, but she nodded. They flew, the nightshades screaming behind. Lacrimosa felt them tug at her soul, and she squinted, howled, and blew fire at them.

Kyrie was lagging. His wings stilled, and his eyes rolled back. A nightshade flew behind him, reaching out tendrils of smoke to Kyrie's tail.

Lacrimosa raced toward Kyrie, grabbed him, and shot fire at the nightshade. It screeched, blinded, and Lacrimosa caught Kyrie. She slapped him hard with her wing. He gasped as if jostled from sleep, narrowed his eyes, and flew again.

A nightshade wrapped itself around Benedictus's leg. He roared fire at it, and flapped his wings, but could not free himself. Gloriae raced toward him, and blew fire at the nightshade.

"I am your mistress, Gloriae of Osanna!" she screamed. "You will leave this place."

The nightshades laughed mockingly. The Vir Requis shot more flames, and Benedictus managed to free himself. They kept flying. Lacrimosa tried to blow more fire behind her, to blind to nightshades, but only sparks left her mouth.

"My fire is low!" she shouted. The others seemed in the same predicament. When they blew, only small flames left their mouths. They would need rest and food to rebuild the fires inside them.

"We're almost at the clouds," Benedictus shouted over the wind and screeching nightshades. "We'll lose them in the storm."

With the nightshades shrieking and tugging at them, the Vir Requis shot into the storm.

Rain and wind lashed Lacrimosa. She screamed, but her voice was lost. Lightning flashed. She could barely keep her eyes open. She flapped her wings, but could not move forward. Wind caught her, she spun, righted herself, and strained to keep flying.

"Ben!" she shouted.

She could see him just ahead, and then winds caught him, and he flew backwards and spun. Lightning flashed again. The rain felt like a million daggers. The sound was deafening. Nightshades flew around her, screeching, spinning, tossed around like rags. Lacrimosa saw a flash of golden scales ahead.

"Gloriae!" she called, but heard no answer.

She flapped her wings, snarled, and tried to reach her daughter.

That was when she saw the tornado.

It spun before her, horrible in its sound and fury. It looked to Lacrimosa like a great nightshade, or like the terror in her heart, the pain that ran between her and her countless kin beyond the stars. It spun toward her, and Lacrimosa shut her eyes. She flew in the roar, wings useless, and Lacrimosa saw before her silver harps, and flowers on marble tiles, and sunlight between birches. She floated as on clouds, and a smile found her lips.

"Daughters," she said with a smile, reaching out her arms, and the toddlers ran into her embrace. They laughed, sunlight upon them, clad in silk, flowers in their hair. The marble columns rose around them, and hills of trees bloomed.

Lightning rent the world

Thunder boomed.

She opened her eyes, and saw rain, and saw nightshades screeching and fleeing. Lacrimosa flapped her wings, eyes stinging, the wind and rain and memories crashing against her.

"Lacrimosa!" cried a distance voice, barely audible. A black shape flew toward her, burly, reaching out.

"Ben!" she shouted.

Their claws touched, and then the storm blew them apart. Nightshades swirled around them, dispersing into wisps. The tornado sucked up some of the creatures. Others it tossed aside. Lacrimosa managed to grab Benedictus, and she clung to him.

The storm spun them and finally cast them out into a world of soft rain, grumbling thunder, and rainbows.

Lacrimosa looked around her. She saw the tornado a league away, moving westward and away from her. Nightshades spun within it. One nightshade broke free and flew toward her. Lacrimosa and Benedictus blew fire at it, the last flames they could muster. Alone, the nightshade dared not face the firelight. It screeched and fled.

"Where are the young ones?" Lacrimosa shouted. The wind was still roaring.

Benedictus pointed. "I see Kyrie and Agnus Dei."

The blue and red dragon came flying from above. They had flown above the storm, and soon hovered by Benedictus and Agnus Dei.

"Where's Gloriae?" Lacrimosa asked, looking around frantically.

"Gloriae!" Agnus Dei called, also searching.

Lacrimosa flew back toward the storm, seeking golden scales. The others flew around her, also seeking. Few nightshades remained. What nightshades attacked them, they beat back with firelight. The tornado was retreating rapidly, leaving a land of puddles and shattered trees. Was it taking Gloriae with it?

"Gloriae!" Lacrimosa shouted. "Can you hear me?"

She flew, scanning the ruins below, and her eyes caught a glint of gold. She flew closer and gasped. A golden dragon lay upon a burned tree below, legs limp, head tilted back.

"Gloriae!" Lacrimosa called and dived. The other dragons dived with her. Lacrimosa reached Gloriae first. She hovered above her daughter, fear claiming her. Was Gloriae, only recently returned to her, taken from her again?

No. Gloriae was alive. Her left wing moved, and her eyes fluttered.

"Mother," the girl whispered.

Lacrimosa touched her daughter's cheek. "I'm here, Gloriae, I'm here, you're fine now."

Benedictus helped lift Gloriae from the burned tree, and they placed her on the ground.

Gloriae blinked, and her lips opened and closed several times before she could speak. "I fell. I'm... I'm not good at flying."

When Lacrimosa examined her daughter for wounds, she found bruises and scrapes, and an ugly gash along her thigh, but no broken bones. Soon Gloriae was able to stand, gingerly test her limbs, and walk.

Benedictus scanned the skies. "The nightshades are gone for now. But they'll be back soon. Shift into human form, everyone. We'll be harder to spot. Those bastards still hate firelight, but they now tolerate the sun."

They turned human again, and Lacrimosa saw that bruises covered Gloriae, and blood seeped from her thigh. She tried to tend to the wound, but Gloriae held her back, eyes icy.

"I'm fine," the girl said. "I've suffered worse."

Lacrimosa shivered. She knew when Gloriae had suffered worse wounds; it had been when she still served Dies Irae, and Kyrie had gored her with his horn. She shoved the thought aside.

When she turned to the others, she saw that Kyrie too was battered. A bruise was spreading beneath his eye. His lip was fat and cracked. He clutched his side, as if he'd been hurt there too.

"Kyrie, did you also fall?" she asked in concern.

Kyrie glanced at Agnus Dei, who shot him a venomous stare.

"Uh, yeah," Kyrie said, looking away from Agnus Dei. "I also fell."

"Fell onto Agnus Dei's fist, maybe," Benedictus muttered to himself.

Agnus Dei glared at him and clenched those fists. "Did you say something, Father?"

"Yeah," he said, voice gruff. "I said let's go. We walk from here. We go to Osanna, and we seek the tombs of her kings."

They walked through the puddles, mud, and ruins, tattered and bruised, heading into the east.

BENEDICTUS

They travelled off road. The forests of Osanna lay wilted. The trees were white and shrivelled up, like the limbs of snowbeasts. Most had fallen over, spreading white ash across the land.

"There, in the distance," Benedictus said. "Two of them."

The others muttered and lay down, pulled cloaks over them, and lay still. Leafy branches, mud, and thorns covered their cloaks, sewn and fastened with string and pins. Soon the Vir Requis appeared as nothing but mounds of leaf and earth.

The nightshades screeched above. Benedictus lay under his cloak, still, barely daring to breathe. Finally the shrieks disappeared into the distance, and he stood up. The others also stood, looked at one another uneasily, and resumed walking.

"There are more every day," Kyrie said.

Benedictus nodded. "And they're larger, too. Irae is changing them. I don't know how, but he is. He's making them stronger, faster, tougher. Next time they attack, firelight won't daunt them."

Kyrie shuddered. "How is he doing that?"

"I don't know. But I'm hoping he doesn't know about the Beams. They're our last hope."

They continued to walk, not speaking, their boots rustling the dirt and snapping branches. It was their twentieth day of walking since leaving Requiem's ruins.

Twenty days of hiding under cloaks, of seeing the ruin of the world, Benedictus thought. They had seen barely any life. Few animals remained. People were even fewer. Sometimes they saw armored soldiers travelling the roads, even several knights on horseback. Mostly they saw nothing but toppled forts, bodies, and devastation.

Benedictus looked at Lacrimosa. She walked by his side, leaves in her pale hair. Her lavender eyes seemed so large, bottomless pools of sadness. He took her hand.

"I'm sorry," he said to her.

She looked at him. "For what?"

The young ones walked behind, speaking in hushed voices; they could not hear.

"I'm sorry that you must walk like this, Lacrimosa. Wearing leaves and dirt. Eating old rations and whatever skinny beasts we can hunt. You should be wearing silk, and dining on fine foods, and living in a palace."

She laughed softly. "Is that who you think I am? A pampered queen? Ben. I'm your wife. I'm your love, and you are mine. I would walk by you even through the tunnels of the Abyss."

He lowered his head. "You are strong, and brave, and I love you. But I've failed." He looked behind him at his daughters. "I've failed them."

Lacrimosa narrowed her eyes. "You are keeping them alive. You are leading them."

Benedictus looked ahead, to the leagues of rolling ruin, the wilted trees, the toppled walls, the animals that lay rotting on the earth. "I could have killed Dies Irae at Lanburg Fields. I pitied him. I let him live. I could have killed him under the mountain, but I was not strong enough. I'm weak, Lacrimosa. I don't know what strength I still have."

She squeezed his hand. "I know, Ben. We'll do it together. We'll find the Beams. We'll make the world safe for the young ones. I'm with you, now and always."

Benedictus turned to look at the youths.

Agnus Dei walked with a crossbow on one hip, a sword on the other. Her brown eyes were narrowed, forever scanning the world for a fight. Benedictus knew that among the youths, she was the most like him. She had his dark eyes, the black curls of his hair, the fire in her belly. Dies Irae thought she was his, that he had fathered the twins when raping Lacrimosa. When Benedictus looked into Agnus Dei's brown, strong eyes, he knew that was false. He knew she was of his blood.

Next Benedictus looked at Gloriae, and he sighed. Gloriae was twin to Agnus Dei, but she looked more like Lacrimosa. She was light like her mother, of fair hair, of pale skin. But there was none of Lacrimosa's frailty to her. This one was strong like her sister, but her strength was of ice rather than fire, a strength Dies Irae had forged into her. *She's still a stranger to me,* Benedictus thought. He wanted to earn her love, but she rarely spoke to him, and when she looked upon him, there was no feeling in her eyes, only that ice.

Benedictus then looked at Kyrie, and sighed again. Kyrie walked with muddy clothes, and his shock of yellow hair was unkempt. He held a dagger drawn in each hand. Kyrie Eleison. The son of his fallen lieutenant. The boy Benedictus had sent to die upon Lanburg Fields. But Kyrie was no longer a boy. He was seventeen now, a grown man, a warrior under his banners like Requiem's warriors of old.

"Can I make the world safe for them, Lacrimosa?" he asked.

"I don't know. But you lead them. You inspire them. That is the best you can do for them now. Look, Ben. Beyond those trees. The tombs of Osanna's kings."

Benedictus looked, and saw a valley between the dead trees. The grass was dead, splotchy with patches of snow. The sky was tan and gray. Tombs rose in the valley, the size of temples, hewn of rough bricks, beaten down and smoothed through centuries of rain and snow.

"The Valley of Kings' Glory," Benedictus said. He stopped walking and stared. Years ago, he had visited this place and seen green grass, flowers, and rustling trees. The land was ruined now, but the tombs remained, as they had for millennia. The youths caught up with him, stood at his sides, and stared into the valley. Wind played with their hair.

"A king whose name begins with T," Benedictus said. "His title will end with 'ite'. Our search begins. Let's stay together. Weapons drawn. If the nightshades arrive, hi—"

"Hide in your cloaks, pretend to be mounds of dirt, we know the drill," Agnus Dei said. "You say that once an hour, Father."

They walked into the valley, crossbows and blades in hand. The wind moaned. Snow began to fall, the flakes clinging to their hair and clothes. They approached the closest tomb, a monolith of rough bricks. Large as a castle, it was shaped like a griffin. The griffin's beak had fallen years ago, and now lay at its talons. Those stone talons rose taller than a house, dead grass rustling between them. A stone door stood at the griffin's breast. Letters were engraved into it, filled with gold.

The letters were in Old High Speech, and Benedictus read them out loud. "Here lies King Tenathax the Blessed, Defeater of Gol, Son of Tarax the Red. May the Earth God protect his soul."

Below the golden letters, in smaller words, appeared the story of Tenathax's life, a tale of battles won and temples built.

"Not our guy," Kyrie said. "His name starts the right way, but ends wrong." He scanned the smaller letters. "And it says nothing here about any Beams or Loomers. Just talk of him defeating that Gol place."

Benedictus nodded. "Let's keep looking."

They left the towering griffin of stone, and walked along the valley, until they reached a tomb shaped like a warrior. The stone warrior stood as tall as a palace. Its base alone was thirty feet tall. They found a stone door there too, also engraved with golden letters. Again, Benedictus read aloud.

"Here lies King Tarax the Young, Defeater of Fidelium, son of Talin the White. May the Earth God bless his soul."

Here too did smaller words appear below the main epitaph, telling the story of Tarax defeating the kings of Fidelium, and destroying their temples and palaces, and annexing their realm to Osanna.

Kyrie rolled his eyes. "Every King of Osanna was named Tarax the Something, or Talin the Whatever, son of Taras the Who Cares."

Gloriae spoke softly, cheeks pink in the cold. "All but Dies Irae."

Benedictus pointed at the letters. "Look at our friend King Tarax again. See who his father was? Talin the White. Could that be the king we're looking for?"

Agnus Dei, snow in her hair, unrolled the scroll from Requiem's tunnels. She showed them the passage again.

"In the days of the Night Horrors, King T_____ite journeyed to the southern realms of G_____nd sought the Loomers o_____olden pools."

Agnus Dei rolled up the scroll again. She nodded. "Talin the White, yes. Father of King Tarax. Let's find his tomb."

They explored the valley for several hours, moving from tomb to tomb. The oldest tombs were shaped as pyramids, their rocks beaten down, their letters almost effaced. Finally they found a tomb labelled "Talin the White". It was one of the simpler tombs. It stood only three stories tall, surrounded by columns engraved with dragons.

Kyrie and Agnus Dei jumped up and down. "Finally."

Benedictus examined the letters engraved into this tomb. "King Talin III, known as the White."

Smaller letters were engraved beneath his name. They all leaned in, and this time, Gloriae read them out loud.

"Born in the year 476. Rose to the throne in 482. Died in the year 489. His reign was peaceful and prosperous."

Gloriae leaned back and raised her eyebrow. "The king who tamed the Nightshades, the hero from the book, was a child? He died in childhood after a peaceful reign? That doesn't make sense."

Kyrie moaned. "Stars. We've been searching this graveyard for hours. I'm tired. Will we find no king to help us?"

Benedictus grunted. "I'm tired too, kid. Let's take a break. We'll eat what food we have."

They camped below Talin III's tomb and unpacked their supplies. They didn't have much. Lacrimosa had found some mushrooms a while back. Agnus Dei had managed to shoot two rabbits. They had pilfered turnips and some ale from a roadside tavern. They shared the food and drink, which left them still hungry and thirsty, and considered.

"We came here for nothing," Kyrie said.

Benedictus shook his head. "No, kid. We just have to go older. We've been exploring the newer tombs."

Kyrie snickered so loudly, a bit of turnip flew from his mouth. He gestured at Talin III's resting place. "New tombs? Benedictus, this is from the year 489. That was...." He counted on his fingers. "2,756 years ago."

Benedictus nodded. "2,766, actually. But our friend here is the third Talin the White. I say we find his father and grandfather."

They stood up, bellies still rumbling with hunger and throats still parched, and kept moving down the valley. Soon they reached tombs so old, they could have been mistaken for hills of scattered rocks. These tombs were mostly buried in the earth, only their roofs showing. Dead grass rustled around them.

Benedictus knelt by a stone roof which rose from earth, grass, and snow. He dug around it, tossing back dirt and snow, until he excavated the top of a doorway.

"Here, look," he said.

Faded letters appeared on the stone door. Unlike the other tombs, no gold covered these letters, and they were roughly hewn.

"King Talin the White," Benedictus read. "Wielder of Beams."

Agnus Dei leaned against the structure. "Wielder of Beans?" she asked. "Because if he has any beans around here, I'm still hungry."

Benedictus glared at her. "Agnus Dei, show more respect among the tombs of the dead. We finally found our man, and you can only make a joke? Let's dig."

They dug in the earth, until they revealed more of the doorway. However, no more letters appeared there, as had on the other tombs. The door was bare.

"Great," Agnus Dei said. "All the other kings had bloody epics written on their doorways. We finally find a match, and his door just has his name on it. Just perfect."

Benedictus nodded. "In the Gray Age, when Talin the White ruled, the tombs were simpler. It is only in later years that the kings of Osanna built great, towering tombs in the shapes of beasts and warriors, and gilded letters on their doorways. Let's step inside. We'll find more answers within."

Agnus Dei raised an eyebrow. "Are you sure, Father? Do you remember what happened last time we entered a mausoleum? You almost got a skeleton as a son-in-law."

Benedictus grunted. "Sometimes I think I'd prefer the skeleton to Kyrie."

A screech sounded above. The Vir Requis spun around to see ten nightshades in the distance.

"Into the tomb!" Benedictus hissed. "Before they see us."

He dug frantically, revealing the rest of the door. The nightshades shrieked, moving closer. The youths snarled.

"Don't shift!" Benedictus whispered through strained jaws. "They haven't seen us yet."

He leaned against the doorway and pushed. It didn't budge. Kyrie added his weight, they grunted and strained, and finally the door creaked. It took the twins to help too, and the door inched its way open.

"In, quickly!"

They scurried into the tomb. It was dank, cold, and dark. The nightshades screamed outside, louder now. Soon Benedictus saw their shadows in the sky outside.

"Did they see us?" Lacrimosa whispered, clinging to his arm.

Benedictus shook his head. "I don't think so. Their eyes must be weak in the day. We're safe."

Breathing out shakily, he surveyed the tomb. The chamber held jewelled swords, golden vases, a suit of armor, and stone chests full of gems. Golden coins covered the floor.

Agnus Dei whistled. "Nice little place Talin's got here. But where's the king himself?"

Lacrimosa pointed at a second doorway in the back of the chamber. "In there."

Benedictus stepped toward the doorway and pushed it. Something screamed.

The doorway crashed open, and a creature leaped at him.

Benedictus fell back and raised his sword. The blade hit rusty rings of steel, bolts, and spinning wheels. It shattered, and a shard scratched his arm.

"Father!" Agnus Dei cried. Benedictus heard her crossbow fire. He saw its quarrel slam into the creature, but it ricocheted off its metallic face. The creature's hands were spinning blades, reaching for Benedictus.

He rolled aside, and one of the spinning blades cut his shoulder. He grunted and kicked, and his leg hit the creature's ribs, which seemed made of bronze. The bronze was old, green and tarnished, and it shattered. The creature leaned back and screeched, a sound like metal gears.

The other Vir Requis were stabbing it, but blades seemed not to hurt it.

"Move back!" Benedictus roared. The others stepped back, and for the first time, Benedictus saw the creature clearly. It looked like a skeleton made of metal. Its body was all gears, wheels, rusty bones. Its eyes burned with firelight. It swung its arm, and a blade flew from its hand. Lacrimosa ducked, and the blade nearly cut her.

Benedictus kicked again, hitting the creature's bronze skull. The skull shattered, raining rust. The creature tried to attack again, but Benedictus kicked its remaining ribs. They shattered, revealing a pumping heart of leather. Benedictus stabbed the heart with his dagger. The leather burst and spilled hot, red blood.

The creature twitched, then leaned over, dead. Benedictus noticed that chains bound it to the doorway.

"What the abyss was that?" Kyrie said, panting.

"A machine," Benedictus said. "Built of elder knowledge now passed from the world."

Kyrie shuddered. "And a good thing, that is."

Benedictus grunted and examined his wound. It was ugly, and full of rust, but he'd worry about it later. He kicked the metal creature aside. It shattered into pieces that littered the floor. Beyond the doorway, a staircase led down into blackness.

"I'll go take a look," Benedictus said. "If it's safe, I'll call you down."

"Ben, I'll go with you," Lacrimosa said.

He shook his head. "No. In case there are more of these machines. Stay here, all of you."

Not waiting for an answer, he stepped downstairs into the darkness. The stairway was thin, and Benedictus placed his hand against the wall.

The stairway led to small chamber. There wasn't much light, and Benedictus lit his lamp with what oil remained. He saw several more mechanical skeletons, but they lay broken on the floor, rusting. Between them lay a sarcophagus shaped like a king with a long beard. The stone king held a stone shield and sword.

"King Talin is down here," he called up the stairway. "Come take a look."

The other Vir Requis stepped down. They crowded around the sarcophagus. Benedictus brushed dust and cobwebs off, and found letters engraved onto the stone shield.

Agnus Dei, leaning over the shield beside him, gasped.

"It's the text from the scroll!" she said. "Only all the letters are here now."

She unrolled the scroll from the tunnels below Requiem. She compared them side by side and nodded. They all leaned over the shield, and Agnus Dei read the words aloud.

"In the days of the Night Horrors, King Talin the White journeyed to the southern realms of Gol, and sought the Loomers of the golden pools. The Night Horrors stole the souls of Osanna, and cast them into the darkness, and Talin the White sought the counsel of the Loomers, who were wise above all others in the land. He spoke with the Loomers, and prayed with them, and they crafted him the Beams. Talin the White returned with the Beams to Osanna, and shone them upon the Night Horrors. He tamed them, and drove them into Well of Night in Confutatis, and sealed it. He placed guards around it, armed with Beams, so the Night Horrors can nevermore escape."

For a moment, they all stood in silence, considering the words. Benedictus stared into the stone eyes of the king, trying to imagine him fighting the nightshades, those same nightshades that now screeched outside the tomb. Finally Benedictus noticed that the others were all looking at him, waiting for him to speak. He scratched his chin.

"The Beams are from Gol," he said. "I've studied many maps, but seen no realm called Gol. The first tomb we saw, the one shaped as a griffin. It spoke of Gol; King Tenathax defeated it. Gol might no longer exist."

Kyrie tapped his cheek. "Gol... I wonder if it's related to Gilnor. We had a few maps of Osanna back at Fort Sanctus. I used to read them for fun; there wasn't much else to read. Gilnor lies to the southwest. It's nothing but swamps."

Lacrimosa nodded. Dust, rust, and cobwebs filled her hair. "I remember a song of Gilnor. Bards would sing of it in the halls of Requiem. I haven't heard the song in years, but... I remember. The lyrics spoke of the swamps of Gilnor. They said that once, thousands of years ago, a mythical kingdom stood there, a land of silver towers and bridges. The song spoke of creatures of darkness destroying the silver towers, and—"

Kyrie jumped and slapped the stone shield. "Creatures of darkness!" he repeated. "Night Horrors. Nightshades. These are all different names for those things that hunt us. They must have destroyed that kingdom of silver towers, which stood where Gilnor's swamps are. I bet you Gol was that ancient kingdom."

Benedictus grumbled. "Stop your jumping up and down, kid. Some old song of some silver towers doesn't mean anything."

Kyrie jumped again, as if in spite. "It means everything. Gilnor must mean Gol. You know the land of Tiranor?"

Benedictus nodded. "It lies far south, near the deserts."

"Well," Kyrie said, "the word 'Tira' used to mean 'fortress' in Old High Speech. Thousands of years ago, High Speech was a little different. I know the word 'Tira' from those old maps I told you about. It was written on the maps beside drawings of fortresses. Tiranor, in the south, had many forts in it; they formed a border along the desert. 'Nor' must mean 'land of' in Old High Speech. Tiranor means 'land of forts'. If I'm right, and I'm always right, 'Gilnor' means 'land of Gil'."

Agnus Dei spoke up. "But we're talking about Gol, pup, not Gil."

Kyrie was speaking so quickly now, his tongue could barely keep up. "Yes, but we're still talking about Old High Speech. That's what people used thousands of years ago, right? Old High Speech, when written down, had no vowels. Only High Speech today has vowels. The elders just wrote down consonants; they assumed you'd know how to read them. So the elders would just write 'GL', and figured you'd know how to say it properly. I'd wager people found the old books, maybe a thousand years later, and forgot how to pronounce the place names. They saw 'GL', and just read it 'Gil' instead of 'Gol'. The new name caught on. When people started writing vowels, they wrote it the wrong way. Gol must have become Gil, and Gil became Gilnor. Land of Gol." He took a deep breath. "It all fits."

Benedictus put a hand on Kyrie's shoulder. "Very clever, kid. But Gol was destroyed. Tenathax destroyed it, remember? It said so on his griffin tomb. Gol's a swampland now, and part of Osanna."

Kyrie looked giddy, rolling on the balls of his feet. "You know what? I say that's griffin dung. I bet you Tenathax was a bloody liar. See the text on Talin's shield. The nightshades attacked Gol. You've met our dear friends the nightshades. You know what they're capable of. I bet you the nightshades destroyed Gol, just like they destroyed Osanna. Years later, Tenathax merely had to walk into the ruins, annex them, and claim that he conquered the place in some glorious battle."

"You're assuming a lot, kid."

"I'm reading between the lines. You think Dies Irae is the only king to have glorified himself? They all did it, each and every one of the bastards. But these Loomers... I'm not sure who they are. Survivors of the nightshade attack on Gol, I'd guess. These Loomers found some way to survive in the ruins of Gol—the Beams. Talin must have stolen the Beams from them."

Agnus Dei punched Kyrie's shoulder. "Pup, you're making up half of this."

He shook his head. "Again, I'm reading between the lines. It says here the Loomers gave Talin the Beams. Really? *Really?* I think not. The Loomers lived in nightshade country. They'd never give up the one weapon they had. When the nightshades turned from Gol to Osanna, Talin must have heard of these Loomers surviving, and sought them out, and stole their Beams. And that's how he sealed the nightshades, and there was peace for thousands of years, until our friend Gloriae freed them."

Gloriae glared at him, but said nothing.

Benedictus grunted. "Kyrie, I don't know how you get all that. There are many pieces missing from this puzzle, and I'm not sure you have the right picture."

Kyrie grinned over the sarcophagus. "Well, there's only one way to find out." He began walking up the stairway, paused, and spoke over his shoulder. "Come on! We go to Gilnor. We seek the Loomers."

AGNUS DEI

As they entered the swamps of Gilnor, Agnus Dei couldn't stop glancing at Kyrie and Gloriae.

The mud was knee deep, and Agnus Dei sloshed through it. Kyrie was walking several yards away, mud covering him. He held a dagger in one hand, which he used to cut vines and branches in his way. Gloriae walked beside him, her hair caked with mud from a recent fall, the jewels and gold of her breastplate brown with the stuff. Once more she slipped, and Kyrie caught her. She lingered a moment too long in his arms, Agnus Dei thought, before righting herself and walking again.

Agnus Dei stifled a growl. She told herself that she should love her twin. After all these years, they were reunited; Agnus Dei knew she should feel rejoiceful. But whenever she looked at Gloriae, she wanted to punch her perfect, pretty face.

Lichen brushed Agnus Dei's cheek, and she slapped it aside, and now a growl did escape her lips. She tried not to, but kept imagining Kyrie touching Gloriae, their bodies naked together.

Don't think about it, she told herself. *You promised Kyrie that you still love him.*

Gloriae slipped again, and made a joke to Kyrie, who laughed. Agnus Dei bit her lip. Yes, she might still love the pup. But could she ever love Gloriae now?

Mother came to walk by Agnus Dei. She placed a hand on her shoulder, and when Agnus Dei looked at her, Mother smiled sadly.

"I think if you stare at her any harder, she'll burst into flames," Mother said.

Agnus Dei lowered her head. Kyrie and Gloriae were talking now, too busy with each other to notice the others.

"I know, Mother," Agnus Dei said, still watching the pair. "But I don't trust her. Even now."

Mother placed an arm around her. "She saved your life. When the nightshades grabbed you, it was Gloriae who saved you."

Agnus Dei sighed. The swamp water was deeper now, going up to their waists. "I know. It's just that...."

Mother nodded. "Gloriae and Kyrie."

Agnus Dei looked up at her mother, and saw warmth in the woman's eyes and smile. "Oh, Mother. He's just a pup, I know it, but... he was my pup."

Mother laughed. "I know, sweetness. He still is. The boy is madly in love with you."

"Are you sure he's not in love with Gloriae? Or she with him?"

Mother squeezed Agnus Dei's shoulder and kissed her cheek. "I'm sure. A mother knows these things. Agnus Dei, I don't know what happened between you three, but... try to forgive your sister. Please. We all must forgive one another now. We are all that's left of our race. If we can't live together, we won't survive."

Agnus Dei hugged her mother. "Okay. I'll try. It's hard, but I'll try."

Now that she wasn't staring at Kyrie and Gloriae, she looked closer at Gilnor's swamps. Where were these Loomers? She saw nothing but logs, lichen, trees, water, and more than anything—mud. Herons and frogs seemed to live everywhere. Mice scurried between the trees. Agnus Dei began collecting the frogs, lifting them from logs and lilies, and placing them in her pouch.

"Frog legs for dinner," she mumbled as she lifted a particularly fat one.

Movement ahead caught her eyes, and Agnus Dei stared, hoping to catch a heron for dinner too.

She gasped.

It was not a heron that moved ahead, but a huge eye protruding from the mud. The eye was the size of a mug, topped with scaly skin.

"Uh, guys?" Agnus Dei said. "There's an—"

The creature burst from the mud, roaring.

Agnus Dei shifted at once. She growled at the swamp beast. It looked like an alligator, but was the size of a dragon, fifty feet long and thin. It rushed at her, its teeth like swords.

Agnus Dei spun and lashed her tail. She hit the creature, knocking it into a tree.

The other Vir Requis shifted too. The five dragons surrounded the swamp creature, who howled and snapped its teeth. It lunged at Gloriae.

Gloriae, now a golden dragon, snarled and swiped her claws. Her claws dug into the creature, spilling blood. It screeched and bit Gloriae's shoulder, and she cried in pain.

Father snarled and leaped onto the creature's back. He bit its neck and spat out a chunk of flesh. The creature crashed into the mud, kicked its legs, then lay still.

"Are you all right?" Father asked Gloriae, blood in his mouth.

She nodded and clutched her shoulder. "It only nicked me."

They stood panting for a moment, staring at the dead creature.

"It's some kind of alligator," Agnus Dei said. "But I've never seen one so large."

Gloriae nodded. "And the thing almost r—"

Shrieks shook the swamp, interrupting Gloriae. A dozen other swamp creatures burst from the mud, howled, and charged at the Vir Requis.

Two charged toward Agnus Dei. She blew fire at one, and it screeched and fell back against a tree. The second clawed at her. Agnus Dei dodged the claws and swiped her tail. She drove her tail's spikes into its side, then pulled back, dragging the creature. She slammed it against a tree.

The burned gator charged, smoking. Agnus Dei snarled, and they crashed into each other. The creature snapped its teeth. Agnus Dei held it back with her front legs, and flapped her wings against it. It howled so loudly, Agnus Dei thought it would deafen her. Its drool splashed her. She kicked its belly, and it crashed back. She blew flames at it, and it screeched.

Teeth sank into her shoulder.

Agnus Dei screamed and reached back, digging her claws into the head of another gator. It opened its mouth to roar, and she spun around, and drove her horns into its neck. That stopped its roaring.

She kicked its body down, and looked around wildly. The other Vir Requis had killed all but two gators. The pair growled, whimpered, and sank into the mud. They began swimming away.

Agnus Dei tried to leap at them, but Father held her shoulder.

"Let them flee," he said. "And stay in dragon form. We're hidden here under the trees and moss. If those things return, I'd rather we met them as dragons."

As blood spread through the swamp waters, the five dragons began wading forward. Agnus Dei had no idea where they were going. Father walked at their lead, but she suspected he just moved aimlessly. "Gol" was all the text on the shield had said. As far as Agnus Dei could tell, the swamps of Gilnor spread for dozens of leagues.

"Maybe those gators were the Loomers," Kyrie said, walking beside her. Lichen draped over his scales.

"Don't be stupid, pup," Agnus Dei scolded him, though secretly, she was relieved to see that he now walked beside her, and not by her sister. "Did those look like Loomers to you?"

Hanging moss went into his mouth, and he spat it out. "So you know what Loomers look like now?"

"Well, I reckon that they're... old men."

Kyrie nodded. "Very old, since they crafted the Beams thousands of years ago."

Agnus Dei twisted her claws. "And they probably... have looms."

Kyrie whistled appreciatively. "Agnus Dei, by the stars, you've got it. Old men with looms. Why didn't I think of that?"

She growled and glared at him. "All right, pup, don't get smart. So I don't know what Loomers look like. But I'm pretty damn sure they're not oversized alligators."

He lashed his tail, splashing her with mud. Agnus Dei screamed like one of the gators, lashed her own tail, and splashed him back. He ducked, and the mud hit Gloriae, who gave Agnus Dei an icy stare. Soon Kyrie was slinging more mud, a twinkle in his eye and a smirk on his lips, and Agnus Dei fought back with equal fervor.

"Vir Requis!" Father thundered. "Stop that."

Agnus Dei rolled her eyes and tossed more mud at Kyrie. "Oh, Father, I'm just teaching the pup a lesson."

Kyrie froze and stared over her shoulder. "Uh... Agnus Dei? You might want to listen to your old man."

Agnus Dei frowned; Kyrie was gaping. She turned around slowly, and her mouth fell open.

Agnus Dei had once sneaked away from Mother and visited a town fair, disguised in a cloak and hood. She had seen a stall selling balls of twine. The creatures ahead looked like great balls of twine, the size of barrels, glowing bright blue. Every thread in their forms seemed filled with moonlight. They hovered over the swamp, pulsing, their light reflecting in the water.

"The Loomers," Agnus Dei whispered.

There were seven. Two appeared to be children; they wobbled as they floated, no larger than apples. The Loomers seemed to turn toward Agnus Dei and regard her, though she couldn't be sure; they had no eyes. They nodded, tilting in the air.

They began to vibrate, and a hum grew within them, until the sound formed words.

"We are Loomers. We are elders' light. We are weavers."

Agnus Dei sloshed toward them in the mud. She felt so coarse, dirty, and clumsy compared to these creatures of light.

"Do you know about the Beams?" she asked, panting.

The Loomers nodded again.

"We are Loomers. We are weavers. Our elders wove the Beams of Light. Our elders blinded the Night Horrors."

Agnus Dei couldn't help but laugh, and she fell back into the mud. "We found them! We found the Loomers. Now we can defeat the nightshades."

Tears filled her eyes. Finally, it seemed, their pain was over. Finally they could reclaim the world—for Requiem, for Osanna, for her and her loved ones.

Father approached the Loomers. He bowed his head. "Loomers of the Golden Pools," he said. "I am Benedictus, King of Requiem."

The Loomers flared. Their light turned white and angry, and they crackled and hissed.

"King?" they said, voices like lightning splitting a tree. "King Talin stole our Beams. Our elders were great weavers. Our elders crafted the Beams. Our elders blinded the Night Horrors. King Talin stole from our elders, stole the light of Gol. We have no love for kings. Have you come to steal from us, King Benedictus?"

Father kept his head bowed. "I seek not to steal from you, wise Loomers. I seek only your aid and wisdom. The Night Horrors have emerged again, and have overrun our lands."

The Loomers flared brighter. They spun so quickly, they appeared as pulsing stars.

"The Night Horrors!" they cried, voices like storm and steam. "The Night Horrors fly again. This is blackness, weavers. This is deep blackness."

Agnus Dei rose to her feet. She sloshed through the mud. "Can you weave us new Beams?" she asked the Loomers. "We need new ones."

Father nodded. "Noble Loomers, we seek knowledge of the Beams."

The Loomers were still spinning, their light flashing across the swamp. "We cannot weave new Beams."

Agnus Dei gasped. "Why not?"

Father touched her shoulder. "Agnus Dei, please, hush." He turned back to the Loomers. "Loomers, please share your knowledge of the Beams. The Night Horrors have covered the northern realms, and we fear they will soon cover the world with their darkness. What more can you tell us? Why can no new Beams be woven?"

The Loomers stopped spinning, and dipped two feet, so that they almost touched the mud. They seemed defeated. Their light dimmed, and Agnus Dei could see the intricate network of their glowing strands.

"We are elders' light," they said, glowing faintly. "The elders lived many seasons ago. The elders wove the Beams. We are elders' light. We have not the wisdom of the old age. We cannot weave new Beams."

Agnus Dei shut her eyes. "So the knowledge of the Beams is lost. Only your ancestors knew how to make them."

The Loomers flared, their light blinding her. "Not all knowledge is lost, youngling. We have knowledge of the old Beams, the Beams of the elder Loomers. The knowledge of weaving them is lost. The Beams still shine."

Gloriae inhaled sharply. Agnus Dei looked at her, and saw that Gloriae's eyes were narrowed, her jaw clenched.

"Loomers," Father said to the beings of light, "where can we find the elders' Beams?"

The Loomers' light dimmed further, until they barely glowed at all. "We do not know. Talin stole them. Talin stole from Elder Loomers."

Gloriae stepped toward them, and spoke for the first time. Her eyes were narrowed to slits. "Loomers, what do the Beams look like?"

The Loomers seemed to regard her, shining their light upon her golden scales. "The elders built golden skulls, and placed the Great Light within them, so that the Beams will shine from the eye sockets, and look upon the world, and tame the Night Horrors."

Gloriae turned to the other Vir Requis. Her eyes seemed haunted, and her wings hung limp at her sides. For a moment she only stared, silent, and Agnus Dei thought she might faint.

Finally Gloriae spoke.

"I know where the Beams are." She winced and covered her eyes with her claws. "Of course. Of course they are there."

Agnus Dei stepped toward her sister and clutched her shoulder. "What? You knew all along?" She shook Gloriae. "Why didn't you tell us? Where are they?"

Gloriae allowed herself to be shaken. She looked at Agnus Dei with wide, pained eyes. "I saw them, but didn't know what they were. The nightshades were sealed in the Well of Night, an abyss in the dungeons of Confutatis. A doorway guards the chamber. There are golden skulls embedded into the doorway, eyes glowing in their sockets. I... I remember looking at them, but... I didn't realize they were the Beams until now."

Agnus Dei laughed and screamed. She turned toward Kyrie and her parents. "Of course! Where else would King Talin put the Beams? Once he sealed the nightshades, he put the Beams near them, so people could use them if the nightshades escaped." She began sloshing through the mud, heading north. "Come on! We go to Confutatis."

BENEDICTUS

They lay on their bellies in human forms. Burned tree branches creaked above them, and their cloaks of leaves, twigs, and mud covered them. Ahead, beyond fallow fields, Benedictus saw the Marble City.

"Confutatis," he whispered.

He stared with narrow eyes. He knew the others were staring too. Here Dies Irae ruled. From here did his nightshades and the shadow of his arm stretch across the land. Benedictus saw thousands of those nightshades over the city, even now in daylight. They screeched, nested on walls, and coiled in the air.

"How do we sneak into the city?" Lacrimosa whispered. Twigs and thorns and dirt covered her cloak. From above, she'd look like a mound of brush and mud. She peeked from her hood at Benedictus, fear in her eyes.

Benedictus watched nightshades swarm over the fields outside Confutatis, as if seeking surviving peasants. The creatures roared and returned to the city, where they landed upon a wall. Men too covered those walls, Benedictus saw. They were too small to see clearly, but their armor glinted in the sun. He estimated there would be hundreds of troops there, maybe thousands, armed with bows and crossbows.

"We can't sneak in," Benedictus said. "We've been watching for hours. Nobody's entered or exited the gates. The city is locked down. Dies Irae is waiting for us."

Agnus Dei growled beside him. "Nightshades? Thousands of soldiers? Dies Irae? Come on. We can take 'em. We'll shift into dragons and burn the bastards."

Gloriae too snarled. "Agreed. Let's attack. Head-on. No more sneaking around. We fly, we burn, we destroy. We kill Dies Irae, grab the Beams, and seal the nightshades."

Hidden under his camouflaged cloak, Kyrie pumped his fist. "Troll dung, yeah! I'm in. We fly at them by surprise. They won't know what hit 'em."

Benedictus scowled at the youths. "No. And that's final. If we fly into Confutatis, we die. There are five of us. There are thousands of nightshades; they'll tear us apart. That is, if they can reach us before those archers' arrows. I see a hundred archers from here, maybe more."

Agnus Dei clenched her fists. "I can take those archers. I'll burn them alive. I'm tired of slinking around. I could use a straight fight."

"Me too," Gloriae said.

"Me too," Kyrie said.

"Me too," Lacrimosa said.

They all turned to face Lacrimosa in shock.

"Mother, are you feeling all right?" Agnus Dei said. "*You* want to fight? You're always on about finding the peaceful solution, of using our brains instead of our brawn, of hiding instead of getting killed. You want to fight now too?"

Benedictus looked at his wife as if she were mad. She stared back at him, jaw tight, chin raised.

"My love," he said to her. "Are you sure? Tell me what you're thinking."

Lacrimosa stared at him, eyes solemn. "Yes. We fight. We charge them head-on. The time for hiding is over. We need those Beams, and an attack on the city is the only way we'll get them. But we won't fly alone." She pulled from her cloak the golden candlestick. Its emeralds glinted. "We fly with the griffins."

Kyrie and Agnus Dei's eyes shone. Gloriae, however, looked worried.

"Mother," she said. "I... I use to ride a griffin. Wouldn't they hate me now?"

Lacrimosa touched Gloriae's shoulder. "We all enslaved the griffins. Requiem and Osanna. They're free to make their choices now. They will fly with us. They will fly to thank me for healing their prince. They will fly to defeat the nightshades and Dies Irae; they hold no love for them. We will summon them. We will fly alongside them, not as their masters, but as their allies. We will charge the city, take the Beams, and defeat the nightshades."

"And face Dies Irae," Benedictus said in a low voice. That was what it all came down to, he thought. Once more, he'd have to face his brother. Dies Irae. The man who'd raped Lacrimosa.

The man who'd killed their parents. The man who'd hunted the Vir Requis to near extinction.

Once more, I will meet you in battle, brother, Benedictus thought.

He remembered meeting Dies Irae upon Lanburg Fields, biting off his arm, sparing his life. He remembered duelling Dies Irae in the same place, ten years later, this time taking the man's eye.

This time, only one of us walks away, Benedictus thought. *You or I will die in this battle. We cannot both live.*

The Vir Requis retreated behind the cover of wilted trees, and Lacrimosa placed the candlestick on the ground. She inserted a candle and lit it. It flickered, nearly perished in the wind, and raised blue smoke.

"Did it work?" Agnus Dei whispered.

Nobody answered. The candle kept burning. They watched silently, until the candle began to gutter, its last drops of wax dripping. Benedictus lowered his head. He wasn't sure what he'd expected. A flash of light? The roar of griffins?

The flame gave a last flicker, then died.

The wick hissed, and the blue smoke rose. It curled, dispersed, then regrouped into the shape of a tiny griffin. The griffin of blue smoke opened its beak, flapped its wings, and flew away.

"It works," Benedictus whispered. "Aid has been summoned."

He stood up, collected his belongings, and led the others deeper into the wilted woods. He walked until they found a rocky slope that led to a stream. They climbed down, and washed their clothes, and bathed. Dead trees reached over them, their branches like knobby fingers. Three cloven shields, several copper coins, and the bladeless hilt of a sword lay on the stream's bank. A battle had been fought here.

"We wait here," Benedictus said. "Stay under cover of the trees. Stay with your camouflaged cloaks over you. Do not speak loudly, do not light fires, and do not shift."

They nodded, and for once the youths didn't argue.

"Good," Benedictus said. "Kyrie, I have a task for you. I saw an abandoned, smashed farmhouse a distance back. Go see if they have any food. No hunting. I dare not risk a fire. Get us bread, fruit, vegetables, dry meats."

Kyrie nodded, drew his sword, and headed off between the trees.

Benedictus turned to the twins. "Gloriae and Agnus Dei, I have a task for you too." He pointed between the trees. "See that toppled fort?"

Gloriae nodded. "It still stood last year. The nightshades toppled it. It looks abandoned now."

Benedictus nodded. "See if you can find new quarrels for our crossbows. If soldiers chance upon our camp, I'd rather we kill them with quarrel than roaring fire."

The twins drew their blades, nodded, and soon disappeared between the trees.

Once the youths were beyond earshot, Lacrimosa laughed softly, and touched Benedictus's arm. The sunlight danced in her eyes and smile.

"You're good at finding us quiet time."

He couldn't help but smile. "I do what I can." He embraced and kissed his wife. "Lacrimosa, you're as beautiful as the day I met you. I don't tell you that enough."

She touched his cheek. "I remember that day. I was fifteen. It was my debut. We danced in the hall of your father—I, the daughter of nobility, and you, my prince. All knew that we would marry."

He held her, and they swayed as if dancing again in those marble halls.

"I was too old for you," he said. "And I'm too old for you now. You're still young and beautiful, Lacrimosa. And I'm aging. And I'm tired. You've deserved a better life."

She kissed his lips. "You've given me the life I wanted. A life by your side. A mother to your children. I could ask for no more. We will rebuild that hall, Ben. We will dance there again, as we did twenty years ago."

He cupped her chin in his hand, and kissed her again. She looked into his eyes, and her beauty pierced him. Her skin was fair, smooth, white as snow. Her eyes were lavender pools. He streamed her hair between his fingers. Those fingers were so coarse, calloused, and her hair was like silk, a blond so pale it was almost white. They kissed again, her arms around him.

"I would make love to you," he said, "a final time."

She ran her fingers down his cheek. "We will make love many more times, my lord."

He held her. "I don't know if we return from this flight. But let us live for this moment. Let us fly for this memory."

They lay on their cloaks by the water, and Benedictus undressed his wife slowly, marvelling at her pale skin, her slim body that was bruised and scarred from all her battles. He kissed her, and held her, and lay with her by the water.

"I love you forever," he whispered to her. "I will be with you forever, if not in this life, then in the halls of our forefathers beyond the stars."

When the youths returned, supplies in their hands, Benedictus and Lacrimosa were sitting by the water, holding each other.

"Here—quarrels," Gloriae said, and spilled them onto the dirt.

"A string of sausages, apples, and two cabbages that aren't too moldy," Kyrie said, and placed the food on a boulder.

"You're getting it dirty, pup," Agnus Dei said and shoved him. He glared at her, and dumped dirt down her shirt, and she growled and leaped at him. Soon Gloriae joined the fray, laughing as she tried to separate the two.

Benedictus watched the youths, and he smiled. It was so rare to hear Gloriae laugh.

"Her laughter is beautiful," he said to Lacrimosa. "Our daughters are beautiful."

He held his wife close. She leaned her head against his shoulder, and they sat watching the young ones, waiting for the griffins.

DIES IRAE

He hovered over his throne, wreathed in nightshades. They
flowed around him, through him, inside him. He could see
through their eyes, the multitudes of them that covered the land.
He saw the weredragons cowering outside the city, covered in
leaf and filth. He saw them peeking, whispering, fearing him.

"Let us fly to him, master." The nightshades hissed,
flowing into his ears.

Dies Irae shook his head. He patted the nightshade that
flowed by his right arm. "No, my pets, my lovelies. Let them fly
here. Let them crash upon my walls and towers."

The nightshades screeched, and he patted them, soothed
them, cooed to them.

"Let us fly to them, master," they begged. "Let us suck
their bodies dry."

Dies Irae shook his head. "They are like rats, my pets.
They run. They flee. They hide. If you chase them, they will
scurry into holes. Wait, my lovelies. They will come to me.
They will try to kill me; they've been trying for years. When they
fly to our city, we will be ready."

A knock came at the doors of his hall, and Dies Irae raised
his eyes.

"Ah," he said, "your dinner has arrived." He raised his
voice. "Enter my hall!"

The doors creaked open, and soldiers stepped in, clad in
mail and bearing axes. They dragged peasants on chains. Dies
Irae saw old women, young mothers holding babies, and a few
scrawny men. When they saw the nightshades, the peasants' eyes
widened, and a few whimpered. The nightshades screamed,
writhed, and licked their lips with tongues of smoke.

"The nightshades have destroyed your farms," Dies Irae
said to the peasants.

One of them, a young woman holding a boy's hand,
nodded. "Yes, my lord. They toppled our barn and their
screams wilted our crops. We have nothing now, my lord.
We're starving."

Dies Irae nodded sympathetically. "If you have no more farms, you are useless to me. You cannot grow my crops. You cannot pay my taxes."

Another peasant, a tall man with black stubble, stepped forward. "Please, my lord, we'll do any work. We'll serve you however we can."

Dies Irae smiled. "Exactly! You will serve me the way I demand. You will feed my nightshades. They shall feast upon your useless souls."

They cried. They screamed. They tried to flee. They fell, the nightshades upon them. The creatures of inky darkness swirled over their bodies, tossed them against the walls, bit into their flesh. The peasants thrashed, weeping. The nightshades sucked out their souls, and spat out their empty bodies onto the floor. Dies Irae sat on his throne, watching, a smile on his lips.

The nightshades crawled back to him, bloated, and coiled at his feet. Dies Irae patted them.

"Full, my lovelies? Good. Good. And soon you will enjoy your main course. Soon you will feed upon weredragons."

KYRIE

He walked with Agnus Dei between the bricks of a fallen fort. They walked alone, seeking supplies; the others had remained at camp.

It was, Kyrie realized, the first time he'd been alone with Agnus Dei since their fight in Requiem. He looked at her and his heart skipped a beat. She was scanning the ruins, eyes narrowed, lips scrunched. Her mane of curls bounced.

She's beautiful, Kyrie thought. *More beautiful than anything I've ever seen.*

She noticed him staring, frowned, and punched his shoulder. "What, pup?"

He put an arm around her waist, pulled her close, and kissed her cheek.

"Not now, pup!" she said, wriggling in his grasp. "We're on an important mission to find supplies."

"I know," he said, refusing to release her. "We really shouldn't."

He kissed her ear, then her cheek, then her lips. She struggled a moment longer, then placed her hands in his hair, and kissed him deeply. He held the small of her back, and whispered, "Do you know what else we're not allowed to do?"

She was breathing heavily, cheeks flushed. "What?"

"Shift into dragons."

She raised an eyebrow. "You can't be thinking...."

"Think it's possible?"

She gasped, but her eyes lit up. "You are one disturbed pup."

He nodded. "It would be horribly wrong, wouldn't it? In so many ways."

She clutched a fistful of his hair and stared at him, eyes fiery. Then she placed both hands against his chest, pushed him back, and shifted. She stood before him as a red dragon.

Kyrie shifted too. Blue dragon stared at red as they circled each other. She blew wisps of fire. Her scales clinked. Kyrie roared fire, and grabbed her, and she growled. Her scales were hot against him, and her claws dug into the earth. He clutched her shoulders, and pushed her down, and blew smoke. Bursts of flame fled her lips. Her wings flapped. His wings wrapped around her. Her tail pounded the dirt, and their necks pressed together. Smoke and fire enveloped them.

He pushed against her, again and again, and she moaned. Their scales rubbed together, chinking. Her wings flapped, but he held her down. Their smoke rose. Their tails lashed, knocking down trees. She tossed her head back, and a jet of flame left her maw. He dug his claws into her shoulders, and roared fire too. The ruins of the fort shook, and bricks rolled loose. Flames covered his world.

When he came to, they were lying on the ground, cuddling together as humans. Their clothes were singed and their faces ashy. Kyrie kissed her head.

"That was new," he said.

She nodded. "I like being a dragon."

He brushed a lock of hair off her face. "I love you, Agnus Dei. I'm so glad you forgave me. I'll always love you, and only you."

She punched his shoulder. "Oh, quiet, pup. I know you're madly in love with me. I always knew." She kissed his cheek. "Now let's get back to camp. Let's get this war over with, so we can do this again and again."

BENEDICTUS

Benedictus was teaching Kyrie to duel with swords when shrieks sounded above.

He and Kyrie, both panting, raised their eyes to the sky. They saw only the dead, snowy branches of trees. The sun was setting, burning red above the naked canopy.

"Those were griffin shrieks," Kyrie said, clutching his sword.

Lacrimosa and the twins were sitting by the stream, drawing maps of Confutatis in the dirt. They stood up and joined the men.

"They're here," Lacrimosa whispered, watching the skies.

Benedictus narrowed his eyes in the sunlight and saw them. He clutched the hilt of his sword. A thousand at least flew there, maybe two thousand. They darkened the eastern sky like a cloud.

Screeches sounded to the north.

"And those are nightshades," Benedictus said. "They've seen the griffins too."

He looked at the others, one by one. Lacrimosa stood with tightened lips, eyes staring back at him. Kyrie held his sword, eyes dark. Agnus Dei bared her teeth, and Gloriae stood expressionlessly, her hand on the hilt of her sword. Benedictus wanted to tell them that he loved them—all of them, even Kyrie. But today he would not be their father and husband. Today he would be their leader.

"Shift!" he said. "We fly. The battle begins."

The twins shifted first, becoming the red and golden dragons. Kyrie shifted only a second later, turning into a blue dragon. Lacrimosa gave Benedictus a last, deep look, then shifted into a silver dragon.

Benedictus nodded and shifted too, becoming the black dragon, and flew. He crashed between the branches and emerged into the sky. The others followed.

He saw the griffins clearly now. They flew from the east, shrieking, the thud of their wings like thunder. The sunset painted them red. When Benedictus looked north, he saw a thousand nightshades flying to meet them.

"We fight among griffins today!" Benedictus called over his shoulder.

The dragons flew toward the griffins, and Benedictus saw Volucris there, the King of Leonis, who had served as Dies Irae's mount. They met in the air, and stared into each other's eyes. The other dragons also took position among the griffins.

They turned to face the nightshades.

The creatures flew not a league away, moving fast. Their hissing rustled the dead grass and trees below. Their arms of inky smoke reached out, talons like shards of lightning.

Benedictus spoke to Volucris, not tearing his eyes away from the nightshades.

"These beasts work for Dies Irae. In the dungeons of his palace, he guards a weapon to defeat them. We must find that weapon."

Volucris nodded, screeched, and clawed the air. His eyes said to Benedictus, "We will find it."

Benedictus snarled. Only moons ago, he had fought Volucris above this city. Now they would fight here side by side.

The nightshades howled and lighting flashed between them. They were five hundred yards away now, eyes blazing.

"Dada, I love you," Agnus Dei said at his side. "I fight by you."

Kyrie nodded, roared, and blew fire. "Requiem flies again!" he called. "Hear the Black Fang's roar. King Benedictus has returned."

Benedictus roared too, and blew flames into the skies, and then the nightshades were upon them.

Benedictus swiped his claws, ripping through two nightshades. Another wrapped around him, and Benedictus felt it tugging, sucking his soul. He shook himself wildly, freed himself, and blew fire into its eyes. It screeched and fell back.

"To the city!" Benedictus shouted to the others. "We fly to Flammis Palace. We need those Beams."

Several griffins fell soulless to the ground. The others were ripping into nightshades with claws and talons. A few nightshades screamed in pain, and fell back, but did not die. Their inky bodies reformed, and they attacked again.

"To the city!"

They flew, the nightshades coiling around them, tugging at them, biting and clawing. The dragons blew fire, burning a path through their darkness. The nightshades were thicker than storm clouds, their eyes like stars, their claws and teeth everywhere. Darkness covered the sky.

From the corner of his eye, Benedictus saw three nightshades wrap around Lacrimosa. He flew at them, clawed their smoky bodies, and grabbed his wife. He pulled her free, and blew flame at the nightshades. They screeched, fell back, and Benedictus shook Lacrimosa. Her eyes opened. Her soul refilled her. She breathed fire.

"Come, Lacrimosa, to the city."

Kyrie and the twins were shooting fire in all directions. They were young and strong, their flames bright. The nightshades closed their eyes and screeched, blinded. The griffins did less damage, biting and clawing and tearing into nightshade smoke, but they were great in number, and clove a path forward. Many griffins kept falling, wrapped in nightshades, empty shells.

"Over the walls, into the city!"

They were approaching the city walls. Benedictus blew more fire—he was running low, but still had some in him—and cleared a passage between the mobbing nightshades. Soon the walls of Confutatis were beneath him.

But they flew too low. The nightshades would not let them fly higher; they covered the sky above. On the walls, the archers drew their bows.

"Kill the archers!" Benedictus shouted, but was too late. Hundreds of arrows flew. Benedictus swerved aside, but an arrow pierced his leg. Another cut through his wing, and he howled.

There's no ilbane on these arrows, he realized, but somehow that only chilled him. *Does ilbane ruin our taste for feesting nightshades?*

Those nightshades grinned; the arrows passed through them, doing them no harm. They attacked him, wrapping around him. Benedictus beat them off, flapping his wings to break their bodies. He felt them tug his soul, but he gritted his teeth, refusing to release it.

More arrows flew. Griffins screeched; a few fell dead. An arrow hit Kyrie's tail, and he roared.

"Stop those archers!" Benedictus cried. He blew flame at the walls. The archers caught fire. The other dragons blew fire too, clearing the wall of them. Griffins swarmed the city battlements, biting and clawing. The surviving archers drew swords and hacked at them.

Benedictus quickly surveyed the battle. Half the griffins had died. Cuts covered the Vir Requis. Lacrimosa flew with a wobble, and Kyrie's tail bled. The nightshades were unharmed; not one had died.

"To the palace!" Benedictus cried. "Hurry, we're being slaughtered. We need those Beams."

He hadn't much fire left. He blew weak flames, scattering the nightshades, and shot over the walls. The ruins of Confutatis spread below—toppled buildings, nightshades flowing through the streets, and soldiers at every corner. Crossbows fired, and quarrels hit Benedictus, knocking off scales. Griffins screeched and fell, thudding dead against streets and rooftops. Their blood splashed.

Benedictus saw the palace ahead, rising from a pile of rubble. Nightshades swarmed around it, forming a cocoon. One of its towers had collapsed. The rest of the palace seemed held with the inky smoke of nightshades. Their lightning crackled across the towers and walls, and their eyes streamed like comets.

Benedictus blew fire and swooped toward the palace. Arrows flew around him. They hit his chest, leg, and wing. Roaring, he ignored the pain, barrelling between nightshades, wreathed in fire, howling and biting.

Shouting, Kyrie flew at his side. His flames blazed, and his claws and fangs ripped through nightshades. Arrows clanged against him, shattering against his scales, nicking him, and he blew more fire. He swooped, scooped up archers as they reloaded, and tossed them against the parapets. The twins and Lacrimosa still flew above, wrapped in nightshades, biting and burning them.

Nightshades swarmed at the palace gates. Soldiers stood behind them, armed with pikes.

"Kyrie, the gates!" Benedictus called. "Fire!"

Kyrie nodded and blew flames at the nightshades and soldiers below. Benedictus added his own flames. The fire roared, and the soldiers below screamed. They fired crossbows and tossed javelins. Benedictus and Kyrie flew aside, dodging the missiles. Nightshades came flying at them.

Three nightshades wrapped around Benedictus. Three more grabbed Kyrie.

Darkness.

Stars swivelling.

Benedictus saw endless spaces, chambers like worlds, his soul ballooning, fleeing, flowing like night skies. Eyes burned there, and tar, and moons that fell beneath him.

Shrieks around him. Feathers. Beaks.

Griffin talons ripped smoke, and Benedictus saw his body there, an old black dragon, missing scales, scarred, bleeding. Nightshades wrapped around him, and griffins were clawing, trying to reach him, and talons grabbed his legs, and—

His body sucked his soul back in. He gasped. His eyes opened, and he saw the battle around him, the fire below, the nightshades that roared.

"Kyrie!" he called. The boy was fighting at his side. Lacrimosa and the twins swooped at him, clad in flame.

"We enter the gates!" he called to them.

He swooped, tearing into the soldiers below with his claws. They screamed, slammed at him with swords, and died between his teeth. He spat their bodies out, and drove his shoulder into the gates. They shattered, and Benedictus rolled into the palace.

He stood up to see a hundred charging soldiers. He blew fire, scattering them, and ran down the hall. He swiped his tail, knocking over several men, and bit another soldier in half.

Kyrie burst into the palace behind him, roaring fire. Blood flowed down his side, and his claws swiped, knocking over soldiers.

"Where are the others?" Benedictus asked, biting and clawing at swordsmen.

"Right behind you," came Gloriae's voice. She tumbled through the gates, a golden dragon. Agnus Dei and Lacrimosa followed.

Soon all the soldiers in the hall lay dead. Benedictus grunted; a sword had sliced his back leg. It hurt badly, and he limped. Ignoring the pain, he surveyed the others. Cuts covered them, but they were alive, panting, and awaiting his orders.

"Gloriae, do you know the way to the Well of Night and the Beams?"

She nodded. "The tunnels are narrow. We'll have to go in human form."

She shifted back into human. Blood and ash covered her, and her eyes were cold. She drew her sword, pulled down the visor of her helmet, and stepped toward a doorway. Agnus Dei and Kyrie shifted too, drew their swords, and joined her.

Benedictus looked at Lacrimosa. "Are you all right? We go underground. Are you ready?"

She looked at him, still in dragon form. Cuts covered her, and pain filled her eyes, but she nodded. "I'm ready. Let's go find those Beams. And then find Dies Irae."

Benedictus was about to shift when a voice spoke behind him.

"You have found me."

He turned slowly.

Wreathed in nightshades, his empty eye socket blazing, stood Dies Irae.

GLORIAE

She saw Dies Irae enter the hall, and their eyes locked.

"Father," she whispered, sword in hand.

But no. He was not her father anymore. She did not know if Dies Irae had fathered her when raping Lacrimosa, but she knew that he'd banished her. Hurt her. Lied to her. She snarled and raised her blade. She would kill him.

Dies Irae gave her a thin smile. She saw nightshade maggots in his empty eye socket, squirming, their tiny eyes blazing.

Then Benedictus blew fire at Dies Irae, encasing him with flame.

"Gloriae, get the Beams!" Benedictus shouted. "Take Agnus Dei and Kyrie. I'll hold him off. Go!"

Dies Irae laughed, the flames crackling around him. He raised his arms, collected the fire into a ball, and tossed it at Benedictus and Lacrimosa. The two dragons leaped back, howled, and charged.

Gloriae wanted to join the fight. She forced herself to turn away.

"Come, Kyrie! Come, Agnus Dei. We get the Beams. That's the only thing that can stop Irae now."

As she raced into a narrow hall, she thought, *I only pray that Benedictus and Lacrimosa can hold him off long enough.*

She raced down the hallway. Agnus Dei and Kyrie ran at her sides, swords drawn. Five soldiers charged at them, brandishing blades. Gloriae ran at them, screaming, Per Ignem in her right hand, a dagger in her left. She sidestepped, swung her sword, and cut one man open. A second soldier attacked at her left; she parried with her dagger, then stabbed her sword, impaling him. Agnus Dei and Kyrie swung their blades, and soon the five soldiers lay dead. The three Vir Requis leaped over their bodies and kept running down the hallway.

"In here," Gloriae said, opening a door. A stairwell led into darkness, lined with torches. She ran down the steps, Kyrie and Agnus Dei behind her. A soldier ran up from below.

Gloriae tossed her dagger and hit him in the throat. Not slowing down, she ran past him, pulled her dagger free, and kept racing downstairs.

The stairwell led into dank, dark tunnels. They twisted underground like the burrows of ants. Gloriae's sword and dagger flew, cutting down all in her path. Their blood washed the floor. The Vir Requis ran down narrower, steeper stairwells, delving into the world's belly.

Finally Gloriae reached a wide tunnel, its walls cut from solid rock. The Beams lay ahead, she knew. Last time she'd been here, a hundred men had guarded the place. Gloriae tightened her lips. She would shift. She would burn them. *And once I have the Beams, I will kill Dies Irae.*

She burst into the chamber. She saw the towering, iron doorways that protected the Well of Night. Three golden skulls were embedded into the doors, their sockets glowing. *The Beams.* The chamber was empty.

Gloriae skidded to a halt. Agnus Dei and Kyrie ran to her sides and stopped, panting. They held their bloodied blades high.

"A hundred soldiers once filled this chamber," Gloriae said, staring around with narrowed eyes. "The Well of Night, where we must seal the nightshades, lies behind those doors."

Agnus Dei struggled to catch her breath and said, "Those skulls. Are they the Beams?"

Gloriae nodded.

Agnus Dei made to run at them, but Gloriae held her back. "Wait. Something is wrong."

Kyrie nodded. "Everything is wrong. Benedictus and Lacrimosa need us! I'm getting the Beams."

He shoved past Gloriae and made a beeline to the doors.

Shadows scuttled on the ceiling.

"Kyrie, wait!" Gloriae shouted.

She looked up at the ceiling and froze. Her heart thrashed, and tears sprang into her eyes. No, it couldn't be. Couldn't! She clenched her teeth and her sword, and struggled not to faint.

Kyrie saw the creatures too. He froze and stared at the ceiling, the blood leaving his face. Agnus Dei looked up and let out a shrill cry.

"What the abyss are those?" Agnus Dei whispered.

"They are us," Gloriae whispered. "Molded at the hand of Dies Irae."

The three creatures scurried down the walls like spiders, and stood facing the Vir Requis. They were sewn together from old, rotting flesh. Limbs of bodies had been attached with strings and bolts. The limbs, heads, and torsos were mismatched; they came from different bodies. Blood and maggots covered the creatures, and their teeth were rotten. Their eyes blazed.

Two were female. One had long, matted, yellow hair that swarmed with worms. The other had dank, stinking black curls. A third creature was male, a youth of yellow hair, rotting flesh, and one leg that came from a goat.

The females looked like decaying versions of Gloriae and Agnus Dei. The male looked like Kyrie.

"Welcome, living sister," said the rotting Gloriae. She opened cracked, bleeding lips to reveal sharp teeth. Maggots rustled inside her mouth. "Welcome, Gloriae."

Gloriae screamed, nauseous.

"Shift!" she screamed. "Kill them!"

She tried to become a dragon, but the magic failed her. She strained, but remained human. She looked at Kyrie and Agnus Dei; they too were struggling to shift, but could not.

The creatures laughed. "Your curse will not work here, no, darlings. You are in our realm now. We are mimics. We love you. You will join us."

Gloriae screamed and charged toward the creatures. Kyrie and Agnus Dei screamed too, and attacked their rotting doppelgangers.

Gloriae's sword drove into her mimic's chest. Its blood spurted, black, foul. The creature laughed, maggots spilling from its mouth. It dug its claws into Gloriae's shoulders, and Gloriae screamed. Poison covered those claws; they sizzled and steamed.

She pulled Per Ignem back and swung it. The blade sank into the creature's neck, and worms fled the wound, squirming up the blade onto Gloriae's hand.

She screamed, shook the worms off, and kicked. Her mimic caught her foot and twisted, and Gloriae fell.

Her mimic fell upon her and bit Gloriae's shoulder. She screamed. The creature's stench nearly made her faint. She kicked and struggled, and managed to punch her mimic's face. Her fist drove into the soft, rotting head, spilling blood and cockroaches. The creature laughed, and its claws clutched Gloriae's chest.

"You will be one of us soon," it hissed. "We will take you apart, and stuff you, and put you together again. Then we'll be together. Then I'll be with you always, Gloriae." Its bloated, white tongue left its mouth and licked Gloriae's cheek.

Gloriae kicked its belly. It grunted, and she grabbed its head and twisted. The neck, already cut from her sword, tore. The head came off, and Gloriae tossed it aside. She pushed the creature's body off her, rose to her feet, and stared down at it.

The body writhed, claws scratching. The head laughed in the corner, spurting blood. Gloriae drove Per Ignem into the torso, again and again, but it would not die.

She ran to the wall and grabbed a torch. The torso came crawling toward her, and she tossed the torch onto it.

It caught flame. The head, several yards away, also caught fire. It screamed horribly. The bugs inside it screeched too, burning. Smoke rose, and the stench nearly made Gloriae pass out.

She looked and saw that Kyrie and Agnus Dei still fought their own mimics.

"Burn them!" she cried. She grabbed another torch and tossed it at the rotting Kyrie mimic. It caught fire, screamed, and fell. She tossed a third torch at the final mimic, the maggoty Agnus Dei, and it too burned. The mimics twisted on the floor.

"It burns!" they hissed. "Why do they burn us? Why do our mothers hate us? Oh, they burn their children. How it hurts! You will burn with us soon. You murdered your children." Smoke and fire rose from them. "You will burn with us in the abyss."

Gloriae helped Agnus Dei to her feet. She had fallen, tears on her cheeks. Kyrie walked toward them, fingers trembling, eyes haunted. The three watched the mimics burn, until they were nothing but piles of ash.

Gloriae stared, eyes dry. Then she tightened her jaw and pointed at the Beams. The golden skulls seemed to stare at her, lights flickering inside their eye sockets.

"Help me pry those from the walls," she said. "We go kill nightshades."

BENEDICTUS

Dies Irae's arm swung. Nightshade smoke flowed from it,
slamming into Benedictus. His scales cracked. He flew, hit a
column, and fell to the floor. Marble tiles cracked beneath him.

Dies Irae stepped toward him, the nightshades swirling
around him.

"My my, brother, you seem to have fallen," Dies Irae said.
Veins flowed across his face, blue and pulsing. The nightshade
maggots squealed in his eye socket.

Lacrimosa flew at him, screaming, her talons glinting.
Dies Irae waved his arm, and the blow knocked her against the
ceiling. Bricks showered down. Lacrimosa fell, hit the floor, and
whimpered. Blood covered her scales. Dies Irae laughed.

"Damn you, Irae," Benedictus growled. The sight of his
wounded wife blazed in his eyes, drowning his pain. He pushed
himself up, his wounds aching. His eyes burned, and blood
dripped into them. He could barely see, but blew fire. Dies Irae
waved his arm, and the flames flew around him. Tapestries
caught fire. They crackled, and black smoke filled the hall.

"Damn me, brother?" Dies Irae asked. "I am already
damned. My daughter Gloriae damned me, infested me with
these creatures. But I am powerful now, brother. More
powerful than you ever knew me."

Dies Irae swung his left arm, the mace arm. The steel hit
Benedictus's chest and knocked him down. Pain exploded. He
saw only white light, then stars over blackness. He flicked his
tail, and felt it slam into Dies Irae, doing him no harm.

Outside, Benedictus heard the griffins and nightshades.
The griffins were shrieking in pain. The nightshades laughed.
Benedictus blinked, and he could see again. He saw a window.
Outside the griffins were falling from the sky.

"Yes, Benedictus," Dies Irae said. "They are dying for you.
Once more, you've led thousands to die under your banners."

No, Benedictus thought. He could not allow another
Lanburg Fields. He could not let Dies Irae win again.

"You murdered our father," he said, mouth bloody, and struggled to his feet. "You murdered millions. I hold you to justice now."

Dies Irae laughed again and swung his mace. Light and pain burst. Benedictus fell onto his back, cracking more tiles. He smelled his blood.

"Ben!" came Lacrimosa's cry, a world away, hazy, echoing. A streak of silver flew. Lacrimosa, a dragon of moonlight, leaped at Dies Irae. He slammed his mace into her, nightshades swirling around it. The blow tossed Lacrimosa across the hall. She hit a column, cracked it, and fell. She moaned, her eyes closed, and she hit the floor. Blood flowed from her head.

"Lacrimosa!" Benedictus cried. Tears filled his eyes. Was she dead? The blood dripping from her head horrified him, yanked his heart, pulsed through his veins. He tried to run to her. Dies Irae, still laughing, lashed his arms. Nightshades flew from them, knocking into Benedictus, tossing him against the floor.

Benedictus lay, bloodied, aching, tears in his eyes.

"Lacrimosa...," he whispered and struggled to his knees.

Dies Irae stood above him. "Lacrimosa," he said. "That is her name. That is the name I called as I raped her. She was only fifteen, did you know? I hurt her then, Benedictus. I hurt her badly. She bled and wept, and—"

Screaming hoarsely, Benedictus charged forward. Dies Irae swung his mace into Benedictus's head.

Light.

Pain.

Benedictus hit the floor.

The pain shattered his magic, returning him to human form. He lay bloodied and moaning.

"So sad, Benedictus," came Dies Irae's voice. "You've fought for so long... only to die now. Your daughters have died too. They seek the Beams. Yes, Benedictus. I know of your plans. I have known for many days, and have been waiting for you. I have placed a horror to guard the Beams, a horror I crafted especially for your children."

Benedictus struggled to rise. Dies Irae placed a boot upon his neck, pinning him down, that boot made of Vir Requis scales.

"They won't die so easily," Benedictus managed to say.

Dies Irae pushed his foot down, constricting Benedictus. He could no longer speak, could barely breathe. "Oh, they are dead already, dear Benedictus the Black. Rest assured, too, that they suffered greatly before dying. My special pets made sure of that. Your wife too is dead."

Benedictus could just make out Lacrimosa's form. She was human again—which meant she was dead, or badly wounded. She lay in blood, unmoving. Benedictus wanted to call her, to tell her of his love one last time, but Dies Irae's boot suffocated him.

Benedictus drew a dagger from his belt. Dies Irae's boot left his neck and stepped on his wrist. The dagger fell.

Benedictus took ragged breaths.

"Why, brother?" he managed to say. "Why? Gloriae, whom you loved, is Vir Requis. You too are Vir Requis, you—"

"I am no such creature!" Dies Irae screeched. His voice was inhuman, impossibly high-pitched and loud. Stained glass windows shattered across the hall. Dies Irae's face burned with green light, and the nightshades swirled around him, lifting him two feet in the air. "You are cursed. You are wretched. You are weredragon. I am pure, a being of light."

Benedictus struggled to his knees. Dies Irae kicked him down.

"No, Benedictus. You stay on the floor. You are a serpent. Serpents crawl in the dust." He raised his steel arm. "Do you see this deformity? You bit off my real arm. Do you remember, brother? Do you remember Lanburg Fields?" He cackled. "When you bit off my arm, did you ever imagine I would grow another one? A steel one that would kill you? Yes. You will die now, creature."

Benedictus looked into his brother's eye—one eye now an empty socket rustling with nightshades, the other bright blue and milky.

"Our father loved you, Di," he said.

Dies Irae froze. Di. His childhood nickname. The name their parents used to call him. The name Benedictus himself would use when the two were children.

Dies Irae stared down, face frozen. "What did you call me?" he whispered.

Benedictus lay at his feet, blood seeping, pain throbbing. "He... he could not give you the Oak Throne, brother. I know he hurt you. He did not know. He did not realize your pain. He loved you, Di. Our father loved you more than life. More than Requiem. He—"

Dies Irae trembled. His chest rose and fell like a hare's heart, thrashing. His voice was nothing but a whisper. A frightened whisper. The voice of a child. "What did you call me?"

Benedictus pushed himself to his knees. "We used to play in the temple, do you remember? The priests had left a chandelier there, out between the trees. We took the crystals from it, and pretended they were jewels, that we were rich. Us, the princes of Requiem, playing with fake jewels, when we could have a thousand real ones! Yet these were somehow more valuable; childhood's joy lit them." Now his own voice trembled, and tears filled his eyes. "Do you remember? Do you remember the trees, and the crystals? You are my brother, Di. I loved you. I don't know you now. But you can come back. You can remember. You can—"

Dies Irae kicked him. Benedictus doubled over, coughing.

"Silence!" Dies Irae screamed, "I do not remember. That boy is dead. Gone!" His voice was like a swarm of wasps. "There is power now, and light and darkness across the world. That is who I am. I am a god, Benedictus. I am a god of wrath. You are a worm. You die. You die groveling at my feet."

Black tears flowed down Dies Irae's cheeks. His veins pulsed, darkness swarming within them. Teeth bared, his good eye wild, Dies Irae raised his mace over Benedictus's head.

KYRIE ELEISON

Embedded into the doors, the three golden skulls stared with glowing orbits. When Kyrie reached toward one, its glow brightened, and its jaw moved. Its glow was the glow of Loomers, blue and white and warm.

Kyrie wasn't sure how he'd pry the skull from the door. It was embedded deep into the iron. When he touched the skull, however, it clanked and fell into his hands. Its glow brightened, nearly blinding him, and a hum came from its jaw, a sound like spinning Loomers.

Kyrie turned to the twins, the Beam in his hands. The light bathed the girls; they appeared angelic, ghostly, beings of starlight.

"It's warm," he said. "There are two more. One for each."

Gloriae sheathed her sword and took a second skull. It hummed in her hands. Its glow suffused her face and billowed her hair.

Agnus Dei took the third and last skull. Her hair too flew, she tightened her lips, and her eyes narrowed.

"How do we use them?" she asked.

Kyrie hefted the skull in his hands. "In *Mythic Creatures of the Gray Age*, the drawing shows a man holding them up. Rays of light shoot out and tame a nightshade."

He turned the skull in his hands, so that it faced a wall. He held it high, hoping rays of light would burst from the eye sockets and sear a hole through the stone. The skull still glowed, but there was no great, searing beam of light.

"Do we need to utter a spell?" Gloriae asked. "*Ancient Artifacts* said nothing about that."

Agnus Dei marched toward the tunnel they'd come from. "Father and Mother are in trouble. We'll figure it out on the fly. Come on."

Holding the skulls, the three ran up the tunnels and staircases. They sloshed through blood and leaped over the bodies of soldiers. It was a long climb, but eventually they emerged back overground. They entered a wide hall, its tapestries tattered, its walls bloody. Bodies, broken shields, and shattered blades covered the floor. Outside the windows, nightshades screeched, lighting flashed, and thunder rolled. Griffin bodies covered the ground.

"Benedictus and Lacrimosa are behind those doors," Kyrie said. *Stars, I hope they're still alive.* He began running toward the heavy oak doors.

A hiss rose, and a nightshade slithered from a shadowy corner. It screeched and rushed at them.

Heart thrashing, Kyrie raised his Beam.

Light exploded. The sound cracked the walls. Beams of light shot from skull's eye sockets, drenching the hall. The world was nothing but white light, searing, blinding him. Kyrie nearly dropped the skull; his hands burned. He screamed, but heard nothing; the humming light overpowered all sound.

He could see the nightshade, wisps of bright gray in the light. It screeched. Its eyes burst into white fire. It struggled as if trying to flee, but seemed caught in the beams. It howled like a dying boar, hoarse, horrible. Walls shattered. It flipped onto its back, writhing, screaming.

Kyrie jerked the golden skull sideways. The beams from the orbits veered, tossing the nightshade against the wall. The bricks shattered. The nightshade wept. Kyrie had not imagined they could weep. He waved the skull again, and the beams tossed the nightshade into the corner. It lay there shivering, shrivelled up like a slug sprinkled with salt.

Agnus Dei too pointed her golden skull. More light blazed, spinning, screaming. Walls shattered. The nightshade's eyes melted. It howled. It begged them.

"Please," it cried, its voice like ripping flesh. "Please, mercy, please."

Gloriae raised the third golden skull. Beams shot from its orbits, and the nightshade burst into white flame. Smoke rose from it, it wept and shivered, and then collapsed into ash.

The Beams dimmed.

Color returned to the world.

The sound died.

The skulls vibrated gently, and once more, their eye sockets glowed a delicate, moonlight glow.

"Well," Kyrie said, "that sure beats dragonfire."

For a moment silence blanketed the world.

Then a thousand nightshades screeched outside, crashed into the hall, and swarmed around them.

Kyrie lifted the Beam, and it burst into light again. A nightshade swooped. Kyrie pointed the beams of light at it, and it screeched and flew back. More nightshades flew to his right. He spun the beams around, and they sliced through the nightshades. They screamed and curled into the corner like halved worms.

The twins were also spinning their Beams. The light seared the world, and nightshades screamed. Once caught in the light, they could not escape. They sizzled, trapped, weeping and begging for mercy in beastly grunts. Kyrie swung his Beam like swinging a club, tossing the nightshades aside.

"Don't bother killing them now!" he shouted over the roaring Beams and dying nightshades. "Knock them aside. We must reach Benedictus and Lacrimosa. They're behind those doors. They need us."

He began plowing forward, step by step, knocking nightshades aside. They screamed and fizzed and shrivelled up around him.

"Agnus Dei, beside me!" he shouted. "Gloriae, watch my back."

He could barely hear himself, but the twins seemed to hear him. Agnus Dei stood to his left, Gloriae to his right; both swung their Beams forward and backwards. They formed a sun, casting light to all sides. His golden skull trembled so violently, Kyrie clung with all his strength. For every step, he battled a dozen nightshades. Their screams and smoke filled the hall.

It seemed ages, but finally Kyrie reached the doors.

"Stars, please," he prayed as he kicked the doors open. "Let Benedictus and Lacrimosa still live."

The Beams drenched the hall beyond the doors. Agnus Dei and Gloriae behind him, he stepped through.

Kyrie's belly went cold.

The room was a mess. The columns were smashed, a wall was knocked down, the tiles on the floor were cracked. Blood covered the floor.

"Where are they?" Agnus Dei shouted. The Beams still rattled and hummed. The nightshades crowded at the doorway behind, but Gloriae held them back with her Beam.

Kyrie stared. There was a stain of blood below a cracked column. Lacrimosa's bluebell pendant lay there, its chain torn. Kyrie lifted it.

"Lacrimosa was hurt here," he whispered.

He moved down the hall. By another stain of blood, he found black scales and a fallen dagger. Kyrie could hardly breathe. The horror pulsed through him, spinning his head.

"Benedictus was hurt here. This is his dagger."

He looked up at the sisters. Both stood with Beams in hands, holding back the nightshades. Both stared at him with wide eyes.

"Are they dead?" Agnus Dei whispered. Her voice trembled, and tears filled her eyes.

Kyrie looked at bloodied footprints. They led from the hall out the doors, into the city.

"Those are Irae's prints," Kyrie said. "They're too large to be Lacrimosa's, and Benedictus has flat boots; these are heeled." A nightshade swooped through the window, and Kyrie tossed it aside, searing it with his Beam. He spoke with a quivering voice. "Dies Irae hurt them. He took them from here."

"Where?" Agnus Dei demanded. "Where did he take them? Are they dead?" She trembled. Nightshades screeched and fell around her.

Gloriae tightened her jaw and began marching toward the palace doors. Nightshades fell and sizzled around her. She looked over her shoulder.

"Follow me," she said. "I know Dies Irae. I know where he took them."

She left the palace and ran down the shattered streets between dead men and griffins. Nightshades covered the skies, howling under the Beams.

Kyrie and Agnus Dei ran behind her, waving their Beams at the walls of attacking nightshades, clearing a way between them.

"Where?" Kyrie demanded, boots sloshing through griffin blood.

Gloriae looked at him, her eyes blank. Her face was pale.

"To his amphitheatre," she said. "He's putting them on trial."

LACRIMOSA

"Court is in session," screeched the voice.

But no, she thought. This was no *voice.* It was whistling steam, and steel scratching against steel, and demon screams—an inhuman cacophony that formed words. She convulsed at the sound. Lacrimosa tried to open her eyes, but darkness tugged her. Where was she?

"All hail Judge Irae!" spoke the voice, impossibly high pitched, a voice that could shatter glass. A thousand screeches answered the words, a sound like a thousand slaughtered boars.

Lacrimosa felt something clammy wrap around her. She felt herself lifted overground, and she moaned. Her head pounded. Her eyelids fluttered, and she finally managed to open her eyes.

She gasped.

Above her floated a figure from nightmares. It was Dies Irae, but more monstrous than she'd ever seen him. Nightshades wreathed him, holding him ten feet above her. He wore a judge's black robes and a wig of white, squirming snakes. He held a circle of jagged metal, Osanna's wheel of justice, its spikes cutting his hand. Storm clouds thundered above him.

"The trial of weredragons begins!" he cried, that sound like steam and metal leaving his mouth. The veins of his face pulsed, as if insects tunnelled through them. Pus and blood dripped from his empty eye socket. Nightshades screamed around him, holding him in the air, coiling around his legs, wrapping around his shoulders. He banged his left arm, the steel mace, against his breastplate. The sound rang out even over the screeches.

"Ben," Lacrimosa whispered.

She saw him across from Dies Irae. Nightshades wrapped around him, holding him upright. Blood dripped from his mouth and leg, and his left eye was swelling, but he lived. He saw her. He tried to speak, but nightshade tendrils covered his mouth. Lacrimosa tried to reach out to him, then realized that nightshades wreathed her too. They pinned her arms to her sides, and held her an inch above the ground.

Dies Irae laughed above them, his wig of snakes hissing. "Here, in this arena, before this crowd, we shall judge the weredragons for their crimes against mankind."

Lacrimosa looked around her, and saw that they stood in the amphitheatre, the same place where Dies Irae had once unleashed beasts upon her. All around, upon the rows of seats, nightshades slithered and grunted and watched the trial. Lightning crackled between them.

"Benedictus," Lacrimosa said again, pleading, and tried to reach out to him. She couldn't free her arms from the nightshades that encased her. One nightshade licked her cheek with an icy, smoky tongue. She shivered.

Dies Irae slammed his mace against his breastplate again. "Silence in the court! Today we judge Benedictus and Lacrimosa, the Lord and Lady of Lizards." His voice was howling winds, raising his words' last syllables into screeches. Clouds thundered and crackled above him. The snakes on his head hissed.

"Dies Irae!" Lacrimosa called, finding her voice. "Cease this mockery of justice. You only mock yourself."

"Silence her!" he screeched, an electrical sound rising into a crackle.

The nightshades covered her mouth, and she shouted into them, but no sound escaped. Dies Irae cackled. He unrolled a scroll and read from it.

"Your crimes, Lizards! I shall read you your crimes. You are charged, verily, of burning alive the children of this city, and eating them, and roasting them, and biting into their innards to suck upon them." He laughed hysterically. Nightshade maggots filled his mouth. "How do you plead, Lizards?"

Benedictus managed to free his head from the nightshades cocooning him. "Dies Irae, you are no judge. Stop this show."

Dies Irae slammed his mace again. "Silence in my court! Silence, I say. Bring forth the children." His voice was a tornado, buzzing with electricity. His 'r's rolled like a rod dragged against cage bars. "Bring forth the victims."

The nightshades across the amphitheatre—there were thousands—squealed. Three swooped from the high tiers to the dusty arena. They carried burned, bloodied bodies in their smoky arms. They tossed the bodies at Dies Irae's feet.

Lacrimosa looked away too late. The image seared her. Three children, burned and twisted, black and red. Who had done this? Had Dies Irae murdered these children as mock evidence for his mock trial?

He was fully mad now, Lacrimosa realized. He knew not fantasy from reality. The nightshades had festered in his brain and broken it. Did he truly believe she and Benedictus had burned these children?

"I find you guilty!" Dies Irae cried. The nightshades lifted him higher. Lightning crackled around him, and the snakes on his head screamed.

"Dies Ira—" Benedictus began, but the howls of nightshades and the booming thunder overpowered his words.

Dies Irae floated upon the nightshades ten feet back, and approached a structure hidden beneath a black curtain. *What horror lies there?* Lacrimosa thought. What more could Dies Irae reveal to still shock her?

Dies Irae ripped off the curtain, and Lacrimosa wept.

It looked like a gallows heavy with bodies. But these bodies were not hanged. They were gutted, bled, and hung on meat hooks. Some bodies were but children. A makeshift butcher shop for humans.

"Behold!" Dies Irae cried. "The weredragons have prepared these bodies to feast upon them. They stole our women, our youths, our children. They butchered them. They planned to eat them. They dined upon them in their halls of scales and flame."

Lacrimosa lowered her head, shut her eyes, and wept. How could such horror exist? How could such evil fill a man? How could a human, for Dies Irae had been human once, sink into such insanity? She shivered. All she had ever wanted, ever fought for, was the song of harps, a life of peace, of leaves and earth and sunlight and stars. How had she come to here, this trial, this stench of blood and fire?

"Ben," she whispered. She would die here, she knew. Close to him, but unable to hug him, to kiss him one last time. The nightshades tightened around her, and she opened her eyes, and looked to Benedictus.

Their eyes met.

"I love you," she whispered to him. He mouthed the same words back to her.

Nightshades flowed into her mouth, but she kept her eyes on her husband. *I wanted to grow old with you. To watch our children get married, have children of their own. That's all I ever wanted. But we end here in pain and horror.*

"I find you," Dies Irae said, "guilty. Guilty! Guilty as charged!"

He banged his mace against his breastplate, and the nightshades howled as if cheering. Winds flowed among them, and the clouds roiled.

Dies Irae kept reading from his scroll. He read of the earthquakes they caused, of the temples they toppled, of the illnesses they spread. He shouted about how they destroyed the world, and stole the souls of millions. As he read, he laughed and screamed.

"Guilty! Guilty to everything!"

Finally he tossed the scroll aside, and pulled a sword from his robes. It was a black sword, raising smoke, a jagged sword that sucked in all light.

"Behold the sword of the executioner," he said, and held it aloft, presenting it to the crowd of nightshades. "Behold the bright blade of justice."

Benedictus was struggling against the nightshades. His face was red. He was trying to shift; Lacrimosa saw scales appear and vanish across him. The nightshades were crushing him.

She saw her husband, and she heard the birches rustle. She could see them again, wisps of golden leaves, and harpists between them, and columns of marble. She saw Benedictus in green and gold, and she walked with him arm in arm, as dragons glided above through blue skies. Tears streamed down her cheeks, and she clung to that memory, those ghosts of a land destroyed and burned. She would die with those memories, that love of her home, that love of Requiem.

"Goodbye, Benedictus," she whispered. "Goodbye, Requiem. May our wings forever find your sky."

Wreathed in nightshades, Dies Irae floated above Benedictus.

"Now, in this arena...," Dies Irae said, speaking slowly, theatrically, savoring every word. "Now, we carry out the punishment. Death. Death. Death!"

Silence fell.

The thousands of nightshades leaned forward, licked their lips, and stared.

The clouds ceased to grumble.

Dies Irae smiled a small, thin smile.

"Death," he whispered.

He raised his sword above Benedictus.

Lacrimosa closed her eyes. She would not watch this. She would remember Benedictus among the birches, smiling and strong, her king. That was how he would remain forever in her memories.

Light fell on her eyelids, and she smiled as she wept, for it seemed to her that the light of Requiem's stars glowed upon her.

A buzz hummed, angelic in her ears, like the sound of dragon wings.

"I'll be with you in our starlit halls, Ben," she whispered. "I'll watch over you, Agnus Dei and Gloriae. I'll watch you from the stars, and be with you always."

"Mother!" they cried. "Mother!"

She smiled. The memories of their voices seemed so real.

"Mother, you're alive!"

Lacrimosa opened her eyes... and she saw them.

She shouted and wept.

"Agnus Dei! Gloriae! Kyrie!"

At first, Lacrimosa thought that she floated through the starlit halls, the spirit Requiem beyond the Draco constellation. White light washed the world, bleaching all color, banishing all shadow. But no. This was still the amphitheatre, now drenched in light. Three dragons were flying toward the amphitheatre. Gloriae. Agnus Dei. Kyrie. They held the Beams in their claws. Lacrimosa knew they were the Beams; great light burst from them, spinning and singing. The world hummed and glowed.

The Beams' light hit the edge of the amphitheatre. The nightshades there, upon the top tiers, screeched and writhed. They turned sickly gray and thin in the light, and their screams shook the amphitheatre. Cracks ran along the stones.

"It's over, Dies Irae," Benedictus shouted over the shrieking nightshades and humming Beams, his voice almost lost. "We have the Beams. It's over."

A nightshade still wreathed him, but it was hissing and squirming. The nightshade holding Lacrimosa spun around her, grunting. The Beams did not shine on them directly, but the light still burned them.

"Mother!" Agnus Dei cried above. She, Gloriae, and Kyrie had almost reached the amphitheatre now. The Beams' rays were moving down the rows of seats, like light through a temple window travelling across a floor.

"When the light reaches you, you're dead, Irae!" Lacrimosa screamed. "You've filled yourself with nightshades, and now you're going to burn."

Dies Irae was staring at the dragons. The nightshades around him squirmed and grunted and screeched. The snakes of his wig blistered, then burst. His good eye blazed, and his skin seemed stretched nearly to ripping. The beams had moved down the tiers of seats, leaving seared, dead nightshades. They were now travelling across the arena floor, stirring the dust. The beams were a hundred feet away, then fifty, then ten, then five....

Dies Irae screamed. An inhuman scream. The defeated cry of a demon.

He turned to stare at Lacrimosa, his good eye burning, his empty eye socket gaping.

"We will meet again, Lacrimosa," he said.

Then he turned and stabbed Benedictus through the chest.

"Ben!" Lacrimosa screamed.

"Father!" came a cry above.

"Ben! Ben!"

The nightshades wrapped around Benedictus burned and fled. The nightshades around Lacrimosa smoked and flew from her. She fell to her knees, weeping.

"Ben!"

She saw Dies Irae open a trapdoor in the arena floor, that door tigers, bulls, and other beasts would once emerge from. He disappeared into the tunnels. Lacrimosa rose to her feet, ran to her husband, and knelt by him. She held him.

"My love." Tears streamed down her cheeks.

He lay in her arms, the sword buried to the hilt in his chest. He looked upon her with glassy eyes, and a soft smile touched his lips.

"L— Lacrimosa," he whispered, blood in his mouth.

The beams washed them. Nightshades screamed and flew around them. Lacrimosa clutched her husband, touched his cheeks, wept into his hair.

"Please. Don't leave me."

He held her hand. "Watch over the young ones," he whispered. "I love you, Lacrimosa, daughter of Requiem."

Sobs shook her body. She embraced him. "I love you forever, my lord."

When his head fell back, and his eyes stopped blinking, Lacrimosa raised her head and howled, a dragon's howl, a cry she thought could rend the heavens. She did not know how much time passed. Nightshades screamed. Beams blazed. There was a great battle. Lacrimosa was aware of nothing but her husband. She cradled his body in her arms.

It seemed that ages passed, the turns of seasons and the reigns of kings, as she held her husband, until the nightshades fled the world and only soft light washed her.

Still holding her king, Lacrimosa looked up. In the soft light she saw her daughters approach, walking in human forms, their steps slow. Kyrie walked behind them, bathed in dying light.

The Beams dimmed.

Darkness covered the world.

Agnus Dei saw her father, and she let out a cry like a wounded animal. She ran forward and knelt by his body, weeping. She held his hand, saw that he was dead, and cried to the sky.

Gloriae stared, face pale, silent. Her mouth was open, her eyes confused, shocked, her hands open.

Kyrie fell to his knees by his king, and shook him, and cried his name. Tears streamed down his cheeks.

"Dada!" Agnus Dei cried through her sobs. Lacrimosa held her, desperate, digging her fingers into her shoulders. Kyrie embraced them. Gloriae knelt by them, looking around, dazed. They wept as one, trembling, their tears joining, falling upon the body of Benedictus.

"My king," Lacrimosa whispered to him. "My husband. My love."

"Dada," Agnus Dei whispered, running her hands over his face.

Lacrimosa kept waiting for Benedictus to open his eyes, to cough, to wake up, to hold her. She kept checking his breath, again and again, finding it gone, his life fled from her forever.

Eyes blurred, she saw Volucris lead the surviving griffins into the arena. *So few remain.* Blood covered them. The beasts saw her holding Benedictus, tossed their heads back, and cried in mourning. Their shrieks thudded against her ears, and Lacrimosa sobbed and held her husband.

Arrows flew. They clattered against the ground around them. Lacrimosa looked up, and through her tears, she saw soldiers streaming into the arena. They fired arrows and drew swords.

Agnus Dei and Kyrie howled, shifted, and blew fire. Gloriae and Lacrimosa soon joined them. Flames filled the arena that night, and blood washed it, and dozens of soldiers died by fang and claw. But many more soldiers streamed in, a city full of them, and Lacrimosa knew they could not win this fight.

She lifted Benedictus's body in her claws. He seemed so small, so light. She flew with him, the arrows whistling around her, until she was out of their range. Her daughters and Kyrie flew at her sides, tears flowing down their cheeks.

The Vir Requis fled the city, and flew over burned fields, over toppled farmhouses, over wilted forests, over the ruins of the world. No more nightshades flew here. Their darkness was gone, but the darkness of Lacrimosa's world seemed greater than ever, and she did not think any light could banish it. The light of her life had been doused.

The dragons flew into dawn, into night, into dawn again. Their wings scattered clouds, their roars pierced the sky, and the tears of Requiem fell as rain upon a ruined world.

The world, Lacrimosa knew, could no longer be mended. Not for her. Not for her children. Never more for Requiem and her life.

King Benedictus had fallen.

AGNUS DEI

They buried her father in the ruins of Requiem.

She stood above the grave, wrapped in her cloak. Snow fell. It filled her hair, turned her black cloak white, and covered the shattered statues, columns, and memories. The snowflakes glided, swirled in the breeze, and stung her cheeks. The world glittered under a soft sun.

"Requiem is beautiful again, Dada," she whispered.

Her tears fell, and she knelt in the snow, and placed a lock of her hair upon his grave. A ribbon held the strand, bright red, a single piece of color in a white world. Her tears made holes in the snow.

She straightened and stared at the grave. They did not bury him among kings; those mausoleums were gone now. Agnus Dei buried her father in a graveyard of soldiers, so he would rest forever in the company of bravery, and sacrifice, and other men of sword and fang.

"You were a hero to your men," she whispered, and a sob shook her. "A leader. A great king. You were a father to them too. You were a father to us all. Goodbye, Dada."

It seemed unreal, but a dream. How could he be gone? How could she carry on without him? How could she find strength within her to continue this war? Father had always known what to do, where to go, how to fight. How could she live without his wisdom, his strength, and his love? Anguish clutched her, so that she could not breathe.

With trembling fingers, Agnus Dei clutched the hilt of her sword. "I swear to you, Dada. I will rebuild Requiem. I will rebuild our home. I will continue to walk in your path, and not stray from it to the left or right. I love you, Dada. Forever."

She backed away from the grave, tears on her cheeks, snow on her lips. Her mother embraced her, and Agnus Dei buried her face against her shoulder. They wept together, trembling.

Gloriae stood by them, staring at the grave, eyes wide, disbelieving. She had not spoken since leaving Confutatis. She kept looking from the grave, to Agnus Dei, to Lacrimosa, and back to the grave. Finally a sob fled her lips, and tears sprouted from her eyes.

"Mother," Gloriae whispered and joined the embrace.

Kyrie stood, face hard, tears on his cheeks. He stared at the grave, lips moving silently. Agnus Dei left her mother, and clutched him, and wept against him. He held her, gently at first, then desperately.

"I'm going to look after you," Kyrie whispered. His tears fell. "I don't know how to carry on without him. He was my king, my compass. I don't know how to fight this war without Benedictus. But I promise you, Agnus Dei. However I can, I will look after you, and Gloriae, and Lacrimosa. You have my word. You have me forever."

"Oh, Kyrie," she said, and clung to him, her tears on his shoulder. Her heart seemed like a ball of twine, too tight, and she trembled.

She left Kyrie's embrace, and took a step back, and shifted into a dragon. She knelt before the grave, and tossed her head back, and blew flame. The column of fire rose into the snowy sky, spinning and crackling.

The others became dragons too. They stood in a ring, tears on their cheeks. They blew four pillars of fire, a farewell of sound and heat and light... for one fire extinguished.

BOOK THREE:
LIGHT OF REQUIEM

TEETH

The three boys swaggered down the streets, arms pumping, eyes daring beggars, urchins, and other survivors to stare back. The dragons had left this city; so had the nightshades. In the ruins after the war, new lords arose. The Rot Gang ruled now.

"Slim pickings today," said Arms. The wiry, toothless boy was seventeen. He crossed the arms he was named for—arms long and hairy as an ape's. "We've been searching this cesspool all morning. These streets are clean."

Teeth glowered at him. "Shut your mouth, Arms," he said. With a long, loud noise like a saw, he hawked and spat. The glob landed at Arms's feet and bubbled.

Arms glowered back, spat too, and muttered.

The third Rot Gang boy—a gangly youth named Legs—watched and smirked. Drool dripped from his heavy lips. He towered seven feet tall, most of his height in his stilt-like legs. He was dumb, even dumber than Arms, and useless in a fight. Teeth kept him around because, well, Legs made him look normal. *So what if my teeth are pointed like an animal's? Around Legs, nobody notices.*

"You like that, freak?" Teeth asked him. "You like me yelling at old Arms here?"

Legs guffawed, drooled, and scratched his head. He had a proper name, though Teeth didn't know it. He didn't care. Freaks didn't deserve proper names.

"Yeah I like Arms angry, I do," said Legs. "Makes me laugh, his little eyes, all buggy like so." He brayed laughter.

Arms turned red. His eyes did bulge when angry. He trundled toward Legs and punched his face. The lanky boy screamed. Tears welled up in his eyes. He swiped at Arms, but the wiry youth dodged the blow.

Teeth spat again. "Useless in a fight, you freak," he said to Legs. "I don't know why I keep you around. Come on, break it up! You want to eat tonight? Let's keep looking. You too, Arms. There are bodies left in this city. We'll find them. And if we can't, we'll make our own."

Legs was crying and Arms muttering. Teeth snarled, pushed them forward, and the Rot Gang kept moving down the street. Blood dripped from Legs's nose, leaving a trail of red dots.

Confutatis lay in ruins. Fallen bricks, shattered statues, and broken arrows covered the city. The nightshades had done their work well; the dragons had finished it. You could go days without seeing a soldier, priest, or guard, but you always saw urchins. They huddled behind smashed statues, inside makeshift hovels, or simply under tattered blankets. When they saw the Rot Gang, they cowered and hid. Teeth smirked as he swaggered by the poor souls. On the first week after the dragons, when survivors were claiming their pockets of ruin, many children had challenged him, adults too. His sharpened teeth had bitten, severing fingers, ears, noses. One boy, he remembered, had tried to steal a chicken from him; Teeth had bashed his head with a rock, again and again, until he saw brains spill. The memory boiled his blood and stirred his loins. He missed killing.

Legs guffawed and pointed. "Hey boss, look here, you see them, little ones, hey." He snickered and wiped his nose, smearing blood and mucus across his face.

Teeth stared. He saw them. A gaggle of urchins—little girls, eight or nine years old by the look of them. They hid behind a fallen statue of Dies Irae. One cradled a dog in her arms. When they saw the Rot Gang, the girls froze. Then they began to flee.

"Catch them," Teeth commanded.

Arms and Legs took off, the former lumbering like an ape, the latter quick as a horse. Teeth stood and watched. Three girls disappeared into a maze of fallen columns. Arms hit one girl with a rock, knocking her down. Legs grabbed the girl with the dog.

"Bring her here," Teeth said.

The girl was kicking and screaming, but Legs held her tight. Arms approached with his own catch. He held his girl in his arms; she was unconscious, maybe dead.

"Let go, help, help!" The girl in Legs's grasp was panting, face red. Her dog shivered in her grasp.

Teeth stepped forward. He snatched the dog from the girl. He clutched it by the neck, squeezed, and held it out.

"You want your dog back, you little whore?" he said. His blood boiled. A smile twisted his lips. The mutt was squirming and squealing, but powerless to escape.

The girl nodded. "Give him back. Let go!"

Teeth slammed the dog against the ground. It whimpered. Teeth kicked it hard, and it flew toward Arms. The apelike boy laughed, and kicked it back, and blood splattered the cobblestones.

"Kick dog!" Legs said. "Kick dog, I want to play it."

The girl screamed and wept as they played. Finally Teeth grew bored. The dog was no longer squealing, and the game was no longer fun.

"Enough," he said. "We've come seeking bodies, not whiny little whores. Legs, let her go."

The gangly boy dropped the girl. Her knees hit the cobblestones, and her skin tore, but she seemed not to notice. She raced forward, lifted her dead dog, and cradled it.

Teeth laughed. "You idiot. The damn thing's dead. What kind of freak wants a dead dog for a pet?" He scratched his chin. "I wonder if Irae would pay for a dead dog."

Arms shook his head. "Nah. No way. You know Blood Wolves?"

Teeth glared at him. "You know I do. You know I hate Blood Wolves. You calling me an idiot, Arms? If that's what you're doing, I'll play some Kick Arms, and have a nice body to sell."

Legs laughed, spraying saliva. "Kick Arms, Kick Arms, I like to play it."

Arms picked his nose. "I ain't calling you nothing. Cool it, Teeth. But Blood Wolves, you see, they've been bringing dead dogs, and horses, and what not. I hear the soldiers speak of it. Even brought a whole dead griffin, they did, Sun God knows how they dragged it. Worth coppers at best, the dogs. A griffin might fetch gold, maybe, but not dogs and horses and all that rubbish. He needs limbs most, human limbs. Heads too. Men, you know. With brains and what not. That's how you make mimics, not dogs." He snatched the dead dog from the girl and tossed it. It flew over a pile of bricks, and the girl ran weeping to find it.

Teeth knew that Arms was right. Sometimes he saw mimics with animal parts—a horse's hoof here, a dog's head there—but they were rare. Human bodies were what the Rot Gang specialized in, but pickings *were* slim lately, other gangs were growing, and their pockets were light. Teeth knew it was a matter of time before they'd have to stop hunting bodies... and start making bodies.

But who *could* he kill? The urchins were too small, mere children with frail limbs; Dies Irae wouldn't pay much for them. And it seemed everybody else in this city had joined larger gangs, arming themselves with daggers, clubs, even swords. *And I only have one knife, an apelike oaf, and a skinny giant who'd piss himself in a fight sooner than kill a man.*

"All right, let's go, north quarter today. Lots of ruins there. Bodies underneath them, rotting maybe, but they'll still fetch some coin, good bronze too."

They continued through the winding streets, passing by fallen forts, crushed hovels, and cracked statues of Dies Irae. Old blood stained the cobblestones. The ash of nightshades, and the fire of dragons, had blackened the ruins. Teeth remembered the battle, not a moon ago. The five dragons had swooped upon the city, blowing fire. Benedictus the Black had led them, and he led griffins too. Nightshades had fought them, and Teeth had never seen so much fire and blood; it rained from the sky. The next day, as men lay rotting in the streets, Teeth had begun to collect.

Finally they reached the smaller, northern quarters, where there were barely streets anymore, merely piles of bricks and wood.

"Dig," Teeth barked at the other boys.

They climbed onto the piles of debris and began rummaging. Wind moaned around them, smelling of rot. Teeth cursed as he worked. If there were no bodies left in the city, there was no money either. He'd have to escape into the countryside like so many others.

I could become an outlaw... live in the forests, hunt travellers, grab plump peasant girls when I can find them. That didn't sound too bad, but Teeth knew little about the forest; he had spent his life on these streets.

I could join the Earthen too, if they're real, he thought. Folks whispered about the Earthen sometimes—wild Earth God followers who lived in caves. Some said they were building weapons, preparing for a strike against Dies Irae, the man who had toppled their temples and banned their faith. But Teeth didn't care much for gods or holy wars, no more than he cared for the wilderness. *This city is a cesspool, but it's all I know.*

The smell of decay hit his nostrils with a burst, so strong he nearly fell over. Teeth spat, dizzy. He pulled aside two bricks and saw a rotting head. He pulled it up by the hair; it came loose from its body. The head was pulsing with maggots, so bloated it looked like a leather sack. Teeth tossed it aside in disgust, and it burst.

"Bah! These bodies are useless now." He clenched his fists. "They're too old, too swollen, no good for anyone anymore. How would Irae sew these together? You just look at them, and they fall apart. Nothing left of them but rot."

Behind him, Arms brayed a laugh. "I tolds you, Teeth. I tolds you. We need to bring animals, dogs and what not, and those little girls maybe, they have teeth that can bite."

Teeth growled. He marched across the pile of bricks and grabbed Arms's collar. "Dogs? Little girls? I want silver, Arms. Gold if we can get it. Not copper pennies. I'm not a beggar like the Blood Wolves."

Arms stared, eyes burning. "I should join the Blood Wolves, I should. Look at you. This is your gang? A group of freaks. You with your dog teeth, and Legs with those stilts of his. It's pathetic, it is."

Legs guffawed and drooled. "Dog teeth, dog teeth! I like to see them."

Teeth growled, drew a knife from his belt, and held it at Arms's throat. Arms stiffened, and his eyes shot daggers.

"You don't like it here?" Teeth hissed. His stomach churned, and rage nearly blinded him. His hands shook, and his heart pounded. "You want to join the Blood Wolves?"

Arms snarled, the knife at his neck.

"Yes," he hissed.

Teeth swiped the knife across his throat. Blood spurted. For an instant, Arms seemed not to notice. He merely stared, eyes narrowed. Then he grabbed his throat, trying in vain to stop the blood. He fell to his knees, and suddenly he was weeping, and trying to speak, trying to breathe, but he could do neither.

Teeth stared down at him. "There's your blood, Arms. Blood's what you wanted. Blood's what you got. And I got my body. A body with nice long arms."

He could have given Arms a better death. He could have finished the job—stabbed him in the heart, or bashed in his head. But Teeth wanted to watch. He stood over the thrashing boy, until Arms merely twitched, stared up with pleading eyes, then gurgled and lay limp. For several moments he merely whimpered and his eyelids fluttered. And then Teeth had his body for the day.

The wind moaned as Teeth and Legs carried the body through the rubble. It cut through Teeth's clothes and pierced his skin. The blood was sticky on his fingers. The sun was setting when they saw Flammis Palace ahead. Two of its towers had collapsed, and several walls had crumbled. It wasn't much better off than the rest of the city, but Dies Irae still ruled there. His banners, white and gold, thudded atop the remaining towers. His guards covered the standing walls, bows in hands.

Teeth and Legs approached the front gates. The bricks were blackened from fire, and the doors were charred. The dragons had breathed most of their fire here when storming the palace. Guards stood at the gateway, clad in plate armor, swords in hands. Their skin looked sallow, and sacks hung beneath their bloodshot eyes. There wasn't much food in Confutatis anymore, and folk whispered that some of the guards had taken to eating the bodies. The stench of rot hung heavy here.

"New body for the Commander," Teeth told the guards. "Fresh, this one."

Legs nodded, holding Arms's other end. "Fresh, fresh! We like them that way. Yes sir we do."

The guards grunted. "All right, boys. Looks better than your last catch. In you go."

Teeth tugged the body, moving past the broken doors. Legs followed. They stepped into a hallway, its northern wall fallen. Bloodstains covered the floor and ash coated the ceiling. One column was smashed and stained red. Teeth knew the way. Hoisting the body, he turned left into a stairwell. The stairs wound into shadows. Torches lined the walls, but most were unlit. Teeth and Legs delved into the dungeons of Flammis Palace, the stairway leading them down and down into the cold and darkness. The palace was twice as deep as it was tall, and Teeth climbed down to its deepest chambers.

Screams, creaks, and squeals echoed through the tunnels. A man laughed. A saw grinded. Screeches rose and fell.

Teeth and Legs walked down a hallway, its floor sticky with blood, and entered a towering chamber. Torches lined the walls, flickering against rows of tables. Body parts covered the tabletops. Rows of legs covered one table, arms another, heads a third. A pile of torsos rotted in the corner. Uncarved bodies hung on walls and filled wheelbarrows.

Dies Irae stood at the back of the room.

Teeth froze. On previous visits, he had met underlings, not the Commander himself. He had not expected to meet Dies Irae here. Once emperor of a mighty realm, Dies Irae now ruled a wasteland of desolation, death, and disease. His skin was grey. Blood stained his clothes. He stood by a table, hunching over a rotten torso. Sleeves rolled back, he was gutting it.

Teeth cleared his throat, blinked, and tried to quell the shake that found his knees.

"Commander," he said. "We brought you a body. A fresh one, my lord."

Legs brayed. "Fresh, fresh, that's how we like them, yes sir we do."

Dies Irae looked up from his work. His one eye blazed blue. A patch covered his other eye. Teeth knew the story. Benedictus the weredragon had taken that eye from him, as he had taken Dies Irae's left arm; a steel arm grew there now, its fist a spiked mace head.

"A fresh one?" Dies Irae asked. His voice was hoarse. Wrinkles creased his brow. "Yes. Yes, very fresh."

Teeth and Legs placed the body on a table. Teeth stifled a cough, struggling not to gag from the chamber's stench. Maggots were crawling on some of the bodies. Worms filled others.

"A fresh body, and look at its arms," Teeth said. "Look at how long they are, my lord. Long and strong, like an ape's. This one's worth two silver coins, one per arm at least, my lord. A good body. Strong and fresh."

Dies Irae examined the dead body, furrowed his brow, and touched those long arms. He smiled, his lips twisting like worms. "Yes. Yes, strong. Fresh."

Teeth didn't like this. He wanted to leave. On previous visits, underlings would examine his finds, mutter, and pay. But Dies Irae seemed... too quiet, lost in his own worlds. Teeth noticed that specks of blood covered the man's lips. He shivered. Had Dies Irae been eating the bodies?

"My lord?" he said. There were bite marks on the body, he saw. Now Teeth definitely wanted to flee. "My lord, two silvers would be our price, if it please you. We'll find you more bodies. We're the Rot Gang."

Dies Irae walked around the table and approached him. He was tall, Teeth saw. Not as tall as Legs, maybe, but heavier, all muscle and grit. Dies Irae stared at him with his good eye.

"Those are good teeth you have there," he said. He licked his lips, smearing blood across them. "Sharp. I bet they can just... *bite* into somebody." He snapped his own teeth, as if to demonstrate. "I could use teeth like that."

Beside them, Legs guffawed. "Dog teeth, dog teeth, I like to see them. Yes sir I do."

Dies Irae turned to face him, as if seeing Legs for the first time. "Well, young man, aren't you a tall one. Look at those legs you've got there. I bet they could just...." Dies Irae stamped his feet. "*Run!* Run like the wind, I bet they can."

Legs brayed. "They run, Legs they call me, yes sir they do."

This was all wrong. Teeth found that he no longer cared about the coins.

"My lord, if you'll excuse us, we'll be on our way," he said. He turned to face the doorway.

A mimic stood there. Not a dead body, but an animated thing, patched together, sewn from the strongest parts. A creature with worms for hair, claws on its fingers, and death in its eyes. It blocked the doorway, grinning. Insects bustled in its mouth, and its eyes blazed red.

"They are strong," Dies Irae said. "They are made from the best. The best parts. I build them myself."

He swung his mace at Legs.

It hit the boy's head, crushing it.

As Legs collapsed, Teeth ran to the wall and grabbed a torch. He held it before him as a weapon.

"Don't touch me, old man!" he warned, waving the torch.

Dies Irae's lips curled back; Teeth couldn't decide if it was a snarl or a grin.

"But I *will* touch you," he said. "I will make you stronger. I will give you the right parts."

Teeth lashed his torch.

Dies Irae sidestepped.

The mace swung.

Pain exploded against Teeth's chest. The mace swung and again hit his chest. His ribs snapped. He couldn't breathe. Blood filled his mouth.

He fell to his knees. The last thing he saw was Dies Irae grinning, and the mace swung again.

Light exploded. Blood and pain flowed across him... and faded. He knew nothing more.

GLORIAE

She flew over snowy trees, a golden dragon in the wind, when her magic died and she turned human.

Gloriae yelped. The forest rushed up toward her. She tumbled. The firewood she had collected fell around her. She uselessly flapped her arms as if she still had wings. Wind howled. Gloriae gritted her teeth and tried to become a dragon again. Nothing happened. Her magic was gone.

Pain exploded.

She crashed into a snowy treetop. Branches cracked. They snapped against her breastplate, tore her leggings, and lacerated her arms. For a moment she hung between two branches, and then they too snapped. She fell ten feet, and her helmet hit another branch. White light flooded her. The pain was so intense, she couldn't even scream.

With a crack, more branches splintered, and Gloriae hit the forest floor.

She lay in the snow, moaning. Everything hurt. She dared not move, fearing the pain of broken bones.

Thank the stars for my armor, she thought. *Without my helmet and breastplate, I'd be jackal food.*

She moaned and took slow breaths. *What happened? How could her magic fail?* For thousands of years, the children of Requiem could become dragons at will, could breathe fire and soar over forest and mountain.

Gloriae pushed herself onto her elbows. Her head spun, and she blinked several times, trying to bring the world back into focus.

That was when she heard the growl.

Wolves, she thought. She leaped to her feet, which made her head spin more wildly. She drew Per Ignem, her sword of northern steel, and looked around. If she could not breathe fire, she could still swing her blade.

She heard the growl again. It came from somewhere between the trees ahead. It was no wolf, Gloriae realized. This growl was too deep, too... twisted, wrong, cruel. She had never heard anything like it, and despite herself, she shuddered. A stench filled the forest, like rotting bodies and sewage, so heavy Gloriae nearly gagged.

She wanted to call out, to ask "Who's there?!", but forced herself to remain silent. Whatever creature growled ahead, it might not have seen her yet.

Slim chance, she thought. Anyone around would have seen her fall from the sky, but Gloriae was a warrior, and stealth was beaten into her like the folds in her blade. She narrowed her eyes. Her body still ached, and the world still spun, but Gloriae could still kill if she had to.

The growl rose again, and a second growl sounded at her right, this one closer. Gloriae spun around, sword raised, and finally saw the creatures.

One stepped out to her right, one from ahead, and one from her left. She knew them at once.

Mimics.

"Damn it," Gloriae whispered.

For a moment, terror froze her.

They walked toward her, rotting, rustling with maggots. Dies Irae had sewn them together from body parts, mixing and matching. One had the torso of a woman, bare breasted and gutted, flies breeding in the cavity of its stomach. One of its legs was the bent, hairy leg of a man, while its arms were tiny, the arms of babies. Another mimic had the torso of a man, but the legs of a goat, and arms that ended with blades instead of hands. The third had two torsoes of children sewn one atop the other, and its four hands held knives. Each was different, but each had long blond hair. Each stared with baleful blue eyes.

Each looked like her.

"Hello, mother," they whispered as one. "Hello, first Gloriae. Your father sends his regards."

Their voices—twisting, screeching imitations of her own—snapped Gloriae out of her paralysis. She screamed and charged.

Per Ignem swung, slicing through one mimic's neck. Its head, stitched on, fell and rolled. Black blood splashed the snow. Its body, headless, lashed at Gloriae with claws.

Gloriae stepped back and stabbed a mimic to her left. She ducked, dodging another mimic's blades. The headless creature reached out its claws. Gloriae leaped forward, drove her helmet into its chest, and swung her blade, slicing another.

Claws grabbed her shoulder, bending her steel armor as if it were mere leather. Gloriae screamed, spun, and kicked. She hit the mimic's leg, snapping it. She brought down her sword. Black blood flew. The other mimics attacked.

As she jumped, dodged, and swung her blade, Gloriae remembered. The one time she had seen mimics before, she had tried to shift into a dragon, but could not. *Their magic undoes my own.*

The severed mimic's head bit her boot, and Gloriae screamed and kicked it. A severed arm grabbed her leg, cutting her with fingernails like blades. She stabbed it, freed herself, and turned to run.

She could not kill these beasts with steel, she knew. She remembered. *Fire kills them.*

As she ran, she heard them following, grunting like rutting beasts. Gloriae reached into her leather pack and grabbed her tinderbox.

Fingers grabbed her legs, and she fell. Her face hit the snow. The tinderbox flew from her hand.

Gloriae flipped onto her back, shouted, and kicked. Her boots knocked back a mimic's head. Its mouth opened to scream, and maggots fell from it. She kicked again, and its head caved in, spilling centipedes and blood onto Gloriae's face.

Her tinderbox lay three feet away in the snow. Gloriae scurried for it.

A second mimic kicked the tinderbox aside, then walked toward her, grinning. Her sword had split its torso in half, from shoulder to navel, but still it moved, each half of its body swaying. Gloriae drove forward, swung her blade, and halved the mimic's head like a grapefruit, ear to ear. Only its jaw remained, and it squealed. Its claws sliced her shoulder, but Gloriae ignored the pain. She leaped five feet, landed by her tinderbox, and grabbed it.

Mimics screeched behind, lurching toward her.

Gloriae opened the tinderbox, gritted her teeth, and began rubbing flint against steel. *Light, damn you, light!*

A mimic grabbed her helmet and pulled her to her feet. It snarled, and drool sprayed from its mouth, green and thick with small white worms.

Gloriae frantically slashed flint on steel.

The mimic leaned in to bite.

Her tinderbox crackled with fire.

Gloriae drove it forward, shattering it against the mimic's face. The tinder spilled onto the creature, and its hair caught fire. It blazed.

She leaped back, watching the mimic burn. Cockroaches screeched and fled from it. The mimic tried to run toward her, but stumbled and fell.

The other mimics lunged at her.

Gloriae kicked the burning mimic's arm. It came loose and burned in the snow. She grabbed the arm, as if it were a torch, and swung it. The mimics cried like slaughtered pigs. Gloriae swung the arm into one's head, and its hair—blond locks like her own—caught fire. Soon its whole head burned.

One mimic remained. Gloriae stared at it, and though her wounds ached, she managed a small, crooked smile.

"Let's play," she said.

She swung her sword in one hand, the burning arm in the other. She dealt steel and fire. Black blood and maggots flew. Body parts fell, burned, screamed, and twisted.

"Gloriae," the last mimic hissed, a mere head with spilling brains, its body burning five feet away. "Gloriae, your father wants your head, and your arms, and your guts, and your—"

Gloriae stabbed it through the face, burned it, and watched it die. The stench of rotting meat and burning grease filled the forest.

She tossed the burning arm aside, disgusted. She breathed deeply, sword still in hand, blood covering her.

Mimics. Stars.

Gloriae looked around for more, and when none arrived, she examined her wounds. A finger had punched a hole through her armor, cutting her under her shoulder blade. More cuts ran along her calf. The fall onto the treetops had covered her with scratches and bumps; tomorrow bruises would cover her.

"Damn you, Irae," she whispered, staring at the burning bodies. She had killed three mimics a moon ago in the dungeons under Flammis Palace. She had never imagined Dies Irae would create more. How many mimics crawled the world now? Were more heading here, into the northwest, toward Requiem?

She had to warn the others.

She had to fly.

When she stepped far enough from the dead mimics, she found her magic. Wings sprouted from her back, scales covered her, and soon she roared as a golden dragon. She flew, crashed through the treetops, and found the sky.

She looked around, and in the distance, she saw trees sway and creak. She narrowed her eyes. Figures moved between those trees, many of them. Soon they moved into a clearing, black and red under the sun, and then disappeared into more trees.

Mimics. A hundred or more—an army of perverted humanity created by the man she had called Father. And they were heading home, to Requiem.

Gloriae cursed and flew.

KYRIE ELEISON

Kyrie was on guard duty, and he was freezing.

Snow fell, flurried in the wind, and covered his world. Kyrie saw no end to the horrible stuff. A blue dragon, he perched atop an orphaned archway, the walls around it long fallen. Below the mountaintop where the archway stood, ruins spread into the horizons: toppled walls and smashed columns and burned trees, the snow covering them all. Winter had come to the ruins of Requiem.

Kyrie shivered and wrapped his wings around him, but found no warmth.

"Stars, I hate guard duty," he muttered and spat. Snow covered him, and he shook it off, but more soon coated him.

He looked north to a valley between a cliff and mountain. Boulders rose from it like teeth, and a frozen river snaked through it. Benedictus was buried there—Kyrie's king, mentor, and brother-in-arms.

"I miss you, old friend," Kyrie whispered. "I wish you could have lived to see this, to see us back in Requiem." A lump filled his throat. "Our home still lies in ruins, but we're back, Benedictus. We've defeated the griffins, and we've defeated the nightshades, and we'll rebuild our home. The home you died to give us."

His eyes stung, and Kyrie shook his head, swallowed, and looked away. Thinking about Benedictus was too painful. *I'm the only male left. I must be strong. I'll be like him.*

Kyrie turned and looked down from his perch. A courtyard covered the mountaintop below him. Once a fortress had stood here, and warriors of Requiem had manned it. Draco Murus, they had called this place; the center of Requiem's military might. It had withstood Dies Irae's griffins longer than any other fort... but it had fallen too. Today only this archway still stood, a hundred feet tall. The rest of Draco Murus lay shattered across the mountain, buried in snow. The skeletons of a thousand Vir Requis lay buried there too.

A hole gaped open in the courtyard, and smoke rose from it. Kyrie smelled sausages and baking bread. He licked his lips. If the fortress had collapsed in the war, its dungeons were still sturdy, a network of cellars and tunnels. Lacrimosa and Agnus Dei huddled there now, Kyrie knew. They'd be warm and cozy by the fire, while he shivered here.

"Where are you, Gloriae?" he muttered. She had flown seeking firewood hours ago. Once she returned, she would guard, and Lacrimosa would fly for firewood. Then he, Kyrie, could enjoy a precious few hours in the cellars, alone with Agnus Dei.

For the first time all morning, Kyrie felt warm. He lived for those moments alone with Agnus Dei. He could already imagine it. While Lacrimosa and Gloriae were away, he'd hold her by the fire, warm under blankets. They'd whisper of losing Benedictus, and rebuilding Requiem, and of their love. They'd comfort each other with kisses and caresses, then undress with trembling fingers. He'd smell her hair, embrace her, and kiss her lips. She'd kiss him back eagerly, seeking healing from pain, fire to melt the world's ice. Her fingers would dig into his back, and her breasts would press against his chest, and—

With a roar, a golden dragon emerged from the clouds, flying toward him.

His dream shattered, and Kyrie started.

Gloriae panted. She all but crashed into the courtyard.

"Gloriae!" Kyrie said. "No firewood? No game? What happened?"

She looked at him, eyes fearful. Blood stained her scales.

"Gloriae, are you——?"

"Mimics," she panted. "I killed three. More are on the way."

Kyrie froze. Terror stabbed his gut, colder than the snow and wind. He remembered.

"Stars," he whispered. His heart pounded.

He leaped off the archway, landed by Gloriae, and shifted into human form. Gloriae shifted too and stood before him as a human girl. Snow filled her blond curls, her leggings were torn, and her breastplate was dented. Blood dripped from her calf and shoulder, and scratches covered her arms. Her cheeks were pink.

"They're not ten leagues away," she said. "A hundred of them, maybe more. They'll be here by nightfall."

Kyrie swallowed. His chest felt tight. He had seen mimics only once, the day Benedictus had died. They still haunted his nightmares.

He grabbed Gloriae's wrist. "Come. Underground."

They crossed the courtyard and reached a makeshift trapdoor they'd built of branches and rope. Kyrie pulled the door open, revealing a staircase leading underground. He raced downstairs, nearly slipping on the damp stone, and emerged into a cellar full of firewood, jugs of ale, and sacks of flour and lentils. He hurried into a tunnel, ran past more cellars, and entered a chamber with a crackling fireplace.

Lacrimosa, Queen of Requiem, sat there upon a fleece. The firelight danced against her pale cheeks and turned her fair hair red. Agnus Dei was rustling the fireplace with a poker. She turned toward them, her mane of black curls bouncing, her eyes wide.

"Gloriae!" Agnus Dei said. "You're hurt."

Lacrimosa rose to her feet. "What happened?"

Still panting, Gloriae sat by the fireplace. Lacrimosa sat beside her, removed the girl's armor, and began tending to her wounds. Agnus Dei sat at Gloriae's other side, smoothed her hair, and looked at her with worried eyes.

"What happened, Gloriae?" she asked.

They all listened as Gloriae spoke of meeting three mimics outside Requiem, of losing the ability to shift, of seeing many more mimics travelling west. Kyrie and Agnus Dei cursed and muttered throughout the story, but Lacrimosa only listened silently, face blank.

Once Gloriae had finished her tale, and her wounds were bandaged, Lacrimosa stood up. Kyrie approached her and stared into her lavender eyes.

"Lacrimosa," he said, "we must flee. Requiem is no longer safe. I've fought griffins and nightshades a hundred times, and mimics only once, but it's that last battle that haunts me most. Let's run. Now."

Lacrimosa took a deep breath and tightened her lips. She stared into the fireplace. The twins sat by the hearth, holding each other, looking at their mother. For a long time, Lacrimosa said nothing. They all waited.

Finally Lacrimosa spoke. "What would he have done?" she said, gazing at the crackling flames. "That's what I always ask myself. I miss him so much. He'd know what to do." She took a shuddering breath. "But we must continue without him." She turned to stare at Kyrie, her eyes large and haunted. "He died for Requiem. He would want to stay and fight."

At that moment, Kyrie felt such love and pain for Lacrimosa, that he wanted to embrace her. But no; she was Queen of Requiem, and she needed no embraces from him, but strength and courage.

"I'd fight for you anywhere," he said. "But... we've always fought as dragons. We can't shift around mimics. Are you sure, Lacrimosa? There are other places to hide, places safer than Requiem's ruins."

Agnus Dei chewed her lip. She opened her mouth, shut it, clenched her fists, and finally spoke. "I want to fight! I do. I've never run from a fight. Ever! But... Mother, I'm scared." Her eyes dampened. "I was never afraid of a fight before, not against all the griffins and nightshades in the world. But I'm scared now. I... if something happened to you too, Mother, I...."

Suddenly Agnus Dei was crying. Gloriae embraced her, and patted her hair, and Kyrie held her hands.

Lacrimosa squared her shoulders. The firelight danced against her face. "I might die in this fight, Agnus Dei. I might join Father in our starlit halls. I can't promise you that we'll all live. But no place is safe anymore. We've been running and hiding for over a decade, and Dies Irae sends his creatures to all corners of the world. Where more can we run? We promised Father that we'll rebuild Requiem. We promised it to him when we buried him. We cannot run forever." She gestured to a doorway, beyond which lay their armory. "We knew Irae would attack. We've stored bows and arrows, blades, and armor. We don't have much, but we've prepared."

Kyrie shook his head. "Lacrimosa, I want to fight too, but... we have only four bows, only a hundred arrows. We have only a few pieces of armor, and only Gloriae has a breastplate. We're not armed well enough. To beat two or three mimics, yes. But a hundred? We never expected that many."

Lacrimosa took a deep breath. Her eyes stared at nothing, reflective, as though staring at a memory of her husband. "We'll build more weapons." She gestured at piles of firewood that filled the chamber. "We'll build javelins and arrows and torches. We can't shift around mimics, but we can still fight them. Dies Irae is weakened now. It's time to make a stand. We will tell him: You cannot keep hunting us. Requiem is reborn, and we will defend her."

Gloriae rose to her feet and drew her sword. "Yes," she said. Ice filled her green eyes, and her cheeks flushed. "Yes. We fight. We kill. We bring fire to our enemies. I'm ready."

Agnus Dei stood up too, looked at Kyrie with uncertain eyes, then at her mother. She bit her lip, gazed to the fire, and whispered something so quietly, Kyrie could not hear. He thought he heard her say "Father". Then she clenched her fists and nodded.

"Yes," she said. Her dark eyes burned. "Yes, I'll fight too. I'm a fighter. It will be a day of flame."

Kyrie looked at the others, one by one. He loved them all, Kyrie thought; even Gloriae. He loved them so much, that his chest ached. *The last Vir Requis. I will defend them. I will fight for them, and if I must, I will die for them.*

"A day of flame," he repeated. "Let us make torches, and let us make arrows of fire."

AGNUS DEI

As she worked, she couldn't stop her fingers from shaking. Piles of firewood, kindling, and jars of oil filled the underground cellars. They had been collecting it for weeks from beyond Requiem's borders, enough to last all winter, to warm their bones and cook their food. As Agnus Dei carried log after log outside, she couldn't help but shiver. She had never imagined they'd use this wood for war... to kill mimics.

Mimics. Even in the chill of winter, sweat washed her. She hated mimics. She had seen them only once, but still woke most nights, out of breath and sweaty, memories of their rot and worms filling her mind.

"I miss you, Dada," she whispered as she carried four logs upstairs, out of the cellar, and into the snowy courtyard. A pile of branches, twigs, and logs rose there, ten feet tall.

Mother stood by the wood, frowning toward the east. The wind filled her hair and fluttered her old, tattered dress. Her eyes seemed dead; no fear, pain, or mourning filled them. Agnus Dei wanted to hug her, but something held her back. She was not only her mother now, but Queen Lacrimosa of Requiem. Ruler of these ruins. Widow.

A lump filled Agnus Dei's throat.

"Here, Mother," she said and added her logs to the pile. Her sister Gloriae stepped out from the cellars behind her, also carrying wood. Finally Kyrie emerged and added more wood to the pile.

Mother seemed not to notice. She kept staring into the snowy horizons, as if imagining the mimics that approached.

"Mother," Agnus Dei whispered. Gingerly, she touched her shoulder. "We've brought the last wood from the cellars. What now?"

Mother turned to face her, and Agnus Dei realized she'd been wrong. Mother's eyes were not dead. Pain saturated them, but steel lived there too, a strength that held the mourning at bay like a breakwater holding back the waves. The passing clouds reflected in those lavender eyes. For a long moment Lacrimosa was silent, and when she spoke, her voice was soft and cold as the snow.

"You will build spears, Agnus Dei. Spears with tips of kindling, to burn mimics."

Agnus Dei nodded. She lifted a long, narrow branch from the pile. Her knuckles turned white around it. "This one will do. I will kill mimics with it."

Mother turned to Gloriae. "And you, daughter. Take our hundred arrows, and wrap their tips with kindling, and soak them with oil. Then make more arrows from straight, strong sticks; they won't have blades or fletching, but they'll still fly and burn."

Gloriae nodded. Her lips were tight, her fists clenched at her sides. The wind fluttered her golden locks and pinched her cheeks pink.

"Yes," she said. "I'm ready for fire. I'm ready to kill."

Mother then turned to Kyrie. "And you, Kyrie, will help me. We'll build a ring of fire around the fort. When the mimics arrive, it'll shield us."

Kyrie nodded. "I'm good at building fires. We'll soak the wood in oil, and crack it, and stuff kindling into it. When the mimics arrive, it'll catch fire quickly, and burn high." He touched Mother's shoulder. "We'll be safe, Lacrimosa. I promise you. I... I'm no great warrior like Benedictus, but...." He swallowed and squared his shoulders. "I'll do all I can to protect you and your daughters."

Agnus Dei smiled sadly. She was better than the pup in a fight, and Gloriae was too, but she knew what he was doing, and she loved him for it. She approached Kyrie, embraced him, and kissed his cheek. He held her, his gloves sticky with sap.

"I love you, pup," she whispered, her head against his shoulder.

Another pair of arms held her, and Agnus Dei saw that Gloriae joined the embrace. For a moment the three stood, warm in their embrace as the wind blew. Then they broke apart.

"We prepare for fire and for war," Agnus Dei said.

She began collecting the long, straight branches from the pile. She placed them in a corner of the courtyard, in the shadow of the archway. *They'll make good spears,* she thought. *Not strong spears like those of soldiers, carved from the heart of boles and tipped with steel, but they'll do.* Gloriae was collecting the smaller sticks, and placing them at the courtyard's other end. Kyrie and Lacrimosa were collecting logs, crooked branches, and any pieces the twins could not use; they began arranging them in a ring around the courtyard.

As she worked, Agnus Dei kept scanning the horizon for the mimics. From here upon the mountaintop, she could see leagues of ruins. The land was dead.

When will the mimics arrive? The wind howled, and Agnus Dei shivered. The sun was setting, and it was getting colder. The clouds thickened.

When evening fell, a ring of wood and kindling surrounded the fort's courtyard, soaked in oil. Torches stood in the ground in an inner ring, two feet apart; wherever mimics attacked, the Vir Requis could grab one to swing. Piles of javelins tipped with oiled brushwood lay around the courtyard for easy access. Each Vir Requis wore a steel helmet, greaves, and vambraces. Gloriae wore her breastplate too. They each held a bow, and their quivers held arrows tipped with oiled straw.

"We're ready for battle," Agnus Dei said, surveying the scene. Splinters, sap, and oil covered her gloves.

Kyrie raised an eyebrow. "Ready? No. This is not what I'd call ready. If we had a hundred men, I wouldn't call us ready. But it's as ready as we'll be this night."

Snow began to fall again, and Agnus Dei cursed.

"Will the wood light when wet?" she asked.

Kyrie frowned. "We soaked it with oil. I hope so." But his eyes didn't look hopeful, and his fists tightened.

The sun sent a last flicker of red light, then sank behind the horizon. The wind screamed, and Agnus Dei shivered. She clutched Kyrie's hand.

"I'm scared," she whispered. "Where are they?"

Gloriae and Lacrimosa came to stand by them. They held their bows.

"Do not light fires yet," Lacrimosa whispered. "We don't want a beacon for mimics to see."

Agnus Dei held Kyrie's hand so tight, he grunted, but she would not let go. She kept scanning the valleys around them, but saw nothing in the darkness. The wind pierced her cloak. She wanted to shift into a dragon, to blow fire, to rush into battle, but dared not. Her magic would fail once those creatures arrived. Agnus Dei gritted her teeth.

"I wish they'd show up already," she said, struggling not to scream out challenges to them. "I hate the waiting. I hate the dark. I want a fight. I want—"

A howl rose in the distance.

Agnus Dei squeezed Kyrie's hand.

For a moment nobody spoke.

"A jackal?" Agnus Dei finally whispered.

A second howl answered the first, distant but loud, gurgling and rising to a squeal.

"That's no jackal," Gloriae said. She hefted her tinderbox. "It's them."

Agnus Dei scanned the night, but saw only shadows. "I can't see them!"

"Quiet," Gloriae said, voice like silk. "Do not speak."

The wind moaned, and another howl sounded. Agnus Dei snarled. Her fingers trembled, and her heart thrashed. Suddenly she wanted to flee, to shift into a dragon and fly for leagues, to disappear into the west.

Stay strong, she told herself. *For my family, and for Kyrie.*

"Come on," she whispered and growled. "Come on, you bastards. Show yourselves."

Grunts sounded in the distance, and squeals, and thumping feet. A creature screamed, a chilling sound like a slaughtered animal. A rumble answered it, and a shrill cry like a dying cat.

"Weredragons!" rose a cry, high-pitched and inhuman. "We smell them. Yes, brothers. We smell them ahead. We will suck the marrow from their bones."

Agnus Dei release Kyrie's hand and reached into her pack. She clutched the tinderbox she kept there. Strangely, her fingers no longer trembled, and her heart steadied. Now was not the time for terror. Now was the time for battle, for fire, for blood.

"Be brave, Kyrie," she whispered, speaking to herself more than to him. "Be brave for the memory of Father."

The howls grew closer, and a stench hit Agnus Dei's nostrils, a stench of bodies. Countless feet thumped up the mountainsides. Screams curdled her blood.

"Weredragons! We smell them, brothers. We smell sweet blood and marrow. Ahead! On the mountaintop!"

Agnus Dei opened her tinderbox. She placed its flint against firesteel, prepared to strike a spark.

A night of fire. I will be brave, Father. For your memory. I will fight well.

A light flickered—Gloriae lighting her own tinderbox, and soon an arrow blazed in her bow.

Agnus Dei sparked flint against steel, drew an arrow from her quiver, and lit it. She nocked, drew her bowstring, and aimed.

"They have fire, brothers! Fire ahead. They seek to burn us! Feed upon them. Make them as we are!" The squeals and screams filled the darkness.

A third light flickered; Kyrie igniting the ring of fire. It burst into flame around them, a towering wall of light and smoke and heat. Lacrimosa was hurrying from torch to torch, lighting them too—hand-to-hand weapons, should the creatures breach their defenses.

Agnus Dei could see the mimics now, and she couldn't help it. She screamed.

A hundred scurried up the mountainsides like cockroaches. They were creatures of rot, worms, maggots, bones and stitches. Blood covered their teeth. Their eyes blazed, and their claws reached toward them. Their leader bore two swords, and when it held them out, Agnus Dei saw that its arms were eight feet long; each was sewn together from three normal arms, like a string of sausages.

"Weredragons!" this mimic cried, voice guttural and thundering. It brandished its swords. "I will feast upon your entrails."

Another voice rose, commanding and deep, and Agnus Dei realized it was Mother.

"Burn them!" she cried and fired a flaming arrow. "Burn them dead."

Her arrow pierced the night, a comet of fire, and slammed into a mimic's chest. The creature screamed and fell.

First blood spilled. The mimics screamed and charged.

MEMORIA

Memoria had never gotten used to living in an ice palace.

Even after all these years, she remembered and missed her house in Requiem. She remembered walking upon mosaic floors, stepping over dolphins and elks and dragons, and how the colorful stones tickled her bare feet. She remembered the rafters of her attic, where she'd hide and read books. In her mind, she still saw the balcony over the vineyard, where she'd paint the sunsets. Most of all, she remembered the southern warmth, how she'd lie in the garden and soak up the sun, hear the birds, and watch the dragonflies.

Here there were no birds or dragonflies, no gardens or trees, no warmth. She lived in a palace now, but it was built of ice. The floor, the ceiling, the columns that rose two hundred feet tall; nothing but ice, cold and glimmering and cruel to her southern bones. She could see the sun through the ceiling, blurred and small, but even it seemed cold, like the glimmer of icicles.

She walked across Whale Hall, her slippers silent. Few elders came to Whale Hall anymore; it was an ancient place where ice crystals rose like a whale's ribs. It had become her sanctuary, her place of prayer. At the edge of the hall the ceiling was thin, and sunlight fell like raining fireflies. Memoria knelt in the sunbeams, the ice hard against her knees, and closed her eyes. She wrapped her seal furs around her, this raiment of exile, and whispered to her stars.

"If you're up there, Kyrie, know that I love you. If you watch over me from Draco's stars, hear my words." She hugged herself, and her eyes stung. "I love you forever, little brother. I miss you every day."

She heard footfalls behind her, opened her eyes, and turned to see her second brother. Terra was walking toward her, clad as always in his old armor. Frost coated the filigreed plates, his horned helmet, and the silver scabbard of his sword. He wore a walrus moustache in the style of the bellators, Requiem's noble warriors; he was the last of their order, but still clung to their symbols. A fur cloak draped over his shoulders, a single piece of the north over his steel garb of southern glory.

"Sister, I worry for you." He sighed. "You spend hours here, speaking to him every day. I miss our brother too. I loved him. But... Memoria, how do you know that he hears?"

Memoria stood up and glared at him. Terra was tall and broad, and she was short and slim, but she glared at him nonetheless. His hair was fair like hers, but already white kissed his temples. His eyes were brown like hers, but sadder, she thought; weary eyes that had seen too much. He was two years her senior, thirty this winter, but looked forty. Youth's hope and grace had left him. She remembered him a dozen years ago, always laughing, bronzed from working in their vineyard. She had not heard him laugh since.

Not since our baby brother left us, she thought. *Not since Kyrie died at Lanburg Fields. My sweet, small Kyrie, the light of our family... forever extinguished, forever a hole inside us.*

"Kyrie's spirit shines among the Draco stars," she said softly. "I know he can hear me. So I speak to him, and I will speak to him every day. You should too, Terra." Tears stung her eyes. "Kyrie needs your prayers too."

Terra sighed again. His hands closed around hers, gloved in leather, warm despite the cold around them. "Sister, I was a knight of Requiem. I devoted my life to helping the living. I know nothing of the dead." He squeezed her hands. "Today the living need us. The icelings are hungry. We must fly. We must hunt."

They walked down the hall between its columns of whorled ice. They stepped between two crystals, then walked through chambers that rose three hundred feet tall. Crystals glimmered around them, larger than dragons. Through towering windows, like windows in a cathedral, Memoria saw a thousand more palaces. They spread for a league across the iceberg, built of ice and snow, glistening like stars. Most of those palaces were abandoned now, she knew, only ghosts left to haunt their halls. Only two hundred icelings lived today, but their ancestors' palaces still stood, their ice never melting, their beauty never fading.

These remaining icelings glided around Memoria between the columns. Their sealskin robes swayed, and their hair was white as snow, even the hair of the children. Their eyes were azure, like clear pools under the sun, and they bore whalebone staffs crowned with their birth crystals.

Memoria wore furs now too—her woollen clothes from Requiem had gone threadbare years ago—but she bore no staff like the icelings. Like her brother, she wore a sword of Requiem at her hip, a glimmering shard of steel she had named Luna Nova.

Why do we still wear these swords? Memoria thought, as she thought every day. *We swung them in Requiem's tunnels, in darkness too narrow for dragonfire. But they couldn't hold back the enemy. They couldn't save our parents... and they couldn't save Kyrie.* So many times, Memoria had wanted to toss her sword into the ocean, watch it sink forever from her memory, but she could not. She was still a soldier, even after all these years, even as Requiem lay in ruin. She still had a soldier's pride.

"Sky friends!"

The words echoed across the hall. Memoria looked up to see Amberus, the Elder of Elders, walking toward them. His flowing robes hid his feet; he seemed to float. His beard was so long, it trailed five feet behind him like a wake. A necklace of icicles hung around his neck, and he held a staff crowned with a garnet the size of a man's heart.

"May your hunt today bring you much fortune," he said, "better than the days before it." His bony fingers tightened around his staff. He looked around at the other icelings, who moved silently between the frozen chambers. "They do not run or laugh, not even the children. They are hungry. They are thin."

Memoria bowed her head. "We will fly far today, Amberus. We will fly close to the Jet Mountains, but we dare not fly beyond them."

The elder's eyes darkened. "If the giants keep eating, we must abandon the Ice City."

Memoria's eyes widened. She gasped. "Abandon it? But Amberus, the icelings have lived here for a million years, since the dawn of ice. How could you abandon it?"

Amberus swept his arms around him, his bracelets of icicles clinking. "We have already abandoned it, sky child. Countless icelings once lived here. Two hundred remain, their bellies tight. I will let no more starve. The day will come, and we will have to leave, to move north, to the very feet of the Jet

Mountains where seals still gather. We cannot let the giants eat so many. Their appetite is greater than that of snow craving clouds."

Terra placed a hand on the elder's shoulder. "Do not move north, Amberus. The giants hunger for more than seal flesh. You know how many icelings they've killed for sport. You cannot fight them."

The old iceling shook his head. The icicles strewn through his beard chinked. "No. But you can. When you take the sky spirit forms, you are mighty warriors."

Memoria took a deep breath. "May it never come to that. Let us fly on one more hunt. The giants would not eat all the seals, or they too would starve. There are more. We'll find them." She turned to her brother. "Come, Terra, we fly."

Even here, a thousand leagues north from her home, the Draco stars blessed her. Memoria drew her magic, the magic of Requiem. Scales flowed across her body, green like the forests of her home, glimmering in the morning light. Wings grew from her back. Claws, white as bone, grew from her fingertips and toes. She flapped her wings, took flight as a dragon, and flew between ice columns into the sky.

Terra shifted too. Soon he was flying beside her, a bronze dragon with white horns, his scales frosted. They flew north, leaving the Ice City, gliding over sheets of ice and snow toward the cruel Jet Mountains that marked the end of the world.

Memoria breathed deeply, relishing the wind. True, it was too cold here in exile, at the northern fringe of the world. And true, she missed seeing forests and rivers below her, not endless leagues of white. But at least she still had flying. To spread wings, feel fire tickle her nostrils, dive and swoop and be free... this was happiness to her.

"Do you remember how we'd fly with the herds?" she called to Terra. He flew at her side, gazing forward with those brown, weary eyes. "Do you remember how we'd sing as we flew over Requiem?"

He did not answer. She knew he remembered, but Terra preferred to forget. *Let him seek solace in the ice*, she thought. *My solace remains in the whispers of warm, southern past.*

They flew for a long time, over gleaming sheets of ice, dunes of snow, and boulders that rose grey and black like ancient goblins turned to stone. The world was white, grey, and black.

Her green scales, and Terra's bronze ones, were the only colors for leagues.

At noon, the Jet Mountains appeared on the horizon, great walls of black stone, ice, and snow. *The home of giants.* Memoria had never seen a giant, but she had seen their footprints, three toed and six feet long. She had seen the blood, bones, and offal they left behind after killing those icelings who ventured beyond the Ice City. And she saw them in her nightmares, shadows always at the corners of her eyes.

"Memoria, look," Terra said. He gestured ahead to a sheet of ice behind a ridge of boulders.

She looked, and her heart leaped.

"Seals!" she said.

A dozen of them, fat and lazy on the ice! This was rare. This time of year, seals normally swam under the ice, and Memoria had expected long hours of searching for their breathing holes. To find a dozen on the surface.... She laughed. If she caught them all, they would feed the icelings for days. Their fur would make warm blankets and clothes; their bones would be carved into blades, buttons, and needles; their sinew would make thread; their teeth would make necklaces and bracelets. This was a treasure.

She dived toward them, reaching out her claws, her heart racing for the hunt. Flames flickered between her teeth. Terra dived beside her, his claws extended.

The seals weren't fleeing.

Memoria frowned. They weren't moving at all.

Something's wrong.

She landed, claws digging into the ice. Terra landed beside her.

"They're dead," Memoria said. She nudged one with her claws. "But there's no blood, and they're gutted. Who would do such a thing? Kill seals, and place them on the ice, and...."

She froze.

Terra finished for her. "Bait," he said. "Whoever did this was laying out bait."

Memoria looked wildly from side to side, seeking giants. *They must have done this.*

"I see nobody," she whispered. She sucked in her breath, prepared to blow fire at any enemy who might appear, but she saw nothing for leagues; nothing but plains of ice.

Terra frowned. "I hear something. Listen."

She listened, and she heard it—a low rumble beneath her feet. The ice creaked. Memoria opened her mouth to speak... and her magic vanished.

She gasped. Her wings pulled back into her. Her scales disappeared. Suddenly she stood on the ice as a human. Terra's magic vanished too, leaving him human and looking just as confused. He tightened his jaw, drew his sword, and stared from side to side.

"What happened?" Memoria whispered. She had never heard of Vir Requis losing their magic. She too drew her sword. The ice shook wildly now, and a shriek sounded from below it.

"Let's get out of here," Terra said. "Go!"

But before Memoria could move, a hole burst open in the ice, and three creatures emerged from underwater.

Memoria screamed.

They were dead bodies, bloated and pale. But no; they were not mere bodies, but creations, sewn together from bits and pieces. She saw the stitches holding their limbs and heads to their torsos. Even in the cold, they stank so powerfully that Memoria gagged. The creatures squealed like walruses. Blood stained their teeth. Their fingers ended with the claws of bears, and those claws swiped at Memoria.

She leaped back and lashed her sword.

Memoria had been a soldier once. She could still fight, even in human form. Her blade severed the creature's hand, but it kept charging. It barrelled into her, snapping its teeth. Its claws slashed her shoulder.

Memoria fell onto the ice. She kicked one creature's head. Its neck snapped back, and worms spilled from its mouth.

"Agnus Dei," it hissed at her. "Dies Irae wants you, Agnus Dei. He sent me to you."

What is it talking about? Memoria drove her sword's grip into its face, crushing its nose and knocking out its teeth. She scrambled to her feet, lashed her blade, and sliced off its head.

She turned to Terra, and saw him swinging his sword, battling two more creatures. His eyes were narrowed, his jaw tight; he was the bellator again, a knight of Requiem. He had shattered one creature's face, but it was still trying to bite. Memoria ran and slammed her sword into its head. Blood and maggoty brains spilled, but the creature only laughed.

Pain blazed on her calf. Memoria looked down, and saw the head she had severed. It was biting her. She screamed, kicked it off, and hacked at it. The head cackled. She stabbed again and again, breaking the head into a jaw, teeth, bits of skull, but still the head moved and gurgled and laughed. Memoria kicked the pieces into the hole in the ice, and they sank. The rest of the body kept creeping toward her. Memoria screamed, stabbed it, and kicked it into the hole. It floundered, and its fingers grabbed the rim of ice. She sliced them off and kicked them underwater.

Terra was swinging his sword, keeping the other two creatures at bay. His mouth was a grim line under his moustache. Frost covered his blade; it glinted like a shard of ice.

"Kyrie Eleison," the creatures hissed at him. "We come to kill you, Kyrie Eleison. Our lord, Dies Irae, commands that you die."

Memoria growled. How did these creatures know her dead brother's name? How dared they utter it? Memoria shouted, her heart racing, her head spinning. She leaped to her brother's defense. Their blades swung together. A severed arm leaped from the ice, clutched her shoulder, and scratched deep. Memoria ripped it off and tossed it underwater.

Terra was wounded too, she saw. Grooves ran down his armor, revealing bloody flesh. *What kind of creatures can claw through steel?* Still he fought, eyes narrowed, until the creatures were cut and crushed like butchered seals. The fingers, feet, heads, and other pieces kept writhing and trying to attack. Memoria and Terra kicked and stabbed, tossing them into the hole in the ice, where they sank.

Memoria kicked the last finger underwater, then leaned over, struggling for breath. Blood covered the ice. The stench of rot made her gag.

Kyrie.

She looked at Terra. Blood dripped from his wound. He stared back, silent.

Kyrie Eleison.

Tears stung Memoria's eyes.

"They... they spoke of Kyrie," she whispered and trembled. The memories flooded back, so powerful that her head spun, and for a moment she was back in Requiem, back in the war that had flooded her home.

"Kyrie!" she had cried, weeping, a youth who had seen too much fire and death. "Kyrie, where are you?"

The bodies had spread below her, thousands of them, covering Lanburg Fields. Where was her brother? Where was Kyrie?

"Kyrie!" Terra had cried too, searching the bodies with her, until they found the remains of a burned child, and wept over it, and buried it, and fled... fled here to exile, to endless ice, to endless memories.

Kyrie Eleison, the rotting demon had said.

Kyrie. My baby brother. The light of our family.

"What were those things?" she whispered, eyes stinging. She stared at the hole the creatures had emerged from. Her wounds ached and bled, but she ignored them. "Why did they speak of Kyrie?"

Terra's breath frosted before him. He stared darkly at the blood upon the ice. "They must be Dies Irae's new pets, something even worse than griffins. These creatures were built to kill Vir Requis. That's why we couldn't shift around them."

Memoria hugged herself. A chill washed over her, as if she'd swallowed too much snow. "So the war still rages. He's still hunting dragons."

Terra lowered his head and clenched his fists. Icicles were forming on his moustache. His voice was strained. "It's still going on. We've been hiding for eleven years, and the war still rages. And now it's here. He found us, Memoria. Dies Irae found us."

She shook her head, her heart racing, and she could barely see. *Could it be? After these years... is it possible?*

"The creatures were seeking Vir Requis, yes," she whispered. "But not you or me. They called me Agnus Dei. Does that name sound familiar?"

He stared at her. "Of course. Agnus Dei was our princess. I met her several times—a young girl with a mane of black curls. She gave me a favor, a single bluebell, before the battle of Draco Murus."

Memoria nodded. "You see, Terra? These creatures were seeking Requiem's survivors. We're not the only ones." Tears filled her eyes. Something halfway between sob and laughter fled her lips. "Others lived and fled into hiding too, Terra. The princess Agnus Dei did... and so did our brother."

KYRIE ELEISON

The mimics charged uphill, howling.

The Vir Requis fired their arrows. Shards of flame shot through the night. Screeches rose from the mimics, and two fell burning.

"Keep shooting!" Lacrimosa cried, an unnecessary command; they were all already nocking new arrows. Four more flaming arrows flew, and more mimics fell.

"Burn, that's right!" Kyrie shouted, excitement pounding through him. His fingers shook and his heart thrashed. The smoke stung his eyes and lungs, and the flames drenched him with sweat. He loaded a third arrow. This was no dragonfire, but it would do, he thought. He could still burn and kill these creatures.

A swarm of mimics reached the ring of fire that surrounded the ruins of Draco Murus. They tried to cross, but leaped back and hissed. The Vir Requis fired arrows through the flames, and the mimics screeched.

"Break the fire," howled their leader, the towering mimic with arms sewn together like strings of sausages. "Into the flames. Scatter them."

As Kyrie kept firing arrows, his stomach knotted. Mimics plunged into the ring of fire, tossing logs left and right. They burned, screamed, and fell. Others replaced them.

"Kill them, those ones!" Kyrie shouted and shot a arrow. He hit one mimic who was scattering the burning logs. His arrow entered its head, and it fell.

"Stack more logs, quick!" Lacrimosa shouted. She ran toward the broken ring of fire. Three mimics were stepping through it, grinning and drooling. They swiped their claws at Lacrimosa.

Kyrie ran, dropped his bow, and grabbed a torch. He swung it and clubbed one mimic's head. It screamed and lashed claws. Kyrie leaped back and swung his torch again, and the mimic burned. Bugs screamed and died inside it.

The twins leaped forward, thrusting burning javelins. Claw marks ran down Agnus Dei's thigh.

"Seal the ring of fire, stop them from entering!" Lacrimosa shouted, face flushed, hair damp with sweat. They all began tossing burning logs into the breach, and soon new flames crackled, showering sparks.

Screams rose behind them, and Kyrie spun around to see mimics breaching the ring twenty feet away.

"Over there!" he shouted. He grabbed a javelin, dipped its tip into the flames, and tossed it. The burning missile flew and sank into a mimic's chest. It screamed and fell.

The twins charged, screaming and swinging torches. They clubbed and burned mimics, who fell before them. Kyrie and Lacrimosa tossed flaming logs onto the new breach, sealing it.

The Vir Requis looked from side to side, panting and coughing. Smoke and sparks covered them. The mimics were now attacking a third location in the flaming ring.

"Shoot them down!" Lacrimosa shouted, voice hoarse. They grabbed their fallen bows, loaded more arrows, and shot. Mimics fell and rolled down the mountainside, blazing. The stench of smoke and rot filled the night.

"Look!" Kyrie shouted. He pointed across the courtyard to the western side of Draco Murus. "They're over there too, more mimics. Lacrimosa, with me! We'll guard the west."

Leaving the twins to defend the eastern mountainside, Kyrie ran with Lacrimosa across the ruins. The ring of fire was thinner here; they had expected the bulk of the attack from the east, whence the mimics had travelled. And yet a dozen of the creatures were attacking the flames here. Their eyes blazed, and their grins oozed drool thick with worms.

Lungs burning, Kyrie shot more arrows, hitting the creatures, but more kept coming. His stomach curdled. They were low on arrows; he had only five left in his quiver. He shot one more, but missed and cursed.

"Girls, you all right?" he shouted while nocking another arrow.

Agnus Dei shouted from across the courtyard. "They're breaching two places. They're pouring in!"

Kyrie cursed, coughed, and spat. His eyes burned with the smoke; he could barely see. He shot an arrow, hit a mimic, and spun around. He loaded another arrow and saw two mimics charging across the courtyard. He shot, hit one, but the other reached him before he could reload. Its claws swiped, and Kyrie leaped back. It jumped onto him and bit his shoulder.

Kyrie screamed, wrestled it off, and reached for a flaming log. Fire scorched his hand, and he shouted but managed to swing the burning stick. It hit the mimic's face.

Kyrie jumped to his feet. His hand throbbed. Mimics were breaching the flaming ring beside him; Lacrimosa was swinging a torch, holding them back. Kyrie nocked an arrow, fired, and hit the mimic closest to her. He grabbed another arrow, fired again, hit another mimic. When he reached into his quiver for more, he found it empty.

"Great," he muttered. He dropped his bow and grabbed two torches, one in each hand.

"Kyrie!" Gloriae shouted from somewhere across the courtyard. "Kyrie, we need you! Twenty mimics broke in."

Kyrie looked at Lacrimosa. She stood at the breached ring, swinging her torch, holding back four rotting bodies.

"Go to them!" the queen shouted. "I'll hold these ones back. Help the girls!"

Kyrie cursed. He didn't want to abandon Lacrimosa, but the twins needed him. His hand throbbing, dread twisting his gut, Kyrie ran east across the courtyard. The twins were fighting back to back, swinging torches and stabbing javelins. Blood dripped down Agnus Dei's thigh and Gloriae's left arm. A score of mimics surrounded them.

Swinging his torches, Kyrie leaped into the battle. He clubbed one mimic's head, then another. The creatures howled and burned. One swung a sword. The blade whooshed, and Kyrie ducked. The blow glanced off his helmet and rang in his ears, dazing him. Kyrie managed to thrust his torch, striking the mimic's chest. It fell back, and Kyrie chased it, swung his torch, and burned it until it fell.

Two more mimics slammed into him, and Kyrie hit the cobblestones. The breath was knocked out of him, and claws slashed his chest. Pain blazed, and he couldn't breathe. All he could see was darkness and fire. Teeth bit his arm.

No. Don't die now. Not yet. Benedictus would not give up so easily. Kyrie couldn't allow himself to do any less. He shoved himself to his feet, though the world spun, and lashed his torches. Sparks flew in curtains. Kyrie screamed, and the mimics fell back.

Blood trickled down his chest, and the night blurred. He didn't know how long he fought. Dimly, he was aware of the twins tossing flaming javelins, pushing mimics back. He saw Lacrimosa swinging a torch in each hand. Deformed, stitched bodies burned and fell around him.

It seemed ages before the mimics stopped charging. Kyrie lowered his torches, panting, ready to collapse. Piles of burning bodies rose around him, raising black smoke. The stench was so heavy, Kyrie could barely breathe.

He looked around. The twins stood side by side, covered in ash, blood, and mimic drool. Lacrimosa approached them, helmet dented and clothes charred, fire-tipped javelins in her hands. The Vir Requis moved to stand back to back, looking around cautiously.

"Are they all dead?" Agnus Dei said, voice hoarse.

Kyrie narrowed his eyes. The fires still crackled and shadows danced; it was hard to see. But no mimics stirred. Their bodies burned, unmoving, across the ruins and mountainsides.

"They're all dead," Kyrie said. "We—"

A howl shook the ruins.

A figure stepped through the orphaned archway, seven feet tall. It unfurled its arms; each was seven feet long, sewn together from three normal arms. It held a sword in each hand. It grinned at them, baring wolf fangs.

"Not all dead," the chief mimic said and approached them, brandishing its blades.

Agnus Dei charged forward first, swinging her torch and screaming.

The mimic swung one link of arms, hit her helmet with its blade, and knocked her down.

"Agnus Dei!" Kyrie screamed and ran toward the mimic. Gloriae and Lacrimosa ran with him, lashing their torches.

The mimic's arms shot out. Kyrie ducked, and an arm swung over his head. Gloriae screamed. The mimic laughed. Lacrimosa ran and drove her torch forward, but the mimic's blade halved it. The top half, still aflame, landed at Kyrie's feet.

He kicked it, and it hit the mimic. Kyrie held his breath... but the creatyre didn't catch fire. Instead it lumbered toward him, swinging its blades.

Kyrie leaped back and raised his arms, protecting his face. A blade hit his vambrace and sparked.

"Agnus Dei!" he shouted. She was struggling to rise, blinking. Kyrie grabbed her and hoisted her up.

"Careful, Kyrie!" she shouted and pulled him back. The mimic was laughing, and its blades swung inches from Kyrie's face.

A scream of rage tore the air. Gloriae was charging, a lit javelin in hand. She drove the javelin into the mimic's back. The tip burst from its chest, still burning.

Kyrie gasped. Would it finally die?

No. Its torso did not catch fire. It turned to stare at Gloriae and laughed. Drool dripped down its chin. Maggots covered the javelin that thrust out from its chest.

"Gloriae," it said, voice guttural. Worms squirmed between its teeth. "Your father seeks you."

It swung its blades at her.

Gloriae ducked, drew her sword with a hiss, and parried. She swung her blade and severed one of the creature's arms.

Kyrie's heart leaped. He charged forward with his torch. Agnus Dei and Lacrimosa ran too, screaming and waving torches.

The severed arm squirmed toward them, leaped from the ground, and slammed against their chests.

Lacrimosa fell and knocked into Agnus Dei, who knocked into Kyrie. Gloriae charged at the mimic, but it swung its remaining arm and drove her back. Its blade whirled.

The severed arm squirmed, and its hand caught Lacrimosa's hair. It pulled her to her feet. Lacrimosa wriggled and tried to pry herself loose, but could not. Unnaturally strong, the arm tugged her toward the body it had been attached to. The creature snarled at her, spraying her with drool.

"Lacrimosa," it hissed. "I was made with the blood of your husband." It spat a glob of blood onto her chest. "Do you recognize it? My master took it from his blade."

Agnus Dei, screaming and weeping, ran forward. She barrelled into the mimic, and it fell. It howled, and its teeth sank into Agnus Dei's shoulder, but she seemed not to notice. She grabbed its head, and slammed it against the floor again and again. The skull cracked, and centipedes spilled from it.

Gloriae slammed her blade down, severing the mimic's second link of arms. Kyrie set fire to it. The arms squirmed and screamed like a blazing snake.

Lacrimosa still struggled with the first severed arm; it was clutching her throat now. Kyrie rushed forward, set it ablaze, and its fingers opened. Lacrimosa breathed raggedly.

"Agnus Dei!" she whispered, hoarse.

The mimic's head had shattered. Blood and bone fragments spread across the cobblestones. And yet its jaw would not release Agnus Dei's shoulder. Kyrie grabbed the jaw, twisted, and managed to pry it off. He tossed it down and stomped on it until the teeth broke off.

Agnus Dei was screaming and sobbing. She drew her sword and began stabbing the mimic's torso, again and again. Its legs kicked, and cockroaches fled from it.

"You have to burn it!" Gloriae said, but Agnus Dei seemed not to hear. She kept stabbing and weeping and screaming.

Kyrie touched her shoulder, but she seemed not to notice him.

"Agnus Dei," he said. "Kitten."

She spun toward him, eyes red and puffy. "It said... about Father, did you hear? It said...."

"It was lying, Agnus Dei," Kyrie said. "Don't listen to it." He handed her a torch. "Burn its body, Agnus Dei. Finish it."

Agnus Dei took the torch and stared down at the mimic. There was nothing left but twitching legs and a shredded torso.

A voice rose from it.

Kyrie gasped. How could it still speak? And yet its blood bubbled, and strange, gurgling words rose from it.

"We will... return... more of us... thousands... we will make you mimics too...."

Agnus Dei tossed the torch onto it.

The remains caught fire, and a scream rose from them, high pitched. Kyrie covered his ears and grimaced. The scream went on and on, and the ruins shook.

Finally silence fell.

Kyrie breathed out shakily.

His wounds ached, his lungs burned, and he nearly collapsed.

"It's over," he said hoarsely. Agnus Dei crashed into his arms, and he held her. Gloriae and Lacrimosa joined the embrace. Blood and ash covered them.

"We beat them," Kyrie whispered into the embrace. Agnus Dei's hair surrounded his face like a pillow, scented of smoke. "We defended our home."

He looked to the eastern horizon. Red wisps spread across it. Dawn had arrived. It looked to Kyrie like rivers of blood.

One battle had ended. The war against the mimics, he knew, was only beginning.

LACRIMOSA

The young ones huddled under the archway, embracing one another. She had washed their wounds with spirits, bandaged them, and prayed for them. Now, as the youths whispered in the dawn, Lacrimosa could be alone with her thoughts, her grief, and her memories.

She walked to the edge of the courtyard. A bit of old wall, three feet tall, jutted there like a last tooth in the gums of an old dragon. Lacrimosa climbed atop it and stared into the dawn. Wind played with her hair. Snow fell lightly, kissing her cheeks. She looked toward the valley where her husband lay buried.

"I miss you, Ben," she whispered.

She missed his strong arms around her; his laughter, deep and rolling like distant thunder; the stubble on his face; the softness in his eyes when she kissed him.

"Watch over me, Ben. You walk now in our halls beyond the stars, with our parents, with our siblings. You're at rest now. I continue the fight for you."

The wind gusted, opening her cloak, chilling her. Lacrimosa hugged herself. It would be so easy, she thought, to lie down in the snow, close her eyes, and wait for warmth to take her. It would be like falling asleep, and she would be with Benedictus again. But Lacrimosa turned her head, and looked back at Kyrie and her daughters, and knew that she must be strong for them.

"I must survive," she whispered into the wind. "I must guide them, and heal them, and fight for them. Who else would?"

They had so much to live for, she thought. Kyrie and Agnus Dei wanted to get married, to raise a family. Gloriae still dreamed of becoming a great leader, a queen of Requiem and defeater of Osanna. The youths spoke of rebuilding Requiem, of killing Dies Irae, of changing the world. In all this darkness, they saw light.

And what of myself? Lacrimosa thought. *Do I still see light in the world? My light died and lies buried in that valley. My children are my light now—my daughters, and Kyrie, my adopted son.*

"I don't know what strength I still have, Ben," Lacrimosa spoke to the distant valley. "But so long as I can, I will carry your torch. I will keep our children alive and their hope burning. I will do this for them and for you." Suddenly she was trembling, and tears flowed down her cheeks. "I miss you, Ben. I wish you were here with me. I love you."

When the wind gusted again, ash from a mimic's body swirled around her boots. Lacrimosa looked at the burned body, which lay in the courtyard, and saw a red glint. She frowned.

Wrapping her cloak around her, she stepped off the wall and approached the body. It was but a pile of ash and old bones. She stirred the ash with her boot, and saw the glint again—something red and glistening like a ruby. Thankful for her leather gloves, Lacrimosa reached into the ash and retrieved a gemstone the size of a chicken's egg.

She brushed it off and held it up. It sparkled strangely in the light. Shadows and stars seemed to swirl inside it, blood-red. It was heavy. Though small enough to fit in her palm, it felt much larger, like lifting a gourd.

"What's that, Lacrimosa?"

Gloriae walked toward her, eyes narrowed. Inwardly, Lacrimosa winced. *She still won't call me Mother. I saved her from Dies Irae moons ago, but I'm still only Lacrimosa to her.*

She hid her disappointment. "A gemstone," she said, holding it out. "I found it inside a mimic's body."

Gloriae frowned at the stone. "This looks familiar. I've seen this before somewhere." She scrunched her lips. "Yes. *Artifacts of Wizardry and Power* spoke of glowing red stones."

Lacrimosa nodded. "Gloriae, would you stay here and watch? You have the sharpest eyes. Call us if more mimics arrive. Kyrie, Agnus Dei! Come downstairs, into the cellars. We have some reading to do."

Soon the three stood underground by the hearth. The cellars looked strangely empty without the wood they'd been collecting for weeks. Her footfalls echoed. Sap, twigs, and pine needles covered the floor. They had few furnishings: A table and chairs Kyrie had built, a bearskin rug, and beds of straw. They had no shelves; their belongings, including their books

Mythic Creatures of the Grey Age and *Artifacts of Wizardry and Power*, lay in the corner.

Lacrimosa set the gemstone on the table, then fetched *Artifacts of Wizardry and Power*. She placed the ancient, leather-bound tome beside the gemstone, blew off the dust, and opened it.

"Let's see," she said and sat by the table. Kyrie and Agnus Dei stood behind her, looking over her shoulders at the book.

"Does it say anything about gemstones from mimic guts?" Agnus Dei said. She reached toward the pages. "Give it here."

Lacrimosa slapped her hand away. "Be patient. I'm looking." She flipped to the first chapter. "This chapter is about the Griffin Heart."

Agnus Dei groaned. "We know all about the Griffin Heart. We destroyed it already. Come on, Mother, get to the gemstones."

Lacrimosa turned her head and glowered at her daughter. "Agnus Dei, calm down. I'm looking."

She flipped the parchment pages and reached the second chapter. "And this chapter is about the Summoning Stick...."

Agnus Dei groaned louder. "Mother, we already used the Summoning Stick when fighting the nightshades. Give me the book. I'm a fast reader."

Lacrimosa glared at her daughter. "Agnus Dei, you're making me angry. Will you please let me—"

Lacrimosa froze.

The table was shaking.

"Earthquake?" she whispered. The gemstone and book rattled on the tabletop.

Kyrie shook his head. "Only the table is moving. Look! Its legs."

Lacrimosa gasped. The table legs were curling inward, forming a shape like animal legs. Before her eyes, the table began to creep across the floor, insect-like.

"What the—?" Kyrie said. "Agnus Dei, look what you did. Even the table is mad at you."

"I did nothing!" Agnus Dei objected.

Lacrimosa rose from her chair and stared. Her heart raced and her fingertips stung. She didn't like this. The table crawled, reminding her of a spider. It seemed to... turn to face her. The book and gemstone slid and fell onto the rug.

The table froze.

"Look, the rug!" Lacrimosa said.

They crowded around it and watched. The bearskin rug twisted. Its head rose to glare at them with its bead eyes. Its mouth opened, fangs glinting, and roared. The body of the rug squirmed, as if the bear were struggling to rise, and surprised to find that it had no bones left.

Kyrie whistled. "First the griffins and nightshades. Then the mimics. And now the furniture is turning against us. Can't we ever win?"

Agnus Dei punched his shoulder. "Pup, this is no time for being smart."

Lacrimosa lifted the gemstone off the rug. The bear gave a last growl, then fell flat onto the floor. Once more, it was still, its eyes dead and its mouth shut. The gemstone was now ice cold, nearly freezing Lacrimosa's hand. Red liquid swirled within it; it looked like blood.

"The gemstone brings things to life," Kyrie whispered, voice awed.

Agnus Dei snorted. "Sir Obvious saves the day again."

He glared at her. "You sound just like your sister, do you know?"

They raised their fists, and their eyes flashed. Lacrimosa stepped between them.

"Children! Stop fighting."

Agnus Dei flushed. "I'm not a child, Mother, I'm *nineteen*. The pup is only seventeen. He's a child."

Kyrie opened his mouth to object, but Lacrimosa put a finger against his lips.

"Kyrie, not now. No arguing. You two *are* children, and intolerable children at that." She placed the gemstone in Kyrie's hand. "Hold this. Now let's try this book again—quietly this time."

Lacrimosa turned several more pages, then nodded. "Here we are."

This chapter was entitled "Animating Stones". It featured an illustration of a battle. On one side fought knights, swordsmen, and archers. On the other side, a wizard commanded an army of statues. The statues seemed to move; they were tossing javelins and waving swords.

Lacrimosa read out loud.

"As there is no greater crime than taking a life, so is there no greater Magik than giving it. In all the lore of Ancient Artifacts, the Animating Stones are the most powerful, and the most dangerous. An Animating Stone can cause a river to rise like a serpent; a statue to march and fight; a corpse to escape the grave; or any other dead matter to take life, to move, to serve its master. Such is their might, that around Animating Stones, all other Magiks and Artifacts lose their power, and—"

"Look at this part," Agnus Dei interrupted. She pointed at the next paragraph. "About the Ancient Days."

Lacrimosa sighed and skipped forward. She kept reading. "In the Ancient Days, when the world was in chaos, the Ocean Deities created the Animating Stones, so they may mold the species from fire and water, and create a male and female from each. First they created the fish, then birds, and finally creatures to crawl upon the earth. They created Man and Woman last, him of fire and her of water, and placed the last two Animating Stones within their hearts."

Agnus Dei scrunched her lips. "It doesn't say when they created Vir Requis."

Kyrie shoved her. "The Draco stars created us, not any Ocean Deities. You should know that."

"Pardon me, oh wise scholar pup."

Lacrimosa continued reading. "When all creatures swam, flew, crawled, and walked, the Ocean Deities collected all the Animating Stones. They took them to a dark forest, and dug deep tunnels, and scattered them underground. None have seen them since."

The chapter was finished. Lacrimosa closed the book.

"So where is this dark forest?" Agnus Dei demanded. "How did Dies Irae find the buried Animating Stones?"

Kyrie mussed her hair. "If the book told us that, it would be too easy. And things are never easy. Haven't you learned that yet?"

"Stop messing my hair, pup."

Lacrimosa stood up. She looked at the youths—Agnus Dei with her flushed cheeks and flashing eyes, and Kyrie who was like a son to her now. She thought of Gloriae, her golden daughter, who guarded above, strong and brave. For the first time since the mimics had attacked, Lacrimosa saw hope for her children.

530

"Let's return to the courtyard," she said. "We have Animating Stones to collect... and life to create."

TERRA

"Kyrie!" he called, flying over the hills of dead. "Brother! Kyrie!"

Lanburg Fields lay below him, a field of blood, shattered weapons, and shattered bodies. Five thousand dead Vir Requis lay here, the last of their kind, cut with arrows, talons, and griffin beaks.

Dead. All dead.

"Kyrie!"

Terra's eyes stung, and his wings shook so badly, he could barely fly. His sister flew beside him, weeping.

"Kyrie!" she cried too, flying over the desolation, trembling. "Kyrie, where are you?"

They landed among the bodies and shifted into humans. The stench of blood and death rose around them, spinning Terra's head. His fingers shook. Desperate, he began to rummage through the bodies, turning them over, shoving them aside.

"Kyrie!"

No. He couldn't be dead. Couldn't be.

"We should have been here," he said hoarsely. "We should have died with them."

But the tunnels had collapsed around him and Memoria. The darkness had trapped them. The Poisoned had fought them. They had spent a day digging for light and life... only to find darkness and death.

"I should have been here with you, Kyrie," he whispered, limbs shaking. He remembered bandaging Kyrie's knee only a week ago, after he had fallen. *When you needed me most, I wasn't here.*

He pushed over the body of a child, but it was a girl, her body burned, her face torn. As he held the girl, the wind died.

For a moment, the killing field was silent.

Memoria spoke behind him, her voice strangely soft, strangely beautiful.

"Terra... I found him."

He turned and saw her looking toward him, but not at him. She seemed to be staring a thousand yards away, her eyes huge and glistening. She cradled a small body in her arms. It was burned so badly, Terra could not recognize it.

But it had yellow hair. It was the right size. It wore the same orange scarf.

Terra... I found him.

Terra clenched his fists.

No.

He took a deep, shaky breath. *Do not remember, Terra. Memories are wrong. Memories are pain. That life is behind you. Kyrie has been dead for eleven years; let him rest in peace.*

Terra looked around him. No blood. No fire. Just ice, snow, and frost. Whale Hall rose around him, its pillars like ribs. The sun shone softly, a mere smudge behind the ceiling of ice. *An end to pain,* he thought. No more memories. No more blood. His life was ice now. He would fill his memories and soul with nothing but this endless ice.

Pain stung him. He winced and cursed.

Amberus, the Elder of Elders, smiled and clucked his tongue. He was sprinkling green powder into Terra's wound; the stuff burned like ilbane. As he worked, the old man chanted prayers to the Wind Goddess, or maybe it was the Sky Eagle or Old Walrus. Terra no longer cared about deities, not those of the north, nor the stars that had abandoned him.

"You will heal now," Memoria said, voice soft. She sat beside him, wrapped in furs, a hood pulled over her head. "Amberus is a wise healer."

Her eyes, large and brown, brimmed with concern. Terra felt his pain melt, both the pain of his wounds, and the pain within him. No, not everyone lay as burned skeletons. Memoria still lived. *And it's for you that I still live,* he thought. *It's for you that I don't walk into the ice and never return. I'll stay alive for you, sister, and watch over you.*

Amberus bandaged the wound and furrowed his brow. "Your wounds will heal, Son Terra, but an evil caused them. The Ice Mother weeps for them. There is dark magic in them, and poison, and secrets from far away. What caused these wounds, Son Terra? They trouble me greatly."

"Demons from under the ice," Terra said. His throat tightened at the memory, and he swallowed. "They were like dolls, sewn together from the body parts of dead men. They seemed to have dark magic to them, yes. Memoria and I could not become dragons around them, as if their magic undid ours."

Amberus closed his eyes and mumbled prayers. His feet tapped, silent against the ice. He chanted to Father Whale, a god of ancient times, and to Mother Turtle, whose northern lights glittered upon the Ice City.

Terra looked at his sister. Memoria stared back, her doe eyes so large, so sad. He could see his fear reflected in them. Was Dies Irae back? Was he hunting them again?

Finally Amberus opened his eyes. They were startling blue and glowed like the moon. Staring at nothing, he drew black powder from a hidden pocket, tossed it onto the floor, and slammed down his staff.

Terra watched, eyes narrowing. He caught his breath. The black powder stirred, swirled, and raised smoke. The smoke rose, flowed toward the distant ceiling of the palace, and raced around the columns of ice. Moaning like wind, the smoke dived to the floor, gathered, and formed into ten figures like men. *No, not men*, Terra decided. The smoke looked like mismatched bodies sewn together, their hair swarming like worms.

"The creatures we saw," Memoria whispered. She clutched her fur cloak.

The smoke dispersed, swirled in a maelstrom, then formed new figures. This time it formed thousands of small, smoky creatures that marched across the ice. *More rotting demons*, Terra thought. *An army of them.* The creatures howled, then dispersed into snakes of smoke. The smoke rose, swirled and raged, and finally collapsed into powder again.

Silence filled the hall.

"What does it mean?" Terra asked, looking up at Amberus.

"They are mimics," Amberus said. Wrinkles deepened around his eyes. "Mimics of life... and mimics of death. They flow with the stench of it. They hunt your kind, the sky warriors that you call dragons. They do not sleep. They do not tire. You cannot kill them. They will never stop hunting you and your kind."

"Do you see more of our kind, Amberus?" Memoria asked. She clutched Terra's hand. She looked at him, and Terra knew she was remembering the names the creatures had spoken.

Agnus Dei.

Kyrie Eleison.

Amberus shook his head, his necklace of icicles clinking. "That is hard to see now, as it always has been. If there are more dragons, they hide well; the Mother Turtle cannot see them. But these mimics... they hunt for dragons everywhere. Most flow to the old ruins, the place you call Requiem. If there are more dragons, they hide there."

Terra closed his eyes. His chest tightened, and cold sweat trickled down his back. He could barely breathe, and his pulse pounded in his ears. War. Destruction in Requiem again.

Terra... I found him.

For years he had struggled to forget, to banish those words from his memory. Now, once more, Terra felt the fire around him, smelled the stench of death, saw the small burned body.

"We have to go back," Memoria whispered.

Terra opened his eyes. "What?" he demanded. "Memoria, we do not return. Not now. Not ever. When we left, we left for good."

Memoria breathed heavily and her cheeks flushed. She glared at him. "Terra, when we left, we thought that we were the last. That they all had died at Lanburg Fields. But they didn't. Two at least still live. Agnus Dei... and our brother."

Terra clenched his fists and shook his head. His chest felt tight. "Kyrie is dead, sister. We buried him."

Memoria's eyes flashed. Her chest rose and fell as she panted. "We buried a body. The body of a burned child his size, with the same hair and scarf. But we don't know it was him." She clutched his shoulders, tears in her eyes. "Kyrie is alive, Terra. Kyrie and the princess Agnus Dei. I know it."

He looked away, throat burning.

Terra... I found him.

He looked back at Memoria, her face so pale, so sad. He couldn't let that happen to her. The loss of his brother still haunted him. How could he lose his sister too, see her body also burned, cry over her grave?

"Memoria," he said, and for a moment he could say no more. He tightened his jaw. For the first time since he'd buried

Kyrie, he felt ready to cry. He refused to. He would shed no more tears. He had vowed to remain strong. It was a long moment before he could speak again, voice strained. "Memoria, I led us here to protect you. To hide you. To—"

"You fled here to escape death!" she said. "You came here to escape memory. To escape pain. To escape... to escape what we found at Lanburg Fields."

He shouted, voice echoing in the ice hall. "We ran to save our lives!"

She shook her head wildly, hair swaying. "That doesn't matter anymore. Our lives are threatened here too. Those creatures found us even here, a thousand leagues north of Requiem."

"Three mimics found us. Thousands march to Requiem."

"So we will return to defend it!"

Terra laughed mirthlessly. "With what? Our swords? We couldn't shift around those things, Memoria. Their claws tore through my armor as if it were wool." He looked at Amberus, who was watching them silently. "Elder of Elders, please. Tell her it's dangerous. Tell her she cannot go chasing that evil."

The old man nodded slowly, lips pursed. He looked at the powder on the ice, and his brow furrowed. His eyes darkened, and his wrinkles deepened. His knuckles whitened around his whalebone staff. Terra had never seen the old man look so troubled.

Finally Amberus looked up, nodded, and spoke in a low voice.

"It is time to reclaim Adoria's Hands."

Terra stared at him. "Adoria? Is this another deity of the north?"

Ambrus shook his head. His voice was soft, as if lost in memory. "She was an iceling sorceress who lived many seasons ago. She created magic to stop other sorcerers from casting spells upon her. She could hold out her hands... and stop magic. Fearing sorcerers, the giants killed Adoria and cut off her hands. The Giant King wears those hands as amulets; they hang on a chain around his neck. They still repel magic."

Terra felt the blood leave his face. "The Giant King...."

Amberus stared at him, his eyes suddenly blazing. "You cannot shift around mimics. Their magic stops your own. But if you owned Adoria's Hands, mimic magic would not touch you.

You could become dragons around them. You could burn them all with dragonfire. If you want to save your friends, you must face the Giant King... and reclaim Adoria's Hands."

Terra turned away from Amberus. He looked at his sister—his small, frail sister, the person he loved most, the person he was sworn to protect. He lowered his head and embraced her.

"How can I face this again?" he whispered. "Memoria, how can I face the dead, their souls that still hover there? I was a bellator, a knight of Requiem. I vowed to defend them. How can I face their ghosts?"

Memoria held him, her grip tight, fingers digging. She whispered into his ear. "We don't return for the dead, Terra. We return for the living."

Kyrie! he had cried. *Kyrie, do you hear me?*

Could it be?

Could he still live?

Terra took a deep, shaky breath. His stomach knotted, and he could barely breathe. Kyrie, a child with yellow hair, only six years old, a somber child who saw too much war, too much pain. Kyrie, who'd be seventeen now, a grown man. Kyrie, who lived forever in his mind, even here, even as he struggled to forget.

Are you still out there, Kyrie? Do you still need me?

He tightened his jaw.

He nodded.

Agnus Dei. Kyrie Eleison.

"We'll need Adoria's Hands." He held his sister's shoulders. "We'll need to kill the Giant King."

GLORIAE

As Gloriae worked, collecting Animating Stones, she did not speak. The others conversed excitedly, imagining where Dies Irae was mining the stones, and how they could animate their own warriors, and about finding more firewood, and... Gloriae ignored it. She kept separate from the others. As they scoured the courtyard for Animating Stones, she walked along the mountainsides, rummaging through the ashes of the mimics her arrows had killed.

Mimics. Monsters. Creatures of death. Dies Irae's latest creations.

Before them, he had sent nightshades upon Requiem, creatures of darkness and evil.

And before the nightshades... he had sent her. Gloriae the Gilded.

For the first time she understood. She looked at the ruin around her, the ashes of demons, monsters, rotting things. She had just been one of his monsters.

"I am Gloriae the Gilded!" she would cry from her griffin. "I fight for light and life."

And thus she had killed. Thus she had tortured, and burned, and dealt death to Requiem. To her own people. Thus she had let Dies Irae mold her into just another monster, a creature of darkness and death. No different than the nightshades. No different than the mimics.

Gloriae came upon the burned, smoking body of a mimic. It rustled at her feet in the breeze. She kicked it, and the body scattered. She reached into the ash—it was still warm—and found another Animating Stone. The stone's innards pulsed red in her hand like a heart.

My heart too was made of stone, she thought. *I was a creature like this.*

Gloriae looked into the stone. Liquid seemed to swirl inside it like blood. In its patterns, she imagined the eyes of a child, a young Vir Requis wounded by griffin claws.

"Kill it," Dies Irae had said to her. "Draw your sword and kill the weredragon."

Gloriae had not wanted to. She wanted to go home. She wanted to look away from the child's weeping eyes, from the blood on his stomach.

"Run the creature through, daughter," Dies Irae had said.

"Yes, Father," she told him. He was a father to her then. She drew her thin sword, and stabbed the child, and stared at the blood with dry eyes. She was six years old.

Gloriae looked back at the ruins of Draco Murus. Her sister was chasing Kyrie, yelling at him for getting ash in her hair. Lacrimosa was trying to stop the girl, but it was like trying to stop a charging mare. Gloriae wanted to smile. She wanted to run too, to laugh, to play. But... those were fragile emotions, weren't they? Emotions regular people felt. Not warriors of ice. Not maidens of steel.

If I smile, if I laugh, if I love... I am human. I am guilty. My hands are bloody.

She stared. She kept her face still. She had to remain this warrior of steel; warriors did not feel pain, guilt, or shame.

"I must remain Gloriae the Gilded," she whispered to herself. "Hard as steel, ruthless as my blade. I will allow no weakness. I will not allow those child's eyes to haunt me. Dies Irae raised me a killer; to change would hurt too much, confess too much blood. I will remain what he made me. But I will not kill more Vir Requis." She turned to look east, toward the distant lands where Dies Irae ruled. "I will kill you, Irae. You made me a killer, and this killer will be your death."

"Gloriae! Gloriae, have you found the last ones?"

Lacrimosa was waving from the ruins, calling her. Gloriae stared back, hand on the hilt of her sword, and nodded.

Stay strong, she told herself. *Even if she is your mother. Even if you love her. Love leads to joy, to memory, to guilt... and then pain.*

"I found them," she called back. She walked uphill, the Animating Stones in her pack, and joined the others in the ruins.

They brushed off a few ashy cobblestones and placed their Animating Stones there. Gloriae counted them. A hundred shone and trembled at her feet. What ash blew toward them formed strands like snakes, which writhed until the wind blew them away. The cobblestones beneath them trembled.

Kyrie stared down at the Animating Stones and shuddered. "Nasty things, they are. Black magic."

Gloriae looked at him and raised an eyebrow. "Black magic, Kyrie? According to our book, they created early life in this world. Death and life are closely linked; they are sides of the same coin. Or stone, in our case. Don't judge so quickly what is evil, and what is good."

She stared back to the stones, and wondered: *Am I talking of this magic, or of myself?*

Lacrimosa lifted one stone and held it to the light. It glimmered. "If we create life with them, will our creations serve us? Or will their loyalties still lie with Dies Irae?"

Gloriae remembered her days at Flammis Palace, serving the man she thought of as Father. Hunting for him. Killing for him.

She put her hand on Lacrimosa's shoulder and stared into her eyes. "Whatever beings we animate—they will not serve him. He animated creatures from dead soldiers who feared him; their loyalties continued in their mimicry of life. But we will animate the stones of Requiem. Our creations will fight for us." She nodded. "Broken statues cover this land. Let us find what statues are still whole, even if ash and dirt cover them. They will be Requiem's new soldiers."

Lacrimosa nodded. "King's Forest lies several leagues north, nestling the ruins of our palace. We will find statues there. Most will be smashed, but we might be lucky and find some whole. Kyrie. Agnus Dei. You two travel there, and take fifty Animating Stones with you. Raise us soldiers of stone. Gloriae, you will travel with me south, where our old temples once stood. We might find more statues among their ruins."

Gloriae nodded. "When Dies Irae returns with more mimics, and he will, he will find us ready this time. I hope he himself leads the next charge." She drew her sword and raised it. The light of Animating Stones painted it red. "If he does, he will meet this blade."

They collected the Animating Stones into packs, and with quick embraces, they parted. Gloriae and her mother began walking down the southern mountainside. Her sister and Kyrie disappeared down the other way.

For a long time, daughter and mother walked in silence.

They walked across valleys strewn with shattered blades, arrowheads, and cloven helmets. They moved through forests of charred trees, skeletons, and fallen columns. Silently, they passed by mass graves, where the wind whispered and yellow weeds rustled. Gloriae tried to imagine Requiem in her glory days: Proud columns of marble rising among birches, stone pools and statues among flowers, and white temples where priests played harps. Mostly, she imagined herds of dragons in the sky, roaring their song, a stream of color and fire and music.

I destroyed this land, she thought, remembering the dragons she had slain in her youth.

But no. She had been only a child when Dies Irae started his war. Three years old, that was all. By the time she was eight, most dragons were dead; only a handful of survivors remained for her to hunt.

"He did this," she whispered and clenched her fist around Per Ignem's hilt. "Not me. Him alone."

The memories swirling through her, Gloriae had forgotten about her mother beside her. Lacrimosa now touched her hair and smiled sadly. There was no accusation in her lavender eyes, only pain and love.

"I know, sweetness," she whispered.

For the first time, Gloriae realized that she looked like her mother. Lacrimosa had the same pale skin, the same golden hair, the same face Gloriae knew people said was beautiful.

"What do you know?" she whispered, and a tightness gripped her chest. She had spoken little; she had thought a lot. Could Lacrimosa see into her heart?

Lacrimosa took her hand. "You are my daughter, Gloriae. You don't have to speak for me to know your pain. You shield this pain in ice, but it pulses red as fire, and I can see its light."

Gloriae stopped walking. A tremble took her knees. "I hide nothing," she whispered.

But suddenly Lacrimosa was embracing her, and Gloriae allowed it. Suddenly tears stung at her eyes.

"I love you, Gloriae," her mother whispered into her ear. "You don't have to speak of your pain. Not until you're ready. I know what he did to you. I know what he made you do. And I still love you. I always did, and I always will." She pulled back and looked into Gloriae's eyes. "You are forgiven, Gloriae."

Something salty touched her lips. She was crying. She, Gloriae the Gilded—crying. Her fingers trembled. *No,* she told herself. *Stay strong. You are Gloriae the Gilded. You are a killer. You are a warrior of steel. You... you....*

She fell to her knees, and another tear flowed, and Gloriae reached out to clutch at something, anything, and Mother was there kneeling beside her. She clung to her.

"I'm sorry," she whispered, her tears on Mother's shoulder. "I'm sorry, please. Please. I didn't know, I...."

She bit back her words. She knuckled away her tears.

"No," she said. "No pain. Not now. I'm not ready. We still have to be strong. To kill him. We must kill him, Mother."

Lacrimosa nodded and brushed back locks of Gloriae's hair. "We will kill him. Now let's keep moving. We have statues to find."

They continued walking through the ruins. Crows cawed above, the first sign of life Gloriae had seen all day. She look at Lacrimosa, this woman of pale frailty like starlight, and realized: *For the first time, I called her Mother.*

AGNUS DEI

"Pup, you're walking too slowly," she said. "Can't you hurry up?"

Kyrie glared at her. He looked to Agnus Dei like a porcupine, all bristly with weapons. A sword hung from his right hip, a dagger from his left. A bow, a quiver of arrows, and two torches hung over his back. Dented armor covered his forearms and legs, and he wore a helmet that was too large. With all this covering him, he sloshed through the snow like a drunkard.

"Agnus Dei," he said, "I swear. If you complain about one more thing, I'm going to—"

"What, give me a black eye?" She smiled crookedly. "Maybe a fat lip? I'd like to see you try, pup. I'm stronger than you, deadlier than you, faster than you—well, obviously faster than you, seeing how slow you're walking. Look at me. I'm bearing just as much armor and weapons, but I'm walking straight and fast."

"I might be slower, but you're whinier," he said, adjusting the strap of his quiver. "That's for sure."

"Who's whiny?" she asked and mimicked him. "Ow, Agnus Dei! My feet hurt. I'm hungry. I'm thirsty. I love you so much, that my heart aches, and my loins are about to burst into flame."

He groaned. "And what about you?" He spoke in falsetto. "Oh pup, I want to fight! No wait, I want to fly now. Actually let's kiss and roll in the hay!"

She snorted. "You wish." But in truth, she did want to fight, and fly, and... as Kyrie put it, roll in the hay. Any one of those things beat crying. Sometimes Agnus Dei felt that no more tears could flow from her, that no more pain could fill her. And yet the pain was always there, a rock in her stomach, ropes around her heart, smoke in her eyes. Fighting, flying, loving—that was better than pain. Wasn't it?

She sighed and took his hand. It was gloved in leather, and she squeezed it.

"All right, pup," she said. "I'll walk a little slower to match your small puppy steps."

They walked through the ruins, snow swirling around their boots. Soon they passed the mossy boulders that reminded Agnus Dei of dragons, and she looked to her right and saw the cemetery there. The ropes around her heart tightened, and she gave Kyrie's hand another squeeze.

I'm still fighting, Father, she thought. *I'll be strong like you. Like you taught me.*

Tears filled her eyes, and she wiped them with her fist. Kyrie saw, and his eyes softened, and for a long time they walked in silence. She looked at him once, and wanted to pester him, tease him, kiss him even... but none of it felt right. Not before, not now. How could she still find joy in this world, when her father lay buried, and monsters crawled the ruins?

But there was something she could do. *I can fight.*

"Do you think we'll find any statues?" she asked. She hefted her heavy leather pack, where she carried Animating Stones. "I've seen only pieces of statues in Requiem, feet or hands or heads."

Like the body pieces Dies Irae sews together, she thought with a shudder.

Kyrie scanned the northern horizon, as if he could see statues from here. "I don't know. But the ruins of Requiem's palace are a good place to look. If we find them anywhere, we'll—"

A howl pierced the air.

Agnus Dei and Kyrie drew their swords with a hiss.

A second howl sounded—closer this time.

Scanning the ruins, Agnus Dei lowered her blade.

"Wolves," she said. "They would roam my old mountain hideout; I'd recognize their howls anywhere."

She wished she could shift—she'd rather face a hungry wolf pack as a dragon—but the Animating Stones in her pack meant facing them as humans.

"Those aren't wolves," Kyrie said. He stared from side to side, as if seeking them. "There are no more wolves in Requiem."

A third howl rose, this one even closer. More howls answered. They still sounded like wolf howls, but... deeper, crueler. Agnus Dei shivered.

"Look!" Kyrie said and pointed with his sword.

Agnus Dei saw six figures in the distance. They seemed like men—they ran through the snow on two legs—but they howled like demon wolves.

"They saw us," she said. "Kyrie, let's light some arrows."

He already had his tinderbox in hand. "I like the way you think."

They switched from swords to bows, lit their arrows, and nocked them. The figures raced toward them. Their stench carried on the wind—the stench of bodies.

"More mimics," Agnus Dei said, jaw tight.

When the creatures were close enough to see clearly, she nearly gagged. Their bodies were from dead humans, stitched and stuffed. Their heads were the heads of dead wolves, sewn onto human necks, fur matted and eyes dripping pus.

"Let's burn those bastards," Agnus Dei said. "Fire!"

She loosed her arrow. Kyrie did the same. The flaming missiles flew in an arc. Agnus Dei cursed; her arrow missed. Kyrie's hit a mimic's leg. It screeched, fell, then rose and kept running.

"Fire again!" Agnus Dei shouted.

They lit more arrows. They shot again. This time, Agnus Dei hit a mimic in the chest, and she shouted in rage and triumph. The creature fell, and the fire spread across it. Kyrie's arrow grazed another's shoulder, searing but not killing it.

"Agnus Dei, light your torch!" Kyrie shouted. He was busy lighting his, and soon swung it as a flaming club. Agnus Dei managed to light hers as the five surviving mimics reached them.

She swung her torch and hit a wolf head. Sparks blazed. A second mimic bit at her left. Its stench stung her eyes and twisted her stomach. She leaped back and raised her arm. Its teeth banged against her vambrace, and it howled. She shoved the torch against its face. Its fur kindled and it screamed.

From the corner of her eye, she saw Kyrie battling his own mimics. Then one leaped onto her, knocking her down. She hit the snow and crossed her arms over her face. Wolf teeth bit at her armor. Drool dripped onto her face, thick with dead ants. Agnus Dei grimaced and kicked the creature's stomach.

The mimic fell off, and Agnus Dei jumped up. She slammed the torch into the fallen mimic, but another one leaped onto her back. Teeth ripped at her shoulder, and she screamed. Her thick, woollen cloak absorbed most of the bite, but those teeth still tore flesh.

She spun, swinging her torch, but was too slow. The mimic barrelled into her, and she fell again. Teeth closed around her forearm, pressing into the armor. The creature snarled, steam rising from its nostrils. Worms filled its fur.

The words of the mimic last night returned to her. *We were made with drops of Benedictus's blood....*

Rage filled Agnus Dei. She dropped her torch, drew her dagger, and shoved it into the wolf's eye.

It screamed and released her. She scrambled to her feet and shoved her torch into its rotting face. The head caught flame, and soon the whole body burned and writhed. She stared down at it, the fire stinging her eyes, and spat onto its body.

"Agnus Dei," Kyrie said, panting. "Agnus Dei, you're hurt."

She turned to see three mimic bodies at his feet, burned dead. Teeth marks peppered his arm; he clutched the wound.

"I hate these bastard mimics," she said and tightened her jaw. The smoke and heat stung her eyes. "I hate the damn things. I *hate* them."

He nodded. "I know. I do too. More than anything—other than Irae, maybe."

Agnus Dei tossed her torch aside, took three large strides, and embraced him. He held her in the snow and smoke, and she rested her head against his shoulder. His hand, bloody, smoothed her hair.

"I hate them, by the stars," she whispered, throat tight. "I hate their lies. I want to burn them all."

"We will," Kyrie promised.

She stared into his eyes. She touched his cheek, smearing ash and blood across it. "I love you, Kyrie. I'm sorry if I tease you sometimes, or call you a pup. You're a good fighter. And you're strong. Don't forget that, Kyrie."

"Okay, kitten," he said, and gave her a smile and wink.

She couldn't help but laugh. It felt good. She kissed his cheek, and pushed him back, and said, "Let's bandage these wounds, then keep walking. And try to keep up this time."

LACRIMOSA

The mimic scurried toward them like a starfish. It had no torso, no legs, no head. It was nothing but five human arms growing around a mouth.

Nausea filled her, and Lacrimosa screamed.

The creature raced toward her on five hands. The mouth in its center snapped open and closed, making sucking noises.

Gloriae shot her bow. A flaming arrow flew and hit an arm. That arm collapsed and burned, but the creature kept racing on its four good arms.

Lacrimosa wanted to gag. She wanted to run. Instead she raced toward the creature, shouted, and swung her torch.

The flames hit the creature between two arms, and it squealed, a sound like a child crying. She had expected a howl of rage; this high, pained mewl shocked her, and Lacrimosa lowered her torch.

The mimic leaped and wrapped its arms around her. It hugged her, crushing her, and its mouth came in to bite.

"Get off her!" Gloriae cried and stabbed it. The mimic squealed—a child's squeal. Blood gushed from it.

Lacrimosa struggled. The arms felt like they could snap her ribs. The mouth opened before her face, screaming, full of teeth. She tried to push it back, but it pinned her arms to her sides. Her torch fell to the ground.

"Burn, you freak," Gloriae said, lifted the fallen torch, and held it to the creature.

It screamed. The flames rose, intolerably hot. Lacrimosa grimaced and closed her eyes. She struggled and writhed, freed an arm, and shoved the burning mimic off.

It curled up at her feet, scurried, and fell. Flames and smoke rose from it. Still it cried, the sound of a human girl.

Gloriae nocked another arrow. Lacrimosa wanted to stop her. *No,* she wanted to cry. *No, it's only a child! Don't kill it.* But she knew that death was mercy for this thing, this starfish of arms growing from a crying mouth.

Gloriae shot her arrow into that mouth.

Blood flowed, and the creature convulsed, then lay still.

"Hideous thing," Gloriae said and spat onto it. "Disgusting."

Lacrimosa said nothing. She stared down at the burning mimic, wondering who it had been in life. Who had given it these five arms, this mouth? Soldiers? Farmers? Was one a child?

She forced a deep, shaky breath. "Let's get its Animating Stone."

Once they had its stone, they continued to walk between the ruins. Snow began to fall, coating their cloaks. Soon they entered the Valley of Stars, where the temples of Requiem had once stood.

Lacrimosa walked silently, head lowered. This was a holy place. Bricks lay strewn around her, white mounds under the snow. The capitals of columns lay fallen, glimmering with icicles. Part of a wall still stood, as tall as Lacrimosa, still showing the grooves of griffin claws. Lacrimosa clutched the hilt of her father's sword. Diamonds shone in that hilt, arranged like the Draco constellation. In the Valley of Stars, the diamonds seemed warm against her hand. *This place still has some power, even as it lies in ruin.*

Gloriae looked around with narrowed eyes, her mouth open, her cheeks kissed pink with cold. She turned to Lacrimosa.

"I remember this place!" she said. "I... I remember temples. They stood tall, as tall as Flammis Palace, all of white stone. Birches grew here." She knelt, reached into the snow, and lifted a glass crystal. "This crystal! It was part of a chandelier. Many of them hung in the temples. I remember."

Lacrimosa looked at her daughter, and memories flooded her too, but not memories of temples and crystals. She saw again a laughing toddler, her hair all golden curls, her eyes green and full of wonder at the world.

"I love you so much, Gloriae," she said, tears in her eyes. "Then and now. My heart broke when Dies Irae stole you. Let our hearts heal now. Together."

Gloriae opened her mouth to speak, but seemed to see something. Her eyes widened, and she pointed behind Lacrimosa. "Look!"

Lacrimosa turned, and a smile spread across her face. She had missed the statue at first; snow and icicles covered it. She walked toward it, cleared off the snow and ice, and her smile widened. It was a statue of a dragon, six feet tall. One of its wings had fallen, it was missing a fang, and a crack ran along its chest, but it was otherwise unharmed. It was the most complete statue she had seen in these ruins.

"Do you think it would work?" Gloriae whispered, coming to stand beside her. Snow sparkled in her hair.

Lacrimosa nodded. A tingle ran through her. "This one will be a warrior of Requiem."

She ran her fingers over the crack along the dragon's chest. It was the work of a griffin talon, or perhaps a knight's war hammer. *In this wound, I will place its heart.*

She took an Animating Stone from her pack. It thrummed in her palm, glowed, and its red innards swirled. It felt hot, so hot it almost burned her. Lacrimosa wedged the stone into the crack, until it stuck. It pulsed and glowed in the statue's chest, a heart of stone.

Lacrimosa took her daughter's hand, and they stepped back, watching.

The dragon statue was still.

Lacrimosa exhaled, feeling deflated.

"It's not working," Gloriae whispered.

"Just watch," Lacrimosa said, still daring to hope.

She stared and frowned. Was Gloriae right? The Animating Stone still glowed and swirled, but....

The stone dragon's wing creaked.

Gloriae gasped and squeezed Lacrimosa's hand.

The statue moved its head, just an inch. The stone creaked, and for an instant Lacrimosa thought the head would snap off. But the stone moved like a living thing—creaky and stiff, but alive.

Then the dragon lifted its arms, and arched its back, and snow fell from it. The icicles on its arms snapped. It tossed back its head and roared, and Lacrimosa wanted to draw her sword or flee. Would it attack them?

"Stone of Requiem!" she called to it. "I am Lacrimosa, Queen of Requiem. Do you hear me? I raise the stones of our land. Requiem calls for your aid."

The stone dragon looked at her, and its eyes narrowed. The Animating Stone in its chest blazed. The statue's mouth closed, opened, and then it roared again.

It was a roar of pain, of grief, and of joy.

"It's thanking us," Lacrimosa whispered, her eyes moist. "It saw the death of this land. It sings for memory, and for new life."

The clouds parted, and beams of sunlight fell upon the ruins of Requiem. The stone dragon, chipped and broken, roared its song.

Lacrimosa turned to face her daughter, and saw that Gloriae's green eyes shone. The girl panted, her hair golden in the sun.

And there is new life here too, grief and pain and finally some joy. As I bring life to the stones of Requiem, let me bring new life to my daughter, to my beloved, to my Gloriae.

She smiled at her daughter, and Gloriae smiled back, the rarest of smiles. *She has a beautiful smile, a smile like sunlight on snow.*

"And now, daughter," Lacrimosa said, "we will build an army."

AGNUS DEI

They entered King's Forest at dawn, five days after leaving their mountain ruins, and Agnus Dei's throat tightened.

"The hall of Requiem's kings," she whispered.

Kyrie took her hand. They stood on a hill and gazed silently upon the ruins. Dead, burned trees lay covered with snow. Requiem's palace lay fallen between them, the palace where Father had once ruled. It had once boasted a hundred columns. They lay smashed now, buried in snow. Only one still stood, two hundred feet tall, its capital shaped as bucking dragons. It rose from the ruins into sunbeams, kissed with light, its marble brighter than the snow.

"King's Column," Agnus Dei said, voice soft. "That is what it's called. They say even Dies Irae himself, atop his griffin Volucris, could not topple it. They say it is star blessed. I thought it a legend."

Kyrie nodded. "It won't fall so long as there are living Vir Requis. While it stands, there is hope for Requiem."

Agnus Dei lit her torch. "Let's move carefully. We might find statues in the ruins. We might also find mimics."

Kyrie lit his torch too, and they walked downhill toward the palace ruins. The snow glittered under the dawn like a field of stars. It was quiet. Agnus Dei heard only a soft wind, the crackle of their torches, and the crunch of snow under their boots. Lumps rose under the snow. Agnus Dei and Kyrie began brushing snow aside, searching. They found many bricks, fallen blades, a broken lance, a shield, the skeletons of men, and even a griffin's skeleton. They found statues too, but they were smashed: a marble head here, an arm there, pedestals with feet still attached, but no more.

"Do you think we can repair them?" Agnus Dei asked. She lifted a statue's hand, twice the size of her own, and held it.

"With what?" Kyrie said, his clothes white with snow. "We have no tools."

Agnus Dei sighed. It seemed hopeless. Some of the war's largest battles had been fought here. Everything here was smashed, aside from King's Column.

She turned to look at the pillar. It towered above her, so wide three men could not hug it. Scenes of flying dragons were engraved into the marble. Agnus Dei walked toward the column and touched the stone. It was cold, colder than ice; she could feel that even through her gloves. She ran her fingers over old words carved into the marble. *Requiem! May our wings forever find your sky.*

"King Aeternum built this column," she told Kyrie. "He was the first of our line, and among the greatest kings, Father would say. Father was descended from him, did you know? Aeternum ruled seventy-four generations before Father, and his line ruled continuously until the war." She swallowed.

Kyrie put an arm around her. "The line still stands. You are descended from Aeternum too. When you or Gloriae are crowned, you will be the seventy-seventh monarch of Aeternum's house."

She raised an eyebrow. "Me or Gloriae—queens? Pup, we are fighters. Survivors. We are no queens. What is there to rule here?" She swept her arms around her. "Nothing remains."

Kyrie jutted his chin toward King's Column. "That remains. Aeternum's pillar. And we remain, don't we? You and I. Your mother and sister. Lacrimosa is our queen; this is her pillar now, her place to rule. And after her, you and Gloriae will rule."

Agnus Dei laughed and pinched his cheek. "Pup, you'd hate me as your queen. If you think I'm bossy now, you'd be running to the hills then. And if Gloriae is queen, I think you'd hate that enough to jump off a cliff."

He grinned. "Maybe you're right. I think a rebellion is in order. I think it might be time for Kyrie Eleison to take power." He laughed, then sighed and took a deep breath. "You're right, kitten. There's not much left here, and not much point for queens, and kings, and palaces. But I like talking about it. It makes me feel like... like it's honoring old Aeternum, if he's watching from the Draco stars. And I feel like we're honoring Benedictus too. When we remember their prayers, their customs, and their lines of power, we're keeping their memory alive. We're carrying their torch. Even if Requiem lies in ruin, and we can never rebuild her, I'll keep carrying this torch. For him. For Benedictus. I loved him."

Agnus Dei looked at him with damp eyes. She sniffed and nodded. "I loved him too. More than I ever told him in life. I wish he were here, that I could tell him that. I wish.... Oh, pup. There are so many things I wish for. The world seems so dark sometimes, doesn't it? But I'm not giving up." She took his hand and held it tight. "And I'm glad you're with me. I love you too, Kyrie. Don't forget it. If anything happens... if mimics arrive, or Dies Irae himself, and if we lie wounded and dying... know that I love you."

Her lips trembled and she took deep breaths. Kyrie shoved their torches into the snow, embraced her, and kissed her. She wrapped her arms around him, and her body pressed against him. They kissed deeply, desperately, and it was long moments before they drew apart and stood, silently holding hands, staring at the ruins under the snow.

Suddenly Agnus Dei gasped. "Look, Kyrie!"

The clouds parted, and the sun emerged. It shone behind King's Pillar, casting a long shadow. The shadow stretched five hundred feet across the snow, like a path. It ended at a hillock of snow beneath burned trees.

"King Aeternum is showing us something," Agnus Dei said. "Let's look."

They followed the path of shadow. It led them out of the palace ruins, and into deep snow where birch trees once grew. The way was tricky, with many bricks, old helmets, and shattered weapons hiding under the snow to trip them. When they reached the path's end, they found piles of snow that rose five feet tall. Just then the clouds gathered, and the shadowy path vanished.

Agnus Dei cleared some snow away. She found herself staring a woman's marble face.

"A statue!" she breathed.

They kept clearing away the snow, and soon revealed the rest of a statue—a nude woman holding a jug.

"She's perfect," Kyrie said.

Agnus Dei frowned at him. "Perfect, huh? Keep your eyes off her naughty bits, pup."

"I mean she's not damaged. There are a few chips, but... the statue is whole. Let's keep digging."

They kept clearing away snow, and found many pieces of statues—hands, heads, legs, torsos, and pedestals. They placed these parts aside and kept digging. Soon they unearthed a second, complete statue—a warrior holding a marble sword and shield.

They kept digging and finally found a third complete statue. This one was a king; he sported a crown, robe, and beard.

"This one is a statue of King Aeternum," Agnus Dei said. "See the two-headed dragon on his shield? It was his sigil."

Kyrie lifted a hammer and three chisels from the snow. "This place must have been a workshop. A sculptor lived here. King's Column knew we should look here." He closed his eyes. "Thank you, King Aeternum. If you truly watch over us, thank you."

They found no more whole statues. Grunting and straining, they dragged the complete statues into clear snow and stood them side by side. A nude maiden. A warrior in armor. A proud old king.

"The girl looks just like you," Kyrie said and reached toward the statue's breasts. Agnus Dei slapped his hand away and glared.

"This isn't time for jokes, pup," she said. "Give me that chisel and hammer."

"Hey, what did I do? Don't hammer me over the head."

"It's not for you, pup. Not yet, at least. We need to give these statues their hearts."

She began to chisel. It was slow, careful work. She hated damaging these statues, but knew she must. *You will be warriors of Requiem.*

Finally she had carved chambers in their chests, where hearts would pulse in living beings.

"Ready, pup?" she whispered. "I'll animate the warrior and the king. You can animate the girl statue you're so smitten with."

He nodded. Fingers tingly, Agnus Dei pulled two Animating Stones from her pack. They trembled and thrummed. The light inside them, like red liquid, swirled and reached toward the statues, as if craving new homes. Suddenly Agnus Dei was fearful; sweat beaded on her forehead, and her pulse quickened. If the magic worked, would these statues attack them?

The Ocean Deities created these stones in the Age of Chaos, she thought. *They are as old as the world, and all that's in it. And I hold them in my palm.* She took a deep breath. *I am a princess of Requiem. Gloriae and I are the last of King Aeternum's line. I will never fear the stones of Requiem.*

She placed one Animating Stone into the marble warrior. Before her courage could desert her, she placed the second Animating Stone into the king. Kyrie planted his stone into the woman, and they stepped back.

The statues were still.

"It didn't work," Agnus Dei whispered.

"Just a moment," Kyrie whispered back. "It—"

A shrill scream, like crackling ice, rose behind them.

Agnus Dei spun around, waving her torch.

Mimics.

"Oh, stars," she said.

Kyrie was already nocking an arrow. "More like star*fish.* Ugly bastards."

The mimics were emerging from the ruins like spiders from under an upturned rock. They had no heads or torsos; they had only human arms, sewn together into rotting creatures like nightmarish starfish. They squealed and raced across the ruins toward her and Kyrie. There were a dozen at least.

Agnus Dei lit and fired an arrow. Kyrie fired too. The two arrows shot like comets, but the creatures moved too fast. Both arrows missed. Agnus Dei loaded another arrow, shot again. Her arrow grazed one mimic starfish, but it kept running. Kyrie's second arrow missed.

They had no time for thirds. The mimics leaped and flew toward them.

Agnus Dei swung her torch. She hit one starfish as it flew. It squealed, pulled its arms together, and fell into the snow. A second starfish jumped and wrapped around her.

Agnus Dei screamed and struggled, but the starfish pinned her arms to her sides. One arm was hairy and broad. Another was the thin arm of a young woman. She could not see the others. They squeezed her, crushing her. She dropped her torch and couldn't breathe.

"Kyrie!" she whispered. She could speak no louder. "Kyrie, help!"

She managed to turn her head. Stars floated before her eyes. She saw Kyrie lying in the snow. Four mimic starfish wrapped around him. She could see only his left foot and some of his hair. They were biting, squealing, *eating* him.

"Kyrie, no!" she cried, eyes burning. "Please...."

She fell to her knees. Three more mimics jumped and wrapped around her. One's mouth—they had mouths in their centers—opened before her. Its tongue licked her cheek, and its teeth came in to bite.

It screamed and pulled back.

Agnus Dei took a ragged breath, kicked, and shouted. The mimic was ripped from her body. Its fingernails scratched her, clinging to her, then were torn free.

The stone warrior stood before her, its Animating Stone pulsing in its chest. It held the mimic in marble hands, regarded it blankly, then tossed it aside.

"Get the others!" Agnus Dei shouted. Two other mimics were wrapped around her, one around her stomach, the other around her legs.

The stone warrior regarded her. Its Animating Stone glowed so bright, it nearly blinded her. With stone fingers, it cut into the mimic around Agnus Dei's stomach. Pus, worms, and black blood spilled from it. The statue pulled it back. The mimic's fingers clung to Agnus Dei, ripping her cloak and tunic, but the statue managed to pull it free. It ripped two arms off, and blood showered. It tossed the rest aside.

Agnus Dei kicked and clawed at the starfish around her legs, and managed to free herself. Her legs were scratched and her pants shredded. She found her torch extinguished in the snow. Mimics scuttled toward her. She drew her sword and swung it. Rotting arms flew.

"Kyrie!" she cried.

The stone girl was pulling the mimics off him. He was alive, coughing in the snow, bloodied. The third statue, the stone king, was fighting mimics beside him. They wrapped around it, but it kept tearing their limbs off.

Agnus Dei kept hacking her blade. The severed arms did not die, but kept crawling through the snow toward her. Finally she managed to beat them back long enough to reignite her torch. Snarling, she began to burn them. The arms twitched, hissed, and curled up.

Finally all the mimics were torn apart, burned, and dead.

Kyrie rushed to her, blood trickling from a gash on his forearm. "You're hurt."

She nodded. Her clothes were tattered, her skin bleeding. "What are a few more scratches?"

They shared a quick embrace, splashed their wounds with spirits, and bound them. Pain filled Agnus Dei, but she ignored it. She was a warrior. She could take pain and keep fighting. Kyrie was pale, and sweat soaked his brow, but he too stood straight, ignoring his wounds. *We've become like statues too*, she thought. *We barely feel pain anymore.*

She turned to look at the statues. The three stood together, splashed with black mimic blood. They stared back, faces blank.

"We'll need more," Kyrie said, voice hoarse. Mimic blood soaked his clothes.

Agnus Dei looked at the smashed columns. They lay everywhere, their segments as large as boulders. She gave Kyrie a crooked smile.

"We have marble. We have tools. We have three statues who will work hard." She patted Kyrie's helmet. "They will build more."

Would it work? she wondered. It seemed crazy, but... this whole war was crazy. She lifted a hammer and chisel and shook the snow off them. She approached the statue of the king, her ancestor, and placed the tools in his hands. The statue's fingers closed around them, and he stared at her with stone eyes.

"For years, you lay hidden in ruin," she said to him. "For years, Requiem lay fallen. Today her stones will live. Today you will build brothers and sisters. The fabled columns of Requiem lie smashed now. We cannot rebuild them, but we can raise them to life. Carve them into men and women. Carve them into warriors who can reclaim our glory."

The statue stood still. Agnus Dei exhaled slowly, feeling like a deflated bellows. *He doesn't hear,* she thought. *Or he doesn't understand. He can move, but not help us.*

She turned to Kyrie. "I don't know how Dies Irae commands them. I don't know how—"

Kyrie's eyes widened and his mouth fell open. "Look."

Agnus Dei spun around. The stone king was walking through the snow, steps slow and creaking. He approached a piece of fallen column. It was larger than him. The statue stood over it, tools in hands.

"Go on," Agnus Dei whispered. "You know what to do."

The statue turned to look at her. Agnus Dei stared back. Light filled the king's eyes—starlight. The statue turned back to the marble and began to carve.

Agnus Dei felt a lump in her throat. She put an arm around Kyrie and kissed his cheek.

"For the first time in years," she whispered, "Requiem will have an army."

DIES IRAE

He stepped onto the parapet, stared down to the courtyard, and beheld an army of rot and worm.

"Mimics!" he shouted and raised his arms. "Soon you will feast on weredragon flesh!"

They howled, shrieked, and slammed swords against shields. Pus dripped from their maws. Maggots swarmed across them. Congealed blood covered their bodies like boils.

My children, Dies Irae thought. *My lovelies.*

"Hail Dies Irae!" one mimic cried, a creature with six arms and blades for hands.

"We will feast!" cried another, a creature with a bloated head like a rotting watermelon.

A thousand screamed below. Their stench rose to fill Dies Irae's nostrils. He breathed it in lovingly. It was the smell of dead weredragons, of victory.

"The weredragons murdered your brothers," he called down to them. "With cowardly fire, they burned all mimics who drew near."

They hissed and screamed. They banged their blades, and their teeth gnashed.

"But you are not mere scouts!" Dies Irae cried over the din. "You are an army. You are an army bred to kill weredragons."

Their howls rose. They waved their weapons and screamed for blood.

"You will eat their bodies! You will suck up their entrails. But bring me their heads. I will sew their heads onto the bodies of women, so that you may take them, and hurt them, and plant your seed inside them. They will be your slaves."

The mimics screamed and drooled. Some dropped their shields and began rubbing themselves, moaning and screaming. Dies Irae watched and smiled.

"Who do you serve?" he cried.

"Dies Irae! Hail Dies Irae!" Their voices shook the ruins.

Smiling thinly, Dies Irae turned and stared at the mimic who stood beside him on the parapets. His most beautiful mimic. The crown jewel of his army. His proudest creation.

"And you, Teeth, will lead them," he said.

The mimic stared back, bared its sharp teeth, and hissed. Its burly, hairy arms reached out and flexed. Centipedes crawled over its stilt-like legs. Dies Irae touched its cheek.

"You are my sweet killer," he said. "Built fresh. Of young bodies. Young freakish bodies. You are strong. You will lead. You will kill."

It snarled. A worm crawled between its teeth. "Yes, master."

Dies Irae smiled when he remembered building this mimic. The two boys had come to him with a fresh body, a friend of theirs, one of their gang. The dead one had long, hairy arms like an ape's. The leader had sharp teeth and a powerful jaw. The third one was stupid, but had long legs made for running, for towering over enemies.

The Rot Gang, that was their name, he remembered. An appropriate name.

He plucked a worm from Teeth's head and crushed it between his fingers. It squirmed, its juices spilling. Dies Irae tossed it aside and licked his fingertips. Teeth snarled.

"Take your army," Dies Irae told him. "Take these thousand warriors. Lead them to Requiem... and to triumph."

Teeth tossed back its head and howled, saliva spraying from its mouth. It raised twin blades in its hands. They caught the light and seemed to shine with the Sun God's fury.

Dies Irae stood on this crumbling wall of Flammis Palace, crossed his arms, and watched his army leave the bloody courtyard. The mimics snaked through the ruins of his city. *Yes, Confutatis lies in ruins now,* he thought. *The weredragons destroyed it. I will make them suffer for it.*

When the army disappeared into the distance, Dies Irae descended the wall and entered the ruins of his palace. He walked down halls smeared with blood, rotting guts, and the old ash of dragonfire.

He stepped down a stairwell, plunging into darkness. The air grew colder. Frost covered the walls and stairs. The smells of fear and blood filled his nostrils. The stairwell kept twisting, burrowing into the darkness that lurked under his palace. Finally he stepped into the dungeons. The old kings of Osanna had kept barrels of wine here. Dies Irae kept sweeter treats.

Torches crackled, lighting a craggy hallway lined with cells. Dies Irae stepped toward a cell with iron bars. He heard the prisoners whimper, and he smiled.

"Yes, darlings, you should whimper," he said. "I like it when you whimper."

The keys hung from a peg on the wall. Dies Irae opened the cell's door and stepped inside.

Five women stood chained to the walls. The torchlight danced on their nude bodies. Dies Irae felt his blood grow hot and his loins stir. The women were ripe, with rounded hips, teary eyes, and trembling lips.

"My mimics are creatures of rot and worm," he said to them. A smile spread across his lips. "When I sent them on the hunt for ripe women, I didn't know what they'd bring. Crones? Corpses? But it seems mimics have the lusts of men. You are like summer fruit, full of sweetness and juices."

He stepped toward one woman, a peasant girl by the look of her. Her hair was red, and tears filled her grey eyes. Dies Irae caressed her cheek.

"Please, my lord," she begged.

Dies Irae touched her hair. "Please?" he asked. "What do you wish to beg of me?"

She trembled. "Please, my lord. Is my father.... The creatures dragged him away, and.... Please release me, my lord, I beg you."

He kissed her forehead. His hands travelled down her body, caressing her. Her flesh was icy but soft. Goosebumps rose under his fingertips.

"You should be proud, sweetness. You will do what so many have dreamed of. You will hurt weredragons. When my mimics bring me their heads, I will sew one onto your body."

"My lord, please...." Tears streamed down her cheeks.

"I think for you, the boy Kyrie will do. His head will look nice on your soft, ripe body. When my mimics take you, and hurt you, and plant their rotting seeds inside you, Kyrie will know more pain and terror than any being before him. Does it not please you, precious, that your body will hurt a weredragon so?"

Sobs racked that body and she could not speak. Finally she blurted out, "Silva will kill you! The Earthen will save us!"

Dies Irae nodded with a smile. "Ah yes, the Earthen, the group of ragtag Earth God followers who've been killing all those mimics." He grabbed the girl's cheeks and squeezed them. "They are pesky flies, and my creations whisper that this Silva, this leader of theirs, has some skill with the blade. He will make a good mimic some day."

The girl opened her mouth to speak more. Dies Irae backhanded her, so hard that blood splattered, and he felt her jaw crack. Her eyes rolled back and she hung limp on her chains.

He left the girl and turned to another prisoner, an angel of soft blond hair and red lips.

"I think... the weredragon Lacrimosa should work for you. She has always been so thin, and you are luscious. Yes. Her head will be for you."

This girl too wept, and begged, and Dies Irae smiled. What a glorious end it would be for the weredragons! He licked his lips.

A voice spoke behind him, soft and cold.

"And I want the head of the golden weredragon."

Dies Irae turned, eyebrows rising. One of the women had spoken. She stood chained like the others, but did not weep. She did not tremble. Her dark eyes stared at him, simmering with anger.

"The golden weredragon?" he asked her. "Gloriae the Gilded?"

The woman nodded. "When the dragons flew upon this city, it was the golden one who torched my home. The weredragon Gloriae killed my brothers. She killed my husband. Cut my head from my body, my lord. Place her head upon me and make me a mimic. Let the others hurt me. I will do this to make Gloriae suffer."

Dies Irae approached her and examined her in the torchlight. Among the chained women, this one was the fairest. Her hair was black satin, hanging down to her chin. Her eyes were pools of midnight. She looked older than the others—a woman, while the others were mere girls. Her body was lithe and strong, decorated with several knife scars. This was no peasant.

"Who were your brothers?" he asked her, narrowing his eyes. "Who was your husband?"

She raised her chin. "Blood Wolves," she said, eyes spiteful. "Will you kill me for that? I think not. Not if you want my body fresh for your dear Gloriae."

Dies Irae nodded, eyebrows raised, and scratched his chin. "Common thieves, you mean."

She spat onto the floor. "Blood Wolves are no common thugs. We are the shadows in the night. We are the daggers in the alley. We are the terror that strikes in darkness."

Dies Irae ran his fingers along her chest, tracing a scar. It ran from her left collarbone, between her breasts, and to her bottom right rib. He touched her hip, and traced the length of a second scar, which ran down her thigh. She stared back at him, chin raised, lips tight.

"Terror in darkness, you say." He pursed his lips. "Shadows in the night. Perhaps I could find other use for you."

She gritted her teeth. "From the way your fingers touch me, I know how you would use me. I have no interest in serving you so, great emperor. I am a Blood Wolf too. I can fight like my brothers and husband, the men the weredragons slew. I will hurt them."

Dies Irae nodded and rubbed his chin. Five women were chained here. But only four weredragons remained. Benedictus was dead, his body stolen. *Yes. Yes, I can spare this one. The four others will be toys to my mimics. This one will be mine.*

He unchained her wrists from the wall, and then her ankles. She moved her limbs, hissed, and gritted her teeth. She rubbed the raw flesh, and sweat beaded on her brow. A snarl found her lips. Dies Irae couldn't help but smile. This one was feral. A wolf indeed.

"What is your name?"

"Umbra," she said and glared.

He grabbed her wrist. "Come with me."

She pulled her wrist free and bared her teeth at him. "I will walk. You will not drag me."

Yes. Yes, I like this one.

They left the dungeons, climbed the stairwell, and walked across the crumbling halls of Flammis Palace. Everywhere were strewn bricks, stains of ash, smeared blood, and guards with sallow eyes. Those eyes lit up when Umbra walked by, still nude.

Umbra stared back at them, chin raised, as if challenging them to speak. Her eyes said, *Make a move, and I'll tear out your throats.*

He led her upstairs and into his bed chamber. The nightshades, griffins, and dragons had destroyed half the palace, but this room remained untouched. It was a large chamber, large enough to house a dragon. Golden tapestries covered his walls. His bed was ten feet wide, made of pure gold inlaid with diamonds. His tables, chairs, and vases were gilded and shone with emeralds, rubies, and sapphires. Priceless swords of steel and jewels hung everywhere.

"Like gold, do we?" Umbra asked. Her eyes darted from gemstone to gemstone. They lit up like the eyes of a starving man who stumbled upon a feast. She reached toward a jewelled dagger which lay on a giltwood table.

Dies Irae caught her wrist. "Do not touch anything. You will have gold too, if you earn it."

She looked up at him. A crooked smile touched her lips. "And how do I earn it, my lord?"

He twisted her wrist and pulled her close. "I will show you."

She spat in his face. "Let me go. My husband hasn't been dead a moon."

He slapped her face. He'd wanted to knock her down, but she stayed standing... and punched him.

Her fist hit his cheek, and he fell. White light blinded him. He blinked and struggled to rise, but Umbra pressed her foot against his chest, pinning him down. She grabbed the dagger, drew the blade, and pointed it at him.

"This dagger is mine," she said. "I take payment in advance. I will kill for you with this dagger. Give me a name, and he is dead. But I will not be your slave. Those women underground? Rape them if you will, not me."

Dies Irae lay looking up at her. His blood pulsed. "I do not want those women underground. I want you. I want your daggers in the night. I want your hands covered in the blood of my enemies. And I want your body under mine."

He reached up, grabbed her waist, and pulled her down toward him. Her dagger scratched his side, but he barely noticed. She snarled, and he rolled her onto her back, and lay atop her.

"Get off me," she said.

"No."

Dies Irae was not a young man. He was twice this woman's age, but she made him feel young. He reached down and found her ready for him. She moaned beneath him, and snarled, and wrapped her arms around his back.

"You will kill weredragons," he hissed as he thrust into her.

"I will cut off their heads!" she cried and panted.

"We will kill the beasts and make them suffer like none have suffered."

She screamed.

Their voices echoed.

He rolled off her and stared at the ceiling. Gold and jewels covered that ceiling too. These chambers were the only place where glory and light still shone. The weredragons had destroyed the rest of the empire. *But they will pay. They will pay.*

Umbra nestled against him and ran her fingers across his chest. "For an old man, you have a lot of fire in you."

Dies Irae looked at her, silent. Suddenly he did feel old. Here beside him lay a woman half his age, a woman of midnight beauty. Her hair was silk, her eyes pools of shadow, her body lithe and tanned and intoxicating as summer wine. And him? An old cripple. Benedictus had taken his left arm; he wore a steel mace there instead. His brother had taken his eye too. Yes, he felt old. He felt ugly.

I should have beaten her, he thought. *I should have made her bleed, made her fear me, and raped her as she screamed.* Then it would not matter that he was old or deformed. Then he would be powerful, a tyrant to fear. But this.... She had given herself willingly. She had *enjoyed* it. That meant that she could judge him, see not only his power, but his weakness too.

Dies Irae looked away and gritted his teeth.

"How many men have you killed?" he asked.

"In bed?" She considered. "Three."

"I mean in a fight."

She snorted. "Your common soldiers fight. They hack and slash with clumsy blades, and wear armor that slows them. I don't fight, my lord. I sneak in the darkness and stab in the back. I poison and strangle. I have killed thirty men. Now I will kill weredragons."

Dies Irae rose to his feet. He stepped toward his window and looked outside at the ruins of his city. "A thousand mimics march toward Requiem. I know the weredragons. They will not all stay to defend their home. They will leave. And I know where they will go."

He turned to look at Umbra. She lay on his rug, staring up at him hungrily.

"Where, my lord?"

"To darkness," he said. "To death. And to your daggers."

MEMORIA

They flew over plains of ice, snow, and rock. The clouds stretched like fingers above them.

"Remember your training," Terra said. Frost and icicles covered his bronze scales. "We've killed griffins. We can kill giants."

Memoria nodded. She let fire fill her mouth and dance between her teeth. Yes, she had fought, and she had killed. She had blown her fire, and lashed her claws, and bitten with her fangs. She had let blood wash her.

"We can kill giants," she agreed.

Her wings were steady and her jaw tight, but her insides trembled. Would giants beg for mercy too? Would they look at her with wide, terrified eyes like the boy she had killed? And, when their eyes met hers, would she find only hatred in her heart and fire on her breath?

Memoria stared ahead at the plains of ice and rock. *No. Do not remember that boy. You had to kill him. If he was old enough to ride a griffin, and old enough to kill dragons, he was old enough to die. Giants will not have such large, frightened eyes.*

They flew for hours. They crossed leagues. They soared over plains of ice, snow, and black boulders; over seas where whales swam; over icebergs where seals would once gather and now only snow whispered. They flew through wind and cloud. Frost covered their scales and icicles hung from their mouths. Finally, after what seemed a lifetime of flying, they saw the Jet Mountains ahead.

They rose like fortresses, black as memory. No snow covered them. Their surfaces were polished, like shards of black glass glued together. When the light caught them, it nearly blinded Memoria. She remembered Amberus's parting words. *The Giant King lives upon the mountaintop. It's him you must face. He has Adoria's Hands.*

"Remember your training," Terra repeated. "We've killed griffins. We can kill gia—."

A howl tore the air.

Memoria narrowed her eyes, and her heart pounded. She looked around but saw nothing.

"Giants," she whispered.

Terra nodded. "Keep flying."

The Jet Mountains were getting closer. The sunlight blazed against them, shooting toward the two dragons. Memoria grimaced and squinted. She could barely see.

The howl rose again. A second, then a third howl answered it. The mountain seemed to shake. Memoria covered her ears with her claws. The howls were deep, guttural, and ached in her chest. Memoria had heard armies of griffins shriek, but she had never heard anything so loud, so cruel, a sound like tumbling boulders.

"Do you see them?" she called over the roars.

Terra flew beside her, eyes narrowed. The light from the mountains turned his bronze scales white. He growled and blew fire.

"No!" he called back. "They've seen us. They—"

"Terra!"

Something came flying through the light toward them. She could barely see it. She grabbed Terra and pulled him down. Air whooshed above them.

"What was that?" Terra cried.

"Fly up! Higher."

They soared and emerged from the blinding light. Snow and ice rolled beneath them. When she looked ahead, she saw the Jet Mountains closer than she'd ever seen them. Shadows raced across them. Panes of stone moved, and light drenched her again.

"They're using some kind of stone mirrors," Terra said and cursed.

The giants' howls rose. A boulder flew from the mountains, tumbling through the beams of light toward them.

"Watch out!" she cried. She swerved right. Terra swerved left. The boulder passed between them, flames coiling around it.

"Not the most pleasant welcoming," Terra said.

Memoria flew higher, shooting up in a straight line. The air grew thin and cold. She could barely breathe. She looked down and saw giants scurrying across the mountainsides, adjusting their stone mirrors. Memoria had always imagined giants to be slow, lumbering beasts, but these creatures were so fast, her eyes barely caught them.

"Higher, Terra!" she shouted. "Fly out of their boulders' range."

He flew beside her, and they kept soaring, until Memoria gasped for breath, and darkness clawed at the corners of her eyes. She had never flown so high.

Are we safe? she wondered... then saw more boulders flying toward her.

She cursed and swerved, but a boulder hit her leg. She screamed. Pain blazed, and tears sprang into her eyes. More boulders flew. She dived, whipped around them, and swooped.

"New plan," she growled, the wind roaring around her. "Let's burn the bastards."

Terra swooped beside her, flames dancing between his teeth. The giants howled below them. Beams of light blazed, nearly blinding Memoria. The clouds swirled. From the mountains, twenty flaming boulders came flying.

Memoria spun. Three boulders missed her. One grazed her back. A second boulder slammed against her wing. She screamed and tumbled, plummeting toward the mountains.

"Terra!"

More boulders flew. Though her wing blazed, she forced herself to fly. She dipped sideways just in time. Boulders shot around her, their flames licking her. She swerved, dived, spun, and swooped.

"Memoria! Fly with me."

Terra swooped beside her, claws outstretched. His scales were chipped along his left side. They veered left and right, up and down, dodging the boulders. The beams of light kept hitting them, blinding them. A boulder hit her tail, and she screamed, but kept swooping. She saw two giants scurrying across the mountain beneath her.

She was close enough.

She blew flame.

The giants leaped behind boulders. Her flames rained against the mountain. The giants screamed.

Terra blew his own fire. The flames hit the mountainside and cascaded like a river of lava. A giant burst out from behind the boulders, hair blazing, a club in his hands.

For an instant, Memoria faltered. It was the first giant she had seen up close. *He's hideous.* The giant stood thirty feet tall, each foot covered in boils and coarse white hair. He wore only a ragged loincloth, and a stench of stale sweat rose from him. His nose was bulbous and red, sprouting white hair from the nostrils. Crooked teeth, each the size of a sword, grew from his mouth. His eyes were small and mean, the color of dried blood.

Howling, the giant swung his club at her.

Memoria flew backwards and blew flame.

The inferno hit the giant. He screamed and fell back, skin crackling.

"Watch out!" Terra said, grabbed her, and pulled her down. They landed on the mountainside. A boulder flew overhead, missing them by an inch.

Terra shot a jet of flame. A giant screamed behind Memoria. Three more giants ran ahead, boulders raised in their hands.

Memoria bathed them with fire. Two dropped their boulders. A third tossed his. Memoria leaped aside, and the missile grazed her shoulder. She grunted with pain. Her leg still throbbed.

"I don't like this," Terra said. Memoria whipped her head from side to side. A hundred giants were emerging from holes, tunnels, and the cover of stone outcrops. They bore clubs studded with bones, boulders that crackled with fire, and gleaming stone daggers. They climbed from below, from above, from each side.

"Fly!" Memoria said and leaped into the air. She flapped her wings as fast as she could. "Over the mountaintop."

Terra flew beside her. Boulders shot after them. One hit Terra's wing. He howled.

"Terra!" Memoria cried. She spat fire down at the giants and flew to her brother. He was wincing, but still flying. She held him and helped him fly higher. All around them, the barage of stone continued. Memoria swerved, dodging most of the boulders. One slammed into her side, knocking the breath out of her. Pain bloomed. She could not breathe. She could not see.

No, don't kill me! the boy had cried. *I beg you, please. I have parents and a sister. Please. Please....*

Only a boy. No older than fifteen. A boy with scared eyes, with soft cheeks that had never grown stubble. A boy in armor. A boy riding a griffin. A boy who flew for Dies Irae, who killed and destroyed.

He is old enough to die.

She burned him.

He screamed. He screamed for what seemed like eternity.

Die already, stop screaming and die! Memoria wanted to cry, but she only watched him burn, until finally he screamed no more. A boy. With parents, with a sister. Silenced.

"Memoria!"

She wept. "I had to do it. I had to."

"Memoria! Fly! *Fly!*"

Her eyes snapped open. Terra was shaking her, struggling to fly with one hurt wing. Boulders still flew around them, and giants howled. Memoria gritted her teeth and flew.

They soared up the mountainside. Their reflections raced along the smooth, black stones—one green dragon, one bronze. More giants emerged from holes and behind rocks. There were thousands.

Blue sky burst before her. They reached the mountaintop, flew over it, and saw the city of giants.

Memoria's breath died.

LACRIMOSA

"No more tears," she whispered to herself. "Now is my turn to be strong. To lead. For our children, Ben. For you."

She stood under the orphaned archway, above the ruins of the fort where they made their home. The wind streamed her hair, kissed her cheeks with snow, and whispered of the growing threat in the east. *There will be war,* she knew. Dies Irae knew they were here; she did not doubt that now. Hundreds of mimics would march here. Blood would spill.

"Mother," Agnus Dei said. She came to stand beside her. Her mop of curls was white with snow. Her clothes were tattered, and bandages covered her wounds. Shadows filled her eyes, and she looked too thin to Lacrimosa, too weary, too haunted.

"Are you eating, Agnus Dei? You look thin."

She narrowed her eyes. "We're mustering forces for war, and that's what you worry about? That I'm not eating?" She sighed. "Mothers will be mothers."

The snow flurried. Lacrimosa shielded her eyes with her palm and stared down the mountainsides. Their forces seemed too few. *They cannot stop the tide,* she thought. *Am I mad to stay here? Am I mad to make a stand? Will this be another Lanburg Fields?*

"We used every Animating Stone we have," Lacrimosa said. "One hundred and twenty. Will it be enough?"

The stone dragon she had animated stood on the eastern hillside, unmoving, a sentinel of stone. Kyrie and Agnus Dei had animated three more statues. The stone maiden stood to the north, the warrior to the south, the king to the west.

Between them stood over a hundred warriors carved from the smashed columns of Requiem. They were crude figures; they had only the rough shapes of men, their surfaces craggy. The four true statues had carved them, and they were ugly things, but Animating Stones pulsed within them. They lived. They would fight.

"Time for dinner," Kyrie announced, climbing out from the cellars. He held two steaming bowls. "I cooked. Gloriae helped a bit. Tonight we have a delicious, lovingly simmered stew of turnips, oats, and sausages."

Gloriae emerged from the cellars behind him, holding two more bowls. "Kyrie, have we eaten anything but turnips, oats, and sausage stew for the past month?"

He nodded, handing out bowls. "Yesterday was more of a soup, what with all the water you added."

"Soup with some Gloriae hairs added for flavor," Agnus Dei muttered. "I nearly choked on one. Sister, you might be the deadliest warrior among us, and you are also the deadliest cook."

Soon the four sat in the courtyard, wrapped in their cloaks, eating as the sunset painted the world red. Lacrimosa was glad to see them eating hungrily, even Agnus Dei. *They'll need what strength they can get*, she thought. *More than ever.*

As they ate, the statues moved across the mountainsides, arranging firewood in a ring around the ruins. *Fire and stone,* Lacrimosa thought, watching the statues work. *This is how we fight in the ruin of the world. This is all we have left. Fire and stone.*

She looked at her children, one by one. Agnus Dei, of fiery eyes, of skinned knees, of grumbles and tears and kisses and flames. *She looks so much like Ben.* And Gloriae... her lost daughter, finally returned. Gloriae, of icy green eyes, of pain, of fear, of hidden love and light. Finally, Lacrimosa looked at Kyrie, who was like a son to her now. Kyrie, the boy who'd survived Lanburg Fields; no, not a boy but a man now, full grown, a man who would father her grandchildren.

I will protect them, Ben, she thought and looked up to the sky. *I won't let them die.*

They were still eating when howls sounded in the distance.

They froze. Lacrimosa lowered her spoon, rose to her feet, and stared east.

"We can't even enjoy one good meal," Agnus Dei said. She grabbed a torch from the ground. "My stars."

The howls rose, some deep and guttural like dying boars, others high like the screeches of ghosts.

"Weredragons!" they cried. "We will eat you alive. We will have your heads."

Lacrimosa drew an arrow from her quiver, tightened the kindling around its tip, and lit it. She walked toward the eastern ruins of the fort, to war, to blood.

"Fire and stone," she whispered. "They fight for us today."

She stepped onto the remaining few bricks of the fort's wall and saw the mimic army.

She felt the blood drain from her face.

"Bloody stars," Kyrie said, coming to stand beside her, bow in hand.

Even Gloriae, always stony like a statue, seemed shaken. She gritted her teeth.

"So many," she whispered.

Agnus Dei snorted, blowing back a curl of her hair. "Come on, we can take em," she said, but Lacrimosa noticed that the girl's fingers trembled around her bow.

She returned her eyes to the mimics. A hundred had attacked Draco Murus last time, and nearly killed them. A thousand now howled ahead, charging through the snow. Their stench carried on the wind, the stench of rot and worms and old blood. They bore swords and shields. A towering mimic ran at their lead, his legs like stilts, his arms ape-like and swinging.

"Weredragons!" this leader of mimics howled. "Your heads are mine."

Lacrimosa smiled a crooked, mirthless smile.

"Let them taste fire first," she said. "Then stone."

She loosed her arrow.

The three young Vir Requis gave wordless cries and shot three more arrows.

The flaming missiles flew through the sky, and each hit a rotting torso. Those mimics screamed, pulled the arrows out, and kept running.

"Damn," Agnus Dei said. "These ones are tougher than the last."

Lacrimosa nodded. "We'll see how much fire they can take."

She ran toward the ring of fire, which surrounded the fort, and lit it. It crackled into life at once, flowing around the fort like a flaming serpent. The mimics screamed and kept charging.

Lacrimosa climbed onto a pile of fallen bricks. She saw the horde closer now, three hundred yards away. She shot an arrow and hit a mimic's shield. It kept running.

"Statues of Requiem!" Lacrimosa shouted. The statues stood outside the ring, unmoving. Kyrie and the twins were still firing arrows, but their missiles did not faze the mimics.

"Statues, hear me!" Lacrimosa shouted. "I am Lacrimosa, wife of King Benedictus, Queen of Requiem. Fight for Requiem. Fight the enemy, tear them apart, destroy them! Fight them now."

The statues began to move. They walked slowly, limbs creaking. The crude statues, those carved from the columns, barely moved at all.

"Charge at them!" Lacrimosa shouted. "Give them no mercy. Fight for the Draco stars, for the rebirth of your home."

They began to move faster. Soon they were running. Their feet thundered, kicked up snow and dirt, and they shouted. Their cries were like cracking stone, like weeping forests, like the pain of Requiem. It sounded almost like the deep, mournful cries of dragons.

"Fire, then stone," Lacrimosa whispered, and watched the statues crash into the army of mimics.

Blood, chips of stone, and gobbets of flesh flew. There were ten mimics for each statue. The rotting creatures hacked at the marble warriors, breaking off arms, heads, and legs. The mimics were made of flesh, but their blows bore the strength of ancient magic. The marble statues swung at them, their arms tearing through rotted flesh, scattering limbs and heads. Black blood and rot sprayed the snow.

Hope filled Lacrimosa. *We can do this. We can defend our home.*

Then she heard cries that chilled her blood.

"For Requiem!" Gloriae cried. She brandished her sword in one hand, a torch in the other.

"For Queen Lacrimosa!" cried Agnus Dei and Kyrie, raising their own swords and torches.

The three youths leaped over the fiery ring, howled, and charged into battle.

"No!" Lacrimosa shouted, horror clutching at her. "Stay with me. Here!"

They did not hear. Swinging their weapons, the youths crashed into the battle and began hacking at mimics.

Lacrimosa cursed and began running across the courtyard. *Stupid children!* They had raised warriors of stone so they would not have to fight themselves. *If the mimics don't kill them, I will.*

She reached the ring of fire. The flames rose around her, blocking her view. They were lower in one spot; that is where the youths had jumped out to battle. Cursing the foulest words she knew, Lacrimosa jumped over the fire and ran toward battle. *The children might be dumber than doorknobs, but I must protect them.*

She drew Stella Lumen, her father's sword. Its blade hissed and reflected the firelight. Two mimics rushed at her, pus oozing from the stitches that held them together. They swung jagged blades.

Lacrimosa was no soldier. She had not trained in swordplay like Gloriae. But she had fought enough battles to muster courage if not skill. She parried left and right, screaming. She swung a torch in her left hand, her blade in the right. She let them taste steel and fire. They fell back.

"Daughters!" she called. "Kyrie! Back to the fort. Do not meet them in open battle."

She could not see them. Everywhere around her, the statues and mimics fought. Severed mimic limbs crawled across the battlefield, clutching her boots. She stomped them and burned them with her torch.

"Requiem!" Kyrie called somewhere in the distance, his voice nearly drowned under the roar of battle. Lacrimosa did not know what she craved more; to kill mimics, or to clobber the boy over the head.

A mimic skirted around two statues and raced toward her. Lacrimosa cursed and raised her blade. The mimic was shaped as a monstrous centaur. Its lower half was a headless, rotting man running on all fours. Sewn onto the man's shoulders, rose the nude torso, arms, and head of a woman. Her hair was made of snakes, and her teeth were jagged metal. In each hand, the rotting woman wielded an axe.

Horror, white and burning, spread through Lacrimosa. She tightened her grip on her sword.

"Stella Lumen, burn with the light of stars," Lacrimosa whispered, holding the blade before her. "Father, be with me today."

The strange centaur charged toward her, squealed, and swung an axe.

Lacrimosa dropped to her knees and slid forward through the snow. The axe whistled over her head. As she slid, Lacrimosa swung her blade and cut the mimic's leg.

It screeched, a sound that seemed to shake the mountain. Snow cascaded. Lacrimosa leaped to her feet, and the mimic charged toward her. It swung both axes at her head. She leaped back. The centaur raced toward her.

Lacrimosa lobbed her torch. It hit the centaur's upper half, then fell into the snow. The mimic screamed. Its chest reddened and crackled. Before it could recover, Lacrimosa shouted, ran toward it, and swung her blade.

Stella Lumen opened the creature's stomach. Snakes spilled from it like entrails. They squirmed around Lacrimosa's feet, hissing.

An axe swung. Lacrimosa parried and sparks flew. She thrust her sword and hit the mimic's neck.

Blood showered. The mimic screamed. Lacrimosa slashed again, and the mimic fell. She stabbed it again and again, but still it kicked and squealed.

Fire. Lacrimosa thought. *I need fire.*

Her torch had extinguished in the snow. She grabbed it, looked up, and saw Agnus Dei fighting beside her. A mimic with four arms was attacking her. Lacrimosa ran and touched her torch to her daughter's. It crackled back into flame.

"Agnus Dei, you are the most numbskulled girl I've ever seen!" Lacrimosa shouted.

Agnus Dei grunted. "Not now, Mother. I'm busy."

The centaur mimic, lacerated and burned, was struggling to rise. Worms squirmed across it. Lacrimosa ran and shoved the torch against its head. The snakes of its hair caught fire, and soon the entire creature burned. It twisted and screeched in the snow.

Lacrimosa did not stay to watch it die. She ran back toward Agnus Dei, and found that the girl had slain the four-armed mimic. Statues and mimics still battled around them.

"Where's your sister?" she cried. "Where's Kyrie?"

Agnus Dei pointed. "There."

The two were fighting back to back, five mimics surrounding them. Beyond them, dozens of mimics and statues lay smashed and burned. Dozens more still fought in every direction.

"Gloriae! Kyrie!" Lacrimosa called. "Back to the fort."

She ran toward them. Agnus Dei ran too. With swords and torches, they slew mimics that clawed and bit from each side.

"Back to safety," Lacrimosa commanded, her head pounding, her limbs shaking. "The statues will finish our work here."

Cuts and scrapes covered the youths. They nodded, panting, and began heading back uphill.

A thundering howl rose before them.

Snow cascaded.

A great mimic came running downhill toward them, shoving aside statues and other mimics. It towered over the others on freakishly long legs, and had hairy arms that rippled with muscles. When it opened its mouth to scream, it revealed sharp teeth like a wolf's. It seemed sewn from three bodies—the legs of one, the arms of another, and the torso and head of a third. In each hand, it held a flanged mace.

The mimic's leader, Lacrimosa remembered.

"Kyrie! Agnus Dei!" she yelled. "Attack it from its right. Gloriae! We'll take its left side."

The mimic grinned. Drool dripped down its chin and steamed when it hit the snow. With a mocking howl, it swung its maces.

Lacrimosa leaped back, but Gloriae charged and swung her sword. A mace hit her breastplate and dented it. Gloriae cried and fell.

"Gloriae!" Lacrimosa cried. She ran and swung Stella Lumen at the mimic.

It swung its mace, and Lacrimosa ducked and raised her arm to protect her face. The mace hit her vambrace, and she screamed. One flange dented the steel and bit her arm.

"Mother!" Agnus Dei cried and attacked at the mimic's other side. She swung her torch at it, but it lashed its mace, holding her back.

"Lacrimosa, down!" Kyrie said, nocking a flaming arrow.

She fell to her knees, and the arrow flew over her head. It slammed into the mimic, plunged through its chest, and extinguished. The mimic grinned and ran toward Kyrie, swinging its maces.

Kyrie shot another arrow. He hit the mimic, but the creature only grunted and kept charging. Lacrimosa and Agnus Dei slammed their swords against its back, but the cuts did not slow it.

Was Gloriae alive? Lacrimosa had no time to check. The mimic reached Kyrie and swung a mace. Kyrie ducked, and the mace glanced off his helmet. He fell into the snow, and his eyes closed.

"Pup!" Agnus Dei screamed, eyes widening. She jumped onto the mimic's back and pushed it into the snow. She began slamming her sword's pommel into its head. The mimic thrashed and howled.

Lacrimosa ran. The mimic rose to its feet and shook Agnus Dei off. It dropped one mace, clutched Agnus Dei's throat, and began to squeeze.

"Let her go," Lacrimosa said, snarled, and swung her blade. Stella Lumen severed the mimic's arm with a shower of blood and starlight.

Agnus Dei fell to her knees, scratching at the hand that still clutched her throat. Lacrimosa helped pry the fingers loose. Agnus Dei sucked in breath and coughed. Her face was deep red.

"Behind you!" she managed to say.

Lacrimosa spun around and hurled her torch. She hit the advancing mimic in the face. It howled, dropped its second mace, and brushed the sparks off its face.

"Pup, pup, get up!" Agnus Dei was crying, shaking Kyrie. The boy was coughing and struggling to rise. *Hurt but alive,* Lacrimosa thought in relief. *What of Gloriae?*

The mimic lashed its remaining arm at her. Lacrimosa ducked and swung her sword. She sliced the creature's elbow. It snarled and reached its claws toward her.

A flaming arrow slammed into its head.

Gloriae came walking downhill, already nocking a second arrow. Her eyes were ice, her face emotionless. The wind streamed her hair. She drew the bowstring.

My daughter. She's alive. Such relief swept over Lacrimosa, that her eyes blurred.

The mimic screeched.

Gloriae shot her second arrow. It pierced the mimic's neck, and it fell to its knees.

Lacrimosa stepped toward it. It snarled, oozing pus and rot.

"Fire," she told it. "Stone. And steel."

Lacrimosa swung her blade and severed its head.

The other Vir Requis burned its body with their torches, until it did not move. But Lacrimosa held onto the head, keeping it at arm's length. It shouted and snapped its teeth. An arrow still thrust out of it.

"We will keep this piece alive," she said. "Now back to the fort."

Holding the head, she raced up the mountainside. The other Vir Requis followed. Around them, as if disheartened by the loss of their leader, the mimics were falling fast. The statues were tearing into them, killing them left and right. Only twenty statues remained standing; the rest were smashed and lay still on the ground. Many lay in pieces no longer than a foot.

The Vir Requis stepped back into the ruins, looked down the mountainside, and watched the statues kill the last mimics. Lacrimosa tossed the severed mimic head onto the cobblestones, then turned to face the youths.

"You three are the stupidest Vir Requis who ever lived. If Ben were here, he'd clobber you harder than the mimics."

Lacrimosa had promised herself she would stop weeping; she could no longer cry, not now, Benedictus having left her to lead. Tonight she could not help it. The tears filled her eyes, and she embraced Kyrie and her daughters.

"Never do anything so foolishly brave again," she said as she embraced them. "I love you too much to see it."

Agnus Dei squirmed in the embrace. "Mother, really."

They broke apart and breathed deeply. Lacrimosa's body ached. The fire crackled in the night, raising sparks likek fireflies.

Laughter sounded in the shadows.

Lacrimosa turned and saw the severed mimic head. It lay on the cobblestones, glaring at her. Its sharp teeth reflected the firelight as it cackled.

"You have won this battle," the mimic said and spat out blood. "You killed a thousand of us. Fifty thousand are gathering as we speak. With each he builds, our master makes us larger, stronger, smarter. You cannot win, weredragons."

Lacrimosa walked toward the head. She pointed her sword at it.

"Where do the others gather?" she asked. "Where does Dies Irae find the Animating Stones?"

It cackled and spat at her. Its gob of spit landed on her boot.

Lacrimosa placed the tip of her sword against its face, but did not break the skin.

"Talk to me," she said, "or you will die."

It cackled. "Kill me, weredragon. It will not save you."

Lacrimosa felt a hand on her shoulder. She turned to see Gloriae. The young woman was covered in blood, ash, and mimic gore. She stared down at the statue, her eyes emotionless, her face as cold as one of the statues.

"I will make it talk," she said, her voice strangely soft. "Mother, take Agnus Dei and Kyrie into the cellars. Leave me with it. I promise you; it will tell me all it knows."

Lacrimosa shivered. What would Gloriae do? Had she tortured prisoners before? Lacrimosa did not want to think about it, did not want to imagine what skills Dies Irae had taught her daughter.

"Gloriae, are you sure?" she whispered.

The young woman nodded, eyes icy.

Lacrimosa looked away. Her eyes stung. *I must be strong. For you, Ben. For our home.* She took a deep breath.

"Agnus Dei," she said. "Kyrie. Come with me underground. We'll bandage your wounds. Gloriae will join us soon."

As they walked downstairs into shadows, Lacrimosa looked back one more time at Gloriae. The wind streamed her daughter's hair, swirling snow around her. Then Lacrimosa stepped into the cellars and saw nothing but darkness.

GLORIAE

She stood among the ruins, staring down the mountainside at the battlefield. A thousand mimics lay burned and torn apart. Nearly a hundred statues lay smashed. The last few statues, including the stone dragon, were searching for mimic body parts and crushing them.

It smells wrong, Gloriae thought. *I was raised to savor the smell of fresh blood. To dream of it, crave it. Yet here I fight, in a field of rot and stone.*

She raised her eyes from the carnage and stared into the eastern horizon. Dawn was rising, sending pink tendrils across a cloudy sky. Beyond that horizon lay home. *What used to be my home, at least.* The empire of Osanna lay many leagues from here, across crumbled cities, burned fields, and wilted forests. The nightshades had ravaged it, but Dies Irae still ruled over the ruins.

"He's still out there somewhere," Gloriae whispered into the wind. "The man I called Father. The man who banished me. The man I will kill."

Hoarse laughter sounded behind her. Gloriae turned. The severed mimic head lay on the cobblestones, oozing its juices. It cackled, eyes mocking her.

"You will not kill Dies Irae," it said, coughed, and spat. "He has a new body waiting for you, Gloriae the Gilded. Yes, I know your name. And I know your fate. He will cut off your head, and sew it onto a new body, and turn you into a mimic. Then he will let a thousand other mimics thrust inside you, until you bleed and beg for a death that will never come."

Gloriae stared at it silently, waiting for it to finish speaking.

"You like talking," she said. "That is good. You will talk more. You will tell me everything you know."

It spat a glob of maggoty spit. "I know that you will be a slave to mimics."

"How lovely," Gloriae said. "But enough about me. Let's talk about you, my toothy friend. Tell me about that Animating Stone that gave you life. Where did Irae find it?"

She knelt before the head, torch crackling.

"Will you torture me now?" it asked. "Burn me? Cut me? Pull out my teeth? Do it. I fear no pain."

A centipede emerged from its mouth and scurried along the cobblestones. Gloriae watched it flee into shadows, then stared into the mimic's eyes.

"Pain won't make you talk. Memories might." She narrowed her eyes, examining it. "Who were you?"

It cackled. "I am mimic. I am death and despair. I am rot and worm. I am your future."

Gloriae shook her head. "That is what you are now. Who were you once?"

It glared at her. "Weak."

"Life," she said. "You were life once. Real life."

It coughed blood onto her boots. "What would you know of life? I know you. All beings do. You killed children when you yourself were a child. You killed countless in your chase of weredragons. You unleashed the nightshades. You destroyed the world."

Gloriae stared at it with dry eyes. *Stay strong. No feelings. No pain.*

"Yes," she said. "I am a giver of death. I deal in blood and steel. I have killed many, and I will kill many more before they burn my body in a great pyre." She touched the mimic's head, leaned down, and whispered to it. "But I was not always a killer. Once I too was life. I too was a child."

The head hissed and tried to bite her fingers. "You will beg for death, mortal. You will be one of us. You—"

"You were a child too once," she said. "You were a boy."

"I am mimic! I am stronger than life. You will join us. You—"

She clutched its cheeks, lifted the head, and stared at it levelly. "Who were you? You have rotted less than the others. You were killed fresh. Who were you in life?"

"Teeth!" it screeched. "I— No. I am only death, I..."

She brought its face close to hers. "Teeth? What does that mean?"

"They... Teeth! Legs. Rot Gang, and Arms. He betrayed us. He had to die. I had to kill him. Teeth! It hurts, Teeth. It hurts. He hit our head with his mace. He lied to us. Silver! I brought you death, I brought you rot, we are Rot Gang. We are three. Pay me my silver."

She shook the head. "Who was to pay you? Who hurt you? Was it Dies Irae?"

Blood filled the mimic's eyes and flowed down its cheeks like tears. "Do not speak of him! He will hurt us again. He wields a fist of steel. He hit our head. He killed our Legs. He.... He...." The head trembled in her hands.

"What did he do?" Gloriae demanded. "Did he kill you?"

The creature wept its tears of blood. More blood poured between its sharp teeth. "I have teeth. Sharp teeth. Teeth, they call me. I had to kill Arms. Long arms, he had, arms for silver, silver coins, that's what I asked of him. But... his fist of steel. He took my head. He hurt Legs. It burns! He burns us."

Gloriae held the head steady, through its blood covered her hands. "He killed you," she whispered. "And he made you into a mimic."

The head shook. "No, master! Not the needles. Not the strings. It burns in our chest, the stone. Not his legs! Give him back his legs. I don't want them. Not his arms, please. I don't want his arms. I killed him for silver, not arms. Where are my legs? Where are my arms? The needle burns!"

Gloriae stared at the weeping, trembling, bloody creature. Was this what Dies Irae planned for her too? To kill her and sew others' parts onto her?

"How many were you?" she said.

"Three. Rot Gang. Rot. We deal in death and silver. Not needles. No, please not needles, and not stones that burn."

She shook the head. "Animating Stones. Where are they from? Where is he finding them?"

"I must serve him. I must kill for him. I must never betray him. He will hurt us, Arms. He will cut us. He will burn us, Legs. We must not tell her. We must never speak of the stones."

"You will speak," Gloriae said. "You will tell me everything."

It cackled, spraying saliva. "You cannot hurt us like he did."

Gloriae shook her head. "No. I cannot. But I can end your pain, Teeth. I can free you. I can separate you from Legs and Arms."

It froze.

Its breath died.

For a long moment, it stared at her with narrowed eyes.

"We... we were Teeth once. We do not want his legs. We do not want his arms. They scream inside me. They still burn! I hear their voices in my skull. Free them from me. Cut them off me! Cut them off. I will speak to you then."

Gloriae glared. "First you will speak to me. Then I will end your pain. Then you will be a boy again, only Teeth. No more mimic."

It wept like a child. "Only Teeth. No Legs. No Arms. No silver. No rot. Just Teeth. Only Teeth, Rot Gang, yes."

"Will you speak?"

It nodded, seeming to wilt in her hands. "We will speak of stones, yes. Animating Stones. Things that burn. Stones of fire; they bind us, they move us. They serve him. Oh, they serve him, Arms. They do not stop. We cannot stop it inside us, clawing us, moving us."

Gloriae narrowed her eyes. "Where did Dies Irae find them?"

The bloody tears kept flowing; Gloriae could not believe it had so much blood. "I have seen them, Arms. Yes, I have. A wagon driving through the city. A wagon that glowed red. Animating Stones were there! They took them into his dungeon, Legs. He took one. He put it inside us. He took my legs. He took my arms. He used yours, he sewed us together, Rot Gang, no silver, only mimic. Only mimic."

"Where did the wagon come from?"

"A mine! A mine in a burned forest. A mine where Animating Stones glow. A mine of mimics, yes. A mine of stones. A mine of pain, and death, and rot. Rot Gang. Free them! Cut them off me. Cut off his legs. Cut off his arms."

Gloriae dug her fingers into the head. "Not yet. Where is the mine?"

It bared its bloody teeth. "Master would laugh of it. The same forest, he said, where the weredragon king once hid. He mined for Animating Stones in a crater, a crater where no trees could grow, and where the earth sank. And he laughed, Arms. Yes, how he laughed."

"The weredragon king? Do you mean Benedictus? Is the mine in Hostias Forest, where Benedictus once hid?"

The head coughed and trembled. "We don't know, Legs, do we? We don't know, Arms. Hostias Forest, he called it, yes, right under the crater where King Weredragon hid. And he laughed. But we only screamed. Our stone burns. It burns us. He hurt us. He laughed and sewed us. Free us!"

Gloriae tossed the head aside. She turned to leave.

Hostias Forest. The crater. Gloriae clenched her jaw. The place she had burned when hunting Benedictus and Kyrie. She would have to return there.

"You promised!" the head screamed behind her. "She promised to free us, Legs. She promised to make us Teeth again, to make us Rot Gang."

Gloriae drew an arrow and lit it with her tinderbox. She nocked the arrow in her bow.

"You lied!" the head shrieked, eyes blazing. "You swore to free them, to cut them off!"

Gloriae shut one eye, drew, and aimed.

"Yes," she whispered. "I lied."

She loosed her arrow. It shot like a comet and hit the severed head. It burst into flame.

"You will burn with us!" it screamed from the fire. "You will burn too, Gloriae. You will burn forever. You will burn in the Sun God's fire."

The flames overcame its words. Gloriae watched it burn, until it was nothing but a skull. Still its jaw moved, and its teeth clacked. Gloriae walked toward it and kicked with her steel-tipped boot. She kept kicking until the skull shattered.

"I did not make you a boy again," she said. "But I freed you. I ended your pain. That is more than what Dies Irae will do to me, if he catches me." She clenched her fists. "But he will not catch me. He will burn too."

She turned around and stepped underground into the cellars.

TERRA

His wing and leg blazed in pain, but Terra kept flying. The city of giants spread beneath him.

"Stars," Memoria whispered.

She flew beside him, blood staining her green scales. Terra clenched his jaw. The sight of her blood hurt him more than his wounds. *I will not let her die too. I will fight and burn and die if I must, but I will protect her.*

He returned his eyes to the city. It spread like a labyrinth. Leagues of grey brick walls wound across the mountaintop. Giants ran between them, shouting and howling and pounding their chests. There were thousands, maybe tens of thousands.

"Look," Terra said. He pointed a claw and grunted with the pain; his knee felt swollen and burned. "The fort."

"I see it," Memoria said, eyes narrowed. "The king must live there."

The fortress loomed taller than an Ice Palace, taller than the old courts of Requiem; Terra guessed that it stood a thousand feet tall. Built of grey, frosty bricks, it was a simple structure; it had no bridges, towers, or courtyards like the forts of men. It was but a great cube of stone. It rose from the city, a sentinel over the mountain.

Hundreds of spikes lined the fort's parapets, holding the decapitated heads of icelings. The heads gazed with eyeless sockets, their mouths open, their skin frozen blue. Giants stood there too, boulders in hands. They howled, and soon those boulders flew toward the two dragons.

Terra cursed, flew sideways, and dodged a boulder that grazed his leg. More boulders flew.

"Fly above the fort!" he shouted. "We'll be harder to hit."

Memoria nodded. They flapped their wings hard, shooting between the boulders. They flew higher and higher. The cold, thin air spun Terra's head. He righted himself, flew north, and circled above the stone fortress.

One giant tossed a boulder. Terra and Memoria scattered. The boulder flew between them, reached its zenith, and tumbled down. The giants below howled, and the boulder crashed between them, punching a hole into the fort.

The boulders ceased flying.

"Good," Terra said, flapping his wings. "We're safe if we hover right above them. I..." A closer look at the fortress made his breath die.

"Stars above," Memoria said, flying beside him. "Look at the *size* of him."

Terra clenched his jaw. Ice seemed to form along his spine. Fire filled his mouth, flicking between his teeth.

"I see him," he said, voice low. "He's a big boy, that one is."

A massive, deformed creature stood atop the fort, howling and pounding his chest. He towered over the giants who manned the parapets around him, twice their size. Tufts of hair grew from his squat, misshapen head. His body was all muscles overgrown with boils and scars. Claws grew from his fingers, each the size of a man. He wore a loin cloth, a belt decorated with iceling heads, and a crown of icicles.

"He must be a hundred feet tall," Memoria whispered.

Terra nodded. "Twice our size. He's their king."

The Giant King howled and reached his claws toward them. His cry shook the air; Terra could feel it pound against his chest. In his mind, he heard the howls of dragons, and the shrieks of griffins, and Memoria's voice. *Terra... I found him.*

"Look at his neck," Memoria said.

Terra frowned and stared. A golden chain hung around the giant's neck. Two small, white objects hung from it. When Terra squinted, they came into focus. Hands. A woman's hands, pale and dainty, folded into fists.

"Adoria's Hands," he said. "Those are the toys we want. Let's burn him, then grab them."

The smaller giants leered and waved their arms. The king pounded his feet, snapped his teeth, and cried out to them in a guttural language.

Memoria shook her head. "No fire, Terra! What if flames burn Adoria's Hands?"

The Giant King spat and shouted. His eyes blazed. Terra imagined that he was insulting them, calling them weak, inviting them to fight. Terra's head spun. He grinded his teeth.

What am I doing here? he thought. *I vowed to never more fly to war. To never more see fire, blood, a loved one die.* He wanted to turn and leave, to fly back to the ice palace. To hide from war. From pain. From those soft, echoing words.

Terra... I found him.

But had she found him? Had that small body, burned beyond recognition, truly been Kyrie?

Are you still there, Kyrie? Still in the ruins of Requiem, waiting for me to find you?

"If you're alive, Kyrie, I'll help you," Terra whispered, quiet enough that Memoria could not hear. "I'll burn the mimics who hunt you. I'll take Adoria's Hands."

His sister flew around him, green scales splashed with blood. "Ready, Terra?"

He nodded, staring down at the giant. "We dive. I'll fly to his front, you to his back. Let's claw out his neck."

Terra bared his fangs, outstretched his claws, and swooped.

Dragons! To me!

Requiem, rally here!

Griffins! They killed the children, they—

The words of old battles screamed in the wind. Terra snarled and swooped. He swooped like in the old days, like he would swoop against Osanna, diving to kill, to burn, to fight for his life. To death. To glory. To pain.

Kyrie! Kyrie, do you hear me?

His howl rang. He reached the Giant King.

Claws flashed. The giant swung his fist. Terra dipped, flew under the blow, and lashed. His claws hit the giant's thigh.

Nothing. No blood. No mark. The giant's skin was tough as the thickest leather armor. Memoria flew behind the giant. She bit his shoulder, then cried. Her fangs would not pierce his skin.

The Giant King roared. Terra and Memoria flew up. The giant's fists swung, and one hit Terra's tail. It knocked him into a spin.

"Terra!" Memoria cried. The lesser giants cheered around them.

The king reached out, fingers thick and bloated like dead seals. Terra flapped his wings, narrowly dodging the blow, and soared.

"The damn thing seems made of boiled leather," Terra muttered. He circled a hundred feet above. The giant howled and stamped his feet below, grinning and drooling. Boulders flew. Terra flew left and right. One boulder grazed his side, chipping a scale.

"Leather? It felt like biting into iron," Memoria shouted. She flew beside him, wincing.

Terra growled. "Let's burn the beast."

"No fire, Terra! We can't harm Adoria's Hands."

"Then we'll burn the smaller ones."

Terra soared, spun, and dived. Boulders flew around him. One hit his left horn, knocking it off. He howled in pain and blew fire at a row of lesser giants. They blazed. More boulders flew. Terra soared, spun, flew at them again. He roared more fire. More giants burned and fell.

"Memoria, you all right?" he shouted.

She flew alongside the fort's parapets, blowing more flame. Giants caught fire. Their boulders fell, cracking the parapets.

"I'm fin—" she began, and a boulder slammed into her side.

She fell.

"Memoria!"

Terra flew across the fortress, moving toward her. He flew too low. The Giant King reached out. Those bloated fingers grazed him. Terra flew higher. For an instant, he thought he was free. Then the king's hand closed around his leg.

The giant pulled him down like a man tugging a struggling bird. Terra howled and lashed his tail. He hit the king's face, but the giant only laughed. His fingers tightened around Terra's leg, nearly breaking the bone.

"Memoria!" he cried. Where was she?

The king pulled him near. His mouth opened, showing rotten, yellow teeth. His breath assailed Terra, as foul as mimics. His tongue reached out. *He's going to eat me alive.*

Terra blew fire, not caring if he harmed Adoria's Hands. His flames hit the king's face, crackling and showering sparks. The king howled, released Terra's leg, and brought his hands to his face.

Terra flapped his wings. The giant was rubbing his eyes, slapping the fire off his face. Terra swooped, shouted, and drove his remaining horn into the Giant King's left eye.

The giant roared so loudly, Terra thought his eardrums would tear. He pushed, driving the horn deep into the giant's head. The giant howled. His hands clutched him.

Terra couldn't breathe. The giant wrapped his arms around him and squeezed. Terra had never felt such pain. His ribs creaked. He felt one crack. He thought his organs would burst. The world turned black. Stars floated.

I'm dead, he thought. *It ends here. I'm dead and so is Memoria. I'm sorry, sister. I'm sorry. I love you.*

He flapped his wings. Somehow he kept kicking. He scratched, but the arms kept squeezing.

His eyes rolled back.

"Terra!"

He heard thudding wings. He heard cries, howls, tearing flesh. The arms released him.

Terra fell to the floor. He looked up and saw Memoria slashing the giant's face. She was like a raven attacking a bear. Her fangs and claws dug into the giant's eyes, nose, mouth. The king howled and swiped at her. Blood covered her scales; she was more red than green.

Up. Up! Fly, dragons of Requiem!

Howling, Terra pushed himself to his feet. His chest blazed. It felt like knives were digging inside him. He flapped his wings and soared.

He slammed into the giant, lashing his claws. One claw caught the giant's slobbery lip, and tugged, and tore. Blood showered.

"It won't die!" Memoria shouted.

"It will! Bring it down!"

The king's hands thrashed. One fist hit Memoria. She cried and fell back. Another fist thudded into Terra's side, but he ignored the pain. For an instant, he saw the king's face. There was barely anything left; his head was a mess of blood and burned flesh. Disgust filled Terra. He flew, spun, and lashed his tail.

His tail's spikes drove into what had been the giant's head. One pushed through the ear, deep into the brain.

The king howled.

Terra pulled back. Memoria flew beside him. They hovered, panting, staring.

The Giant King swung his arms uselessly. He mewled. Mucus and blood flowed down him. He took one step toward them, knees shaky. He took a second step... and faltered. His knees hit the fortress roof, shaking the structure. He reached out feebly, swinging his hands as if swatting flies.

"Let's put him out of his misery," Terra said.

He flew to the giant's right. Memoria flew to his left. They lashed their claws, lacerating the giant's neck.

The Giant King gave one last, gurgling yowl. He clutched his face and mewled like a demonic baby.

Then he fell.

He hit the fortress, cracking the stone. He kicked his legs, then lay still.

Terra collapsed beside the body. Breathing hurt. Memoria landed beside him and nudged him.

"More giants are climbing the walls," she said. "Let's grab Adoria's Hands and get out of here."

Terra nodded and grunted. He limped toward the dead Giant King. The body lay facedown, hiding Adoria's Hands beneath it. Terra shoved the body, but it felt like shoving a mountain.

"Come on!" Memoria shouted, shoving with him.

Giants howled behind them.

Boulders came flying.

Terra and Memoria leaped aside. The boulders hit the Giant King, shoving the body several feet back.

Terra roared fire. The flames shot across the fortress and hit a dozen giants. Memoria blew fire behind him, burning more giants. More boulders flew. The two dragons scattered, and the boulders hit the dead king again.

"Terra, the hands!" Memoria shouted.

The boulders had shoved the king, revealing Adoria's fingertips. The king's body still buried the palms.

"Hold them back!" he shouted to his sister.

Memoria nodded and flew in circles, blowing fire at the climbing giants. Flaming rocks flew around her. Terra shoved the giant's body, pushing with his feet. He howled with the pain. The body barely moved.

"Hurry, Terra, more are climbing!"

Terra grunted, shoving, driving forward. White pain blinded him. He shouted... and the body moved a foot. Terra reached down, snapped the chain, and tugged it. The hands came free.

"I've got them!" he called hoarsely. "Fly!"

Clutching the hands, he flapped his wings, shooting straight up. Memoria flew beside him, eyes narrowed, blood trickling. Boulders blazed around them like flaming comets.

In his mind, Terra saw the flaming arrows, the hordes of griffins, the fire upon Requiem. He saw their old home: the mosaic floor, the balcony in sunrise, the vineyard at sunset, the garden where he'd play with Memoria and Kyrie.

"I never left you," Terra whispered as he flew. His eyes stung. "You're still with me, Requiem. Now. Always."

If Memoria heard him, she said nothing, but she gave him a sad smile.

They flew from the Jet Mountains. They flew over plains of ice and snow. They flew over this land of exile, this frozen world where they hid from fire and pain. Blood had spilled here today, and fire burned, and for the first time in years, Terra felt the ice inside him melt.

I remember. I was a soldier. I was a brother. I am that man still.

He looked at Memoria, his little sister, the person he'd stayed alive for. He nodded at her.

"It's time to go home."

GLORIAE

She knew this place. She had hunted here. She had burned here. She had shed her mother's blood here and nearly killed her father.

Hostias. Once a shadowy, ancient forest. Today it was a land of burned trees and memories of war.

I rode my griffin Aquila over these woods, she remembered, *cutting the sky, the wind in my hair. I was a warrior of glory, of gold, of grandeur... and of lies.*

"Are you sure you know the way?" Gloriae asked her mother. "The land looks different now."

Lacrimosa nodded, walking beside her. "I know. I visited your father here every new moon. I will find the crater."

Her mother's tunic and leggings were tattered, her cheeks were ashy, and her lavender eyes looked too large, her face too thin. When Gloriae looked at her own body, she saw more dirt, more tatters, more scratches and bruises and thinned limbs.

I was a huntress of jewels and might, a light upon Osanna, a champion of justice. And now... now we are humble, and dirty, and gaunt. Gloriae missed those old days, missed the glory. But what glory had that life truly held? *Only glory to the blind,* she thought. *And I was blind. Dirt and hunger, when suffered for truth, are nobler than gold and lies.*

Gloriae looked over her shoulder and drew comfort from the sight of their host—marching statues with pulsing Animating Stones in their breasts. Roughly hewn from boulders and columns, they were craggy, bulky things, slow to move and rough to touch. Frost and snow covered them. Their features were mere chips, eyes narrow slits, mouths harsh lines. Though their first statues—the dragon and the maiden—had carved them only recently, they seemed to Gloriae like ancient things, gods of earth and stone and wisdom. The age of the stone appeared in every nook and bump upon them.

"They make a bloody racket," Agnus Dei muttered, walking beside Gloriae. The statues crackled with every step, a sound like grinding rubble. "The mimics will hear."

Kyrie was walking with an arrow in his bow. He snorted. "Let them hear. Our statues beat them to pulp last time. They can do it again."

But last time we fought on our turf, and now we march upon theirs, Gloriae thought, but said nothing. She knew that attacking a place was harder than defending it. Kyrie would learn that today, she suspected. She pulled down her helmet's visor, a gilded mask of her own face. Behind it, she felt like a statue herself, blank and expressionless, made for killing.

"I recognize this place," she said. She pointed at a frozen stream that snaked between craggy boulders shaped like trolls. Rushes had once grown along it; they had burned away in the war, but the boulders were unmistakable. She had camped here with her griffins once. "We're almost there."

Lacrimosa nodded. "Ben's hut was near. We would walk here many times."

And this is the place where I nearly killed Kyrie, Gloriae thought, but said nothing. It seemed so long ago. *Dirt for gold. Truth for glory.*

They kept walking. The charred trees rose around them, creaking in the wind, heavy with snow and icicles. Soon Gloriae heard a sound from ahead: creaking, hammering, grunting. She sniffed and smelled rot on the wind. *We're near.*

"Gloriae," said her twin, and placed a hand on her shoulder. "You are a brave warrior. You will fight well today."

When Gloriae turned her head, she saw Agnus Dei staring at her with somber eyes. *She's afraid,* Gloriae realized. *And so am I.*

She nodded. "You will as well. You are a warrior, Agnus Dei. I've seen you fight. I have fought you myself. Yours is a steel heart."

The sounds grew louder as they walked. *Thump thump* and *twang.* Hammering. The creaking of ropes. And above it all the grunting, squealing, and screaming of mimics.

"Stop," Gloriae said, raising her hand to halt the others. The statues too ceased walking; when still, they looked like nothing but boulders with the hint of men's shapes.

"What is it?" Kyrie asked.

"We make too much noise. I'll scout ahead. Wait here."

She left them between the burned trees. As she walked, she drew Per Ignem, and the blade caught the light. *My blade is thirsty for your blood, Irae,* she thought as she walked. *You gave me this blade. You gave me these steel tipped boots. You gave me this steel armor and this steel soul.* A snarl found her lips. *If you are here today, these weapons you gave me will be your death.*

The sounds from ahead grew louder. *Thump. Twang.* Squeals and shouts. *Move faster, maggots. Get this dirt out of here.* Screams and clashing metal. And above it all, a stench of rot that filled Gloriae's helmet and made her growl.

She stepped over a fallen bole, climbed a hill of burned birches, and beheld the Animating Stone mine. She knelt behind fallen trees and watched.

A ditch and wooden palisade surrounded the mine. Behind these crude fortifications, Gloriae saw a crater the size of the amphitheatre in Confutatis. It was clear of brush and dust rose from it. Tents, scaffolding, and wagons of dirt covered the crater. In the center, a shaft led underground.

Gloriae narrowed her eyes, examining Dies Irae's forces. Mimics patrolled the crater, their arms burly, their chests broad. Some seemed to be workers; they carried shovels and buckets. Others were warriors; their arms ended with blades instead of hands. Gloriae counted thirty workers and fifty warriors.

"Is that all?" she whispered, raising an eyebrow. *This mine is the key to Irae's power. Are these all his guards?*

Frowning, she walked back to the others. She found them ahead of the statues, lighting their torches and arrows. Their faces were somber, their eyes dark, their fingers tight around their weapons.

"What did you see?" Kyrie asked her. Ash and mud covered his face.

"Fewer than a hundred mimics," she said. "This worries me."

Kyrie snickered. "You're worried about a hundred mimics? We smashed a thousand back in Requiem."

Lacrimosa seemed to understand faster. "Exactly, Kyrie," the queen said. "That's what worries Gloriae. This mine is valuable to Irae. Why guard it with a mere hundred mimics? Where is his army?"

Kyrie rolled his eyes. "Didn't you hear me? We smashed his army in Requiem."

Agnus Dei groaned and punched his arm. "Pup, you are denser than a statue's backside. Don't you remember what the mimic head said when Gloriae questioned it? Irae has thousands of mimics left. Why aren't they guarding the mine?"

Kyrie rubbed his arm and glared at her. "Because they're preparing to invade Requiem, that's why. Maybe they're invading it already, while we're here in Osanna. Dies Irae underestimates us. He always has. So he guards this place with a hundred mimics and thinks it's safe."

Gloriae nodded slowly. "Maybe, Kyrie. Maybe. But I'm worried. Let's proceed cautiously."

"You mean, let's be extra careful not to die?" Kyrie snickered again. "I think we've all become rather good at that already, Gloriae. If you think it's some elaborate trap, and want to turn back, say so. Otherwise, let's storm the damn place and smash it."

Gloriae looked at Lacrimosa. "What do you say, Mother?"

Lacrimosa stared toward the mine. Her lips tightened and she drew Stella Lumen. She nodded.

"We need that mine. Whatever horrors await us in its darkness, we will face them." She raised the blade, and stars seemed to shine within its steel. "Fire and stone."

Gloriae bared her teeth. "Fire and stone."

She spun around and drew Per Ignem. She raised the blade in one hand, her torch in the other. With a shout, she began running. The others answered her cry, and she heard their footfalls behind her. The statues ran too, their feet shaking the earth, their cries like mournful thunder and cracking mountains.

Waving her torch, Gloriae leaped over a fallen bole and charged toward the mine.

The mimics below howled. Their stench hit Gloriae like a fog. Balls of flame flew over the sharpened stakes that surrounded the mine. Gloriae batted one aside with her torch. Another hit her breastplate and fell to her feet. Gloriae spat. It was a flaming human head.

"Bring down the walls!" she shouted. A thousand statues of Requiem ran around her. "Knock them down!"

The statues jumped into the ditch that surrounded the mine. As they crashed down, the mine shook. They began smashing the palisade, cracking and toppling the sharpened logs. More flaming heads flew from within the mine. Gloriae snarled as she dodged them.

Soon the palisade fell, and statues filled the ditch like stones filling a mote. Behind the smashed fortifications, Gloriae saw the mimics waiting. They waved blades, howled, and leered.

"Kill them all!" Gloriae shouted and ran toward them. She ran over the mimics in the ditch, as if they were stepping stones, and leaped through the smashed palisade.

Two mimics ran toward her. They had no hands; their arms ended with blades. Those blades swung at her. Gloriae ducked, dodging one blade, and parried the second with her sword. She tossed her torch and burned one's face. She leaped up, spun, and swung her sword. The second mimic's head flew. Before the first mimic could recover, she thrust her blade and pierced its chest. As it howled, she lifted her torch and swung it left and right. Soon the mimics burned.

The battle raged around her. The other Vir Requis were swinging their torches and swords, holding back dozens of the undead. The statues were pouring into the mine behind her, and their stone hands tore mimics apart.

Three mimics raced toward her, only three feet tall. Gloriae grimaced. Were they children or dwarves? She could not tell; their heads were too rotten. They lashed at her with daggers. Gloriae parried and swung her weapons. Soon they lay dead around her, oozing pus. She stared down at them. *If they were children, well... I've killed children before.*

It only took moments. Gloriae slew two more mimics, these ones with the heads of horses, and it was over. The mimics all lay torn across the mine. Their limbs, torsos, and heads still twitched and crawled. The statues moved across the crater, stomping the mimic parts and grinding them.

"Is that all?" Agnus Dei said and laughed. She kicked aside a crawling arm. "Is that all Irae's got?"

Gloriae stared around, eyes narrowed. *This was too easy.*

"All right!" Kyrie said. He began walking toward the shaft. "Into the mine. Let's kill whatever creatures crawl down there and be done with."

No, Gloriae thought. *No, this is wrong.* She knew Dies Irae. He would not leave this place so vulnerable. This had to be a trap, or—

A grumble sounded below.

The crater trembled.

Kyrie paused outside the shaft. He took a step back and raised his weapons. Gloriae clutched her sword and snarled.

"Here we go," she whispered. "Whatever terror Irae prepared for us... it's waking up."

A stench rose from the mine, worse even than the dead mimics across the crater.

"Come near me," Lacrimosa said, voice strangely calm. She raised Stella Lumen, her sword of Requiem steel and diamonds. "Let us stand together."

The crater trembled. The strewn mimic arms began to crawl toward the trees, as if fleeing what evil lurked below.

Gloriae moved to stand at her mother's left. Agnus Dei and Kyrie moved to her right. The queen of Requiem held her sword before her, and its blade glimmered.

Gloriae raised her own sword, Per Ignem, a blade of northern steel and gold. "I fight beside you, Lacrimosa, Queen of Requiem."

Agnus Dei and Kyrie had no ancient, legendary blades. Theirs were common swords found in abandoned castles, their steel unadorned, their grips simple leather. Kyrie had named his "Irae's Fate", and Agnus Dei had dubbed hers "Pup Killer" after an argument with Kyrie. Common swords, but as the two raised them, they shone with just as much light.

"For Requiem," Kyrie said.

"For Father," whispered Agnus Dei.

A howl rose from the mine.

Cracks ran along the crater. Burned trees snapped and fell. Red light beamed out of the shaft. Thousands of cockroaches fled from it and scurried across the crater. Thunder boomed and lightning rent the night.

A shadow rose from the shaft.

Gloriae gasped. Her legs shook. She panted and growled and hissed. Beside her, she heard the others curse.

"What the stars is it?" Agnus Dei asked, disgust twisting her words.

"Irae's insanity," Gloriae answered softly. "And all his malice."

The creature unfurled before them, and Gloriae screamed.

KYRIE ELEISON

"Stay near me, kitten," he whispered. "I'll look after you."

Beside him, Agnus Dei clutched her sword and torch. "Pup, focus less on protecting me, and more on killing that thing. All right?"

Grimacing, he watched the creature unfold itself, rise to its feet, and roar to the heavens.

"Deal," he said.

The creature from the mine stood twenty feet tall, maybe thirty. It was a mimic, but unlike the others. It seemed stitched together from gobbets of flesh. Its limbs were huge, ten feet long, wide as barrels. They were made of many smaller limbs braided together. Its muscles were woven of human legs and arms bundled into strands of oozing flesh. Its torso was stitched together from a dozen rolled up bodies; Kyrie saw three faces peering from its stomach like fetuses trying to emerge from a womb. A helmet the size of a barrel covered the mimic's head. Kyrie was grateful; he did not want to see its face.

For a moment, the world was silent. The mimic giant stood before them, watching them.

Then Lacrimosa's voice pierced the night.

"Burn it."

Kyrie nocked a flaming arrow and fired.

It slammed into the mimic's chest, and it roared. Bricks rolled and the earth shook. The other Vir Requis shot arrows too. They slammed into the mimic, and it screamed and pulled the arrows out.

"Statues of Requiem!" Lacrimosa called. "Bring it down."

The statues raced toward the undead giant. Howling, it swiped its arms, and statues flew. Kyrie cursed and leaped aside. A statue flew over his head, a missile of chipped stone. He glanced behind him and saw the statue crash into its brothers, scattering them.

"Damn thing's going to ruin my day," Kyrie muttered and nocked another arrow. He aimed at the giant mimic's head. The helmet had only a thin slot for the eyes. *If I can only shoot my arrow in there....*

The giant kept moving, lashing its arms at statues. Kyrie stayed still. He closed an eye. He aimed. He caught his breath... and fired.

The flaming arrow pierced the night. It slammed into the helmet, an inch above the eye slot, and fell.

"Stars damn it!" Kyrie said. He gritted his teeth and reached for another arrow, but had no time. The giant howled and leaped toward him.

Kyrie cursed and jumped back. The mimic giant swiped a hand at him. Each finger, Kyrie realized, was made of a man's arm. He ducked, and the hand flew over his head. He raised his sword and sliced into the hand. Blood showered.

"Pup!" Agnus Dei shouted somewhere in the battlefield.

The giant tossed back its head and howled. Kyrie leaped, ran, and sliced his sword across the giant's calf. It roared, and Kyrie ran behind it. Before it could turn toward him, he nocked an arrow. When it started racing toward him again, he had aimed and fired.

The arrow glanced off the giant's helmet.

"Damn it all!" Kyrie shouted.

He raced across the crater. The statues were hacking at the mimic's legs, but it kept kicking them away, like a man kicking away nipping dogs. Lacrimosa and the twins were firing arrows, but they barely fazed the giant. A dozen arrows soon covered its torso, but it seemed not to feel them.

"Aim for its eyes!" he shouted at the girls.

Agnus Dei groaned. "Pup, I don't tell you how to kill mimics."

The giant heard her and ran toward her, feet cracking the earth. It swung its hands at her. One finger slammed into her shoulder, knocking her down.

"Agnus Dei!"

Dread filled Kyrie like a bucket of ice inside him. He shouted, ran, and leaped onto a pile of fallen statues. He vaulted forward and landed on the giant mimic's back.

The stench assailed him. Kyrie thought he might pass out. The mimic bucked and reached over its back, and its hands slammed against Kyrie. He grunted. Each blow felt like a hammer. He dug his fingers into the mimic's flesh. Its back was woven of a dozen human bodies slung together, a jumble of arms and legs and gasping faces. The giant kept leaping, and the blows fell onto Kyrie, but he clung on. He drew his dagger. He drove it into the mimic's back.

Rot sprayed. The giant screamed. Kyrie grimaced and twisted the blade.

"Pup!"

"Kyrie!"

The giant thrashed and its hands slammed against Kyrie's back. The pain bloomed. Kyrie thought he might pass out. Statues kept attacking the giant's legs, but it kept kicking them aside. Arrows kept piercing its chest, but it barely noticed. It kept reaching over its back and lashing at Kyrie, knocking the breath out of him.

"No way," Kyrie managed to say, the blows raining against him. "No way, my friend. You are going down."

He pulled his dagger free. Blood and halved worms covered the blade. Kyrie shoved his fingers into the creature's back and pulled himself up, until he reached its neck. With a cry, he shoved the dagger down.

Blood flowed from the giant's neck.

It wobbled.

It pitched forward.

"Pup!" Agnus Dei cried.

The giant hit the ground. The world shook. Kyrie tumbled off it, rolled across the ground, and stopped at Agnus Dei's feet. She knelt over him, ran her fingers over his cheek, and her eyes were red. He could barely see her. His eyes fluttered and stars floated before him. Gloriae and Lacrimosa rushed to him too.

"Pup, are you alive?" Agnus Dei shook his shoulders. "Get up! Get up, pup, or I'll kill you!"

Kyrie pushed himself to his feet. He turned to face the fallen giant. It was struggling to rise. Its arms, each one woven of a dozen severed limbs, flexed as it pushed itself to its knees.

"This one's mine," Kyrie said hoarsely.

He reached over his back and took his last arrow. Legs trembling, he walked toward the giant mimic.

It stared at him. Kyrie could see red, blazing eyes inside its visor, each the size of a human head.

He lit and nocked his arrow.

The giant roared.

The arrow flew.

This time Kyrie shot true. The flaming arrow flew through the slot in the visor—it was only three inches wide—and drove into the giant's eye.

Its scream was so loud, that the crater cracked, and Kyrie fell. He grunted, struggled to his feet, and walked forward. The mimic giant floundered at his feet, its head burning. Kyrie drove his sword into its visor, and clenched his jaw as the blood poured.

The giant gave a last cry, and its limbs hit the dust.

It lay still.

Covered in its blood, Kyrie stared down at it, sword in hand.

"Bastard," he said.

And then Agnus Dei was hugging and kissing him, and Lacrimosa was tending to his wounds, and even Gloriae gave him a curt nod that said, *Well done.*

When they burned the giant's body, it raised black smoke that seemed to never end. Kyrie watched it burn, and thought about the men, women, and children who had died to form it.

"We have to kill Irae," he said, jaw clenched. "We have to kill him once and for all."

Agnus Dei stood by him, her arms around him. "We will."

AGNUS DEI

She raised her sword. Pup Killer, she had named the blade after a fight with Kyrie. A silly name, she knew. A silly fight. Tonight she wished she had a legendary sword like Gloriae's Per Ignem or like Mother's Stella Lumen, swords with history, glory, and might. Tonight she would need all the might she could get.

"We enter the mine," she said. "If we find Animating Stones, we'll take them. If we find Dies Irae, we'll kill him. I'll climb down first. If Irae is down there, I want him to meet my sword first."

Gloriae stepped up beside her. "I'll enter behind you. We are twins. We will wield twin blades."

With a small smile, Gloriae raised Per Ignem and touched its steel to Pup Killer.

Agnus Dei nodded. "Time of the twins."

Lacrimosa joined her blade to the salute. "The statues will enter behind you. I'll bring up the rear. Kyrie, you go with me. If anything enters the mine behind us, we'll kill it."

Kyrie touched his blade to the other three. Thunder rolled. It began to rain.

Agnus Dei approached the shaft leading into the mine. When she listened, she heard nothing from below. No hammering. No cries. Silence.

"There are more mimics down there," she said. "They're waiting. I'm ready for them. Come, Gloriae. Behind me."

With a deep breath, Agnus Dei climbed into the shaft.

A ladder led into darkness. Agnus Dei held the rungs with one hand, her sword with the other. She began to climb down. Cold air blew from below. When she looked down, she saw nothing but darkness.

Gloriae climbed above her. "Do you see anything?" she said.

"Yeah, I see your smelly feet above me. Nothing but darkness below."

It seemed that she descended forever. The air became so cold, Agnus Dei's teeth chattered. Wind moaned around her, ruffling her hair. The stench of rot grew as she descended. Above her, she heard creaking and thumping, and dirt rained onto her.

"Gloriae, what's going on up there?" she asked.

Gloriae's voice answered in the darkness. "The statues are digging their hands into the sides of the shaft. That's the only way they can climb down."

"Just make sure the bloody things don't make the mine collapse, all right? At least, not before we grab some Animating Stones."

They kept plunging into the darkness. Agnus Dei remembered the last time she had plunged underground. She had crawled through caves in Fidelium Mountain. Father had been with her. Dies Irae and his nightshades had waited for them.

I wish you were with me here too, Father, she thought. *The darkness seems colder without you. Your spirit now dines in our halls beyond the stars. If you can see me down here, please watch over me.*

Finally the shaft ended. Agnus Dei let go of the ladder and stood on shaky feet. The darkness was complete. When she held her hands before her face, she couldn't see them.

"The shaft ends here," she said. "Be careful, Gloriae. Come stand beside me."

She felt in the darkness. Her hands touched craggy walls and slats of wood. She inched forward and found herself walking into a tunnel.

"Let's light some fire," Gloriae said.

Agnus Dei nodded and rummaged in her pack for her tinderbox. Soon she and Gloriae held crackling torches. The light revealed a tunnel that sloped into darkness. Wind blew from it, cold and rank with the smell of mimics.

"I used to come to this crater every moon," Agnus Dei said. "Mother and I would travel here to meet Father. I never understood why no trees or grass grew from it. Now I know. It's because Animating Stones pulsed beneath it. This place is evil."

Gloriae shook her head. "No. Animating Stones are only tools. Tools are rarely evil; the men who wield them often are."

"So let's find our man. Let's shove our swords into him."

She began walking down the tunnel, her torchlight dancing against craggy walls held with wooden slats. As she walked, she couldn't help the thoughts that whispered. *Our man. Dies Irae.* Was he... could he be... her father?

Agnus Dei growled. No. Impossible. True, Dies Irae had raped her mother nine moons before she and Gloriae were born. True, Dies Irae believed that he was the true father, not Benedictus. But Agnus Dei refused to believe.

"I am nothing like him," she whispered, jaw clenched. She had brown, fiery eyes like Benedictus. She had black hair like him, a temper like him, skin that tanned gold like his. And Gloriae... true, Gloriae had blue eyes and golden hair like Dies Irae, but so what? Lacrimosa was fair; Gloriae must have inherited her eyes and hair from her, not Dies Irae.

I will never believe that he's my father, she thought. *And even if he is... I don't care. I still hate him, and I'll still kill him.* She couldn't wait to thrust her sword into his flesh and watch him die.

Her footfalls echoed down the tunnel. When she looked over her shoulder, she saw statues walking behind Gloriae. She could only see several feet into the darkness; if Mother and Kyrie walked behind, the shadows hid them.

A growl sounded ahead.

Agnus Dei whipped her head forward and snarled. She raised her torch but saw nothing. She stopped walking and stared.

The growl sounded again.

The tunnel shook.

Dust fell from the ceiling and wooden beams creaked. More growls filled the tunnel, and something cackled.

"Time to kill," Agnus Dei said. With a wordless battle cry, she ran into the darkness, swinging her torch and sword.

A beam snapped to her right. A boulder crashed above. Dust rained.

"Come face me!" she cried. Shadows scurried ahead, laughing. She ran toward them, but they fled. All around her, wooden beams snapped, dust showered, and rocks fell.

"Agnus Dei, back!" Gloriae cried behind her. "Turn back."

"I can see them ahead!" Agnus Dei answered. "They're running away. After me, Gloriae!"

She raced into the darkness, leaping over falling stones. The tunnel shook violently. Agnus Dei fell, scraping her knees.

She pushed herself up and kept running. She saw a mimic ahead. Its eyes blazed, it leered, and then it turned and fled.

"Come face me!"

Gloriae shouted behind her. "Agnus Dei, the mine is collapsing! Boulders are falling."

Agnus Dei looked over her shoulder and gasped. The ceiling was crumbling, burying the animated statues. Boulders crushed them.

"Mother!" Agnus Dei screamed. "Kyrie!"

Boulders crashed and began rolling toward her.

"Run, Agnus Dei!" Gloriae cried.

Agnus Dei ran deeper into the darkness. Rocks buffeted her back and helmet. A boulder crashed ahead of her. She leaped over it and kept running. More boulders rolled behind. The mimics were gone. She couldn't even hear them laughing anymore.

"Gloriae!"

She grabbed her sister's hand. The two ran together, heading deeper into the tunnel. A beam crashed before them, and dust blinded Agnus Dei. She leaped over the wood and rocks and plunged into darkness. She fell. Rocks rained. Dust filled her nostrils. Statues cried behind her.

"Mother," she whispered.

A rock hit her shoulder, and she fell onto her chest. Gloriae fell beside her.

Her hand opened.

Gloriae's hand slipped from her grip.

Rocks covered her, and Agnus Dei reached out, trying to grasp something, anything.

"Pup. Pup...."

Mimics laughed in the darkness.

Stars shone.

A blow struck her helmet, and her face hit the ground. All sound and light faded from her world.

LACRIMOSA

She had reached the bottom of the shaft, and begun to walk down the tunnel, when the mine collapsed.

My daughters.

Stones fell, beams snapped, and dust rained.

My daughters!

No other thought filled her mind. She raced forward. Debris crashed around her. A rock hit her shoulder, and she shouted. She had to get through. She had to save them.

"Agnus Dei!" Kyrie shouted beside her. He began tossing rocks aside.

"There, move that boulder!" Lacrimosa said. A boulder the size of a man blocked their way. "Help me."

My daughters. No. Please, stars, please, don't take them from me.

She grabbed the boulder and pulled. Kyrie strained beside her. It wouldn't budge.

"Statues of Requiem!" Lacrimosa called. "Do you hear me?"

Had any statues survived? They had all entered the mine before her. Were they all crushed, as dead as the burned mimics?

"Statues, come help us," Kyrie shouted, but they did not emerge from the wreckage. A few more rocks tumbled, and then the dust settled.

Lacrimosa released the boulder she'd been pulling.

"It was a trap," she said.

Kyrie was still tossing rocks aside. In the light of her torch, Lacrimosa saw that his eyes burned and his cheeks were red.

"Agnus Dei!" he shouted. "Do you hear me? Gloriae!"

Lacrimosa wanted to scream too, to attack the wreckage, to cry and shout. *No.* She steeled herself. She refused to panic. *Stay calm. Think. If the twins are alive, I have to stay calm to save them.*

"It was a trap," she said again. Her fingers trembled, but her voice was steady. "This was not the main entrance to the mine. It was built for us."

"What are you talking about?" Kyrie demanded. "Lacrimosa, come on, help me move these boulders. Hurry!"

She clutched his shoulders and forced him to stare at her. "Kyrie Eleison! Listen to me. Think. Dies Irae knew we'd come here. He knew we'd crawl down the shaft. He rigged the tunnel to collapse onto us. But he wouldn't destroy his only entrance to the mines, not if he wants more Animating Stones. There must be a back entrance somewhere. If the girls survived... if they're trapped somewhere down there... we have to find it. Now come, hurry! Back to the surface."

Kyrie's eyes blazed. He looked ready to argue. Then he squared his shoulders and nodded.

"Let's go."

They began climbing the ladder out of the collapsed mine. Scratches and bruises covered them, but Lacrimosa barely felt the pain. *My daughters.* A vision of them crushed and broken flashed through her mind. Lacrimosa tightened her jaw and banished it. *Don't panic. Stay calm. Save them. There must be another entrance to the mine. There must be. If the girls are alive, I'll find them.*

Soon she and Kyrie climbed back onto the crater.

Mimic dogs awaited them there.

The creatures howled and lunged at them.

They were stitched together from various dead animals. Their heads were canine, but some had the bodies of goats, and one had human arms instead of legs. One had the body of a flayed pony, and another had an arm for a tail. They all barked, drooled, and bared their teeth.

Lacrimosa swung Stella Lumen, slicing into them. Kyrie fought beside her. They swung their torches too, burning the creatures. The dogs swarmed and leaped, their eyes blazing in the night. Their fur burned, but they kept attacking. One bit Lacrimosa's arm, and she screamed and beat it off.

"Lacrimosa, look!" Kyrie said. "Between those burned trees. It looks like a path."

Lacrimosa torched another dog and stared. *Yes.* She had missed it earlier, but now, with the blazing dogs casting their light, she saw it. A rough path led from the crater between the burned trees.

"You think Irae made the path?" she shouted over the howling dogs.

"It might lead to another shaft. Let's go! This dog and pony show is getting boring anyway."

They began to run, slicing and burning their way between the throngs of mimic dogs. Her arm bled, and her head spun, but Lacrimosa forced herself to keep running. They raced out of the crater and onto the path, the dogs in hot pursuit. Burned branches snapped under her boots.

My daughters. Please, stars, please. Don't let me lose them like I lost my husband.

The dogs yapped behind her. As she ran, Lacrimosa nocked an arrow. She spun, knelt, and fired. A dog yelped and fell. She kept running.

"Damn it!" Kyrie shouted and skidded to a stop.

Lacrimosa fired her last arrow. Another dog fell. "What is it?"

"A hole in the ground. I nearly fell in."

Lacrimosa ran forward and held her torch over the ground. Hidden under charred logs, a shaft led underground.

"Climb down," she said. "I'll hold back the d—"

Before she could finish, three dogs leaped onto her. She beat one back with her torch. The other two knocked her down. They snapped their teeth, and Lacrimosa banged one's face with her sword's hilt. The other bit her arm before Kyrie stabbed it. A hundred more mimic dogs came running from the forest.

"Into the mine!" she shouted. "Hurry."

Kyrie nodded and climbed down. "Come on, after me."

Lacrimosa clubbed two dogs with her torch, then leaped into the shaft. A ladder led into the darkness, and she began scurrying down. The dogs surrounded the opening, barking, but dared not jump down.

"Think we'll find the girls down here?" Kyrie shouted below her. She could barely hear him over the howling dogs.

Lacrimosa closed her eyes as she climbed into darkness. *Please, stars. Please. Don't take my daughters from me.* Her fingers trembled around the rungs of the shaft's ladder.

"I don't know, Kyrie. Hurry."

The ladder seemed endless. She descended into darkness—the darkness of the earth, and of her fears. She had only just buried her husband. If she now had to bury her daughters, how would she continue? How could she revive

Requiem, if only she and Kyrie now lived? How could she find strength to live on?

"No," she told herself again. "No, don't despair. Not when your daughters might still breathe, might still need you."

She forced herself to think only of every new rung, every new step into the belly of the earth. They descended until finally, shivering with cold and fear and injury, they reached solid ground.

"Agn—!" Kyrie began, but Lacrimosa elbowed him.

"Quiet, Kyrie," she whispered. "Let's move quietly."

They ran down a tunnel, struggling to keep their footfalls as soft as possible. Soon they heard hammering, grunting, and digging ahead. Red light glowed in the darkness. They rounded a corner, and Lacrimosa cursed and leaped back.

"Wait," she whispered and held up her arm, stopping Kyrie. "Peek."

They stuck their heads around the corner, and Lacrimosa exhaled slowly. *Stars.*

"There must be hundreds," Kyrie whispered, knuckles white around his sword hilt.

Lacrimosa nodded. "And hundreds more get their hearts here every day."

The cavern ahead was as large as Requiem's old halls. Torches and scaffolding covered its walls. Wooden bridges criss-crossed its depths like spider webs. Iron wagons screeched in and out of a dozen tunnels, moving on tracks, their wheels sparking. Everywhere she looked, Lacrimosa saw mimics. They covered the walls like bats. They dug in the cavern floor. They rode the wagons and manned the bridges and hollered as they worked.

"Look, Lacrimosa," Kyrie said and pointed. "That tunnel, over there."

Lacrimosa squinted. A fist seemed to grip her heart and squeeze. Far below and across the cavern, twenty or thirty mimics crowded around the entrance of a tunnel. It was hard to see in the darkness, but it seemed like the tunnel was blocked. Rocks and boulders filled it, and dust still poured from it.

"That must be the tunnel that... that...."

That my daughters escaped from? That my daughters died under? She did not know how to finish that sentence. Before she could say more, the mimics around that collapsed tunnel shifted, and Lacrimosa glimpsed two figures on the ground.

"No," she whispered, tears budding in her eyes. "Please, stars, no."

Lying on the ground by the tunnel, covered in dust and blood, were her daughters.

Kyrie made to race down into the cavern. Lacrimosa grabbed him and pulled him back.

"No, Kyrie!" she hissed.

He looked at her with wild eyes. "Lacrimosa, they... stars, they might be hurt, they need us, they...."

"We can't help them by dying," she said. "Wait, Kyrie. We watch. We hide. If we rush into this cavern alone, we're dead. If they're still alive, we'll save them, I promise you, Kyrie, I promise you. Now is not the time to rush to battle."

Panting, Kyrie knelt beside her. His fists clenched around his weapons. Lacrimosa placed her hand on his shoulder, and they stared silently from the darkness.

As they watched, a figure emerged from shadows and walked toward the collapsed tunnel. Cloaked in darkness, the man stood over the bloodied girls. A mimic held a torch near him. Its light glinted on jewelled armor and an arm of steel.

Lacrimosa's heart seemed to shatter inside her.

"Dies Irae," she whispered.

DIES IRAE

He stood in the cavern, arms crossed, and stared down at the girls.

The twins.

His daughters.

Finally, after all this time, he had them.

Gloriae was unconscious. Blood speckled her armor, and when Dies Irae removed her helmet, he saw her eye and forehead swelling.

My beautiful sweet Gloriae, Dies Irae thought. *Why did you have to disobey me? You were once so beautiful, so pure. You could have ruled this glorious empire at my side. Now you will serve me as a mimic.*

He turned to look down at Agnus Dei. Blood trickled down her forehead. Her eyelids fluttered weakly, and her mouth kept opening and closing. Bandages covered wounds on her arms and legs. Fresher scrapes peeked from the tatters of her clothes.

And Agnus Dei, my freakish daughter. You have never served me. You have always hated me. You will too will become a mimic of rot and worm.

Dies Irae turned to stare at Lashdig, chief of his miners. The hunchbacked, warty mimic stared back, his one eye large and blue, the other squinty and black. Matted red hair grew between scars on his head.

"Tie them up," Dies Irae told him. "And gag them."

Lashdig bowed his head. "Yes, master."

The stooped mimic barked a few commands, mimics shuffled, and soon ropes bound the twin girls. Lashdig stuffed bloody cloths into their mouths, which he secured with more rope. The girls began coming to, and started to struggle, but their screams were muffled, their limbs too weak to break free.

Dies Irae caressed Gloriae's cheek. "Why do you struggle, sweetness? You will become a beautiful mimic, a slave girl to my warriors' desires."

Her eyes blazed with hatred, and Dies Irae laughed. He turned to Agnus Dei, the dark twin.

"And you, Agnus Dei, why do you struggle so?" He chuckled at the sight of her squirming and screaming into her gag. He leaned down and kissed her forehead. "You too will become a beautiful mimic, Agnus Dei. Lashdig himself here will enjoy thrusting into you, he and all his miners."

He straightened and faced Lashdig again. "What of the other weredragons?"

Lashdig stared from his mismatched, rheumy eyes. "The tunnel swallowed them, my lord, as you planned. Their beastly stone mimics are crushed too."

"Find me bodies. If you have to scrape them off stones with a shovel, do it. I want their blood. I want what's left of their bones. Find me the weredragon whore and the boy."

Lashdig bowed. "Yes, my lord." He turned toward his workers. "Mimics! Dig. Dig well. Find us the weredragons. Their blood will feed our new children."

A voice spoke behind him.

"The blond one. Is that Gloriae?"

Dies Irae turned to see Umbra, the Blood Wolf assassin, walk toward him. She held a drawn dagger, and her eyes blazed. In his chambers, at his insistence, she was always nude. Today she wore black leggings, a black bodice, and five more daggers around her waist.

"This is her."

Fast as a panther, Umbra pounced atop Gloriae. She snarled and backhanded the young woman's cheek. Gloriae grunted into her gag. Her lip split, and blood trickled from it.

"You murdered my husband," Umbra hissed. "You burned my brothers." She backhanded Gloriae again. "I will make you suffer." She brought her dagger close to Gloriae's face. "I will make you suffer like they did."

"Umbra!"

Dies Irae's voice rang across the cavern. He grabbed her shoulders and pulled her off Gloriae. She struggled in his grasp, but he held her tight.

"Umbra, control yourself. That is an order."

She hissed and spat. "She will pay for her crimes."

Dies Irae nodded. "But not at your hands, Umbra. If you kill her, her pain ends. Once we make her a mimic, her pain will last forever."

Gloriae moaned, blood trickling down her chin. Agnus Dei screamed into her gag and thrashed. Umbra laughed.

"Very well, Irae," the Blood Wolf said. She tossed back her hair and sheathed her dagger. "I will keep her alive. But once she is a mimic, Irae... I will hurt her, again and again, a thousand times for every Blood Wolf she slew."

Dies Irae nodded. *And I will hurt you, Gloriae, for every nightshade you released from the abyss. And I will hurt you, Agnus Dei, for every man a weredragon has slain.*

He turned toward Warts and Bladehand, two of his finest warrior mimics. They rustled with bugs and stared at him with bloodshot eyes.

"Lift the girls," he told them. "While Lashdig and his miners dig for the others, we'll take these two to the camp. We'll dissect and stitch them there. Soon you will have fine, rotting bodies to enjoy."

Warts and Bladehand hissed and drooled. "Yes, master. As you command."

Bladehand grabbed Gloriae and slung her over his shoulder. Warts lifted the writhing Agnus Dei. Both girls screamed into their gags, a beautiful sound. Dies Irae began walking across the cavern, and the mimics followed behind. All around him, the miners dug, tunnelled, and sifted for Animating Stones. The red crystals glowed in wagons, thousands of them, thousands to keep building his armies.

One will be for you, Gloriae. And one for you, Agnus Dei.

As Dies Irae walked across the mine, the twins screaming behind him, he smiled thinly.

GLORIAE

Everything hurt. Bruises and cuts covered Gloriae. Her head pounded. Stars shone above between naked branches. As the mimics carried her through the burned forest, every jostle shot pain through her.

"Move faster, my lovelies," Dies Irae called out, marching ahead of the column. "I want to hit the camp by sunrise."

The mimics growled around him. Fifty of them, maybe a hundred, snaked through the forest. They carried crackling torches. Tied up and gagged across one's shoulder, Gloriae couldn't see much, only burned trees, thumping mimic feet, and glimpses of Agnus Dei tossed across a second mimic's shoulder. She kept trying to meet her sister's eyes, but only caught glimpses of the girl's flopping, dusty hair.

Are Mother and Kyrie dead? Or are they captured too? Worry for them gnawed on her, worse than her pain. The entire tunnel seemed to have collapsed behind her. It seemed unlikely that Mother and Kyrie could have survived.

"You will be my slave," hissed the mimic who carried her. His hand grabbed her thigh and squeezed. "I will take you deep, and break you."

Gloriae glared down at its chest, the only part she could see. Oozing wounds stretched across that chest, slapping against her cheek as it ran. Gloriae closed her eyes and tried to ignore the stench and pain.

If Mother and Kyrie are dead, so is Requiem, she thought. *Kyrie is our last male. Unless... unless his child truly quickened within me, and is a boy, and can still survive.* That too seemed unlikely to Gloriae. She had not bled since lying with Kyrie two moons ago, or was it three now? But she had also barely eaten, barely slept, barely rested from battle. Those more likely dried her blood than any life within her. Tied and gagged across a mimic's back, Gloriae lowered her head, and her soul seemed to sink into her belly.

So it's over. We lost the war. And soon... soon I and my twin will be mimics too, maggot-ridden and cursed for eternity.

Gloriae wanted to find hope. She struggled to grasp any ray of it she could find. But how could she? How could she escape death yet again?

A bird cawed.

A second bird, across the road, answered it.

Whistles cut the air.

With thuds, flaming arrows slammed into a dozen mimics.

"The *Earthen*." Dies Irae spat the word in disgust. "Mimics! Find them."

More flaming arrows flew. Gloriae grimaced. One arrow flew so close, it singed her hair. She stared through narrowed eyelids, but saw only shadows in green cloaks darting between the trees. *Green cloaks. Earth God priests.*

Twenty mimics raced into the woods, firing their own arrows and swinging their swords.

"Bring me their heads!" Dies Irae shouted. "A hundred slaves to any mimic who brings me Silva."

Gloriae sucked in her breath. Silva the Elder? She had heard his name whispered in the halls of Flammis Palace. Dies Irae had called him an outlaw, a crazy old man, a disgraced follower of a false god. He had killed Silva's siblings, toppled his temples, hunted him across the land. Did the priest still live?

More arrows flew. Three mimics fell dead. The battle raged through the forest, mimics and Earthen clashing swords and firing arrows.

Green shadows leaped from the burned trees, racing toward Gloriae with raised swords. *Will they free me from the mimics? Or will they kill Gloriae the Gilded, she who had hunted and killed so many of their number?* She remembered the tavern last summer, where she had hunted Kyrie; she had killed an Earth God priest there, one Tilas, or Talis, or Taras. She had forgotten his name, but would these Earthen remember her crime?

Bladehand grunted and tossed her down. She landed with a grimace, banging her elbow against a rock. Warts tossed Agnus Dei down; her sister slammed against her, yelping. The two mimics snarled and clashed blades with the Earthen.

She lay, Agnus Dei atop her, watching the fight. It only lasted minutes. Growling, Bladehand tore into an Earthen's face, then stabbed his chest. Warts sliced off a woman's arm, grabbed her throat, and clawed out her eyes. Soon they were feasting on

Earthen entrails. The other mimics came walking back from the forest, carrying severed heads, chewing on human organs.

Dies Irae nodded. Blood covered his mace and splashed his armor.

"Good, lovelies, good," he said. "Now grab the weredragons. Our camp lies just ahead. Soon the weredragons will taste needle and stitch."

They began to march again. Dawn rose around them, spilling red stains across the sky. The burned trees creaked in the wind, their icicles glimmering red. *A dawn of blood,* Gloriae thought and closed her eyes. *Perhaps the last dawn of my life.*

The mimics crested a hill and began to descend. They grunted and howled around her, and Agnus Dei screamed into her gag. Gloriae opened her eyes to see a camp sprawled across a valley below. Stench rose from it like steam. A palisade of sharpened logs surrounded the camp, protecting dozens of huts. Chained humans shuffled between those huts, mimics howling and whipping them.

Dies Irae led them into the valley, and soon they marched through the camp. Gloriae looked around, nausea twisting her gut. Blood soaked the snow and the huts' walls. When a mimic cracked a whip and entered one hut, Gloriae glimpsed prisoners inside, thin and shivering, their backs lashed. Many prisoners were missing limbs, their stumps wrapped with bloody bandages.

Between the huts rose piles of body parts, sorted into arms, legs, torsos, and heads. The piles rose thirty feet tall. Mimics walked atop them, rummaging through them, like ants scurrying over hives. Gloriae saw one mimic lift a woman's arm, lick it, and toss it aside. She gagged and coughed, her head spinning.

What has he turned into? she thought. How could Dies Irae, an emperor once devoted to gold and light and beauty, sink to such evil? This was not the man she had known. True, the Dies Irae who'd raised her had hunted, killed, and brutalized his enemies. But he had done it for order, light, and justice. This... there was no light here. There was no glory or justice. *You became worse than any enemy you've imagined.*

Past the piles of bodies, Gloriae saw ditches where fires burned. The mimics were tossing body parts into the flames: limbs that were frail, torsos that were thin, heads with no teeth.

They crackled in the fires. Gloriae understood. *He collects what he needs. He burns the rest.*

Finally Dies Irae stopped by a group of chained, whipped prisoners who stood barefoot in the snow. He raised his hand, and the mimics carrying Gloriae and Agnus Dei stopped too.

"Put them down," Dies Irae said.

The mimics tossed Gloriae and her sister onto the bloodied snow. They rolled, grunted, and shivered in the cold.

"What have we here?" Dies Irae asked, examining the prisoners. He caressed the hair of a chained toddler. "Why, this one is too small. He is useless to me. Burn him." He moved on to a woman with a bruised face. He squeezed her arms. "This one is strong. Take her limbs. Her teeth are crooked; burn her head." Next he frowned at an old man. "Burn this one, all of him."

He went from prisoner to prisoner, choosing parts to keep and parts to burn. Gloriae watched, her head spinning, the taste of vomit in her mouth. She struggled against the ropes binding her, but only chaffed her skin bloody. Beside her, Agnus Dei also struggled. She screamed into her gag, and her eyes were so wide, Gloriae could see white all around her irises.

I will kill you, Dies Irae, Gloriae swore again. *This is not the empire I fought for. This is not the vision you taught me. I will break free and I will kill you.*

When he had finished reviewing the prisoners, Dies Irae walked toward Gloriae and Agnus Dei. His boots, made from the golden scales of a young dragon, stood a finger's length from Gloriae's face.

"And now... these two."

His voice was soft, almost loving. He knelt and caressed Gloriae's cheek. She glared at him. His face was so different now. She remembered his face being strong, cold, and tanned gold. Now his face was gaunt, deeply lined, and ghostly white. A patch covered his left eye, and his right eye seemed paler too, a watery blue. He smiled at her, his lips like squirming worms, and touched her hair.

"This one... this one is strong. This one is steel. But she is treacherous, yes. A betrayer. Use what parts of her that you will, but leave me her head."

Next he knelt by Agnus Dei. She floundered in her bounds and her eyes shot daggers. Dies Irae leaned down and kissed her cheek, leaving a line of saliva on her skin.

"And this one... this one too is strong. Stupid, yes. Beastly and cursed, certainly. But *strong*. Use her body for your warriors, Warts and Bladehand. Leave me her head too. I will take their heads back with me to Confutatis."

Bladehand, the mimic who had carried Gloriae, nodded. "Yes, master. We will be building a new batch today, master. Their bodies will make good warriors." He knelt on all four, leaned in, and licked Gloriae's cheek with a bloated tongue.

"Excellent," Dies Irae said. "Toss them in with the others for now." He smacked his lips. "Right now, it's time for breakfast."

Bladehand lifted Gloriae, and Warts lifted Agnus Dei. Grunting and licking their chops, the mimics carried the twins to a hut, opened the door, and tossed them in. The lock snapped shut behind them.

Gloriae rolled across the floor, and her head hit somebody's leg. Agnus Dei rolled too, cursing behind her gag, and came to a stop beside her. At once, hands covered the two, feeling and grabbing. One hand held a rusty shiv near her head. Gloriae began to struggle, but these hands did not hurt her, and the knife did not cut her.

"Hush, girls, we'll remove your gags."

The shiv worked at the rope around her face, and her gag came free. Gloriae coughed, sucked in breath, and coughed again. Prisoners crowded over her, wearing rags. They shivered in the cold, gaunt and sickly. Their skin draped over their bones, and their faces were skeletal. Their eyes were sallow, their hair wispy.

"Thank you," Gloriae whispered hoarsely, finding that she could speak no louder.

The prisoner with the shiv began cutting the ropes around her ankles and wrists. Gloriae moved her limbs only an inch, and pain blazed. She gritted her teeth. Every movement shot bolts through her. She massaged her wrists; they were chaffed and bleeding.

"Drink," said a prisoner, a young woman with large grey eyes. She held melted snow in her palms, and Gloriae drank. Another prisoner was busy freeing Agnus Dei.

"Gloriae!" her twin said once her gag was removed.

Gloriae crawled toward her—she felt too weak to walk—and the two embraced. Agnus Dei had tears in her eyes, and Gloriae felt her own eyes sting.

"Oh, sister," she whispered. "It's horrible, isn't it?"

Agnus Dei trembled. "Do you think Mother and the pup are here? I... I tried to look for them as they carried us through the camp, but I couldn't see them. I'm worried."

Gloriae looked around her, and for the first time, she got a close look at the hut. Its walls were frosty, splashed with blood, and lined with bunks like shelves. A single slop bucket stood in one corner, a pile of frozen bread in another. It was a small hut, smaller than her old bedroom at Flammis Palace. And yet hundreds of prisoners filled it. They covered the floor, shoulder to shoulder, or lay in the bunks. Many were missing limbs. Their eyes were glassy, their skin sweaty, and bloody bandages covered their stumps. Some lay mumbling, feverish, their wounds green with infection. A few were dead already. *Their limbs are now attached to mimics,* Gloriae knew.

The prisoner with the grey eyes, who had given Gloriae water, gestured around her. She smiled a sad, crooked smile.

"Welcome," she said, "to Dies Irae's imagination."

KYRIE ELEISON

It began to snow, and Kyrie cursed.

The trail had been easy to follow until now. A hundred mimics had marched from the mine, cutting a path through the snow. Kyrie and Lacrimosa had been following their trail for several hours now. It led them through lands of dead trees, frozen streams, and rocky hills. Kyrie remembered walking here last summer, fleeing griffins and seeking King Benedictus. Trees had rustled here then, and hope still filled the world. Dies Irae had burned these trees, and little hope filled Kyrie now.

"Damn it," he muttered. The snow swirled around him. He could barely see through it. Worse, the snow was covering the mimics' footprints.

Lacrimosa shivered and tightened her cloak around her. "Let's move faster. We can still see the trail. Hurry, Kyrie."

They ran through the snow, their torches crackling. Around them among the burned trees, creatures howled. *Mimics,* Kyrie thought. This time, if they attacked, he didn't know if he'd survive. They had no statues left; they lay smashed and buried in the mines. They had no Gloriae and Agnus Dei with their swords and arrows.

Gloriae. Agnus Dei. Kyrie's heart twisted, and ice seemed to fill his belly. He had never felt such anguish. It churned inside him, spun his head, and tightened his throat. They had been alive in the mines. He had seen them thrashing in their bonds as the mimics carried them off. But were they alive now? Kyrie shivered, cursed, and ran as fast as he could. Lacrimosa ran at his side, eyes narrowed.

Please, stars, Kyrie prayed silently. *Please protect Agnus Dei. Please.*

He loved her so much, that he felt his insides could crumble, his heart stop beating, and his lungs collapse. He wanted to hold her, protect her, kill anyone who harmed her. If she died, he thought he would die too.

"Be strong, kitten," he whispered into the snow. "I'll be there soon."

If the stars heard his prayers, they ignored them. The snow only fell harder, a blizzard that stung his face and buried the mimics' trail. Kyrie cursed and stumbled forward, but soon stopped, backtracked, and realized he was lost.

He cursed and looked from side to side. Screeches rose in the blizzard around him, moving closer. Kyrie raised his torch, eyes narrowing. Lacrimosa did the same.

"Kyrie," she said, "I don't like this."

"Me ne—"

A dozen shadows flew toward them from the trees.

Kyrie couldn't help it. He cried in fear. They were mimics, but more hideous than any he'd seen. They looked like oversized bats. They had human heads and outstretched human arms. But below the shoulders, their bodies tapered into nothing but a spine. Skin stretched from their wrists to their tailbones, forming wings. They flapped toward Kyrie, shrieking.

He screamed and lashed his torch.

How can such terrors exist? The creatures' eyes blazed red. Their teeth snapped at him, and one bit his arm. Kyrie's head spun. He screamed again and lashed his blade and his fire. Lacrimosa screamed and fought beside him. The world was crackling fire, swirling snow, and everywhere those terrors, those bats, those things that had once been human.

No, he found himself praying feverishly. *No, please, stars, it can't be. They can't have been human. No mind can be sick enough to create these things. Please, stars, let me wake up from this nightmare. Let this all be a dream. How can this be real?*

"Kyrie, look!" Lacrimosa cried. She pointed, and Kyrie saw a tatter of green cloth hanging on a tree. Agnus Dei had worn a green cloak when captured.

"I see it!" he shouted and clubbed at the flying bats.

"The mimics carried the girls that way," Lacrimosa shouted back. "Let's go."

They ran through the snow, clubbing the mimic bats. One flew onto Kyrie's arm, flapping its wings against him. He tore it off, and grimaced when he saw its face, the face of an old woman. He kept running, swinging his torch and sword. The bats were everywhere, screeching, swooping, crying.

"Broken ice, over there!" he shouted. A frozen stream lay ahead, its surface cracked and splintered in one place. Kyrie ran over it, and he saw a path of broken branches through the forest. "The mimics took the twins this way."

Lacrimosa swung her sword and cut a bat. Its blood sprayed the falling snow. "Keep going!"

They ran, the broken branches scratching them. Kyrie raced between two trees, and suddenly the ground sloped. He found himself tumbling down a ravine, snow cascading around him.

"Lacrimosa!"

She fell beside him, covered in snow. The bats screeched above, but did not follow. Kyrie tried to grab something, but found no purchase. He seemed to fall forever, before he finally hit a mound of snow, and was still. Lacrimosa rolled to a stop beside him, shivering, her torch extinguished.

Kyrie leaped to his feet and helped Lacrimosa up.

"Where's the path?" she demanded.

Kyrie looked up the slope they had crashed down. They had fallen a long way. The bats fluttered above between the trees, but dared not leave their cover.

"I don't know," he said, and suddenly his eyes stung, and his throat swelled. "I don't know, Lacrimosa. I'm... I'm scared. I don't know if... if...."

If Agnus Dei will become one of those bat things. Or if she is one already. If I will become one too. I don't know if this is real, or some nightmare. I don't know what to do.

But he could say none of these things. How could he? Benedictus had died, and he—Kyrie Eleison—was the last man of Requiem. It was his task to be strong, his duty to protect the others. Only... it seemed impossible. Even Benedictus, always strong and brave, had never dealt with humans twisted and cut and sewn into these horrors. How could Kyrie face them?

He only lowered his head, and his body shook. "I'm not strong enough, Lacrimosa. I'm trying to be like him. Like Benedictus. But...."

She grabbed his shoulders. She stared into his eyes.

"Kyrie," she said. Her face was so stern, her eyes so angry. He was sure she'd yell at him. But then her face softened, and her eyes watered, and she embraced him. They stood in the snow, shivering together, holding each other.

"I'm sorry, Lacrimosa. I feel weak."

She touched his hair and kissed his cheek. "You were never weak, Kyrie. You are good, you are scared, you are in love with Agnus Dei. If you were cold and heartless, well, you wouldn't be a man I wanted fighting by my side. And you are a man now, Kyrie."

He took a deep, shaky breath and squared his shoulders. The snow fell around them. "Let's find them, Lacrimosa. Let's find the twins. The path was leading south. We'll move south along this ravine, at least until those flying creatures are gone, then pick up the trail."

Lacrimosa wiped away tears and took his hand. They ran together through the snow, the wind whipping their faces.

AGNUS DEI

She nibbled on her bread. It was stale and frozen, but she forced herself to chew it into mush, then swallow. *I'll need my strength to kill Irae,* she thought. *And I will kill him today.*

Her eye kept wandering to the prisoners around her, especially those missing limbs. One was a young woman, no older than her own nineteen years. She was missing an arm. The bandage around her stump was bloody, and her face was sweaty, even in the cold. *She will die,* Agnus Dei knew. *And then the rest of her will become a mimic.*

"There is a rebellion brewing," whispered a frail man, clutching Agnus Dei's arm. "The Earthen, they're called. Silva the Elder leads them, a great Earth God priest. They'll save us, child. They'll save us."

The man's eyes spun wildly. He was mad, she realized. Soon he retreated into a corner, where he hugged his knees and rocked.

It seemed forever that Agnus Dei huddled here among these prisoners—some of them mad, most of them dying. Gloriae huddled by her, her eyes closed, her lips mumbling. Agnus Dei leaned against her, embraced her, and laid her head on her shoulder. She felt a little safer this way, but not much. There was no safe place here. The prisoners wept, moaned, and prayed around them. Agnus Dei did not know if prayers could be heard from a place like this.

Soon she had to make water. She was no pampered princess—she did not mind going in the bushes—but how could she truly go here, in a bucket, before everyone? And yet she lined up. And she did. And then she returned to Gloriae's side, and embraced her again, and closed her eyes lest her sister saw her tears.

"Sometimes... sometimes I think they're dead," she whispered to Gloriae. "Mother and Kyrie."

Gloriae opened her eyes and touched Agnus Dei's cheek. "Don't say that. This is no time to despair."

"When else is time for despair then? I'm so scared, Gloriae. I want to be strong. But I'm scared."

Gloriae smiled wanly. "That's why you're strong. Strength is conquering your fear. Dies Irae taught me that."

Agnus Dei shuddered. She huddled closer to her sister. "I don't know how you could have lived with him. He's a monster."

Gloriae sighed. "He was not always like this. He was always cruel, yes. And violent. Not toward me, but toward his enemies. And he was always so strong, so stern, so sure of his ways. But this? No, he was never like this. He followed the Sun God. He fought for light. For order. For his own brand of justice. Most of all, he fought for glory. But that was before the nightshades infested his mind. Before a shard of metal drove into his eye. He's insane now, Agnus Dei, which he had never been when he raised me. If we can kill him, it will be a mercy to him. He's trapped in his own insanity, helpless to stop it. The mimics he creates are reflections of his madness and nightmares."

"We *will* kill him." Agnus Dei clenched her fists. "We have to. Not only for Requiem, but for the entire world."

The door swung open.

The prisoners whimpered and screamed.

Dies Irae stood at the doorway, armored in steel, gold, and jewels. Umbra stood beside him, clad in her black leggings and black bodice, her eyes blazing. Four burly mimics stood behind them, carrying chains.

Agnus Dei snarled and leaped to her feet. "You die now, Irae."

She leaped toward him.

Dies Irae didn't move. Umbra did, however. Fast as a falcon's shadow, she crouched, slid forward, and reached out her leg. Agnus Dei tripped over it. She pitched forward. Umbra grabbed her hair, pulled her head back, and knocked her onto her back. Agnus Dei screamed and punched. She hit Umbra's face, but the woman only snarled, and a dagger gleamed in her hand. The blade pressed against Agnus Dei's throat, and she froze.

"Good girl," Umbra whispered. She licked blood off her lips. "Stay nice and still or I'll gut you like a fish."

A shadow leaped, and Gloriae crashed against Umbra, shoving her off. Agnus Dei leaped up and kicked. Her leg hit Umbra's side. The dagger slashed the air. *If I can only grab the blade....* She reached, caught Umbra's wrist, and twisted. Umbra screamed and punched. The blow slammed into Agnus Dei's cheek. White light flooded her. She kicked blindly. Gloriae screamed.

"Stop this!"

Dies Irae's voice filled the hut. Agnus Dei blinked and saw him standing above the fray, glaring.

"Mimics," he said, "grab the twins."

Agnus Dei tried to fight them. She kicked and punched and even bit a mimic's maggoty flesh, but only fire could hurt them. Soon she kicked and squirmed in one's grasp. A second mimic held onto Gloriae, its hand covering her mouth.

"Face me like a man, Irae!" Agnus Dei screamed. "You and me. Or are you a coward?"

He laughed, though there was no joy to it; it was a cold laughter, a cruel laughter that made Agnus Dei shiver.

"Dear Agnus Dei," he said. "Feisty as ever. Beastly as ever. You will go first. Mimics, bring her to the block."

Gloriae screamed into the hand that gagged her. Agnus Dei growled and kicked, but could not free herself. The mimic holding her began carrying her to the doorway. She screamed, struggled, and kicked the air. The mimic's grip was iron.

"Gloriae!" she cried, eyes burning. "Gloriae!"

Her chin bloody, Umbra laughed. "Your sister can't save you now. She'll go next." She spat onto Agnus Dei. "Scream louder. I want to hear it."

Dies Irae left the hut, and the mimic carried Agnus Dei after him. Umbra followed, laughing, spinning her dagger in her hand.

Stay strong, Agnus Dei told herself. *Stay strong. Stars, whatever happens, stay strong. For Kyrie. For Mother. For Gloriae.*

She saw the block ahead.

She felt the blood leave her face. Ice seemed to wash her belly, and she trembled.

"Stars, no...."

It was made of wood. Oak, she thought. Blood stained it. The block rose from the snow between the huts, iron rings embedded into it.

"Chain her down."

Agnus Dei kicked. For an instant, she thought she could break free. But two more mimics grabbed her. They forced her to her knees before the block.

"Irae!" she screamed. "I'll kill you! Fight me! Fight me, I dare you."

Umbra laughed again, grabbed Agnus Dei's hair, and pulled her head down. The block was cold and smooth against her cheek.

"Oh yes, you are a loud one," Umbra whispered, her cold lips brushing against Agnus Dei's ear. "I'm going to enjoy watching this. I bet you'll squeal like a pig."

The mimics surrounded her. Manacles were placed around her wrists. More chains bound her legs.

"Gloriae!" Agnus Dei screamed, eyes burning, throat aching, belly roiling. Tears sprang into her eyes.

Umbra grabbed her wrist. She pulled Agnus Dei's arm across the block and chained it down. *Stars, no, please,* Agnus Dei prayed. *Please. Stars, no....*

She heard the hiss of a sword being drawn.

"Mother," Agnus Dei whispered. "Mother, please...."

Through burning eyes, she saw Dies Irae walk toward her, holding a drawn sword. His face was blank. His eye looked dead. His face was pale, a white mask. *There is no humanity left.*

He raised his sword.

"Mother!" Agnus Dei cried, tears in her eyes.

The blade swung down.

Pain.

Blood.

She screamed.

Stars. It's gone. It's gone. My hand is gone. How could it be gone? Mother, please....

Umbra laughed.

Agnus Dei wept.

Dies Irae turned and walked away. Blood stained the snow, and distant trees creaked under a mournful wind.

KYRIE ELEISON

He crawled up the snowy hill, teeth chattering, clothes icy. Snow filled his mouth and clung to his stubble. At the hilltop, he lay on his belly behind a fallen tree. He parted the tree's branches and gazed into the valley below. He felt the blood leave his face. He turned his head.

"Lacrimosa!" he whispered down the hillside. "Come quick."

She nodded and crawled up beside him. She stared into the valley too, and her lips trembled.

"Stars," she whispered.

The camp sprawled across the valley below. A ditch and a wall of sharpened logs defended it. Beyond the palisade, blood stained crude huts. Every few moments, mimics would drag a prisoner from a hut, chain him against a butcher's block, and swing a sword. The severed body parts were sorted into bloody hills. Kyrie saw one pile of legs, another of arms and hands, a third of heads. The hills rose twenty feet tall. Some body parts—those deemed too frail, it seemed—were burned in ditches.

Kyrie had seen enough.

"We have to save them," he said, voice strained. "We can't wait a moment longer."

What if Dies Irae dismembered Agnus Dei and Gloriae while he hid here, watching helplessly? Kyrie stood up and made to run downhill.

"Wait, Kyrie!" Lacrimosa said. She grabbed his tunic, pulling him back. "Hide."

He spun to glare at her. She stared up from the cover of burned branches, her face pale but her eyes determined. He shook himself free.

"Lacrimosa," he said, "they're building mimics down there. And not just from old bodies now. He's *killing* people and sewing mimics out of them." He drew his sword. "We have to save the twins before it's too late. Stars, we have to save *all* these people."

He couldn't help but imagine Agnus Dei turned into a mimic, stitched together with foreign body parts, drooling, rotting, hunting him. He shuddered.

Lacrimosa pulled him down behind the fallen logs. "Kyrie, if you run down there brandishing a sword and torch, they will kill you, and they will turn you into a mimic, along with my daughters." Her voice was strained but steady, her eyes red but dry. "If the girls are alive, we'll save them. But not by rushing to our own deaths."

Kyrie raised his chin. His heart thrashed. "I'm willing to die for Agnus Dei."

"And some good that would do her." Lacrimosa opened her pack, revealing a hundred Animating Stones. "I didn't grab these from the mine because I think they're pretty. We'll build new warriors."

"From what?" Kyrie gestured around him. "I see no statues here, Lacrimosa. I see nothing but snow, ice, and burned trees."

Lacrimosa gave him a small, mirthless smile. "Dies Irae burned these trees and killed the Earthen who worshipped them. I believe that today, these trees will fight for us."

Kyrie stared at her in silence. She stared back. Finally Kyrie sighed and nodded. *If it can save the girls, it's worth a try.*

They crawled back downhill and began to move among the trees: old oaks, twisted and blackened, but still strong; thin birches, their bark burned off; charred pines, their roots still deep. *These trees are dead, but we will give them new life.* Kyrie and Lacrimosa moved silently, placing Animating Stones into holes that had once held birds, squirrels, and insects. Trees creaked. Icicles snapped and fell. Branches rose. A mournful cry like wind passed through the charred forest, a rustling of twigs, a shifting of roots, a sadness and rage.

Kyrie thought of Fort Sanctus, where Lady Mirum had raised him on fish, bread, and tales of the ancient days. In several of those tales, the trees would rise to fight the wars of men. Those trees always rustled with green leaves, and could talk and sing. There was nothing as beautiful here, but Kyrie still felt like a hero from one of Mirum's old stories.

As the trees creaked and moved, he whispered, quoting from one of her tales. "We are the children of the earth; our hosts are the rocks of the field, the trees of the forest, and the song in the wind...."

Lacrimosa came to stand beside him. She drew her sword and raised her torch. The trees crowded around them, raining ash and snow, their icicles snapping, their boles creaking. Their roots spread around them like the legs of spiders, twisting and seeking purchase.

"Stay near me, Kyrie," Lacrimosa said softly. "We'll find the girls."

They began to march.

The trees' roots groaned, dug into the snow, and dragged the boles forward. Their branches kept snapping, falling black and broken. They were frail things, burned and mournful, moaning in pain. But they marched. A hundred charred, twisted trees raised their howl, and gained speed, and soon began to charge downhill. Hostias Forest rose in rage.

Kyrie snarled. He waved his sword and cried with them. He ran among the trees, boots kicking up snow. Lacrimosa ran beside him, Stella Lumen raised in her hands. Snow flurried. The hillside shook. At the camp below, mimics squealed and rushed to the walls.

Kyrie shouted. The trees roared. They crashed into the palisade under rain of blood, steel, and fire.

GLORIAE

When she heard Agnus Dei screaming outside, Gloriae snarled, clenched her fists, and trembled. Prisoners pushed against her on every side; she could barely move between them. Elbowing and shoving them, Gloriae managed to reach the hut's door.

"Agnus Dei!" she shouted, eyes stinging. She slammed her shoulder against the door. It wouldn't budge. She slammed again, and her shoulder throbbed with pain.

"Dies Irae, let her go!" Gloriae shouted. She slammed against the door again and again, and kicked it, but couldn't break it.

"Fight me, you coward!" she shouted.

She heard Umbra laughing outside. The mimics howled. Agnus Dei's screams faded. *Is she dead? Stars, did he kill her?*

"Dies Irae!" she screamed and slammed against the door again. Her shoulder ached, but she didn't care. She needed to get out, to save her sister, to kill Dies Irae. She spun toward the other prisoners.

"Help me," she demanded. She panted and her hair covered her face. "Come on, help me break down the door."

The prisoners only watched her sadly. They were all too frail. They shivered in their rags, feverish, nearly dead with disease. *They cannot help me,* Gloriae realized, her chest rising and falling.

The door's lock clinked behind her.

Gloriae spun back toward it, growling, ready to kill whoever stood there.

The door opened, and Gloriae was about to leap... then froze.

"Oh stars," she whispered, and her knees shook. "Oh stars, no, please no...."

Dies Irae stood at the doorway, holding Agnus Dei before him. His face was icy, his eye dead, his mouth like a slit in leather. Blood stained his armor. Agnus Dei was unconscious, her chin against her chest. Her left arm ended with a bloody, smoking stump.

"Stars, Agnus Dei...," Gloriae whispered.

Dies Irae stared at her. He smiled a small, thin smile.

"The weredragon king took my left hand," he said. "So I will take the left hands of his followers. Yours will be next, Gloriae. But first, make sure this one lives. I want her alive and screaming when I cut the rest of her."

He tossed Agnus Dei forward. Gloriae caught her, held her, and lowered her onto the floor.

"I'm here, Agnus Dei," she whispered and touched her sister's cheek. "I'm here with you, I'll look after you."

Agnus Dei did not wake. Her breath was shallow, her forehead hot.

Rage blazed inside Gloriae. Her teeth clenched, and she spun around to leap at Dies Irae... but he slammed the door shut. Gloriae crashed against the door, but it was locked again. She could not break it. Outside, she heard Umbra's voice.

"Let's build a nice new mimic with her hand," the woman said and laughed.

"Very well, come with me," Dies Irae answered. Gloriae heard their footfalls leave the hut, and their voices faded in the distance.

"Glor... Gloriae...."

Agnus Dei was whispering, voice hoarse. Gloriae rushed to her side, knelt by her, and touched her hair.

"I'm here, Agnus Dei."

Her sister's eyes fluttered. She struggled to raise her head. A tear streamed down her cheek. Her lips moved, struggling to speak, but then her head fell back, and her eyes closed.

Wincing, Gloriae examined her wound. Dies Irae had cauterized it, burning the stump to staunch the blood flow. Gloriae had seen this done in battle before. The fire could close the arteries and kill infection, but it left a messy wound of sizzling, raw flesh. Gloriae gritted her teeth.

"I need bandages!" she called out.

A prisoner hobbled toward her, holding a rag. Gloriae grabbed it and wrapped Agnus Dei's stump.

"This isn't enough," she whispered. "I've seen such wounds before. It will fester. Blood will keep trickling. It will not heal this way." She looked around the hut, panting. "We need to file down the bone, so it doesn't cut the wound. We need to remove the burned flesh, and sew the arteries shut, and seal the stump with a flap of skin. We... we need medicine, and tools, and healers." Gloriae's eyes stung, and she rubbed them. "Bring me some tools! She'll die if we don't treat her. Why don't you move?"

The prisoners only stared at her. Gloriae trembled. She looked at them; so many others suffered the same amputations. So many others were already infected, bleeding, dying. The same would happen to Agnus Dei, she realized. *And the same will happen to me.*

Gloriae lowered her head, jaw clenched. *So this is how it ends,* she thought. *He'll cut us piece by piece, and turn us into a dozen mimics.*

She cradled Agnus Dei's head in her arms and kissed her forehead.

"I'm so sorry, sister," she whispered. "I'm so sorry we only had this short time together. I love you, Agnus Dei. I'm with you now. I'll be with you always."

Her twin's lips moved, and her brow furrowed, but she wouldn't wake. Snow and sweat drenched her tunic. Blood stained her bandage. Gloriae wished she had a blanket for her, a roaring fire, and water for her to drink. *Will she die today in my arms? If she does... that will be a kindness to her. If she lives, Irae will drag her out again, and cut off more.* Gloriae shuddered. *And soon he will cut me.*

Roars sounded outside. Feet thumped through the snow. A mimic squealed.

"Man the palisade!" Dies Irae shouted. "Man your posts, mimics."

Gloriae crouched, cocked her head, and listened. Further away, she heard another sound. She couldn't recognize it. It sounded like moaning wind and creaking wood, but almost human, a cry of sadness and rage.

"Agnus Dei!" shouted a voice in the distance. "Gloriae!"

Gloriae jumped, shouting. Tears filled her eyes.

"Kyrie!" she cried, jumping up and down, jostling the prisoners around her. She laughed and wept. "Kyrie, Kyrie!"

Eyes blurry, Gloriae knelt by her sister. She wept over her and cupped her cheek.

"Kyrie is alive!" she said, her tears splashing Agnus Dei's face.

Agnus Dei's eyes fluttered opened. She smiled wanly. "I knew he would be," she whispered.

Gloriae leaped back onto her feet. She shoved her way between the prisoners toward a window. It was a small window, only several inches tall and wide. Gloriae stared outside and gasped. Charred trees were moving through the camp, swinging their branches against mimics. The mimics hacked at them, but the trees kept charging, breaking through them.

"They animated the bloody forest!" Gloriae shouted and jumped up and down. "Agnus Dei, they brought a hundred trees!"

Gloriae looked back at Agnus Dei, and saw her twin smiling weakly from the floor. She turned back toward the window, stuck her face against it, and shouted.

"Kyrie! Kyrie, we're in here! Break open the door."

Where was he? Gloriae couldn't see him. She saw only dozens of trees crash against the mimics. Blood flew. Branches snapped and fell. She glimpsed Umbra racing between the trees, torching them.

"Kyrie!" she shouted.

A voice answered her. "Gloriae! Gloriae, is that you?"

Mother! It was Mother's voice!

"I'm here, Mother!" Gloriae shouted. "In the hut by the ditch. Get the trees to break the door down."

Across the hut, Agnus Dei cried out: "Mother!"

The lock creaked. The door swung open.

Gloriae rushed toward it, prepared to see Kyrie or Mother. Instead, she found herself facing Dies Irae and a group of mimics.

"Kill the prisoners," Dies Irae told his mimics. "Kill them all."

The mimics rushed into the hut.

Gloriae growled and leaped toward them.

One mimic swung an axe down toward Agnus Dei, who lay at its feet. Gloriae growled and slammed into the mimic, knocking it back.

The mimic Warts swung a sword at her. *Per Ignem! My own sword!* Gloriae ducked, and the blade whistled over her head. She grabbed Warts's arm and pulled it down. Per Ignem's blade hit the ground. Three more mimics rushed toward her. Dies Irae stood behind them, watching with a hard face.

Warts bit Gloriae's shoulder. She screamed. A spear lashed toward her. She dodged it and twisted Warts's wrist. Per Ignem fell. Warts's teeth pushed deeper into her flesh. Gloriae knelt, grabbed Per Ignem, and slammed its crossguard against Warts's head.

The mimic opened its mouth, screamed, and Gloriae's cut off its head. She swung the blade, and mimic blood sprayed.

"Pull her back!" Gloriae shouted to the other prisoners. "Get my sister back against the wall."

A dozen mimics faced her at the doorway, drooling and hissing. She slashed at them, spinning her blade, eyes narrowed, lips tight. Gloriae lived for this. She was a decent archer. She knew how to fight as a dragon. But swordplay... she had been born for swordplay. Per Ignem moved like a part of her. She snarled as she hacked and maimed. Mimics piled up at her feet, their arms and legs crawling and grabbing at her. She kicked them aside, shouted, and barrelled between mimics and through the doorway.

"Irae!" she shouted. She glimpsed him marching away, disappearing into a crowd of mimics. "Irae, you coward! Come fight me."

A shadow flew, and Gloriae raised her sword. Her blade hit a flying dagger, knocking it aside. The blades sparked.

"Hello, sweetheart," said Umbra. She came walking toward Gloriae, a dagger in each hand. Her black, chin-length hair swayed in the wind, and a crooked smile played across her lips. A second dagger flew.

Gloriae leaped sideways. The dagger glanced off her helmet, then hit the hut behind her. She snarled and ran forward.

A third dagger flew. Gloriae leaped, waving her sword and growling. The dagger hit her breastplate and fell. She swung her sword down.

Impossibly fast, Umbra drew two new daggers from her belt, crossed and raised them, and blocked her sword. Gloriae pulled her blade back, and a dagger slashed. She leaped aside, but the dagger sliced her arm. She growled and lashed her blade. Umbra parried. The woman was smiling, her eyes flashing.

"Do you know who I am, girl?" she asked.

Gloriae swung her blade. Umbra parried again. Sparks flew.

"One of Irae's pets," Gloriae said. She bared her teeth and lunged with the blade.

Umbra parried, sliced, and drove Gloriae a step back.

"I was a sister. I was a wife. You burned my husband and my brothers."

The sword and two daggers slammed together, showering sparks.

"Good," Gloriae said. "I hope they screamed loudly when my fire rained upon them."

Umbra snarled. Her eyes blazed. She leaped forward, daggers flashing.

"My husband and brothers never harmed you," she said, teeth bared. "They were Blood Wolves, warriors of the alleys. You burned the city with your dragonfire. You killed innocent people, Gloriae the Gilded."

Gloriae snickered. "I don't care." She lashed her sword, slamming it against a dagger. The dagger fell from Umbra's hand.

Umbra snarled and leaped carelessly, driving down her remaining dagger. Gloriae raised her arm, blocking the blow on her vambrace. The two women fell into the snow, Umbra atop Gloriae.

"You will suffer now, Gloriae," she hissed. She raised her dagger and brought it down.

Gloriae swung the hilt of her sword, hitting Umbra's wrist. The dagger drove into the snow, an inch from Gloriae's face. Umbra screamed and tried to bite, but Gloriae kicked her stomach, knocking her off. She leaped to her feet and swung her sword down, but Umbra rolled. The sword hit the snow.

Umbra crouched, eyes blazing, snarling like a wild animal. She tossed her last dagger. Gloriae rolled aside, and the blade sliced her thigh. She screamed and ran toward Umbra, sword waving. Umbra snarled. Her daggers gone, she leaped back and disappeared into a crowd of mimics.

Gloriae tried to chase her, but the mimics blocked her way, howling and slamming their blades against Per Ignem.

"I will burn you like I burned your husband!" Gloriae shouted after her, voice hoarse. "Run, Umbra. Run from me and cower. I will find you, and I will burn you."

The mimics shouted and waved their blades. Gloriae narrowed her eyes and parried left and right. *I will kill these mimics. And I will kill Umbra. And I will kill Dies Irae.* Her blade spun, raining blood.

"Gloriae!" Lacrimosa cried, leaping into battle beside her.

"Mother!"

Mother and daughter fought side by side, hacking at mimics.

"Where's Agnus Dei?" Lacrimosa shouted.

"She's in the hut! She's hurt. Go to her, Mother. I'll hold back the mimics."

Lacrimosa nodded and ran to the hut, hacking her way between mimics. When Gloriae looked around, she saw animated trees crashing into the huts, freeing the prisoners, and knocking mimics aside. The prisoners were limping toward the breached palisade that surrounded the camp; some were already fleeing into the forest.

"Hullo, Gloriae," Kyrie said, leaping into the battle beside her. Snow, ash, and blood covered him. He swung a sword and torch at the mimics.

"Hullo, Kyrie," she answered. She stabbed a mimic and kicked it down. "About time you showed up."

Kyrie torched a mimic who leaped at him. "Thought I'd drop by and save your backside."

Gloriae sliced off a mimic's leg, then drove her sword into its neck. "You haven't saved it yet. There are hundreds of these damn mimics around."

Kyrie nodded. "It was fun, but I think it's time to leave this party."

"Agreed."

Swinging their weapons, they pulled back toward the hut. As she fought, Gloriae stared around, seeking Dies Irae. When she saw him, she growled. He stood across the camp upon a hilltop, Umbra at his side. They were watching the battle from safety. Gloriae snarled, wishing she had her bow or crossbow.

"Oh stars," Kyrie said beside her. His voice was choked. "Stars, Agnus Dei. Oh stars...."

Gloriae gritted her teeth and kept fighting, her back to the hut. Her eyes stung. She heard Lacrimosa cry in mourning. Gloriae snarled. Rage bloomed through her. She looked up at Dies Irae, the man who had maimed Agnus Dei, who had killed her father, who had brought her family this pain. More than anything, Gloriae wanted to rush through the army of mimics, reach Dies Irae, and kill him.

But no, she thought. *My family needs me now. They need me to lead them to safety.*

"Come on!" she shouted over her shoulder at them. Kyrie and Lacrimosa were huddling over Agnus Dei. "Help her up. Follow me. We're leaving."

More mimics kept pouring toward her. She saw no end to them. Their teeth snapped, their claws slashed, and Gloriae's arms ached. She couldn't hold them back much longer, and few trees remained standing to help her.

"Let's go!" Kyrie shouted. He and Lacrimosa held Agnus Dei between them. She was conscious, but sweat matted her hair, and pain filled her eyes.

Gloriae gestured with her chin. "The palisade is breached over there. Let's get her out of here."

Five trees crashed into the crowd of mimics, kicking their roots, lashing their branches. Mimics fell and rolled. Gloriae used the diversion to drive between them, clearing a path with her blade. Mimic limbs and blood flew. The other Vir Requis followed her.

She reached the breached palisade. Other prisoners were limping through it. Mimics were leaping onto them, killing those who were too slow.

"Come on, hurry!" Gloriae shouted. She stabbed and kicked a mimic. It crashed against a pile of amputated legs. The bloodied limbs rolled, tripping the other mimics.

"Put me down," Agnus Dei said. "I can run. I can fight!"

"Kitten, come on," Kyrie said. "We're leaving."

Agnus Dei growled. She managed to walk on her own, then run. She leaped out of the breach, holding the stump where her hand had been. Kyrie and Lacrimosa leaped after her, swinging their torches at mimics. Gloriae stayed a moment longer, fighting inside the camp. She saw no other prisoners; they had all fled or died.

She looked up and stared at Dies Irae. He stood atop the hill across the camp, arms crossed—the real arm, and the steel one. He stood three hundred yards away, but it seemed to Gloriae like their eyes met.

She growled. "We'll meet again, Irae. This isn't over."

Then she turned and leaped out of the camp. She ran with the other Vir Requis through the snow, mimics howling and chasing them.

They ran fast, even Agnus Dei. They ran until they lost the mimics between the trees and boulders. They ran until the curse of the Animating Stones faded in the distance.

Gloriae roared and shifted into a dragon. Her wings thudded. Her maw roared fire. She leaped up and flew. Her tail lashed and her fire bathed the world. It had been so long since she had flown. She sounded her roar.

Three more dragons flew up from the forest: Lacrimosa, silver and slim, blowing blue flames; Kyrie, blue and fast, roaring fire; Agnus Dei, a red dragon missing her front foot.

Gloriae dived toward her sister, held her, and helped her fly. The four dragons roared, blew fire, and flew into the clouds. They streamed over burned forests and fallow fields, heading west, heading to Requiem.

Gloriae shut her eyes. *We should never have left*, she thought. *We should never have attacked the mines. Now Agnus Dei is hurt, and we've lost our Animating Stones. What will we do now?*

She swallowed, opened her eyes, and looked at her sister. Agnus Dei stared back, wincing, jaw tight with pain. Her wings roiled the falling snow.

"I'm so glad you're alive," Gloriae said to her. That was what mattered, she knew.

Agnus Dei blinked back tears. "I never thought we'd make it out in one piece. I guess I was right."

Gloriae laughed and sobbed. The sun began to set. The dragons flew into its dying beams.

MEMORIA

She flew over plains of ice, bloodied and bruised. The giants had chipped her scales, pummelled her body, and nearly killed her... but she still flew. For Requiem. For Kyrie.

"Terra, we're almost there," she said.

He flew beside her, grunting. He was hurt, but still he flew, eyes narrowed.

They each wore one of Adoria's Hands around their necks. They had split the Giant King's chain and hung the segments around their own necks. As Memoria flew, she looked at the hands. They were so small, pale, folded into fragile fists. They swayed on the chains like worms on a fishing line. *Could such dainty things truly hold back the mimics' curse?*

The Ice City was never where she left it. It forever floated on its iceberg, moving with the currents. Finally she saw it ahead, its hundred palaces glistening like crystal shards.

Home, she thought, and the thought surprised her. On the eve of her return to Requiem, did her place of exile become her home? She would miss the icelings, she realized. Old Amberus, with his long beard and wise eyes. Small and silly Gif, only five years old, who would carve ice sculptures with her. Her friends, Illa and Oona, who were shy around Terra and giggly around her. *Yes, this too has become a home to me,* she thought, and she smiled sadly. The Ice City was cold, lonely, and far from Requiem, but it had been a good home.

"Amberus will heal our wounds," she said to Terra. "And then we'll fly to Requiem. We'll fly to Kyrie. He's alive. I know it."

Terra only grunted, eyes wincing with pain. They dived toward the iceberg, snow gusting around them, and flew between its palaces. All but one were abandoned now, their towers still, silent, and glistening. The two dragons, one green and one bronze, flew between the steeples of ice, kissed with snow. They glided toward the tallest palace, the place Amberus ruled, the place where they'd hidden for eleven years.

They landed outside its gateway, and Memoria's breath died.

Blood stained the ice at her feet.

Memoria growled.

Grunts sounded inside the Ice Palace. A screech echoed. Wind blew, carrying the stench of bodies.

"Mimics," she said.

Terra grumbled and fire crackled between his teeth. "Looks like we're still in for some fighting today."

Memoria kindled flame in her maw and ran into the palace.

The front hall, a towering chamber that dwarfed even two dragons, was splashed with blood. Bodies of icelings lay strewn across its floor, torn apart. Mimics leaned over them, feasting.

Memoria screamed and ran forward.

"Get off them!" she cried.

They raised their bloody faces from their feast, glared, and hissed. Their curse hit her with a thud, like air from a bellows. Memoria gasped and faltered. She felt their magic crash into her own, wrestle it, shove it, try to claim it.

"No!" she cried and gritted her teeth. If she became human now, she could not defeat them all. Not with only her sword. Her scales began to melt off. Her wings began to fold into her body. Her fangs retracted into her gums.

Around her neck, Adoria's fist began to uncurl.

Memoria shook her head wildly, struggling to cling to her magic. The mimics began racing toward her, drooling and hissing, brandishing swords.

Adoria's Hand opened.

It felt like a wave crashing forward. The power shoved back the mimics' curse, and Memoria's magic refilled her. She was fully dragon. She was fang and claw and fire.

Her jet of flames blazed across the hall, spinning and crackling, and crashed into the mimics. They burned and squealed and fell. Terra shot flames beside her. A few mimics reached them. The dragons lashed their tails and claws, sending them flying. Adoria's Hands rose on the chains, holding back the mimics' curse. The flames filled the chamber, and the walls wept.

It only took moments, and the mimics across the hall lay burned. Memoria ran from iceling to iceling, but they were all dead, their innards eaten.

Screeches rose from other chambers across the palace. Memoria raced between the rooms, shooting flames, burning mimics, lashing them with her tail, clawing them open. Iceling bodies filled every chamber.

"They're all dead," she whispered. "All dead."

Kyrie! she had called. *Kyrie, do you hear!*

Lanburg Fields stretched around her, drenched in blood, piled with bodies. She was rummaging through them again, searching for her brother, weeping over his body.

Kyrie!

Terra ran up behind her, flames dancing between his teeth.

"A hundred mimics are streaming into Whale Hall. Come, Memoria."

They ran across the ice, flapping their wings to steady themselves, and burst into Whale Hall. A hundred mimics ran toward them, bloated and rotten, hideous creations that were part men, part beasts. Terra and Memoria blew their fire. The hall blazed. Water streamed down the walls. Mimics screamed.

Finally the flames died. The mimics lay twitching and burned. And among them....

Memoria ran forward, tears on her cheeks.

No.... Stars, no.

But it was him. Amberus, kindly old Amberus with the long white beard, the elder iceling who had become a father to her. He lay in the corner, his belly split open, his entrails consumed. Mimic drool covered him. He had tried to shield his followers; the bodies of iceling children lay in the corner behind Amberus. Young Gif, whom Memoria would sculpt with. His sisters. So many others.

"All dead," she whispered.

She turned to Terra. Her throat was so tight, she could barely speak.

"They came here searching for us," she said. "It's our fault."

Terra stared at the bodies with dark eyes. His claws shook, and he dug them into the ice floor. "We will avenge them. We will kill the man who sent them here." He looked up at her. "We will kill Dies Irae."

She shook her head. "I don't care about Irae." Tears welled up in her eyes. "I just want to save whoever I still can. Agnus Dei. And Kyrie. My Kyrie."

They pulled the bodies outside, and placed them on the ice, and prayed for them, and wept for them, and let the sun and moon shine upon them.

"The last of the icelings," Memoria whispered. "The end of a race. A people extinguished, but forever in my memory, forever in my soul."

She had never prayed to the northern gods, but she prayed to them now. She whispered to Father Walrus to bless the memory of the ice people. She sang to the Wind Goddess, to Sky Eagle, to Sister Moon. She prayed to Mother Turtle who glowed green and purple upon the horizons. She wept as she lowered the icelings into the water, one by one, until they sank into the embrace of Old Whale, their guardian of afterlife.

They bound their wounds. They mourned for days. And they flew. Terra and Memoria, soldiers of Requiem. Exiles. They flew over icebergs, over oceans, over plains of snow and lifeless rock. They flew over forests of pines, the first trees they had seen in eleven years. They flew over fields of grass, over herds of deer, over fields and villages of men.

They flew home.

DIES IRAE

"They are beautiful," Umbra said.

She stood beside him on the walls of Confutatis, staring down into the field. The wind swayed her black hair. Her eyes were narrowed. A small smile twisted the corners of her mouth. She placed one hand on her hip, the other on his shoulder, and licked her lips.

"They are beautiful," Dies Irae agreed, "they are strong, and they will kill the weredragons."

The army roared below in the field, the greatest army he had ever mustered.

"Come," he said to Umbra, "let us walk between the troops. Let us inspect them."

They descended the city wall and walked into the field. Umbra slung her arm through his, a wolf's grin across her face. They approached the army's vanguard—thousands of howling mimics—and walked between their formations.

"Fifty thousand mimics scream here," Dies Irae said. "The world's greatest soldiers."

The mimics bared teeth, screeched, and banged their blades against their shields. Stench rose from them, and their eyes blazed. Some had the heads, legs, or claws of animals. Others sprouted many arms. A few towered twenty feet tall, giants stitched from gobbets of leftover flesh.

Dies Irae stopped by a burly mimic with a bull's head and four arms. Its hands held an axe, a spear, a sword, and a warhammer.

"Look at this one, Umbra. Look at the hand holding the axe. Do you recognize this hand?"

Umbra gasped. Her grin widened. "It's *her* hand. The hand we cut."

Dies Irae nodded, smiling silently.

Umbra laughed. "Brilliant, my lord! I hope that hand cuts the rest of Agnus Dei."

"Come, I will show you more."

For long moments, they walked by the lines of howling mimics, until they emerged from the vanguard and approached the left flank. Thousands of snowbeasts drooled here, towering creatures of white, loose skin hanging over knobby bones. Seven feet tall, they looked to Dies Irae like great white spiders, or perhaps furless cats with six legs.

"Their legs are fast, and their jaws will tear into weredragon flesh," he said.

Umbra caressed one. "They are beautiful."

They continued walking. Past the snowbeasts, they reached a battalion of skeletons. Wispy beards, flakes of old skin, and rusty armor clung to them. They held spears and their eye sockets glowed.

"The skeletons of Fidelium," Dies Irae said. "I have freed them from two thousand years of underground shame. They will fight for me now."

Umbra's own eyes seemed to glow. Her breath grew heavy. "I love them, my lord. Show me more."

They walked between the skeletons, passing row after row of them. Finally they reached an army of great reptiles, the size of dragons, who growled and snapped their teeth. A thousand of them roared as Dies Irae and Umbra walked between them.

Umbra's cheeks flushed, and her lips parted. "What are they?" she breathed.

"Swamp reptiles," Dies Irae answered. "Terrors from Gilnor. They are as large as dragons, and with larger teeth."

"Show me more," Umbra begged. "I want more, my lord."

He nodded. They kept walking. They reached a field where twisted, scaly creatures stood. They looked like men, but fish scales covered them. Their eyes bulged. Some had eyeballs that hung on stalks. Their fingers were webbed, their arms long and twisted. Blood dripped from sores on their faces.

Umbra bit her lip in delight. "What are these things, my lord?"

"They are the Poisoned," he answered. "Years ago, with green smoke from my dungeons, I turned many weredragons into these things. Today I found peasants, prisoners, soldiers who were once men; they are the new Poisoned, and they will fight for us with tooth and claw."

Umbra trembled in delight. "Show me more."

He took her past the Poisoned, and to a field where thousands of nightshades coiled. They shrieked, took flight, and roiled above them. They looked like storm clouds, creatures of black smoke, thunder, and lightning. Their eyes blazed like stars. Their mouths snapped, showing and hiding smoky white teeth.

"They hunger for weredragon souls," Dies Irae said. "The weredragons will not have a chance to use their Beams this time. The nightshades will swoop from the clouds and break them."

Umbra panted. Her cheeks were red. Her eyes closed. "More, my lord."

He led her past the nightshades into a field drenched with blood.

"Here, Umbra. My proudest creations."

She screamed in delight. "Sun God!"

Five thousand mimic dragons roared before them. They took flight and circled above, showering droplets of blood. Their wings were made of human skin. Their bones and flesh were sewn together from thousands of bodies. Fifty Animating Stones pulsed inside each one's breast. When they screamed, the sound shook the earth.

He looked at Umbra. She held her hands to her chest, gasping.

"This army will descend upon Requiem," he told her. "The weredragons have defeated scattered enemies before. Now they will face an army such as the world has never seen. Soon we will have their heads."

She stared at him, eyes blazing, lips parted. She panted. *Such cruelty in this one,* he thought. *Such strength, such hatred, such fire.*

When Gloriae had served him, she had never shown fire, only ice. Gloriae had always been so cold, so calculating. But Umbra... this one was a demon's daughter, a creature of shadow and malice. Dies Irae pulled her toward him, clutched her throat, and squeezed her body. She gasped and her eyes shone.

"You will bear me sons," he said.

She bared her teeth. "Sons who will lead. Sons who will bring fear to the world." She clenched her fists. "Sons who will rule a land with no weredragons."

He pushed her to the ground. She lay in the dust and mimic blood, looking up at him. He tore her bodice open, exposing her goosebumped flesh, and she growled. He took her violently, until she screamed, and the mimic dragons screamed above. When he was done, he dragged her through the mud, and returned with her to the city walls. They climbed atop the tallest guard tower. They stood above this grand army, this sea of dark wonders, this glory and power and lust and blood. He raised his arms, and they howled. The mimics brandished blades, the snowbeasts snapped their teeth, the skeletons clanked, the swamp lizards growled, the Poisoned screamed, the nightshades screeched, the dragons roared.

Dies Irae smiled.

He put his arm around Umbra's waist.

"We march now," he said. "We march to victory and glory. You will march by my side."

She drew her daggers and snarled. "I will kill by your side."

"We march to Requiem!" he called to his army. Their howls shook the city. The sun itself seemed to tremble.

With dust and noise and fury, they marched.

LACRIMOSA

She wiped Agnus Dei's forehead, kissed it, and lifted the bowl of soup.

"You must eat, Agnus Dei. Kyrie made soup."

She held the bowl up to her daughter's lips. Lying on a pile of furs, Agnus Dei sipped, winced, and spat it out. She coughed.

"The pup... he's flying too slow. We must reach Salvandos. We have to keep flying."

She coughed again and trembled. Her face was pale, and her eyelids fluttered. More sweat beaded on her brow. Lacrimosa had lit a fire at the cave's entrance, but it was still cold here, so cold that she was always shivering. She rearranged the furs covering Agnus Dei.

"Salvandos is far away, sweetheart. You flew there already with Kyrie, do you remember? It was in the summer. Drink the soup, Agnus Dei. It'll help you."

She held the bowl up again, but Agnus Dei only coughed when she sipped and shivered. Her forehead was so hot. Lacrimosa kept the bowl up, and sip by sip, Agnus Dei managed to drink half the bowl.

The campfire cast flickering light against the cave walls. This place lay far north in the ruins of Requiem, in the mountains where few dragons had ever flown. It was a hidden place, but Lacrimosa did not feel safe here. *We hide, but he'll find us*, she thought. *Dies Irae's armies will scour this land, and they will find us anywhere we hide.*

She touched her daughter's cheek. "It's time," she whispered.

Agnus Dei shut her eyes, mumbled, and nodded.

Lacrimosa pulled back the furs, revealing Agnus Dei's left arm. It ended with a wet bandage, one of only two bandages they owned. Blood and pus painted the bandage red and yellow. It smelled of infection.

Wincing, Lacrimosa unpeeled the bandage. Agnus Dei grimaced and clenched her fist. Sweat poured down her face.

"This will hurt," Lacrimosa whispered.

But Agnus Dei did not hear. She had lost consciousness again. Her eyes moved under her lids, and her lips mumbled.

Lacrimosa had only one bottle of spirits left; Gloriae had found it in an abandoned inn ten leagues east. Lacrimosa took a deep breath and splashed the wound. In her sleep, Agnus Dei winced, trembled, and mumbled.

"Dada," she said. "Dada, please, they'll hurt you. You have to fly. You have to fly, Dada."

Struggling to keep her fingers steady, Lacrimosa replaced the old bandage with the new one, then wiped the sweat off Agnus Dei's brow. They had done all they could. They had filed down the bone's sharp edges, removed the burned flesh, and sewn it over with skin. And yet the stump still festered. For the past two days, Agnus Dei only woke briefly from unconsciousness. Lacrimosa worried that soon, she would not wake at all.

She shut her eyes. *Please, stars. Please. I lost my husband; don't let me lose my daughter too.*

Wings flapped, and Lacrimosa looked outside the cave. She saw two dragons block the stars. Soon Kyrie and Gloriae landed at the cave, shifted into humans, and walked in.

"More spirits," Gloriae said. She held out a bottle. "We flew for hours, and finally found the bottle in a town two leagues east of the border."

"And another blanket," Kyrie said, holding it out. "Warm fur. We also found flour, a jar of honey, and three jars of apple preserves; they're in my pack."

They walked to Agnus Dei and knelt by her. Kyrie kissed her lips, and Gloriae wiped her forehead.

"Watch over her," Lacrimosa said. "Call me if she wakes up."

Before they could answer, she stood up and stepped outside the cave. Her eyes stung and she shivered. The night was cold, and her breath frosted before her. She stood on the mountain and looked at the stars. The Draco constellation shone there.

"Winter has come," she whispered. "It has covered Requiem in snow, and it has covered my heart in ice. I'm scared, Ben."

She looked at the Draco stars. They seemed so cold, so far from her.

"He's coming here to kill our family," she whispered. "He'll have armies, greater than any we've seen. And... I don't know how to face them, Ben. I don't know how I can protect our family." Her eyes dampened. "Agnus Dei is hurt, and her fever won't break. I'm scared." She tightened her cloak around her. "Are you up there, Ben? Are you watching over me? If so, give me strength. Guide me, Ben, for I'm afraid and lost."

The stars glistened, casting rays of light, blurring behind her tears. Lacrimosa rubbed her eyes, but the stars still seemed misty. Strands of starlight spread out from them like cobwebs. Lacrimosa gasped. The strands moved through the night and connected the stars in her constellation, forming the shape of a dragon. In the star maps she'd read in childhood, scribes would connect the stars with lines, accentuating the shape of each constellation. *Does some scribe now paint these lines in the sky? Ben, are you up there, pulling a great brush between our starlit halls?* As she watched the starry dragon, Lacrimosa felt peace spread through her like those strands of starlight.

She stepped back into the cave.

"Children!" she called. "Come outside. Come see."

Gloriae and Kyrie leaped to their feet and drew their swords.

"What is it?" Kyrie said.

Gloriae snarled. "Mimics."

Lacrimosa shook her head. "No mimics. Come look. Let's carry Agnus Dei outside. I want her to see this."

Gloriae and Kyrie exchanged uneasily glances, and cautioned that Agnus Dei could not be moved, but Lacrimosa insisted. Alcohol and bandages had not staved off infection; if anything could save Agnus Dei, maybe it was this miracle.

Agnus Dei moaned when they carried her outside, and her skin burned, but once the starlight hit her, her face seemed calmer to Lacrimosa, her skin cooler. They lay her on a fur blanket in the night air.

"Look, Agnus Dei," Lacrimosa whispered, holding her daughter's hand. "Your father is up there. He's watching us."

Agnus Dei's eyes fluttered open. She looked at the dragon in the stars. A smile touched her lips.

"Hi, Father," she whispered. "I'd wave, but... Mother's holding one of my hands, and I think Dies Irae is holding the other."

Gloriae gaped at the sky. The starlight glinted in her eyes, painted her hair silver, and kissed her cheeks. "What does it mean?" she said, voice awed.

Lacrimosa pulled her close and kissed her cheek. "Hope," she whispered.

DIES IRAE

They marched through the empire, feet shaking the earth, howls splitting the sky.

Dies Irae rode before his army upon a black mimic horse, its fur matted and its mouth foaming. When he looked over his shoulder, he snarled and grinned. A hundred thousand warriors marched behind him, covering the countryside like spilling oil, swallowing the empire beneath them. Thousands of nightshades and mimic dragons circled above, shrieking.

"We draw near Requiem, my lord," Umbra said, riding her mimic horse up beside him. She wore no armor and bore no sword. She was a Blood Wolf, and she rode to war as one, garbed in black. Her leather boots rose to her knees over her leggings, and six daggers hung from her belt.

Dies Irae nodded. "The ruins of Requiem lie beyond the mountains ahead." He scanned the horizon and saw a town below those mountains. Chimney smoke rose in fifty columns; there would be survivors there. His grin widened. "We will stop before crossing the mountains, and we will dine."

Umbra licked her lips.

They rode toward the town, the army roaring and drooling behind. When they got closer, Dies Irae saw a hundred cottages, a temple, and several fields. Soon he rode through the streets, Umbra at his side. His army surrounded the town like ants around a fallen piece of fruit. The streets were empty.

"The peasants are hiding," Dies Irae said.

Umbra looked around, eyes narrowed. "Like rats."

"Burn them out, Umbra. Burn these rats' nests."

Soon she held two torches, and ran from house to house, setting their thatch roofs afire. The rats began to flee. They ran out of their houses, haggard peasants, their clothes tattered, their faces gaunt. Some began to run to the mountain, wailing.

"Dine, my lovelies!" Dies Irae called. "Dine upon them."

The mimic dragons swooped. The nightshades flowed between them. The mimics and monsters stormed from house to house, grabbing whoever they could. It only took moments, and the lucky ones feasted. The unlucky creatures, those who could not catch a peasant, growled and screamed. Some began to eat one another. Blood splattered the town.

Umbra emerged from the smoke, manhandling a peasant girl. She held a dagger to the girl's neck.

"I found one for us to dine on," she said.

Dies Irae smiled. The girl was thin but comely, about the same age as his daughters. She had red hair, white skin, and teary eyes.

"We too will dine," he agreed.

He dragged the wench to the town square, backhanded her, and shoved her against the well. Umbra sat on the well's edge, smirking, and held the girl down as Dies Irae lifted her skirts. The girl struggled as he took her, and Umbra laughed. When he was done, he tossed the weeping girl toward a group of mimics.

"Enjoy," he told them.

They leaped upon her, drooling and howling, and she screamed.

Soon his army moved again, marching, shuffling, crawling, flying. They howled, they drooled, they screeched and moaned and growled and hissed. They oozed into the mountains, leaving the light of Osanna behind, spilling into the mountains of Requiem's ruin.

"Soon I will have you, Lacrimosa," Dies Irae whispered as he rode at the van. "Soon I will hurt you, Agnus Dei and Gloriae. Soon I will break you, Kyrie Eleison. You will be my basest mimics, pathetic slaves to my warriors' lusts."

Umbra fingered her daggers. "Your glory will soon cover the world."

The ruined town faded in the distance. Requiem rolled ahead.

AGNUS DEI

Strange dreams filled her world.

She saw strands of starlight form a dragon in the stars. She saw mimics bearing her face, fifty thousand strong, marching through snow and ash. She saw her father, clad in dark green and silver, ruling in a marble palace, his eye sockets empty and bleeding. They smiled at her, this dragon, these mimics, her father, smiles that flowed around her head. When she reached for them, they vanished and laughed, flowing into the sound of sad pipes and wind through tunnels.

"Mother," she whispered. "Mother, the Poisoned... I have to burn them. I have to. I have to save the scrolls."

Mother held her hand. "They're gone, sweetness. The Poisoned are gone."

Agnus Dei blinked. "But we need to find the Beams, Mother. They're in a swamp, I think. The pup said something about a swamp."

He touched her cheek, that pup, his face blurry. Was he truly there? She heard him.

"Rest, kitten. Don't worry about the Beams."

She tried to see him, to blink, to clear her eyes. But she saw only tunnels stretching before her, diving under mountain and ruins. Skeletons surrounded her. Was Father one of these skeletons? She tried to find him.

"Father! Father, don't worry. You can be a skeleton. I'll be one soon too. I don't care, but Mother will say I'm too thin."

Her left hand hurt. She could feel the fingers twisting. Someone was burning it.

"No, Umbra, please," she begged and wept. "Let me go."

But the woman only chained her down, and *stars, no, please, no....*

She heard the hiss. A sword being drawn. *His* sword.

"Please, Irae... Mother, help me!"

Stars, it's gone. My hand is gone. How could it be gone? Where is it?

She had to find it. She had to. *The pup will hate me without a hand. He'll leave me. He'll go be with Gloriae.* She had beautiful hands.

Tears streamed down Agnus Dei's face, so hot. *I'm like him now. I'm like Dies Irae.*

"He'll take my other hand," she whispered, trembling. "Please, Mother, he'll take my leg. Please don't let him."

Arms embraced her. "I won't let him, sweetheart. I promise."

Where was she? Who was holding her?

"Mother!"

She fell into tunnels. She wanted to stay with her mother, with her sister, with her pup. But the tunnels pulled her down. Pain! Fire on her hand. The fingers moved.

I am mimic. My hand is cruel. My hand will hurt me. Stars, it's gone. How could it be gone? Please, Irae, please.

She saw her hand before her. It rose from the shadows, speckled in blood. It wielded an axe toward her. *Please, don't cut my other hand....*

The hand grew from a mimic with four arms and a bull's head. Its hair was long, black, curly, rustling with bugs. Its eyes mocked her. It smiled, showing pointed teeth and a slobbering tongue.

"Agnus Dei," it hissed. "He will cut your head. He will make you a mimic like me." It tightened her hand around the axe. Worms crawled over the knuckles.

She trembled. She tried to kick, to fight it, but was too weak. The darkness pulled her. The heat! Fire burned her hand, her forehead, her lungs. Sweat drenched her.

"The nightshades broke me," she whispered. "They're pulling me into their worlds, into the shadows."

The darkness shattered her, tugged her into pieces, drowned her. Fire everywhere. Pain and fire. Her eyes rolled back. *I'm sorry, Mother. I'm sorry, Gloriae. I'm sorry, Kyrie. I don't want to leave you. I love you all so much.*

Golden light rolled across her, like the hint of dawn over a swaying field.

"Mother?"

The heat left her.

The pain vanished.

When she opened her eyes, she saw light like feathers. It tickled her face. Blue wisps floated above them; bits of sky. She heard rustling leaves, and saw rolling hills, rays of light between birches, and columns of white marble. Figures robed in white floated before her, harps in hand.

"Requiem?" she whispered.

Snowy mountains and valleys of pines spread before her. A great mountain soared ahead, all in gold, dragons flying around it, bugling, sunlight on their scales. They were true dragons, wingless, limbless, flying serpents of brilliant colors, of fluttering white beards, of crystal eyes.

"Salvanae!" she said. She smiled softly under their light. "I am here again, in Salvandos. I remember flying here with Kyrie."

Tears flowed down her cheeks. Was this the afterlife—to spend eternity with the salvanae? Hope welled within her and she wept. This was a good place to die.

I'll wait here for you, she swore to her family. *One day we'll fly here together.*

A golden salvana flew toward her, coiling and uncoiling. His white moustache and beard fluttered in the wind. His eyes were the size of melons, spinning and glowing.

"Nehushtan!" Agnus Dei cried. "It's me. Agnus Dei. Do you remember?"

She found herself lying in grass in human form. Nehushtan floated above her. He lowered his head, so that his beard brushed against her. His head was larger than her human body. His eyes blinked, his long white lashes fanning her.

"Wake, daughter of stars," he said, his voice like harps. "The song of Requiem calls you."

Stars floated around her, spun, streamed. *But I am awake,* she thought. *I live among the stars.*

Somebody squeezed her hand, and she heard Mother's voice.

"Wake up, Agnus Dei. Open your eyes. It's not yet your time to leave me."

But my eyes are open, she thought. *I can see beauty and light.*

Yet she managed to open them again. New light shone. She gasped, and cold air filled her lungs, scented of mountains. Nehushtan seemed to smile at her, teeth glinting, moustache fluttering. His golden scales chinked and glimmered as he floated. Behind him, thousands of other salvanae hovered in the sky, their long bodies undulating like snakes in water.

"Mother?" she whispered. She looked to her right and saw Mother sitting there, the salvanae's light against her face. Kyrie and Gloriae sat there too, their eyes soft.

"Agnus Dei." Mother kissed her forehead and caressed her cheek. "How do you feel?"

She blinked. "I feel better. I... am I dreaming? I see the true dragons, Mother. Thousands of them. Are we in Salvandos?"

"You are in Requiem still," said Nehushtan, his voice like crinkling old paper and the wind in pines. "We saw the strands in our stars, and sang to them, and heard your prayers sing with ours. So we flew here, daughter of Draco, and we will help you again. We sang too for your healing."

Agnus Dei gasped and raised her left arm. For an instant, she hoped to see her hand regrown. That hope crashed. Her arm still ended with a stump, though the wound was healed. Instead of infected stitches, she saw pale, smooth skin.

"Thank you," she said softly, though she could not feel joy. She felt, instead, only shame. Her wound was healed, but her arm looked strange to her, deformed. Tears stung her eyes. She was still crippled. Impure. Ugly.

Agnus Dei looked at Kyrie, her pup. *Does he think I'm a freak now? A gruesome cripple? Will he still love me? Or will he leave me for Gloriae, who is whole and still beautiful?* Suddenly she wished he'd look away. She wanted to hide her arm, to never show it to anyone again. She lowered her eyes.

"Oh, pup," she whispered. "I'm sorry."

He shifted closer. "Sorry for what?"

That I'm like this, she wanted to say. *That I'll be forever different.* But she could not bring those words to her lips. Instead, she looked up at him, her pup, her love, her best friend, and she said, "I love you."

His eyes softened, and he scooped her into his arms, and kissed her. His hands held her head, and she placed her good hand on his back. They kissed in the light of the true dragons, and tears flowed down her face.

"I love you too," he said, holding her. "I'll always love you, Agnus Dei."

Laughter burst from her lips, surprising her. She pinched his cheek. "You really are a pup, do you know that?"

She looked over his shoulder at the mountains and valleys of Requiem. The snow was melting. Winter would soon end. Beams of dawn fell between the thousands of salvanae. War would come here, Agnus Dei knew. Dies Irae would march into these lands with all his might and malice. *But that is tomorrow,* she thought. *Today... today life is beautiful.*

Gloriae leaned down, kissed her cheek, and smiled. Mother held her good hand. They sat on the mountainside, embracing one another, watching the sunrise.

TERRA

When he saw the army in the distance, he felt the blood leave his face.

"Stars," he whispered. "Down, Memoria!"

They dived, landed on a snowy mountainside, and shifted into humans. Wind moaned, flurrying snow around them, sneaking under his armor like the fingers of ghosts.

"There are thousands," Memoria said, gasping. "A *hundred* thousand."

Terra narrowed his eyes. It was hard to see from here. The army moved leagues away, a black stain upon the ruins of Requiem, oozing forward. He could hear faded roars and battle cries, a sound like an angry sea. Creatures flew over the army, thousands of them, like murders of crows. They were too distant to see clearly, but they had to be massive, the size of dragons.

He scowled. "This army was mustered to kill the last Vir Requis."

Memoria clutched the hilt of her sword, as if that sword could defeat such an army. "To kill Agnus Dei, and to kill Kyrie," she said.

Terra stared at this spreading black puddle, his stomach twisting. He was no stranger to war. He was a bellator, a knight of Requiem. He had fought griffins at Draco Murus, the Poisoned in Requiem's tunnels, the giants of the north. But this.... Terra had never seen forces that chilled him so. Strange things moved there. He saw the shapes of great beasts towering over smaller troops, and he saw stars and lightning crackle between the creatures that flew. This army marched with dark magic.

"They move slowly," he said. "We fly fast. Let's find Kyrie."

Memoria nodded. "The ruins of Requiem's palace. King's Column. So long as Vir Requis live, that column will stand." Her eyes dampened. "I know Kyrie. He's there."

If he's alive, Terra thought, but said nothing. Memoria believed. *Let her cling to hope while she can. Hope might be all we've got.*

"Let's fly," Memoria said. "I remember the way. Follow
m—"

Before she could finish her sentence, a distant shriek rose.
Terra cursed. A dozen flying beasts, the size of specks from
here, disengaged from the army and came flying toward them.

"They saw us," he said. "Damn it. Let's fly!"

He shifted into a dragon, roared fire, and soared. Memoria
flew beside him, snow flurrying around her green scales. They
flew west, the clouds streaming around them, the snow slapping
their faces. The mountaintops rose around them. When Terra
looked over his shoulder, he saw his pursuers gaining on them.

"Those things are fast," he said.

"So are we. Fly, Terra!"

He narrowed his body, flapped his wings mightily, and
shot forward through the wind and snow. He growled and fire
filled his mouth. He looked behind him again and cursed.

"Damn it! They're gaining on us. What *are* they?"

Jaw clenched, Memoria looked over her shoulder, and her
eyes narrowed.

"They look... they look like dragons," she said.

Terra shook his head. "No. Not dragons. But whatever
they are, there are six of them, and two of us. Fly higher. We'll
lose them in the clouds."

They soared and crashed into the snow clouds. Wind, ice,
and snow stung Terra's eyes. He lowered his head and narrowed
his eyes to slits, pushing himself forward. He couldn't see ten
feet around him.

"Memoria, are you with me?" he shouted.

Her voice came from the clouds to his left. "Right beside
you. Fly against the wind; it'll take us to the ruins of the palace."

And maybe slow down those creatures following us, he thought.
He kept flying, driving through the clouds, and heard the
screeches behind him. They were closer.

"They're fast bastards," he said.

Green scales flashed beside him between strands of
clouds. "What the stars *are* those things? They were leagues
away only moments ago."

Terra grunted. "Friends of Dies Irae."

The siblings kept flying, driving through the storm, until
the clouds parted. They found themselves over valleys of
toppled ruins and fallen trees. Marble columns, each a hundred

feet long, lay fallen like so many sticks below them. Snow dappled the ruins like patches of leprosy. The cries sounded again behind them, like the sound of butchered elephant seals. When Terra turned his head, he saw the creatures emerge from the clouds, only five hundred yards away.

"Bloody stars," he muttered. Beside him, Memoria gasped.

They were dragons, or at least, shaped as such. They were sewn together from the dead. Men's bodies, trussed up like hams, formed their necks. Their wings seemed made of human bones and skin. Their tails, their bodies, their limbs, their heads; all were patched from body parts, sewn together, rotting and wormy. They opened their maws and squealed.

Mimic dragons. Lovely.

He felt the Animating Stones; their curse slammed against him, tugging at his magic. Memoria grimaced; she felt it too.

Around their necks, Adoria's Hands opened.

The mimic dragons shrieked and flew at them, claws extended.

Terra and Memoria blew their fire.

The streams of flame roared, crackled, and hit two mimic dragons. They screamed and burned, their skin peeling, their flesh blistering. The four others flew around them, lightning fast, and blazed toward Terra and Memoria.

Terra had no time to muster more fire. The things moved so fast, he could barely see them. Two crashed into him, their claws—they seemed made of sharpened femurs—lashing at him.

Those claws scratched his side. He growled and bit. His teeth sank into soft, rotten flesh. It tore free easily, filling his mouth with juices and dead flies. The taste made him gag. He spat and clawed, hitting the beast's head.

It growled and bit, and its teeth broke several of Terra's scales. Roaring, Terra flapped his wings, kicked, and pushed himself back. He swiped his tail, hit the creature's head, and blew fire.

The mimic dragon burned. Its skin peeled back as it screamed. Its stitches melted. The bodies composing it came loose and began falling from the sky—men, women, children, pale and rubbery.

"Terra!" his sister cried.

He growled and flew toward her. Three mimic dragons surrounded her, scratching. Terra roasted one and swung his tail at another. Before it could recover, he swiped his claws, bit, and tore its head off. Memoria burned the last mimic dragon, and it fell to the ruins below, coming apart into two dozen bodies.

"That was easy," Terra muttered, rubbing a wound at his side.

Memoria growled. "I hear more."

Terra heard them too. It sounded like hundreds were flying in the clouds, moving closer. *Once they emerge from the clouds, they'll see us.*

"To the ground," Terra said and began to dive. "We continue on foot, as humans."

They dived, the air whistling around them, the snow stinging them. The clouds growled and the mimics screamed in the distance. They landed by a fallen tower, shifted into humans, and crawled under the ruins.

"Damn," Memoria whispered, peaking through the ruins to the sky. Snow filled her hair and kissed her cheeks pink.

Terra grumbled. A hundred mimic dragons emerged from the clouds above, squealing. Their wings creaked and roiled the snow. *How are we to defeat so many, even with Adoria's Hands?*

Memoria clasped his hand. "Do you think... do you think these things found Kyrie?"

Terra shook his head. "If Kyrie survived this long, he's good at hiding, at fighting, at *living*. If he's alive, we'll find him." *Terra... I found him.* He grabbed his sword. "We'll look in the west. We'll look at King's Column."

The mimics above shrieked and flew over them, soon disappearing into the distance. Terra and Memoria hid for long moments, shivering in the cold. Finally they crawled out of hiding and began to walk. Their feet ached, their teeth chattered, and their limbs were weak with hunger and wounds.

When Terra looked behind him, he saw that black puddle oozing over the horizon. He cursed and quickened his step.

KYRIE ELEISON

He walked through King's Forest, holding Agnus Dei's hand. The snow glided around them.

"Oh, pup," Agnus Dei said, head lowered. "This place feels so sad, doesn't it?"

The trees were fallen now, burned and toppled years ago. It seemed to Kyrie like all the horrors of the world had been born here.

Twenty years ago, Dies Irae raped Lacrimosa here. Four years later, he stole the griffins here, and toppled these columns. Five years after that, Requiem's survivors gathered in this place, and marched to Lanburg Fields. Kyrie sighed. *And now... does Requiem fall here now?*

Kyrie raised his eyes and looked at King's Column. It rose in the distance from the ruins, two hundred feet tall, its marble bright. Salvanae coiled above and around it, bugling their song.

"It is sad," he said, "but look, Agnus Dei. New dragons fly here now. And we're still here. We still fight. We can win this war."

Agnus Dei raised her head and looked at him. Her eyes seemed so large to Kyrie, pools of sadness.

"I'm so afraid," she said. "I lost Father. And... at the camp, when...." She swallowed and hid her left arm. "It feels like somebody else died. I grieve for my hand, the same way I grieve for Father. Is that strange, Kyrie?"

He shook his head, touched her cheek, and kissed her forehead. "It's not strange."

She lowered her eyes, her eyelashes brushing his cheek. "I'm so scared of more loss. Of you dying, or Gloriae, or Mother. Kyrie, I... I want to be brave again. I want to growl and shout for battle. But I can't feel that way anymore."

He nodded. "You're growing older and wiser." He tapped her head. "Maybe soon you'll be as wise as me."

Normally she would punch him, wrestle him, and pull his hair for such a taunt. Today she did not even smile. She sighed, and he held her, his arms around her. She held him with her good hand, but kept her left arm hidden behind her back.

"Oh, pup, I can't even hug you properly now."

"You can."

She shook her head, and Kyrie felt her tears on his cheek. She trembled.

"Kyrie, I'm ashamed. I'm sorry. I don't even like holding you now. I don't like when you hold me." Her voice shook. "I used to like you looking at me. It made me feel funny and good. I wanted to be beautiful for you, as beautiful as Gloriae. But I can't now. Not without my hand, with this arm that... that just ends with a stump. It looks so ugly to me. I hate it. I'm ugly now, and I'm so embarrassed whenever you look at me. I'm so sorry that I'm like this for you."

He laughed softly, and she stiffened. She pulled back an inch, looking at him with narrowed eyes.

"Why do you laugh at me?" she asked.

He caressed her cheek. "Agnus Dei. You have the largest, most beautiful eyes I've seen, with the longest lashes. You have the softest, bounciest, curliest hair I've seen, like lamb's fleece. And most importantly, you are good, and brave, and kind. You are beautiful, Agnus Dei. You are the most beautiful woman I know, inside and out, and you will always be beautiful to me. No matter what. I will always think this, and I will always love you." He held her hand tight. "If you ever doubt this, I'll beat you up."

She sighed again, lowered her head, then raised her eyes. A soft smile touched her lips. "Oh pup, you're such a poet, do you know? Not a very good one, but an earnest one." She touched his cheek. "And you know that you can't beat me up. I can still beat you in a fight, even with one hand."

She kissed his lips. They held each other, kissing deeply, the salvanae coiling and singing above.

"Come with me," he said. They walked through the forest, and found a hollow between three fallen columns. He lay down his cloak, and they sat upon it, holding each other. They pulled her cloak above them and huddled for warmth. He kissed her lips, her ear, her neck. She moaned and dug her fingers into his back.

They undressed each other, trembling with cold, goosebumps rising across them. His lips moved down her neck, and he kissed her breasts, then pulled her atop him. She sat in his lap, and tossed back her head, so that her mane of curls cascaded to his knees. She wrapped both arms around him, her eyes closed.

Soon Kyrie was no longer cold. He remembered the first time he made love to Agnus Dei, in the summer on the border with Salvandos. It seemed so long ago. Back then, Agnus Dei had confused him, taunted him, teased him, seemed so much older and mysterious and intoxicating. Today she was more to him: a kind, brave, sensitive woman he loved, a woman he wanted to be with forever. They kissed and swayed in the cold, their furs draped over them.

They were walking back to King's Column, hand in hand, when they heard shrieks and thudding wings above.

Agnus Dei's eyes widened. "Griffins! The griffins are here!"

Kyrie looked up, shielding his eyes with his hand. He gasped. Thousands of griffins flew above, snow clinging to their fur, their eyes bright. Volucris flew at their lead, King of Leonis, Dies Irae's old mount. Rays of sun fell between them, and their shrieks seemed to shake the world.

"They too have seen our stars," Kyrie whispered. "They too have come to fight." He squeezed Agnus Dei's hand.

She nodded. "The great battle of our generation will be fought here, I think. All the nations of the world gather. To fight Dies Irae. To fight darkness." She swallowed, tears in her eyes. "Salvandos, Leonis, Requiem... we join together to fight for life. This war is not only about us anymore, Kyrie. Irae's evil has crawled to all corners of the world, I think... and the world is fighting back."

The griffins began to land in the forest. They stood atop the fallen columns, the smashed walls, the shattered mosaics that lay buried in snow. Kyrie passed by one, a golden female with yellow eyes, and placed his hand against her fur. She cawed and tilted her head at him.

He kept walking with Agnus Dei and approached King's Column. It rose before him, its capital glimmering in the sun like a beacon. Lacrimosa and Gloriae stood below the column, wrapped in cloaks, talking in hushed tones.

A man and woman stood by them, speaking with them. Kyrie frowned. Something about these strangers made him freeze.

The two strangers had not seen him yet. The woman was short, slim, and fair-haired. She wore furs and bore a sword in the style of Requiem blades. Tall and board, the man bore a similar sword, and wore plate armor and a horned helm. His face was haggard, sporting a walrus moustache like Kyrie remembered his father wearing.

"Who are they?" Agnus Dei whispered, eyes narrowed.

"I... I don't know," Kyrie said, but somehow he did know, or used to. He knew these people. He knew that the man had a deep laugh. He knew that the woman had brown doe eyes, though he could not see them.

"Kyrie!" Agnus Dei said. "Your hand is trembling."

He wanted to walk forward, but could not. His insides roiled. He saw a vineyard, not far from here, kissed with sunlight and humming with dragonflies. He saw a mosaic floor, dragons and dolphins and griffins all twinkling with thousands of stones. He saw a balcony, and tasted wine, and he saw these people; he knew them, he loved them.

Lacrimosa saw him first. She looked toward him from King's Column, and her eyes softened. Gloriae looked at him too, and then—slowly, almost hesitantly—the two strangers turned to face him.

Their eyes. I know their eyes. Brown eyes like his own, the woman's kind and round, the man's weary and haunted. Both pairs stared at him, piercing him.

The two walked toward him. Kyrie stood frozen, half of him wanting to disappear, the other half burning for answers. He held Agnus Dei's hand tight.

When the strangers reached him, their eyes turned soft and damp.

"Kyrie?" the woman whispered. Her voice shook, and a tear streamed down her cheek. "Kyrie, is that you?"

Kyrie! she called. *Kyrie, the geese are flying outside, come see them. Kyrie, I wrote you a story, come hear. Kyrie, I love you.*

He breathed heavily, staring at her through narrowed eyes. He turned to stare at the man, the tall man with the walrus moustache and the plate armor, a man who looked so weary, so haunted... and Kyrie saw him younger, happier.

Go on, Kyrie! Pull the line, you've got him. It's a trout, and a big one. You caught him, Kyrie. He saw the sunlight on the water, smelled frying fish, heard his brother laugh as they wrestled.

My... brother?

"Kyrie?" the man said. He stepped forward and held Kyrie's shoulder, examining him, his mouth opening, his eyes widening.

Yes, I had a brother once. And I had a sister. But they died. They died years ago, along with my parents, with my friends, with everyone I've ever known.

"Who are you?" he whispered.

The woman smiled—a warm, teary, loving smile. "It's Memoria, Kyrie. I've come to you again. Do you remember me?"

He shook his head, mouth hanging open, eyes still narrowed. "I... no. I'm sorry, but I don't."

"She's your sister," said the tall man. "And I'm Terra, your brother."

And suddenly they were embracing him, and crying over him, and saying so many words he did not understand. They spoke of a tunnel trapping them, and of seeking him in Lanburg Fields, and fleeing into an Ice City, and something about a sorceress and a giant, and a palace built all of ice, and mimic dragons.... Kyrie understood none of it.

"Don't you remember us, Kyrie?" Memoria asked, tears spiking her lashes. "Do you remember our home?" She touched his cheek. "You were so young. You were only six years old when we lost you. Do you remember?"

"I... I remember having a family. I remember my parents. I remember having many cousins, and friends, and older siblings. But... I've always only remembered blurry images, sounds, smells. I...."

Suddenly his knees felt weak, and he had to sit down on a column. Everything spun around him. Memoria and Terra kept holding him, and laughing, and crying over him. Lacrimosa laughed and cried with them, and Agnus Dei still held his hand, and Gloriae moved silently around them. They all blurred around him, becoming smudges of color and sound like his memories.

"I have a sister?" he whispered. "I have a brother?"

It was impossible! *I'm the last Eleison. I've always been the last. Dies Irae murdered my family. He....*

Terra.

Memoria.

He remembered those names. He remembered! They pounded through him. He remembered the mosaic floor, the balcony, the vineyard, the stream where Terra would take him fishing.

"I have a sister. I have a brother."

He shook and his eyes dampened. Terra patted him on the back and laughed again, that old laughter Kyrie still remembered, and Memoria hugged him, and he was confused, so confused, and he could barely tell memory from reality.

Memoria kissed his cheek, trembling, sobbing now. "I'm so sorry, Kyrie. I'm so sorry we left you. I'm so sorry you had to survive without us for so long. But we're back for you now. You'll never be alone again."

I have a sister. I have a brother.

He looked toward Agnus Dei. She looked into his eyes, her smile trembling.

"Is this real?" he whispered. "Am I dreaming?"

She laughed and mussed his hair. Her eyes sparkled. "It's real, pup. They look just like you."

Kyrie looked at them. Terra. Memoria. With the same sandy hair, the same brown eyes, survivors, fighters, siblings. He lowered his eyes.

"I'm sorry," he said. "I want to remember more. I... I didn't know your names until you told me. I didn't even remember your names. I thought you had died so long ago. I'm sorry that I never found you, that I never.... You know who I am. You have all these memories of me. I wish I could say the same." He lowered his head, ashamed.

But they only laughed, and hugged him again, and they cried together.

"We found him, Memoria," Terra whispered. "We found him."

Kyrie held them. The dragonflies hummed in his mind, and the vineyard rustled, and the stream splashed with fish.

It's real, pup. They look just like you.

"It's real," he whispered. *I have a sister. I have a brother.*

The griffins cawed around them, and the salvanae bugled, a song of reunion and joy, of light and hope and love... before the fall of night.

DIES IRAE

His black horse grunted beneath him, rot seeping through its stitches, foam dripping from its mouth. Dies Irae dug his spurs deep.

"Weredragons were here," he said. He tossed back his head, and his nostrils flared. "I smell them."

Umbra rode beside him, scanning the ruins with narrowed eyes. Night had fallen, and only a glimmer of red light remained in the west. She sniffed too.

"I smell nothing but rot," she said.

Dies Irae pointed up the mountainside that loomed before them. An orphaned, crumbling archway crowned the mountain, the remnants of a weredragon fort. *Draco Murus, they called it,* he remembered and snickered. The greatest of Requiem's fortresses—smashed upon the mountain.

"This is where my pets found them. Let us seek them there."

He kneed his horse, leading it up the mountainside. Umbra rode at his side. Behind them, his army marched, crawled, and flew, a hundred thousand creatures all howling and drooling. Stones tumbled, but the undead horses plowed on, stronger in death, faster and needing no food or rest.

"The place is an utter ruin," Umbra said, disgust and glee mixing in her voice. "It's worse than Confutatis."

Dies Irae nodded. "Confutatis will rise again, stronger and more glorious than before. This place, this Requiem, will sink further into ruin and pain."

Soon his forces covered the mountainside, like worms covering a body. The snowbeasts smashed down the archway, squealing. Its stones cascaded, hitting several mimics, incurring laughter from their comrades. Dies Irae dismounted on the mountaintop, his boots scattering snow from the cobblestones of an old courtyard. Umbra dismounted beside him, drew her daggers, and hissed.

"The air is rank with the stench of reptile," Dies Irae said. He spat. Mimics howled around him, waving their blades.

"A hole," Umbra said, pointing her dagger.

Dies Irae nodded. "A rat hole. Light a torch and follow me."

He climbed into the darkness, Umbra behind him, torch crackling in her hand. A stairway led him into a network of cellars. *Do you hide here, weredragons? Do you cower from me?* He couldn't wait to find Lacrimosa, to tear off her clothes, hurt her, take her, crush her, to pull her hair and see her tears. He licked his lips.

"Where are you, my lovely?" he whispered. "Where do you cower, my lizard whore?"

Tree bark, broken branches, and sap filled some chambers; wood had been stored here. A second chamber held a bear rug, a table, and four clay bowls.

"Where are they?" Umbra demanded.

A tattered dress hung on a peg in the wall. Dies Irae lifted it, held it to his face, and inhaled deeply. *Lacrimosa's dress. Yes.* She had worn this the night he caught her in the field. He savored the scent of it.

He turned and began walking back upstairs, the dress in his hand.

"They went to King's Column," he said. "They retreated to the only place their light still shines." He clenched his fist around the dress, gritted his teeth, and smiled. "That's where we'll find them."

Umbra snarled. "They will be our mimics soon. Slaves for our warriors to torment. I will hurt them too."

Dies Irae nodded. He stepped out onto the courtyard and stood on the mountaintop. His army spread around him, line after line of mimics, snowbeasts, the Poisoned, swamp lizards, skeletons, rotting dragons, and coiling nightshades. Their cries shook the earth.

"We will smash King's Column!" he shouted. "We will destroy the weredragon curse forever. Their bodies will be yours!"

They howled. The clouds roiled. Dies Irae mounted his horse, spurred it, and galloped down the mountain.

LACRIMOSA

Lacrimosa flapped her wings, circling above the burned trees and shattered halls of King's Forest.

It felt good to fly. She had barely flown all winter, and she needed to feel the clouds around her wings, the wind in her nostrils, the fire in her belly.

"Requiem!" she said. "May our wings forever find your sky."

The words of her fathers, of her priests, of her life. She still flew for her fathers, for her priests, and for life—her life, the life of her children, the life that still flickered in Requiem.

"I still find your sky. And I will fight for you. Give me strength, stars of Requiem. Give me strength, Ben. The great battle of our time comes to us. I pray that I can withstand its tide."

She circled above King's Column, the last pillar of their halls. She remembered a hundred griffins slamming against it, trying to topple it, but the Draco light still blessed it; so long as Vir Requis lived, it would stand. *I will not let it fall.*

The griffins now flew around her, her allies. The salvanae flew here too, coiling and uncoiling, their eyes spinning, their scales glimmering. Volucris flew at her right, shrieking, wings churning the clouds—King of Griffins. Nehushtan flew to her left, a hundred feet long, his moustache fluttering and his scales like molten gold—King of Salvandos.

"Thank you, my friends," she said to them. "Thank you for flying with me, with Requiem."

Nehushtan bowed his head to her. "The evil of the tyrant spreads across earth and heaven. The stench of it has carried to our land. It poisons the glow of stars. We have come to fight. For Requiem. For Salvandos our home. For Leonis, realm griffins. We fight for all lands of civilization."

Lacrimosa remembered travelling across the ruins of Osanna, the empire of men. She had crossed it by foot, and taken ship from Altus Mare on the sea. She had seen ruin, death, desolation. Cities lay crumbled, farms burned, forests wilted, bodies rotting. *And who will fight for Osanna?* she wondered. *Who will fight for the realm Dies Irae rules, enslaves, and burns?*

The griffins shrieked, and the salvanae bugled.

Drums and trumpets sounded in the north, answering her.

Lacrimosa stared and gasped. She blew fire, and her eyes stung.

They marched from the burned forest, thousands of them, bearing banners of green and brown. They flowed forward like a snake emerging from a basket. A hundred horsemen rode at their lead, clad in armor, bearing lances and standards. Behind them walked thousands of women, children, and old men, all wrapped in cloaks, huddling together for warmth. Thousands of men surrounded their grandparents, mothers, wives, and children. Some wore armor and bore swords. Others wore peasant tunics and carried pitchforks and torches.

"The Earthen," Lacrimosa whispered. Children of Osanna. Followers of the Earth God. *Friends.*

She flew down and landed on a snowy, fallen column. She stood, wings folded against her back, and watched the Earthen approach.

An old man led them, she saw. He rode a brown horse and wore a green cloak over chain mail. His hair and beard were long, and more white than brown, but his back was still straight, his eyes still bright, his hand still steady on the hilt of his sword. He rode up to her, two armored riders flanking him.

Lacrimosa bowed her head to him. "Silva the Elder," she said. "Welcome to Requiem. May our stars, and your Earth God, bless you."

The priest nodded to her. His face was deeply lined, his voice hoarse. "Queen Lacrimosa of Requiem. A great host approaches. Our scouts have seen them. They cover a league, and they march fast. It's an army of beasts and demons, abominations to the Earth God and to your stars. They'll be here soon."

"Our own scouts have seen them," she replied, remembering what Terra and Memoria had reported. She swallowed. "An army of mimics, snowbeasts, nightshades, and all other creatures of darkness. We stand ready to fight them."

Silva gestured to the riders beside him. "These are my sons. At my right is Silva the Younger. And here is Silas, my second son, a great priest like his brother."

The two men drew their swords.

"We stand ready to fight with Requiem," said Silva the Young.

"We fight for the Earth God," said Silas, snow in his hair.

Lacrimosa looked over their heads at the people they led. Horsemen. Footmen. Peasants. Women and children. *Dies Irae has hunted them for years. Here is their final stand. Will this be their Lanburg Fields? Will this be death to us all?* A few of the children began to cry, and Lacrimosa looked back to Silva.

"Lead the mothers and children into the trees west of King's Column. They are burned and many have fallen, but they will give some shelter. Place armed men around them. Take the fallen logs, and build what palisades you can. Then take what men you can spare, and what women can wield a weapon, and rejoin me here at the pillar. We will hold council."

She took flight, soaring as high as she could, until the air thinned, her lungs hurt, and her head spun. In the east, she saw them approach, a league away, a shadow falling over Requiem. Fear coiled in her belly. There were so many, a vast host like she had never seen. Countless nightshades and mimic dragons flew there. Fifty thousand mimics marched below, howling and banging war drums. Behind them moved endless skeletons, reptiles the size of dragons, herds of snowbeasts on gangly legs, and mobs of oozing Poisoned.

And one man I must kill. One man who has haunted my life. The man who raped me, murdered my husband, murdered my parents, murdered my people. One man I must face today. Lacrimosa tightened her jaw. *Be strong, daughter of Requiem,* she told herself. *Now is your hour.*

She looked below her, surveying her forces. Five thousand salvanae, the true dragons, creatures of fang and lightning. Five thousand griffins, their talons bright, their beaks sharp. Ten thousand soldiers, followers of the Earth god, protecting ten thousand women and children.

"And us," she whispered. "Six Vir Requis."

She saw the others below, huddling together by King's Column. Her daughters, the lights of her life. Kyrie Eleison, who was like a son to her. Terra and Memoria, new hope for their race.

That was all. A small force, she thought. A sparrow against the swooping vulture of Dies Irae's wrath. *But we will meet them still.*

She dived toward King's Column.

"Nehushtan!" she called. "Volucris!"

They flew to her, and landed with her in the shattered hall of Requiem's kings. Silva joined them, tall upon his horse, his sword in hand. King's Column rose above them into the rays of setting sun. Darkness was spreading fast, the stars emerging.

Lacrimosa shifted into human form. She placed a hand upon Stella Lumen, her father's sword.

"Daughters," she said, turning toward the twins. "Kyrie. Do you have the Beams?"

They nodded. Gloriae opened a sack and spilled out three golden skulls, each twice the size of a man's skull. Their orbits glowed and their jaws grinned.

"You have wielded Beams before," she told them. "Today you will wield them on griffinback. Choose your griffins and ride them against the nightshades. Burn them with the Beams and scatter them."

Gloriae nodded and lifted one skull. Snow filled her hair, scratches ran down her arms and cheek, and most of the gold had peeled from her breastplate. And yet her eyes were still strong, ice and fire. Once she had worn samite and jewels, Lacrimosa remembered. Once Gloriae the Gilded had hunted for Osanna, had killed and maimed for the glory of the Sun God. Today Lacrimosa saw a woman of justice, of honor, and of starlight.

"We will kill them," Gloriae said

Agnus Dei lifted the second skull. At first she held it awkwardly with one hand. Then she steadied it with her left arm, tightened her lips, and stared solemnly at Lacrimosa. Her leggings were tattered, her bodice was torn, and her cloak was shaggy. She wore only rusty pieces of armor: a pauldron on her left shoulder, vambraces on her forearms, dented grieves, no breastplate or helmet. Her sword hung on her hip. Lacrimosa remembered Agnus Dei not a year ago, full of rage and sadness, a beast trapped in a cage. Today she saw not an angry youth, but a strong woman.

"We will kill them all," Agnus Dei said, standing by her sister.

Kyrie lifted the third Beam. He too wore rags and dented armor, but his eyes were solemn, his face hard. Lacrimosa remembered meeting a boy in the summer, a boy who ran and hid from those who would kill him. Here in the winter snow, a man stood before her, a man who had fought and killed for those he loved.

"We will wield them for you, and for Requiem," he said.

Lacrimosa turned to face Nehushtan, ruler of the salvanae. The true dragon hovered several feet in the air, his serpentine body undulating. He blinked, his eyelashes fanning the snow. His moustache swayed in the breeze, and his crystal eyes glowed.

"Nehushtan," she said and placed a hand against his cheek. His scales were cold and smooth like mother-of-pearl. "I ask you to lead your salvanae against the flying mimic dragons. They are fast demons and do not die easily. Burn them with your bolts of lightning, and tear them apart with your fangs."

He nodded, his beard dipping into the snow. "They have woken the wrath of Salvandos. The Draco stars call us to war. We will fight them, Queen of Requiem. We will fell them from the sky, or die defending our stars."

She turned to Volucris next. The great griffin knelt in the snow before her, head lowered. Lacrimosa walked toward him, placed her hand against his beak, and rested her head against his.

"Volucris, my old friend," she whispered. "I'm proud to fight by you again. I ask of you this. Lead your griffins against the crawling beasts of Dies Irae. Fall upon his skeletons, his reptiles, his Poisoned, his snowbeasts, and all his horrors. Tear into them with your beaks and your talons, and kill them all."

He nodded, his eyes narrowing. They seemed to tell her: *We will kill them all.*

Lacrimosa nodded and turned toward Terra and Memoria. She wanted to be stern, but when she saw them, she couldn't help it. She felt her face soften, and she smiled.

"Terra," she said. "Memoria." She took their hands, and her eyes stung. "You have blessed us today. You have brought us new life, new love, new hope. Thank you."

They bowed their heads to her.

"My queen," Terra said, voice deep and gruff. He was only thirty, Lacrimosa knew—five years her junior—but she saw that white already invaded his temples, and lines already marred his brow.

"How should we serve you?" Memoria asked, fear and determination in her eyes. *She's so small,* Lacrimosa thought. *So delicate. But she was a soldier of Requiem. She will be a soldier again.*

Lacrimosa stared at the siblings. New Vir Requis. New survivors. *Will they die today, leaving us so soon?*

"You two wear Adoria's Hands," she said, nodding at the hands they carried on chains. "You two can shift around mimics, which we cannot." She squared her shoulders. "Tonight, fly as dragons, and swoop, and blow fire. Shower the battlefield with flame. Burn all mimics who march upon the ground of Requiem."

"We have burned them before," Memoria said.

"And we will burn them again," Terra finished.

Finally Lacrimosa turned to face Silva, priest of the Earth God. He stood by his horse, his hand resting on the pommel of his sword. The wind blew his long beard and green cloak, and his eyes stared at her steadily.

"Silva," she said. "For many years, Dies Irae hunted your priests, and burned your temples, and now he has murdered your people and turned them into his mimics. He murdered many of my people too. I'm proud to fight with you against him. Tonight let us fight side by side. We will lead the ground forces of our camp. The others will fight from above; we will face Dies Irae on the field."

His sword's grip and crossguards were made of twisting roots, like the old roots that had formed Requiem's throne. He drew the sword. Lacrimosa drew Stella Lumen, and they touched their blades.

"We will face him on the field," Silva agreed.

The sun disappeared behind the horizon. The Earthen lit torches, and the salvanae blew lightning above. War drums thudded in the east. Howls rose, a hundred thousand voices. The earth trembled. The squeals and grunts of beasts echoed among the ruins.

"It has come to us," Lacrimosa said. She took a deep breath, fighting to steady her fingers and the thrashing of her heart. "The great battle of our war is here. May we fight it well."

And if we must, may we die well.

She looked them over one last time. Her daughters. Kyrie and his siblings. The true dragons, the griffins, the children of

Osanna. They stared back, eyes solemn, lightning crackling above them.

"It begins," she whispered.

She looked to the east and saw countless red eyes and shadows.

The battle of King's Forest began.

GLORIAE

She ran, boots kicking snow, as the howls and shadows descended upon King's Forest. Men were running and griffins taking flight around her.

"We need griffins!" she shouted. "Griffins, hear us."

But they were soaring from the ground, shrieking, flying into battle. Gloriae cursed and tried to shift, but could not. Mimics were near.

"Volucris, give us griffins!" Kyrie shouted, running beside her. Snow flurried around him.

Great wings thudded, billowing Gloriae's hair. Volucris landed before them, talons digging into the earth. *Dies Irae's old mount.* He towered over her and lay down his wing.

"Agnus Dei, ride him!" Gloriae shouted. "He's strong and swift."

Agnus Dei nodded. Clutching her Beam, she ran up Volucris's wing and sat bareback upon him.

"Fly, Volucris!" Agnus Dei cried. The golden skull glowed and hummed in her grasp. His wings blowing snow, his talons digging, Volucris took flight. The griffin king soared into the night, screeching, and drove into a storm of mimic dragons and nightshades. Already Agnus Dei's Beam blazed, shooting a ray that seared the storming nightshades.

Standing beside Gloriae, Kyrie pointed. "There's another griffin."

They ran through the snow. Men ran around them, shouting, swords drawn. Mimics crashed into the battlefield, roaring, their teeth and eyes red in the torchlight. Lightning blazed above them as the salvanae roared and fought the mimic dragons.

"Kyrie, you fly this one," Gloriae said when they reached the griffin. "His name is Malathor; he was one of Lord Molok's griffins. Fly, Kyrie! Fly now!"

Kyrie nodded and leaped onto Malathor. With shrieks and thudding wings, they soared into battle. Fire and light blazed around them. Kyrie's Beam seared through the night, and nightshades screamed and burned.

Gloriae scanned the battlefield, but the griffins had all taken flight. She saw them above—crashing into mimic dragons, swooping down to cut swamp reptiles, slashing at nightshades. On the ground around her, men and mimics still fought.

"Griffins!" Gloriae shouted. "I need a mount!"

"I'll mount you, girl," hissed a mimic, lunging toward her. She recognized the hunchbacked, warty form and matted red hair. *Lashdig, the chief miner.* It swiped its claws at her. Gloriae growled, leaped back, and swung her sword. Lashdig's arm flew, then came crawling through the snow toward her. She kicked it aside, spun, and cut Lashdig's legs at the stitches. The mimic fell and began crawling forward on its arms.

Gloriae raised her eyes. The nightshades were everywhere. They swarmed between the salvanae and griffins, wrapping around them, sucking their souls like a glutton sucking marrow from bones. Salvanae and griffins rained from the sky, helpless to hurt the nightshades. Agnus Dei and Kyrie shot the Beams in all directions, slicing through the demons of smoke, but they were overwhelmed.

Lashdig grabbed her leg and cackled. "You will be our slave, Gloriae." Spiders spilled from its mouth.

Gloriae kicked the creature, swung her sword, and cut off its head. She ran through the snow, hacking at mimics.

"Griffins!" she shouted.

A golden figure swooped.

Tears sprang into Gloriae's eyes.

Feathers flurried, talons glinted, and she saw her griffin.

"Aquila?" Her voice was small, hesitant. The griffin looked at her and lowered her wing.

"Aquila!" Gloriae shouted. She ran and embraced the griffin's head. "You've returned to me, girl. I thought you were dead."

The griffin cawed and tilted her head, anxious.

"Yes, Aquila, there's no time. We fly." She looked around her, ran forward, and grabbed a fallen branch the length of a lance. She leaped with the branch onto Aquila, her Beam held tight in her other hand.

"Now fly, Aquila!" she shouted over the roar of battle. Fire, blood, and lightning filled the night. "Fly like in the old days. To battle. To war. To glory. Fly!"

They soared.

The snow and blood dwindled below them, and they crashed through swarms of mimic dragons, swooping nightshades, roaring salvanae, and shrieking griffins. Blood, feathers, scales, and smoke blazed around her. Flaming arrows flew; mimics were firing them from below. Lightning flashed. Gloriae glimpsed Terra and Memoria flying to her north, raining fire upon the battle. Agnus Dei flew to the south, and Kyrie to the west, their beams renting the night. The roars, shrieks, and howls nearly deafened her.

"There, Aquila!" she shouted. "To the east. To those nightshades."

The demons of smoke and shadow were wrapping around salvanae, and the true dragons were falling fast. Gloriae snarled and dug her knees into Aquila. They shot through smoke, fire, and darkness. Gloriae nearly fell off, and she tightened her legs around Aquila as hard as she could.

She raised her Beam.

Lights shot from the skull's orbits, searing the night, slamming into nightshades.

They howled. The light turned them grey, and they shrivelled up, smoking, curling, falling. Gloriae spun the skull from side to side. Nightshades flew at her, maws opening, eyes blazing. She cut them down.

"I am Gloriae!" she shouted. "I fight for Requiem. I am her daughter. You will die before me."

Her armor was dented and dulled, its gilt chipped away, its jewels fallen. Her clothes, once priceless and embroidered with golden thread, were tattered and muddy, revealing more skin than they hid. Her lance was but a charred stick. Her griffin no longer wore gilded armor or a saddle; she rode bareback and wild. And yet Gloriae felt more powerful than ever. This was true power, she knew; this was justice and righteousness. This was the war she had always craved.

"I am Gloriae," she cried, "daughter of King Benedictus and Queen Lacrimosa, heir to Requiem. I kill for her tonight."

Flaming arrows blazed around her. One slammed into Aquila, and the griffin screeched but kept flying. As she swung the Beams, slicing through mimics, Gloriae scanned the night.

"Where are you, Irae?" she hissed. Where was the man she had called Father? Where was the man who had kidnapped her, who had murdered her friend May, who had murdered her true father?

Salvanae roared around her, scales flashing, lightning shooting from their mouths. Mimic dragons screamed and darted and bit. Flaming arrows flew, and smoke filled the air. The battle for Requiem raged, but Gloriae cared for only one man.

"I will kill you, Irae," she swore. "You die tonight."

MEMORIA

Fire, lightning, and beams of light shot around her, a storm of war. Arrows whistled, mimics roared, wings flapped, dragons swooped. The night spun around her, darkness and light, fire and blood.

"Terra!" she cried. Three mimic dragons mobbed him, slashing and biting. She flew, eyes narrowed, and slashed at one. Its flank opened, spilling snakes and cockroaches. When it turned to bite her, she blew her fire.

Terra shook off the others, growled, and torched them. A gash ran down his side, bloody. Salvanae, griffins, nightshades, and more mimic dragons spun around them, battling in the air.

"They need us down there," Terra said. "With me, Memoria! Let's burn the battlefield."

They growled, pulled their wings close, and swooped. The ground rushed up to meet Memoria, bristly with mimics. Their lines stretched into the night, endless formations of rot. She righted herself several feet above them and blew fire, raining the flames upon their ranks. They howled and fell, blazing. Javelins and arrows flew. One arrow shot through her wing, and she screamed. For a moment, she could not see with pain. A javelin grazed her leg.

"Memoria, fly! Higher!"

Terra flicked his tail, guiding her. She growled and flapped her wings, soaring into the clouds. Flaming arrows flew around her. She crashed into a nightshade, and it began to suck at her soul. She screamed. She felt the creature ripping pieces of her, laughing, lapping them up. And then Kyrie swooped forward on his griffin, his Beam blazing, washing her with light. The nightshades screeched and scattered.

"Terra, let's dive!"

She swooped again, Terra at her side. They broke apart near the ground and raced over the lines of mimics. They rained more fire, and more mimics burned. They soared, arrows snapping against their scales, and Memoria surveyed the battle.

She cursed. The mimics were tearing into the lines of Earthen, slashing their limbs off, digging into their bellies to feast. The Earthen lines were crumbling, and more mimics kept flowing forward. Lacrimosa fought there, swinging Stella Lumen, hacking at mimics. Blood splattered her.

"They need us!" Memoria shouted. "Down there, by the column."

Terra heard and nodded. Memoria steeled herself, drew flames into her mouth, and dived toward King's Column.

Ten mimic dragons soared toward her, claws outstretched.

Memoria blew her flames, hitting one dragon. It screamed and fell. The others crashed into her, lashing their claws and biting. She whipped her tail around her, and bit into their maggoty flesh, and cut and burned them. But they kept swarming. When she glanced below her, she saw more Earthen dying.

"The mimics are getting near the women and children!" she shouted.

Terra was battling a mob of mimic dragons. He roared and blew fire in a ring, scattering them, and dived. Memoria joined them. She drew fire and torched the line of mimics. Another arrow hit her, and she roared and flew higher, only to crash into a biting mimic dragon. She tried to dive for another round of fire, but could not. The mimic dragons filled the sky around her, protecting their comrades below

"Nehushtan!" she cried. "Cover us."

She stared above and saw the salvanae blazing all around, shooting lightning and biting into mimics and nightshades. They too were overrun.

A dozen mimic dragons flew at her from all sides. She blew fire in a ring, cursing. She could not shoot fire forever. Soon her reserves would dwindle, and she'd need rest to rebuild them. Would Lacrimosa and the Earthen survive until then?

A mimic dragon bit her calf, and she screamed and beat it with her wing. It opened its mouth to roar, and she slammed her tail into it, breaking it into a dozen bodies that rained onto the field. More flew at her. Memoria lashed her claws and tail, cursing.

LACRIMOSA

Her sword was a beautiful thing, she thought, a work of art, its blade filigreed, its grip glimmering with diamonds in the shape of her constellation. *But today... today there is no beauty to Stella Lumen. Today my blade deals death and blood.*

She swung that blade, cutting into mimics, their pus and blood and rot spraying. She screamed as she fought—for her children, for all free people, and for all her fallen.

Silva fought at her side, his beard fluttering in the wind, his eyes blazing, his sword bloody. His men fought around them, eyes solemn, green cloaks covered in snow and gore.

"Fight, friends!" Silva called over the din of battle. "Fight for the Earth God. We will kill the tyrant."

The enemy kept coming at them. Lines of flayed mimics burst forward, their bared muscles glimmering with blood, their internal organs shiny and pulsing. They looked like men turned inside out, and they swung jagged blades. One slashed at her, its eyeballs bulging from its skinned face. Lacrimosa parried, shouted, and swung her blade into it. Blood sprayed her.

"Terra!" she shouted to the sky. "Memoria! Burn their lines. Scatter them!"

Yet when she glanced up, she saw the mimic dragons mobbing the siblings, biting and lashing at them. More mimics and nightshades filled the sky all around. Lacrimosa cursed and parried another mimic's blade. Three attacked her at once, flayed and dripping, their teeth sharpened. She parried left and right, stabbed, thrust, and suffered a wound to her arm. She screamed and kept fighting until they lay dead.

For only a moment, she could catch her breath. Then new horrors burst from the battlefield.

Snowbeasts.

They towered seven feet tall, lanky things with six legs, flaps of white skin draping over their bones. They snapped their teeth, spraying the field with drool, and shoved between the mimics, charging toward Lacrimosa.

She ducked, dodging a blow from one's leg, and swung her blade. She hit its other leg, it fell, she leaped, she stabbed. Black blood sprayed. Another rose behind her, jumped, and slammed into her. She fell and its teeth came down. She raised her sword, screaming, and stabbed it through the mouth.

Lacrimosa lay on her back, panting, bleeding, her head spinning. More snowbeasts scurried around her like spiders. Silva cried commands to his men. Swords swung, horses thundered, and arrows blazed overhead. Above in the night sky, rays of light, pillars of fire, and streams of scales and shadow flowed.

They're too many, she thought in a haze. *We can't defeat them. We have to run.*

Bodies lay around her. Men and women of Osanna, come to fight here and die. Dead salvanae, the light of their eyes extinguished. Dead griffins. Everywhere—death, darkness, despair. Her eyes stung, and she felt herself sinking into the snow and blood.

The nightshades, salvanae, and dragons parted briefly above, and between them, Lacrimosa saw one of her stars. Its light was soft. She could almost not see it beyond the battle. But its glow seemed to call to her. *Lacrimosa. Child of the woods. You are home, you are home.* The words of her fathers.

Lacrimosa tightened her lips. *Not yet. I still fight for you, Requiem.* She leaped to her feet, shouting, and swung her blade.

Poisoned charged across the battlefield, shrieking in high-pitched, tortured voices. They had been men once, Lacrimosa knew, men twisted by green smoke and dark magic. Fish scales covered them. Their arms had grown long and twisted, their fingers clammy and webbed. Their eyes hung from their sockets on bloody stalks, slapping against their cheeks as they ran.

Lacrimosa fought them. She fought with blade and torch. She fought for Requiem. For her dead parents. For her husband. For her children. She fought as griffins and salvanae rained from the sky, dead or dying. She fought as men fell around her. She fought because her stars still shone, and life still filled her, and Lacrimosa would fight so long as she could. *Until my last breath. Until my last drop of blood. I will die fighting for Requiem, and then I will be with you again, Ben, in our halls beyond the stars.*

The creatures howled before her, blood rained from the sky, and Lacrimosa swung her blade.

AGNUS DEI

Flaming arrows whistled around her. Nightshades swooped in every direction, eyes blazing, maws dripping smoke. The mimic dragons bit and lashed their claws. Volucris spun between the enemies, three arrows in his breast, his wings roiling smoke and flame.

Agnus Dei wished she had a second hand to hold onto Volucris. Her good hand held the golden skull, pointing its beams at swarming nightshades. Her left arm hung uselessly.

"Careful, Volucris!" she cried when he swooped, soared, and swerved. She nearly fell, and she pressed her legs against him so hard, she thought they could break.

Flaming arrows blazed around them, and one hit Volucris's leg. He howled and bucked, and Agnus Dei screamed. She slid down his back, tightened her knees, but kept sliding. She had to push the Beam against her chest with her left arm, then grab Volucris's fur with her right hand.

"Damn it!" she shouted. Her Beam dimmed, then extinguished.

The nightshades howled with new vigor, cackled, and swooped toward her. Their eyes burned like collapsing stars. Their maws opened wide, revealing white teeth. She felt them tugging at her soul, tearing piece by piece from her body. She growled and screamed.

"Not again, you don't," she said and gritted her teeth. They had stolen her soul once, and the memory still flooded her with terror.

Damn my missing hand! If I had two hands, I could hold on with one, and fire the Beam with the other. She howled in rage. *I'm crippled now. I can't even fight any more.*

Arrows flew, mimic dragons bit, and Volucris swerved and soared and dipped and spun. Agnus Dei bounced atop him, flew into the air, and fell back onto him. The ground spun below her, distant, swarming with mimics and monsters. Rays of fire and smoke shot around her through the sky. The Beam began to slip from under her arm, but she dared not release her fistful of

Volucris's fur. The nightshades howled and flowed around her, brushing her with their icy bodies, and she screamed. She felt her soul being ripped away, pulled from her like stuffing from a torn doll.

She shook her head wildly, struggling to cling to herself. *I need my hand.*

"Volucris!" she screamed. "Catch me."

She released his fur and leaped off his back.

She fell through fire and smoke and raining blood, the battle spinning around her. The nightshades yanked her soul, and she saw her body tumbling below her, shouting in the night.

Volucris's talons caught her, knocking the breath out of her, nearly knocking the Beam from her grasp.

Her soul slammed back into her body.

She grabbed the skull with her good hand.

Rays of light blazed out, spinning and crackling, bleaching the world. They seared nightshades, slicing them in half. More nightshades screamed to her left, and she spun the Beam, burning them.

Kyrie flew by her on his griffin, waving his own Beam. "The damn things keep coming," he shouted. "Agnus Dei, you all right?"

She nodded, held in Volucris's grip. "Take the north, Kyrie! I'll deal with the south. The nightshades are tearing into the salvanae. We've got to do better."

He nodded and flew off, firing rays of light.

"Fly into them, Volucris," she shouted. "The cluster of them in the south. Let's burn them."

The griffin shrieked and flew, crashing into hundreds of nightshades. Their screams nearly tore her eardrums. She held her Beam before her, cutting into them. White smoke rose from them, and they crumbled and rained like ash.

Agnus Dei glanced below her and cursed. Dies Irae's forces spread into the distance. She could see no end to them. Mimics and snowbeasts swarmed closer to King's Column, tearing into the lines of Earth God followers. She saw Mother fight there, surrounded by mimics. Every second, another Earthen fell dead.

Lights blazed below. The mimics were lighting arrows. The flaming missiles shot into the sky. Hundreds blazed around her like comets. Three flew so close, she felt them stir the air.

One arrow grazed her thigh, tearing her skin, and slammed into Volucris's belly.

The griffin shrieked and bucked, tossing Agnus Dei in his talons. More arrows flew. One whistled an inch from Agnus Dei's face, sliced through her hair, and slammed into Volucris's neck.

Three mimic dragons swooped upon them, and Agnus Dei gritted her teeth.

Fire, blood, and darkness exploded. Mimic claws of steel scratched. Eyes blazed. Feathers fell and blood streamed down Volucris.

"Fly, Volucris!" Agnus Dei cried. "Get out of here, fly south."

He tried to flap his wings, but the mimic dragons tore into them, biting, tearing off feathers. Flaming arrows flew. They slammed into his belly, his neck, and one into his head. The Griffin King roared, but still he held Agnus Dei in his talons.

Smoke and tears filled her eyes, and Agnus Dei screamed.

"Let me go," she shouted. "Let me fall. Use your talons!"

But still he held her in his left talons, fighting only with his right. The mimic dragons cackled and flew at his left side. Agnus Dei pointed the Beams at them, but they were not nightshades; it would not burn them. They bit into Volucris, tore off chunks of his flesh, and began to eat.

"Volucris!" Agnus Dei screamed. She dropped the Beam and caught it between her legs. She drew her sword and swung it, but could not reach the mimic dragons.

The nightshades howled and wrapped around Volucris's neck.

Arrows whistled, slammed into Volucris, and fire blazed across him.

"No!" Agnus Dei cried, horror pounding through her. Her eyes burned so badly, she could barely see. "Volucris!"

Flaming arrows peppered him... and Volucris, King of Griffins, fell from the sky.

The ground spun, racing up toward her. Agnus Dei cursed, freed herself from the talons, and scurried up Volucris's leg. She leaped onto his back, but he was still falling. She clung to his fur with her good hand. Her Beam tumbled, and the night swallowed it.

"Fly, Volucris!" she screamed and tugged his fur. The air roared around her. Fire and smoke churned everywhere. They spun. "Fly, damn you, *fly!*"

His eyes rolled back. He gave her a last stare. He cawed softly.

The ground rushed up, black and white and red, mimics racing across it.

Volucris's wings flapped once. He managed to steady himself, to slow his fall.

Mimic javelins flew.

They slammed into him. One tore through his neck, emerging bloody near Agnus Dei's cheek. She cried. Volucris slammed into the ground.

At once, mimics came rushing forward. They began to hack the griffin, climb upon him, and eat his flesh. Agnus Dei howled and leaped to her feet, standing atop Volucris, swinging her sword.

"You will not touch him, scavengers!" she cried. Tears in her eyes, she leaped off Volucris's body, slamming herself into the ranks of mimics.

She fought against hundreds of mimics, snowbeasts, and skeletons. They surrounded her, and she sprayed their blood upon the snow. She could not see her forces. Mother fought across the forest, hundreds of yards away. The others flew above between the flaming arrows and bolts of lightning. She stood alone.

"But I will not die alone," she said and growled. "I will take hundreds of you with me."

Her sword swung. For Requiem. For her parents. For her sister. For Kyrie. She fought. A mimic cut her leg with a blade, and she fell, screaming. She swung her sword, cutting it down. Salvanae lightning rained from the sky, white and purple, torching the dead trees. Fire and smoke filled the air, melting the snow, intolerably hot against her cheeks. She coughed and snarled and narrowed her eyes as she fought.

A howl rose above the din of battle.

A great shadow emerged from the flames, shoving mimics aside.

It came marching toward her, snarling and drooling blood. Mimics fled from it. It was a mimic too, but taller and burlier than the others. It had a bull's head and four arms. Its four hands held an axe, a spear, a sword, and a warhammer.

The bull's lips opened, and it spoke in a growl. "Agnus Dei...." It raised the hand holding the sword. "Do you recognize this hand, Agnus Dei? I thank you for it."

Agnus Dei stared, eyes narrowed. Its hand was long and slender, a woman's hand. *My hand.* Ice washed her belly.

"No," she whispered, shaking her head. *Stars, no.*

The bull mimic smirked. "I will kill you with your own hand, weredragon."

It lunged toward her, its four weapons swinging. Agnus Dei screamed, a howl of horror and rage. *My hand. It has my hand.* She ran through the blood, leaped, and swung her sword.

The mimic's sword clanged with her own. Sparks rained. Its axe swung over her head, narrowly missing it. Its warhammer glanced off her vambrace, and its spear grazed her shoulder.

She screamed, pulled back, and slashed her sword again. The mimic swung its blade, parrying, and thrust. Agnus Dei blocked the blow, but barely. It glanced off her shoulder, tearing her shirt. Its warhammer swung, and she ducked, dodging it. She lashed her blade and hit the mimic's chest. Blood spurted, but it only laughed and swung its axe and sword.

I can't beat it. Stars, I can't win this battle. We can't win this war.

The mimic growled and lashed its spear. She parried, driving it aside, but the axe swung too, and she leaped. It hit her pauldron, denting the steel, sending pain through her.

No! Don't give up. Never give up. Not until death. I will fight so long as I live. She screamed and thrust her blade. The mimic parried, laughing, blood and centipedes spilling from its wound. Hundreds of mimics formed a ring around them, howling, watching the fight.

Agnus Dei leaped sideways, and the axe clanged against her armor. The sword nicked her hip, drawing blood. She spun, swinging her blade, and slammed it into the mimic's leg. She cut deep into its flesh, and when she pulled it free, bugs spilled. The mimic laughed, spraying saliva, and advanced toward her. It lashed all four weapons.

She ducked and parried, and the spear ran down her thigh, scraping skin. The warhammer hit her blade, shattering it.

Agnus Dei fell onto her back, staring up in horror.

She clenched her jaw.

Goodbye, Mother, sister, Kyrie. I love you all. Goodbye.

Its axe came down.

Agnus Dei screamed and raised her arm.

The axe hit her vambrace, shattering it. The blade cut her skin, but the armor had blocked most of the blow. It did not reach bone. *I won't lose my second hand so easily.*

She tossed the hilt of her sword. The broken shards of blade slammed into the mimic's eyes.

It howled.

Agnus Dei leaped to her feet, grabbed its axe, and pulled it free.

The mimic pulled the shattered blade from its face. It had pierced its forehead and right eye. The creature grinned, worms and drool dripping from its maw.

Agnus Dei swung her axe and cut off its hand—*her* hand. It landed at her feet.

"How does it feel, bastard?" she screamed and swung her axe. The blade drove into its neck, tore through the stitches that held the bull's head to the torso, and emerged dripping from the other side.

For a second, the mimic stood still.

Then its head slid off its body and splashed against the ground.

Agnus Dei swung her axe, opening its skull. Snakes filled the skull instead of brains. They fled. The mimic's body tried to keep fighting, but was blind. Agnus Dei hacked at it, screaming hoarsely.

"How does it feel, you bastard?! You will feel this too, Irae. You will feel my blade."

She hacked at it until it fell, cut to pieces. She grabbed a burning branch and tossed it onto the body. Soon it blazed in a pyre, drying her tears.

Her hand burned with it.

Agnus Dei wiped her eyes and spat onto the burning body. She looked around her, panting. Countless mimics still surrounded her. They howled, brandished their blades, and attacked.

TERRA

The battle raged around him, a song of light and fire in the night. Salvanae and mimic dragons battled above. Griffins and nightshades streamed at his sides. Beasts crawled and grunted below him, slamming against Lacrimosa and her troops. Everywhere he looked, he saw flame, smoke, and lightning.

The battle is lost, he realized. *We are overrun.*

He growled, remembering the war that had killed his people, that had shattered his family. His growl turned into a roar.

I am the last bellator. I will defend Requiem to my last breath. If we die here tonight, I die with blood on my talons, and the flesh of my enemies in my jaws.

He howled and dived, knocking between the hordes of flying mimics, and blazed fire across the ruins of King's Forest. Skeletons withered in his flames. Poisoned ran like living torches. And yet more kept coming, wave after wave of them, their ranks stretching into the darkness. Mimic giants, each limb woven of dead bodies, charged through the ranks of Earthen, tossing men and women aside, roaring to the sky.

Terra swooped toward one giant, readying his fire. Before he could reach it, squeals rose in the night around him. A hundred creatures burst from the shadows, shooting toward him. They looked like great bats, but they were mimics. Terra grunted with disgust. Dies Irae had taken men and women, stripped their bodies away below their shoulders, and left them with only heads, outstretched arms, and spines. He had pulled skin between their wrists and tailbones, crafting them wings to flap. They flew at him, biting, their eyes blazing red.

Terra blew his fire, spraying it in all directions. He fought down nausea; he had never seen anything so hideous.

They were people once. Stars, they were people. He clenched his jaw. *But they are not people now. The only mercy I can give them is the mercy of fire.*

He roared, summoned more flame, but had no time to shoot it. More bats emerged from the darkness, smoking and screeching, and flew onto him. They covered his back and crawled along his wings, biting and scratching.

Terra roared and flapped his wings, but the creatures clung to him. Their teeth bit, and he howled in pain. He shook and flapped his tail against them. They scurried across him, screeching. When he knocked one off, three more swooped from the darkness onto him.

"Terra!" a voice cried above.

"Kyrie!" Terra shouted. "Get out of here. You fight the nightshades."

Kyrie swooped down on his griffin, his sword drawn. Ash painted his face and hair. Blood trickled down his cheek. *I remember him a boy,* Terra thought through the haze of pain. *He is a warrior now.* As the mimics bit him, and as the fires burned, Terra felt pride well inside him. *My brother is a warrior of Requiem.*

"You've got something on you," Kyrie said, hovering over him. His griffin leaned sideways, and Kyrie swung his sword, hacking off the bats. They shouted and fell into darkness.

Terra shook himself and turned around, and Kyrie hacked at the other bats, slicing them and knocking them off. Terra's wings blazed in pain. He could barely flap them. He felt the wind rushing through holes the bats had left.

"How are those nightshades?" he called over the roar of battle.

Kyrie ducked, dodging a salvanae that roared above him, flying at a mimic dragon.

"We're handling the nightshades," he shouted back. "It's the ground I'm worried about. The Earthen are being butchered down there."

Terra nodded. "Going to swoop again. I—"

A great dragon of rot and stitch burst from the clouds, tumbling toward them, blazing. It crashed into Terra with smoke and heat and howls, and he saw nothing but fire and darkness.

"Kyrie!" he shouted. He tried to flap his wings, but they burned, and he grimaced. The mimic dragon blazed, but still lived, snapping its teeth and clawing at Terra. He growled and bit into its neck, tearing out a chunk of arms and legs, but could not shake the beast loose. Its weight shoved him down, and he tumbled. He crashed against a salvanae who flew below, and then more mimic bats were on him, biting his tail and legs.

Terra roared, tumbled upside down, and crashed into the ground.

The mimic dragon rolled off him, and Terra shoved himself up. He swung his tail, knocking the mimic's head aside, then spun to face a horde of skeletons racing toward him.

He lashed his tail, knocking them over, and slashed his claws, hitting leaping wolf mimics.

"Kyrie!" he shouted. He looked up, but saw only smoke, coiling salvanae, and flaming arrows. He tried to flap his wings, but the mimic bats were covering them again, biting and weighing them down.

Roars pierced the night, and footfalls shook the ground. Terra turned to face the sounds. From the smoke and fire, three towering reptiles charged forward, each the size of a dragon.

"Perfect," Terra muttered, howled, and roared fire.

He had been blowing flames for hours, and could muster only a weak spray. It barely fazed the reptiles. They crashed forward, stepping onto mimics, and leaned in to bite.

Terra lashed his claws and lacerated one's head. He swiped his tail, hitting another's flank. The third bit his arm and tugged him down.

Growling, Terra kicked and hit one. It fell back, and he blew whatever fire he still had, hitting a second reptile. Each was his size, with claws and fangs like swords. Claws scratched along Terra's back, and he rolled over, kicking and biting.

A reptile crashed down onto him, knocking his breath out. Terra clawed at its face. He pushed it off and tried to fly, but could not. The bats tugged on his wings, pulling them to the ground.

"Here goes nothing," Terra said... and shifted into a human.

The bats fell off him. The reptiles crashed around him. Terra ran between one's legs. He drew his sword as he ran and swung it, slicing the creature's hamstrings. It fell behind him, and Terra ran through the snow. He jumped into the air, shifted, and flew.

The reptiles howled. Terra spun, swooped, and rained his last reserves of fire. The creatures blazed and fell, burning.

Terra soared into the aerial battle, flying through smoke and fire and battling creatures. He gazed over the battle and his heart sank. Thousands of salvanae and griffins lay dead upon the ground, mimics tearing into them. Dozens were falling around him from the sky, bitten, bristly with arrows, crackling with fire. Terra searched the air for the other Vir Requis, but couldn't see them through the smoke and lightning.

When he looked below him, Terra's spirits sank deeper. Dies Irae's ground forces still covered King's Forest, stretching as far as he could see. Lacrimosa and Silva still stood by King's Column, swinging their swords, but their forces had been decimated. Hills of dead Earthen rose around them.

Terra swooped. He had no fire left, but he lashed his claws at skeletons, at mimics, at the dark forces that kept charging. He roared in the night.

KYRIE

His griffin plummeted, blazing. The smoke flew over Kyrie, stinging his eyes, entering his nostrils, choking him. He coughed and clung to the griffin. He wanted to shift, and tried to summon his magic, but too many Animating Stones pulsed around him.

"Gloriae!" he shouted. "Agnus Dei!"

Where *were* the twins? He could see nothing, nothing but smoke, darkness, and the ground rushing up toward him.

"Oh stars," he said, tightened his jaw, and winced.

His griffin crashed into the field, landing atop mimics and skeletons. Bones snapped beneath it. The griffin slid over bodies, snow, and blood, and finally crashed into a fallen log, dead.

Arrows flew.

Kyrie cursed, leaped off the griffin, and crouched behind it. He clutched his sword and gritted his teeth.

"Oh bloody stars, this is bad."

The ground shook. Mimics galloped toward him, centaurs sewn from dead horses and dead women. Their hair was woven of snakes. Their arms ended with bloody blades. They swung those blades at Kyrie.

He crouched, slid through the snow, and hacked at one's legs. He rose and ran, shoving his way between skeletons, bashing them with his blade.

"Lacrimosa!" he cried. "Where are you?"

He saw King's Column rising ahead from smoke and flames. He ran toward it. Hooves galloped behind him, and he turned to see the mimic centaurs chasing him. He cursed, grabbed a spear from a dead man, and tossed it. The spear pierced one centaur's chest. Kyrie ran at the other and clanged swords with it. He ducked, sliced at its legs, and ran.

"Lacrimosa!"

Was she alive? Mimics surrounded him—starfish, centaurs, giants, dogs, bats. He saw no end to them. Dead salvanae, griffins, and Earthen covered the ground. The mimics were feasting upon them, or leaping over them to kill more.

Ten mimic centaurs came galloping toward him from the smoke, bearing lances. Kyrie cursed. He gritted his teeth and raised his blade.

A horn blared. A hundred Earthen leaped from the flames and swung swords.

"For the Earth God!" cried Silva, their High Priest. "Kill the abominations."

Kyrie swung swords with them. Blood spilled and mimic limbs burned. Lightning fell from the sky, hitting more mimics. The salvanae swooped, biting, clawing, killing. Mimic dragons flew around them, tearing them apart with their claws. Blood splattered.

Kyrie glimpsed Lacrimosa ahead, only a hundred yards away. She seemed to glow in the battlefield, her blade bright, her hair sparkling, her face like glimmering marble. King's Column rose above her.

"Lacrimosa!" Kyrie cried again and ran toward her, hacking his way through skeletons. He had to step over the bodies of men, his boot even stepping on one's head. He winced but kept running. Enemies surrounded his queen; he had to protect her.

The skeletons parted before him.

A woman emerged from the shadows.

Kyrie growled. "Umbra."

She gave him a mocking smile and placed her hands on her hips. "Weredragon."

Kyrie knew this one. He had seen her capture the twins in the mine. He had seen her battle Gloriae at the camp. He knew about her chaining down Agnus Dei's hand so that Dies Irae could sever it.

"You might have escaped Gloriae's sword," he told her, "but you won't escape mine."

He raised his dripping blade. Umbra drew her daggers. The skeletons and mimics formed a ring around them, like spectators eager to watch the fight.

Umbra tossed a dagger.

Kyrie parried with his blade, knocking it aside.

Snarling, Umbra tossed two daggers.

Kyrie knelt and raised his blade. He knocked one dagger aside, and the other glanced off his helmet. He ran forward, swinging his sword.

The mimics howled. Umbra slid through the snow, drew two daggers, and crossed them. Kyrie's sword slammed into them, and Umbra twisted her daggers, yanking the sword from his hand. The mimics cheered and Kyrie's heart leaped with horror.

He jumped back, defenseless, as Umbra lashed her daggers. One bit under his arm, grazing him, drawing a line along his ribs. The second dagger hit his raised arm, glancing off the vambrace.

"Are you ready, boy?" Umbra said, smirking.

Kyrie leaped back, dodging her daggers. "I'm not dying yet."

Umbra laughed and winked. "I didn't ask if you're ready to die. I asked if you're ready to become my mimic." She lashed her dagger, nicking his shoulder, and Kyrie cursed. "I will carve you like a pig, and sew you back together into my slave."

Kyrie fell to one knee, grabbed snow, and tossed it at her face. Umbra shook her head, snow in her eyes, and Kyrie jumped forward. He barrelled into her, knocking his shoulder hard into her chest. She grunted, and Kyrie grabbed her wrists and twisted them.

Umbra snarled and clenched her fists around her daggers, pointing their blades toward him. Kyrie grunted, struggling to push her arms away, shocked at her strength. She was as strong as him—maybe stronger—moving the daggers closer and closer.

Kyrie kicked her shin. She grunted and he headbutted her.

Umbra screamed and fell back. She lashed a dagger. Kyrie ducked, and the dagger hit his helmet. He grabbed his sword and swung it, but Umbra parried. The blade hit the snow. A dagger lashed. Kyrie blocked it with his vambrace and pulled his sword up. It sliced Umbra's thigh, she screamed, and she stabbed her blade.

The dagger scratched Kyrie's neck, and ice flooded him. For an instant, he was sure he was dead. Umbra's eyes widened, and a smile found her lips.

No. It only cut skin, Kyrie thought. He could still breathe, still shout, and he swung his blade.

Umbra parried with both daggers. She tried twisting the sword between them again, but Kyrie pulled his blade back. Umbra lunged at him, leaping through the air, howling, daggers gleaming.

Kyrie thrust his sword forward.

Umbra twisted, parried with one dagger, and brought the other down hard.

Turning sideways, Kyrie dodged it and punched Umbra's shoulder. He knocked her down and stepped on her wrist. She screamed and tossed her second dagger. Kyrie ducked. It flew over his head.

The skeletons and mimics howled. Kyrie placed his sword against Umbra's neck.

"You will be the mimic, Umbra," he said. "Once I cut you, Dies Irae will have no other use for you."

She kicked hard, hitting his knee. The pain suffused him. He fell, cursing, and Umbra leaped up. She drew another dagger, and the blade flashed down.

Kyrie raised his sword.

The blade pierced Umbra's stomach.

The mimics and skeletons roared. Kyrie sucked in his breath, stars floating before him, his blood dripping. Pain spun his head. He pushed himself up, Umbra impaled on the sword, and shoved her down.

She fell and curled up, clutching her stomach. She glared up at him, snarling, a wild animal.

"Weredragon!" she screamed and spat at him. "I curse you. I curse your kind. I curse you all to the abyss, and to pain, and to eternal slavery. You are monsters. You killed my family." Blood filled her mouth and her eyes blazed. "I curse you, weredragon! My lord will destroy you!"

Her clothes soaked with blood, she leaped to her feet and jumped at him. Her daggers lashed. Kyrie parried, thrust his blade, and pierced her chest.

She fell to her knees.

Blood poured down her clothes.

She stared up at him. Kyrie stared back, panting. He expected her to rage, to curse, to spit... but tears filled her eyes. She whimpered.

"Why?" she whispered. "Why do you do this? I miss my husband. I miss my brothers. I'm sorry I couldn't avenge you. I'm sorry."

She fell to her knees, then fell forward, and her face hit the snow. She lay still.

Kyrie knelt by her, surprised to find pity fill him. He placed a hand on her head.

"You fought well," he said softly. "Whatever your pain was, I'm sorry if we caused it. May you find some peace in the world beyond... with your husband and brothers."

He rose to his feet and looked around him. The mimics and skeletons were screeching and fighting the Earthen. Blood and fire filled the night. He looked above him. The nightshades had scattered, but many mimic dragons and bats still flew. Salvanae kept falling; they covered the battlefield, sliced and battered and burned.

"Pup!"

He turned, and his heart leaped to see Agnus Dei running toward him. Snow, blood, and ash covered her. She hacked at a skeleton, jumped over a dead salvanae, and came to fight beside him. They swung their blades, holding back attacking mimics.

"Agnus Dei, what do you know?" he shouted over the din.

"It's bad, pup. Silva's troops are falling fast. Most are dead already. Half of the salvanae have fallen, and most of the griffins."

Kyrie cursed. "Lovely. How's our friend Irae?"

Agnus Dei pierced one of the Poisoned with her blade. "I can't find the bastard. But his troops keep coming at us. There's no end to them. Pup... what do we do?"

A snowbeast leaped at them. They hacked at it, chopping off its legs, and stabbed its mouth until it died.

"I don't know," Kyrie said and cursed again. The monsters kept slamming against them, endless in the night. He looked at Agnus Dei. Blood filled her hair and smeared her face. Her armor was dented and her clothes were mere tatters.

"I love you, Agnus Dei," he said.

She looked at him, fear in her eyes. "I love you too, Kyrie. In this life and in our starlit halls."

They fought back to back as the shadows and horrors of the night surged toward them.

DIES IRAE

He swung his mace, crushing an Earthen's head. The man's helmet was weak. The spikes in Dies Irae's mace punched through it. When he yanked his mace back, it came free with a spurt of blood.

A swordsman attacked at his right—a mere peasant garbed in Earth God green. The man's chipped blade slammed against Dies Irae's plate armor, glancing off with sparks. Dies Irae swung his mace. The man tried to parry, and the mace shattered the blade. Dies Irae smiled and clubbed his head. When the man fell, he swung his mace down, finishing the job.

Pathetic, he thought. These were no warriors. This Silva had brought farmers to fight, their armor weak, their weapons chipped, their bodies fragile. He swung his mace side to side, shattering bones. Their blades could not pierce his armor. Their bodies piled up at his feet.

"Where are you, Lacrimosa?" he said softly. "Where are you, my lizard harlot? You will be mine, Lacrimosa. I will burn your body, and sew your head onto one of my women, and you will warm my bed every night."

He scanned the battlefield, seeking her. *She will try to defend King's Column.* He turned northward and saw the column rising from smoke and flame and lightning. Yes, she would be there.

Smirking, Dies Irae began cleaving a path through the enemy, clubbing them, tossing them left and right. His mimics fought by him, burly beasts, each with four human heads sewn together at the napes, so they could see in every direction. They swung bloody war hammers, shattering their foes' bones.

They drove through the lines of Earthen, and Dies Irae saw a sight that made him grin. A ring of Earthen surrounded a hill, guarding a makeshift palisade. Behind the palisade, thousands of women and children huddled atop the hill.

"Look at them," Dies Irae said to his mimics, laughing. "Once more, the weredragons bring women and children to fight their wars."

His mimics laughed, spraying blood and drool from their maws.

Dies Irae clenched his fist. "We smashed their women and children at Lanburg Fields. We will crush these Earth God peasants too."

I will join you soon, Lacrimosa. First I will whet my appetite.

He began driving a path toward the hill, grinning savagely. The Earthen seemed desperate. They crashed against him, shouting, thrusting their spears like madmen. They fell fast. For every mimic they slew, they lost three men. Dies Irae grinned as he clubbed at them, breaking knees, ribs, arms, heads.

He reached the palisade, a frail wall of thin logs, and clubbed it with his mace.

"Tear it down!" he shouted. "Tear down the wall."

His mimics attacked the logs with their war hammers. Within moments, they had breached the palisade. Earthen soldiers crashed against them, howling, torching and cutting them. Mimics fell blazing. The women and children on the hilltop screamed, sobbed, and held one another.

Mimic bodies piled up at the breach in the palisade, smoking. *Weaklings,* Dies Irae thought in disgust. He stepped over their bodies, the smoke rising around him, stinging his eye and filling his lungs. Laughing, he swung his mace at the Earthen who attacked him. Their blades sparked against his armor. He drove forward, mace swinging, and crossed the palisade.

"Mimics, after me!" he bellowed and pointed his mace at the hilltop. "Kill them all."

The women and children screamed.

Roaring, his mimics stormed through the palisade behind him, clashing against the Earthen soldiers. Dies Irae drove forward. The women and children were trying to flee, but the hill was too crowded, and the palisade locked them in. They fell and cried and shouted. Dies Irae laughed. *They doomed themselves.*

He tore through the last line of soldiers, and saw the women and children fleeing. He ran forward, grabbed a child by the hair, and pulled it around. The young girl stared at him with huge, teary eyes. Dies Irae clubbed her head and kicked her body aside.

Her mother knelt and wept over her, and Dies Irae slammed his mace into her skull. The others fled, trampling over one another, a mad rout. Dies Irae grinned and moved between them, swinging his mace. They didn't even fight back. They died around him; it was like slaughtering lambs.

Dies Irae laughed. He had not enjoyed himself so much in many days. He grabbed a baby from its mother, and was about to club it, when a shout rose behind him.

"Let the child go, Irae. Face me instead."

Dies Irae's smile widened.

He turned around slowly.

"Lacrimosa!" he said in delight and tossed the baby aside.

She stood before him, covered in blood and ash. Her armor was dented and nearly falling off. Her clothes were mere tatters. Her hair was singed. She stared with blazing eyes from a blackened face. When she raised her sword, it caught the light and glowed like the stars of Requiem.

"Dies Irae," she said. "Your crusade of death ends here."

He licked his lips. "It's only beginning."

She leaped toward him, swinging her sword.

LACRIMOSA

Stella Lumen hit his breastplate. It sparked and glanced off the steel, shooting pain up Lacrimosa's arm. Dies Irae swung his mace. She leaped back, and the steel arm of Dies Irae swung before her.

Do not parry, she told herself. *He will shatter your blade. Jump. Dance. Attack where his armor is weak.*

His mace swung again. She leaped back, hitting a fleeing child, and bounded forward. She swung her blade toward his helmet, its visor shaped as a monstrous beak. He parried with his arm, and her sword scratched along the steel, showering sparks. He thrust his mace again, and she ducked, dodging it.

Do not parry. Jump. Dance. He is slow and you are fast.

She sprang up, swinging her sword. She aimed for the chain mail under his arm; it was weaker than his plates of steel. But he twisted, and her blade hit his breastplate, not even chipping it.

"You are feisty, lizard whore," he said, eyes blazing behind the slits in his visor. "Will you be feisty in my bed too?"

She growled and thrust her blade. *Do not waste words on him. Jump. Dance. Kill him.* She aimed again for his armpit, but he moved, and the blade slammed against his pauldron. He swung the mace again, and this time Lacrimosa did have to parry. The mace glanced off the base of Stella Lumen, and she caught her breath, sure it would shatter. But her father's blade was strong, stronger than most blades of steel; it glowed and rang. She swung it and hit Dies Irae's helmet. He grunted but did not fall.

"Did you hear the sound your husband made when I butchered him?" Dies Irae said, swinging his mace. "He sounded like a pig in heat. You will make the same sound every night when I thrust into you."

Lacrimosa's eyes stung with smoke. Her limbs shook with weakness. The mimics had cut her, and blood stained her left leg and trickled under her ribs. She did not know how bad the wounds were, but she could still stand, still breathe, still kill.

Leap. Jump. Dance.

And they danced. It was the dance of her life—against death, against evil, against blood and darkness. She danced for life, for the light of her stars, for the love of her family—because she could not stop dancing, she could not give up, not when her children needed her, not when her people cried to her from the earth. She was Queen of Requiem. She was a widow. She was a mother. So she swung her sword, and cried to her stars, and lashed her blade at the man who'd raped her, who'd killed her family, who'd shattered the halls of her home. She danced and cried and pierced his armor below the arm, so that he screamed and his blood spilled.

"It's over, Irae," she said, face drenched in sweat. He clutched his wound, glaring at her. "It's over. I end your reign this night."

She swung her sword.

Snarling, he raised his mace and slammed it against her wrist.

Lacrimosa screamed. She felt the bones in her wrist snap. The blade fell from her hand. Dies Irae swung the mace again, and she could not breathe. Pain filled her, white and blinding. Her shoulder shattered. She fell to her knees, gasping for breath. She tried to leap, to run, but he kicked her, and she fell.

Stars of Requiem... give me strength. Help me rise.

He stepped onto her neck, his boot bloody, made from the golden scales of a Vir Requis child. She could not breathe or speak. He lifted her sword with bloody fingers.

"My my," he said. "You still struggle beneath me?"

She tried to speak, but his foot constricted her, nearly snapping her neck. *I'm sorry, Ben. I'm sorry, Gloriae, Agnus Dei, Kyrie. I love you all so much. I love you.*

Blackness was spreading before her eyes. Through blurry tears, she could see that the women and children had fled the hill. She smiled softly. *I saved them. He will kill me now, but I saved them.*

He lifted Stella Lumen above her. The Draco Stars shone above between the smoke and flames, glittering across the sword.

"I'll kill you like I killed your husband, whore," he said. "I'll butcher you with your own sword."

Stars floated around her. Stars glowed on the hilt of her sword, and in the sky beyond the fire and shadow—the stars of her life. The light of Requiem fell upon her, waiting for her. *I will join you soon, Ben. I will join you soon, Mother and Father.*

Dies Irae lifted his foot off her neck.

"Will you plead for your life now, weredragon?" he asked. "Beg for it."

His boot crushed her shattered wrist, pinning her down. She saw her husband again, her love, her eternal companion. They danced in the halls of Requiem among marble columns. They raised their daughters in the light of stars and the song of harps. They fled together, hid together, fought together. She sat with him again by the stream outside Confutatis, the night they had summoned the griffins. *The young ones went seeking supplies, and we kissed, and he loved me by the water.*

She smiled softly. It began to snow. The snowflakes glided, so beautiful to her, and coated her.

"I do not fear death," she whispered, staring up with blurred eyes. "I do not fear my father's blade. But yes, I beg you, Dies Irae. If you still remember Requiem... if you still have any pity in you... spare me. Spare me for the child that I carry within me."

His eyes widened.

"Pregnant," he whispered. "With his child."

Her lips parted. The blade slammed down, a streak of starlight.

She gasped.

Blood bloomed across her breast, poppies in the snow.

She tried to speak, but no words left her lips. He stood above her, boots crushing her. He twisted the blade, his eyes alight. But Lacrimosa felt no pain, only love and warmth. She smiled softly and her fingers uncurled.

Harps played, and the stars seemed so close, their light no longer cold and distant, but warm against her. She looked at King's Column, which rose from the fire, and it seemed to her like the halls of Requiem stood again, all in white, awash with light. The birches rustled around her, their leaves silver.

"I return to you, Ben," she whispered, tears in her eyes. "I love you."

She held his hand as starlight flooded her.

KYRIE ELEISON

He was running uphill when he saw her fall.

His heart froze.

He gasped.

Lacrimosa. Stars, no.

"Mother!" Agnus Dei shouted beside him, voice torn.

Stars, no, Kyrie prayed. *She lost a father already, don't let her lose her mother too.*

"Lacrimosa!" he shouted and ran uphill, his eyes burning. Smoke flowed around him. Fire licked at his boots. He ran, shouting, horror pulsing through him. *Stars, no, please.* He shoved his way between battling Earthen and mimics.

He reached the hilltop and saw Dies Irae laughing, Stella Lumen bloody in his hand. Lacrimosa lay at his feet, eyes glassy and staring. Kyrie shouted, eyes blurred, and leaped at him. He swung his sword.

The blade slammed against Dies Irae's breastplate. Rubies flew from it. Dies Irae laughed and swung his mace, and Kyrie leaped back, dodging it.

"Murderer!" Agnus Dei screamed, swinging her blade at Dies Irae. Her hair was wild, her eyes blazing. "I'll kill you, bastard! I'll kill you!"

Her blade slammed against his helmet, knocking his head sideways, but he stayed standing. He swung down his mace. Agnus Dei leaped back, and the mace grazed her thigh. She screamed and thrust her blade.

Shouting, Kyrie swung his sword too. He wanted to go to Lacrimosa. *Is she dead? Oh stars, is she dead?* But he dared not. He leaped onto Dies Irae, screaming, the world turned red. He slammed the pommel of his sword against Dies Irae's visor, a monstrous beak of steel. It dented, but Dies Irae only laughed.

Agnus Dei whipped around him and slammed her sword behind his knees, where his plates of armor joined. Dies Irae shouted. Agnus Dei swung the blade again, tears on her cheeks, shouting hoarsely. Blood splashed down his armor.

Dies Irae fell.

"You killed her!" Agnus Dei screamed, weeping. "You killed my parents, bastard."

Dies Irae was on his knees, blood seeping from his legs. More blood poured from his armpit, trickling over his armor.

"Knock him down!" Agnus Dei screamed and swung her sword into his helmet.

Dies Irae swung his mace at Kyrie, but missed. Kyrie hacked at his helmet too, and kicked, and Dies Irae fell onto his back. His blood darkened the snow.

Wet, gurgling laughter came from his helmet. "Yes, weredragons, fight me. I like it when you fight me."

Kyrie placed his foot against Dies Irae's chest, holding him down. He slammed his sword against the beak visor, knocking it open.

Bloody stars.

Kyrie froze, nausea filling him. For a moment, he could not move.

Moons ago, Benedictus had taken Dies Irae's left eye in battle. Today Dies Irae wore a new eye, sewn into his face with bloody stitches. It was the eye of a horse, three times the size of his right eye. It spun madly. Blood poured down his forehead, seeping into it.

"Stars," Kyrie whispered. "What have you done to yourself?"

Dies Irae opened his mouth and cackled. His human teeth were gone. Instead, wolf teeth were screwed into his rotting, bleeding gums.

"I am strong now," Dies Irae said, blood bubbling in his mouth. "I am mimic. I will live forever. I am too strong for you to kill."

He struggled to rise, but Kyrie kept his boot pressed against his breastplate. Agnus Dei stepped on his mace, pinning it down. Roaring, she ripped off his helmet and tossed it aside. Kyrie placed the tip of his sword against Dies Irae's neck.

"Call off your troops," he said.

He laughed, spraying blood. "Weredragon, you—"

"Call off your troops!" Kyrie shouted, pushing down his blade enough to tear the skin. A bead of blood trickled down Dies Irae's neck.

Dies Irae laughed and coughed. His chest rose and fell. "Mimics!" he shouted. "You heard the weredragon. Place down your arms. This is between the weredragons and me now."

The mimics grunted, howled, but obeyed. They tossed their weapons into the snow. The blades clanked against one another. The Earthen paused too from battle, panting, their cloaks red and black with blood.

Kyrie stared down at this man, this beast, this wretched creature who bled and cackled. *He's no longer a man,* he thought. *He stopped being a man moons ago, maybe years ago.*

"Agnus Dei, go to Lacrimosa," he said, never removing his eyes from Dies Irae.

Agnus Dei ran to her mother, knelt, and cradled her in her arms. She cried to the sky, a wail so heartbroken, that Kyrie knew that Lacrimosa was dead.

He tightened his fingers around the hilt of his sword, keeping the blade pressed against Dies Irae's throat.

"You killed her," he said. "You killed so many. Why, Irae? Why?"

The creature cackled, his horse eye spinning wildly. Blood dripped down his teeth. "You...," he said, coughed, and laughed. "You are weredragon. You infested this world. You will die. You will be my mimics. You will be my slaves."

He tried to rise, but Kyrie held him down, his boot against the creature's breastplate. Agnus Dei cried and howled behind him. Kyrie realized that the entire battle had paused; the armies watched from a distance, smoke rising between them. From the corner of his eye, he saw that Terra and Memoria had joined the hill. They knelt by Agnus Dei in human forms, watching him.

"No, Irae," Kyrie said softly to the creature below him. "No. You failed. You murdered so many. You destroyed so much. But you failed. It has already ended for you."

The creature laughed, spitting blood. Maggots squirmed in his mouth. "Try to kill me, weredragon. You cannot. You are a lizard. You are weak." He coughed.

Kyrie shook his head, and suddenly his eyes stung, and he could see Benedictus again, hear the man's voice, feel his spirit with him.

"No, I will not kill you," he said. "King Benedictus wanted to put you on trial. He wanted the world to know your sins. I will not give you the honor of dying in battle." His took a deep breath. "I will honor his wishes. Dies Irae, you will live today, and you will watch Requiem be reborn, and you will stand trial in her halls. If you are found guilty of your crimes, you will spend your life as our prisoner, and rot in a cell as our nation blooms."

Agnus Dei raised her head, her eyes red.

"Yes," she whispered, holding her mother's body. "He will stand trial."

Terra and Memoria held each other, covered in blood and ash, their eyes huge and haunted. Fires burned behind them, and they both nodded. *Yes,* their eyes told him. *He will stand trial.*

Fire crackled. Smoke unfurled. Mimics and Earthen whispered and bustled.

A long shadow fell upon the battlefield. Covered in ash and blood, Gloriae emerged from the smoke and fire.

She walked forward, her eyes green ice, her face blank, her sword drawn in her hand. Her hair flew in the wind, black with smoke.

"Gloriae," Dies Irae whispered, choking on his blood.

Gloriae the Gilded, the Light of Osanna, Heir to Requiem, walked toward the man she had once called Father. She said nothing. Her face was a dead mask

"Gloriae," Kyrie said softly, and she shoved him.

He fell off Dies Irae and stumbled two steps. Before he could leap back, Gloriae pointed her sword at Dies Irae's neck.

"Stand back, Kyrie," she said quietly. "This is between me and him."

"Gloriae, he—"

"Stand back, Kyrie!" she shouted, and her eyes blazed. Kyrie froze.

For sixteen years, Gloriae lived captive to this man, he reminded himself. *Let her say what she will.* He stood watching.

"You murdered May," she whispered.

Dies Irae nodded. "I raped her too. What is your point?"

She bared her teeth. Her knuckles were white around the hilt of her sword. "You murdered my parents."

He shook his head. "But I am your parent, child. I created you when I took the lizard queen. You are mine, child. You are mine."

Her voice shook, and her eyes burned. "I am not your child."

He raised a bloody hand to her. "Gloriae. Leave these weredragons. Join me. We will rule again. You are forgiven, child. You are still beautiful and pure. Leave these creatures who corrupted you. Let us rule together like we used to. Look at you. You wear rags now. You hide in mud and grime. Join me, and I will forge you new armor of gold, and you will rule a great empire again, not these piles of ruin."

Gloriae stared down at him, her lips tight, and her eyes dampened. She shook her head. Her voice trembled.

"I believed you once," she said. "I loved you once. I fought for your ideals. For glory, light, order and justice." She gestured at the battlefield. "Look around you, Irae. Look at the creatures you created, that you brought to war. There is no light and justice here. You always told me that you fought monsters. But you have become the monster, leading a host of them. I still believe in light and justice and glory. But I found it among the mud and ruins. You will pay for what you've done. But you will not stand trial; I will not allow it."

Dies Irae stared up at her, eyes widening. "Gloriae. Please. Gloriae, I—"

Gloriae screamed.

Smoke unfurled and fire crackled.

"You will die on the blade that you forged me." She drove Per Ignem into his neck.

Blood painted the snow.

The stars glowed.

Dawn rose in the east, and Kyrie fell to his knees, and held the body of his queen, and wept. His siblings held him. His beloved cried with him. Sunrise flowed over King's Forest, a dawn of blood, tears, and light.

Kyrie lowered his head. *All victory is vanished; all joy is forever lost.* His queen had fallen.

GLORIAE

She stood apart from the others. With dry eyes, she stared at the grave, and at the last survivors of Requiem who huddled together with tears and whispers.

Another funeral, she thought. *Another sacrifice for our nation, our life, our sky.*

The wind blew, ruffled her hair, and stung her cheeks. It sneaked under her breastplate to kiss her skin. The wind too seemed to cry, but Gloriae could not. She could shed no tears, could whisper no whispers, could not embrace with the others and share their pain. Her mourning was her own. *They will think me cold,* she knew. *Gloriae the Gilded, the warrior of ice.*

Her pain was a private thing; it always had been. The pain of her exile. The pain of losing May. The pain of finding her true parents, only to lose them like this, so quickly, a flash of stars soon overcome with clouds.

Gloriae rested her hand on the hilt of her sword. Her mother's sword. Stella Lumen, diamonds upon its grip, shaped like the Draco constellation.

"I will carry this sword, Mother," she whispered.

Crows flew above, circling the sky. *The crows have returned. Winter is ending.* Gloriae took slow steps toward the grave. The others saw her approach and pulled apart silently, tears in their eyes. She saw the tombstone behind them. It rose beside the grave of Benedictus—twin stones.

It was tall and white, taller than Gloriae, carved of marble from Requiem's fallen columns. Kyrie had carved text upon it.

> *Queen Lacrimosa*
> *and her sleeping child*
> *lights of Requiem*
> *our guiding stars*

Now tears did sting Gloriae's eyes. She thought of this unborn child, the sister or brother she would never know.

"He would have been a great son of Requiem," she whispered. "I would have taught him. But he would not have been a warrior. He would not kill like I have killed. He would have been a ruler of peace. I would have loved him."

Agnus Dei approached her, and placed her arms around her, and leaned her head against Gloriae's shoulder. Gloriae held her sister, lowered her eyes, and found tears streaming down to her lips.

"I'm glad I have you, sister," Agnus Dei whispered. "I love you."

Gloriae's tears fell, and she held her sister tight. "I love you too," she whispered.

The others joined their embrace. Terra, Memoria, and Kyrie. Young, brave, foolish Kyrie, the boy who had grown up in fire, the warrior whose promise whispered within her. She looked at him over Agnus Dei's shoulder, and he met her eyes.

They flew over Requiem. Five dragons, streaming over ruins and snow. The last of their kind, diving through the clouds, roaring their fire. The wind filled Gloriae's nostrils, streamed under her wings, and stung her eyes. She blew flame and flew, like she would fly on Aquila, and she roared for her new home.

This is my home now, Gloriae thought. She who had lived in palaces, who wore gold and samite, who killed for light and glory... she lived now among ruins and whispers, but this was her home. *This is who I am. This is where I find my strength.*

No bones remained here. They had buried and burned the slain mimics and Earthen. The living beasts had fled with the death of their master; Silva and his men still hunted them. For this day, peace had come to Requiem. Only ruins. Graves. Wind rustling the last snow. Gloriae roared her fire.

She found herself flying to King's Forest. Memories would always haunt this place, but Gloriae would not avoid them. She had seen horror there, and anguish like she'd never known... but there too pulsed the heart of Requiem, and she flew toward it through her fire and the icy wind. The others flew around her. *We are a new herd, like the herds of old.*

She landed by King's Column. Even in dragon form, she felt dwarfed by this column; it towered above her. The other dragons landed around her, their claws silent in the snow.

Gloriae shifted into human form, drew her sword, and place its tip on the earth. She knelt before the column, and she prayed.

"Draco stars," she whispered. "I have never prayed to you before. But I beg that you hear my words now. I am Gloriae, daughter of Benedictus and Lacrimosa, a warrior of Requiem. Let me serve you now. Let me defend you with sword, claw, fang, and fire."

The others knelt around her and whispered their own prayers. For Requiem. For their constellation. For the memory of the dead and their souls in starlit halls.

Gloriae closed her eyes and lowered her head. "And for you, Father and Mother. For you, the brother or sister I never knew. I will restore this land for your memory. I swear this to you. I love you always."

When she rose to her feet, she found the others looking at her strangely, their eyes soft.

"It is time," Memoria whispered and smiled sadly.

Kyrie nodded. "It is time," he agreed.

Gloriae frowned. She looked from them to Terra and to her sister. They stared back, solemn.

"It is time," Agnus Dei whispered.

"For what, sister?" Gloriae asked, sword still drawn. "Tell me."

Agnus Dei approached her, smiling sadly, her eyes soft. She placed her hand on Gloriae's shoulder.

"It is time that we crown a new queen of Requiem."

Gloriae couldn't help it. She laughed. "Sister, I... do you mean to crown me?"

She nodded. "You were born before me, Gloriae. Only a few minutes before me, but you are still the rightful heir."

Gloriae laughed again, though her eyes stung. She looked at the others, one by one, but they all stared back solemnly. She shook her head in bewilderment.

"My friends... the Oak Throne is burned. It burned years ago. Our halls are shattered."

Kyrie shook his head. "King's Column still stands. We stand in the hall of Requiem's kings, as many generations have stood before us."

Gloriae swept her arm around her. "I see ruins. Only five of us remain. Would I rule over a single column, a sister, and three friends? There is no more meaning to ceremony, to titles, to queens or kings."

Agnus Dei nodded. "Maybe, Gloriae. Ceremony and titles might be meaningless now. But not to me. Not in my heart. Not if we're to survive, and honor the memory of our fathers, and rebuild this land. For seventy-six generations, since King Aeternum, we have passed down the reign, and ruled here. For our stars, and for those who died, let us continue their tradition." She looked at King's Column, and she took Gloriae's hand and squeezed it. "Maybe ceremony and titles are still worth clinging to."

Gloriae lowered her head, and her throat felt tight. She remembered her arrows, lance, and crossbow. She remembered leading her griffins on the hunt, killing and burning. She remembered the child she had killed, a young boy with teary eyes, and how her blade had pierced him.

"I... I cannot be queen," she whispered. "I do not have a good heart. I am not just, or righteous, or gentle. I am not like you, Agnus Dei, or like you, Kyrie. You two have kind souls. You feel love, you feel compassion. But I am cold. I am steel; all I know is war. My hands are stained with the blood of innocents, even children. I killed children when I myself was a child. How could I, who sinned, who killed, who did such evil... how could I rule Requiem?"

Kyrie approached her, eyes somber. A scar ran along his forehead, a lingering whisper from the Battle of King's Forest. A beard was growing over his cheeks, frosted white, and Gloriae found herself wondering at how he had grown. She had fought a boy once, and mocked him, and hurt him; the war had killed that boy.

"Many kings and queens of Requiem have sinned," he said. "They enslaved griffins. They cast out Dies Irae from their court, and scorned him, and drove him to his rage. From the fire, we are reborn, purer, stronger. This is true of Requiem herself. It is true of you too, Gloriae. You have been raised to destroy Requiem. Let your hands be those that rebuild it. This is just." He knelt before her and lowered his head. "My queen."

Agnus Dei knelt too, tears in her eyes. "My sister. My queen."

Terra and Memoria knelt next, their heads lowered, their drawn swords held with tips in the snow.

"My queen."

"My queen."

Gloriae looked at them kneeling around her, and looked up at King's Column, and looked at the sky strewn with winter's last clouds.

I am no longer Gloriae the Gilded, she thought. *Let that woman fade into the wind. I am Gloriae of Requiem, of starlight and fire.*

She whispered softly, and the others whispered along with her, echoing her words.

"As the leaves fall upon our marble tiles, as the breeze rustles the birches beyond our columns, as the sun gilds the mountains above our halls—know, young child of the woods, you are home, you are home. Requiem! May our wings forever find your sky."

KYRIE ELEISON

He stood alone in the snow, the burned trees icy around him. He wrapped his cloak around him and watched the sunrise. It spread pink and yellow fingers across the sky, rivers of dawn.

"I miss you, Mirum," he said softly. "We used to watch the sunrise together from Fort Sanctus above the sea."

He sighed, his shoulders heavy. Requiem was free now, beautiful under the snow, and they had defeated their enemies... but Kyrie couldn't stop thinking about all those he had lost in this war. His parents. The Lady Mirum, his foster sister and best friend. Benedictus, his king and mentor. Lacrimosa, his queen, his inspiration. So many had died. So much pain still filled him, even in this victory.

He looked over the valleys and hills and took a deep breath. *But I have Agnus Dei,* he thought. *I have my brother and sister. And I have Gloriae.*

He tightened his cloak around him. Gloriae. Who was she to him? He had hated her once. He had fought her. He had watched her laugh as Dies Irae murdered Mirum. And... he had lain with her in the ruins of Osanna. He had sworn to defend her with his sword. She was his queen, his friend, and....

"Kyrie."

He turned his head and saw her emerge from the ruins. Gloriae no longer wore her armor. Today she wore a green dress Silva had given her, a silver cloak lined with fur, and a pair of moleskin gloves. Her golden locks cascaded over her shoulders, and her eyes stared at him, solemn.

"Gloriae."

She approached him, stood behind him, and placed her hands on his shoulders. She lay her head against him.

"Kyrie," she said softly, "do you know what I want to tell you this morning?"

His throat itched and his fingers tingled. "Yes."

She walked around him, faced him, and held his hands. "It's been over three moons now, four I think. You remember that night, when autumn leaves covered the ground."

He nodded, and his heart thrashed against his ribs. His eyes stung. "I remember," he whispered.

She embraced him and kissed his cheek. "I told Agnus Dei," she said. "She's happy for us, Kyrie. She won't let this change what you two have. I won't either. This is a great blessing."

Her eyes were soft, and she smiled. He smiled too, his breath shook, and he held Gloriae as they watched the sunrise.

"Are you still ready, Kyrie?" she whispered.

He nodded. "I am. I've never wanted anything more."

They walked through the ruins and frosty trees, and saw King's Column before them. Terra and Memoria stood there, garbed in green and silver, their swords at their hips. They smiled at him, eyes damp.

When he saw Agnus Dei, Kyrie's breath caught.

She stood between his siblings, head lowered shyly, arms behind her back. When she looked up at him, her eyes were shy, questioning, trembling with tears. She was more beautiful than he'd ever seen her. She wore a green gown and flowers in her hair. She smiled through her tears, and reached out to him. On her left arm, she wore a giltwood hand Silva had carved her, its fingers moving on invisible joints.

Kyrie approached his bride and held her hands, one hand soft and warm, the other hard and smooth. They walked to stand before King's Column, and gazed over the shattered hall of Requiem's kings. Snowflakes fell around them, filling their hair.

Terra and Memoria stood at their sides. Gloriae stood before them, eyes solemn.

"This is a sad day," the Queen of Requiem whispered. "This is a day when we still mourn those we lost. But I know that Benedictus and Lacrimosa are watching over us. They stand now in our starlit halls, and they smile."

Agnus Dei nodded, biting her lip. Tears spiked her lashes.

Kyrie could never afterwards remember Gloriae's words. She spoke of love, and joy, and a future for Requiem. And he spoke too—spoke of meeting Agnus Dei, of loving her always, of growing old by her side. But words glided like snowflakes, and he thought only of her eyes, and her smile, and the light in her hair, and he marvelled at how much joy she gave him, and how the mere touch of her hand spread warmth through him.

He kissed her, arms around her. She mussed his hair and laughed.

"Pup," she said, and winked, and cried.

They walked through the forest, hand in hand.

The snowflakes fell, and melted, and the ice left the trees. They planted gardens, and for the first time in years, life grew in Requiem: sweet peas, and mint, and squash, and enough flowers for Memoria to pick every day, and place inside the cave where they lived. And they lived—like the wild dragons of old, nesting upon cliffs, sleeping in caves, roaring in the dawn and herding across the sky.

"It's a new spring," Kyrie said as they planted birches around the ruins of their temples. He brushed soil off his hands. "These trees will be saplings next year, and the year after that. But when our children pray here, tall trees will shade them, and countless leaves will rustle around them."

The twins smiled and placed their hands upon their bellies.

Under summer's blue skies, Gloriae lay in their cave, and shouted and clutched Kyrie's hand. Memoria delivered their child, and held up the squealing, red creature that Kyrie thought looked so ugly, he couldn't help but laugh and cry.

"It's a girl," Memoria said. "A golden haired girl."

Gloriae took the baby into her arms, and nursed her, and kissed her head. "Her name is Luna."

Autumn winds blew, and Kyrie found himself in the cave again, holding Agnus Dei's hand and she shouted, and cursed him, and swore to beat him bloody. When Memoria held up the child, Kyrie thought this one ugly too, wrinkled and red and squealing. This babe had curly black hair, like lamb's wool.

"It's a son," Memoria said, smiling, and place the baby in Agnus Dei's arms.

Agnus Dei nodded, her brow and hair sweaty, and kissed the child. "His name is Ben."

Once he had lain in blood, dying. Once he had hidden in a tower, trapped and frightened. Once he had fought wars, and killed, and seen those he loved die. Two years after he escaped Fort Sanctus, flying over the sea with Dies Irae in pursuit, Kyrie found himself waging a new war—battling soiled swaddling clothes, and cleaning baby sickness off his shoulders, and nursing sick and crying creatures that he loved deeply. *I am happy,* he often thought, even when bone tired after hunting, farming, tending to the babes, and fleeing Agnus Dei when she chased him for breaking a plate or forgetting to weed the garden.

I am happy.

And yet... at nights, he often lay awake, and those memories returned to him. Lady Mirum, her skull shattered, falling upon the tower. Benedictus, dead in his arms. Lacrimosa, blood pouring down her chest, soaking the snow around her. When night fell, and the others slept around him in the cave, he stared into the darkness, and still saw the mimic bats, and the eyes of the nightshades, and the fire and blood of Lanburg Fields.

He would gently remove Agnus Dei's arm which draped over him, and tiptoe out of their cave, and stand in the darkness. He would stare into the horizon, and wait for sunlight, and he would miss them. Mirum. Benedictus. Lacrimosa. His friends. *I am happy. I've never been happier.* And he knew then that time did not heal all hurts. Not all memories faded. The scar on his forehead would remain; so would these terrors in the night, and this pain in his chest.

He'd return into the cave, and sneak back into their pile of furs, and kiss Agnus Dei's cheek as she mumbled and shifted. *I love you, Agnus Dei. Now. Forever. I am happy so long as I have you.*

When the first snow fell, they gathered in their cave. The twins, holding their babes. Kyrie and his siblings. Seven Vir Requis, the last of their kind. They ate the sweet peas, and the squash, and the turnips, and the other crops they grew in their garden. And they ate the game they hunted beyond Requiem's borders, in the forests of Osanna where Silva now reigned.

And for the first time, they spoke of it.

"What happens when they grow?" Kyrie said softly, watching his children.

The twins looked up at him, rocking their babes in their arms. Terra and Memoria looked at each other, then back at him.

Agnus Dei answered him. "I don't know," she said softly.

Kyrie touched Ben's cheek. The baby reached out and held his pinky finger.

"They... they have nobody but each other," he said. "Brother and sister. How will... well, I mean...." He tongue felt heavy. "Being related, how would...."

Agnus Dei groaned. "Pup, I think the babies are more eloquent than you. You want to ask how they'd *breed*. How our people will continue, if the entire next generation is brother and sister."

He bristled and felt his cheeks redden. "Well, I might have phrased it better than that, if you'd have given me a chance."

Agnus Dei rolled her eyes, but it was Gloriae who answered.

"He was terrified of it."

They all looked at her. She stared at them over her meal, face blank.

"Who, Gloriae?" Kyrie asked her. "Terrified of what?"

"Dies Irae," she answered, and Kyrie shuddered. He saw the others shudder too. They had not spoken his name since he had died.

"Terrified of what?" Kyrie asked softly.

She stared at him, eyes icy. "Of our magic. Of our curse. He claimed that weredragons would rape the women of his empire, and infect them with reptilian blood. That their disease could spread." She caressed Luna's hair and sighed. "Many men and women of Osanna died too; they too want to rebuild the world."

The all looked at one another, the words sinking in. Terra laughed softly. Memoria raised her eyebrows, then laughed too. Agnus Dei looked at them all in shock. Kyrie only sighed—a deep, contented sigh.

Yes, he thought. *I am happy.*

Gloriae—the Light of Osanna, the Maiden of Steel, the Queen of Requiem—smiled. She rocked her baby, and her voice was warm.

"It's time to mingle with the people who feared us, hated us, and hunted us... and give them a bit of our magic."

THE END

NOVELS BY DANIEL ARENSON

Standalones:

Firefly Island (2007)
The Gods of Dream (2010)
Flaming Dove (2010)

Misfit Heroes:

Eye of the Wizard (2011)
Wand of the Witch (2012)

Song of Dragons:

Blood of Requiem (2011)
Tears of Requiem (2011)
Light of Requiem (2011)

Dragonlore:

A Dawn of Dragonfire (2012)
A Day of Dragon Blood (2012)
A Night of Dragon Wings (2013)

KEEP IN TOUCH

www.DanielArenson.com
Daniel@DanielArenson.com
Facebook.com/DanielArenson
Twitter.com/DanielArenson

CPSIA information can be obtained
at www.ICGtesting.com
Printed in the USA
LVHW090954070321
680804LV00010B/233